# SCARLET SOLSTICE

B.O. Folarin

# SCARLET SOLSTICE

Copyright © 2015 Bo Folarin

All rights reserved.

ISBN 10:1514271850
ISBN-13:978-1514271858

# DEDICATION

Dedications… so many people, but the obvious are to my fantastic parents, Kunle and Joyce, without whom, none of this would have happened and let's not forget my dear Aunty K who accommodated me all these years and my darling sister, she's just great.

Finally I would like to thank my friend Ken Tsang a.k.a. "Cookie" in Hong Kong whose friendship, when tempestuous, allowed my imagination to soar as I contemplated what to do to get even, but because he's a true friend (and I never fancied spending time behind bars and I actually like his wife and kids) I kept my thoughts where they were till I wrote this book.

See everyone, there is a use for repressed anger after all.

Enjoy!

# ACKNOWLEDGMENTS

I would like to express my gratitude to Andreas B. Kønig, Martin Gæbe, Gabi Pickett, Agust Karlsson, Jelena Bozic (YES, she does exist), Alex Blumlein, Mama Balder and Mama Gaash, Marleen Geneste for being my inspiration, along with The Balder Lysen, Jackob Visscher, Kenneth Clausen, Martin Søberg and Shane Watt for their inspiration and help.

Forgive me if I forgot to mention some of you, but my head hurts but thanks for buying this book. Your support has gone a long way to make my dream come true.

# 1

*8 October 2010*

Gabriela was driving home when a sense of fulfilment came creeping over her, her mind and body resonated with the melodic music playing on the radio. It was as if her whole being was responding to every smooth guitar lick reverberating through her speakers, that and the fact that her work was becoming less stressful.

She felt tranquil, confident that she was finally getting somewhere with her work. The recent conviction of Javier Lopez, the minister for education, imprisoned for receiving kickbacks from parties bidding to construct the regional schools had meant there was one less fraudulent prick that she had to deal with.

She had become immune to the caricatures in the newspapers, labelling her as Gabriela Pickett, the 48 year old laughing hyena. She had given up any chance to find a meaningful relationship and a family and instead became a matriarch of the justice system, purging her territory among the countless vermin that dwelt in it. These vermin she had to deal with on a day to day basis bore a resemblance to the corrupt politicians inhabiting the upper cesspool of the Spanish justice system. Each time she saw them, she would sigh. It wasn't easy being a female judge in the Constitution Española.

As she turned off the highway, she allowed herself a faint smile and considered the latest conviction of the minister. With the six other members under investigation, she was officially kicking more ass than her male counterparts. She couldn't wait to see their faces and receive their fake celebratory handshakes when she returned to her chambers after the weekend; it was all her doing, and now it was her time to shine.

Well before all the congratulations set for Monday, she intended to dedicate her weekend solely to relaxation. Approaching the road leading to her home, she checked her rear-view-mirror to ensure she was still being followed. The state security thought it was necessary to keep her under observation, for her own good apparently. Once certain her 'protectors' were still there, she searched for a place to park.

"Mierda" she swore, as she saw the horrid parking attempts executed by inconsiderate drivers who likely thought the lines demarcating the spaces were for decorative purposes only.

It was beginning to look like relaxation would have to wait until she could find a decent parking spot. She yearningly looked at her front door as she drove by hoping she wouldn't have to drive to the other end of Spain to find a parking spot. Finally, about three blocks away from her house, she was able to park.

Pleased with her exceptional parking skills, she fumbled for her keys and noticed her state allocated protection drive past her. She looked at her watch; it was already eleven at night. Her minder's shift was over, meaning the others were set to arrive anytime soon.

She was eager to get home and being outside her car made her feel vulnerable. She wondered if her feelings of anxiety and vulnerability were a subconscious reaction to the death threats she had been receiving over past few months. She was getting used to the threats, hell she would even read them sometimes just to laugh at the creativity-absurdity of the writing; however she received one over the past week that had unnerved her.

This most recent threat was different. It was personal and detailed; the note explained a plot to turn her daily coffee run into a bloody show for the public to enjoy. It stated exactly the perpetrator's intent. Her guilty pleasure of caramel infused cappuccino with a double shot would, this time, be served with blood and brains on the side at her local coffee shop La Cocotte in Barcelona.

Shaking off her paranoia she reminded herself that this type of thinking wasn't the best way start to the weekend. She locked her car, and started the short walk to her apartment.

As she rounded the corner, a sense of unease lingered and made the distance to her flat seemed longer than usual. She quickened her pace, trying to mask her fear and her great desire to be home. A couple of meters down the street she heard a car door close and some feet scuff on the pavement.

Gabriela looked back nervously, a tall and handsome man with a chiselled face, and dressed in a clean cut suit was fast approaching behind her. As her eyes laboriously worked down his broad shoulders, she froze. He was wearing gloves! Normally she wouldn't pay any attention to such a mindless accessory, but it wasn't a cold night.

Her already heightened sense of discomfort and the sight of his gloved hands sent alarm bells blaring in her mind. She immediately quickened her pace to the point of speed walking down the street. To her horror, instantaneously, he began to walk faster as well. "Is this the end?" She asked herself, was her moment of glory going to be snuffed out by some gangster on the street.

Gabriela gasped as she stumbled forward; the stock of her 6 inch heel of her left shoe got caught in a crevice between two pavement tiles. However she managed to keep her balance. She instinctively tensed, grasping her keys by the head with the teeth poised to strike if required. She was bent forward and almost ready to swing her improvised weapon when she heard his footsteps come up from behind. She was about to turn to face him, thinking it better to die looking him in the eye, but when she did, he just walked by, almost leisurely, without even a glance in her direction nor paying attention to her plight.

Gabriela regained her composure, and was appalled by the lack of chivalry the stranger demonstrated, not even stopping to help a lady in distress. "Men these days" she said aloud, trying to calm down her nerves.

Arriving at her apartment block, Gabriela finally felt at ease. Closing the door, she took off her shoes that had been hurting her feet and ascended up the stairs to her apartment. Halting for a moment, she placed her hand on the railing and bent over; laughing at how foolish she had been. She couldn't believe that she could have been so paranoid yet she was happy to be home.

Once in her flat, Gabriela opened the cloakroom and tossed in her coat and designer heels that had so annoyed her for nearly giving her a mini-heart attack.

Walking into her kitchen for a glass of water, a tsunami of fear washed over her and a cold sweat began rolling down her neck as she saw that on the kitchen table were two cups. It was La Cocotte take away coffee.

Gabriela stood as still as a statue, not knowing what to do when a voice said "Well you took your bloody time". Gabriela gasped; she hadn't noticed the woman sitting on her windowsill, wearing nothing other than her towels. "I was tired of waiting, so I decided to freshen up a bit just before your arrival, but it seems as if you've caught me quite off-guard" said the stranger.

A billion questions were rocketing through Gabriela's mind; most notably she wondered why the fuck there was a near naked lady in my apartment. Eventually, Gabriela was able to relax a little as she took into consideration the limited harm a women wrapped in towels could do. Since the unwanted guest had already made herself at home, Gabriela asked "Well I hope everything is to your liking dear?" with a somewhat feigned confidence.

The woman rose from her perch proclaiming "Oh don't worry, it most certainly is... Dear." As the stranger stood, Gabriela took an opportunity to study the woman that was intruding upon her sacred personal environment. She was just over 6 feet tall, olive green eyes, her hair were bundled in a towel, as was her waist and it wrapped around just barely able to cover her private parts. Her large breasts and a near hour glass figure created a flawless combination which Gabriela envied. It was a figure that would have any man or woman taking a second glance to behold her beauty.

Despite the growing familiarity, it didn't negate the obvious danger Gabriela knew she faced. Unarmed; Gabriela surveyed her kitchen for any items that would be useful means of defence should this conversation turn towards a more violent direction.

Gabriela spotted the large knife on the table she had used the night before, however, the trespasser caught on and her eyes suddenly changed as if she just turned into a predator with her sights set on Gabriela who had begun to sweat. It was as if Gabriela could physically feel the menace of the lady in the room.

The sense of irony was not lost on the judge as she wondered how quickly she could reach the cooking utensils. The unwanted guest in Gabriela's kitchen remained motionless and remarked in an ominous tone, "It's funny how people have a false notion of safety once in their home. You seemed perfectly happy until you saw my gift waiting for you. Hopefully you enjoyed that notion of safety, if only for a moment. I'll admit that I only sent Juan to rile you up".

"Juan?" Gabriela asked.

"Yes, the fine piece of ass you met downstairs". Gabriela had a flashback, the man with the gloves.

Adjust herself on the heater, on which she sat, the intruder continued "You know why I'm here don't you?" "Frankly I don't have a clue" Gabriela pretended. She did not like where this conversation was going and was caught between taking hold of the knife and looking frantically for any opportunity of escape. Gabriela was losing her cool faster by the second.

The woman continued "I guess you expect me to say you pissed off the wrong people, the kind of people who don't like it when you go on meddling in their business, but you would be wrong. You are just a means to an end and I am ever so sorry for that." Her apology, though it seemed genuine, meant little to Gabriela who was still distracted, wrangling with her choices.

Suddenly, the women's towel gave up its important task of maintaining its grip. As the intruder bent down and fumbled to retrieve the towel, Gabriela seized the opportunity to turn the tables on the stranger.

Gabriela immediately leapt toward the kitchen knife on and grasped it and ran towards the woman. The intruder abandoned her quest for the towel and was now, rather unexpectedly, adjusting the towel covering her hair. The knife arched back and forth as Gabriela swung it wildly but then a short whistling sound pierced the air, the woman miraculously drew a gun with a silencer on it's nozzle from what seemed to be out of nowhere, when in reality, it was hidden in the towel which she had wrapped around her hair but was now on the floor, exposing he long thick damp hair.

Gabriela, seeing this, halted her advance and she felt a sharp pain cut through her gut. "Ah darling, I wished you didn't do that. Now you left me no choice. Of course you were going to die, just not like this". Gabriela lost the power in her legs and fell on her knees to the floor.

"Yes, there is pain, but it's still possible I could survive this", Gabriela thought, but the optimism was short lived. The intruder politely continued "Believe me darling, it's nothing personal." before firing the gun right in her face.

Gabriela slumped sideways, her head violently hitting the floor she could now easily see the face of the stranger, a now naked women, with auburn hair. Gabriela continued to watch as her assassin picked up the towel and walked over her as she died slowly and silently.

Prior to her departure, the intruder went over to the table, to collect one of the now blood stained coffee cups. She took a sip to quench her thirst and exhaled as she remarked "not bad."

## 22 October 2010

A fortnight had passed until Gabriela's lifeless body was found on her kitchen floor. It didn't bother her colleagues or long suffering aides that she was absent for so long without reason, but it did bother the neighbours that a foul smell emitted from her flat, the source of which was her decomposing body, the process spurred on by the heating being turn up to the highest.

When the new broke in the media, unlike her colleagues, Spain was on fire with outrage. A prominent judge that made their name by standing up for the common man had been murder and no one in authority seemed to care, but with the public opinion swinging against their aloof stance, politicians of every colour began to point fingers.

The usual suspects, the once violent separatist groups, were quick to wash their hands of the incident, coming on air to wave the signed peace accord before any camera turned at them to ensure that the world knew that they had nothing to do with it or had an interest in Gabriela's demise. With the police not giving any clear information and politicians keeping their distance, the population began to smell a rat.

There were protests in all the major cities of Spain. People pinned the blame for her death on the government, whom they branded as murderers and assassins, believing that those in the cabinet had more to gain now she gone.

In any other country, any member of the parliamentary opposition worth their salt would have tried to make some gains on the back of this popular revolution, but even they didn't dare show their face or raise their voice because their leader had also been under the late judge's microscope for using his position to get jobs for friends and family.

Painted into a corner with accusations of guilt, the state gave the judge a state funeral in all but name believing it was what the people wanted. Though the crowds did turn out, the television coverage showed the most awkward moment where the preceding bishop underlined that Gabriela had no immediate family and her only relative was a second cousin in Italy who, when the cameras turned on him, looked as though he had been forced to attend the send-off of a person he had never met.

If anything hammered home the late judge's dedication to her job, that was it, "sacrificing personal happiness for that of her community" underlined the cleric.

Though the small protestant church in Girona that could hardly hold a hundred people within its walls there were double the number of mourners and media. The media broadcasted the proceeding to every set in the land and also to the crowd gathered across the street and down the boulevards numbering three hundred thousand strong.

No politician dared show their face out of fear of being lynched by the populace. In turn, it was seen, by the very same populace, as a snob by the political establishment.

This act of self-preservation was s spectacular own goal which the royals, with the best counsel money could buy, didn't wish to replicate and, with heavy security, the princes, princesses, lord and ladies sat amongst the judges and high ranking members of the police force who once thought she was an overbearing busybody, now sobbing, repeating to themselves, "that could be me."

Even the young dean could barely contain his grief as the coffin was brought in. The coffin cut a lone figure before the alter. The presiding priest captured the mood of the nation when he called her a martyr and reminded everyone it was now up to the young people, those he labelled "Gabriela's Children" to keep up the good fight, to bring peace and prosperity to the land regardless of their denomination and political leanings because, he added "We are all Gabriela's Children!"

Following the service, the people's outrage over her death roared through Girona.

When it was time for her body to be laid in the vault with her parents, the people followed to pay their last respects before returning to the street to vent their anger on public buildings, pouring scorn upon officials who failed to attend the interment of the Judge.

The prime minister's appeal for calm on television fell on deaf ears as government buildings were torched, political party headquarters ransacked and effigies of state officials set alight in front of the parliament building. The King made an appearance on television as well, begging the people to return to their homes, confirming that he had been given assurances from the police that the case would be investigated.

One had to pity the poor monarch. His plea was taken by each individual with a lorry load of salt. The King himself had a member of his family under investigation for syphoning off funds set for charities and, as expected, his pleas fell on deaf ears. In the minds of the protesters, the thieves were asking a frail old man to speak on their behalf and they considered that a low and cowardly act, prompting the storming of more public buildings and the eventual deployment of the army on to the street.

Crisis talks were held by parliament. Everyone in the building knew that should anyone get killed in the riots it would be their head on the block. The government could see their doom as did the opposition. They hastily appointed an independent judge to investigate the murder and put all the facilities available at the judge's disposal.

The judge was then shoved before the media to announce his own appointment. He promised to bring those who killed his "beloved friend" to justice. He continued by explaining he would be working with Commissioner Portilo, whom the judge had standing next to him, and Superintendent Menendez, who was camera shy, to make that happen.

The government was mistaken to feel it could quell the mistrust that was firmly cemented into the minds of every Spaniard. The protesters who had occupied some government buildings remained as the Judge and his team set to work. On his first day, the Judge and the two policemen appointed to head the investigation were summoned to a private meeting with the King flanked by each leader of every political party present in parliament to be told in no uncertain terms to act quickly and not to "leave any stone unturned to save Spain from anarchy." and that was enough to motivate them into action.

*29 October 2010*

Twilight in the fields outside Tarragona never looked better. The birds were on their way to the tropics as winter approached and it made spectacular displays in the orange sky.

It didn't matter whether they were skylarks or swifts, the birds numbered in the thousands. It didn't matter either to the fairground worker, Jose, who watched them, where they were going, all he knew was that what he was witnessing was simply stunning and a befitting end to a very profitable day at the fair.

Despite the misery of the economic depression that loitered around over the past two years or the recent spate of strikes and protests following the Pickett affair, business was booming for the amusement industry and for those who were making money from the "We are all Gabriela's Children" T-shirts and banners. Perhaps everyone needed a distraction from their problems, assumed Jose.

Having had his fill of watching the aeronautic display, Jose set about his duty of locking up the two rides he had been allocated before going to bed.

Every year, for the last twenty three years, he had worked on the rides. Despite the threats from all the video games that kept people at home, the ability to have an unforgettable moment with your friend or child; meeting a date at a neutral place or the thrill of the rides and the lure of the snacks brought the crowds coming, leaving behind piles of rubbish all over the place, the latter being the only down side.

Having cleaned up the love tunnel and locked it up, he went about doing the same with his pride and joy, the bumper cars, housed in a movable tent held upright by ropes and ten steel poles which were nailed into the ground.

As he picked up wrappers and cans, Jose reflected on his working life. Using a stick to take a condom off the ground, he marvelled at how liberal his homeland had become, so much so that nothing surprised him much anymore.

Once done cleaning, Jose did a final test to check if the bumper cars were working correctly. Content, Jose locked up the wooden door. Despite believing that nothing could get the better of him, Jose certainly didn't expect that after having checked the locks, a cloth soaked in chloroform would be pressed firmly over his mouth and nose. He struggled until, having taken a few deep breaths, he fell unconscious.

*30 October 2010*

Jose woke the following morning as a result of a bucket of water being poured over him. He had a slight headache and despite all his denial, Jose could not explain to his boss why he was found next to the portable-loo reeking of alcohol, with an empty bottle of whiskey resting by his side.

He had received many warnings about his drinking before and was told again that this was his final one. His only saving grace was that he had secured all the rides and nothing was missing or seemed out of order.

Despite knowing he had been framed, Jose could not find a defence other than the fact that, if he did wish to go on a bender, wine would have been his preferred method, whiskey was far too harsh.

Unfortunately there was no time for him to prove his innocence, the fairground was to open early due to the growing popularity of the imported festival of Halloween and it was set to be busy. This was one he just had to take on the chin.

Manning his post at the ticket collection booth for the bumper car ride, Jose remained baffled and could not shake off his headache. The ticket booth was a boring, thankless job which required a strong constitution to bear all the standing, rowdy children and even rowdier adults but he was managing so far.

At six in the evening, nine hours into his shift with three more to go, Jose was looking forward to the end of the day and his bed. The last thing he wanted was trouble. However trouble arrived in the guise of a smartly dressed man in a raincoat with a stern face who walked past everyone else in the queue causing a little ruckus amongst those who had been waiting for a considerable period of time.

The man stood in front of Jose with a smug grin. "You can't cut the line like that, go to the back please?" Jose ordered. The man did not respond, rather, he reached into his pocket and presented him with a picture identity card. "Juan Luiz Menendez, Inspector from the Catalonian Police…" Jose read and his hand went clammy.

With a shady past to hide, Jose asked "So you want to ride?" The police man simply nodded. Jose pressed the button to allow the man to go through the turnstile into the ring. The policeman progressed onwards still without speaking. "Manner-less swine" Jose remarked at the audacity of the man before apologising to the little girl who had to wait as a result of the queue jumper.

Inspector Menendez did indeed overhear him, but wasn't bothered by Jose's perception. Menendez had come to the fair on business and with some plain dressed colleagues inconspicuously scattered amongst the crowd for good measure, he looked for a red car to sit in and wait for the call, all in accordance with the potential informant's instructions.

Jose had a trick up his sleeve and secrets to hide. With all the cars occupied, he proceeded to check if everyone had fastened their belts and as he did, he took the opportunity to speak to a young boy alone in his car across from the policeman. He offered him free rides for the rest of the evening so long as the boy keeps aiming to hit the rude inspector. With the deal made, Jose returned to his post.

Oblivious to the fact he was a target in a fiendish plot. Menendez took out his mobile phone waiting for the message from the person planning to meet. She claimed she had information relating to the death of a prominent Judge, killed in her flat three days earlier.

Normally, he wouldn't have bothered with a lot of people claiming they know things about events, but this lead was different. The woman knew far too much to be ignored. During their call she was able to divulge a lot of background data that no one, except someone associated with the deceased, could have known.

For example she told him where the Judge had been prior to being murdered, execution style, even describing the bullet used and the entry points of the two shots, the first to the belly and the other through the nose. She even detailed the make of the clothing worn by the deceased when Gabriela met her end. Everything checked out, this was real.

The potential informant had agreed to meet Menendez at 6pm at the bumper car ride at the fairground. He was to board a red bumper car and wait to be contacted. She said she knew the killer and those behind the murder and wanted to make a deal.

Menendez had his own selfish interest in getting this information even though he knew he wasn't authorized to make any deals. His career would greatly benefit from cracking this case; hence he had nothing to lose.

The music came as did the lights of the car signifying the start of the 5 minutes allocated to the willing crash test dummies behind the wheel. It was then Menendez received a text. As he tapped on the screen to read it, he was shunted to the left from a hit by the giggling child chosen to make his stay in the ring miserable.

Menendez gave the boy a cold look and proceeded to drive to the corner of the ring as the child reversed to give himself enough space to create enough ramming speed. As the boy maneuverer into position Menendez had a moment to read the text.

"Call me on this number" it said. Menendez pressed the button to instigate a call.

From the corner of his eye, he could see of the oncoming bumper car and quickly moved out of the way causing the boy to crash into the wall. Menendez had no choice but to drive whilst calling.

It took a few seconds before the phone started to ring. Jose heard the melody of a ring tone for a slight moment before it turned into a loud bang that snapped one of the supporting metal beams and within less than three seconds, more blasts were heard in quick succession.

Jose instinctively jumped out of his booth but was hit by the shrapnel of the flying steel. As he reeled in agony on the floor with pieces of metal sticking out of his limbs, onlookers screamed and gasped. People rushed forward towards the heavy tent roof top that had come down on the drivers within the ring.

The efforts of those rushing forward were thwarted when bright blue sparks emitted from corners of the fallen structure electrocuting all within. This precluded the fire that began to consume the tent and its inhabitants and along with the smell of sausages, popcorn, candy floss, caramel and toffee, the odour of burning flesh and canvas filled the air.

Many ran fearing the flames would spread, others had to be restrained from entering to save their loved ones whilst others, immobilised by shock or by flying bits of debris were whisked off or left where they fell. Jose screamed in horror, stunned by what he was witnessing.

Through all this commotion, someone stood in the distance watching the pandemonium, not out of horror but more out of what seemed contentment. After bearing witness to the efforts of others to contain the situation for over an hour, she picked up her mobile phone to make a call.

As she scrolled through her contacts in search of a British number under the name 'Purple', the person whom she was set to call was busy in his home in Ruislip pouring some mini chocolate bars into a bowl in preparation for the evening.

It was to be a busy Saturday. Halloween was on Sunday but the residents of the street had decided that the ritual of treat giving should take place the day before to, allow the children to stay up late without affecting their school day. It was also his birthday and he expected guests to show up about 9pm after he finished his Halloween rounds with his son.

As the man disposed of the empty bag, there was a knock on the door.

He raced to open it and as expected, there stood his son, dressed as count Dracula and his wife, Caroline holding her gown in her hand. "Happy birthday, daddy!" the boy cried. He picked up his son and kissed him on the cheek.

"Thank you." The man replied

"Happy birthday." Caroline said handing him a card.

"Yeah, thanks… thanks for coming." He added.

Caroline entered without further exchange of words, the cold war had returned. The man and his wife had been separated for two years but she only moved out a year ago.

Things were amicable. They both agreed not to tell anyone of their decision and agreed to have custody of the boy on a weekly basis. Part of this "tell no one our marriage is on the rocks" agreement was to keep a façade of normality by attending and, as in this case, hosting events together.

The order of the night was simple. He would take their son out trick or treating and return home after to join her in hosting his birthday party.

The man could see the excitement on his son's face. It was Halloween's eve after all and there were a row of houses from which sweets lay to be harvested, it was his task to make sure he didn't miss a door whilst his wife sat by his to distribute chocolate to passing children.

Excited, the boy asked his father "Why haven't you changed yet?"

"I was waiting for you. I need your help getting ready so that I can look at as good as you. Let's go upstairs!" The child cheered and ran up the stairs leaving his parents for a brief moment. "Are you alright?" He asked Caroline as she entered and shut the door.

"Yes, I am fine." She replied. "Come on, go get ready before he comes back and drags you."

He quickly kissed her on the cheek and ran up to his bedroom where his son was already there trying out his father's sunglasses. "Looking cool." He remarked to his son.

"Daddy are we going to get more chocolate this time?" the boy asked

"I don't really like jaw breakers."

"Let's make a deal; I'll give you my chocolate if you give me your jaw breakers." The father proposed as he took off his shirt.

"Deal!" cried his son.

"Cool. I won't be long; I need to get my face on." The father said as he went to the bathroom to apply the white face paint that would transform him as the second part of the father and son blood sucking team.

Whilst smearing on a coat of make-up, he heard his mobile phone ringing. Unwilling to be distracted, he called out to his son "Tim could you answer that for me?"

Following his father's orders, Tim answered the phone. The father soon realised that his son was having a friendly chat with the person. In order to prevent anything from being revealed, the father asked who was on the phone. "She didn't tell me, but she called you 'Purple'" Tim replied.

There was no longer any need for whitening the skin by using stage make-up, the man lost all colour at the mention of the name. He stopped what he was doing, went back to his bedroom and took the phone from his son. "Could you go downstairs for a moment? Please?" he didn't want Tim to overhear this conversation.

With Tim out of earshot, the man proceeded with the conversation in Russian "Hello."

"Good evening my evil eyed monster. How are you Purple?" the colour was the nickname given to him by a woman he had known for over eight years. A very intelligent creature who seemed to be always one step ahead of him and was not shy to flaunt it.

He had many nicknames growing up; 'Smarty' at primary school for knowledge, 'Tuff' at university because of his accent, 'Cat' when he started his career, then "Pussy" because his colleagues considered him a cat with nine lives having survived many near scrapes with death and finally 'Purple', the name he hated the most and what's worse, used by just one person, the woman who branded him with the name.

"Purple?" she called again after a moment of silence. Just saying the colour brought a shiver to his core. Yet, he knew whom he was dealing with and thus needed to remain composed asking "Oh… it's you. To what do I owe this pleasure?"

"I just wanted to know how you were celebrating your birthday? I see Tim is visiting."

"Yes, he is and I plan to have a party." Purple replied.

"That sounds great. You know, I had an event here in your honour. I took out a target on your birthday, just for you."

"I'm flattered." He lied, he was actually terrified.

"I knew you would be." the caller replied in a sarcastic manner. "You may not care, but I am about to perform a "Scooby doo" without the meddling kids capturing me and explain to you what I did."

"If you insist…" He replied

"Oh, but I do Purple, I do. I think you would be proud of me." Her portentous tone was certain to be the prelude to an ominous tale and he knew it. Yet, his fascination could not let him see reason and he urged "Do go on."

The woman on the phone began by posing a question "You must have heard on the news of Gabriela Pickett, the Judge found dead in Barcelona?" He confirmed that he did hear about her and wondered if she was responsible for her demise "Yes, and I kind of feel bad. She was an upstanding person who only fought for people's right to good governance."

"So, for getting your target, you called to seek a shoulder to cry on as you seek penance for your sins?" He enquired sarcastically. She laughed. "Oh Purple, you are so funny. Of course not, I only felt bad for half an hour and no, she wasn't the target, she was the bait. The target I got rid of a couple of hours ago, actually, he got rid of himself after I asked him to perform a few tasks, what a performance. Actually, I lie; he wasn't the target, more another stepping stone to my goal."

Although he heard what she said, he struggled to concentrate due to the noise in the background. Purple then said "You know, I can't really hear you, there's a lot of activity out there. Want to call me later? Or find somewhere quieter?"

She apologised and asked for his patience as she made her way further from the scene. "This should be better. The noise you heard was the main event and I have been dying to tell you all about it.

I just got rid of a policeman and few others, but they don't matter. I got him to come to a fair with promises of information on the murder of our dear Gabriela and asked him to meet me at the bumper cars. He was quite obliging and even sat in one of the cars; he looked out of place in his Armani suit. I just wondered how he could afford it on a policeman's salary."

"Anyway, I then told him to call me on a number which I had diverted to another phone, which was then diverted to another phone and was continuously diverted till it went to ten handsets, each attached to a batch of plastic explosives placed inconspicuously and strategically on the supporting posts that held up the roof and the electrified grids all without interfering with the power supply.

So when our member of the Mossos d'Esquadra gave me a buzz, the phones rang and set off the explosives. He brought the roof down and gave himself and the others in the tent the shock of their lives." She laughed at her own pun, but the disclosure of this disturbing information almost sent the man she called Purple into a state of silent distress.

Purple had broken into a sweat which caused his makeup to run down his face as he replied "It must have been quite a site."

"Yes it was. I can see them collecting the bodies right now. 13 so far and I dedicate each one to you on your birthday."

Masking his weakening resolve, he replied "That's thoughtful of you… Please, tell me, who you were told to get rid of this time?"

"Well, I know I shouldn't, but since you asked ever so nicely and it is your birthday, I will, yet before I proceed, I am amazed by your question. When was the last time I ever took out one person?

Anyway, it's not a person, or a group of people… it's much bigger Purple, much bigger. Expect to see those who rule to lose their jobs…"

"So, you're after governments now?" He concluded

"You catch on fast." she replied.

Tim could hear his father was still on the phone as his mother arranged the snacks for the party. He was growing impatient having seen some children already strolling past the house in costume. He ran back up to his father's room and called out "Dad? Hurry up!"

After his demand for haste, Tim entered his father's room to find him standing there, still on the phone. Tim, like most children, was perceptive. He could tell all was not well.

On over hearing Tim's voice, the caller concluded "I best not keep you any longer. Send Tim my love and have a fabulous birthday. As you usual, you can try to trace the call, but I'd be long gone by then." She hung up.

The tale of the helpless being burnt alive filled Purple with horror. Few things were scarier than a professional assassin who may have lost touch with reality. He returned to the room where he met his son waiting.

Looking at his father and in a lowered tone Tim asked "Daddy? Are you okay?" He could see the concern in Tim's face. It was time to do some more pretending. He immediately smiled, went forward crouched down and kissed his son on head and said to Tim "I'm sorry, I'll get changed."

## 31 October 2010

The early Halloween celebrations were not just isolated to a small corner of northwest London. In Berlin, someone's Halloween celebrations had come to a definite end in the early hours of the day itself.

In a large, metal dumpster behind a nightclub just off Joachimstaler Strasse, laid Stefan; mangled, bashed and in a critical state. Mortally wounded, Stefan pondering his final thoughts. He was not overwhelmed by feelings of hatred or anger towards his attackers; that was the last thing on his mind.

Stefan accepted he had had a short yet very fulfilling life. "So let the end come!" he initially called; a challenge to Azrael, the angel of death to come for him before the stench of his surroundings grew. The smell was overwhelming, forcing him to think of ways to get out of this maggot infested den.

As he shifted his position in the dumpster, using every fragment of his body and spirit, the only thing that preoccupied his consciousness was his family. Not his biological one, but the one he grew into. Stefan's was flooded with scenes of Khoi, Mikel, Marcel, Paul, Jeroen, Joel as well as his adopted parents Georg and Anita and his long lost friend Ben. It caused a happy sense of warmth which overflowed his body, his memories drowning the pain.

Then worry set in, a sense of unease wavered, he knew how Georg and Paul dealt with anger and grief. Their violent nature could be horrendous if not checked. Stefan's heart ached as he knew he didn't want them to harm themselves, such was his nature, warm hearted and altruistic in his dying moments. He knew that the two would have it hardest, unable to keep a hold of their emotions, too disturbed to deal with them, let alone show it.

A nauseating dizziness initiated by swallowing too much of his sweet metallic blood brought him back to his own immediate reality. Disgorged blood, beer and half-digested peanuts covered his left chin and shoulder. Stefan's breaths continuously became softer and intermittent. His bones were broken, he was bleeding severely, and he knew he was not getting out of this dumpster alive. Yet he did everything to get up and putting his broken arm behind his back, leaning forwards grimacing at every small movement. It was the dying hours of the night; no one was usually out in this area, not even the wrong kind of people.

Stefan was frantic and he had one thing on his mind; he wanted his dying wish to reach them, the people he lived for and soon would die for. He didn't want to betray them or cause them harm. He was resolute about that and it was obvious he'd rather die than let their secrets be known. Though his body was mangled and useless, Stefan allowed his spirit to drift as though it wanted to put him at peace. It began to paint a picture in his mind that gave him a moment of respite as the cold set in.

A sound from the outside of the dumpster caused his slowed heart to beat just a bit faster. Stefan called out into the enveloping darkness, with each dwindling breath it seemed as if the air dimmed. He was out of it, his strength lapsed, slowly tilting his head back, he felt comfort knowing he gave his all. His organs were failing, his senses closing down, this would be the last time he would close his eyes... but he was determined not to die in a dumpster at least without someone familiar to comfort him.

Stefan gasped, grasping and holding onto his last dying breath, using all his power to keep his eyes open. Somewhere in the far reaches of the alleyway something slammed into a dumpster. This was it, his final moment. Some force had granted him his dying wish. Stefan felt a last surge of adrenaline creeping slowly towards his heart. It was the jumpstart he needed. "He...hey .... You over there" Stefan managed to say. Whatever that was making the noise froze. Stefan feared it was some stray feline scouring for a late night snack, yet he pleaded "Oh please I need you, you heavenly being... if you can understand me come to my voice". Stefan was overwhelmed with emotions; a tear ran down his cheek. "I need you, come to me, oh please, don't let me down, not now".

Silence... then as he was ready to give up a second time he heard a small but firm hand grasped the dumpster. "Oh yes, you... you can save them, please..." But the hand stayed there, subtly gripping the edge metal container, as if to exemplify the hesitance and shyness of the person that the hand belonged to. "Hey come on now... Don't be shy!" a little sternness crept into Stefan's voice; he did not want to have his last words fall on deaf ears.

A head gradually emerged. "Mister, I hear you". The words came from a shadow. The lid opened. Stefan's sight was slowly failing him, as the person leaned forward the glow of a street lamp shone upon a girl's features. She had two frightened eyes, a chiselled dirty, yet beautiful face, and long hair. A girl not older than 12 was standing over of him, close enough to touch him, her anxious eyes voiced the unspoken hardships that she had gone through.

"Please listen to me; I need to tell someone something" began Stefan to the terrified child.

"Why are you lying in the dumpster sir? And why can't you tell them yourself? If I don't get back home soon, I'm afraid that I won't be able to speak in the morning" the girl said.

"Come closer dear" Stefan begged.

"Oh sir you're hurt… Please don't tell me you're dying. I'm going to cry if you are" she said.

"No please don't cry. I'm not a person to lose tears over". Stefan's eyes closed, fearing he wasn't going to open them again. Yet, he still had his faint voice. "Little girl, tell me your name and then listen".

"It's Nylah, sir" she whimpered.

"Nylah, you have a beautiful name…" He cringed in pain yet needed to speak "As you can see, I'm dying. But I can't let my friends down. Sweet Nylah can you do two things for me?" Stefan said as his time was dwindling.

"Yes, of course…" she replied

"Reach into my breast pocket" She hesitated, he knew she needed prompting "don't be afraid of the blood, it will wash off… please get my cigarettes".

She grabbed the pack in his pocket, the smokes he bought from Old Jazz also known as "OJ", and the welcoming bar that he and Khoi frequented. "Please put one into my mouth and light it… the lighter is in the packet". She complied and did so hurriedly using the jade covered lighter.

Stefan hated smoking. He only took them with him to give to those who asked and used it as a good way of meeting girls. He had shared his first stick with Khoi, it was a horrible experience and because of it he steered clear from smoking for the rest of his life, until now. He wanted to share this experience as he had with so many others with his friend and he wanted to share his very last one with Khoi.

He inhaled deeply, his lungs hurt as he coughed. Nylah took it out of his mouth. Once he was able to speak, Stefan said. "Nylah it is important you listen to every word I say, do not forget anything, Look for Khoi, he lives at 23 Eisenacher Str. There is gallery there. Look for Khoi and give him the lighter, he will understand, tell him his good friend is waiting for him at OJ's." Stefan coughed again, the smoke choking the last space left in his lungs. "I beg you, come closer, because this may be the last thing I shall say for a long time to come". Nylah jumped upwards, allowing her midriff to cover the edge of the dumpster, leaning her head towards Stefan's disfigured face. He whispered "Tell him it was Lefty... Tell him Stefan sent you."

Then he added passing words which Nylah didn't fully understand, and yet she jumped back down and ran into the gloomy night with Stefan crying out with his last breath "Go my angel, my friend awaits" he said, hoping he'd die with smoke in his lungs and a smile etched on his face because his friend was soon going to find him.

Stefan started imagining what Khoi was doing. Khoi was probably showering, which was usually a quick and systematic routine, was now a rare and thoughtful occasion. He knew Khoi would have felt in his core that something was wrong. Khoi probably reached out of the shower to check his phone though usually when checking his phone he would not get the gut wrenching feeling which he had now. What would have bothered Khoi was the silence.

Putting his hand against the wall he'd use the other to rub his face, as if to alleviate the feeling of dread even though if he would have checked his phone he would have found no message from him. Stefan knew Khoi would panic because generally, Stefan was always careful and would notify Khoi if he had returned successfully from OJ's, the so called jazz bar where Khoi and Stefan shared many great memories, from their adolescent and mischievous teens until just recently.

Since Stefan had promised to come by after the party was over at 2am; it was around 2:30am now and it was expected that Khoi would worry.

Having been in the shower for too long, Khoi would have grabbed his towel dried off, and dressed in something smart, even though he was going to bed shortly; he always aimed to look his best.

Khoi would have craved something desperately, anything to preoccupy his mind while he waited for a response to his frantic message to Stefan. Khoi would have gone to read daily newspaper which he always abandoned by the door under normal circumstances, but this time things would be different. Bending down he would have also felt he was being watched because he was always intuitive.

Stefan hoped Khoi would sense someone standing across the street staring at the direction of the gallery over which Khoi lived. He hoped Khoi would look through the window and find, standing there, a lone girl. A girl who looked concerned, and against his better judgement Stefan prayed that Khoi would go downstairs and open the door.

The idea of a girl wandering about so late at night would normally set alarm bells ringing in anyone's head. Always cautious, Stefan could have put money on it that, Khoi's main concern was not to get involved with any angry parents, or a runaway child. Yet, Stefan banked on Khoi's intuition that he would feel as if she was there for a reason.

Stefan imagined Khoi strolling to across to the opposite sidewalk, looking both ways not just for oncoming cars. When he deemed the area safe, Khoi would call out to the sobbing girl "little lady, what's wrong?" waving her over with his hand. She'd approach him slowly, her face showing signs of concern, pacing as though scared of what was to come. As she drew closer Khoi would have asked "hey, what is wrong". Initially, Stefan expected that Nylah would have said nothing; rather, she would drop the lighter at his feet and turned to dart off. But Khoi is quick; he would have nabbed her before she could have taken her third step. "That isn't nice; don't be frightened, what brought you here?"

She would have whimpered and tears would start rolling down her petite face. Khoi would have looked down and froze, as if a ghost had walked over his shadow. On the floor would lay the jade lighter he gave Stefan for his birthday.

Khoi would bend down and pick it up, his fingers touching the rough but moist carving of the Buddha on the lighter. He'd turn and faintly ask the girl "Stefan?" Nylah would nod. Perhaps it would be then that Khoi would realise that the moisture he felt wasn't due to the mist of the night settling on the lighter, but blood, the sight of which would throw him into a state of shock beyond belief with all the worst scenarios rampaging through his mind.

Khoi would probably hold back the vomit as he wondered what had happened with Nylah whimpered "Mr, he told me to find you and give the lighter to you".

"Was he still alive when he gave this to you?" Khoi would ask repressing every urge to flip and scream at the girl demanding she tell him where Stefan was. But he'd remained calm knowing Stefan wouldn't want him to.

"Yes, he was but he was hurt, bad" Nylah would sheepishly reply.

Stefan could almost hear Khoi shout "Where is he?" terrifying Nylah to cry back "The alley behind OJ's! He said that you would know where it is."

Stefan could visualise Khoi ready to sprint with the lighter in his pocket and as he passed the girl, this time it was the girl that held him back from running. "He said I should tell you this."

Khoi would have been lost in his emotion as he heard the words Stefan said fleetingly. Each word would bring a sob rocking throughout his body. He'd turned and the girl would add her own thoughts "Don't be sad, sir, he was happy, I could see it, please remember that."

In that split second she'd have looked wise beyond her years. Khoi would give the girl a kiss on her forehead, sweetly thanking her.

Knowing him, Stefan guessed Khoi would have said something along the lines of "I shall remember you, and if you stay I will repay your kindness, I'm going to go meet my friend now". Nylah would let go of his arm allowing Khoi to sprint as If his very life depended on it. Stefan could feel Khoi running as fast as his black loafers could carry him. Khoi wouldn't have cared about his shoes; all that'd be on his mind was his beloved Stefan.

It was that feeling of being that kept Stefan going as his vital life signs shut down one after the other. He let his is imagination take over, as though he was watching Khoi in real time running down the street screaming "Of all people, why?", his nose dripping as he wiped tears away with his sleeve, Stefan's words stinging his soul as though being dragged through the thorns of anguish and guilt based on the premise that even though he was mortally wounded, Stefan's thoughts were with his friends and adopted family.

Khoi wished it could've been him instead whilst clinging to a sliver of hope that it was all a joke. The girl said that he was still alive when she left, however the message that she told him sounded as ominous Stefan's message was: "I love you all so much, I'll watch you all from the stars above, just please promise me... don't do anything rash". Khoi picked up his pace, petrified yet eager to be with his friend.

It would have taken Khoi 15 minutes of running before seeing OJ's up ahead. What normally would have taken him 35 minutes was being done in no time. Stefan dreamt of his friend rounding the corner into the alley. Stefan thought he could hear Khoi checking and rattling the back door of the bar, frantically. "Fuck this shit, fucking stupid locked door" Khoi would have screamed in desperation. Probably as he walked backwards, Khoi would back onto the opened dumpster and choose to look inside and there he'd find his friend.

Stefan could almost hear Khoi scream out "STEFAN!!! NOOOOOO!! WHY!! FUCK SAKE! WHY" as reached into the dumpster to touch his body that had beaten to a pulp, head caved, legs and arms broken, his face unrecognizable, his jacket the only thing to identify him by. Khoi dragging him out, resting his body on the floor as he buried his head in Stefan's bloody neck letting out a lengthy sob. "No, no, no, this can't be, not you". Khoi turned around in grief, opened the WhatsApp group and typed "Stefan's dead, come quick" before sharing his location.

In sadness Khoi smashed his phone on the floor, grief overcoming him. He dropped to his knees holding Stefan's face, slapping it gently trying to revive him; Khoi's warm hands would have been a welcomed feeling, if only it were true.

There was no Khoi coming to his side, nor was there any Nylah, there was no one, it was all a lie, an elaborate rouse created by his now still mind. The warmth he felt was the left over kebab an unsatisfied customer thought was better in the bin than in their stomach; Nylah was just a cat that managed to get into the dumpster before leaving and the cigarette, left over butts with the lingering smell of burnt tobacco in them.

All this he knew but chose to allow his mind to create a happier picture where he didn't spend his last minutes alone, at least that's what he told himself. What he saw was what he wished would happen, what he wanted to happen, he wanted to have his friend with him, he wanted Khoi, but Khoi wasn't going to come.

Stefan took his last breath with hot sauce running down his face, mingling with his blood and his last sensation was a cockroach crawling over the back of his hand while he imagined his grandmother whom he loved so much as Nylah appeared to him again, this time with a smile on her face reaching out to him "Time to go Stefan. Khoi will sort it out. You can rest now."

Stefan was finally able to smile and die in peace, safe in the assurances given by Nylah, the angel.

Eight hours after Stefan had taken his final breathe, in the "Hollow Gallery" two kilometres away, Julien was in his office totalling up the figures from the previous exhibition which had closed the day before and despite his best efforts, he found it nearly impossible to concentrate due to lack of sleep.

Everything seemed to conspire, all at once, to ensure he was unable to rest starting with the exhibition held in his gallery ending three hours later than planned, at 11.32pm. The gallery and his office, formed part of the four storey building which included abasement area used for storage, it was a building Julien inherited, and was a complete mess when the initial 50 people invited thought it would be nice to bring friends and thus tripled the number in the space. He decided he would leave all the cleaning until the following morning when the cleaner showed up and went to bed at midnight.

Two hours into his sleep, he heard stumbling sounds and giggles. Khoi, his boyfriend, returned home heavily drunk, making a ruckus as he tried to find his way in without bothering to turn on the lights. He walked through the flat that formed the upper two floors of the building, tipping over a vase on the side table next to the wall. As it crashed to the floor, Julien woke and wondered why he placed another new breakable item there when it always faces the same fate in the end.

Khoi usually returned in such a state every three weeks. As usual, Julien got up, took Khoi to the kitchen and sat him down by the dining table whilst he used a brush and dustpan to clean up the fragments of the vase.

As Julien got up, he heard the sound of Khoi wrenching his guts. This wouldn't have bothered him normally, if it weren't for the fact that Khoi had chosen the kitchen floor to deposit his bile and alcohol infused vomit. This meant more cleaning up for him to do.

Julien went down to the gallery collect the mop and fill the bucket with some water and detergent with the intention of clearing up the spew on the kitchen tiles, thanking his stars that he installed a lift. He walked into the kitchen to find Khoi seated in a daze.

Julien proceeded to start cleansing his kitchen when Khoi got a bit amorous and tried to steal kiss by walking up to Julien from behind, turning him around and forcing his lips on those of Julien. The thought and, much worse, the taste of Khoi's vomit was repulsive. Julien pushed Khoi away and vaulted to the toilet to puke in disgust.

Oblivious to the true reason for Julien's reaction, Khoi felt spurned, he became emotional and started to sob as he heard Julien heave loudly and the sound of the toilet flushing. Julien emerged from the bathroom, slightly traumatised to find on entering the kitchen to find Khoi absent. He could hear movement in the living room and assumed Khoi was there.

Julien filled a glass with water and went to the living room to hand it to Khoi. He found him there in floods of tears serving himself a glass of 18 year old single malt whiskey which, as his favourite, Khoi always drank neat when he felt sorry for himself. "Oh no." Julien remarked running over to relieve Khoi of the alcohol in exchange for water. "You've had enough. Take this."

"Leave… leave me alone." Khoi replied shoving him aside, in the process nearly losing his balance staggering and pointing as he added "You don't love me… no one does."

Julien rolled his eyes at the monthly rendition of what he called 'nobody cares about me' story which always, without fail, follows Khoi's binges. Julien resorted to the tried, tested and now memorised phrase that always seemed to appease the needy beast that dwelt in Khoi "As I said before, I do love you and you don't need to worry, life isn't fair, you don't deserve all that's happened to you, but I'm here now and that's all that counts. OK? Now give me your drink please?"

Khoi didn't seem convinced "why didn't let me kiss you?" he asked sipping his drink. "Do I disgust you?"

"You just regurgitated your dinner and about half a month's wage of an average worker in booze on the kitchen floor and then wanted to kiss me with that mouth? How would you feel? Was that meant to be romantic?" posed Julien. Khoi paused, swayed a bit in his inebriated state and then laughed at how funny the situation was. He unsteadily passed the glass of whiskey to Julien, spilling some on the way as he remarked "You know you always make sense… I'm sorry; I have to go to sleep now."

Julien shook his head as Khoi wobbled out of the living room, his steps stamping hard on the stairs up to his bedroom. With a sigh, he considered the worst was over and turned his attention to the kitchen. Before the mop could touch the floor, Julien heard the distinct sound of Khoi orally purging himself of the rest of his stomach contents again. Julien deduced that Khoi failed to make it to the nearest toilet or even his bedroom. "Oh shit!" he heard Khoi cry raising Julien's concerns.

Julien raced and moaned "oh lord" as he witnessed Khoi collecting some his vomit with his bare hands and then race into the bathroom to fling, the remainder that didn't drain through his fingers, into the toilet.

Exasperated, Julien cried out "KHOI!" Khoi jumped in fright, his foot trotting in what he was trying to clear up and froze, his puppy eyes lowering Julien's anger which was soon brushed away when Khoi added "I'm sorry."

Julien sighed again and refrained from dwelling on the matter further as he offered "Why not leave it and I will clean this up. Go for a shower ok?" Khoi nodded like a scolded child and did as his was told, his dripping hand and soiled shoes ferrying the mess into the bathroom. With the bathroom door shut and the sound of running water, Julien went to work with the mop starting with the kitchen. For some reason he got carried away, cleaning not only the kitchen but the gallery as well which took him all of four hours.

Once done, he moved on to the last patch of his flat that needed sprucing, the bathroom. It was just then he noticed that the shower was still running and Khoi wasn't in his room when he went in to vacuum. Concerned, Julien went to the bathroom. He knocked on the door. "Khoi?" Julien called to no reply. He turned the knob and once the steam dispersed, he found Khoi, fully clothed, sprawled out in the bath with the shower spraying warm water all over him.

Fearful of what potential harm may have befallen Khoi, Julien rushed to turn off the water and check on Khoi. Khoi didn't seem to have slipped in the bath; rather, he looked comfortable "Khoi?" he called.

"Leave me alone." Khoi snarled as he turned to get more comfortable in his make shift bed.

At least he knew Khoi was well and out of the way. Julien cleaned the bathroom floor and toilet, Khoi not even stirring amongst the sound of activity around him.

It was seven in the morning when he Julien put the brush down. He was too exhausted to bother waking up Khoi, besides, he wasn't complaining, so there was no need to worry, Julien concluded.

Julien went his room, thanked God it was Sunday and crawled under the covers in anticipation of sleep which came quickly but the sleep was swiftly snatched away by a repetitive tapping sound at his window. A quick check revealed that winter was coming. Hail stones the size of sugar cubes were falling from the sky.

Folding the pillow over his ears didn't work; neither did improvising earplugs by wetting some toilet paper and forcing them into his auditory canals. Even when the hail stones diminished in size and they turned to rain, the intensity of the down pour was equally as loud as the preceding form of precipitation. There was to be no more sleep for him this morning. Perhaps he would try his luck in the afternoon.

With that in mind, Julien went down to his office to do the accounting and that was what he had been doing until now.

The rain had stopped an hour earlier and it was approaching noon, yet he was only half way through what he was meant to finish on Monday with only the digital radio for company which was no solace. Wherever he turned, the channels seemed stuck, as though a gentleman's agreement, on persistent replay of 90's music or the "rubbish they play today" as Julien considered it.

However all that he could tolerate, but when the winning song of the year's Eurovision song contest came on, Julien could take it no longer. The attempt to use the remote control failed, forcing him to rise from his station and physically switch off the set.

Accepting he would have to be happy with silence, Julien returned to his large leather armchair behind his iroko wood desk to continue his work, when he was interrupted by the door's buzzer. "Oooh!" he groaned. Sluggishly, he left his office, walked through the gallery to open the door. Julien was astonished to find a male and female police officer in their smart uniform of various shades of green, their hats under their arm and a sombre look about them.

Julien's first thought went to Khoi, wondering if he had broken the covenant they had established which was, should the police ever come looking for him, their relationship would come to an end. His blood began to boil, but his suspicions had to wait. "Good morning." Said the female police officer in a rather polite manner "Sorry to disturb you, may we see Khoi Nguyen?"

The tone of her voice didn't signify that Khoi was in any form of trouble, it didn't convey any form anxiety which Julien expected and actually they looked subdued.

"Yes, he's in… he's sleeping." Julien replied.

"May we speak to him please?" requested the female officer.

"Of course, do come in." Julien ushered them into the gallery, the two officers looked nervous, which made him more nervous. This wasn't good.

"One moment" he said as he raced up the stairs, neglecting the use of the lift he installed.

He woke Khoi from his booze induced slumber, his clothes wet and stinking as Khoi sat up startled from being shaken so vigorously by Julien who order him to "Get up, the police are here to see you… they are down stairs."

Still sleepy, Khoi rubbed his face and repeated "The police? What for?"

"I don't know. Just get yourself to the ground floor now." With that command, Julien left to meet his surprise unwanted guest.

Hoping that being hospitable would sooth his growing anxiety, Julien offered them a seat and some refreshments, all of which the two officers refused. Now itching to have this over and done with, he called out for Khoi to hurry up.

Khoi attempted to get out of the tub which nearly saw him crashing to the floor, his leg weakened from being cooped up in an awkward position. Still, he managed to escape the bath. He looked in the mirror and saw how scruffy he had become. "KHOI!" Julien screamed "COMING!" he replied in equal measure.

Khoi quickly stripped himself and changed from his soaked designer wear to his t-shirt and shorts. Thinking ahead, he sent a text to Georg with the words "Call me in ten minutes without fail."

It was an insurance that he set in place should he be whisked away, his phone would ring and Julien would be able to answer the phone he left behind in Julien's room and reveal what ever happened to him. Now he was ready to meet the officers.

Khoi took the lift and upon arrival was met by the two officers. They didn't leap to apprehend him, so that was a good start. Then the female officer spoke. "Mr Khoi Nguyen? Mr Julien Kilpatrick?" the pair nodded. The woman stated her name and rank as did her counterpart before proceeding. "Do you know a Stefan Yur?" That was an odd way to speak, Khoi thought, they used the letter 'a' before Stefan's name… that wasn't good. Yet he nodded his confirmation which allowed the woman to proceed. "I'm so sorry to inform you but we found a body that may be that of Mr Yur this morning. He named you both as his next of kin. We need your help in identifying the body."

It was probably a joke, Khoi thought. Stefan wasn't one to get himself killed, he was the one everyone expected to outlive them all.

Khoi giggled in disbelief parrying the officer's statement "you can't be serious right? What do you mean you found Stefan dead? I saw him yesterday."

"I'm so sorry to bring such news to you sir, and we may be wrong, that's why we would like you, as his next of kin, to accompany us and identify the body… let's hope we are wrong and you can carry on with your day."

It was with great reluctance that Khoi went along with the officers and only relented when Julien was allowed to go with them. As they walked down the corridor at the morgue, an officer and a man in a gown led the way. Khoi's hands got clammy; his mouth began to water as a sickly sweet taste formed. Each step made him wish he refused the offer. Khoi longed to turn back and offer them his parent's name and number; perhaps they could take his place.

A hand touched his, holding it tight, an effort by Julien to provide some sort of reassurance. Khoi turned to him and smiled in appreciation of Julien's efforts despite the fact he was failing miserably.

They stopped at a large metal door which was opened to reveal a clean, tilled, sanitised, room with what looked like lockers stacked to the ceiling. It was like the movies, he just hoped it wasn't going to follow a similar script. It was at that very moment Khoi's courage left him. He broke into a sweat and started trembling before halting his progress. "I can't." he remarked as he whimpered stunning those around him. "Will there be blood? If there's blood I can't go."

Though the others were baffled by Khoi's sudden case of yellow belly, Julien was the only one who knew the source of the U-turn and said to Khoi "this is not the time or the place for your complex…"

"I can't do it…" Khoi reinstated with tears running down his cheeks.

Julien could see the intensity of Khoi's fear and unlikelihood of it dissipating; he drew him close and kissed him on the head. For the officer present though, the display of affection was moving but there was a body that needed identifying. "I'm so sorry." Interjected the officer "We need someone to confirm the identity of the victim…"

"I don't think he can do it… I don't mind doing it alone if it's not a problem?" Julien offered.

Excusing herself, the officer went away to speak to her superiors and returned moments later to ask if Khoi was happy with the proposal and without waiting a second, permission was given by Khoi.

Julien was then led into the room. Despite it being expected, the room with lockers was rather colder than he thought. The man in the white overcoat went to a midlevel locker labelled number 27, pulled it open and drew out a tray with a black body bag laying on it, the contents of which was a corpse. Standing by the tray, the man in the over coat smiled at the officer who nodded, the sign to proceed given. The zipper was pulled down half way. Julien the first reaction was to scream out turning away from the site of the corpse.

On the other side of the metal door, upon hearing Julien's cry, Khoi felt his heart pause for a moment as he imagined the horror of the damage inflicted to the body. Julien, however, didn't need to fathom its state. The face was so pounded that Julien initially asked himself how they possibly could expect him to identify this person, it was most certainly not Stefan, a glimmer of hope flourished like the initial spark from a lighter at the initial strike. It was then he noticed a distinguishing feature that ticked a major box. The hair was curly, the body did have the same sort of nose, the same build, same density of hair on the torso… it was him, it was Stefan.

The stench of the body mixed with an unknown number of chemicals and the site of the blood began to terrify him, it cast aside all trauma and grief the view of his late friend initially inflicted. Julien soon began to understand how Khoi felt as the picture of the broken body caused Julien to shake and lose engagement with his surroundings leading to him to subsequently faint. This was enough to allow those present to assume that it was a positive identification.

Returning to the flat, Khoi, in his zombie state, was led in by Julien, who set the grieving fellow on the sofa, speechless with a blankness in his gaze. Unable to contemplate what to do all Julien asked "Would you like a cup of tea?" Tea, the remedy to everything, according to his English grandmother, Khoi didn't reply. This added to Julien's nervousness, he added "I'll go and make you some. OK?"

Julien turned on the television as he left Khoi behind in the living room, Khoi's mind collecting his memories to quantify his loss.

There was a strong bond with Stefan that even over took any emotions Khoi had for Julien.

Each time Julien would criticize the gang and Stefan, Khoi would reminisce, misty-eyed about how much Stefan meant to him. Stefan's history was also his history and it ran deeper than the relationship Khoi shared with his own brother.

Khoi recollect when they first met; he was six and was bullied and alone, always seen on his own, sitting on the swing. He noticed from afar that he was being watched by a curly haired boy with brown eyes, a year or so older than him. Khoi would wonder whether to approach the boy and try to be friendly, ending his isolation, and then again, he could just be another potential tormentor waiting in the wings. So he never approached him. Yet each day, the boy with black curly hair along with his friends and two twin brothers, would watch him and speak amongst themselves.

Paranoia set in after six days of this. He had almost chosen to abandon the swing all together when his watcher walked towards him. Khoi scanned his face but there was no emotion to be found, so he looked away. He had learnt early that looking away would often allow bullies to let you go in peace rather than to be shoved. Khoi said he was about to get off the swing when he heard the curly haired boy, who had left his friends behind, call out to him "Hi… what are you doing?" Khoi looked up at the boy asking the question and wondered what to say, he was worried he may be in for a punch, so he looked back down again when he was set to walk away again the boy spoke "I'm Stefan. What's your name?" Khoi's intuition kicked in, this Stefan didn't sound menacing and, most importantly, he had a gentle smile about him even though he was much bigger.

Cautiously, he responded "Khoi." Stefan stretched out his hand "Nice to meet you."

It was the first hand of friendship he had ever received at that school. With his mother ill at home and his brother acting as his chosen carer, his life was a lonely one indeed. So, despite the risk, he reached out to shake the hand of his new-found friend. Stefan smiled as he added "come and play with us. My friends and I are playing cops and robbers." And that was it, Stefan was his first true friend, he never forgot this and for better or worse, he promised to stick with him.

The twins were Joel and Jeroen, who initially seemed distant but soon warmed to Khoi's presence among them. Stefan was the oldest, biggest and toughest, he saw Khoi as a replacement for his little brother who had died three years earlier, destroying his formerly happy home by throwing his parents into a never ending state of mourning and apathy.

The identical twins, on the other hand, were crazy. They were mischievous and non-relenting; hence they would take on anyone, and, because they had each other's back, they often won. They fit the twin clichés, often finishing each other statements, agreeing about everything, and more interested in doing things together. They even laughed the same way. The most unnerving fact was that one of twins could tell where the other was without a sound escaping their lips. The only way anyone could tell them apart was when they were writing. This led to Jeroen being called "Droit" and Joel being dubbed "the socialist" but Khoi called him "Jojo".

However with Khoi, their differences were exposed. Jeroen was stimulated by Khoi's intelligence, sparking his creativity and encouraging him to increase his knowledge. The effect on Joel was inevitable, if less spectacular. Jeroen and his twin brother, Joel, who were once seen as below average pupils began to take two different routes. Jeroen forged ahead to battle with Khoi to be head of the class whilst Joel made minimal leaps from being below average to simply average.

While Jeroen's growing attachment to Khoi was due to intellectual pursuits and curiosity, Joel had a love hate relationship with Khoi. He could always rely on Khoi to understand how he felt about things. As well as his growing disconnect from Jeroen, Joel found himself even more reliant on Khoi. Khoi knew how to manage Joel's explosive nature by simply walking away when Joel started throwing a tantrum, returning after Joel had exhausted himself. And that was what Joel hated about Khoi as well, he did, however, love was the time they shared.

They both loved football and played well at the fairs. They also competed at the shooting range and at any event that required physical skill rather than brute strength. Khoi found it exhausting to be mentally and physically prepared for every encounter, but with Stefan, it was different. There weren't competing, they were just friends, each spending time together to escape their problems at home which never seemed to end. With Stefan, he was never lonely again and the added numbers meant he never faced being bullied at school again either.

Khoi's reminiscing was brought crashing down, returning him to the horrors of the present by the news that flashed on the television. A heavily made-up woman with a strong Bavarian accent started talking once the jingle was over announcing "This is the news at 3, the headlines; A body was found in a dumpster close to where a twelve year old girl was found dead a week earlier. It noted that the late girl was child prostitute…"

The news could no longer be heard as the realisation impaled Khoi's heart. It was true, it wasn't just a sick joke and he wasn't dreaming. Stefan was dead. Khoi's emotions, repressed by his deluded hope, tumbled down like a crumbling dam. It caused Khoi to howl in pain, falling to his knees, crutching down in a foetal position.

Julien came running in to find Khoi trembling and weeping loudly. In the midst of the wails the newscaster continued uninterrupted "… the body was found in a refuse container in Joachimstaler Strasse, just three streets from where a twelve year old girl was found brutally murdered leading to speculation that there could be a connection between both killings, Frank Karlson reports…" Before the news could expand on the story, Julien switched off the television hoping it would alleviate Khoi's suffering. Julien knelt by Khoi in an attempt to calm him "hey, it's ok. It's ok. Get up…"

Khoi reacted aggressively, pushing Julien aside as he unfurled, rose and ran to Julien's room, Julien followed from a safe distance "Khoi?" He called, with no reply. Khoi picked up his phone, walked past him and went for the stairs "Khoi!" Julien called again with no response as the door slammed.

Initially Julien contemplated chasing after him, but upon reflection, he thought otherwise and instead looked out the window to see Khoi walking down the street into the distance.

Khoi could not stop crying and didn't care if people noticed him weeping; he had to get to Georg's. He hailed a taxi and once in the backseat, Khoi proceeded to make a call. He wanted to deliver the news but didn't want to do it directly; he feared what the results would be if he did, so Khoi chose to give Mikel a call.

Mikel was in a car on an errand, wondering why he was driving in the pouring rain, next to the person whom he considered the most dangerous and grumpiest "Tasmanian devil" in history, Paul.

You never knew when Paul would get into one of his moods. It was no wonder he was the enforcer for the gang. If you were on his side you were relatively safe, just so long as you weren't double crossing him. It was because of his predictable nature that Mikel, despite his objections, was sent along with Paul.

Paul and Mikel had been driving for hours to get to Amsterdam. It was painful, as Mikel had been sitting silently in the passenger seat, Paul's last words to him being "get in the car", and it felt like eons ago. Their job was to secure a new partnership with a hashish dealer that was in The Netherlands, since the previous one was forced to take early retirement from the business and according to Georg and Stefan via a lovely external contractor, for being too greedy.

This time, they were going to set the terms and if everything worked out well, they would create a revenue stream that would be making them millions.

As they drove, Mikel's mind drifted, searching the recesses of his mind to find something to pass the time. He already had counted the stitches of his window, much like the big presenter Jeremy Clarkson of his favourite TV show. His thoughts were interrupted by a buzz in his pocket. It was his phone. He answered but before he could speak Khoi said "Listen, don't say anything, just listen and do exactly as I say."

"Em… ok." Mikel responded sensing the seriousness in Khoi's tone. "Don't start freaking out or shouting, you know what that might do to our friend Paul…" Khoi sighed, summing up the courage to stop weeping. Finally he said "Stefan's dead…he's been killed…come back and I will fill you in. OK."

Mikel went into shock for a spilt second at the enormity of the news before responding "OK."

"Good… what's Paul doing?" Khoi asked. When Mikel told him Paul was driving, he requested that Paul not be told until they had stopped.

"Understood." Mikel said as he hung up.

Initially, Mikel tried to keep his wits about him, but the grief was too much. "Aww shit." Mikel yelled as he punched the dash board, startling Paul in the process.

"What man, what is it?" Paul asked.

Mikel quickly realized his mistake; he did not want to spur Paul's temper, although he was deeply shocked to get the message. "That was Khoi… Pull over at the next gas station, Mikel demanded". "No, tell me now!" Paul demanded sternly.

"I have bad news, Paul, its serious, stop the car and grab your pen and pad". It sounded like a weird request, but Mikel was always weird, Paul thought, so he decided he would oblige him.

Paul pulled off the highway at a gas station. They got out of the car and walked over to the rest stop, Mikel darting ahead. Paul, not far behind with his pad, was now blotted with curiosity and anxiety. They found a wooden bench and sat there under the shade of the large wooden roof.

Paul was waiting impatiently for Mikel to say something; the silence was making him so edgy, that he started staining the blank sheet of white paper with red dots from the tip of the pen which he continuously tapped on to the pad as Mikel paced up and down, contemplating how he would deliver the message safely. Paul knew that Mikel was scared of his short temper, so he tried his best to concentrate on the task at hand. Paul decided to keep himself occupied and took out a pack of cards which he always carried with him on trips when he had to wait alone or with other members of the gang.

Paul began to shuffle them when Mikel asked "Are you ready?"

Paul replied with a stern "yes".

"Ok well stay calm man, because I have some very bad news..... Stefan's been murdered".

Cards flew everywhere. Before Mikel could appeal to Paul to keep his rage in check, Paul had stormed out off to the side of the petrol station and picked up a dumpster, an item a normal person would struggle to grip let alone carry, lifting it over his head and chucking it a few meters away. As distraught as Mikel had been he was still impressed at Paul's superhuman strength.

Paul uttered a primal shout, which vaguely resembled a war cry. When the cashier at the gas station came out to see what had happened, Mikel quickly ran over to her and explained that they had just gotten some extremely bad news and thrust a hundred euros into her hand, asking her to turn a blind eye ,promising that there would be no more trouble. The shop keeper agreed and returned to her post in the gas station as Paul stood there shivering. Mikel watched from a safe distance. He knew that Paul was sad.

Although Mikel's history and bond with Stefan was brief and casual, Paul had a stronger bond with the dude. Paul looked up to him. Mikel was upset as well and he was going to miss the guy, but it was clear that his was sorrow was nothing compared to that of Paul's who said in a roar "How am I going to repay him now?" It was a worst case scenario and Mikel wanted to avoid any injuries so another step back was needed. He also knew it wouldn't be Paul that would be injured but more likely the people around him. However, Mikel knew that Paul was either bravely managing his sadness or was set to turn into a madman.

Mikel could tell from Paul's blank gaze and silence meant that he was going nuts in response to the news of Stefan's death. It was Paul's blind loyalty and unbridled rage that drew Stefan's attention initially.

That was one of the reasons why Stefan had taken him in. Paul was to become his right hand man, and to act as the enforcer of the gang. Everyone knew him around the criminal circuit, and if Paul arrived alone you were a dead man.

No person idolized Stefan more than Paul did and this was his first time dealing with the death of someone close. Paul could be a gentle, if not, disturbed soul, an intelligent man with crippling anger issues, and for the moment, Mikel's heart went out to him.

Yet, Mikel, from a safe distance, let him vent out his anger for over an hour. Amazingly Paul practiced multiple martial arts he had learnt from Stefan in succession. Mikel could see that even though Stefan was dead, Paul did not want to let him down. It brought a tear to Mikel's eye.

After a while Paul stopped, he said "I know you want us to go back, but we aren't. We're still going to Amsterdam … tell them that." Mikel knew that Paul would be planning his revenge every second of the way; he knew that he had to give Paul as much space as possible. Paul took a deep breath and loosened his fists, Mikel asked "Done"? Paul nodded. They returned to their parked car and drove on toward Amsterdam, still without a word between them. Mikel sent a quick text to Khoi relating Paul's decision. Khoi's response was short "Do as he says." Khoi sighed as he hailed a taxi.

Now that Paul and Mikel were notified, he had to tell Marcel, Daniel, Ralph, Joel, Georg, as well as the official head of the gang and one time world class boxer, Anita, the true brains behind the set up. He would also try to contact Georg wife and their twin sons Joel who was currently being groomed as one of the gang leaders and his brother Jeroen, who due to a car accident, had suffered brain damage and was now kept in a sanatorium.

As the taxi stopped, Khoi realised it now a race against time to reach Marcel before Mikel broke the news to him.

Marcel and Mikel had come into the gang as a pair, joining six years ago and with immediate effect Marcel, the Dutch, French, English, German and Russian speaking giant, won his stripes via his actions. Marcel was famous for his sense of fairness; something that was evident the day Khoi set eyes upon him and Mikel in Neukölln.

He remembered the day clearly. A man walked into the grimy pub in one of Berlin worst neighbourhoods. He looked tired, hungry and wet, but most of all, frustrated. He dropped himself onto one of the barstools. "A trucker's breakfast, please" he said.

The barman, a short, thin man scoffed. "Can't you read? No breakfast food served after 11 am, idiot" wagging his finger at a sign above their heads. The wet man's eyes slowly glided across the letters above him on the sign. He then returned his focus to the barman, and suddenly he lunged forward, grabbing the man's fingers tightly in his hand. "Now, I asked you nicely. I'll ask you nicely again." His large hand starting to crush the smaller man's fingers "an order of trucker's breakfast, Please." The bartender yelped and muttered something inaudible. "What?" cried the irate customer "I can't hear you." He leant further across the bar; bringing his face close to that of the bartender who whimpered as the man squeezed his hand even tighter "It's... not breakfast time anymore. The cook..." The blood appeared to rush to the man's face as his vision focused on the wall clock observing "It is 11:06am. It's still breakfast time for me." He yelled, bringing his other hand to the now thoroughly squished appendages, he started to bend back one of the barman fingers.

"Please oh please oh please... stop! I'll make the breakfast, I, aaaaargh" begged the bartender. The customer let go just before the bone snapped, and pushed the barman causing him to fall to the ground before he quickly scurried off crawling into the kitchen.

The man sat back down, breathing loudly in an attempt to calm himself. Stefan and Khoi had been sitting in the bar for the last ten minutes and were, along with the other 17 people present, appalled, yet no one did anything other than mummer amongst themselves.

Despite their disgust, there was something about the guy both Stefan and Khoi liked. It wasn't so much the looks of him, but the "I don't give a damn attitude" which he exuded. It was so obvious he had immediately caught their interest when he walked in. The man had entered through the swinging doors without concern, carelessly allowing the door to hit the face of the person following close behind.

The man was around 190cm tall, broad and thickly muscled. Although the thick coat, worn to keep away the winter chill, hid much of his form, he walked with the grace of those who were in great shape and used to using their body in asserting the principle of "might is right".

Although he seemed pacified as the sounds and smells of something frying filled the establishment, the man still looked angry. He wiped his blond hair away of his eyes as he looked at the drinks menu, his left leg moving up and down as his hunger grew.

"Is that one of them?" Khoi asked Stefan.

"No, I don't think so, unless that's Marcel… but he's meant to be here with Mikel… I hope it's him." Stefan replied, speaking in a slightly raised voice to ensure he was heard over the radio and over the chatter of the people behind him who were all expressing their variant degree of repulsion regarding the man's actions.

It was then that Stefan faintly heard a familiar voice saying "Come on, calm down. It's none of our business." He knew that voice anywhere. He had heard it for the first time when he went to Cologne with Georg for a meeting with the regional head of the crime syndicate of the North Rhine-Westphalia state. They had been invited to see what potential business could be made by joining forces with those in Berlin a year earlier. It was the voice of the person allocated to show him and Paul a good time in the city.

Stefan turned round to find he was right, seated in far left corner of the bar was a tall and lanky guy. He was immaculately dressed and his suit somehow seemed untouched by the rain. His black hair was greying around the temples, giving him the air of a distinguished gentleman. What were most noticeable were his eyes. They were a very dark blue, and always twinkling and glimmering with what seemed a hidden light. It was this feature that made him so popular with the ladies, Stefan remembered the guy, it was Mikel, and he had brought another person with him.

Accompanying Mikel was a man with a red tint to his skin, perhaps as a result of the cold (the bar was poorly heated) or out of anger, Stefan deduced this was Marcel. With his coat hanging on the rack, and the sleeves of his shirt rolled, he had his arms folded and looked furious as well, and by God, it was clear that you didn't want this man angered.

Marcel was tall, at 2.07 metres and he would probably look down on everyone, even Stefan. Stefan noted Marcel's lower arms were completed covered with tattoos and strained his neck trying to see what they depicted with little success. Mikel looked like a twig next to this wavy, golden haired man with his copper coloured trimmed beard, his impressive chest and broad shoulders. His face would have been round and friendly in normal circumstances, but now it was twisted into a snarl of rage.

Stefan's usual smile grew even wider. Stefan remembered how he had bonded with Mikel and found out a lot about his character. Despite his confidence in the decision to invite the pair from Cologne, Stefan could only watch uneasily hearing Marcel's slightly raised deep voice stating that he was not happy with the man he branded the 'breakfast bully'. There were more verbal exchanges in a lowered tone out of ear shot from Stefan before he heard Marcel remark "I don't care."

Mikel raised his hands in defeat and decided to be a spectator to the next sequence of events as Marcel got up and headed straight for the man at the bar who remained unaware of the 'vengeance' approaching.

Just at that moment, the bartender had returned with a plate of sausages and eggs, his eyes darted at Marcel, towering behind the breakfast bully, but he quickly cast his eyes downwards again and placed the plate on the bar. The unsuspecting bully immediately started eating. Marcel taking the spot next to the man and leaning forward. Quietly, but with a voice deep enough, yet still clearly heard in every corner of the bar Marcel said "I think you should say thank you. It was very nice of him to make you that breakfast." The man just hissed. "Piss off" and continued eating. Marcel did not move. "I think you ought to say thank you, and then apologise."

Stefan could now see the muscled bulge beneath the standing man's shirt and his tattoo that covered his lower arms, the one which ran from the length of his left arm read 'Death is the ultimate leveller'. The tattoos were of no interest to Marcel's breakfast bully who taunted "What the Fuck is your problem? You have nothing to do with this." The man turned his barstool so he could face his aggressor. "Wrong move!" Mikel shouted from across the room, prompting Khoi and Stefan to turn and face Mikel, it was then he noticed them "Oh! Stefan." and proceeded to leave his seat to meet them, all without Marcel paying the least bit attention to the cordialities taking place as he had an oppressor to deal with.

Marcel's arm moved as quickly as a snake and grabbed the man's throat pushing him backwards. The back of his head hit the plate of food on the bar. The bully gagged and tried to fight back, clawing at the wrist that held him down, it was all in vain as Marcel repeated "I think you ought to say thank you and then apologise, don't you?" Grabbing the fork the man had just used to gobble up his eggs, while holding the struggling man down with his other hand Marcel threatened "If you don't apologise, I might have to get really rude. Even ruder then you were to the poor worker in this establishment."

Marcel played with the fork in his hand, letting it catch the light from different angles, before jamming it into the wood just next to the bully's head. The man shrieked in fear, and started to turn a faint shade of blue from oxygen deprivation. Marcel pulled the fork out again. "The next time it will be in your throat. Now, do you have something to say to the barman?" Marcel loosened his grip a little bit, the bar tender had been standing in the far corner of his station, watching as the bully whispered, "I'm sorry" to the smug looking bar tender. Marcel finally released him allowing the man to get up and he hurry out of the bar, ketchup and eggs in his hair.

The bartender's courage seemed to return as he came from behind the bar to stand next to Marcel, where he felt safest, to shout after the man "Don't come back here again you bastard." He turned to thank Marcel for his intervention only to feel a force whacking him on the face, flooring him once again. In a daze the bartender said "What's it with people being so violent today?"

"You!" Marcel shouted. "Stop being rude to people. I am surprised he didn't break your face when you called him an idiot. Don't do that again! OK?" Sheepishly, the bartender nodded. Then the friendly smile returned to Marcel's face as he offered him his hand to assist him off the ground.

The crowd applauded and it was then he was introduced to Mikel Nouta Van Bovenlijven and Marcel de Jong, the children of sisters who both decided to marry Dutch men.

Khoi's reminiscing ended as the taxi driver took a sharp left turn, jolting him back to reality and the present. How was he going to tell Marcel without risking him running out on to the street on a rampage? Quickly Khoi called Mikel and once received, didn't wait for the Mikel to speak as he ordered "Don't tell anyone else you hear me?" "Understood." Mikel replied.

Khoi hung up, ran his hand through his hair in frustration. "Turn here." He ordered the taxi driver, deciding to make a detour on his way to Georg and Anita's.

Khoi directed the driver to Nassauische Strasse, stopping at number 56 he requested that the car stay whilst he went to get Marcel.

Upon reaching the building, Khoi pressed the buzzer at Marcel's flat and waited patiently for a reply. When it came, the voice was raspy, proof of a hangover. Even though he was offered the chance to come up, Khoi replied "Get down here in 5 minutes. There is a meeting at Georg's. I have the taxi waiting. Bring some money or your card." Marcel begrudgingly dressed himself and with the quick use of a cap full of mouth wash came down to the door where a pale, stern, yet distracted looking Khoi.

With his long, straight black hair, which he got from his Vietnamese father, fluttering all over the place, his dark green eyes, genetically passed down from his German/Russian mother, revealed a man who was either in distress or lacking sleep. Yet one could never tell with Khoi because for a guy standing 183cms high and in such great athletic shape that got people's heads turning in the summer, Khoi always looked nervous.

As he drew closer, Marcel expected a smile, Khoi always did that, but there wasn't one. Once he reached Khoi, he asked "Are you alright?" Khoi didn't reply. He just shook his head and walked back to the taxi and took a seat in the back. Something was definitely wrong.

It was a silent ride all the way to the suburbs. At one point during the half hour ride, Khoi sobbed which made Marcel even more uncomfortable. Though he had never seen it, Marcel had passingly heard that Khoi was prone to sever bouts of depression. Fearful he was going to witness it and unable to handle the situation, he chose to ignore him and look out the window as they left the city limits. Khoi eventually managed to gain some resemblance of composure upon arriving at the mansion. Marcel paid the €34 for the ride and followed Khoi to the front door.

Anita was observant enough to see them coming up the path and opened the door to greet them. The grim energy radiated by Khoi was strong as he stood there, trembling ever so slightly. "Good morning Khoi… how are you?" she asked. Khoi bit his lip slightly before responding. "Hello Anita, are Georg and Joel in? Something urgent has come up."

"Yes, but of course do come in. They are in the living room." Anita allowed Khoi to pass, but as Marcel followed, she grabbed him by the arm to have a quick word "What's going on?" Marcel shrugged his shoulders to indicate he was equally in the dark.

Khoi walked in to find Georg enjoying his favourite pastime, watching a boxing match in his plush chesterfield leather arm chair commentating to his audience despite having son, Joel, there to share the event. Joel seemed to be struggling to stay awake let alone pay attention to the match unfolding on TV.

Anita had followed and quickly caught up, announcing the arrival of Khoi and Marcel. The old timer didn't even bother to turn around and look at them as he took a sip of his port "This is crazy! He should have blocked that." Georg cried.

"Georg?" Anita called again "We have guests."

"They're not guests! They practically live here." He replied finally turning. "Grab a chair and stop interrupting my match." He retorted.

Khoi couldn't keep it his secret any longer. He walked past a drowsy Joel to the set and turned it off. Marcel gasped witnessing Khoi's apparent death wish. The sudden loss of sound caused Joel to wake "Huh... what?" he said in a disorientated state. Even Anita knew it was ill advised to come between Georg, a former world heavy weight boxer and his live television matches. He made it clear by asking Khoi "Have you gone mad boy?"

"Fuck your boxing! Stefan is dead!" Khoi cried.

Georg froze, as did most of the room. The silence was universal as they marinated in the news. The glass of port slipping out of Georg's hand as Joel slowly rose from his chair. Everyone fought to find the words to express their disbelief, hoping Khoi was just playing a prank. When Khoi repeated, now heavily sobbing "he's dead... they found him this morning." it seemed clear that it was not a prank after all.

"But we all saw him yesterday... We saw him early this morning." Marcel added in a bewildered state, his voice saddled with sorrow.

"Oh God... what happened? How did it happen? Was it an accident?" Anita asked. Khoi found this the most painful part of all. He shook his head and took a deep intake of breath, then began to weep causing him to break intermittently as informed of where Stefan was recovered, the state of his body, and ,most troubling of all ,the fact that it was no accident. "He was murdered. He had been beaten and stabbed before the murderer left his body in waste disposal container... that's where they found him." Khoi concluded.

"NO!" Georg roared banging his fist on the armrest of the chair as his emotions flipped between misery and ire. Anita screamed as she held her head repeating "Stefan, not Stefan!" before slumping on to the ground weeping. Joel rushed to his mother's side, embracing her tightly as she knelt on the floor, rocking her back and forward, trying to calm her whilst attempting to stem the flow of his own tears.

With those present in the room floored by grief, the only one who remained standing as calm as the thin crust over a volcano about to blow was Marcel with his fist clenched as he asked "You said he was murdered… do you have an idea who did it?"

"No." Khoi confessed.

"What are we waiting here for?" Marcel shouted. "We should be out there asking questions till we get hold of the person! If you won't do it you know that I will…."

"No! Stay here!" Khoi ordered

"Why? The killer may have left town by now! What if they are coming after all of us?" Marcel's eruption had begun in earnest and whilst Khoi tried to calm the situation, he was shouted down by Marcel saying "We have to go, we have to show them we won't take this sitting down!"

"We have to wait and reason. We can't just go there and knock a few people around for answers, we'll just get lies!" Khoi replied

"Yeah, the weak man's approach, you never had it in you anyway!" teased Marcel

"SHUT UP!" Georg interjected "Marcel, you talk like that to Khoi in front of me again and I'll break your legs! You are not going anywhere except the kitchen. Go to the kitchen and wait there till you settle down and are ready to apologise…" Georg then turned to find Marcel still there slightly stunned "Didn't you hear me? Go to the kitchen or must I get up?"

Reluctantly, Marcel left the room.

Amongst the background noise of a weeping woman and her son who was trying his best to console her, Georg for once found himself out of ideas. He looked to Khoi and said "I don't know what to do… I feel like I lost my son… What do we do next?"

"I think we best wait for a few hours… we need to know what the police know. They found him before we did. We can't really do anything except try and cover all our tracks. We don't want them snooping into our affairs." Khoi advised.

"But his killers are out there. We have to find them!" Joel interrupted echoing Marcel's sentiment.

Khoi could not keep his own thoughts on the matter to himself any longer. He looked at Joel and Georg declaring "I agree we need to get those bastards, but we've got to do it in a way that doesn't leave us exposed. The police have the body, we wait for their reports and till then we put our ears out, act like nothing happened and should we get a whiff of any scent of guilt on anyone, I give you my word I would join in any search to hunt the murderer down. I swear."

"No, stay out of this. Let the others handle it!" Anita pleaded "Georg, tell him."

Georg knew why Anita spoke. Khoi was the clean one, and he should never get his hands dirty, yet he had never heard Khoi speak with such conviction and wished to have it affirmed "Did you mean what you said?"

"With every fibre in my being." Khoi asserted.

Georg nodded and concluded. "We do what he says. No one goes out there probing people for information. We wait for the report and then we act." Fixing his eyes on Joel he stressed "Especially you! And go tell Mr pepper pot out there the same!" equanimity soon followed "Khoi?" He called "You go home and rest now. Thank you so much for coming to tell us. We'll inform the others, there will be no meeting tomorrow we'll have it on Tuesday."

"Yes Georg" Khoi responded, leaving the house to begin its period of mourning.

Khoi returned home feeling drained. He walked up the steps to his flat. He could hear the television set was on, tuned to the 24 hour news channel. Each step seemed to increase the volume of the question that repeated itself over and over till he reached the living room.

He entered and found Julien sleeping on the sofa, a half drank cup of tea lay cold on the coffee table. Khoi turned off the television set prompting Julien to wake in time to see Khoi pick up the cup. "You're home." Julien remarked. Khoi did not respond. "Are you alright?" Unable to contain it any longer Khoi asked "How did you know it was him? How were you so sure?" Khoi watched as Julien perched himself uncomfortably on the sofa. "Why do you ask?"

"You told me his face was so mangled you couldn't recognise him, so how did you know it was him?" Khoi asked again. Julien felt uneasy discussing the past considering the current situation but he had no choice.

He took Khoi back to the summer of 2006, less than three months after they moved in together. The heat wave was unrelenting and the night temperature was over 22c by the end of July.

As it was every end of every month, Khoi would work late totalling the figures for the gallery's accounts. Julien was alone at home, drinking champagne, the fan on and every window open to get some air circulating as he tried to keep cool at midnight.

He was watching a movie when he was interrupted. In walked the Stefan. His slightly long, jet black, curly, receding hair was slicked back using a great amount of wax. There seemed nothing out of the ordinary about Stefan barring his new hair style. He walked in as he usually did, with long strides to accommodate his height of 2 meters whilst swinging his arms, almost like a model strutting on a catwalk, and he could have been a poster boy for a fashion house as he was tall, dark, athletic, strong and lean.

There was nothing strange about his smile either. It was a warm, inviting, friendly smile which got him noticed by many possible suitors. Even though it masked the intelligent mastermind of a criminal organisation, it was nevertheless genuine because Stefan was almost always a jovial person and a true gentle giant to the point that he when he was able to delegate the dirty physical work required of his status, he didn't hesitate to do so.

Stefan was a fun loving kind of guy, extremely thoughtful and respectful, so it did come as a surprise that he entered the gallery and made his way up to the living room unexpected and unannounced.

At the door, Stefan, in his white cotton t-shirt and his black jeans, momentarily stood still and the smile seemed a bit crooked. He wasn't wearing his glasses, a near permanent feature of his face as far back as Julien could remember, and his eyes were red.

Despite Stefan's initial faux pas of what amounted to trespassing, He was still able to remember his manners "Good evening." he said in a drunken slurred manner, his being and breathe reeking of booze.

"Stefan, nice to see you… I wasn't expecting you. If I had … I could have prepared for your arrival." Julien responded with an undertone of sarcasm he felt the situation merited to underline his dissatisfaction on having his evening and home intruded. "No need… I just came to see you." Stefan replied as he struggled to maintain his smile and the conversation. Julien could see the sweat running down the side of Stefan's face and wondered if it resulted from the heat or his evident nerves.

The answer came when Stefan began to pull off his t-shirt, causing Julien initially to wonder where this was heading. Then Stefan turned to the left to show off his sore, bruised, marked skin. "Look!" he proclaimed. "I got a tattoo."

"And a large one too… wow!" Julien remarked looking at the detail of the imprinted image of a standing man who had been flayed, draping his skin over his extended left arm "Saint Bartholomew."

"Yeah!" Stefan proclaimed, showing pride in his choice "You didn't expect a Jewish boy to get a Christian saint on his body; you don't see that every day do you?"

"I am not sure I follow the latest fad in the Semitic tattoos weekly, but if it is contrast you are aiming for, I have to admit, I have seen several baptised Christians with Arabic phrases on their body, and besides, Bartholomew was Jewish before Jesus came along and…"

"OH SHUT UP!" Stefan shouted. Incensed he added "This is why I hate you; this is why I can't stand you! You are just too smart!"

"Is that really why you came?" Julien challenged.

Julien could see Stefan quake slightly, as though stripped bare in the midst of an autumn breeze. Nervously, the smile returned intermittently till Stefan could no longer keep the pretence. He took a deep sigh and asked "May I sit?" Julien gestured and directed him to the empty leather arm chair.

Stefan began to heave slightly. He shut his eyes for a moment, took a deep breath before expelling what lay heavy on his chest. "Khoi and I had a fight… it was about you, I wanted him to move back in with Paul and I. I wanted him to move back…" Stefan hesitated and began to rock. The strain of his confession was telling. Julien thought he could fill the silence which was quickly developing by striking a conciliatory note "I know you both are very close…"

"Close is an understatement. You don't know what he means to me… When I was 5, my kid brother died, he was 2, I was meant to watch over my brother but I don't remember what happened, all I remember was my mother and father screaming as they held his lifeless body. He'd drank some kitchen cleaning product while I was busy doing something, I can't remember. What I do remember was the effect; it was like the light got turned out in my house. My parents started to distance themselves from me, they wouldn't touch me; they didn't even want me near them." Then a sneer developed on Stefan's face "It was ridiculous, I went from one bar mitzvah to another, constantly being asked when mine was to be held, but it never came. I never got one. It was as if my parents were punishing me.

When I turned 16 and they assumed I could fend for myself they up and left for Jaffa, content that they had fulfilled their duties as parents as required by the state. They abandoned me and though I now shave, and my voice is deep and my balls may have dropped all the way to Australia… I will never be a man." The regret was evident as the tear trickled down his cheek.

Stefan took a deep intake of breathe before he continued "I was lost and I found heaven in Khoi's home. His brother was out a lot; it made it easy to study and stay for lunch and supper as well. We'd do our homework and he'd cook… and as you know, he's a really good cook. Khoi gave me my first taste of ham and showed me how to eat prawns. Eventually, during one of my visits, he was serving me some noodles, and I couldn't help it, I grabbed him and kissed him. I took off his shirt and mine as well drawing him tightly to me, feeling him near me… I gave him a blowjob and wanted to go all the way, but then he stopped me, the bastard stopped me… he told me 'it would spoil our friendship.' I don't know if he was right but I became angry with him… I left and I didn't speak to him for a couple of weeks till I got over it. So yeah, you could say Khoi was my first too."

Julien did hope this shocking revelation would bring Stefan some form of relief, but it failed. Unable to keep his silence, Julien asked "Why… I mean you are straight, so why did you do that?"

"Maybe I am not totally straight…maybe I was desperate and wanted some human contact so badly that I was willing to give up my faith and put aside my sexuality just to have someone hold me… do you understand?"

"Yes." Julien concluded.

Stefan put on his shirt, reached into his pocket and produced the keys to the flat. "I stole them from Khoi earlier this evening during our argument." When asked what it was about, Stefan confirmed "I already told you, it was about you. I tried to get him to leave you and move back in with me remember? Guess that will never happen." Stefan got up and proclaimed "time to go."

As he was about to leave, Julien called out "Stefan?" Stefan stopped, unable to stand still. Julien got off the sofa and wrapped his arms around him giving him a hug. Stefan in turn held him close. "You can come by anytime if you need a hug, but it's up to Khoi to decide if he wants to come back."

"I know." Stefan conceded "just take care of him will you?" He concluded as they released each outer. Stefan proceeded down the stairs, nearly tripping as he left the building. It was the tattoo that was revealed that night that allowed Julien to positively identify the body as Stefan.

Khoi seemed to giggle as he remembered that evening. "You know, he did come to me in the office, he'd said he had been drinking with the guys and started telling me that the flat wasn't the same without me and Paul was becoming reclusive again. He kept asking if you pissed me off in any way, if I was unhappy." Khoi's voice appeared to crack a little with grief as he persisted. "I told him no, I told him I was happy, I would visit and all that. Then he called me selfish and ungrateful… I don't know what I said to him but we both found ourselves shouting at each other, he was crying telling me to shut up and that I was laying into him, I don't even know what I called him, but I was vicious anyway, even though I knew it hurt him. He approached me and wanted to hold me but I pushed him away… I told him to 'fuck off' and he did. I hurt him, I don't know if he ever forgave me." With a mournful lament of regret Khoi concluded "Too late to ask isn't it."

Julien tried to find the right words to calm Khoi's troubled spirit, but remained speechless, he didn't need to bother anyways as Khoi looked down and said "I best wash this cup and go to bed… thanks."

"No problem." Julien replied as Khoi went to the kitchen. He could hear the water running and faint sound of sobbing. He'd had enough of that sound for one day. Julien turned on the television again and tuned in for the late afternoon movie.

.

# 2

*3 November 2010*

The meeting was convened at the spa resort just at the periphery of the city. It was one of the legitimate divisions of the business. It was their venue of choice when they had big projects or situations to address and no situation was bigger than the loss of one of their own.

Khoi had arrived 7am, two hours early. He'd started to sleep walk again and it often led him to sleep poorly. Better busy than bored he decided and he took the opportunity to catch a cab to the resort and do some work from the designated meeting room.

An hour later, whilst calculating the outgoings of the new 24 hour gym, a text arrived from Joel. "Dad can't make it. He's in hospital. Minor chest pains, nothing serious. I will be there on my own though." The news was a bit alarming. Khoi knew Georg never gave up his tough guy act even after he gave up boxing.

The 'nothing serious' was an understatement. He more than likely had another minor heart attack, Khoi contemplated before shuddering in guilt for thinking such bad thoughts.

It was time to stem the tide of negativity with more paperwork. Looking through the pile of papers Khoi noticed one that read "expenses" and it belonged to Stefan. , He could tell how the money was spent and what he bought. He noticed the amount of €10 again and again, it the price of a cocktail called "old smoky" and it was all Stefan ever drank when he went to OJ's. It was odd however, as Stefan never bought the same drinks, he seemed to have some kind of phobia about it. He didn't mind buying everyone the same round at once, but when it came to his own drink, he would purchase it individually. Stefan didn't believe in a bar tab either; he didn't like surprises, even though he was never able to prepare for them.

Holding the expense paper gave Khoi some comfort. The impromptu meeting he had with Georg and Anita earlier had trashed his emotions. They had discussed Stefan's funeral arrangements. He would have a small wake with the gang, just his friends and his 99 year old Grandmother who was in the latter stages of Alzheimer's. Anita had remarked "When I told her the bad news about her grandson, she kept asking if it was safe to come out. She was afraid of being found by the gestapo apparently." Her affliction had resulted in her being sent to a home when Stefan was 17. Yet, the old woman did remember Stefan, but as a 6 year old with a constant runny nose making her incapable of fully understanding her grandson's demise. In spite of that, she was to attend the wake before the body was flown off to Israel, accompanied by Anita and perhaps Khoi who would be met by Stefan's parents and his two younger sisters whom Stefan had never met.

The absence of his family had always been festering wound in Stefan's life. They left him in his grandmother's care when he was 16 and left to start a new life without him in Israel, promising they would send for him.

Prior to the popularity of email, Stefan would write letters in hope that one day they would announce was time to join them. His parents would always claim that something gotten in the way whether it was a lack of suitable accommodations, or that they were still searching for employment, even a pregnancy. When he turned 18, they reasoned, "You are a man now, your grandmother needs you. It would be unfair for you to leave her in her condition. We do not think you should come and live with us; your place is in Germany. We will send you money. Feel free to visit when you can."

Khoi could vividly recollect that day. It was the day before they were to take their math exam in their final year of high school. And Stefan had come over to his place weeping, asking between tears why his family didn't want him.

Stefan didn't go to the exam the next day. Feeling rejected, he wrote to his parents, and told them that he never wanted to see them again, adding he had a new family now; one that cares about him. Before the letter was even able to be ferried into the back of the van to the sorting office, Stefan had immediately left the flat to swear allegiance to Georg and demand his place in the gang.

It was thus surprising the parents insisted Stefan's body be repatriated to a land he had never been to have a proper Jewish funeral. Khoi was invited, but his sense of outrage regarding Stefan's parents was too intense to bring him to take the flight.

Lost in reflection, Khoi was startled when the door opened. Marcel walked in first followed by Ralph and Daniel. "Hey" Marcel said to greet him. Khoi got up to shake his hand, but Marcel drew him in for a hug and a patted him on the back.

Sitting around the table, no one could speak; they simply couldn't find the words. So they stood there for a two minutes avoiding eye contact, each one consumed by varying levels of self-recrimination until Joel walked in. He was feeling a bit awkward watching them all looking sombre, so he asked "Are we having a moment of silence?" They laughed and greeted him then followed up the question as to the whereabouts of Mikel and Paul? It was confirmed that Mikel had stated they were on their way.

They all took their seats, and before Joel could launch into the meeting, Mikel had entered looking flustered. After everyone present gave their thoughts on the murder of Stefan in a few words, everyone turned to their attention to the elephant absent from the room. "Where is Paul?" asked Marcel as Mikel took his usual seat next to Khoi. "He isn't coming." Mikel announced. A pause followed then Joel asked "Does he know there is a meeting?" Mikel nodded prompting a follow up question "weren't you meant to get him?"

"Yes, and I did go and pick him up... let's just say he's not ready for meetings?" Mikel diplomatically summarised.

"What the fuck is wrong with that kid?" Joel began in a low voice which progressively went higher as ranted "Is he the only one that lost someone? I mean we are all here? What does he think we are going to do? Gossip about the latest fashions in Moldova? Selfish idiotic dick head! I am going to go and get him!"

"Jojo, could you calm down before you get yourself all worked up for nothing?" Khoi suggested. "Look, I will go and get him. You know what I think already. You sort out the meeting guys, Mikel and I will sort out Paul."

With that, Khoi got up taking despondent Mikel with him for the journey back to his old pad. On the way, Mikel got a bit of a grilling. Reluctantly, Mikel let it be known that Paul didn't take the news of the death too well. He admitted he and Paul had a chat whilst in the Netherlands, surprising Khoi by adding, "The little bugger had a lot on his chest."

Khoi asked what had happened when Paul was asked to attend the meeting, "I went to get him at the flat and he was plastered, Mikel replied, and he said he didn't see the need to come to the meeting." This was alarmingly and unusual since Paul was obedient to a fault.

Arriving at the building, Khoi used his old key to enter, and ascended the stairs up to the flat. At the door he heard the loud sound of rap music. Khoi recognised the song as one of hip-hop albums from Stefan's collection and currently Stefan's favourite song was playing. It was strange to hear the music being played because Paul couldn't stand hip-hop.

Khoi unlocked the door and upon entering, was hit by the stale smell of alcohol; there was evidence of drunkenness everywhere starting with the uncollected empty bottles that could be seen from the entrance. As they went further down the pathway that had been created by the bottles the music grew louder. In the parlour were the empty containers of take away and pizza and Chinese food were festooned across the carpeted floor. They saw no sign of Paul though.

Khoi could hear something other than the music, but couldn't make out what it was. Reaching the stereo, he turned down the volume and the sound of a running tap could be heard followed by a groan. Khoi ordered Mikel to stay behind. Khoi proceeded to head upstairs to the bathroom where he found the door slightly open.

Through the gap, Khoi watched unnoticed. Paul was there, his lower arm in the sink as though washing something thoroughly, or so Khoi thought before he noticed the droplets of diluted blood running down the side of the white ceramic basin. A more acute observation revealed that Paul was scrubbing his left arm ,using a metal scouring pad normally used to get out burnt food from the bottom of pots, in such an aggressive manner that the metal tour through the layers of his skin.

Paul paused to look and in exasperation cried "Why won't you come off?" before continuing with his task. Periodically he would wince as the pain got too much, but Paul seemed determined. "Come on, come on, leave!" he cried.

Having decided he had seen enough of this unnerving self-mutilation, Khoi quietly called out to Paul "Paul?" he asked. Paul turned and with his lips quivering and his eyes streaming with tears, interrupting his scrubbing and showing off his forearm, the tattooed area rubbed raw, dripping blood. Khoi could hear a tone of insanity in Paul's voice as he said "It won't come off… It won't come off." Paul then quickly returned to his task, placed his arm under the running water and carried on scrubbing. Khoi knew the situation had to be handled with the skill of bomb disposal expert.

Khoi set forth calmly, and stood behind Paul and asked "Why do you need it to come off?"

"I don't know." Paul snapped "It just has to go… it just has to go" he repeated the phrase over and over even when Khoi reached out to him, holding his wrist gently, calmly urging, "It's ok Paul. You'll get it off later."

"It won't come off, it'll never leave me. I'm marked" Paul replied as Khoi slowly pulled the hand that was holding the scouring pad away from his flesh and repeated to Paul "It's alright. It's ok. It'll leave... I promise." Paul seemed pacified and Khoi took the pad out of his hand and left it in the sink, ushering him out of the bathroom.

Paul seemed to have entered a state of abstraction as he was coaxed to his room. He sat on his bed not speaking, the alcohol he had consumed sedating him. It allowed Khoi to leave the room, and with his mobile he called Mikel, instructing him get the car ready for a trip to the hospital adding that no matter what, Mikel must act as though nothing was wrong with Paul.

Mikel did as he was told; he didn't say a word when Paul and Khoi emerged from the building, with Khoi's coat draped over Paul's shoulders. Seeing the misery in the air, Mikel decided to lighten things up as he opened the door to the back of the car. "Hey, you ok? Had a party without me? I thought we were going to cut it in Holland?" Mikel's teasing caused Paul to smile.

Khoi helped Paul in and prior to departure, swore Mikel to secrecy before ordering that Mikel take Paul to the group's private medic for treatment adding "take the medic to your flat and don't allow Paul out of your site till I say so." Khoi promised to join them later.

As the car vanished in the distance, Khoi was able to pay attention to his own condition. The rush of saliva into his mouth, the sweating and shaking, the racing pulse, and disorientation all a prelude to Khoi suddenly finding himself bent forward vomiting heavily and to such an extent that his stomach began to hurt. It left him exhausted as he had thrown up five times in quick succession. Once he had recovered he called the gang and asked that the remainder of the meeting be postponed until the following day.

*7 November 2010*

Khoi was feeling slightly stressed a few evenings later. As he made his way to the meeting, he wondered what sort of a reception he would receive after changing the meeting date again and for having missed the wake organised in Stefan's honour.

One of the reasons for the postponements and absences was Paul's crumbling constitution. Over the past few days Paul had gone mute, and the only sound he made was when he cried. He ate his food and drank water to prevent himself from being pestered by Khoi but once done, he would return to the spare room in Mikel's flat. No matter how much he tried, Khoi could not coax him to talk.

Arriving at the meeting, Khoi began to wonder if the services of a grief councillor might be required, however upon opening the door, he realised that, for now, a peace keeper would be more useful. There was no warm greeting, no hello, just long dagger like looks aimed at him as he entered. "Good evening." Khoi said, although he was expecting no response.

He took a seat next to Marcel, the only one in the room that he felt safe around for the moment, and Joel sat down across from him. Khoi proceeded to apologise to Joel for being twenty minutes late when he was cut short, "Fuck your apology. Where were you yesterday?"

"I'm so sorry I couldn't attend the wake, I had to take care of some pressing issues." Khoi replied

"Oh? Something that couldn't wait, that's why you let my mother fly out to Tel Aviv on her own. That's just disrespectful man. And where are Mikel and Paul? Couldn't they find the time to join us either?" Joel remarked sarcastically.

Feeling attacked, Khoi responded "Paul isn't well, Mikel is taking care of him, your father excused them from attending and that's that. OK? I really am sorry for missing the wake, the pressing issue was Paul. He really isn't well…"

"Is he alright?" interjected the caring voice of Marcel.

"He'll be fine." Khoi was glad the question had been asked; it allowed him to push the topic away from his tardiness and focus on the situation at hand. Khoi began, "So, we are here to review our current positions now that Stefan is gone and we should look at the reassignment of roles… Mikel will be taking over the …"

"Khoi what the hell is this? You came here to talk about positions? Fuck that; let's talk about getting the bastards who caused this change in positions in the first place!" Joel asserted while banging the table with his fist receiving a cheer of support from those around him.

Khoi could see that he could was losing control of the situation and tried to call the meeting to order but Joel still had more to say "While you were busy mothering Paul, exhorting posh boys and sorting out the schematics of your fictitious cooperate structure, we have been wondering what happened to justice. Screw your changes!" Joel's statement led to a short applause from those around. Khoi sat back in his chair and waited patiently for the lynch mob to subside for a moment. "Well, what have you got to say?" Joel challenged.

Khoi knew he had to be diplomatic because Joel's volatility was clearly infectious at the moment and had to be contained, so he chose to surprise them by saying "I agree with you." stunning the room before he added "I don't intend to stop you in your quest for justice, I actually will actively support it. So Joel, do you know the person or persons who killed Stefan?"

"Yeah, it's the damn Ankara boys." Joel asserted with such conviction that it almost brought Khoi on side. Luckily, Khoi's common-sense intervened. "Got any evidence of this?"

"We don't need evidence. They tried to kill him before and even attempted to take my life!" Joel replied

"Yes. And we addressed the matter, I doubt they'd have the balls to give the issue another try..." but in mid-sentence Joel rebuffed "Yeah, yeah, that's what you think. Dude, I know it's them and we have to strike!" Joel exclaimed and the others nodded in agreement, Khoi just sat there his mouth agape in astonishment.

"I can't believe this." Khoi remarked "You can't seriously be going along with this?" Posing the question to the team "The Ankara Boys wouldn't dare it, the code..."

"FUCK THE CODE! Do you think the people who killed Stefan cared about the Code?" Joel. Khoi shook his head remarking "This is stupid." This provoked Joel to retaliate again "What's stupid? Our friend's dead and the killers are out there somewhere and that's stupid? Do you want them to get away with it?"

This touched a nerve in Khoi who felt he was being forced to prove his loyalty "Come on, you know that's not what I meant. I want the guilty parties brought to justice as much as you do..."

"Then approve my request. Grant us permission to go after them and let's make an example it..." this was followed by a cheer of accord. Khoi could take it no more and had to shout out "NO!"

Joel goaded "I knew you would say that you fucking coward. You can't stop me."

"I don't want to stop you." Khoi began as his voice began to grow louder "You usually do what you want anyway regardless of the warnings people give you, look how far that's got you?" Khoi knew it was a low blow by the sight of Joel grinding his teeth, but he had to say what needed to be said to make his point "I'm not saying we shouldn't seek vengeance, I just want us to get the right people. If you go out there and start targeting the Turks without justification you'll have a gang war making all of us a target and as we shed blood amongst ourselves, the real perpetrators will watch with glee as we annihilate ourselves. You can call me a coward, fine, I am a coward, but I want concrete proof of their culpability. If I get that I'll gladly throw away the rule book and back you up. If you can't find proof then you're on your own… and be rest assured that I'll get your dad involved too"

"Fuck you, you bloody dictator!" Joel screamed

"Oh, ok. Dictator, am I?" Khoi stood up and asked "Who wants to go out on a killing spree based on Joel's hunch? Come on? Anyone? Raise your hand?"

There was an utter silence that followed, no one was willing to show their opinion, with the exception of Daniel, who seemed reluctant at first but then raised his hand prompting Khoi to chastise him "Oh come on Daniel, stop being a dick!" Daniel quickly retracted his hand leaving Joel fuming but having no choice but to accept defeat.

Seeing he had caused Joel to lose face, Khoi tried to strike a conciliatory note offering him a handshake "Look, as I said, I am all for getting the bastards that took Stefan from us too… he meant the world to me and you know that, but we need to be wise about this. You get the evidence to back up your suspicions and I am in." Khoi hoped Joel would take his hand to seal the deal, but it was slapped away by a disgruntled Joel who promised "I'll get you your fucking proof." Before storming out of the room and slamming the door behind him.

The others, feeling there was nothing else to add to this fiasco, slowly rose and left the room, the last to leave Marcel who said to Khoi, "You were right to pull the brakes… we're all a bit crazy right now and we needed a cool head to prevail." He walked over and patted Khoi on the shoulder before he left.

Khoi slumped into his chair and shuddered as he wondered what was getting himself into. He realized there was no point trying to work at this point with his mind being so troubled so he decided to straighten things up and return home.

When Khoi arrived home he immediately noticed there were several people wandering around the gallery, taking away packed items... For a moment, he wondered if there were some financial troubles he wasn't made aware of.

He hastily entered the building, where he saw a hive of activity and fittings being removed. In the midst of the chaos was Julien with a smartly dressed, enthusiastic individual on his knees reviewing what looked like floor plans. The man was pointing and gesturing with his hands toward Julien who looked rather sceptical.

Then Khoi suddenly remembered. The proposed refurbishment of the gallery was set to happen soon. Khoi rolled his eyes he had completely forgotten about it. He crept past; try to remain unnoticed by Julien, who, noticing him called out "Hello Khoi." Khoi didn't reply as he went up the steps to the flat. Julien picked up a pencil and drew circles on the paper.

There was no additional chatter from Julian, and with a heavy sigh, Khoi was relieved. Hoping to drive his hunger and angst away, he opened the fridge. He had hoped to find something to consume but was disappointed to find it empty with the exception of some rye bread and ham prompting Khoi to mumble to himself, "The idiot left the bread in the fridge, why does he do that? Well, at least I have supper sorted out"

Having assembled his 'supper', Khoi examined his cup of tea and so called sandwich. Looking at the pitiful meal in front of him was enough for him to lose his appetite. He left the food on the coffee table and turn on the television, sitting there for a moment to watch some random comedy program. Thankfully the TV was enough to distract him.

As he chuckled at the jokes, his eyes caught sight of his knitting needles and wool in the basket beneath the table; it was the half-finished scarf he had been making as a present for Kat because she always seemed to lose hers.

Knitting was a skill Khoi and his brother learned from their mother. Khoi knitted as a means of relaxing, and right now, he was desperately in need of relaxation.

Clutching hold of the pins, he started; the clattering of metal touching one another eased his mind. He was so dedicated to distract his mind from his current situation that knitted so vigorously he finished the project. For the first time, Khoi realised knitting could also be exhausting. Along with the laughter of the audience to the stand-up comic's jokes humming in the background, Khoi fell asleep completely abandoning his food.

After several hours, he was awoken by a shove. Khoi was still groggy when Julien asked "finished with this?" pointing to the left over meal and tepid tea. Khoi nodded.

Khoi, still laboured by sleep, stretched and yawned before reaching for the finished scarf from the table, lifting up in the air and called out to Julien. "Hey! Give this to Kat on her birthday for me will you?"

"Leave it on the bed so I won't forget." Julien ordered as he cleared the food away and decided to consume the sandwich himself whilst disposing of the tea.

Julien continued, "So, have you organised alternative accommodation?" Khoi gave a blank stare as the words floated around in his mind, however Julien could already read the response in Khoi's face and he wasn't at all pleased, remarking "Oh my God, you forgot didn't you?"

"I'm so sorry. I've had a lot happening lately…" Julien wasn't pleased with the excuse snapping "We all have a lot on our plate, but this has been on that very same plate since June! Every week I remind you 'Khoi, the flat isn't going to be habitable for 6 to 8 weeks, as you know Kat and I are off to Asia, where are you going to stay?' was I speaking Greek? We have to leave by the weekend."

"Don't worry about it. I'll sort something out." Khoi replied. Julien gave him a disapproving look which spoke volumes and Khoi quickly added "Don't worry, I promise I won't stay with the guys. I'll find a hotel or something." Khoi got up and left for his room to his bedroom to contemplate his next step.

Julien looked at the well interwoven material. This was something Khoi excelled at, a creativity that Julien often forgot about. It was made from Khoi's favourite colour, royal blue, which he shared with Kat and he bought many balls of yarn of the same colour which Julien considered rather boring, but this time, holding the gift in hand filled Julien with guilt and went to meet Khoi in his room.

Tired of his own perceived nagging, Julien tried to ease the situation "Are you sure you can't take time off to join us? Everyone needs a holiday and Kat would love to see you." Khoi once again declined citing some pending work deadlines as an excuse instead of telling Julien the truth which was his concern for Paul. To be honest, Khoi would have loved to tag along because he missed Kat whom he hadn't seen in over four months.

Kat was the third child of two career diplomats who had served as ambassadors in various countries, she had just moved to Berlin to follow in her parent's footsteps, taking her place in amongst the ADCs in the new capital of are united Germany.

Kat was more like a sister to him. Khoi had known Kat since he was 9 when she frequented the bar his brother worked at called "Tiff's Café". Khoi was allowed to sit in the backroom to do his homework or practice his piano skills as his brother worked. He became so adept on the instrument the owner of the café had it brought out front to a secluded corner of the restaurant where Khoi could play and entertain the guests. In addition to receiving free food, Khoi also received some money from the owner.

Khoi remembered the first contact he had with Kat. He was busy stroking the keys, playing a piece by Chopin. A stylish lady of average height, with blond hair and powder blue eyes, approached. He walked up placing 20 Marks beside his glass of milk and complimented him. "Well done young man." Her smile was so warm it filled Khoi with a freedom had never contemplated. The girl introduced herself as Kat.

He thanked Kat for her generosity and went to show off his acquired funds to his older brother who promptly informed him to return it. When he did as he was told, he realised this girl possessed a fire within her as well. She marched to the kitchen and gave Khoi's brother a good talking too.

Everyone present could hear the scolding being meted out "Don't you wish to encourage his talent? Or is it pride that's getting in your way of appreciating him?" The confrontation worked and Khoi was allowed to keep the money. The consequence being that his practice time soon became a little bit more of a money maker for Khoi. Kat was often there with her friends, employees of the various Embassies and State representatives to enjoy the music and they in turn left him tips.

Eventually, Khoi's brother began to appreciate the additional income, as well particularly with things being so hard at home. Khoi in turn had a sense of accomplishment for having contributed to the family funds.

Khoi started looking forward Kat's visits to the cafe. She made an effort to get to know Khoi better and each additional day drew them closer to one another, particularly when she found out about his family circumstance.

Orphaned at the age of 8, Khoi's only immediate family was his big brother, Vania. Vania was 9 years older and endeavoured keep him and little Khoi together. Vania put his education on hold and with the help of their mother's friend who owned the café near their house he got a job. He was initially washing dishes before graduating to being a waiter and then a chef's assistant.

Khoi admired his brother for his hard work, but like most teenagers, he loathed him sometimes for constantly insisting that Khoi focus on his education. It was his persistence that ensured Khoi always remained top of his class. Of course once Kat knew of this, she regretted being so hard on Vania.

Over the years, the bond between Khoi and Kat grew. Khoi came out to Kat when he was 14, two years before even telling his own brother and it was also her guidance that allowed him to be more comfortable with his sexuality. She wondered why Khoi was so reluctant to speak to Vania "He probably knows already." She surmised. However by the time he did tell his brother about his sexuality, the situation at home was already taking a turn for the worse.

Khoi had turned into a mid-teen terror, disobeying his brother despite his best efforts to curtail his movements and limit his associations. He considered Khoi's new found friendships with Stefan and his ilk a bad influence.

Khoi began to skip classes, though his grades didn't slip and it incensed his brother, causing Khoi to run away from time to time to Kat for comfort, often weeping or in a rage, and she would sooth him. Once he had enough of his brother's complaints, Khoi moved out and their relationship went into terminal decline.

This was in sharp contrast with the relationship he had with Kat. Their friendship had grown to the point that Kat was now the only constant in his life. Even when she found out whose Khoi's associates were, she didn't judge him; all she would say was "please stay safe".

Kat was there for all major moments of his life but none was more important to Khoi than the day she introduced him to Julien. Watching Julien clean the kitchen area brought back the gleeful memories of that day.

It was his twenty third birthday and she had invited him for a night out at a newly opened bar which had rented the skateboard park as part of the evening's entertainment along with some ice sculptures which were melting in the late summer evening heat.

Kat had got them in quickly and the bouncers seemed to know her by name, if only in a cordial manner. The room was cold as a result of the solidified water sculptures and there were people dancing everywhere, the laser lights swinging about causing an astonishing display. Khoi paused to marvel, but Kat held his hand leading him further through the crowd and to the back door that was opened wide leading into the skateboard park with a crowd dancing within it and only a couple of people using the park for the purpose in which it was originally built.

Then Khoi heard Kat cry out "Julien!" Khoi looked around searching for the lady concerned, only to find a guy walking towards them. He was the same height as Khoi and very good looking with green eyes, dressed in a t-shirt and camouflage trousers with baby blue eyes and the same full beautiful smile as Kat often wore. The similarity was justified; they were first cousins. And Julien was the offspring of a German carrier diplomat and New Zealander art professor.

Julien gave Kat a hug, lifting her off her feet. Khoi then got a warm smile from him as he said with a strange almost English accent, in German "so you must be Khoi." Khoi had been stunned by the sight of Julien. He was unable to speak causing Julien to do what became a staple in their relationship "Oh well, let's go to the table. Perhaps you'll have more to say there. Come on!"

Julien led the way to a small table in a booth where there was a bottle of champagne in a bucket of ice and three waiting glasses.

As they sat, Julien served the drinks and asked "So Kathrin, Khoi, how was your day?" But before he could receive a response, a girl came over and called out Julien's name insisting on having a dance. Appearing to be a gentleman, Julien got up and proceeded to dance the tango with the wild lady. Khoi was mesmerised by his movements on the dance floor. Kat was speaking to him, but he wasn't really listening. As the song neared the end, he felt the glass of champagne leave his grip.

Khoi turned and there was Kat who had mischievous grin on her face "Don't just sit there, go and get him!" she ordered. Khoi's heart almost stopped at that point, yet he didn't want to seem rude, he asked "Are you sure?"

"Go, go!" she instructed.

Khoi got up and walked through the crowd as another song began and Khoi drew closer to Julien on the makeshift dance floor. Their eyes met, and Julien gave him a smile again. Julien whispered some words in the ear of his dance partner who laughed and they both walked over to the bar to have some shots.

Khoi continued to follow them until Julien's dance partner spotted Khoi, calling him over and handing him a shot of tequila. At the count of three, they all took the drink in one fluid motion. The shock of the alcohol caused Khoi to close his eyes momentarily, when he opened them, he was being offered another shot, but the girl who had been dancing with Julien was gone.

To be polite, he took the drink from Julien. Before he could make any excuses, he was grabbed and given a deep French kiss from Julien just before he ran off into the chaos of the dance floor. Shocked by this display, he attempted to follow Julien but could not locate him.

Eventually, after five minutes of searching, he heard a cheer from the far side of the half pipe. Intrigued, Khoi walked over and found Julien, on a skateboard, doing some great moves on the ramps, flipping and twisting in mid-air, amazing the spectators. This graceful display only drew Khoi closer to Julien.

As the spectators applauded and cheered Julien, whose display came to a slow end, soon disappeared back into the crowd. After a few more minutes of wandering, Khoi became disheartened and returned to Kat for some moral support.

Taking his seat, Kat noticed he was looking pretty glum. She offered him a glass of champagne. Khoi related the tale of the chase to her and half way through, she began to point. Khoi turned around to find Julien approaching. Julien stopped before him, leaned forward and said to Khoi "May I kiss you?" Khoi struggled to speak, and turned to Kat for instructions. She rolled her eyes and said "For goodness sake, go for it!" Overwhelmed, he held Julien's face and kissed him deeply.

When the kiss had ended, Khoi blushed. Kat started cheering as Julien asked "Great huh?"

Khoi didn't know if it was confidence or arrogance, but remained speechless "He doesn't say much, does he?" Julien Sarcastically added before offering Kathrin a dance. She obliged him and was soon in the centre of the floor grooving.

Khoi didn't know what was happening but he did know he needed to be with Julien. He walked across the crowded floor, shoving the dancers in his way until he reached the pair. He tapped Kat on the shoulder and with a glance and a smile, Kat got the hint and she promptly left the two of them to dance till their lips locked again passionately. Khoi was hoping beyond hope that Julien felt the same way as he did at that moment. Khoi was in love and Kat was happy for him.

Hence Kat was always like that; striving to encourage others to be happy; being the rock others could count on. Troubled at home? Kat was on the scene. Mounting depression? She knew just what to say.

Sadly, when it was her turn for emotional support, she was more than willing to keep her suffering well hid. By the time Kat had found the love of her life and settled down, she struggled to turn her house into a home. For her, a home had children in it and after two failed attempts to have a child; she was fragile and weak, yet she never confined Khoi. Rather she turned to her cousin, Julien and as a result, Khoi felt left out.

The resulting effect of her most recent loss, which took place nine months earlier in the first trimester of her latest pregnancy, was a trip. It was suggested by Julien and approved by all that Kat needed a break from work and frankly life in general. There was no better way than to travel with her best friend and Julien across Asia while he worked and searched for new artists, she would frolic in the available cultural activities and the nights out.

Back to reality Khoi realised it was time to leave the gallery and he was about to be temporarily homeless. He fetched his laptop to scan through any available hotels.

*13 November 2010*

Parking in front of the hotel on Hardenbergstrasse that was to be Khoi's home, Marcel took a moment to marvel in awe at the imposing structure, commenting "Fancy place". Khoi didn't really care about the place, he felt slightly ill from his longing for Julien and Kat who had flown out 12 hours earlier.

Khoi's car door was opened by a porter, greeting them in a grovelling manner which irritated Marcel to the core, but Khoi didn't pay attention to it as he stepped out of the car. The porter took out his things from the trunk allowing Marcel to drive off to the underground car park.

Khoi checked under the name Kyle Tabone, as directed by Anita.

Payment was to be in cash, using €100 notes and at €200 per night; it was going to take a considerable period of time to count the expected amount for an over 50 night stay. Hence he was directed to a private room where the sums were totalled up and the transaction was completed.

As Khoi was accompanied to the counter to be given the key cards to his allocated room, 616, Marcel waited next to the porter who looked as though he couldn't help feeling intimidated by Marcel's stature. The porter led the pair to the room on the sixth floor.

Once inside, Marcel looked around with upturned lips, observing the furniture and layout before remarking "it's nice, but I still don't understand why you couldn't stay with me or Paul?"

"Paul is still in hospital." Khoi replied.

"Oh, I forgot. How did he end up with an infection? Anyway, I have a vacant room?" Khoi said nothing as he unpacked his clothes and Marcel decided to fill the void. "How is Julien? Haven't seen him in a while, is he still into antiques?"

Khoi giggled before he corrected Marcel "Art. Not antiques."

"Oh yeah… I remember when you brought him over. He's fun. You should invite him out with us when he's back." Marcel proposed.

It was nice to hear Marcel speak positively of Julien particularly after the initial tension that persisted between Stefan and Julien. The question turned Khoi's attention to another matter however, "Is Joel still mad at me?" he asked.

"Yeah." Marcel said as he inspected the fridge "Don't worry about it. He's been on a drug fuelled bender in the last few days. Fucking spoilt brat. Hey?" Marcel called out as he shut the fridge "Why don't you come with me for dinner, it's a Saturday and Mikel needs cheering up."

"What's wrong with Mikel?" Khoi asked as he hung his shirt.

"He got dumped again. So will you come? Please?" Marcel begged. Khoi smiled, nodded and agreed to spend the night out with the cousins.

They got to the flat to find Mikel in a cheerful mood, greeting them warmly. His demeanour was not that of a person who was currently smarting from a broken heart. "We have come to take you out!" Marcel proclaimed. Mikel didn't require much coaxing and within minutes, they were out, choosing the nearest bar.

It was empty, except for the man playing the fruit machine, inserting his pension into it in the hope or retrieving more than he was spending. There was a woman seated at the bar as well, smoking as she spoke to the bartender. This meant they had their choice of chairs and they settled on a place in the corner of the room, the light was dim and the music on offer was from the 80's which matched the decor.

Khoi sat there like a spectator as Marcel and Mikel chatted rubbish about their times in Cologne both amusing and shocking Khoi in equal measure. Half way through listening to Khoi's tale regarding some creative accounting, Mikel struggled to keep a happy face as the number of empty beer glasses started to pile up in the corner. The lack of a busboy ensured that they were able to measure what they had consumed. The resulting effect of the alcohol eroded Mikel's acting skills till he could act the part of the happy no longer. Consequently, he bent his head forward and began to sob.

This display of emotion resulted in an awkward silence as the other two waited for the right time to show some compassion. It came when Mikel paused and said "I'm sorry…" Marcel placed his arm over his shoulder as well, comforting him by saying "Don't worry man. You'll be fine. Try and forget about it."

"I can't. I miss her so much…"Mikel admitted

Marcel stressed "Dude, she dumped you. It's the bitch's loss!" Mikel's response was swift as he head-butted Marcel in the face and with a heavy shove, Marcel found himself off his chair and on the floor, Mikel standing over him, scolding him in Dutch "Don't ever call her a bitch again! I love her!"

Immediately Mikel stormed out of the bar. "Mikel!" Marcel called after him as he got up, but Khoi intervened and said "Let me go after him". Khoi dashed out of the bar turning left initially but with no sign of Mikel, quickly turned right and saw him in the distance. "Mikel!" He cried out and chased after him.

When he finally caught up with Mikel, Khoi stood in front of him to halt his progression "What was that? Marcel was just trying to cheer you up." A closer inspection of Mikel's face showed he was weeping.

Khoi drew him close giving him a hug and Mikel began to confess "I'm a fucking idiot! It's my fault! I am such a dick. She told me she was pregnant. I don't know what happened, I just panicked. I didn't know if I was ready or if it was the right time … I don't want to bring a child into the world. I can't look after a plant let alone a child." Removing his head from where it rested on Khoi's shoulder, he looked Khoi in the eye adding "Smart move right? I am so fucking stupid… I chased her away and now I am alone."

"Oh Mikel" Khoi remarked.

Mikel paused for a moment in a reflective mode warning "Khoi, if there is any advice I can give you it's this, don't be alone. You have something good going there with Julien, don't fuck it up, don't do what I did… I'm pathetic." Khoi smiled and gestured that Mikel should look behind him.

Mikel turned to find Marcel apprehensively approaching. Once close enough, though maintaining a safe distance, Marcel stretched out his left hand and presented Mikel with his wallet "you forgot this." Mikel took it and humbly responded "Thanks… I'm sorry. I didn't mean to …"

"It's ok. I deserve it. You owe me a drink though, the night isn't over." With Marcel's conciliatory words, Mikel's mood lifted and the night did progress only ending when they ran out of energy and alcohol at a night club.

*1 December 2010*

Morning arrived with a foggy mist enveloping the city. It had been a month since Khoi had challenged Joel and since then, there had been very little communication between both of them and both seemed dedicated to avoid each other. So when Joel summoned a meeting, Khoi was not amongst the group who sat silently as they waited. None of them wanted to be there, but Joel insisted that they attend; stressing that he had important news.

Lowly followers as they were, despite their grief, they arrived all within two minutes of each other only to find two people missing for their 6am appointment, the organiser and the bean counter.

Joel was 15 minutes late, unacceptable under normal circumstances, but in this misery ridden room, no one took notice. Khoi wasn't going to come. He already had an appointment to see Jeroen; Khoi thought he ought to know what happened to Stefan whether or not Jeroen understood. The seconds ticked by. Occasionally, the stillness was broken by heavy sighs from a reflective mourner, but besides that, they said nothing. Everyone was on the edge particularly around the presence of Paul.

Paul seemed distracted. It was his first meeting since his attempted tattoo removal which was only the start of his problems.

The first attempt to bring him back into the fold was by giving him a job to do, but at the destination, he broke down, blithering in the car in front of Mikel, unable to move as he bawled like a baby. Several days later, Paul ended up with a temperature as a result of an infection to his wounds which he failed to care for. It was then the order came that Paul be made to take mandatory leave.

This made the assembly more auspicious. Paul had only moved out of Mikel's flat just three days earlier and Mikel hadn't seen him since then. Looking at Paul, who remained rather subdued, Mikel whispered across the table and asked "Are you alright?" Paul just looked at him, grinned, and then turned away.

Everyone felt upset. The only person who didn't seem sad was Daniel; he looked bored as he fiddled with his mobile phone chatting with people on WhatsApp silently, often forcing himself not to smile. Paul didn't know how much more of this he could take. He desperately wanted to go back to his flat, sadly he couldn't, the door opened, there stood Joel scanning their faces. Joel entered with a folder under his arm with a determined air about him. "Sorry I'm late." he announced, pulling out a chair and taking seat. "I kind of found it hard to get out of bed… I guess I should learn more from you guys. I am sorry…"

"What did you call us here for? Can we move it on quickly?" Paul snapped echoing the feelings amongst those present.

Under normal circumstance, Joel wouldn't have stood for such behaviour; then again, these weren't normal circumstances. Joel smiled and replied "Glad you are back Paul, I'm sorry, I'll stop dithering." He said and proceeded to open the folder and took out some sheets of paper. "First of all gentlemen, I was wrong, but first, I have here the post-mortem report from the hospital and I wanted to share this with you… it's not pleasant reading. Please pass this round" he instructed, taking out the document from the folder, handing them over to Mikel who sat to his left.

As the papers were dished out Joel closed the folder and added "What you have gentlemen is the list of injuries that were found on Stefan's body." Holding up the folder he declared "This is what those bastards did to our brother." Joel deliberately used the word "brother" to pull on their sense of loyalty and press the extent of their loss. For added dramatics, he tossed the folder across the table. Eyes followed the document as it skidded over the wood, settling in the middle of the table, at arm's length of everyone, waiting for someone to be bold enough to open it.

Joel proceeded to give them a synopsis "The report states that Stefan had received 13 stab wounds to the back, three puncturing his lung, two perforating a kidney. There was a deep laceration across the neck which cut through his veins, gullet… they slit his throat okay? He had a compound fracture …" Whilst listing the injuries, the most grief stricken of them all moved first. Paul picked the folder and looked through the pictures, stoic in manner, but in reality he was just too exhausted to show anymore emotions. Paul flicked through the grisly images then cut into Joel's roll call of injuries said in the manner of a frustrated waiter being requested to list the ingredients of a complicated dish by asking "Where did you get this?"

Joel was caught off guard and thought quickly "It doesn't matter where it came from, what counts is what it contains." Paul said nothing, but Joel was already bothered by his interruptions. Paul closed the folder and passed it to Marcel who opened it, turned instantly pale and couldn't go beyond the first picture before it got too graphic for his constitution.

Hurriedly, Marcel handed it over to Mikel. True to form, Mikel instantly went into shock, almost fuming and incensed by the picture "This is wrong… Oh my God, look what they did to him… We got to do something!"

"Let me see?" cried Ralph, wondering what all the fuss was about. Mikel gave it to him. Ralph took a look at all the pictures and welled up with tears before he closed the folder and offered it Daniel who signalled he wasn't too interested in seeing them. Perhaps it was enough to see everyone's reaction Ralph thought. As he returned the folder to Joel his conviction couldn't be clearer. "We have to find the perpetrators and make them pay."

This was what Joel wanted to hear as he received it, but he had an obstacle "Yes, I couldn't agree more. I finally have the names of the persons involved and yes, those who did this should pay… and I believe I have your support, left to me, I would say go for it, but my hands are tied.

According to father's instructions, all decisions must be made jointly by Khoi and I, or nothing gets done."

"To hell with Khoi! Let's go get them!" Ralph riled

"Get who? Do you know who did it?" Paul asked "all this thirst for vengeance, with no clue as to who did it… save your strength."

"But we have a witness." Joel revealed "He came forward yesterday and offered to talk, for free, I must add…" Joel opened the folder to return the list he had into the folder. "I haven't spoken to him yet. I thought it would be best if one of you did, I don't think I am level headed enough. That's why I would like you to meet with him." Joel proposed to Mikel.

Without reservation Mikel asked "Where is he?"

"He's at the museum café waiting for you. His name is Max. You can't miss him; he's so white, he could pass as an albino. He's wearing a blue hat and coat." Mikel got up and was about to leave when Joel underlined "Remember he's a witness, not a suspect. No roughing him up, simple question "What happened?" and come straight back. OK?"

"Yes." Mikel replied as he walked out the door. An uncomfortable silence lingered again. Paul decided to seek answers. "Once we know who did it, then what?"

"We weigh up our options and see how best to get justice for Stefan in tomorrow's meeting." Joel confirmed.

"What about Khoi? He's soft. Do you honestly see him saying yes?" Paul pressed

"I don't know." Joel concluded by pushing the folder again across the table towards Paul. "May be if you show him this when he gets back from his trip and ask him to call me for more info, he could come around?"

Meanwhile, Khoi was waiting patiently in the visitor's room of the sanatorium. He was nervous yet eager to see Jeroen again. He picked up a magazine, it was four years old. Still he tried to read but was saved when he heard the voice "Hello Khoi!"

He looked up and there was Jeroen being led towards him by a nurse, a role of paper in his hand. Khoi could not hold back, he went to embrace Jeroen who giggled. The pair sat by the table, Khoi reached out and touched his friend's hair "You might need a haircut."

"The nurse said I have been good." He proclaimed in all his innocence.

"Has he?" Khoi rhetorically address the nurse. She nodded. "So what have you been up to?"

"I have been painting. Look." Jeroen offered the rolled up cardboard to his friend.

"Is this for me?" Khoi unfurled it and there was a picture of three figures. He could make out who two of the people were. Khoi pointed with to one with thin eyes and asked "Is that me?"

"Yes. And that's me." Jeroen added "and that is Steven" referring to the tall skinny figure with brown curly hair and glasses drawn on the paper.

There was that slip again "Stefan. You mean Stefan." Khoi corrected. Having to mention his name brought it all back and it only got worse as in his ignorant bliss he Jeroen added "Yeah, Stefan. Is he coming?"

"No Jeroen… no he's not coming anymore." Khoi said struggling to hold back the tears, but it wasn't easy. Jeroen looked confused, then concerned "Is he angry with me?"

"No, he's not angry with you." Khoi wondered how to approach this, but the anticipation for additional information was flashing in Jeroen's eyes. "Stefan is on holiday."

"Oh." Jeroen remarked "Good. I hope he has a good time?"

"He is…" Unwilling to continue on that track, Khoi instantly brought out his phone and showed it to Jeroen "Look at this game I found, it's called settled… want to play?" With Jeroen suitably distracted, Khoi watched over him wondering what the impact of the truth would have been had he told? Soon he prayed for the visit to end.

After an hour, his initial haste to depart subsided as he watched Jeroen play and asking questions. It was comforting to him and a great distraction. In the end it pained him to leave, but he had to.

Once outside the building, he suffered intensely from struggling to keep himself from weeping. All the time with Jeroen brought back the good old days. Now he was in public, it was impossible to cry. This was too much pain and it didn't seem to feel better. The last time he felt like this, Khoi had just lost his mother, but then he had someone to lean on, now he didn't know if he did. Accepting there was little he could do, he decided to return to his office, hoping it would sooth his pains.

Arriving at the 'Fitness and Wellbeing Center' in the heart of the city, he went through the side entrance to enter the office area, passed by the staff and entered his fishbowl private office where he sat to review the day's issues, more financial requests and expenditure but before he could attend to his task, he was soon reminded of his losses when he caught sight of a picture he had in a frame resting on his desk.

Khoi paused to look at the picture with fondness. The photo caught his 15 year old self sitting on step of the entrance of his old block of flats, bursting out laughing with 17 year old Stefan, sitting on the right doing the same, slapping his thighs as the person who had set the camera on automatic just made it to the steps having initially tripping and falling to the floor. It was that accident that caused the hysterical laughter, but the guy made it and he sat in the middle with relief in his eyes as he cracked a smile. The photographer was another lost friend called Ben who, at the time the picture was taken, was 19.

After his own personal trials, Ben decided to leave the city and the country after sustaining his own traumas. Sure he kept in touch via the occasional letters and with the advent of social media, it became easier to track him, yet, it didn't make his absence bearable, Stefan mockingly never called Ben by name, opting to refer to him as "The one who got away."

Khoi couldn't take it anymore, he had had enough of grieving. As he faced the picture down, he sort a distraction and there was plenty to distract him from his grief here, but that was just wishful thinking for a peaceful life as he saw Paul coming towards him, striding like a paranoid wolf, with a laptop bag. Khoi put aside his documents and prepared himself. It was never good news when Paul came alone.

Paul opened the door and stepped in, locking it behind him as Khoi greeted him "Paul, nice to see you." Paul said nothing as he unzipped the bag and pulled out the folder. Paul then appeared to scan the room raising Khoi's apprehension as to what Paul had in store. Homing on what he needed, Paul picked up the plastic waste bin next to the table and presented it to Khoi. "Hold it close. You'll need it."

"Okay." Khoi replied placing the bin on his lap whilst still trying to mask his unease.

Paul handed him the folder and stood back. Khoi still couldn't fathom what was going on. He opened the folder and noticed that the front page had stuck to inner cover as a result of static. Khoi was going to address it if he hadn't come face to face with the picture that startled him, causing him to fling backwards so quickly that he fell off his chair. "What is this? Oh my God!" he remarked as he proceed to use the bin for the purpose Paul had intended. Khoi heaved and gaged.

Paul promptly closed the folder and drew it away from Khoi's range. Noting they were being watched by the eight employees, he opened the door and asked "Could someone please bring him a glass of water?"

It took Khoi an hour to recover from his gut wrenching experience. He sat there with Paul who had to open the window to get the smell of regurgitated food out of the confined space.

Khoi finally regained enough strength to speak. "That was Stefan?" Paul nodded. "Why the hell did you bring me that?"

"Joel told me to… he wanted you to see what they did to Stefan." Paul replied

"Who are the "they" that did this to Stefan?" Khoi queried. Paul softly informed him that a witness had come forward and claimed he had seen two members of the "District 3 crew", as Paul called them, committed the act.

Khoi then asked for Joel's whereabouts and was informed Joel had gone to his home with Ralph to organise things. Khoi got a bit interested in these "things" Paul could not elaborate on. Paul noticed a side of Khoi that he never saw, an enraged Khoi.

Breathing heavily Khoi demanded "give me your gun." Contrary to his best judgement, Paul looked around and slipped the firearm under the folder, pushing it forward. Stealthy Khoi took hold of the gun concealing it by placing it between his belt and back. Khoi took the folder and placed it in his desk and, having found out that Paul had brought his car, demanded that Paul take him to Joel right away.

Having driven Khoi to the house, Paul decided to sit in the car; he wasn't too keen on confrontations and he could see one coming as Khoi left the car straight to the door, entering the house using the spare key given to him by Anita. He could hear Joel discussing the next shipment with Ralph and followed the sound to find them sitting in the kitchen. When he was noticed, Ralph, upon seeing the expression on Khoi's face, instinctively knew it was best not to be there. "I'll go for a cigarette." He said leaving the room and the house.

Ralph regretted leaving, it was drizzling and he was bound to get wet. Ralph noticed Paul's car and went to it. He knocked at the glass to be let in.

Paul allowed him in. Accepting that both Joel and Khoi would have a lot of words to exchange, it wasn't worth the effort speaking at all.

Finally Khoi and Joel were alone. Khoi was seething and he didn't know why, yet he wasn't afraid to express it but first he had to know "Why in God's good name did you send me that fucking file?"

"To show you what happened to Stefan, to show you what they did…" but before Joel could finish, Khoi cut him off in midsentence "Can someone tell me who are these they who did it? I only heard it from Paul that he heard it from you that you heard it from Mikel that there was a witness who saw everything!"

Perplexed, Joel gesticulated "And the problem is? It came from a credible source. Max is one of our mules."

Khoi's intuition was gnawing at him "I know your game. You want to retaliate."

With a grin and opening his arms Joel asked "Is it that obvious?"

"Yes, and so do I, but I can't agree to anything till I hear directly from this so call witness what he said!" Joel almost fell back on his chair; his mouth fell open in shock as Khoi asked "Now where is this guy?"

Joel still found it hard to believe Khoi's stance and thought he best capitalise on it as soon as possible. "Come on." He ordered, picking up his car keys.

Paul had put on the radio to add some variety to the silence. Whilst the occupants of the car were listening to bad music, Joel's car pull out of the park way and whizz past them. "I wonder where they're going?" Ralph asked as he reached into his breast pocket for his hip flask offering Paul a sip of his whiskey. "Do you know Khoi has a gun?" Paul divulged handing back the flask following his swig. "Hmm, let's hope they come back." Ralph remarked having another sip from his flask.

Max was working his patch which was close to the area surrounding Berlin Zoologischer Garten train station. When people vied for spots, they scuffed at the idea of taking the area surrounding the zoo "As if giraffes want to get stoned" someone once told him, but his patch stretched for a one mile radius which, when quantified included Berlin Institute of Technology, a part of Berlin Technical University and where there are students, there's a market and even geeks get stoned.

Max waited patiently for his customer in the under pass on Hertzallee. It was to be a big sale, €350 worth meaning a tidy profit for him. Max had arrived early; it allowed him to catch up on his orders. Whilst reviewing his next appointment, Max heard steps approaching and turned see who was coming.

Max saw two people approaching. He couldn't really see their faces from afar due to his combined case of astigmatism and nystagmus, but he could make out that the tall figures approaching weren't his customers, so he carried on reviewing his list on his phone ignoring the footsteps which drew closer.

Max's inventory taking was interrupted abruptly when he was shunted to the wall of the underpass and held in place by a hand firmly pressed on to his chest with a gun pointing at his face. Max almost froze initially when he found a person he had never seen before holding a pistol to his head, with eyes of scarlet, panting and standing behind him looking a bit uneasy was Joel. "Joel… hey?" Max called but Khoi cut him short "Shut up. You said you saw what happened to Stefan?" Max, shivering and striving not to wet himself, nodded "Did you see it?" Khoi asked again.

"Yes! Please don't kill me." Max pleaded. Khoi faced the gun down and replied "We promise we won't kill you if you tell me the truth." , Returning the gun into his coat pocket, Khoi ordered "Come." and proceeded to lead the way. Max followed with Joel tailing behind him.

As they marched, Max turned to Joel who mouthed "Sorry" at him and signalled he remained calm by waving his hand down. It was easy to tell one's self to "stay calm", but it was hard to remain so when there was a tall Asian looking man with a gun and his friend accosting you and taking you to places unknown.

Soon, they arrived at Joel's car. Khoi opened the door to the back seat and pointed, directing the mule to enter. Max thought it would be far safer to obey.

Khoi followed after him whilst Joel went to the driver's seat, started the car and began to drive. Khoi took out the gun again rested it on his thigh as he began "You are going to tell me everything you told them and I want the truth."

Max found it difficult to inhale let alone form a sentence but with the cold hard steel pressing on his side, he soon recovered his ability to speak. "It was Halloween night. I was waiting outside Kiki's in the backstreet near the sex shop. Don't know if you been there, but it a small path way, flanked by buildings, about fifty metres long. I was at the end leading to Ritterstrasse waiting for my sale. Initially I thought it was my sale, but on closer inspection, I saw Stefan coming, he was walking quickly, looking pretty upset. He took out his phone and made a call, but before he could speak, someone must have been waiting in ambush and whacked him hard on the face with what looked like a bat. Stefan seemed dazed, he didn't respond, he didn't have enough time really. The person stepped out from the shadows and began to beat him mercilessly. It was terrible. He didn't seem to stop; he just pummelled at him raising his arm high before bring the bat down as hard as he could."

"Someone came running forward and said 'Come on Richard, save some for me.' Stefan wasn't moving much by the time the second guy came. Then new person bent over Stefan, pulled out a knife and started thrusting it into his back like he was stabbing into a block of ice with an icepick. You could hear Stefan grunt each time. He must have been stabbed 12, 13 times? Then Richard got edgy, he told the guy to hurry up. I remember the name of the guy; I think it was Ziggy, or something, just a few inches taller than me, fuzzy blonde hair, and crocked smile… that sort of guy. Anyway, the guy pulled Stefan by the hair and drew the knife across his neck… then he got up and ran towards me. I hid behind the bin and they jogged off. That's all I saw."

Whilst providing his version of events, Max had felt the gun steadily press harder and harder into his side as he told the tale till it began to hurt.

Khoi had turned slightly blue having held his breath throughout the story. Khoi drew back the gun he had pushed onto Max's rib cage. He was still a cynic. Yes, there could be an element of truth in Max's narrative but he still wasn't sure.

"Describe Richard." He ordered. Max told him that Richard was a tall guy with orange hair and quite athletic. He also had a tattoo sleeve on his left arm.

Accepting the probability that description wasn't a fib, Khoi then asked Max to explain what the second person looked like and he did, describing a rather generic average blonde bloke. It was then Max said "I have seen Marcel and him together many times." This made Khoi go cold. Khoi knew exactly who was being described and his heart sank, this was not the news he sort after.

With the question nagging in his mind Khoi asked "Tell me, you saw all this happening and you didn't do anything to help? Why?" Max decided to be candid "I'm an albino with dancing eyes; 165cm tall, hardly physically active, afraid of the sun, poorly educated and had various run in's with the law. What could I do? Call the police? Or intervene?"

"Stop the car." Khoi ordered. Joel parked close to winery.

Feeling remorseful, Khoi said "Come by tomorrow to see Joel for your payment." Max remained shaken, so Khoi added "And we'll compensate you for the inconveniences. Thank you."

Max didn't say a word, he was just eager to leave. Max stepped out of the care, Khoi watching him as he gradually accepted Max's excuse for abstaining from interfering, who didn't want to see the morning?

Joel turned to ask "Where too?" Khoi requested he be driven to the hotel. Joel kept glancing at Khoi and could tell he had achieved his goal, but just to confirm, he asked "so, what do you think?" Khoi said nothing. Joel remained resilient. "So you going to let me and the boys handle it?"

"No." Khoi replied. Joel was about to freak out but kept his cool as he asked "No? I thought you were all up for it?"

"I didn't say I changed my mind. Justice must be done, but it's not going to happen without me."

Joel was thrown by Khoi's reply. "I don't understand"

"I'm in on this one. I want to be an intricate part of this. I want these guys gone."

Joel didn't like the sound of this and protested "No, you can't."

"Why can't I? You think I can't handle it?" Khoi challenged.

"It's against the rules. Dad said you should never get your hands dirty!" Joel underlined

"Rules? Rules? The rules state that the heads meet to settle any feud." Snapped Khoi as he added "Can you imagine those fat idiots seating in a room calculating how much they feel is fair to pay for Stefan's life? A life that's priceless? And who would they give the money to? His grandmother in a care home who is as batty as a rabid dog? That's the rule, why don't we follow that?"

Joel could see Khoi getting more and more animated. This wasn't the route Joel wanted, but things had taken a course of their own as Khoi shook his head with determination "No, no… fuck that. You are trying to tell me it is ok for you to break rules and not for me? Fuck you! We do it together or we don't do it at all."

With this ultimatum humming in his mind, Joel began to wonder if he had made a serious mistake, it was finally confirmed that he had when Khoi mumbled "It starts tomorrow."

Joel knew better than to utter anything. He hoped all Khoi's posturing was all a result of his anger and perhaps in the morning it will all be out of his system.

Khoi didn't say anything as they drove to his hotel. Winter was certainly here. It was just seven in the evening yet darkness had arrived. The initial drizzle was now a full blown shower.

Now parked in front of the main entrance, Khoi opened the door. "Pick me up in the morning for the meeting." Khoi instructed Joel rudely as he got out of the car. Khoi went straight to his room and once the door was shut, he was at a loss about how to respond or act. Too many thoughts ran through his mind, it was smothering.

Khoi decided to address this with his tried and tested method and took out one of the pair of knitting kit bags he brought, seized his size 12 needles and proceeded to knit a scarf, spending hours on it and had nearly completed it before falling asleep.

*2 December 2010*

The following morning Joel arrived to find Khoi waiting for him outside the building. Khoi got into the car and didn't even greet him. Joel soon realised that the night had failed to tame Khoi's fury.

Joel chose to remain shtum hoping the awkwardness of the wordless drive would prompt a discussion, but nothing was forthcoming till the reached their destination.

Joel could tell he was losing this one as he reversed into his allocated space with Khoi face void of any feeling. Joel parked the car outside the venue where the meeting was to be held. It's always been the same place, a room on the top floor of their four storey gym in the Dahlem district close to the Ethnologist Museum.

Once the car was still, Khoi tried to open the car door but it remained locked. "Aren't you going to open the door?" Khoi enquired as Joel gazed ahead, almost in a hypnotised state, his hand firmly gripped on the steering wheel. "Joel?" He called. "Do you really want to do this? Once you get your hands dirty, they'll never be clean again." Joel warned in an ominous tone.

Pausing for a moment to contemplate his actions, Khoi balanced his thirst to avenge his loss and satisfy his anger against his promise to Georg not to get involved in "Street politics." But an answer was required. "What's it going to be?" Joel asked for the final time. "I can drive you back and pretend this never happened."

"Open the door." Khoi commanded.

Joel looked startled; he felt a lump in throat. Joel turned to his friend "No one needs to know…"

"Open the door." Khoi demanded.

For the second time in his life he chose to be disobedient. He had to prove himself and punish those that have brought him so much misery. Joel couldn't deny him his wish anymore. He pressed the button to release the lock allowing Khoi to step out of the car. Khoi waited for Joel to join him.

They walked into the building straight past the reception, to the door on the other side of the building. It required a code to open it. Once Joel punched in the code, the door beeped allowing him to shove it open with his shoulder. He stood aside letting Khoi enter before closing it firmly checking to see it was locked. Joel led the way up the flight of steps to the top floor, then to another door which required another access code.

Once the code was entered, the beeping sound signified they could enter again, but Joel hesitated, his hand still on the handle. Khoi lost his patients and pushed the door open, causing Joel to let go of the handle and nearly trip.

Khoi didn't give him a second look. He walked past the small kitchen area before they reached another door. He turned to Joel and asked "Does this need a code too?" Joel did not respond, having shut the main door, he walked to final door and knocked as he turned the handle opening to reveal a long meeting table with eight chairs on other sides and two at the opposite ends with a flurry of noise. Upon entry Khoi noticed Daniel and Ralph on one side laughing at some sort of comment shared. On the other side, seated together were Marcel and Mikel. Mikel was busy explaining something to Marcel, who sat listening attentively. There was a slight hive of chatter with the exception of Paul who sat on chair away from Marcel and

Mikel, pad on the table, pen in hand, but nothing was being drawn or written, he had a gloomy look about him which spelt exactly how he felt.

"Hello everyone!" Joel proclaimed as he went to chair at the end of the table with Khoi who sat next to him and a chair away from Daniel and Ralph. There was a moment of silence as all attention turned to Khoi and his presence, but no one spoke making Khoi perceive the reception as arctic. "Well, what a week it has been hasn't it?" Joel continued. Everyone knew what he meant, but no one wanted to relive it. "We agreed last week that we were going to target those who were responsible and today, we were meant to discuss the game plan, but I guess, as you can see by Khoi's presence, the order of the day has changed as well." The reference to his name resulted to more unneeded attention. Khoi felt scrutinised and Joel knew it, hoping it will do more to deter Khoi's convictions than his pleas. Joel carried on "Khoi wanted to be part of the process should there be proof. And, marking his words, he's here."

The apprehension felt by the others was clear. In their eyes, Khoi was Georg's powder white goose who shouldn't be sullied. They were speechless, but Joel still had more to say. "This must never leave this room. You know exactly what would occur if we let it slip to anyone, especially Dad." Everyone bar Paul nodded in agreement. "So Khoi," Joel called clasping his hands over the table "provided you all agree and based on certain conditions, I see no problem with him being part of it."

This was news to Khoi "Conditions? What conditions are those?" he asked, uneasy as he wondered what Joel had in mind. "Lend me that pad please?" Joel asked from Paul who passed it on to him. A glance at Paul's droopy face prompted him to declare "Cheer up will you."

Joel reached into the breast pocket of his coat and took out his pen, scribbled a few things down. Khoi wanted to crane his neck but he didn't need to, Joel was a fast writer and soon concluded with a heavy tap on the pad marking his full stop. "Pass this on to the others please?" Joel said handing it over to Paul confident that Khoi would never agree to the conditions thus, never take part.

Paul didn't even look at the list provided; he didn't know why he came in the first place. He wanted to be alone, so he passed on the pad to Marcel who looked at it and laughed before handing it over to Mikel. "This is crazy." Mikel proclaimed as he gave it second look. Khoi kept his calm exterior but inside, he was an eager child wanting to cry, "Let me see!" and snatch the pad. Mikel pushed the pad across the table to Ralph. One look and he shook his head before handing it to Daniel. Daniel chuckled and passed the pad to Khoi with the words "Good luck."

Khoi received the pad like and unpinned grenade and considering the content, it might as well have been one. Joel watched smilingly and gawking at Khoi who knew his game and averted his eyes as Joel read the conditions out loud.

"1. All plans must be executed by Christmas.

2. If required, not more than one bullet must be used.

3. Physical contact with any of the intended target must be kept to a minimum."

"Tell me Khoi, what are your aims?" Joel was being snide in his approach. With his eyes firmly fixed on the pad in his hand, Khoi replied "To get those bastards without turning it into a turf war where we all get killed."

"Noble." Joel accepted.

No one else spoke, they, with the exception of Paul, could see a game playing out and remarked "This is stupid. Who will blink first?"

Khoi for once, realised that he may have bitten more than he could chew, but he wasn't intent on giving Joel the satisfaction. "What happens if I fail?" He enquired. Joel replied

"We'll think of something." And from his track record, Khoi knew Joel wasn't a person who held sentiments.

Khoi sat back and despite his gut telling him not to he responded "If you are going to give me conditions, you have to hear mine."

"We're listening." Joel conceded. Khoi then proceeded to list his demands "I'll accept all of this provided you give me full control of the entire process. I'll have access to whatever resources I need including manpower and I expect the entire team's full cooperation on this."

Joel had to bite his lower lip to stop himself from begging Khoi to stop digging himself too deep, but there was unison from the majority, except for Paul who still remained silent, with Daniel leading chorus "Sound's fun. I'm in." the others, one by one, agreed till two were left, Paul and Joel.

Paul who had his head bowed for most of the time looked sternly into Khoi's eyes. "You promise you will get those bastards?" Paul was the one who felt the loss the most. Stefan saved him and it ate at him that he wasn't there for Stefan. Khoi with full conviction responded "With my life." Paul nodded his approval, leaving Joel in a dilemma of his own making.

Joel had been out voted and he couldn't back out now. So he faked complacency "If that's what you want, sure. So when do we get the two walking corpses?" asked Joel

"Who said we were going after two people?" Khoi's question stunned everyone into a state confusion. "I told you that the aim is not to start a turf war. We get two; the others will come for us. Besides, I just don't want to get them, I want to end them. I want "District 3" to capitulate.

"We're not going after the two, I want all the five top guys and we all know who they are." He turned facing Marcel who sat uncomfortably as Khoi homed on him for one particular reason.

Marcel began to regret giving his approval as Khoi added "We must put all familiarities aside, they are nothing but targets now and I will need all the information I can about them, not just their home address and phone number, but what they like, what they hate? Where they go when they are bored, even what brand of toothpaste they use. I need details."

With an idea in his head, Mikel excitedly proclaimed "We could use that girl Ralph and I had to work with when we had to get our hands on the cheat in Rotterdam. You know her Joel, Stefan hired her." Joel wasn't too pleased to be reminded of that fact, yet, excitedly; Ralph continued "Man, she is amazing. She found the asshole with just his phone number, even though he'd changed it. Took her two days, she is amazing! We could use her.' Ralph suggested "What's her name again?"

"Elina?" Mikel proposed.

"Nah, it's Belinda." Ralph corrected.

Jelena, her name is JELENA!" Joel shouted, angered that his plan failed, perhaps this was another opportunity to put it back on track as he tried to dissuade Khoi "She's wild. Anyway, she cost too much. Besides, we have Paul, why don't we use him?" All eyes swung across the room the subject. Paul seemed to perk up in anticipation, but it was misplaced. Khoi shook his head replying

"No, we can't have our prints on this in anyway and I thought you agreed that resource wasn't an issue?" Khoi rebutted with conviction in his eyes he directed Joel "Get me Jelena."

It was all changing and there was nothing Joel could do about it other than to acknowledge his understanding sarcastically with the words "Yes Boss."

# 3

*2 December 2010*

Winter had come early to Storvreta. No one understood why the snow came down so heavily in the first two weeks of October and since then, they have had a dusting every day at various degree, thus ensuring that the snow never melted.

It was just a matter of interest as opposed to anything else in Charlotte's case as she sat on the steps putting on her winter boots. Regardless, it was getting a bit boring considering it's been snowing for two months now and there was no respite in sight.

Ever the optimist, Charlotte considered herself lucky. Despite the proximity of Uppsala, Storvreta still maintained the village mentality and when the call came out to help the elderly and vulnerable, there were no shortage of volunteers which included her.

The trains still ran, the buses too, but individuals would need an off road vehicle to travel to the town centre.

With the snow in some outer reaches of the town standing at over a metre high, trapping most active people, she could only wonder how the infirmed must feel at this point in time.

The emergency services were called in to gather those in need together at the community centre where they could be cared for and that was what Charlotte planned to do this Saturday morning.

With her shoes on, she took a look at herself in the mirror observing how her tightly fitting sweater hugged her curves. Content, Charlotte put on her coat and wrapped her scarf around her neck, moving her long blonde hair from being caught. With the cookbooks and an extra pair of shoes in her bag, Charlotte put on her hat and ventured out of the door of her home which she once shared with her ex-husband but with him gone and her children in university, she now lived alone.

The fact that she lived alone didn't really matter to her. Charlotte was lucky with her genes. At forty-five, she looked thirty and was often mistaken for younger and why wouldn't they? She had her face lifted, her teeth done, her nose straightened and her breast were large and perky, but those were real.

Charlotte had an active sex life which she certainly enjoyed after twenty years with a man whom she once described as "sitting there; doesn't move; doesn't vibrate; doesn't do anything". She was reclaiming her body and loving it.

Walking on the grit scatted on the pavement; the cold gust of wind brought back a longing. Only two months back she was in Varna, by the black sea, spending a hot and sensual week with a good looking Bulgarian man of 24… if only she could remember his name.

Arriving at the community centre, she could see it contained a few people already. Charlotte entered the first door, took off her coat; stuffed her gloved, hat and scarf in the left arm and placed it on a hanger and hooking it on the rack. Off came the snow boots and on came more comfortable plimsolls, she carried her bag under her arm with the book. Now she was ready to help the needy.

She opened the second door and, whilst not paying attention to the fifty odd others who were there talking and making noise, focused her attention on the young, good looking organiser who, if she had to admit it, was the only reason why she came.

She was about to wave to him as she took her fourth step into the hall when Charlotte was stopped in her tracks by a voice. "Excuse me." She heard. Charlotte turned round and found standing there, clutching her bag in her left hand and a white cane with a ball on the end, held in her right. She was blonde, tall, elegantly dressed in designer wear and dark glasses and seemed extremely attractive. Normally Charlotte would have considered her a threat if it weren't for the saving grace that the woman appeared visually impaired. "Could you help me please?" continued the lady.

Charlotte was torn between assisting the woman and chasing after her man of interest. Charlotte then noticed the man looking at her, she considered her options, and it could work in her favour if she was seen to be helping those in need.

Charlotte quickly gave the man a wave and then turned to the lady. "How may I help you?" She said placing a caring hand on the arm of the blind woman.

"Could you please lead me to the toilet? If you take me in and open the door and point my finger to the lock, I am sure I can manage?" pleaded the handicapped woman.

"Oh… Of course. No problem." Charlotte took the lady's arm and placed it on her. "Here we go." Charlotte proclaimed as she led the way.

Rather than taking the shorter route behind the chairs, she walked up the aisle to meet her eye candy. As she passed by him and pretended that it was a chance meeting by saying, "Oh hello Par, how are you?" The young man smiled but wasn't given the chance to reply as she added "I will be back in the moment. Just have to assist our friend here. One minute." Then she walked a bit spritely, trying her best to keep her composure.

As they proceeded, the blind woman asked "You like him?" Charlotte giggled and asked "how do you know?"

"I may be blind but I am also a woman." replied the lady. This made Charlotte warm to her a bit more as they walked out of the hall, through double doors, down a corridor with empty rooms on either sides towards the toilet. On the way Charlotte asked for her name, the lady replied "Alexandra"

Once at the door of the toilet, Charlotte let the lady through and marvelled at the space allocated for the disabled toilet. There was just one toilet in a room large enough for two.

Charlotte directed Alexandra in. Alexandra then asked "Could you show me to where the sink is please?" Charlotte took out Alexandra's left hand and placed it on the sink when some items dropped from Alexandra's handbag on to the floor.

Instinctively, Charlotte reached to pick up the lipstick and the mobile phone and was about to apologise when she felt a hand grab her hair and before she could resist, it was grappled, yanked back and her forehead slammed onto the ceramic sink.

The first bash made her face numb, yet it didn't stop. Her head was slammed on to the edge of the sink in such quick succession that should not put up any resistance.

After the ninth time, it stopped. Charlotte slumped onto the floor, blood oozing from the exposed gash in the front of her head.

Charlotte couldn't scream even if she wanted to, it was a task to keep awake as the final events she saw was Alexandra, panting heavily after that exertion, taking off her glasses, revealing she was not blind. Alexandra placed the shades in her bag before leaving that on the floor and with her gloves still on, she picked up her cane.

Charlotte feared what was to follow as Alexandra bent the cane at the point where it folded from the middle, she pulled and a cheese cutter wire extended across to about two and a half feet before she approached Charlotte.

Alexandra turned her around face down; sat on her back, raise her head by hair, holding it up with her teeth before holding the cheese wire across with both hands using the folded ends of the stick, placing beneath her neck.

Alexandra then released Johana's hair from her teeth and quickly wound the wire around Johana's neck and tightened by pulling at both ends, then tugging causing the wire to tear the skin.

As Charlotte gargled and tried to reach under the wire, the final words Charlotte heard whispered into her ear were "Sleeping with my ex-boyfriend was the wrong thing to do, fucking bitch."

Alexandra pulled and tugged with all her might as the Charlotte tried to toss her off her back. Alexandra resorted to kneeling on her back, tugging from side to side cutting deep into the skin of Johana's neck before changing tactics. Alexandra twisted the wire ends, garrotting Charlotte causing her eyes to bulge out her sockets. Charlotte could feel her windpipe collapsing; there was no way she could breathe now. Charlotte twitched, and even though there was no hope of return, Alexandra continued twisting till Charlotte stopped moving.

Alexandra removed the wire, got off her and stood exhausted for a minute. It was time to leave.

Alexandra pulled on the wire, triggering the spring mechanism that allowed the wire to recoil back into the stick before she put the folded cane into her bag. She took out latex gloves and produced spray bottle containing bleach and some wipes. She cleaned areas of contact vigorously and avoided getting close to the body and its oozing fluids as best as she could.

Once done, she returned everything back into her bag, and in a calm manner, left the toilet. Alexandra then used a flat piece of metal, the size of a small coin and turned the lock from the other side of the door signifying it was occupied before walking down the hall, back into the room slipping out unnoticed by the majority of the people as she changed from her heels to her snowshoes and exited the building.

She walked up the road to her parked hired 4x4 and drove out of town, satisfied with her accomplishments as she threw out her blond wig and shook loose her dark brown hair.

As Alexandra handed back the keys of her hired car at Årlanda airport before she made her way to departure, her phone rang, it was a number she knew, so she answered "Hello Darko. How are you?"

"I am fine." The caller replied. "Jelena, we have a job for you in Germany starting in 24 hours. Think you can spare a month?"

"How big is the deal?" Jelena asked as she handed over ticket to the checking desk, Darko informed her it was enough to get her the seaside villa she wanted by summer. That made her mind up for her. "Hold on." She said to the man at the check in desk "Yes, I packed it myself; No, it doesn't contain any prohibited objects; No, I wasn't given anything by anyone any other questions." The man behind the desk shook his head. Jelena returned to her call. "Tell them I will be there in 48 hours. I still have some unfinished business to attend to."

"Oh no Jelena, are you still on the war part with your Teodor? You broke up, it's over, move on." Darko Pleaded

"Thanks for your words of wisdom and you are right. I'll book a flight and you can arrange for them to meet me." She concluded.

"Very good. So you will be Berlin tomorrow then?"

"No, 48 hours. Take care, Darko." With that she hung up collected her boarding pass and continued her journey.

In the middle of a snow covered field covered with patches of grass protruding, a rabbit emerged from it borrow. It looked around considering whether or not it was safe for it to go out. The last time it went to forage, it bore witness to the death of another rabbit at the hands of a passing fox.

The rabbit sniffed the air, stood on its hind legs to survey its surroundings. With no sign of any present danger, the rabbit left its hole and went forward through the long strand of dying grass.

As it nibbled under the shadow of a large house in the field, the rabbit ventured further away from its hole to enjoy the shoots of grass not covered in snow.

The rabbit saw another of its kind, a female for that matter. Being a male and having been stuck in its hole for the last two day, it wasn't just hungry, but also horny.

The rabbit decided to approach its intended mate. The female turned and started running away. The male rabbit interest could not be quenched by her fleeting departure. It chased after her but she wasn't going to be caught so easily. She increased her speed, running towards the building.

The male was slowly catching up with her and was just a foot away from his sexual prize when fate intervened. The male rabbit found itself being lifted off the ground at full speed whilst the female ran to its burrow right next to the house; watching from a safe distance as a fox turned her intended suitor into a meal.

It was not safe out there anymore, at least not today. The female rabbit went deeper into its burrow next to the house.

The house in the middle of the field was a very nice one. Made from logs, boulders and a lot of concrete, it had a large hunting lodge feel.

Selected for its location close to the mountains and ski resort of Bansko, this four bedroom duplex was fully furnished with all the mod-cons.

Downstairs, it had a huge lounge with an open fire place and enough dead animals to raise a conservationist's concern. It also had a large dining room and a kitchen with both an old style wood burning stove and modern cooker which ran on gas.

The stairs lead to 4 large bedrooms. Each was ensuite and the largest had an open fire place too.

Finally, there was the storage space located in the loft accessible via a point over the landing of the staircase via ladder.

This beautiful home belonged to the dashing young entrepreneur, Teodor Tetov who made his money from advertising and despite none of the rooms being used since his arrival, Teodor was home.

Teodor had fallen asleep, the exhaustion brought about by being starved for over 2 days made him feel weak. It wasn't a comfortable position to be in, but there was no choice in the current predicament. One moment, he arrived at his winter lodge outside the town of Dobarsko getting ready for the skiing season, then, as he inserted the key into the lock of the door, he received a hefty knock on the head only to wake up in the loft of his house where all his winter gear was stored, tied to heavy wooden chair which was nailed to the floor.

The means by which he was bound was quite effective. The rope was wrapped around his person, strapping him to the chair so tightly that it made it difficult for him to breathe deeply.

His legs were bound together before being tied to the chair. This was followed by his upper arm tied with a rope wrapped around his chest, then around each arm before being put through the loop made around his chest then fastened with a knot before being pinned to the arm of the chair knot made around the elbows. His lower arm and wrist were held to the armrest of the chair with several knots, creating a sleeve reaching up to his wrist, which was so restrictive that he could hardly feel his fingers.

Yet, his mouth wasn't covered. Silly of him for picking a lodge where the nearest neighbour was at least 1.5km away. He could have screamed all he liked, and he did, but no one could hear, there was no chance of rescue.

With no access to any form of light, he could not tell what time of the day it was. Teodor hated the dark, it had something to do with when he was a child and getting locked in a cellar which made his imagination run wild. There were noises and growls, shadows and formations of grotesque creatures each threatening to get him. He thought it was left behind in the cellar when he was six, but they never left, before he passed out, he found himself screaming and howling in fear, crying till his voice was hoarse. Hence, sleep was certainly a welcomed relief.

Teodor was awoken by sounds originating from below. The front door opened and shut. This was followed by footsteps coming up the wooden stairs. It grew louder as it drew closer. The heel hitting the plank made his imagination go awry again. Someone was in the house, but whom?

They were downstairs and have been there for over an hour but couldn't pinpoint their location till the whiff of spices came through the floor boards, teasing him.

Teodor's heart raised, he was close to having an anxiety attack as the trap door opened, a gloved hand pushing it open then placing a large handbag on to floor of the loft. The light streamed in as the person mounted further up the ladder, the first sign of the approaching individual was their olive coloured hunting hat, then their face. "Hello darling." Jelena said, announcing her arrival as she came up the final step and pulled herself up to the floor of the loft and turned the switch on the light which emitted from a single light bold dangling over his head.

It wasn't clear whether it was anger or terror that prompted his reaction. Teodor found himself screaming uncontrollably, tousling in his chair.

Jelena took off her hat, placed it next to her bag and walked quickly to meet him. Jelena took off the glove of her right hand, placed it in her pocket and in an attempt to calm him touched his face "Shh, shh, don't scream my dear, I have come to see you."

"Let me go you demented, vindictive cow!" He screamed at her.

"What a warm welcome." She replied sarcastically as she stroked his hair feeling him shiver and shake.

Jelena then stopped, sniffed then looked on the ground to find she had been standing in his faeces. "Oh dear, you soiled yourself."

"You would too if you were locked up in a loft for two days by a psychotic woman!" He exclaimed.

"Come now, name calling? Has it deteriorated to this?" she asked. Her calm approach to the situation was unnerving as she took off her other glove and placed it in her left coat pocket with the other.

"I brought us some dinner. Roast lamb. Your favourite; but I guess you are hungry now." She announced. Jelena reached into her right pocket and produces a pear and a flick knife. She cut out a segment of the pear and placed it close to his lips. "Eat, you must be starving." He looked at her suspiciously before he opened his mouth and received the fruit. "There. Enjoy." She urged smiling and stroking his hair.

Her touch, once welcomed began to repulse him. He couldn't take it anymore. He spat the half chewed pear in her face.

Her creepy smile turned in a medusa like gaze as the knife slipped from her grip. She slapped him across the face, walked away to her bag to get some makeup wipes.

Observing on the sheet how much foundation she had taken off, Jelena laughed she confessed "I met your Swedish girlfriend." The under toned of her voice exposed the fury that she would have to redo all her makeup "Charlotte Lund Bay. You should be ashamed of yourself. The woman is old enough to be your mother." Teodor said nothing as she threw the used wipe on the floor, but she certainly had more to say. She had a reflective almost remorseful look on her face as she added "Why Teodor? Why? I thought we had something good. Why did it have to end?"

This was perplexing to Teodor who decided to set the record straight "What the hell are you talking about? First you cheated on me and then you dumped me?"

"Let's not get into details of who broke up with whom and why, you clearly didn't love me; running off with some floozy only seconds after we split up." She replied as she approached him.

"We broke up nineteen months ago! Is something wrong with your memory woman?" He enquired now certain she was deranged.

She approached him; stopped to pick up the blade she dropped when she went to clean her face and folded it back into its case before placing it back in her pocket.

Once again she began to caress his face and touch his lip. "You don't understand… I miss you." Seeing the potential in her statement, he capitalised on her words as her fingers ran through his hair. "I missed you too." He lied. "We were good together weren't we?" Teodor added "And we still could be." She concurred kissing him on the forehead. "It can still happen…" He said "look at me." She stopped and looked in his eyes as he asserted "It can still happen… but it's up to you. We can be together. I know that's what you want… but it can't happen if I am bound up like this."

She began to look receptive and his heart was lifted when she asked "What do you want me to do?"

"Cut off these ropes… we can put this all behind us and have dinner… please?" It seemed that he may have had her. Jelena touched his right hand and felt the rope around it. She produced the blade flicked it open and knelt before the rope bound hand. "Us together again… is that what you really want?" She asked all doe eyed.

"Yes, it is… now let's go cook together." He fibbed, but it was working, she placed the blade between the hemp rope and the arm rest, placing her hand gently on Teodor's wrist and before she started asked with her hair falling over her face "Do you know what I want?"

"Tell me." He encouraged eager to have her onside, even though he didn't care.

She raised her head, her hair clearing away from her face. Jelena's eyes were over flowing with evil as she replied "I want you dead."

The knife took a different direction; she pulled on his hand to expose the wrist. Jelena sliced the anterior side of the wrist, cutting through all the veins and ligament to the point of touching the bone.

His blood splattered on her chest and face as she smiled, sending him automatically into shock. Her speed prevented Teodor to feel the pain initially. By the time he did, she had progressed to his left hand and calmly did the same.

She watched him scream and remarked "If we were good together, you should have come after me."

"Help me! Please!" he begged knowing the eventualities of her action would be mass blood loss which would lead to his demise.

Jelena threw the knife on the floor, collected her things and proceeded down the ladder. Her final words to him were "Goodbye Teo, enjoy the rest of your evening." She switched off the light and shut the loft access door. She walked down the ladder and then down to the ground floor to clean herself and check on her food.

Teodor's childhood fear had become real. He was going to die in the dark unless someone or something intervened. "Jelena! Jelena! HELP ME!" He cried out over and over. Teodor's screams became the sound track to her evening as she took off her blood splattered clothes and threw the logs into the fireplace along with some kindle.

Teodor began to shake, he wondered if his anxieties could be causing him to lose more blood as his life force oozed from his opened veins. He pressed his wrist on the arm rest hoping it would stem the blood loss. The pain was severe initially, but soon his endorphins were kinking in and for some reason, he knew it was not good. "Jelena! Please... I don't care about dying but please don't let me die alone!" he whimpered as he wept, whaling "Jelena! Jelena!"

Yes, she heard her name being called, but she was too busy setting her clothes on fire. She was sad to see her designer coat go up in flames, but it had to be done.

Now in her underwear, she went to the kitchen to check on the lamb cutlets roasting in the gas oven on a bed of vegetables. The constant reference to her name irritated her. Jelena was forced to turn on the radio and listened to some rock music, playing her air guitar as Teodor gradually realised that she was not coming.

He stopped crying as he started to feel woozy. He had to act. "Our father, who art in heaven, hallow be thy name…" as he commended his soul to God, he was interrupted by a question "Teo, where do you keep your salt?" Jelena asked as she checked the cupboard "There it is." Jelena remarked when she found it behind the jar of olives "Carry on."

Teodor had grown tired, he had been praying for as long as he could till he couldn't get the words out anymore and it turned to moans. Jelena grew weary of hearing him whimper. She wondered when he was going to die as it was well over an hour since her actions and his voice was putting her off her meal.

She went to the front room where she had left her luggage, a tear nearly emerging to her eye as she saw her coat continue to smoulder and burn, but she accepted it was a justifiable sacrifice. She rummaged through the external pocket of her Samsonite bag, took out her earplugs, put them in and returned to the kitchen to finish her dinner.

Once done and she was full, she went to the living room to enjoy the warmth of the room resulting from the fire which made her sleepy. She opened the chest by the fire place where the blankets were kept. Looking at the various patterns fondly, memories of the nice times they once had when they visited the lodge the previous year.

Still, Jelena had to travel the following day and thus needed her rest. Still in her underwear, she curled up under the blankets and nodded off.

In the loft, Teodor too was nodding off as the last drops of blood made their way out of his body. He was feeling cold, his heart rate had reduced and he knew it was the end. He wondered if he could find something meaningful to say, and he did "Help me…" he begged for the last time.

*3 December 2010*

Morning broke and a well-rested Jelena yawned. She walked to her luggage took out a change of clothes before making her way toward the bathroom upstairs. As she ascended the steps, she was met with the sight of congealed blood on the top three steps. She looked up and found that blood had been seeping from the loft. She sighed, resigning herself to having a "towel bath" in the kitchen.

Once she was ready and had fully recovered from the loss of her coat, she took her items to the rented jeep. Jelena returned to the house for the final time with a small can of lighter fluid. Standing in the living room for a moment, she realised she was going to miss this place but was also aware it was just another sacrifice that needed to be made.

Jelena reignited the fire in the fire place and poured the lighter fluid generously on the sofa before setting it alight as well. As the sofa caught fire, Jelena left the living room, the door still ajar and methodically moved around the house to check that the windows were locked.

As she carried on through the house toward the front door she stopped in the kitchen. It was just long enough for her to open the gas valves on the stove before continuing, quickly yet calmly, to the front door, shutting it firmly behind her as smoke began to fill the house.

Jelena started the jeep's engine and drove away. Once she had reached a safe distance she stopped and listened to the shallow blast of the gas explosion as the fire consumed the entire property. She could not wait and enjoy her handy work, her flight left in nine hours and she had four hours of driving and some shopping to do.

# 4

### 3 December 2010

Early evening in Berlin Tegel Airport, standing outside of arrivals, Daniel yawned and looked disgruntled. He wasn't pleased to have been chosen to meet their Serbian contact. He stood there complaining while Marcel searched for the flight details. "Shit. I want to go to bed! Can't she find her own way?" Marcel didn't pay any attention to his whining.

Once Marcel spotted the flight on the overhead screen, and realised they still had some time before the flight arrived, he called Daniel to come along, leading him to a café. Marcel proposed "If I buy you a coffee, will you shut up?" Daniel agreed and was duly given an extra strong cup of java.

They returned to their previous post, Marcel gradually getting more annoyed, Daniel was slurping his drink and it was driving him to distraction. The gate opened and people began to step out. They hadn't been given any means of identifying her, all they were told was "She'll find you."

The disembarking passengers streamed out of the gate all welcomed with various degrees of warmth and cordiality, but no one had yet approached Daniel and Marcel. With his patience slipping away and the slurping getting louder, Marcel resorted to approaching the first person that would fit the bill of a hard edged woman who knew how to handle a man.

Marcel spotted an average height, stern looking woman with a sturdy build, wearing a shirt and heavy hunting jacket, choosing to carry her bag as opposed to utilising its wheels. She reminded Marcel of an Eastern German shot-putter. The woman stood still and looked around as though searching for someone.

Marcel decided to take a chance before he killed Daniel. He walked up to her and asked "Are you Jelena?" The lady looked perplexed and replied in Russian "I don't speak Germany." Marcel then asked again in Russian to confirm the woman was not the person they sought and she confirmed that she was not. He apologised and stood there looking around not knowing if the person they were seeking had found them yet.

Jelena walked up behind them unnoticed. She coughed to attract their attention, and once Daniel and Marcel turned, she most certainly got their attention as they looked her up and down.

A six foot tall, full figured woman, in a body hugging dress which showed her shoulders and stopped above her knees. She had wavy long dark hair, and a beautiful show stopping face enhanced by her full lips and light green eyes. She had a fur coat draped over her left arm, whilst using the other hand to drag her luggage, her long legs encased in black stockings, her height enhanced by the stilettos she wore "You must be Daniel and Marcel. I am Jelena." She said in Russian, stretching out her right hand.

Her confidence was disarming. Marcel reached out and greeted her with a warm handshake.

"Nice to meet you and welcome to Berlin… do you speak German by any chance?" he cautiously asked "Yes, but not very well." She replied in German. Pleased with her response, Marcel introduced Daniel who instantly turned on the charm "Hello." He raised her hand to kiss it but she seemed apathetic to his advance. "Want some coffee?" Daniel offered, shoving it under her face.

"Uh… no thanks, could we make a move please? I am eager to meet with your superiors." She responded.

The word 'Superiors' stumped both Daniel and Marcel but they dismissed it as a cultural thing. "This way… let me get your bags." Marcel offered as he reached for her luggage. She took a step back with a calm rejection "No, I can manage." Perhaps it was a display of independence he thought as he smiled at her and led the way to the car. Leaving her alone with Daniel, who was totally consumed by lust at that point and momentarily sacrificed charm and tact when he inquired boldly "So, do you have a girlfriend?" Jelena didn't bother to give it a response as she paced ahead to catch up with Marcel.

Marcel turned to find her by his side looking straight ahead. He accepted that she certainly wasn't one who believed in the power of first impressions.

Arriving at the vehicle, a Land Rover, Marcel opened the boot. He reached for her bag but found she had lifted it in by herself, she folded her coat and placed it on the luggage without flinching.

"Is the brief here?" She asked Marcel. "They are in the back seat waiting for you." He replied. Without a word of thanks, she turned around and almost bumped into a grinning Daniel whom she began to consider him a nuisance.

Jelena sidestepped him and got in the car. She looked beside her and saw the folder awaiting her inspection. After she closed the car door Marcel shut the boot and they contemplated what to make of her. Daniel already had his views "She's my kind of girl, a fighter."

"She's a bitch." Marcel concluded and walked to the driver's side of the car.

As they drove out of the car park, Jelena took the opportunity provided by the long drive to review the files. It seemed old fashioned to her to have the pictures of the subjects and notes attached to them in a plastic folder. But still, it was nice to be looking at the tablet computer.

Jelena crossed her legs, getting comfortable, as she looked at the first picture. It was one of a middle aged man with wild looking hair and glasses.

He seemed "geeky" and expressionless, like a boring teacher forever doomed to work in a failing school.

His face seemed worn and exhausted; his lips thin and near invisible and his eyes being of a basic blue. She turned the page and read the notes. He was labelled "Mr A", real name Andreas Thill; aged 40, the sight of his age forced her to take another look at the picture, he looked fifteen years older.

Andreas, Mr A, was 5 foot 9 inches tall; from Kiel. He had been a member of a gang, starting at the bottom and moving up the ranks to become the leader. Andreas had a cover as project manager in an engineering company and the last information provided was his number and address.

The second set of pictures and notes were of a man labelled "Mr C". He was a rather angry, scrawny, thin looking, curly red haired guy with green eyes; it was a picture of him with his arms around a friend, showing he partied hard. The picture also revealed the fact that he was tattooed.

His name was Richard Huober. A hand written note over his profile read "The insane one". Jelena noticed they both happened to be the same height. A short history was provided, nothing much. He didn't have a cover story, he was simple a heavy, the person they sent in to strike fear in anyone who crossed them. She wasn't too interested in reading further and turned to the next picture.

"Mr D" certainly got her attention. Robert Steger, there was a picture of him posing in his underwear and a quick look at the notes confirmed that he was a model. He was stunning, 6 foot 4, which was perfect for her due to her own height. She found him totally sexy with his dark hair and blue eyes. Further reading revealed he was a marketing and sales guy, reeling in the clients and keeping them sweet, particularly the high rolling clients.

As she perused the document, Jelena could sense being watched. She looked up over the folder slightly to avoid being noticed and sure enough, whilst Marcel was focused on driving, Daniel was focused on her and her legs using the rear-view-mirror as a means of surveillance.

Not willing to stand such voyeurism, Jelena uncrossed her legs and reached for her bag, she then took out her phone and sent a text message. Jelena stopped looking at the folders and had her sights fixed on Daniel who still hadn't noticed he had been found out.

Five minutes later, Marcel's phone rang. Though it was illegal to do so, he looked at his mobile and decided to answer "Hello Joel."

"Hi, I see you have our Serbian colleague in the car." Joel asked as he sat by Khoi and Paul reviewing the same pictures given to Jelena. Marcel said she was indeed in the car. "Is Daniel sitting next to you?" Marcel confirmed that he was. "Could you be so kind as to stop the car and move our guest to the front seat?"

"But we are on the highway." Marcel protested.

"Please find a place to park and do so. Thank you." Joel then told Marcel the reason for the request.

Marcel had already had his fill of their new guest.

Once the call ended, Marcel drove as quickly as he could down the autobahn till he found a hard shoulder. He put the car in park, walked around to Daniel's side of the car and opened the door "Out." Marcel ordered. "What?" Daniel remarked, rather surprised, as Jelena got out of the car with her files in hand and began to walk toward the front seat "What's going on? Why should I get out?"

"Because you are a perverted bastard." Marcel replied. Daniel caught glimpse of her approaching, it caused him to smile. Marcel thought this was a twisted dance which he didn't enjoy. Daniel disembarked and mumbled "I love this witch."

Once they had changed places, Marcel, exasperated, went back to the driver's seat and declared "Right... let's go." before he hastily returned to the road to continue their journey.

Silently, she carried on her review, pushing Robert's profile aside she moved onto "Mr E", Oliver Fealsch. He looked normal, quite good looking, blonde, with a smart casual sense of dress and steel in his eyes. His gaze could cut through an iceberg.

Jelena took a closer look at the picture. Oliver had his shirt opened to the third button and Jelena noticed that right beneath his shirt, right close to his heart was what looked like a tattoo, closer inspection revealed it was face of a child. There wasn't much information about him, just the basic, address, number and a disclaimer that he was a good shot who could get people anything they needed.

Finally she set upon the last profile "Mr F", Siegfried Weidman. He an average height individual, nothing spectacular that jumped out at her at first until she realised that there were pages and pages of information on him. She didn't have time to read it all however as they arrived at their destination.

Jelena closed the folder, looking outside for a moment, there was a fog settling and she knew it all that humidity would make her hair frizzy. She thought if she walked into the building quickly, she could salvage her hair-do.

Jelena opened the door, and walked out of the car leaving the folders, Marcel and Daniel behind to marvel at Jelena. Marcel at her breadth of her arrogance and Daniel at her breath-taking ass as she stepped toward the front door.

She walked past the receptionist who called out to her "Excuse me? Excuse me?" Jelena ignored the person, continuing to the private door, entering the access code as the receptionist came walking toward her. There was a beep and the door was unlocked "I'm sorry, but you are not authorised to enter there."

"Fuck off." Jelena replied as she went through the door.

The receptionist was about to go after her but heard Marcel shouting from behind her "It's ok, it's ok. She's with us." as he and Daniel entered the building.

Jelena carried on up the flight of stairs until she reached the meeting room and knocked on the final door. "Come in." cried Joel. Joel, Khoi, Paul, Mikel and Ralph looked up as the door opened "Jelena! You are here!" Joel cried. "Hi boys." She said in German.

"Oh she's here, look Paul, she's here!" Mikel announced in the manner of child who just saw Santa Claus.

Ralph, usually the unanimated one, also seemed to be a fan of her as he got up to greet her with hugs and kisses on the cheek while Paul and Khoi waited patiently. "Why didn't you guys come and meet me at the airport instead of sending grouchy and pervy?" She remarked as she gave Mikel a big hug.

Once she was done greeting the familiar people in the room, she proceeded to address the new faces. Paul walked up first, Joel presenting him to her as they shook hands, then he introduced Khoi "Jelena, this is our team leader Khoi." She took his hand as he said "Hello". Jelena gave him a look over and remarked "Perhaps you could have sent him to pick me up."

Khoi didn't understand what she meant by the comment as he took back his hand but Joel did. Joel laughed "He's not for you Jelena" as he proposed they all sit down. Joel offered their guest the head chair closest to the door and Ralph pulled out the chair for her and she sat.

As the others returned to their seats, the door opened, Marcel entered first with the folders in his hand. He walked to Jelena's side and placed the documents loudly and firmly on the table before her. "Your papers." He announced. She looked at him and said "That will be all." Then turned away, looking straight ahead.

Marcel could have crushed her neck at that point. His self-restraint was being tested. Overcoming his urge to provide a physical demonstration of his mental desire to pummel her, he took his seat to the left of Joel, who was seating at the opposite end of the table.

A few moments later, Daniel entered, dragging along with him her heavy luggage. He had lobbed it up the steps and was out of breath as he dropped the bag by her side, announcing, "I brought your bag." She looked, and gave him a smile that lasted a second before looking away again.

That was enough to make Daniel's day. He took the seat right next to Jelena, his eyes focused on her.

With everyone assembled, Jelena looked around, noticing someone seemed to be missing "Where is Stefan?" she asked. The mixture of ecstatic, angry and indifferent faces all turned sombre and uncomfortable. There was stillness in the room which was enough to alert her to the obvious. "Oh... I'm sorry for your loss."

Jelena's sympathies lasted all of three seconds though before she spun them all back to reality. "Although, judging from your welcome, I am clearly loved; however, I believe my presence here isn't because you were all longing for a reunion. What can I do for you?" She asked, directing her question to Joel. Joel corrected her. "Oh no, I didn't invite you here, Khoi did. Over to you Khoi."

Khoi could feel all the eyes focused on him, his ability to speak disappeared as Jelena's gaze tore into him. Everywhere he turned, he found eyes filled with anticipation. Khoi tried anyway "We need..." Then fell silent, losing his voice mid-sentence. "Sorry." Khoi said again, looking away then looking up again when noticed Joel beside him grinning. Khoi could tell his best friend was willing to have him fail and he wasn't prepared for that.

He straightened his back, cleared his throat, and began again "I want... you to perform a data collection exercise for me. We believe... we know that, directly or indirectly, the people whose profiles we gave you were all involved in Stephan's death. Your role will be as a consultant to me and our team, your suggestions and influence will be appreciated, as for the dirty work, we will handle it.

For now, I would like to send you on a fact finding mission. I need to know as much as possible about the people in those files and I need it within a week. After that I will decide how we approach things and what further part you will play in the matter." Khoi didn't know it, but he spoke with an air of authority and clarity. A growing sense of respect began to spring forth from the rest of the group with one exception. Joel watched with an intensifying sense of insecurity.

Jelena began to sense this challenge was one that she was going to enjoy, but she still required her tools. "I am sure I can do it in three or four days. I will require access to two cars, one bought and one rented but the same make, same colour. I'll need three sim cards, pay as you go, topped up with €150 each. I also will need to have a hotel room..."

"Overlooking a river." said Mikel finishing her words for her. She looked at him with an approving smile as he added "I remembered your criteria from the last time you worked with us. Your cars are in the hotel parking space and your sim cards are in your room. I'll drive you there."

"Oh Mikel, you are so sweet, but remember what happened the last time?" She teased. Mikel blushed. She had another person in mind to drive her however and proclaimed "No, I want Marcel to take me."

Hearing her call his name was bad enough, but having to spend more time in her company made Marcel want to leave the room. "That won't be a problem would it Marcel?" asked Khoi.

Marcel was privately seething, he was being goaded and he couldn't fight back "It will be my pleasure." Marcel said, feigning enthusiasm through gritted teeth.

"Ahh…" Mikel moaned childishly at being bypassed.

"Cheer up, I promise once I get all the details required, we'll have a night out… it'll be like old times, and give me a chance to make new friends." She winked at Mikel, who blushed some more. "By the way, how is Bridget?"

"We broke up." Mikel added.

"Pity, she is a great girl." With that she rose to her feet and announced. "I guess I have my work cut out for me. If you don't mind, I need to have a shower and a nap. I had a very tiring morning."

"Doing what?" Joel asked

"Having fun, burning a house down." They all chuckled and thought they knew what she meant, and she knew they were wrong, so she giggled along before enquired "Who should I call?"

Joel was about to speak when he was shot down with the words "that would be me" which came from Khoi.

Jelena was pleased by the prospect. She requested all the relevant phone numbers she needed before kissing everyone on the cheek but Daniel, whose hand she shook instead. She bade them goodnight as she left with Marcel the same way she arrived, like a glorious bird of paradise, a disgruntled Marcel tailing behind with the folders and her bag.

After her departure, Mikel sat laughing to himself. He was also feeling sorry for Marcel if all went wrong. He patted the table and asked if there were any other topics to be discussed. He was met with the gaze from the others fixed intently on him, Daniel led the questions, "So what did she mean by "Remember what happened"?"

"Oh that? Nothing much… we just had a good time experimenting, it was around the time I met Brigette." Mikel stated. Daniel asked for clarification on what he meant by "experimenting". Mikel smiled longingly as he recollected the events of that summer evening last year.

Mikel seemed go into a euphoric state as he began his tale.

Mikel, Ralph and Stefan were driving Jelena to Rotterdam to find their target, however they had set off late and weren't even over the Dutch border until after 11pm.

They decided to stop for the night in the town of Kleve. They drove around for a bit and soon found a hotel just off the main street called Hagsche Strasse which, thankfully, happened to have a few bars and a couple of night clubs. It was a welcome sight. Despite their fatigue they were not completely spent, and besides, they were hungry.

After they checked into the hotel the four decided to venture out into the small town. It was almost devoid of cars and people; however, one would expect that from such a place on a Thursday night.

The first spot they passed was a place that served fast food. The guys slowed but began walking past more quickly when they noticed Jelena was not stopping. Luckily for them, Jelena spotted a brasserie which was across the road from a lively looking student bar. Thankfully the bar was still serving food although it was ten minutes to midnight. Seated at the bar, they gave the barman their orders. Mikel took the time to list all the items he was allergic to in order to ensure he wasn't exposed to it.

The food was mediocre to say the least, but it was filling. Jelena only ate half her serving; she was distracted by the salsa music which she could hear blasting from the bar across the street.

As Stefan asked for the bill, she asked if anyone was interested in a drink before bed. Ralph and Stefan declined but Mikel chose to stay, he felt it was ungentlemanly to leave a lady on her own and accepted her offer of a drink.

The others returned to the, so called, 'four star', in name only, hotel leaving Mikel and Jelena to enter a dimly lit venue called "The Noise".

It had a live acoustic band comprising of a pianist, guitarist, percussionist and a fat jolly man with his accordion, they were playing soft Latin American music whilst the crowd danced. It wasn't Mikel's style of music. He was more of a techno hard beat fan, but when Jelena asked if he would like to dance, he couldn't resist so he pretended instead.

It was the cha-cha, Jelena drew him close, looked in his eyes, and proceeded to stop the dance after three steps, Mikel having stepped on her foot with each movement. "May be we will be better off drinking." She suggested.

The pair hit the bar and ordered shot after shot of hard liquor. They chatted about their experiences and memories for what seemed hours until Mikel finally looked at the time.

"Shit, I think we best head back. It's getting really late." Mikel recommended.

"Just one more drink. Please?" Jelena gave him a pitiful look and fluttered her long eyelashes, forcing him to give in. "Alright. One more drink." Mikel conceded.

"Great. Two shots of tequila, please?" Jelena promptly ordered. Mikel was pleased, she was like him, and she played hard.

Intoxicated by the music and the shots they had consumed, Jelena decided to perform a party trick and ordered tequila. The usual rules are rudimentary. Take your lime; rub it on the side or back of your hand to allow the salt, which is subsequently sprinkled on the citrus wedge, to stay on to your skin. Dependent on how familiar you are with the person, count down or toast the person you are drinking with, lick the salt off your skin, and finally, down your drink and proceed to sink your teeth into the segment of lime.

However, Jelena didn't play by the rules. When the bartender handed them the salt shaker and the two wedges of lime along with their tequila, she took them both and dropped one to the floor. "Whoops… now you'll have to share mine." She proposed.

Mikel waited to see what she had in mind. He licked the side of his hand, picking up the salt shaker, but soon found he didn't need to. Jelena had downed her drink and held the piece of lime between her teeth, raising her brows. He put back the salt shaker and downed his drink, but before he could return the glass to the counter, Jelena had pulled him forward, her face so close to his that he could feel her breathing. It was time to bite the lime.

Mikel drew closer to her and soon realised he wasn't sucking on the fruit anymore, his lips had locked on to hers. It took his breath away like the pulling force of an electro magnet on a paperclip.

Mikel tried to multitask by attempting to place his shot glass on the counter whilst his eyes were closed and lips attached to another, but he missed the counter and the glass dropped to the ground, however, the sound didn't interrupt the mutual lip service.

It was sensual. Mikel had never felt this way before. Seven minutes of none stop lip locking and tongue wrestling, Mikel was starting to feel strained due to the force being exerted on him by Jelena, but he didn't care, he was overrun with lust and he'd be damned if he would stop now. It did stop however, as she halted and took a step back.

They stood there, panting, looking at one another. Mikel wondered what was next. He didn't know who was supposed to make the next move but he didn't have to wait too long. She turned to the waiter and asked for a tall glass of water. After receiving it, she handed it to Mikel and ordered, "Hold this" as she opened her bag and after a quick rummage she produced a small square pack containing four blue pills. "Give me your hand." She ordered.

Somewhat mesmerised, Mikel did as he was told. She pressed it into his palm "Take it." Jelena instructed enthusiastically. Mikel had the sense however to ask what it was. "Viagra" she frankly responded "Take it; we're going to have crazy sex tonight."

Alarm bells rang in his head. He never considered those two words fit together, but he wanted to find out more. He took the pills while he watched Jelena hastily pay the bartender and purchase something else which Mikel couldn't see before grabbing him by the hand and leading him out of the bar.

Once on the street Jelena took off her heels crying out "come on!" and began to run up the street. Mikel gave chase, following her over the small pedestrian bridge and through the town square as the clock struck one. He struggled to keep up with her, "Come on you pussy!" she screamed at him as she increased her speed.

If the words were meant to spur him on through antagonism, it worked. Mikel found the energy to speed up, his hard sole shoes clattering loudly on the street, yet he could still not catch her.

Jelena took a sharp left, he followed, noticing it was the street where the hotel was situated and soon enough she had stopped in front of their hotel at "Number 44". Mikel could not contain himself; he stopped at the entrance and grabbed her by the arms, kissing her tightly "You still want to have crazy sex with me? Let's do it here…"He suggested.

"No, I have a plan." Jelena's hand made its way down Mikel's body settling upon his midsection to check on his erection. "You're ready. Let's go." she said, leading him into the building by the hand, past the bored student manning the front desk whose reading was interrupted by the giggles and the site of both Jelena and Mikel looking sweaty and frazzled.

"Hello." Jelena said to the student, giving him a small wave. "We're going to have crazy sex." Mikel added. Jelena told him to shut up as the student replied in an apathetic voice "I'm happy for you."

They entered the lift, they were on the first floor, but it was enough time for a quick kiss and cuddle. "Your room or mine?" Mikel asked as the door opened. "Yours, and keep your door unlocked." She instructed.

There rooms were on the same side of the hallway, separated only by Stefan's. The twenty four steps that would have normally taken only a minute took four times as long as they indulged their urges kissing in the intervals between steps until they reached their first stop, Mikel's room.

"Wait for me here." She said.

Mikel entered his room, wondering what to do… he had to get ready. He rushed into the bathroom to brush his teeth, took off his shirt and sprayed some cologne.

When he was done, he stepped out to find Jelena in his room with a knife cutting into the side of the large towel provided by the hotel, ripping them into strips. "What are you doing?" He inquired

"Making ropes, it's all part of the game. You still have a hard on?" Jelena asked.

"Won't go down even if I thought of my grandmother." Mikel said reassuringly. He watched her exerting a lot of effort to make the strips, tantalising his interest.

When she finished, she paused to catch her breath, throwing the knife aside. "You said you were allergic to peanuts right?" Mikel nodded. "What happens when you eat them?"

"My face swells up, my throat closes and I can't breathe, it could kill me." He underlined.

"Nice." She acknowledged with a sinister grin that seemed to immediately dull his interest in the proposed sexual encounter. "So you suffer from anaphylaxis. What do you take for that?" Mikel went to his jacket and took out a slim tube like item about 14cm long and handed it to her.

Having examined it she declared "Cool. EpiPen." Mikel didn't understand why but he was beginning to be frightened. "Do you trust me?" Jelena asked. Every ounce of sense in his head told him he shouldn't trust this woman, but he was fascinated by her, so he said "Yes."

Jelena walked around him, examining Mikel as she touched his chest. "You are sexy." Mikel was nervous and she felt it. To temper this, she took off her shirt and her bra and reached for his hand and placed on her bare breast. It worked and he relaxed.

Mikel kissed her and proceeded to continue down her neck, his arousal levels were now sky high "do you want this?" She asked "Yes, God please..." he begged. She pushed him onto the bed, now he was ready for any kinky filth she may have in mind. "I'm going to tie you up. OK?" he nodded. "Move to the centre of the bed." She ordered.

Mikel placed himself in the middle of the king sized bed. She pulled out a condom from her back pocket and another item Mikel didn't notice and left it on the bed side table. He couldn't care what it was though as he was transfixed on the possibilities that awaited him.

Jelena took off her jeans and underwear. Mikel could only gasp seeing how stunning she was in the nude.

Jelena got on the bed. Straddling him with the strips of the towels in her hand Mikel got a chance to have a closer look at her whole body, particularly the lower half. Shaved, just as he liked it. His admiration was cut short however when he felt her take his left arm, stretching it to reach the bed post, attaching it to the metal frame. She used four of the strips, ensuring it was practically impossible to move.

Jelena followed by attaching the right hand. Satisfied it was firmly fastened, she kissed him deeply on the lips before gradually moving down his body, stopping right above his naval. Jelena unzipped his chinos and pulled them, along with his underwear, down to his knees. "Wow, you are big boy." She remarked, making Mikel proud of his genetic inheritance.

Jelena proceed to bind his feet to the posts at the foot of the bed and then, in a cat like manner, crawled up toward his face and said "I don't suck." Mikel could have told her he didn't care, but he was just confused by her, he remained still with the smile on his face. She kissed him again and reached across the bed side table for the condom.

She sat back up and ripped open the packet with her teeth, placing it over his member.

His heart began to race, he was eager to enjoy her. She flung away wrapping of the condom and then reached for another packet, holding it away from Mikel's view along with the EpiPen.

Jelena took hold of his cock, slipping it within her. She moved to a comfortable position and she asked "Do you trust me?" Mikel was in her power, he nodded obediently, willing to indulge all she had in mind. Almost as soon as the phrase left her lips she revealed the other packet to Mikel. It was salted peanuts and she was dangling it in front of him. She continued, "Have you ever imagined what it's like to get close to brink? Going to the light knowing you could always turn back?

Surrendering your life into the hands of another?" She ripped open the small bag of peanuts, poured three pieces into her hand and brought it close to his lips urging him to eat it with the words "Let's go there Mikel, let's go there together."

His carnal desires blinded his intellect. Mikel received the nuts as though it were communion. As he chewed, a cartoon villain grin formed on her face as she said remarked "Good."

Jelena touched his body and began to gyrate moving his member deep within her. She knew what she was doing and did it well. Five minutes of normal, better than average fun, Jelena was being gentle with him, kissing him softly in intervals. Then she stopped and noticed his skin breaking out in a rash. It was then she launched a more intense exertion of effort.

Jelena kept riding but her momentum grew faster. Mikel didn't want it to stop, even though he could feel his nose running and his swallowing was becoming difficult. Jelena had no intention to pause, in fact she increased the speed to a level he didn't think possible. He was frightened of the possibility that his dick may fall out which could end with her sitting on his penis and potentially breaking it, but it didn't happen thankfully.

The feeling was amazing, even as his eyes watered and his nose became blocked, it only got better. Mikel's breathing began to rattle, despite his intentions to see it to the very end, his reflexes had other ideas. Mikel began to twitch all over. His eyes had been forced shut due to the swelling around them, and now, his body appeared to be losing control, quivering hysterically.

Mikel suddenly received huge smack across his face, followed by the order "Calm down and trust me." Mikel felt himself stabilise as his allergic reaction took control of his body.

Despite his desires, Mikel felt his body cramp in pain as it struggled to make do with the ever decreasing amount of oxygen being processed by his lungs. Jelena noticed it as well when Mikel's skins started turning a slight tint of blue under the dim light of the window, but she couldn't stop, not yet, not whilst she was so close.

As his windpipe got tighter and tighter, his instinctual reflexes wanted him to break free, but Jelena had done a good job of securing him and he could hardly move. The pain of his oxygen deprived lungs was unbearable but amongst all his agony, there also came a release of gratification.

The carnality of Jelena's movements made him climax, putting a greater strain on his aching body. But still he remained erect, despite the fact that his airway was now completely blocked all but for a sliver of air.

It's amazing what the mind does in such circumstances. Mikel soon saw the paradox of the situation and drifted off into a philosophical haze. He had heard it said that any real man would love to die in the throes of pleasure, no less in the arms of a beautiful woman and, perhaps, there may be a strong element of truth to that theory.

In Mikel's case, with his life slowly melting away in a flurry of groans, the movements of Jelena's hips and sensuality, his life dimmed out rather than flashed before him.

As the swelling around his face blinded him, the pleasure which persisted soon began to mix with fear with each instinct battled against the other for dominance.

It must have been the Lord's doing he thought as at the moment his airway was about to close completely, she climaxed, bouncing up and down in slower movements till she sighed in satisfaction. Mikel accepted it was all over as his hearing began to get hollow, and then he heard, "Told you, you can trust me."

Jelena pulled off the cap of the EpiPen with her teeth pressing the end of it on the side of his thigh. She pushed the top of it to eject the needle into the skin, flooding his body with lifesaving epinephrine before she dismounted and rested next to Mikel who started to shiver from the cold which had resulted from the shock he received to his system.

Mikel passed out and could only piece together the rest of the evening from information given by Stefan. According to him Jelena came knocking at his door, woke him up and asked for help to take him to the hospital.

Jelena was clever enough to cloth Mikel first, sadly, his erection had failed to subside and that made Stefan suspicious and, of course, caused all sorts of hilarity once he was admitted to recover. Despite Stefan's pleas for details, Mikel kept the events of the night to himself.

As he recovered, Mikel met a trainee nurse from Berlin named Bridget who had been charged to attend to him. She was a simple .yet demure little thing, someone he wouldn't have given a second look to if he passed them on the street, but Bridget was nice, sweet and caring, perhaps that was what he really was looking for. Prior to his discharge, Mikel asked if she would like to have a drink when she was back in Berlin, she agreed. That started a relationship which lasted till early October when his infidelities caught up with him.

And with a sigh of regret for his loss, Mikel concluded "and that's how

I met Bridget."

After Mikel's exposé, a pin drop could have triggered a deafening boom. Everyone was speechless.

Appalled, Joel had to ask "Is that why you had to spend an extra day in that town's hospital? You chose to have a near death experience for the sexual thrill?"

"Yeah!" Mikel unashamedly proclaimed. Daniel couldn't hold back his curiosity, gingerly asking "Mikel, Mikel, how was it?" Slamming his hand down on the table to emphasise his point, Mikel stated "I'd never do it again, but it was awesome"

"Sweet." Daniel said nodding his approval.

"You guys are disgusting. I can't believe you did that!" Joel protested

"Oh shut up and stop your belly aching, you just pissed because you wish it was you she had tied to a bed post." Khoi snapped.

Whilst the others rambled on about their opinion of Mikel's tale, Paul broke his silence and begged "Is this meeting over? Because I'd like to leave now, go home and take some mind altering drugs to help me forget all I just heard."

The meeting was indeed over. They left the room and ventured out into the dark early evening of winter. As Khoi walked with Joel to his car, Paul came jogging towards him holding a rectangular item wrapped up as a gift which he offered to Khoi. "Here". He grasped the item as Paul explained "It was for Stefan… I guess you can have it."

Feeling moved and rather surprised, Khoi gave him a heartfelt thank you. Without a word Paul walked away. Khoi watched Paul's exit, his concentration broken when Joel snatched the gift right out of his hand.

Khoi protested and chased after Joel who unwrapped the item as he ran. He halted at the sight of the gift. "An advent calendar?" Joel exclaimed, in a somewhat confused state. Khoi caught up with him and snatched the gift back. "I guess you are not the only gay one in the group." Joel remarked. Though it was snide, Khoi laughed as he looked at the cover with all its festive decorations.

Khoi opened the first door which had a picture of a snow man and took out the chocolate shaped like a penguin offering it to Joel who gladly ate it. The next door contained a treat shaped like a robin. That was to be his.

Whilst they watched Paul enter Mikel's car, Joel finally asked Khoi "Come on, what's the real reason for getting Jelena here?"

"I just don't think Paul's ready." Khoi replied as they both chewed, Joel posed his next question "So what now?"

"We wait till she gets me some information and we act from there."

Khoi said.

It was then he noticed Joel's shivering hands and added "I need to make you some gloves."

Rolling his eyes Joel instructed "I want blue. The red ones you made me last year were just too… girly"

"Guess you'll have to take me to the yarn shop then?" Khoi concluded.

That was to be his evening, Khoi sitting in his bed, the advent calendar stationed on the bedside table, knitting away with the TV set on as he searched for ideas.

Meanwhile, Kathrine was at the airport, excited as a ladybird in a botanical garden in spring. Kat was so taken by her forthcoming trip she had forgotten Jan was standing there, already missing her. At the departure gate her last words to him were "I'm going to Hong Kong, isn't that exciting?" and gave him a deep kiss.

She promised to stay in touch and send lots of photographs. She also pleaded with him, telling him to try and relax and reassuringly added "The interview will be fine, just try not to be yourself." Advice given, she walked through the first class express gate and didn't even look back to wave him goodbye.

Unlike the sad, gloomy, weeping masses at the departure gate, Jan was actually glad to see the back of his partner.

Jan was a Berliner, born and bred, though his ancestry was mixed and he did grow up in east when the wall still stood tall. He met Kat 19 years ago when he was just turning 18.

Jan was working as a waiter, his first ever job since the wall came down. Kat thought he was friendly and she liked his wit and integrity, not to mention his broad shoulders, great physique and the most inviting blue eyes she had ever seen. Jan was never short of ambition, but like most people, life and circumstance got in the way of achieving them.

Shortly after they met an affair ensued. They moved in together and it was with her encouragement and financial support that Jan left his old job to pursue a career in the police force at the age of 21.

They never married, however, each year he'd propose and each year she'd laugh it off and say "I'll think about it."

Regardless of this constant rejection, Jan felt lucky to have Kat by his side. He was orphaned at the age of 16 and with no immediate family to speak of, she was all he had. It seemed it would remain that way too, because after three miscarriages, Jan didn't see the prospect of them raising a family. Adoption was often mentioned, but all she would say was "I'll think about it".

The last miscarriage had been 8 months ago, and despite Kat's brave face, Jan could tell her spirit was slowly broken as both time and her body had conspired against her.

So when Julien, her cousin and best friend, offered her a chance to get away from it all, Jan encouraged her to take the opportunity not just because she needed the break, but also for the fact that it would take her away from her friends as Jan wasn't particularly fond of the company she kept.

Jan called them the "diplobrats" who had nothing better to do than waste public funds mingling amongst themselves. That aside, he knew Julien's boyfriend and Jan wasn't too happy with how close she was to Khoi, the head of finance for a health and wellbeing chain, which, although only rumoured and no evidence ever brought to light, had links to the criminal underworld. Khoi was special to her though and she made it clear from the onset that she wasn't going to tolerate anyone cherry picking her friends for her.

Kat and Jan reached an understanding that Khoi was never to come to their flat. It was also understood that his name was not mentioned because Jan had no interest in him and would like to keep it that way for the sake of his position on the force. Hence the added bonus of this trip. The further away from the pest called Khoi, the better.

Once Kat was out of site, Jan was left standing there, contemplating what she meant by "Try not to be yourself." It was already past 10 at night. He had work in the morning and was too tired for philosophy. He went home, got into bed and tried to sleep, but couldn't, the bed felt empty without her. He lay there, awake, reflecting on the fact she was gone for the next three weeks.

Jan regressed to his lonely youth for comfort. He went to the storage space in the basement of the building to retrieve his writing pad of unfinished stories and proceeded to work. He was out like a light by midnight.

Whilst Jan rested, Jelena was busy at work. She went through all the information she had available on the internet and social media outlets. She found it remarkable that most of the subjects were so flippant as to have a nonchalant attitude with their privacy online.

From just his profile on social media alone she hacked into several people's accounts and was able to ascertain the usual haunts of Robert, who had failed to turn off his location finder.

Using the same means she was able to map out the diary of Richard's social life. Jelena thought it would be best to dedicate the weekend to Richard and Robert and get as much information on them as she could and by Sunday night.

She looked briefly at the others online though could find very little on

Siegfried and Oliver and practically nothing on Andreas. She settled on the most complicated of the group, Andreas. Jelena decided it was best with him to resort to what she did best, tracking.

Prior to going to bed, she decided to go for a quick drive to accustom herself to the area where Andreas lived and find the best place to observe him from. It was rather annoying that google, which often proved accurate turned out to have miscalculated the distance. Rather than it being half an hour away, it was more an hour adding to her growing fatigue.

# 5

*6 December 2010*

Jelena arrived in the nice quiet neighbourhood with small shops and cafes lining the road. She spotted Andreas' building and noted the key entry points and how much time it would take to get in or out from one of the surrounding streets. She also took mental notes of where the blind spots were and the best vantage points of the premises. Content in her knowledge of the building, Jelena wondered if it was worth the effort returning to her hotel room. She decided against it and instead began an impromptu stake out.

Jelena spent Monday morning tailing Andreas and she found him a most peculiar person. Once he was safely at his office, Jelena broke into his flat. She picked the lock to be sure her visit would remain undetected.

Upon entering she strategically planted several surveillance cameras in and around the flat. Prior to her departure, she sifted through his mail and other documents to collect more data on her subject. It was then Jelena found an envelope from a hospital which aroused her interest, so she took it. Jelena also found that Andreas was still the old fashioned pen to pad type when she discovered his organiser on the bed side table.

It was amazing, it included everything in fine detail, by date, time, even the length of time it would take to complete any given task. The organiser was worth its weight in gold as it not only underlined the pattern of Andreas' life, regardless of how warped it seemed in writing, but it also included the schedule and availability of all the people in his network. There was no point taking pictures of it, the leather bound brown book had to come with her.

In a race against time, Jelena took the book to a nearby print shop and photocopied all the pages for the month of December before sneaking back to Andreas' flat and left the book back where she had found it.

The next two days, as the gang carried on with their day to day activities, Jelena spent time alone in her room going over the dossier prepared for her, noting each and every single detail, determining which of her subjects she should focus on first. Jelena grasped Mr "A's" folder, flipping through the pages, she realised it contained little to no information whatsoever on the man besides his professions, address and phone number. It was in stark contrast to Mr "F" whose folder was over flowing with details. She realised that her first point of focus could be Mr "A", Andreas, and she would have to address this one personally as she put his file aside.

Jelena then took a look at Siegfried's file. Reading page, after page, she concluded that such information could not have been gathered through hearsay and that it must have been obtained from an inside contact. She put Siegfried's file aside as well and drew a question mark on the folder before she continued reading the other profiles.

With six hours of her life gone and a headache on its way, Jelena reached for Andreas' folder and this time laid it side by side with three other folders she had chosen. She proceeded to decide on her course of action.

Richard was the wild one, living off a cocktail of sex, drugs and violence. It was easy to deduce the best way to get to him was via his excesses. There was a paranoid streak running through every word related to the man, therefore, it would easier to have this addressed by her employers. Still she wrote her suggestions on the best method to eliminate him on the inner part of the folder.

Looking at Robert's information, Jelena smiled as she looked at the picture of the man. He was very attractive and clearly very vain. With her keen eye, she could also tell that he was the one who could be lured into a state of false confidence through his vices, just like Richard. She wrote her opinions in the document before casting it aside.

And then there was Oliver. Out of all the information provided, he seemed the most normal, yet the most complicated of them all in many ways, however with her head hurting and her make up feeling uncomfortable on her face, she decided to leave him aside for now. It was time to go to bed, but before she left her desk, Jelena made her decision. She was going to work alphabetically after all and selected Mr "A". He was to be her focus of attention.

Waking up the following morning, Jelena set to work and for the next three days she dedicated her efforts on observing her subject.

The first thing she needed to do was map his movements. She arrived at the park opposite Andreas' apartment block at thirteen minutes past five in the morning with darkness still holding the city in its grip and the cold eating at her resolve. She walked up and down for a moment, ensuring the front door was never out of her sight nor her flick knife out of her grip as she kept an eye on all those that passed her.

The wind blew stronger by the minute. She began to feel the cold penetrate her bones and her attention was momentarily swayed by a woman and her dog exercising together. While she was distracted, a nervous looking man walked out the grey, five storey-block of flats, wearing a camel covered rain coat, dark brown trousers and white shoes. He was walking at a quick pace, in a somewhat disorganised fashion.

Looking over at him Jelena knew this was her target and began trailing him on his journey, keeping a safe distance to avoid detection. Her subject's first destination was the underground station to catch a train. She followed him down the stairs and waited on the other end of the platform.

A train arrived, the U8 to Wittenau, and despite the flow of people, Jelena could still see her target. She was about to step onto the car when she noticed that the man had remained where he was, making no move to enter the train. Realising this Jelena promptly exited back onto the platform. Perhaps the train was not going to the appropriate destination she thought. Jelena looked at the timetable for the next train and noted that the U8 was the only train that served this station.

Another train arrived and the same thing happened. She watched him look up at the timetable and then his watch. She suddenly realised that it wasn't a certain train he was waiting for. The man's main concern was the time he boarded. They weren't his trains because they didn't leave at the time he wanted.

Finally after the fourth train had come and gone, he boarded the fifth and Jelena followed. She watched and giggled as the man performed a sort of ritual before he sat on his seat. As he clutched his leather satchel bag, Jelena noted from her vantage point, now standing just a few feet away, that the man also wore latex gloves to cover his hands which he would remove periodically in order to apply cream to his hands before putting on a fresh pair. They got to their stop, Residenzstr. The man left the station and made his way to his place of work which was not too far from the station itself.

Stage one complete she thought as she returned to the area where the man lived, and again she decided to find out more about her target by returning to his flat to look around.

Using her lock-picking skills again, she got back into the building and into the man's flat once again. Entering the apartment she stood there a moment, amazed by what she saw.

The entire flat from ceiling to floor had been freshly painted bright white and totally void of decoration. She took off her shoes before she ventured in.

There was no furniture present in the living room except a couple of white plastic chairs and matching table. The kitchen was the same situation, with just one of every utensil, neatly placed upon the counter facing up, and all white as snow.

It wasn't until Jelena got to his bedroom that she found some colour. It was in his wardrobe which housed all of his 12 tweed coats, along with 12 of the same white shirts and brown trousers, all pressed and hung ready to be worn. Despite this strange spectacle, Jelena could find nothing of interest in the rooms despite her meticulous search.

There was only one room left to search, the bathroom. Again, it shared the same decor as the rest of the flat, right down to the white bar of soap. The exception was the mirror on the medicine cabinet, which, when she opened it contained boxes of disposable latex gloves on the lower shelf and on the top, tubes of hand cream.

Jelena stood to assimilate what she had just uncovered. Regardless of this fact, there was still very little of interest to be found anywhere and three days of tracking revealed that the man was extremely secretive and very clean. There was no need to tail him anymore. Jelena decided to divert her time to looking into the life of Mr "E".

*7 December 2010*

Though Khoi had arrived 15 minutes late, he was still left waiting in the meeting room for over half an hour. He was a bit upset by the text he received from Joel which read "Jelena and I are stopping for a coffee." Khoi fumed at the fact that Joel didn't even bother to ask if he wanted anything. He sat at the table, deciding to play a word game on his phone to pass the time.

When Joel and Jelena, who clutched her file folder close to her chest, did arrive, at 6:47pm, Khoi had already reached level six having restarted the game five times. The pair entered in a chirpy mood, caught in the middle of a laugh. "Hey man, sorry we're late. I wanted to show her mum's favourite cake shop and we..." Khoi raised his hand to halt Joel's yammering, and it worked as Joel said in a contrite tone "... sorry."

Khoi then pointed to the available chairs "could we get down to business please?" The pair took their place either side of him. "I hear you have some information for us." Khoi began.

Jelena smiled, unzipped the folder and took out the files she had brought. "I have some information on Andreas and Oliver, some suggestions regarding Robert and Richard, and a question relating to Siegfried." She announced passing the paperwork to Khoi.

Khoi picked up the first folder and flipped open the first page as Jelena continued "Regarding Siegfried, who compiled the dossier on him?"

"Marcel. He and Siegfried grew up together in cologne before arriving in Berlin... why?" Khoi ask whilst scanning through the first page.

"That's good... Would Marcel be involved in his removal?" She asked, Khoi confirmed. "I don't think it is a good idea." She added

"There's very little I can do about it. He insisted and I can't deny him." Khoi' response made him sound subservient and left her wondering if he was really the one in charge.

Jelena said "I might need to speak to Marcel..." but before Jelena could complete her statement Khoi, who was now reading through the first paragraph of findings for Mr A interjected "you tell us when we send him down. It says here that "Andreas is repulsed with contact and has a fear of dryness..." Khoi, for Joel's benefit, he read Jelena's findings out loud. When he finished, Joel passed judgement on the man. "He's a freak."

"He's not a freak Joel, he has OCD." Khoi corrected.

"Dude, everything in white and the constant need to wear gloves? Sounds like a freak to me." Joel rebutted.

Ignoring Joel, Khoi proceeded to commend Jelena on her work and added "This will be very useful, I assure you." He picked up the folder for Richard and saw it had a suggestion in one line which Khoi glanced over, initially showing it to Joel who didn't bother to give it a look as he was had become more occupied with the vision of Jelena before him, prompting Khoi to ask "Now, about our friend Mr "C", how certain are you that it will work?"

"It depends on how strong a stomach you have." Jelena replied. "Trust me, if you do it, it will work."

Before Khoi could pose a follow up question, Joel interrupted "That's very impressive, but I am hungry. Want to go for dinner?" directing his question to Jelena.

"I'd love to, but only if Khoi can join us." She proposed.

Khoi was about to make an excuse when Joel butted in with "I'm sure Khoi will be able to come. Right?"

Before too long they all found themselves in a Thai restaurant. They were seated at a table near the back for added privacy and Khoi was feeling like a third wheel on an impromptu date between Jelena and Joel. Khoi braced himself for boredom as he took his place at the table.

Initially the chat was subtle and nothing more than a gush of flattery from Joel, who was trying to play the role of good listener, asking Jelena questions as they waited for their first course. Khoi could sense the strain in Jelena's voice and could see that the constant interrogation was beginning to fray her.

When the soup finally arrived, Jelena and Khoi both secretly hoped it would lead to a rest in the conversation, but they were wrong. With one spoonful in their mouths, as Jelena savoured the flavours of the soup, Joel asked permission to ask a private question. Sensing she may regret it, Jelena, nevertheless replied "feel free to ask anything." Putting his spoon aside and leaning forward for added secrecy, Joel began "So tell me Jelena, what brought you into this line of business?"

Jelena had a smirk on her face. She placed her spoon down and dried her lips.

Khoi stated it was probably the most inappropriate question he had ever heard but Jelena was keen to speak on the matter "It's not the first time I've been asked this question." She sat back in her chair while Khoi looked on uncomfortably. Joel was itching to hear the tale. "Revenge", she said.

The one word answer wasn't satisfactory however as Joel pushed further. "Is there a tale behind it?" Khoi wanted to intervene but she wasn't deterred, rather she seemed eager to share.

"Well." She began as she leaned forward, lowering her tone, as though about to spread some scandalous gossip. "When I was 15, I was walking home when a wealthy smuggler leader snatched me off the road. He raped me several times and then drove me home afterwards." The relaxed manner of her revelation was puzzling "I didn't go home, I went to the police to report it, but the officer simply said "Why are you here? A girl like you should know better than to dress like a common prostitute. Go home."

I went home and told my mother and she, in turn, told my father who went to confront the perpetrator, threatening him, saying he would contact the authorities, but when the man opened his wallet, everything was fine. My father, in effect, sold my virginity for €40,000. They gave me €1000 as restitution. My mother said nothing and supported his action, now she could improve the house.

When I asked why he did it, my father said 'Perhaps if you didn't dress so provocatively…' You know the rest. So I left home. I was on the streets for a while, got into the wrong crowd, however I proved myself and that's what brought me to this point. I did, however, achieve my revenge on the smuggler."

Jelena paused, picked up her spoon and continued eating her soup. "Sorry, don't want it to get cold." Once she had her fill, she drank some of the champagne and without an iota of tension or grief; she began the tale of how she got back her rapist.

In a lowered tone, Jelena went about describing the man. He was a lanky, hairy man who didn't believe in using things like deodorant fearing the harmful effect of the chemicals they contained. In addition, he was a "new age" believer, constantly looking for a means of purifying his body.

This put an image in the minds of Joel and Khoi of a rich guy, driving around in a fancy car across town through the midst of poverty while emitting a terrible body odour. And they surmised he also commanded respect, pulling in the ladies because he could splash a lot of cash around.

Jelena then added that with some intense snooping, she found that the man liked to be clean inside and out. Hence, he had a monthly colonic irrigation at a private health retreat on the banks of the Danube.

When the time did come for his cleansing, Jelena decided to meet her rapist. To enable this to happen, she accosted the staff member in charge on her way to work and took her place temporarily.

Now in the building and the designated private room that housed the relevant equipment, and armed with her tools of vengeance, she set to work preparing the scene and once done, all she had to do was wait for her patient.

The man was an hour late and when he materialised in his bathrobe, he took a look at her and immediately went about lecturing her on the dangers of using makeup.

It didn't bother her that he mocked her lipstick; it was the small, foul, untamed whiff of body odour that angered her. Still, she had a job to do, so she smiled and asked if the man could go behind the screen and put on the gown provided.

He followed the instructions and when he emerged, smiled at her showing his vile, discoloured gold capped teeth. "Haven't I seen you before?" he asked. Without answering, Jelena winced; she pointed to the table and asked the man to lay down on the paper covered surface.

As she inserted the tube into the man's anus, Jelena said "We have a new herbal remedy from Japan today. It injects antioxidants directly into the system. "Sounds nice" the man remarked.

"Yes, it may sting a little" she replied as she switched on the machine releasing the fluids that began to flow into the man.

20 seconds into the process, and satisfied that all was going to plan, Jelena excused herself "I'll be right back". She left the room, locking the man in before stashing the key safely in her pocket. She briskly walked out of the spa to her car and contently drove away.

Once Jelena finished her story, Joel seemed confused "That's it? You left a tube in his ass and left?"

"There's more to that tube than meets the eye." Khoi interjected and his inquisitive mind made him ask "What was in the cleansing fluid?"

"HF", she replied sipping her drink, observing that Joel looked perplexed.

"HF?" Joel repeated "What is that?"

"Fucking genius, that's what it is." Khoi remarked, adding "readily available, easy to handle and the effects are irreversible, that guy was a goner!"

Still perplexed, Joel inquired "What are the effects? What did you use? Can someone clarify?"

"Hydrofluoric acid." Khoi replied and seeing it meant nothing to Joel he repeated "acid?"

Then it clicked, Joel's eyes flung open and expressed his shock whilst struggling to keep his tone down "Sweet Jesus, it'd eat him from the inside.

The guy would have shit out his own liquefied organs."

"That he did." Jelena confirmed with a sinister grin "I attended his funeral." Joel found a whole new respect for Jelena.

Khoi was speechless, his mouth agape. Joel was quicker in recovering his faculty of speech and remarked "Damn, you are hard-core."

"Thank you, but I haven't finished. There was one more person to go." She said; taking more spoonful's of her broth as she progressed. Jelena proceeded to explain how she tracked down the policeman who ignored her request.

I tracked him down one summer's night and found him enjoying the quiet life with his family which she disposed using her silencer, right before his eyes.

Surrounded by his dead wife and his two daughters, the policeman cradled his only son's lifeless body.

Furious, she remarked "Oh, I see that the girls mean nothing to you, you ass. Get up." Jelena ordered. After he reluctantly rose, she hit him over the head with the butt of her pistol, causing the man to fall to the ground again, dazed. Jelena then proceeded to take out a syringe, injecting the cop with propofol, putting him to sleep.

While he slept, Jelena transported him to the roof of an old abandoned warehouse and carried his sleeping body two floors up. Luckily for her the man was light and had a small frame, so it wasn't too difficult.

Placing him on a chair, Jelena made a noose out of fishing wire, attaching it to the end of a rope. She placed it over his head and around the man's neck. The other end of the rope was attached to a flag pole.

She smothered his palms with super glue and placed them on his ears, fixing them firmly using bandages which she had wrapped around his head. She then waited patiently, as a soft breeze carried the dust around the space, causing her some irritation.

The man began to stir after an hour. Jelena thought that enough time had passed for the glue to set. She rushed to remove the bandages and walked the man to edge of the building, leaving him a standing position before waking him up.

The man opened his eyes. Initially, his vision seemed blurred but he soon realised where he was perched and was instantly terrified. He almost lost his balance attempting to spread out his arms to maintain it, however, he realised he wasn't able to stretch his them apart. Still, he managed to maintain his balance with his toes.

He took a step back and tried to take another but felt the cold, hard metal of a gun barrel. Terrified, he turned quickly, nearly bashing Jelena on the face with one of his elbows. Now facing her, she moved the gun to his temple, and laughed before commenting "What delicious irony. You didn't want to listen to what I had to say back then and I guess it's the same situation we find ourselves again today."

"Please, please, let me go." The man pleaded. "I swear I won't tell anyone."

"I'm sorry, I can't hear you." Jelena said as she pushed the man with both hands, forcing him to fall backwards from the edge.

The man screamed, but it lasted only three seconds as the fish wire tightened itself around the man's throat and as the slack ended, his weight led to the inevitable. The fish wire cut clean through his neck.

Jelena then concluded that "It was with great satisfaction to watch the surprised news reporter later that evening as he described the police as being "perplexed" at how a man could be found decapitated, whilst still holding his head in his hands. She had left the gun behind with only his prints on it and because of this; the cops just wrapped it up as a Policeman gone crazy... a murder/suicide.

The shock on the boy's faces said it all, Khoi then asked "Why did you do that?"

"Why not?" she parried.

"Haven't you heard of forgiveness?" Khoi suggested, but she shrugged him off and said "Forgiveness is a very important word in my vocabulary, just never found the context in which to use it."

Just then, the waiter came along to collect their bowls. Only one person had eaten most of their starter, Joel and Khoi had hardly touched theirs.

As she watched the waiter stroll off, she sighed, her carnal interest in the man was abundantly evident. Having revealed her naked truths, she thought it was their turn. "Well I would love to find out how you two got into this, as if I didn't know already. It is the need for justice that brought us to this table. I got my revenge on the person whom I thought deserved it, who do you think deserves it?"

Joel and Khoi looked at each other, Khoi hesitated, but Joel wasn't so coy. "Jürgen Schmude" He instantly replied.

"Come on Joel…" Khoi chided him but the flames of curiosity had been stoked.

"And who is he?" Jelena asked

"The man that took my brother…" Joel realised he was speaking in riddles and expanded "Jeroen and I snuck out of the house to go to an event. I admit we were young and foolish, but the man was drunk. He shouldn't have been behind the wheel. He ran straight into us driving at a high speed in the wrong direction." Joel paused as the events of the night seemed to overcome him and he tried to keep the tears at bay.

It didn't stop him from persisting "Jeroen wasn't wearing his seat belt that night… he flew right out of the windscreen. He was in a coma for five months and when he woke up, I didn't have a brother anymore… or maybe he didn't have me anymore.

He was so brain damaged that he couldn't speak, couldn't walk and couldn't remember anything about me or my family, but he is getting better now, he is improving…" Then he turned to Khoi with envious grin and said "But he remembered you, he never forgot you. That night I had a brother with three broken ribs, whiplash, a broken jaw and arm, a brother who has the mental age reverted to that of a three year old. Not to mention, a father who blames me for everything, blames me for taking away his most promising son because it was my idea to go out that night… I had lured him to his doom."

Joel paused and cleared away a tear before he giggled at the irony. "And you know what Jürgen Schmude got? Six months. He was out in three. He's living his life and we are living with the consequences of his night out." Noting the silence, Joel tried to make lighten things up "Sorry about that. I just brought the whole evening down."

"Don't be silly." Jelena replied "It's a fair choice, now Khoi, it's your turn. Who would you like to get back at?"

Khoi gave a scornful look "I don't want to play this game." His irritation was clear and unashamed. "It's not a game, come on Khoi, tell." Joel urged.

"I don't have anyone I'd like to get back at. Is that so hard to believe?" Khoi lashed out. There was a moment of uncomfortable silence but Joel couldn't help but goad him on and when Khoi refused to comply, Joel spoke for him. "There were these boys called Ingi and Ben, they use to pick on him and beat him up." Joel revealed "Shut up!" Khoi ordered. Jelena detected a weak spot and decided to capitalise on it. "Ingi and Ben, who are they?" She poked him for information.

Exhausted, Khoi caved in and spoke quickly "They were these two individuals who thought I was a punching bag as opposed to a human being. Even though I was keen on martial arts, I couldn't bring myself to hurt others and they knew this, hence, I had a near daily dose of battering till I was fourteen when Joel and the gang saved me. Ah look, dinner is here. Let's try and enjoy our meal shall we?" Using the moment to change the topic as their plates were brought to them.

The arrival of dinner had put a full stop to the round of questions, but before they ate, Jelena grinned and said "I know what I'm getting you both for Christmas."

As they had their dinner of roast duck, Jelena confirmed that she felt she had made remarkable progress with her information gathering exercise. As she fought to find some pleasure from chewing on the piece of dry duck breast she had been served, she asked "I normally never pry, but I am fascinated. You know all these people, you know where they live, could you not just put some metal in them?"

"But that would deprive us of your wonderful company." Joel teased causing her to laugh.

When she had finished her food, Joel also gave up on his meal, pushing his plate away and sighing "It's for our friend here, Khoi. He wants to prove himself and show he can stand shoulder to shoulder with us and save money on what you call 'metal'"

"Ah, a display of brains over brawn." Jelena concluded.

Despite being the centre of conversation, Khoi didn't speak; he kept eating, not feeling the need to defend his actions. Joel was still interested in Jelena. "So where has your business taken you so far?"

As Joel and Jelena spoke amongst themselves, Khoi was bored, very bored. Jelena didn't mind talking about her trips and Joel hung on every word, clearly taken by her graceful manner and beauty. All this gushing made Khoi feel sick and he would have vomited if he wasn't so hungry, so he carried on eating and drinking.

Jelena and Joel found common ground on a lot of topics, from sex to political views, it acted like soul mates, meeting and sizing each other up and since they were fixed on each other, they ignored their food and their wine, and hence didn't need a top up on their drinks.

The waiter was as effective as a watering can. Since Khoi was the only one drinking, he was the only one getting his glass refilled. Seventy minutes and six glasses of red wine later, the dessert was served. It was welcomed with anticipation and near applause by Jelena and Joel who remarked how they both loved warm apple pie.

When the plate was placed in front of Khoi, he waved it away. "I'm fine thanks... I have had too much."

It was then Joel made an observation "You're drunk."

"Of course I am, you would too if you had like... I don't... a lot of wine." Khoi slurred, hardly able to stay on his seat. Feeling guilty, he promptly added "I'm sorry, I'm spoiling the evening aren't I... you two need to be alone... I'll go." Khoi said as he got up, took a few steps before he tripped, falling to the floor to the gasps of the other patrons in the room.

That was officially the end of the evening. Joel helped his friend out of the restaurant through the back door, Jelena trailing, holding his coat. Khoi kept repeating "I'm sorry, really unprofessional of me... I am a light weight, this must be embarrassing." This continued till they reached the car.

Khoi was put in the back seat, left there to giggle hysterically, prompting Jelena and Joel to see the humorous side of the whole event.

Joel started the car and drove. Being that his hotel was closest, the first stop was to be there. Joel tried to revive the conversation, to find out more about her.

"Do you still talk to your father?" Joel inquired

"No. The last thing I asked him was "Did you enjoy the money?" Then I left". She replied without emotion on the matter. Any hopes of reviving a conversation following her chilling revelation was near impossible.

They finally arrived at Khoi's hotel, parking at the front door of the hotel. Jelena and Joel went to open the back door of the car in anticipation that Khoi may need some assistance.

Khoi appeared to have recovered his ability to walk and managed to step out of the car unaided. However, one step away from the car, he seemed to near trip again prompting Jelena to rush forward to prop him up, allowing him to rest his weight upon her shoulders. Joel came to help also and though he wanted to help, Khoi shoved him away.

Buoyed either by curiosity or alcohol or perhaps a bit of both, Khoi's inhibitions evaporated as he turned to Jelena and asked "Will you help me to my room?"

It was a standoff, like Khoi, Joel was eagerly waiting for a response, desperately hoping that Jelena would look upon it as a joke and desperately praying she would leave Khoi to his own devices, allowing them to continue their conversation. He wanted to know her, to have her.

She turned to Joel and she didn't need to speak, but she did, his heart had already sunk before she even said "You know what? I don't live too far away, I don't mind. I'll take care of him. You can join the others."

Joel anxiety heightened. He had to intervene; he wasn't going to lose her so easily. "You're barking up the wrong tree!" He cried. "I know." Jelena replied. "I'll pick up my bag tomorrow at the meeting. Thank you for a wonderful time." She quickly kissed Joel on the cheek as she ordered "Come on Khoi, let's go."

Joel watched on for a moment and was confused, as though he had been played with and it didn't feel right. He decided he wasn't keen on watching anymore and walked to his car, driving home completely discontent with life at that moment. He didn't want to be social anymore; he determined and convinced himself that he was more interested in the happenings on the sports channel.

Jelena was equally unsure what the night was going to bring. She helped Khoi to his room and set him on his bed in a seated position. She helped him out of his shirt and realised he was all together good looking and still rather drunk. "Ok, bed time for you little one." She ordered as she took off his shoes and watched him snuggle up to the pillow. Khoi looked so innocent, and seeing him that way made her initial intention of taking advantage of him melt away. Jelena decided to go home instead and to search on more data regarding Oliver.

# 6

*8 December 2010*

Khoi woke up from his heavy sleep still tired and with a slight hangover. His overactive mind had kept him dreaming all night long and most of the visions weren't so sweet.

It was 6am when his alarm clock rang. He went to the hotel's gym and did his usual exercises before returning to his room for a shower. He turned on the tap and wondered if this could be a means of swift retribution… no, too torturous and ineffective, he concluded, as he walked into the shower stall to cleanse his skin.

Breakfast was dull and it didn't help that he wasn't hungry anyway. He spent time watching television as the weather report confirmed that there was a bracing wind of change set to hit Germany. The meteorologist warning to "say goodbye to the bright nice sunny weather and prepare yourselves for the cold as the mercury is set to drop."

His boring pancakes all of a sudden tasted better as he processed the information about the weather. He decided his breakfast had become a hindrance. Khoi left the table and didn't care how odd it was to be seen running to the lift.

A sense of urgent excitement bore through his mind. He thought he may have had a "Eureka" moment, but he still wasn't certain. Khoi grabbed his laptop, as well as a note pad and all the things he required for extensive research at the University Library.

Khoi arrived at the library before 9 in morning. He was directed to the appropriate department by the hip looking librarian and began to look for toxicology and medical reports, interested in the effects of mercury on the body.

After two hours, Khoi slowly lost hope that mercury was the answer. He read various reports that stated that the amount that one was required to ingest would be too high to use in an incognito manner. Still others confirmed that mercury would be the ideal substance as it could get into a person's system in various ways, but if it was detected, could be treated and he didn't want that. Khoi searched the internet to find other materials that could help him achieve his goals.

Jotting down notes on the pad, he got the usual list, cyanide, arsenic, belladonna, Botox. There was even a plant from India that was so toxic and undetectable that it would have been the perfect item. It would have been perfect if it didn't take two to four months for delivery. He also noticed that death form the substance was near instantaneous and that wasn't what he was looking for. He wanted something that would linger.

Khoi paused for a break. It wasn't that he didn't enjoy the research, all the books littering the table reminded him of his youth, when he was curious about anything and everything. It infuriated him that he couldn't find an answer.

Maybe a break for some air and a moment away from the smelly old books would help, Khoi thought. He collected the articles and books to return them to their relevant shelves.

As he placed back a medical journal, he caught site of an Asian girl, wearing big, round, loosely fitting spectacles with thick lenses. She was dressed in a slightly over sized sweater and donned a very long tartan skirt. Khoi took a book from the shelf next to him and glanced through the literature, pretending to be interested in it.

She drew closer as he placed a book back on the shelf. It was a report chronicling the effects of mass poisoning when an indigenous coastal community ingested mercury from contaminated fish. In it he found out that incubation period of the liquid metal varied from patient to patient, another damper on his slowly dissolving plan he thought.

Khoi was startled when the young lady said "Hi" in English.

"Hello." He replied.

"So, are you a medical student? What year are you?" She had the directness of an arrow.

Khoi had been caught off guard, he thought quickly and replied "I am a research student."

"Oh" she remarked. Then she took a look down at one of the books he held, reading out the title, "Properties of Mercury." What are you researching exactly?"

"The neurological effect of mercury on the human brain." He replied, then, feeling stupid for having actually told the truth, attempted to bring the conversation to an end. She added "Funny thing mercury. It's a very poisonous metal. Some guy I heard about in France had a few drops of an off shoot of mercury on his latex gloves and didn't know it. He was dead within a month."

This must be his lucky day, Khoi thought; he wanted to know more and proposed "That sounds interesting, it could be helpful to my research. Would you care to tell me more over a cup of tea?"

She pushed her spectacles back up on her nose and smiled "Sure, I have another three hours before my next class."

"Good." He said, as he placed the last book he was holding and introduced himself "I'm Khoi by the way, what's your name?"

"Han" she replied with a smile.

Khoi collected his things and allowed her to select a cafe. Playing the tactical game of charm, he asked Han about her background and how long she had been in Germany. She explained that she had been studying medicine at the university on a scholarship programme for over a year now.

It meant money was tight and hence the library was her only source of materials and thus her second home. The fact she was a struggling student was obvious to Khoi just looking at her old laptop which she clutched tightly. Yet she seemed a cheerful and bright person even though she slurped her tea and ate her bun with her mouth open.

Khoi didn't touch his food or drink. Instead he asked for more information about the substance she referred to as 'Dimethyl mercury.' She placed her cup down, her glasses temporarily steamed up by the tea. Taking off her glasses to clean them before shaking her hair which had been cut in a fashion of a pudding bowl, she returned to the topic "mercury itself is poisonous, but it's the methyl group that makes mercury toxic. Generally, mercury has one methyl group, hence its toxicity, but it depends on the length of exposure and quantity. Dimethyl mercury, on the other hand, has two methyl's making it super toxic." Then she took out her pen and writing pad. Khoi could see that this future professor was in her element.

Placing the pad on the table, she began to draw what initially looked like a web. Then she wrote "C" in the centre, followed by three lines facing outwards from the "C" in different directions and at the end of each line she wrote "H". An "Hg" was then placed between the "H" and "C" before she pointed out triumphantly to Khoi what he could only consider scribbles. "This is its molecular structure.

The substance is very lipophilic. That means it loves fat and adheres to it, eventually mixing with it. After time it will dissolve the fat in the body.

Can you guess where there is the large amount of fat?" Khoi gave her a blank look.

Han took out her felt pen and drew a circle on his forehead proclaiming "The brain!" as she drew two dots for eyes and a smile. Khoi didn't understand why he didn't react to this violation of his space... clearly he was disarmed by her intelligence. "The substance will dissolve all the fat there. The effect is irreversible and there is no treatment available. That's what kills the person."

"What happens to the person?" Khoi asked as he rubbed his forehead to clean off her drawing. She explained that a person would basically lose their balance, their mind, their faculties, their cognitive capabilities and would likely die in agony within a few weeks. "Sounds horrible, if you can't touch it, how can it be handled? And what else can you use it for?"

"Very carefully is how you handle it..... And it's otherwise useless" she replied as she finished her sandwich.

Han began to eye his meal which he hadn't touched. Khoi noticed and swapped her empty plate with his. "So you need gloves to hold it?" He continued

"What do they teach you?" she giggled "Ordinary gloves wouldn't be enough to protect you. Some man in France died when a couple of drops fell on his latex gloves. It permeated through it and got absorbed through his skin. I think I told you that already didn't, I?

You would likely need silver lined gloves and protective clothing and a gas mask to handle it."

"It sounds like motion detected bomb. How do you transport it? With a titanium tank?" Khoi inquired. He was totally amazed that such a substance existed.

Han took a bite of the second sandwich and speaking again with her mouth full explained, "Yes, titanium would be effective, but a cheaper means of carrying it around is in a poly-propylene container, you can get those anywhere."

Khoi could not have wished for a better outcome to his day. He was happy having found out what he wanted and he wasn't heartless. He asked how Han was coping in Germany and she was candid with her replies. Han confessed she found Germany tough, telling him she was under a lot of pressure to succeed which has left her in a dilemma.

She explained she only received a small stipend and though it was enough to feed herself, it was still difficult to live comfortably adding, "I can't complain though. I am here to study, not play."

Han finished off her drink as the conversation came to an end.

She reached for her purse but Khoi told her to put her money away, insisting on paying, it was the least he could do for her help.

Whilst leaving the café she asked for his name again, he told her. "Khoi, how nice… sounds Vietnamese" she perceived correctly. Then she asked for his number, contrary to his better judgement, yet seeing her potential, Khoi gave it to her. "I have to go to my class." She proclaimed "Thank you for the breakfast."

They shook hands and parted ways, leaving Khoi feeling a bit lighter with the knowledge he could achieve his goal with relative ease… provided he could get his hands on Dimethyl mercury. Khoi needed to buy the catalyst and, not knowing if or how he could help, he nevertheless decided to call Joel.

In a brothel on the north side of Berlin, a woman walked into a room in her black lace underwear with red trim. She didn't think she could have a client so early in the morning until she was informed that one customer hadn't left. He had been there for their services since one in the morning.

The client had arrived at the brothel, working his way through four girls, three bottles of champagne, two packets of cigarettes and one very large dose of speed and still wanted more.

Despite him being told that he should calm down, the lady was still not interested in attending to such a guy. This wasn't what she had paid €1000 to the people traffickers to get her to the west from Moldova but she had to do it. It was good money and she had almost paid off all her debts and her family was now living well, so perhaps she didn't need to complain. It wasn't like she hated her job, actually, she enjoyed it.

As she entered the room and found the client on the bed, already naked, watching porn on TV while some techno-pop music originating from his IPhone plugged into speakers which blasted the tunes overhead.

He turned to find her standing by the door. She was relieved, he wasn't bad looking and wasn't too large either. "Good morning." She said. The client turned to look at her, his eyes bulging from the drugs and lack of sleep. "Good morning" he replied. She could tell he had certainly not calmed down. "I hear you've been having fun all night. Still have some energy for me?" she asked, amazing herself with her acting.

"Yeah baby, I got more energy than a nuclear power plant." He replied as he played with his member to enhance his erection. "Come in here and give me dance."

"It's only a job. It's only a job." She repeated to herself as she strode in on her high heels and proceeded to groove along to the beat, watching the man getting more and more aroused whilst he touched himself more aggressively.

Halfway through dancing to a track called "Doktor Spiller" the music gave way to a ring tone. "Don't go away." Said the man as he reached over to the bedside table and checked the name on the line. "Got to answer this." He said as he picked up his phone. "Why do you always seem to catch me at the most inappropriate time?" He whined.

"I'm sorry Joel" Khoi apologised "but I have a quick question."

"Make it quick, my boner is becoming a downer." Joel then mouthed to the prostitute "One second please."

"I need to know where I could get some Dimethyl mercury."

"Dimanti what?" Joel tried to repeat the words.

"Dimethyl mercury." Khoi corrected. "I need it for my plan. It's very important. Can you get it for me?"

Though it sounded exciting, Joel's excitement waned as he could see the lady beginning to act bored "Yes, I am certain I can get you whatever you need."

"Really? Well, we must meet up now then." Khoi ordered.

"Now? But I'm busy." Joel lamented.

"What are you doing?" Khoi's question put him on the spot. Unwilling to expose himself, he sighed and gave in "I'll see you in an hour… your hotel?"

"Thank you Joel and sorry for disturbing you, the next whore will be on me." Khoi tried to keep himself from snickering but Joel could hear him and replied "You bastard."

With his pleasurable morning brought to an abrupt end, Joel rolled his eyes, took out his wallet and paid the woman €400 which pleased the prostitute as it was the quickest amount she had ever made in such a short period of time. Watching his intended delight leave the room, Joel sent an angry text to Khoi with the words "You are a dick."

Later that morning, Joel arrived at the hotel as Khoi was having lunch as he reviewed the information and notes he had gathered earlier that morning.

Joel was led to Khoi's table by a member of the staff. Arriving at the table just as Khoi was about to place a bit of chicken in his mouth Joel ordered "Come on, let's go."

"Good day Joel, would you like to join me?" Khoi replied in an attempt to reclaim Joel's manners.

"No thanks. You stopped me from having my meal, now it's your turn to skip yours. Up you go." Joel grabbed him by the arm and literally lifted him off his chair. He marched Khoi out of the hotel barely having the chance to collect his notes, papers and other items he had brought, all the way to the car park, still dressed in only his jumper, jeans and shoes. "I've made an appointment with our contact. It can't wait. Let's go." Joel asserted. Khoi could not argue and entered the car.

Thanks to Joel's seething, repressed anger and Khoi's detection of it, the drive out to the periphery of the city to a science park was quiet.

They waited outside a building patiently. Khoi wondered why they were just sitting in the car but was too afraid to ask because Joel still wasn't in a talking mood. From the rear view mirror, Khoi noticed a skinny man of average height walking at a quick pace towards the car. He walked with marching strides in a quick step which made his angular frame seem cartoon like.

He got to the car and opened the back seat door. "Hello Joel." The man said.

"Khoi, this is Callum. Callum, this is the bane of my life, Khoi." After Joel's introduction, Khoi turned around in his seat to shake the man's hand and found he had piercing, emotionless eyes, hardly smiling through his thin lips and acne ridden face. He proved his credentials by giving the offered hand a look and promptly ignoring it by going straight to business. "So how may I help you?" Callum asked Joel.

"Khoi?" Joel redirected the question.

"Right." Khoi began, "I wonder if you could get me some damormercury?" Callum looked bewildered. Khoi realised that he could have mispronounced it "I mean dimoreanmercury?"

"Is your friend alright?" Callum asked Joel.

Frustrated, Khoi reached into his pocket and handed him the drawing of the molecular structure drawn by Han. Callum took one look and promptly figured it out. "Oh. Dimethyl mercury. Well, that settles it. Your friend is crazy."

"You can't get it?" Joel asked

"Of course I can" Callum hissed "but it's fucking dangerous, once whiff and you're a dead man!"

"How much do you want?" Joel responded as he knew it was only a matter of cash.

Callum paused and looked out the window for a moment before he spoke. "It's going to be risky…"

"How much?" Joel snapped, frustrated by Callum's procrastination.

"Minimum €7,500." Callum answered.

"What? €7,500?" Joel repeated.

He was about to give Callum a display of his anger when Khoi intervened and said to Callum "That's fine, but on one condition, I am going to need to request an additional favour, this should be part of the cost, should it not?"

"I don't know…depends on the favour" Joel turned around and shot a frightening gaze at Callum causing him to capitulate "Ok, ok… yeah, that's fine. How much of the stuff do you need?"

"Two to three drops, in this." Khoi confirmed, presenting Callum with a tube of Nivea Q10 hand cream. Callum took the item and replied "Are you kidding?"

"No, I am not. Can it contain it?" Khoi said waiting for clarification. Callum confirmed that it could safely do the trick. Assured, Khoi calmly replied "You will be paid two thirds on delivery and the remainder once the results of the experiment are in. By the way, we need delivery by Monday please? Oh and get us some protective hand gear and add it the bill will you?"

Shrugging his shoulders, Callum concluded "It's your money. I'll bring it to you tonight, just text me the details." He then took out a pen and scribbled his phone number on the paper containing the molecular structure drawing. He handed it back to Khoi and promptly left the car walking away under the observing eye of Joel.

As Joel drove Khoi back to his meal, he decided to ask "Why did Callum act like he wanted to piss himself when you asked him about the Dimethyl mercury?"

"Wow you are able to pronounce it? I still can't" Khoi remarked, but not willing to give too much away, Khoi replied to the question "All will be revealed in three to four weeks." Joel accepted Khoi's response and with a smile and drove Khoi back to this hotel.

At the hotel, Khoi invited Joel to stay for some food. His reply was "You go finish your meal, I'll go finish mine." He left Khoi standing amongst the exhaust fumes as Joel sped off.

Accepting he would dine alone, Khoi returned to his hotel room. No use going back down to the restaurant, he thought. Khoi placed an order for some room service, a meal of pasta and a glass of red wine... boring, yes, but it was all they had on the menu that he found palatable. He sent a text to Callum with the address of the hotel and his room number.

Khoi turned on the television for his usual background noise then settled down to review his copy of the folder labelled "Robert". Khoi was instantly drawn to the subject's weaknesses, the main one being Robert's vanity, not to mention a love of fine food and even finer women, the latter of which he had plenty.

Robert, "Mr D" was how Khoi remembered him and he clearly didn't grasp the idea of a meaningful relationship. He was an example of the "ugly duckling who turned into a swan" experience. A geeky loner teenager with bad teeth, worse skin and a horrible taste in clothes, if the pictures Jelena gathered of his youth were anything to go by.

But Robert was now, most definitely a swan. He was tall, good looking, fit and Khoi found him totally sexy. What confounded Khoi more was that such vanity existed in the straight world. With the exclusion of Beckham but everyone knew why he was that way. In addition to this, what struck Khoi as strange was that, unlike him, Robert came from an upper-middle class family, and never had to get his hands dirty nor did he need to.

That aside, Khoi thought carefully about which one of his three vices would be the most effective means of getting to his target.

Robert was a social butterfly, always going to the same expensive, high class bars, where all those present were beautiful or trying to look beautiful or out to net someone's shallow greed and that's where Robert met all his ladies. He would lure them to his penthouse for a home cooked meal in the hopes that it would lead to copulation or sealing the deal. Khoi wondered if he ever failed.

Robert dined well, at the finest eateries, tasting the finest wines and foods. Food could work, Khoi thought to himself. He could poison his meal and watch him convulse on the floor before his tongue poked out of his mouth leaving him dead. However that was too risky. Evidence would be everywhere.

Khoi decided to find another way. He took another look at a picture of Robert with one of his many main squeezes and the photos again drew his attention. He looked at all the pictures provided of Robert's many suitors. They showed that Robert had a type which he seldom deviated from. That could be a strong possibility.

A stronger possibility he considered was his gym membership. It had eluded everyone but Khoi, and possibly Jelena, that their target used one of the many gyms owned by Joel's father. They could easily get him there. An incident of some sort leading to a horrible accident… the thought of Robert bleeding on the floor of the workout area as a result of a heavy weight crashing down upon him made Khoi nauseous and when his meal arrived, he requested it be taken back promptly running to the toilet to dry heave.

Once Khoi had fully recovered he decided that he certainly had a clear way to get his man, all he had to do was set out a plan. He still wasn't feeling well, and he noticed his hand shake as he took out the chocolate from the advent calendar.

Khoi thought he could get more information from speaking with his source. He sent a text to Jelena, asking if she would come by for dinner by 7pm, within a minute she responded yes.

All this planning was officially getting to Khoi and so was his lack of sleep.

At just past noon and with just less than seven hours to his next appointment, Khoi decided to try and force sleep through his usual means of relaxation.

Khoi went to his luggage, unzipped it, and took out the bag containing his knitting kit. Khoi opened the bag and as he took out the yarn and needles holding a half done scarf, an item dropped to the floor, rattling as it rolled away. Khoi went after it and found it next to the radiator. It was a medicine bottle which read "Diazepam", one tablet a day and Julien's name typed beneath it.

Initially, Khoi wondered how it had gotten into his knitting case then wondered how Julien was coping without them but soon realised that Julien's loss of pills was his gain.

He opened the bottle and shook out a pill, placing it in the centre of his tongue knowing that he couldn't taste the pill there. He sipped his wine whilst reading the bottle for side-effects, it was then, just before he swallowed, he read "Not to be taken with alcohol."

Lucky for Khoi he hadn't swallowed anything yet. He spat back the wine and pill into the glass. He went to the fridge to take a bottle of water and tried again with a fresh pill.

Done, he went and rested on his bed patiently. Time seemed to go by slowly. To keep himself occupied, Khoi started to knit, but didn't make it past the ninth row before sleep came calling.

7pm arrived in a blink of an eye. At least that was how Khoi perceived it. He was awoken by the phone in his room ringing. The receptionist called to inform him that Jelena was waiting for him in the Lobby.

Disaster, he had over slept. Khoi leapt out of the bed and remembered he hadn't showered. He paused for a quick spray of perfume, not bothering to look in the mirror before putting on his coat. He placed "Mr D"s" folder under his arm and went down to meet Jelena.

Khoi greeted her at lobby with a kiss on the cheek. Jelena was perceptive "Oh dear? Are you ok? You look exhausted." Khoi confessed that he was tired, but that it was best to avoid that topic, rather, he asked "Do you like Vietnamese food?"

As they were being driven to the restaurant, the street lights shining on Jelena was enough to show how attractive she was and it got Khoi thinking. He kept pondering right up till the time they placed their order.

After their order was taken Khoi considered sharing his thoughts about her, but she spoke first. "Thank you for inviting me out. It has been a long time since I had the opportunity to eat in a relaxed setting that doesn't serve champagne… a change, but most welcomed"
"Eloquently put." He responded, as he took the folder from under his chair where he had placed it and handed it to her. "Could you look through this please?"

She opened the folder and flicked through the pictures of the women "Mr D" had dated before wondering, "Why are you showing me this? I organised them." Leaning forward and speaking softly, Khoi began "Initially, I thought the best means of getting our target was via his workout regime, but, having spent some time looking at you, I realised with your long hair, nice tits, full figure and full lips... you are the perfect fit. You are his type."

Jelena closed the folder, instantly figuring out what Khoi was insinuating. "The guy has good taste. One can't deny that all the girls in the picture are pretty good looking..."

"Just like you." Khoi interrupted.

"Oh Khoi, am I converting you?"

Khoi blushed as he leaned back on his chair "I don't know... I never investigated."

"You are such a charmer." She replied waving him off.

"No, seriously." A glance at him was enough to show he wasn't kidding.

"If I weren't hungry, I would have walked out of here by now... ignoring your flirtatious overtures, are you asking me to be the honey trap?" Jelena was clearly aghast, yet Khoi persisted.

"Tomorrow he is going to the fashion week after party at a swanky hotel close to the Brandenburg gates. You could be there and, if possible, net him."

Jelena tapped the table, asserting in a low tone "It was not in my job description."

"I know, it's a lot to ask and you will be adequately compensated..."

"Don't insult me. If I were going to do it, I would do it for the thrill. The money would be a bonus, but basically it would be for the thrill." She confirmed.

Brushing the comment aside Khoi continued "I promise you will not be in any danger. If anything happens, we will be there..."

"I can take care of myself." She snapped.

Feeling he wasn't getting anywhere, Khoi asked "Is there any way I can convince you?"

She kept quiet and looked at her spoon till the meal arrived. Even then, Jelena didn't say much, rather she commented on the food and inquired about Khoi's family. "I have no family." Khoi replied "They are all dead."

"Well that was short." Jelena then changed the topic "I never had noddle soup like this, it's rather spicy."

"Yeah…" Khoi murmured. Khoi never liked talking about his family and Jelena soon realised that she had killed the mood of the evening with her bad selection of theme. They sat quietly to eat their meal till it was done.

When they finished, Khoi paid the bill and as they walked out to their waiting taxi he asked her "So, will you do it?" She said nothing as they entered the back of the taxi from opposite doors.

As the car moved she spoke "I don't like people who lie to me. So why do you do so Khoi?"

Khoi turned to find her looking at him "I didn't lie to you." He protested.

"Oh… tell me about Vania?" Jelena's question caught him off guard

"You have been keeping tabs on me?" He began defensively "Is that part of your job description?"

"That's beyond the point. Tell me about Vania?" Jelena insisted.

Khoi was boiling with indignation, but he was cornered. He looked away from her for a moment, shut his eyes and considered if it was fair to be honest. With a deep intake of breath, he proceeded "He's my brother… my big, better in every way, brother. My hard working, better looking, smarter, kinder, caring, selfless brother; he's my opposite… wouldn't harm a fly while I am the loser, the evil one who seeks revenge with nothing but hate and fear in his mind, always finding it hard to fit in."

The self-reproach gave way to regret "We don't talk anymore and it's entirely my fault.

He brought me up straight, I turned out gay. He taught me what's right, I picked what's wrong and he tried, he tried ever so hard to keep me safe… I just thought it was too much and hated him for that. I left to hurt him and after that he considered me out of his life… now I am the one who is hurt.

Funny how things backfire isn't it?" He asked rhetorically, turning to look at Jelena who was beginning to see his soft underbelly.

She didn't know whether it was compassion, but Khoi's weakness made him irresistibly sexy. She grabbed him and began to kiss him deeply. Khoi was taken by surprise, not because he was being kissed by a girl, but the fact that he actually liked it and was getting sexually aroused by it.

The feeling of her hand going under his coat, touching his chest, made him want her more. His hands ran through her hair, pulling it back, as he kissed her neck slowly, going lower till the car came to a full stop. "€11.45 please?" requested the driver as he parked in front of Khoi's hotel.

Khoi took out his wallet and gave the man €20 telling him to keep the change, opened the door and with a foot outside he hesitated. He was confused yet excited, he turned to her "Come with me… please?" he begged. She held his face and kissed him deeply again, for a moment giving him hope, then she stopped, handed him the folder for "Mr D" and said "Here's your file. Good night Khoi."

Khoi felt rejected. He got out of the taxi and shut the door as he overheard her commanding the taxi driver to proceed. Khoi didn't know what was happening to him. He asked himself how it was possible that a day of indifference and promise could end with such heartache. He wished Julien would come back soon, his resolve was slipping and he knew it.

As he entered the hotel, he passed the reception and the lady behind the desk called out his name and presented him with a delivery. It was a square package, wrapped in brown paper and from the feel of it, a lot of bubble wrap. It had the words 'From Callum' written on it. "Shit." He remarked. He had forgotten about Callum. At least the stuff was here, however it would be more work on his plate.

Khoi proceeded upstairs. Entering his hotel room, he took off his coat, leaving it on the floor. He immediately sat the desk and opened the folder again to consider another means of getting "Mr D" but each time he did, he was taunted by the pictures of the ladies, his mind playing tricks with his vision implanting Jelena's face there… he couldn't concentrate and it drove him to distraction causing him to fling the folder away. He asked himself how he could be left feeling like this. Why did he want her?

His phone beeped. He had received text. He picked it up, it was from Jelena, and it read "I'll be your honey trap". Small consolation, Khoi thought, now he didn't want her to do it. Nevertheless, he replied with the word "Thanks". He then summoned Marcel, Mikel and Paul for a 4am meeting, he had something to execute the following day. With a lot of protest and sounds of discontent, they agreed to be there on time.

Khoi spent the rest of the evening knitting till midnight came and went. He had been working with the wool so vigorously, in an attempt to expel his angst, that the tips of his index fingers hurt having been pressed on the head of the knitting needles. The only satisfaction was that he finished making a scarf.

He put down the needles realizing he had nothing else to do and he still he couldn't think clearly. Maybe another one of Julien's "nighty night" pills would help, but he couldn't bring himself to take one. He needed to act quickly. Rather than taking a pill to get him to bed, Khoi took the chocolate of the day from the advent calendar. Having eaten it, Khoi called on the three members of the team to come to his hotel room without delay. Tomorrow was to be the start of his two pronged approach.

# 7

*9 December 2010*

At 6am, an alarm clock rang. Its job was to alert its owner of the time and wake them, but it wasn't permitted to do its job. The owner of the digital time piece was already awake, as always. He had been conscious for seventeen minutes already. To him, the clock wasn't used to get up on time; it was like the firing of a starter pistol, telling him to prepare for the day.

Andreas Thill reached over with his left hand and tapped the alarm clock on the head before promptly getting out of bed.

He went to the bathroom and turned on the shower, allowing the water to run before taking off his clothes. He proceeded to sit on the toilet for his morning bowel movement, the first of the two he had scheduled that day, as he did every day, one at 6:05am and another at 8:25 pm, none lasting more than five minutes.

He helped get things moving by rubbing his groin as he strained. It took him just over three minutes to empty himself and a further minute to ensure all evidence of his deposit wasn't present on his ass. He still had a minute to spare, so he waited in front of the medicine chest till 06:10. When the designated time arrived, he opened the cupboard, took out a thermometer and his electric toothbrush.

One minute brushing his upper set of teeth and another to clean the lower. He used the water he had left the night before in the cup and rinsed his mouth, gargling eight times and swishing it around in his mouth for another eight minutes before spitting it out into the sink.

Teeth cleaned, Andreas took his thermometer, walked the shower, placed the thermometer under the running stream of water for a minute. A quick check showed it was 40c, a bit more cold water and another twenty seconds; the water was now 38c. That was perfect.

Sponge in hand; he rubbed it nine times on the bar of soap. Every part of the body got its usual five scrubs except his face which got seven. With his body covered in soap suds, he stood under the running water for five minutes to clear his skin. At 6:20am, he went to his room and dried his skin with his towel for exactly one minute. At last he started the longest part of his daily regime. He took out a pot of Nivea body lotion and applied it to his skin rubbing three layers on every inch of his skin.

Part of his OCD was his perpetual fear of his skin drying out. After ten minutes and even though he didn't consider it enough, he had to stop. It was time to put on his clothes.

Andreas walked to his wardrobe, opened the door and took out his set attire for a Wednesday, blue shirt, black suit, blue underwear, no tie and white shoes. He had five minutes to get into his clothes, and the same amount of time to look through his bag in the living room and ensure he had everything. He used his check list, confirming out loud "Files, pen, lip balm, hand cream, laptop, mobile, antibacterial hand gel, wet wipes. Good." He went to his coat and sprayed it lightly with a mild disinfectant and then checked for his spare latex gloves which he left there, as per usual, the night before.

Andreas then went to the fridge to pick up his packed lunch of an orange, banana, and a ham and cheese sandwich he had made the night before. He took a look at his watch; the time was 6:40. He walked out of the door of his third floor flat and stood by the lift.

Taking another a look at his watch, Andreas decided he had the time to wait. His next door neighbour was also making her way out of her flat having just kissed her husband and baby goodbye. "Good morning Andreas." She said to him. He didn't reply. He just stood there, fidgeting with his key in his left hand and holding his office bag in his right. She came and stood next to him, noticing the lift hadn't been called she asked. "Not 06:45 yet?" knowing he wasn't going to reply and being that her watch said two minutes before a quarter to the hour, she called the lift.

It took forty seconds for the lift to arrive. She entered and pressed the button to keep the door open, waiting for him to step in.

06:45 arrived. Andreas pressed the button again and stepped onto the lift as the good natured neighbour continued to hold the door for him. It was a silent trip down. When the door opened at the ground floor Andreas exited first. He ignored the sound of his neighbour calling out "Have a nice day Andreas." He didn't reply as he walked out of his flat in a newly refurbished building in Friesenstrasse.

Andreas had selected that building because it was a south facing building. The flat was a complete rectangle with windows strategically placed the way he liked them. Yes, it was half an hour from where he worked by underground, putting a strain on him, but it was exactly what he wanted, far from his colleagues and their potential germs.

He walked up the road, he was counting his steps. He needed to make it to the junction of Willibals-Alexis Strasse within 50 steps but no less than 40 steps. If he didn't, he would have to do it again and that would eat into his time. Andreas was often walking strangely to ensure he was within the correct range.

He managed it this time in 43 steps just before he arrived at the traffic lights. Relived, he crossed the road. He had to make it to make it to the Arndtstasse junction within the same amount of steps. With some more unorthodox walking, he managed it in one step less to the traffic lights.

Andreas stood at the corner, proud to have achieved his goal. He waited for the light to turn green along with four others who had gathered for the same purpose. . There was a woman with her son in a pram, a man speaking on the phone and a young woman, who also seemed to be in a rush.

Andreas looked at his watch impatiently, wondering how much longer he would have to wait. Suddenly, he felt someone yank his right arm. His bag had been snatched right out of his hand. Andreas looked and saw the culprit running across the road, causing an approaching car to screech to a stop.

Andreas went into shock; his disorder paralysed him. He was unable to cross before the light turned green.

The man on his phone didn't have such hang-ups "HEY!" He screamed as he dashed across the road, giving chase to the thief. Andreas was hyperventilating.

The light had turned green; Andreas walked across the road fearfully taking the proper amount of steps, torn between his instincts to chase the criminal and his need to follow his routine.

Andreas could not control it; he was prisoner to his condition. Once on the other side, Andreas started to count his steps. It was difficult to do as he watched the thief and the hero getting further and further away. The thief took a quick turn into a pathway called Otherland Buchhandlung leading to Bergmannstrasse and out of Andreas' view, followed by the man trying to stop him.

Andreas couldn't scream, he couldn't speak and he literally held his breath as he got closer to Otherland Buchhandlung. The only thing stopping him from losing his mind at the moment was the fact he was still within his range of steps, however his bag was gone and he feared for that.

Andreas was nearing the end of the road just before the intersection of Otherland Buchhandlung when the stranger emerged with his bag and a slightly swollen face.

The man came to Andreas and handed over his bag to him. "Here." Andreas could hardly speak, he was very pleased when he took a quick look at his watch and noted he could still meet his train. "Em… thank you … Good bye."

Andreas walked away, leaving the Good Samaritan to watch him paces off. "That's disgusting. He didn't even say thank you." The Samaritan turned and found that the remark had originated from the woman with the pram, who had seen everything. The Samaritan scoffed "Such people don't live long" and then he turned and looked into the pram declaring "cute kid." After receiving a gratified grin from the lady the man walked away.

The Good Samaritan walked away, stealing looks at the man as he turned left into Bergmannstrasse then took out his phone from his pocket to make a call as he crossed the road entering into Arndstrasse past a pizza restaurant. As it rang, the man saw the thief approaching with his friend. Their eyes met and the thief pointed as the pair came jogging towards him.

Finally, the call was answered. "Hey Khoi, it's done" the Good Samaritan reported as he threw away the tube of cream he had exchanged for the one he brought with him and heavy silver lined glove. "Well done Marcel, sterling effort." Khoi commended and asked "What about the others?"

"They're on their way." Marcel said as Paul and Mikel met him and patted him on the shoulder. "Very good, did you follow the steps laid out?" Khoi asked

"To the last letter." Marcel confirmed as he walked with the others toward the park "Paul was impressive, he came running and snatched the bag, I went after him, we found a quiet place and exchanged the items."

"I'm impressed. One down four to go." Khoi noted. "Well, back to work with you. We have a delivery coming in and we need you, Ralph and Daniel to receive it. May I speak to Paul?"

Marcel handed the phone to Paul who instantly was told "I need you to come to me now. I have another exercise for you. Remind Marcel and Mikel that they must now put into effect the buyout plan. Clear?"

"Crystal." Paul confirmed, before the phone went dead. Paul did not look too happy as he handed back the phone announcing "Sorry guys, I have to go and you've got some shopping to do."

In the underground, Andreas relaxed as the train moved. There were places to sit, but he preferred to stand the whole 23 minutes until his stop. He was frightened of what germs lurked on the surface of the chair, he couldn't take the risk.

There was no greater relief than the safety of the building where he worked and the sanctified sanitised surroundings of his private office thought Andreas. He turned up the heating to 18c, just as he liked it before sitting in his chair.

Prior to sitting down, he took out some disinfectant spray and wiped the surface of his desk, keyboard, chair, phone, computer mouse, computer screen and even his bag with the disinfectant. Once done he returned the spray to his bag and took out another pair of latex gloves and the hand cream.

Andreas gave the tube of cream a quick dusting with the cloth moistened with disinfectant. Once satisfied, he took off the gloves, disposed of them before putting some cream on his hands to keep them from drying out. He hated the idea of his skin losing moisture.

Andreas didn't scrimp on quantity. He usually went through a tube every week having to apply cream to his hands every time he washed them or before he changed gloves which could amount to nine to twelve applications a day and today, this was to be the first of many.

At noon, on the other side of town, Jan sat outside the meeting room, waiting. He wasn't nervous, rather, he was annoyed, aggrieved that Wolfgang, his friend and colleague, had actually concurred with Kat when she said he shouldn't try to be himself. "Stop trying to stir the middle ground. Try and say how you actually feel for once." Wolfgang had suggested. For that Wolfgang was an ass.

It wasn't that Jan didn't want the job; it was because it was all Wolfgang's fault that he was seated on a cold fiberglass chair in his uniform waiting to be grilled. Wolfgang had done the most unforgivable thing, he saw the potential Jan had and put him forward for a promotion.

The door opened and Jan was called in. He was asked the basic questions, namely, why he wanted the job, what would he bring to the role, where does he see himself down the line and so on. Then came the technical questions to test Jan's knowledge of the law. He found them easy and gave direct answers.

Finally, the questions turned to his integrity as the interviewer asked "If you found a friend, member of your family… someone close to you was doing something wrong. What would you do?"

Jan hesitated. Initially he wanted to go with his instinct and give a blunt answer, and then he considered his options. Accepting there was little to lose; Jan decided to speak without thinking. "It depends on what you call wrong. If it was an issue of morals, cheating on his wife or breaking a promise to a child, I would shrug my shoulders and mind my own business, to be honest, who am I to judge? However, if wrong meant breaking the law, again, who am I to judge their motives for their actions? I wouldn't judge them, but I wouldn't let them get away with it."

Having completed his statement, Jan wished he could retract it, sensing it was an indigent response to a loaded question. The stern faces of the three interviewers didn't fill him with confidence either as they scribbled down some words. They thanked him for his attendance.

Jan's feet felt like lead. Once out of the room, he cringed and wanted to swear, asking himself over and over why he was such a fool to have given such an answer. He would have gone for a stiff drink if he didn't have a further six hours and twenty minutes before his shift was over, that was just too long.

As seven in the evening finally came, Jan thanked the lord his day was over. He was met by his colleague, Wolfgang who, over their second beer, assured him that there was no blueprint to a perfect interview and no amount of hindsight could rectify any damage that may have been done. He told him to take heart, since, regardless of the outcome, he would still be employed.

As Jan was licking his wounds in the policeman's bar, Khoi and Paul entered the hotel where Jelena was staying, walking through the lobby. It was the first time they had both been to the hotel and were astonished by the opulence of the place.

As they progressed into the building, Khoi felt the need to venture alone. He was keen to speak to Jelena. As they walked to the elevator, he turned to Paul and said "Wait here." Paul did as he was told as watched Khoi enter the lift to the 6th floor.

Once the lift arrived, Khoi walked on the plush violet carpet to room number 623. He knocked on the door "It's open." She cried out. Delicately, Khoi touched the door, pushing it open, and there she was, in her black and gold lace underwear looking absolutely stunning as she did the most peculiar thing, she appeared to be filing the head of a small metal spike which stood about 8 inches long.

Jelena appeared transfixed by her duties, but not so absorbed as not to notice she had company. She greeted him whilst stroking and using the metal file in one direction, aiming to get a sharp tip before pausing to touch the end to check on her progress. "Nearly done." She announced. Losing his manners to greet her and forgetting what he initially wished to say, Khoi chose to follow his nose "Could I be so forward as to ask what you are doing?"

After a few more strokes of the file, Jelena looked at the tip and nodded to affirm she was satisfied with the result. "I" she began, picking up what appeared to a flat heeled shoe as she began to screw the spike into the base turning it into a stiletto. She slipped them on to try them out before she continued "was getting my protection ready." She concluded. Khoi was puzzled "Protection? Aren't you taking a gun with you?" Jelena put on her other pre-prepared shoe to check if they were both levelled as she added "I never used a gun when fishing, never had the need."

"So you think you can protect yourself using your heels?" Khoi asked again. Jelena walked toward him and as she drew closer, she kicked the air, her feet just centimetres from his face with the sharp pointed heel millimetres from his nose, holding her foot in the air for few seconds to prove her point. It failed however. "You protect yourself by kicking?" Khoi asked. Jelena brought her foot down, shook her head in disappointment, lamenting "And I thought you were the smart one."

Jelena walked to the dressing table and squirted on some perfume. She sighed at the prospect of having to delve deeper into the matter. "You might as well know why I was not so keen on your proposal to act as your bait. The last time I was anyone's bait, it went wrong, terribly wrong." Jelena then proceeded to cover her face with foundation adding "I was meant to get some data from some big shot businessman with loose morals.

My chaperon was meant to keep his bodyguards occupied whilst the man and I slipped away to his hotel and it worked for a while. The guys were drinking with my minder, I and the target headed to a hotel 20 minutes away, then it all went wrong." Jelena then proceed to describe what ensued.

She was alone in the room with the man, stripped down to nothing but her panties and her shoes ,laying on the bed, as the businessman called Francis sucked on her nipples. Forcing fake pleasure only seemed to increase his nibbling, so Jelena resorted to kissing him instead. She took the opportunity to scan around the room and found the laptop she was aiming for on the desk.

Jelena was searching for her bag and remembered she had left it in the entrance of the room. She had to think of an excuse to get it and the syringe containing the drug she needed to knock Francis out. Then Francis' phone rang. The 199cm tall man with tobacco infused breath, stained teeth, walrus moustache, portly belly and heavy set frame, totally unappealing in reality, got off her and said "Don't go away."

Francis walked to the desk where the laptop sat to answer the call. He began to speak in French, convinced that Jelena could not comprehend him. She did and what she heard was enough to tell her that it was time to leave. Overhearing that her cover had now been blown, Jelena got off the bed, picked up her dress and wanted to quickly put it on. As she searched for bra, Francis put down his phone and asked "Where are you going?" as he approached Jelena.

Jelena had to mask the fear and put on a puppy face as she picked up her dress. "I don't feel too good. May be next time?" Francis was now standing close behind her. Jelena turned around and he was upon her.

He held the dress and yanked it out of her hand before tossing it aside. "Who do you work for?" he asked. Jelena was momentarily scared stiff giving Francis the chance to shove to the ground.

The push occurred suddenly and Jelena could not manage to fully break her fall causing her to land on her right hand with a slight cracking sound which Francis heard as well. "Oh, you broke something?" Francis knew he was correct, Jelena had landed hard on the wrist of her right hand and it was truly broken.

She swayed briefly on the ground as she engaged the pain she felt, but before she knew it, Francis was on laying on top of her, immobilizing her using his hefty size "come on baby, we might as well have some fun?"

Francis proceeded to force himself upon her, holding down her arms as he kissed her neck. This was too repulsive to take. Jelena shunted her knee into his groin as hard as she could. Francis cried out in pain, giving her the opportunity to push him away. With Francis temporarily restrained by pain, groaning on the floor, Jelena got up and raced for her dress and hand bag, her speed hindered by her stilettos.

Taking swift small steps, Jelena managed to get hold of her clothes and for a split second she contemplated taking off her shoes, but thought she could do so once she was out of the hotel room.

As Jelena hurried towards the reception area for her handbag, she was brought down again.

Francis had grabbed her by ankle of her right leg and pulled, making her fly for an instant prior to crashing to earth like a lumbered tree.

This time her head hit the floor leaving her vision blurred. She turned round on the carpeted floor and saw Francis crawling towards her, growling, his face ridden with protruding veins visible from beneath his skin.

Accepting she was most likely going to die, Jelena decided that the least she could do is fight and perhaps get him angry enough to kill her now than face any possible torture they may have lined up. Francis placed his hand on her right leg and was going to reach forward to touch her body when she summoned all the strength she had with the intention of kicking him away. Jelena quickly lifted her free leg, drew it back and shoved it forward hoping to stamp on his face.

Francis snarled softly. Jelena was pleased with her success. Then he fell silent and slumped on the floor, his head resting in the space between her legs, yet oddly enough, her left leg felt restricted and unable to stretch out fully, as though inhibited and Francis had stopped moving.

Jelena sat up and found that she had kicked Francis square in the face with her left foot bent at a 45c angle to the left, causing the entire length of the stiletto's heel to force its way through the soft tissue of Francis' left eyeball.

Blood oozed out from the entry point. She initially tried to pull her shoe free using her foot, but it was well wedged tightly in there. The feeling of having to push on his head which was slowly losing colour made her cringe. It was no use. Jelena leaned forward and unbuckled the footwear liberating herself from her now motionless aggressor. His head lurched down, prevented from touching the floor by the shoe. Jelena knew she was pressed for time, but there was no way she could leave such an item behind.

She attempted to turn him over. Francis turned out to be heavier than he looked and after five tries, she gave up. Jelena had to lift up his face and rest it on its chin. She had to brace herself for the pain of using her injured hand as well as hold back her revulsion. She put her foot on his face and pulled as hard as she could, using both hands to dislodge the metal heel of the shoe from Francis' head.

Her morbid fascination made her look into the hole left behind as it filled up with blood. It was clear that the heel must have gone straight through the eye and pierced the brain. Jelena couldn't help herself. She stuck her finger into the injury just to check how wide it was, it felt awful and while her finger had only penetrated half way, she withdrew her digit quickly as what little time she had left dawned on her.

She unbuckled the other shoe, took it off and put on her dress. She left the room and the building with the laptop and waited across the road in the rain, observing the building to note when Francis' henchmen would arrive. They missed her by six minutes.

Though it sounded farfetched, Khoi was inclined to believe her. During the period in which she told the story, Jelena had put her makeup on and proceeded to pull up her stockings. Khoi proclaimed "That must have horrible…"

"Yeah, it was, I was really upset. The cobbler couldn't get the blood off the shoe no matter how hard she tried. They were blue suede, my favourite." With her stocking on, she picked up her shoes adding "that's why I asked him to make this. Now I can detach the heel if I want. Smart, right?" Khoi agreed.

Yet the story seemed incomplete and Khoi asked about her minder. "Him? The guy was a prick. I couldn't believe it. He fled, didn't bother to give me a heads up, I could have died!" Jelena proclaimed as she straightened her dress and pulled the straps over her shoulders. She walked up to Khoi as she continued "When I found him, I realised he needed an emergency tracheostomy."

As Jelena approached and stood in front of him Khoi could only think of how racy she looked with her full lipstick covered lips and wide eyes, her hair tied back and even her fingers could give a person lewd thoughts.

Khoi required clarification "A tracheostomy? Did his lung collapse?"

"No" Jelena calmly said as she turned her back to Khoi showing off her exposed back "I didn't say he needed it for a collapsed lung. Having first nailed him to the floor, I gave him a tracheostomy using a funnel which enabled me to channel the flask full of liquid nitrogen down his wind pipe." Khoi was shell-shocked by the act she claimed to have conducted, not that she noticed.

She had other things to address and she needed help with one of them. "Could you zip me up please?" Khoi sheepishly did as he was told allowing Jelena to take one last look in the mirror before confirming "I'm ready."

"You look beautiful." Khoi remarked with all sincerity. She turned around and smiled. She came up to him and kissed him tenderly on the lips. She picked up her bag and coat and walked to the door as Khoi followed.

Jelena was driven towards the grand looking upmarket hotel where Robert was set to be for his usual pick up and drink after having finished a photo session. As they approached the building, Jelena checked her watch, it was nearly seven. She checked her makeup one last time. Khoi was seated in the back with her, watching her touch up her lipstick.

As she rubbed her lips together, he started developing feelings for her, it was interesting, something he had never thought he would find. She was just a stranger, a visiting colleague at most, so why did he feel so protective over her? He felt confused.

She was now confident she was ready. "Drive off as soon as I have gone in." Jelena ordered.

Khoi was frightened to say what he felt, but knew he had to say it. "Do you think you will have to sleep with him?" Looking in the mirror of her compact case, she clasped it shut responding "It depends, it could occur out of casual indifference... If I have to, then I will."

As the car parked in front of the door, Khoi snapped "You don't have to, so don't." This odd standoff triggered Paul's concern. He didn't expect Khoi to sound in so assertive, neither did Jelena. She looked at him, raised an eye brow, giggled, opened the door and stepped out saying, "See you later Khoi."

Jelena stepped out of the car and walked so elegantly one would have thought she was gliding. She didn't look round to catch the glares of Khoi who appeared to be fuming for no justifiable reason. Yet he watched on as Jelena was greeted by the door man and he didn't stop looking until she was out of sight.

Paul started the engine of the car and was about to move when Khoi ordered him to wait. His eyes transfixed at the door, the thought of her prospective liaison eating him from the inside. He fought to contain it but heard himself shouting out the word "Shit!" and it seemed to do the trick.

"Are you alright?" Paul asked, perplexed by the sudden outburst.

"Yeah, I'm fine. Let's go." Khoi said, faking a smile to mask his insecurities, "Time to clock off. Drop me off at the hotel." He ordered.

Walking on the plush red carpet with a gold peacock woven into the centre, one could not help but be taken by the opulence of the place. Chandeliers, gold plated candle stick holders mounted to the walls, a tasteful blend of modern and old art adorning the walls, all made for a triumphant exhibition of interior decoration.

Although she had seen better in Moscow, it was nevertheless impressive Jelena thought as she turned into the bar and paused. She surveyed the room; it was crowded, filled with a combination of some naturally and unnaturally beautiful people drawn by the stench of money emitted from the passing business men. These people accounted for 50% of those in the room. The rest were either there on business, hotel guests and people on a date, or just the Thursday night drunks out to waste their hard earned cash.

Amongst all this, she was meant to identify the model, and she didn't need to look far. Robert was seating in one of the heavy leather arm chairs placed around a small table in the middle of the room. Robert was not alone. He had three other people with him, they looked middle aged and watched on attentively as Robert spoke, his hand movements seemed to have hypnotised them, then they started laughing out loud and with vigour. Robert had just detonated his bomb of hilarity that he was famous for.

Jelena walked further, she could tell by the way the man had his phone on the table, facing down and by the side looks he gave the person to his left, that it was probably not a casual meeting amongst friends, a deal was on the table.

Jelena needed a good vantage point and found one by the bar. Luckily, there was an empty chair there. As she walked over toward the bar she noticed prospective usurper for the space. Jelena's strut turned into a quicker pace, and she was afraid she wasn't going to make it.

Quickly, she tossed her purse. She threw it just as the man was about to reach the chair and it landed on the cushion. The man saw the silver and black purse land and turned to find where it originated from. His revulsion over losing his place was replaced with lustful desires once he set eyes on Jelena, who returned to her usual poise and came to him slowly and said "So sorry about that. My legs are killing me. Would you like me to buy you a drink in compensation?"

"No, not at all, you don't have to… May I buy you one?" The young man with bad posture asked. Sadly for him, Jelena not only took the seat and rejected his counter offer; she gave him such a cold shoulder that even a well fed polar bear would have felt as she picked up her phone and pretended to make a call.

The man took the hint and was soon on his way, smarting, as he received his order of a large gin and tonic. With the temporary annoyance gone, the bar tender came up to her and asked what she was going to have. She requested a glass of champagne and asked the bartender if he knew what Robert was having. "I don't." replied the man behind the bar. "OK, let's play a game." She said seductively as she reached into her purse for a €100 note and held it before him, "This is yours if you can find out in 2 minutes."

The bartender silently nodded and walked away from his post to go and speak to one of the waitresses. Jelena watched as information flowed from one person to the other before it reached her with 23 seconds to spear. Vodka and lemonade was what Robert was having.

With his side of the bargain fulfilled, the man pocketed the €100. Jelena waited patiently until Robert started laughing again, raising his glass. It revealed that the contents of his glass were soon to be exhausted. It was time for Jelena to set another task. "Get me their bill and serve him a double shot of vanilla vodka with lemonade, be sure to take it to him, personally."

"Certainly madam, one moment." He responded as he dealt with her request for champagne and added "It's on me." Taking the contents of the message at face value, she winked at the man as he tried not to smile, concealing his braces.

It was time to pretend again with her trusty smart phone. She acted as though she was typing a message as the bartender stepped away from his post again the drink on the tray gracefully cutting its way across the crowd to where Robert was seated.

From the corner of her eye Jelena watched Robert frown as another drink was placed before him. She smirked as she read his lips. Robert inquired why he was being served something he didn't request. The bartender then directed Robert and his guest attentions towards Jelena before handing him the bill. "It's all been paid for." The barman added as he picked up his other glass despite though it still having a little liquid in it He placed it on a tray and was set to leave when Robert grabbed him by the arm and asked "She isn't a prostitute is she?"

"No sir. I most sincerely doubt that." The drink merchant replied before leaving them to wonder what was going on.

Jelena carried on her Thespian pursuits whilst maintaining a watchful eye on her subject. Robert was clearly trying to manage an awkward position, but his guest could clearly see the funny side of it and most importantly, the potential that lay ahead.

Robert turned to look at her and gave a small wave in the hopes of getting her attention and inviting her over, but that wasn't her game plan. She took a sip of her drink and carried on the act.

The men seated with Robert didn't want to cramp the style of their host; after all, they were not blind. The meeting was quickly concluded and handshakes were exchanged, the signal of their imminent departure.

She watched the two men pass by as they exited the bar. They exchanged glances at Jelena to see what Robert was getting himself into, giving their approval with a thumbs up. Misogyny had a home in Berlin, she thought to herself as she took another sip from her glass.

Jelena then noticed her glass had been smudged by the lipstick she wore. This instantly diverted her attention. She was angry having bought the rouge on the grounds that it never left any marks when touched. Incensed by her purchase, she checked through her purse to find the product, she intended not to make the same slip up twice.

With her hand just entering her purse, Jelena heard the thud of a glass landing on the wooden surface of the bar. Robert's jeans and light brown moccasins came into her line of sight. Jelena looked up slowly, taking in the pink shirt and black blazer before she beheld his beautiful lips and straight nose, centred between his high cheek bones. His skin was flawless and his eyes sparkled as did his teeth but it was ruined by the sleazy grin on Robert's face. "I believe I have you to thank for the drinks."

Jelena carried on her acting, trying her best to keep her breathing in check, as her heart raced upon seeing such a handsome site. She continued rustling through her purse to avoid eye contact as she replied "Don't mention it."

"So, what are you looking for in there?" Robert asked craning his neck to take a peek. "This…" She declared, holding up the tube of lipstick. "Come on, seriously, you don't need to doll up for me." Robert clearly thought he was funny, but it failed to even raise a smile from Jelena. Rather, Jelena raised an eyebrow and put him straight by saying "Don't flatter yourself."

Feeling deflated, Robert could only watch as Jelena requested the bartender to dispose of the rouge. Robert reeled momentarily from his failed first attempt and tried to recover some sense of dignity by trying another tactic. "I'm Robert." He said offering his hand. "Nice to meet you Robert." She replied, shaking it quickly before returning to her drink.

The nerves were getting the best of him and he didn't know why. Robert often saw himself as being able to charm fish out of the sea, but he was faltering fast. He tried to save the situation by making an observation. "From your accent, I detect you are not local."

"Well done. So you aren't just a pretty face after all. What else do you see?" Her sarcasm made him chuckle, causing him to reply "Wow, I see we have a tough cookie here. So where are you from? And what brings you to Berlin?"

"I'm from Slovenia and I am here on business and in this bar for a quick drink…" things were going fine till Robert cut her short again interjecting "And to buy me one?"

Again, she sighed but continued "Yes, because I find you attractive, even though you seem keener on laughing at your own jokes." She took another sip of her drink and she knew she had his attention "I am here for a month, so I thought I might as well get some company."

The word company lit Robert's carnal urges overcoming his senses and leading to a gush of honesty as he proclaimed "Your honesty is just mind blowing." Jelena finished off her glass of champagne and added "Do collect the fragments of your brain"

Jelena called for the bill, went through the ritual of making her payment. She collected her receipt and then took out a pen from her purse before scribbling something the back of the paper, folding it four ways and offering it to Robert. "I have to go."

"I thought you said you were looking for company?" Robert asked in disbelief.

"Yes." She said dismounting her stool exposing her height. She would have been the same height as him if she didn't have her heels on, Robert observed, as she continued "but I didn't say I needed some company tonight, did I? Are you free Saturday around 6pm?" Robert took hold of the paper being offered to him in near shock and was stunned into silence prompting Jelena to repeat herself. "Well? Are you or aren't you?" Every fibre of his being seemed to advise him to shy away, but he was captivated, never had he seen such arrogance from such beauty.

Robert did have plans that Saturday, he was to have dinner with his mother, but now, the importance of that seemed to fizzle in comparison to the eruption prompted by the beauty before him. When he finally spoke he said "I could be."

"Good. See you then."

With her purse in hand, she walked out of the bar, leaving a shell shocked Robert to try and piece together what had just occurred between him and ... her name, he didn't have her name. Robert raced out of the bar into the vestibule of the hotel and saw her just paces away from the door.

Robert cried out "Hey!" Jelena stopped but didn't turn round to face him. He soon realised he had cause a slight commotion by raising his voice as the entire guest and staff stopped to see who was making the noise. He raced quickly to her and in a low tone he noted "You didn't tell me your name."

"And you didn't read the note." She parried in a cold manner before kissing him on the cheek hard and long enough to leave a smudge. "Good night Robert."

Again he had been disarmed; unable to collect his ability to speak, let alone bid her farewell, not that it mattered. She strolled elegantly in her red coat out the door, waiting a few seconds as a taxi approached. As mysteriously as she arrived, she left, and was gone.

Robert seemed to only regain his composure when the doorman walked up to him and remarked on how stunning she was. Robert opened the note and saw scribbled on it "See you at Uhlandstr subway station. Ulrika."

Jelena didn't need to look back as she boarded the taxi, she knew she had him and it only took eighteen minutes. All that she needed to do now was reel him in. She picked up her phone to make a call and found a message already waiting for her. It was from Khoi, asking "Come over once you're done, I need to talk to you."

Jelena was peeved by the text she received. As soon as she thought she could ignore it, another arrived "Are you done? Are you safe?" it said before another followed. "Shall I send someone over to collect you?" Unable to bear it any longer, she simple wrote back "I'm fine." Any hopes of her two word reply stemming the vibration of her handset survived all of 3 seconds and another text flashed across the screen of her phone. "Good, come over now." Khoi ordered.

Flabbergasted, she exclaimed in her native tongue "Oh my God, who does he think he is?" This time, Jelena decided to ignore Khoi and his messages by turning off her phone.

She asked the driver to stop, deciding to walk to her hotel. The monotony and silence of the night contained a street lamp shimmering on a couple. They were taking a moment from their stroll to cuddle and Jelena began to yearn for company.

Risking a flood of messages, she decided to turn her phone back on and taking her chances by calling the only person she knew close to her current location. Jelena pressed the number and it rang for five times before it was answered. "Hello?" Mikel asked sounding out of breath. "Hello… did I catch you having sex?" She asked.

"Jelena! How are you? No, no such pleasures for me. I was just taking a shower. How are you?"

"Not bad… I am close to your neck of the woods and wondered if you had time for a drink?"

"Em… I was actually on my way out to see Paul… want to come along? We can drink there."

"Sure… I'll see you in about 15 minutes." Jelena confirmed

"Cool, see you soon." He confirmed

She walked slowly, taking her time to enjoy the tasteful vandalism of the graffiti on the wooden panels that covered a building under construction. A small surprise came when she turned into the street that led to Mikel's door. There, in the window of a small shop was a delightful dress of lace and soft shade of lapis lazuli. Jelena examined it and concluded, with some minor alterations, she could make it fit.

She took down the name of the shop and a snapshot of the dress placed on the mannequin before proceeding down Sanderstrasse to number 76. She pressed the buzzer for the 4th floor. "Coming down!" Mikel replied.

Jelena waited patiently watching a man walk his king-poodle. She was given a nod, Jelena smiled in return. Mikel soon emerged from behind the door and after a quick greeting before Mikel observed "I thought you were on a date?"

"I was. I like it short and sweet, as you should know." Her reply made them giggle.

As they began their stroll, Mikel told her that Paul was just a few streets away. Jelena asked if she was expected to bring a bottle of wine to which Mikel said in the midst of laughter "Please God no. We are trying to reduce his consumption. He's usually well stocked."

Considering the time, Jelena was forced to ask "Why are you going to Paul's so late? Business?"

"No, not that, it's just my turn to babysit." Mikel remarked in snide manner. Finding it remarkable, she had to know more "Babysit? Do expand." Jelena could see Mikel's foot-dragging which caused her to add "You don't have to if it's private or something."

Mikel appeared to sigh and pause before he began "Paul didn't take Stefan's death well… almost drank himself to the grave…" Passing by a playground, Mikel pointed to a park bench "Mind if we took a seat?"

"Sure." Jelena replied.

They found a bench and in a somewhat reluctant fashion Mikel went about providing an abridged version of the life of Paul with strife in his tone. "The Stefan you met… the Stefan of old, the lady charming, hand kissing, spectacle wearing, approval seeking geek you saw, the suave, the immense kindness was principally a façade. He was a sadistic bastard. He had an unquenchable blood lust that even caused Stefan to question his own sanity at times. Stefan was methodical in his approach in dealing with people that crossed the gang… locking a person in a box of fireworks just to give him some dazzle to the person's departure… he seemed to try to find innovative means to prevent the act of killing from being boring."

Mikel then described how Stefan realised that he was troubled and Stefan realised it when his work began to overwhelm him. Over the years following the expansion of the EU, we found ourselves competing with the Poles, Czech, Bulgarians and even Russians holding Estonian and Latvian passports, all wanting a slice of our pie and all had to be eliminated, put to heel, or, where possible, assimilated, which seldom happened, this meant that Stefan was very busy in his role as the gangs accountability and punishment enforcer in chief.

The constant need to take someone down began to affect his mood. He drank a lot more and turned grouchy. It was easy to tell he was getting slightly unhinged. On one drunken evening he started to ramble and then he said "I love to be there when people die. I want to know why they die. The Japanese have their death poems; I read a lot of that… quite intriguing. But it means nothing really… because I want to see the moment when people die. That's what fascinates me." Stefan took a moment to reflect and added "I guess I am sicker than I thought."

All this began to tell and it came to a point when the boss told him to tame it down a little, be couldn't, he needed his fix, to get his hands dirty… it helped him sleep at night.

Then Paul came along. He had the right background Stefan required with the perfect mind to mould."

Mikel chose to divulge all he was told in confidence in parts by Stefan but predominantly by Paul. He asked Jelena to picture East Germany, communist time in Erfurt, in the district of Udestedt. In some early winter's day in 1985, someone abandoned a baby at the door of an orphanage, naked, bar the swaddling clothes he was wrapped in with a note attached which read "Unwanted. His name is Paul."

There were many reasons why a baby could have been left at the doorstep of such an institution at that time. The communist state was at a crossroads and facing economic difficulties that even Moscow could not help. This saw a spike in the rate of foundlings. Although possible, it was unlikely that poverty was the main reason for a baby like Paul to be left out in the elements, it was more probably to do with the fact that Paul had an extreme form of a cleft pallet.

Surgery was performed but it was botched. His lip was badly stitched together with one half higher than the other, exposing part of his teeth when he tried to put his lips together and the side-effect of this disastrous act of facial augmentation being that Paul was not a pleasant site to watch when eating.

The managers of the orphanage had a mind-set stuck in the Middle-Ages and seemed to associate physical deformity with mental retardation. Thus not much effort was expended on educating Paul and his ilk with variant degrees of deformities and disabilities.

Education was provided in all it rudimentary forms. Teachers from local schools would volunteer their time and effort to help these children, often leaving disheartened and demoralised.

Then a visiting teacher, Mr Babij, who came twice a week to teach the teenage children literature, came across Paul peeping through the window on every lesson. On one sad day Mr Babij was feeling borderline suicidal whilst viewing the blank faces looking back at him when he asked them where Hamlet was set. Hamlet, the book they had just finished reading over the past month and he might as well had read it to himself. "Can't anyone answer the question?" He begged then a small voice from outside the class that cried out "Denmark." The class turned to face the source of the sound and with all the faces looking at him, Paul asserted "It's Denmark you morons."

Paul was 5 then, but the man saw potential and hope to propagate the seeds of knowledge in the hope they'd germinate wildly in Paul by staying an extra hour to read to initially read to the boy and soon, after half a year got Paul reading to him.

The man would come each week with a new book for him to read and keep. They started with the children's books, followed by a dictionary or two then a book in a foreign language that was paired with a dictionary that translated the words to German for him. An interest in language grew which was an effective distraction that lowered Paul's entrance into the room of punishment for a thrashing because Paul was one who never took any teasing sitting down.

People called him camel lips. Paul would fight anyone who ever said it to his face and always win even against people older and bigger than him because despite his age and size, Paul was freakishly strong. Paul could defend himself; always able to give more than he got to those who dare crossed him which led to him being isolated as violent radical, sent to the quiet room for hours on end.

Paul encouraged and made good use of his segregation. With the constant influx of books and the use of a tape player provided by his scholar friend, Paul taught himself English, French and Russian. He attempted Spanish, but found it a bit too hard. He endeavoured to exceed his station, undertaking mock exam papers and doing all he could to better himself even though deep inside he would wonder what it was all for.

When the wall came down, it still took some time for the East to catch up with the West in terms of care for their children with needs. The westerners flooded in to help the children in the homes but it seemed that no one wanted him at his age and his ugly face especially with his track record for violence, even the special needs kids found homes.

Paul remained in the institution and regardless of the improving conditions, a change in staff and their attitude towards him and those who were left behind, more educational possibilities, the introduction of TV and the constant influx of adverts showing him what he could have in the new society, Paul nevertheless remained imprisoned there till he was 16 when he was told to leave with the little belongs he had, €150 in his pocket and an address for a homeless shelter for disaffected youth.

Paul was now wandering the street, bumping into those who had left before him. They had been reduced to vagabonds, begging on the streets living amongst the trash and addictions of alcohol and heroine. They were the first set of failed children, the classic and expected results of releasing institutionalised people into an alien society. Now many were destitute, insane, or dead.

The other set that he saw from time to time were, in the short term, lucky, if that's what one could call it. They dressed better, looked better but potentially had a shorter shelf life than those who took the narcotic route.

The second set sought safety in numbers and had joined gangs and thus climbed the back of the cold blooded sea snake of criminality gluing themselves to it's scaled back for a ride as it was swam on the surface of the ocean. But a sea snake eats fish which never graze on the surface of the water. Hence, each time it went to retrieve a meal from the depths of the ocean a body would be found with a bullet in to the heart, or mutilated, or, if they were really unlucky, there was no body to be retrieved at all. Yes, as the serpent went to eat, those who rode on his back were set to drown for no one could hold their breath as long as the snake.

Paul spent a week at the shelter he had been directed to. It was filthy and filled with degenerates that he decided to take his chances on the street and keep his nose away from any potential trouble or powder on offer. All he wanted to do was to make his way in peace through the street. His plan was to try and get a job or as much studying as he could when he could and perhaps then, apply to take a college exam, if he lived past the first winter that is.

As autumn loomed, the temperature, like the leaves from the trees, began dropping, Stefan made his way to a meeting at the gang's second spa, the first ever opened in the city centre. A risky venture instigated by Khoi, but with the success of the first one still ringing in their ears, people were confident that this was going to be working out too and it wasn't such a bad thing that they had their meeting closer to their customers.

Stefan always made this journey on foot at around half past four in the morning, using the time to evaluate the establishments around him and see where a potential business opportunity lay. It was on his usual stroll down Otto-Suhr-Allee, in the affluent Charlottenburg district that Stefan found Paul sitting at close to door way of the closed library in the town hall, under the arches by the pillar, illuminated by the street lamp reading a book Dante inferno in French amongst his belongings of a rucksack, bomber jacket, stained jeans, sleeping bag and a sign that perched by his crossed legged and an empty cup by his side with propping up a sign that read "Give if you can, thanks if you can't." he was coughing badly.

Stefan observed the small young man for a while. Paul gave a slight shiver when he finished coughing. It wouldn't have been an odd sight if it wasn't an area where vagrants were few and far between and the fact that it wasn't even 6 in the morning. Too early for the beggars in any part of Berlin, let alone one sitting a library, sober, let alone reading a book in a foreign language.

All these anomalies drew Stefan to Paul and for the next few days. On his way to his daily meetings he would look out for him and as the autumn intensified its grip, there was Paul, still with his sleeping bag, few belongings, reading a book, coughing.

On one cold Thursday, unable to take the sound of Paul's chest convulsions any longer, Stefan went to the nearest store and returned with a bag.

He slowly walked up the steps and presented the items to Paul, expecting some form of gratitude. Rather, Paul took all the items out the bag one after the other. They consisted of some sandwiches, a bottle of fruit juice, a book by Oscar Wilde called "Dorien Grey" and some cough remedy.

Without uttering a word Paul returned all the items into the bag with the exception of the books and handed them all to Stefan. This was an odd, even silly self-defeating attitude. Stefan was furious, but didn't have the time to give a lecture on the benefits of manners; he was going to be late. He left Paul to his books as the first worker came to open the library for the day.

Once at the gym, prior to the meeting, Stefan reviewed the items and wondered if they was something wrong with his selection, was Paul dumb or was he was allergic to one of the items?

The question possessed Stefan so much so that he left the building three minutes before the meeting, surprising those present for his sudden need to take flight.

Stefan went to consult with a pharmacist who explained that the recipient, may be allergic to gluten and perhaps that was why he rejected the food, but there was nothing in the cough medicine to worry about

Stefan went back to the shop the nearby and sought out gluten free products and more books before returning in search of Paul. When he found Paul he was three feet away from his initial spot, he smugly presented him with the bag announcing with pride that the items were gluten free so he can have them.

Again, Paul, this time looking rather bothered, went through all the items, kept the books and returned the rest to Stefan who could take this rudeness no longer. Stefan scolded Paul, calling him ungrateful. Paul watched and once Stefan was done expressing himself, asked "Is the medicine non-drowsy?"

"Does it matter? Just be grateful you ugly little prick" Stefan replied leaving the items behind as he left storming off to his meeting.

In the midst of his rage, he wondered why he even bothered. At the door of the gym, Stefan reviewed the question asked by Paul and it ate at him till he got an epiphany. What a fool he was. A young homeless boy, passed out in the street due to medication would be an invitation for any perverted non-consenting ass banger, murderer or far right skin head. How stupid was he not to check? Stefan asked himself in a moment of self-rebuke.

Humbled, he went back to the chemist, his phone ringing with the calls from the others to request his presence, but Stefan wasn't going back till he made amends. Once he retrieved what he required he slipped in some Euro notes into the box. He returned to Paul and handed him the medicine with the words "non-drowsy, I am so sorry".

Stefan then walked away. Feeling very stupid, Stefan failed to hear Paul thank him from a distance.

The next day Stefan went in search of Paul but he was nowhere to be found and this was the case for the next two days. The following Monday night, he went out after work to look for him again and failed.

Stefan was spent. Three hours of combing the same square mile, from one end to the other yielded nothing, except an oncoming cold. He accepted it was time to go home.

Itching to get there as soon as he could, Stefan decided to take a shortcut via a dark underpass by the fast running canal. He paused to take a cigarette, the first he had had in a year since Khoi banished the burning of tobacco in the house, but he was desperate.

As he stopped in the middle of path, Stefan lit his cigarette illuminating the environment just a little more. Whilst in the middle of inhaling the stress relieving fumes of toxins, Stefan observed a man, clearly in his late thirties and in the mid-stages of baldness, wearing a leather jacket of the same colour of his dark brown eyes and his olive tanned skin, perhaps of Aegean heritage, at the end of the path, a knife drawn in his left hand as he slowly walked towards him.

There was significant distance between them to negate the need to run. So Stefan turned and was set to pick up the pace only to find waiting for him another Mediterranean, but younger, looking man brandishing what looked like a machete.

Flanked by the tracks of the train many feet below to his left, a drop onto which would invoke and inflict extreme pain resulting from any broken bones before the train finished him off, caused Stefan to think again because to his right was a shallow canal. The effect of a fall there would probably be the same with the exception of the train.

Calmly, Stefan took the stick of cigarette out his mouth and disposed of it, there was no point in having something smouldering in your face under these circumstances. Stefan then asked "How may I help you?"

The approaching knife holder paused, as did his partner in crime who seemed stumped by the question. Hedging his bets on who he could potentially reach out to, Stefan turned to the man with the large blade and slowly reached into his pocket.

"Stay cool. I'm just getting my wallet." Stefan announced, hoping the offer of money would end this affair. Then he heard the older man speak in Turkish. Stefan didn't spend many years on the streets of Berlin and not pick up some of the language. This underlined one thing, he was doomed. Yes, they were going to take his money, but they were not willing to let him go. This was a contract killing and he was the target.

Stefan pretended not to show his concern as the younger man's face grew sterner. Accepting that bribery was of no use, he turned back and ran towards older man with the knife, hoping he would be an easier shot to escape. Stefan prayed he could push the older, heftier man away quickly enough, prior to the younger man getting to full speed.

As he ran, the plan was failing; the man braced himself and was ready to strike. Upon reaching the middle-aged man, Stefan grabbed the man by the hand that held the blade and began to tussle with him. But where was his partner? Stefan caught glimpse of the man with sleeping bag on placed over his head as a few punches to the back from a much smaller person, brought the machete holder down.

Stefan wondered who was fighting on his side, but he had more pressing matters on his hands. The knife fell, punches were thrown, and soon he and his potential attacker were on the floor. Stefan over powered the man and pinned him down before ramming his forehead onto the man's face, dazing him.

Quickly, Stefan reached for the blade which was close to the wall and as the man slowly recovered, his nose bleeding badly, Stefan, who still pinned the man down, said in Turkish "So you came to kill me huh? You scream and I will slit your throat." Stefan stabbed the knife deep into his left palm, slicing deep and stabbing hard to ensure there was irreversible nerve damage, severing of tendons as he repeated the process seven times.

The pain could be read on victim's face, swallowing it all without making a sound. Content with the damage he created to the left hand, Stefan proceeded to do the same thing to the right but with an added wickedness.

Having tenderised the area by means of repeated stabbings, Stefan lifted the hand by the middle finger and began to slicing through the webbing that joined the finger he held to the man's index finger. Stefan wanted him to suffer, but he was not that cruel. He ran the blade through, extending the division between the digits two fold as he cut through the flesh to the bone. The man did give a short scream but a quick tap on the head with the blade's handle soon silenced him as Stefan did the same to the skin between the index and the ring finger.

Once satisfied, Stefan got up and threw the knife into the canal. The man struggled to get up under the watchful gaze of Stefan who turned his attention to other man now. He was still being pounded by the person who came to the rescue, sitting on the man's chest, punching the man beneath the sleeping bag.

He could tell from the back of the person's head that he had brown hair. He also observed a brown hunter's jacket which matched his backpack, and most certainly had a strong left hook. With each blow, the man's right leg would twitch. Accepting this was enough, Stefan walked up to him, picking up his wallet on the way, and as the person raised his fist again, Stefan grabbed hold of if, halting its descent.

The person turned, angered about being interrupted and thus revealing who he was. "You." Stefan remarked upon realising that his knight in dirty clothing was the beggar whom he bought the medication for, it was Paul. Recovering from his moment of surprise, he added "It's enough."

Heaving, Paul rose to his feet. Stefan proceeded to pull off the sleeping bag that covered the younger Turk. The damage inflicted by Paul was horrendous, with the man struggling to breath.

Stefan rolled up the sleeping bag and called upon the older man "Come help your friend. He doesn't look good." Stefan was right; the man didn't seem able to get up on his own accord whist his partner was smarting now that his hands had been made useless.

Stefan formalised the conclusion of the event by throwing the blood stained sleeping bag into the canal to be washed away. At the sound of the splash, Stefan got a taste of the force within Paul's arm. Paul then, without warning, gave him a sharp blow to his side. It nearly made Stefan to keel over and he would have if he wasn't posturing like the strong man of the moment.

Paul stormed off, causing Stefan to give chase, leaving the wounded to collect themselves. Once in public, Stefan tried to run but found it difficult to do so due to the lingering pain from the blow. Still, with some long strides, he caught up with the 156cm high fellow and cut him off. "What did you do that for? Where are you going? You didn't allow me to …"

"You threw away my sleeping bag and my money! I had €140 in there!" Paul screamed before pointing at him "You owe me money!"

Stefan noticed Paul's blood stained finger and replied "I owe you more than that… you're bleeding." Paul paused and observed his arm. His jacket had been ripped and he was indeed bleeding. The machete had sliced through the stuffing of his jacket into his skin. "Come with me… " Paul looked at him, the mistrust radiated in his eyes "Please, trust me."

Stefan could see his tension dissipate. Paul held on to his injury and replied "OK."

"Cool, we'll catch a taxi, but one moment…" Stefan said as a sudden rush of saliva filled his mouth leading to him to puke heavily as he grabbed his right side around the lower rib area before stumbling on to a wall to rest his back. His face flushed, he began to sweat as he groaned. Concerned, Paul asked "Did they hurt you?"

"No, you did…" Stefan replied through gritted teeth. "What's your name anyway?" It was then the homeless boy revealed his name was Paul.

Such knowledge did not ease Stefan's pain but had to put on the bravado.

Stefan returned to his feet, lying to Paul, telling him he was fine and hailed a taxi. The driver was reluctant to take them initially, however, after a few words, said in a soft manner by Stefan, the man was only too obliging to have them in the back of his Mercedes.

Driving through the boulevards, the street lamps whizzed by, causing Stefan to feel dizzy as he perspired in silent agony. He glanced at Paul and felt sorry for the poor guy who looked lost. Stefan gave him a reassuring smile, but got nothing in return. He was not going to take this display of indifference as an affront, rather, Stefan let Paul be.

They arrived at the flat, which was actually the amalgamation of the top two floors of the building, to find it empty. This was a complete relief to Stefan. He wasn't too sure how Khoi would have handled things. When Stefan thought about "things", he didn't mean the presence of a destitute looking individual coming through his door; there have been many varieties of those brought home from drunken nights out for Khoi to care anymore. Rather he was more concerned about the drops of blood, dripping from the guest's coat.

Stefan took Paul to the bathroom to perform some first aid to the deep looking cut. His own experiences had made him a dab hand when it came to stitching up gaping wounds with the precision of a surgeon.

With Paul mended, Stefan offered him a chance to use the shower. After being provided the towels, he directed Paul to the soap and showed him how to operate the showers. Most importantly though was when Stefan showed Paul how to lock the door. He savoured the opportunity to bathe in privacy and alone, totally contrary to the usual procedure of showering with several others.

The shower was a near religious experience. Whilst he had to sustain the same temperature of water every day of the year in the home which was basically a few degrees above cold, here, he was in charge of the amount of heat he wanted touching his skin. Paul relished the euphoria the moment provided so much that he forgot himself, only choosing to step out when his skin began to prune.

He opened the door to find some clothes with their tags still on them, waiting for him by the door. Paul picked them up and smelt them before rubbing it to his face.

Stefan had been resting on the sofa with the television on, pressing a cold compress on his aching side when Paul entered. He was looking cautious and confused and walked tentatively over to Stefan. Paul stood before him in the clothes he had arrived in and the new ones under his arm. "Em…" Paul began "Where are my things please?" Stefan stretched, pointing to the backpack out on the balcony. The odour it emitted had forced Stefan to do so. It was now Stefan's turn to ask a question "Why aren't you wearing what I gave you?"

Paul looked rather ashamed as he admitted "I wanted to keep it… may be wear it later." Stefan smiled.

Paul felt uncomfortable in these clean, plush and comfortable surroundings. "I think I will go."

"Where are you going?" Stefan enquired "You can stay here for the night if you want? We have two guest rooms and it's already past midnight…" He could see the Paul's suspicion of strangers had yet to waver. "You don't have to go. You are safe here." Stefan sat up with great agony which he tried to repress. Paul's fortress of caution crumbled when Stefan offered him the remote control of the television saying "You can watch whatever you want." It was a small insignificant event, but a bond was formed the moment when the plastic electronic changed hands, at least in Paul's mind.

Stefan explained how to use the remote to change the channels in a patient, clear and respectful manner which brought back memories of Mr Babij, patiently underlining the significance of the act of Lady Macbeth's prayer to be unsexed. The same man who spent five years encouraging him before seeing a future for himself in Dusseldorf. That was the bitter fact. Mr Babij didn't stay, and because of that, Paul remained cautious, this moment of normality was not going to last. Yet, in an optimistic vibe, Paul accepted that at least for an hour or two, if, someone paid attention, positive attention to him, then he might as well enjoy it whilst he could.

Khoi arrived at five minutes past two in the morning having wined and dined some potential clients.

Walking into the living room, he found Paul sitting there watching cartoons with his eyes wide open, his focus on the moving animation similar to that of a hypnotised snake. His concentration was only broken when Khoi spoke. "Hello." Paul looked up at the Khoi, who looked startled. "How are you?" Khoi asked. Paul froze, unable to say anything constructive. Khoi's impatience was telling "Stefan?" Stefan woke, groggy and still ridden with sleep acclaiming "Oh, you're back."

"Yeah… who's your friend?" Khoi asked.

"Oh, Khoi, this is Paul." Stefan replied

"Nice to meet you." Khoi responded. Paul debated between smiling or responding whilst Khoi rubbed his eyes and added "Sorry I can't stay and watch TV with you guys. I am so tired. See you in the morning Paul." Khoi went to his room locking the door behind him. He didn't mind strangers in his home, he just didn't trust them.

Paul watched as Stefan returned to his slumber. As Stefan snuggled in the sofa, he didn't notice Paul clear away a single tear from his cheek because he wasn't being chased away.

Though normally a light sleeper, the feeling of soft comfortable material beneath him caused him to lose all need for alertness as he snuggled on the second sofa and for the first time in many years, he didn't have nightmares.

When Paul did wake it was to the sound of a lady speaking above the din of applause, he found a blanket had been placed over him and Stefan was gone. Paul followed the sound of the woman talking which was followed by some laughter, into the kitchen. Khoi was sitting there with his laptop, but his concentration was more on the television set and the lady on it who appeared to be hosting a talk show.

He was soon noticed by Khoi "You're up. Come in. Want something to eat?" he offered the guest. Paul shook his head refusing his offer, his speech impeded by coughing. "Ah, Stefan told me about that wheeze of yours and I heard it all last night. We must look into that. Please, come and sit down. We have some fruit, bread, whatever you want. You deserve it for saving Stefan's life."

He could see Khoi was a nice person from just his smile, still Paul had a query "Where is Stefan?"

"Hospital." Khoi replied, revealing that Stefan woke up in tremendous pain. Khoi suspected his ribs might be broken before adding "Your small hands are clearly capable of causing serious damage." Paul sensed the nervousness persisting, Khoi got up and made a plate of food and a mug of hot chocolate. He placed it on the table before an empty chair "Please sit and eat." This warm invitation could not be refused. Paul took his seat at the table.

Khoi took the time to delve very carefully into Paul's past and he was touched by what he had heard. When Stefan returned in less pain, having been medicated for his two broken ribs, Paul was taken aback when Stefan and Khoi began to converse in a strange language.

It was rather rude to have people rabbiting away in a foreign tongue before a guest, who had no inclination of what was being said, but Paul shrugged it off. He relied on facial expressions to try and deduce what was being said. At one point, Stefan raised his voice at Khoi who firmly put him in his place. Then they laughed together, it was odd. In his lonely nights in the home, he often imagined what breakfast with his parents would be like and strangely he had a feeling of Deja vu albeit with the wrong people and the wrong gender.

When the pair concluded with a smile, Paul was coughing as Khoi said "You are unwell. Would you like to stay here till you are better?"

"I'm fine" Paul replied, suddenly losing his appetite. "I don't want charity." He stated.

"Hey!" Stefan interjected "It's not charity. You are sick. You think by saving my ass, there won't be people out there looking for you? It's not safe for you out there anymore. You saved my life… we want to make yours better. Let us and if you don't like what's on offer you could always go."

Paul didn't respond. There was a clear mistrust emitting from him that Stefan and Khoi perceived.

Under Khoi's instructions, Stefan decided to set things straight. "You do know what I do, don't you?"

"Yes, you're a gangster." He replied as he coughed on.

Stefan grinned his confirmation, adding "Smart boy."

"What about you?" Paul asked directing his question to Khoi. "You one of them too?"

"No… he can't be." Stefan clarified "So, want to stay?"

"Only till I get better." Paul replied taking a sip of his drink.

Paul didn't care about the risk involved in staying in a flat with a mobster; all he wanted was to get better. After a week in which he hadn't been thrown out, Paul found common ground with Khoi in their love of books, Paul began to feel more comfortable and it was near impossible to deny what was steadily happening. When Khoi brought him papers to enrol into college, Paul realised he was settling down.

After two months, Paul counted his blessings. What was on offer in this new stable home? There was the food, lax rules and the company which differed from the isolation he endured for many years.

So when Khoi proposed he went to school, he clasped at the opportunity with both hands. Test and trials soon uncovered that he had an advanced mind, but yet it was considered best he stay a year behind to enable him to cope. Enrolled into the school on his own accord, being over 16, Paul started his classes with a lot of promise.

Within a week, he was suspended for ripping out the top of the desk and slapping it into the face of a boy who mocked him.

What Khoi and Stefan had neglected to see, but the school principal and the broken nose class mate had noticed was that Paul had anger issues and it was recommended that it be addressed warning that another act like that would see Paul thrown out of school. The first suggestion from the Principal to Khoi was to find Paul a hobby, one that could help him channel all the energy.

Khoi thanked the school for their understanding and after a silent trip back home. Paul saw how far apart he had becomes to Stefan.

Khoi scolded him for his actions, asking why he did it. "Names are what they are, just words!" He stressed. Stefan, on the other hand, just smirked and laughed and when finally asked to contribute to what seemed like a nauseating example of motherliness, all he could ask was "Did the little fucker cry?"

It was enough to drive Khoi to despair and he diverted his anger to Stefan. Switching tongues again, he let it rip; verbally lashing Stefan till he abandoned all his initial cockiness and offered a compromise "Would you like to try martial arts?"

Kung Fu and taekwondo were selected as Paul's after school activities and Khoi insisted that he join a weekend gardening club. The activities helped control his temper... a bit.

Paul began to excel at school within the year. The bright side was that he didn't get into trouble at school anymore, but the down side was that he had was turning into a green fingered walking assassin who could end people not only with his fist as before, but now with a few nicely placed strategic chops and blows. He showed off these talents when he started entering gardening competitions and punched a judge for his second place ribbon.

Running out of ideas and furious with Stefan thwarting Paul's positive efforts by suggesting "Let me take him in, he'll be better off!" and tantalising Paul by taking him out on business trips like a mascot Khoi could take no more. He gave Paul one final warning before he left the flat and went to calm his nerves, going to the local civic centre for his weekly art class.

Paul noticed the pads on the table before, and by the door in a bag, but never paid attention to their purpose till Khoi returned that night rather late. Sitting in the study with the desk lamp on, Khoi tried over and over to get the perspective of the assignment right. Paul walked past on his way to the toilet and paused to look at him. It was captivating to watch Khoi's stoic dedication, the pencil moving around the pad gracefully for a moment, Khoi's infallible concentration occasionally broken when he noticed a mistake. Paul wondered if it was possible that he could ever give such time and merit to anything.

Paul chose to investigate, and when asked, Khoi passed Paul the pad to give it a try. Khoi became envious at how the boy achieved what he had fraught to attain within minutes. Khoi thought this could be Paul's calling, since art wasn't a competition. It was a means of expression, something Khoi thought Paul could benefit from. Thus he was invited to the next class.

That was it. Paul had a skill, one that he excelled at. His sketches were carnivorous in their technique and punchy in development, art was his way to cope with the trauma that haunted him on a daily basis whenever he looked in the mirror.

Despite the progress he made, Paul was a late developer. His teenage angst didn't propagate at 14 but waited till he was two months after his 18th birthday and at the start of the final term of college. Paul began to grow weary of Khoi's overbearing insistence that he focus on his exams and choose a university, preferably outside Berlin or better still out of the country, and spend less time idolising Stefan or in chat rooms on his laptop.

Arguments, fights and silent treatments became the main stay whilst Stefan was a spectator, somewhat finding some thrill from it.

Then came the day Khoi would live to regret. He had asked Paul to come along with him to the office over the weekend for some paid work. He had a lot of paper work to go through and print, so some assistance was required. He thought it would be nice to show Paul around and half way through the tour, they passed by the boxing ring where Georg was having an impromptu meeting of the team.

As Khoi and Paul made their way through the exercise area, they walked over to Georg in order to greet him. Georg was busy pacing on the treadmill, giving instructions to the team present. Khoi saluted Georg who saw he wasn't alone. "Who is this ugly bugger?" The old man asked.

"He's Paul. He's the one who saved my life." Stefan announced "And I wouldn't call him that, he's vicious." Georg examined him and admitted "I can see that." Then Marcel made the mistake of sharing his opinion by rolling his eyes. Georg saw him and asked "You don't think so?" Marcel didn't say a word, "Come on Marcel, do you think you can take him?"

"I don't think I want to. It wouldn't be fair. He's already ugly" Marcel replied

Georg sniggered and with conviction in his voice focused on Paul he said "I think he can take you. He could kick your ass in the ring. Don't you think so son?"

Khoi attempted to avoid any confrontation and began "I think we have some paper work to…" when Georg interjected "Shut up Khoi. So, you think you can take him?" Paul could feel the man's words pressing his confidence. He had no choice, Paul nodded. Georg grinned and replied "Lace him up." Khoi tried to convince Stefan and Joel to intervene using Jekorian, this annoyed Georg who roared "Don't use that devil language here. Ralph, sort out the boy."

Paul entered the ring, itching for a fight, but kept his eagerness in check. He felt like a caged predator, yet was capable of standing perfectly still. Marcel ducked under the ropes and stood up tall with an aura of arrogance and a smirk, a tell-tale sign of his callous attitude that this was all a joke to him.

The two men locked eyes, Marcel smirking, Paul keeping his dead face and gaze hoping not to reveal the far too familiar all-blinding fire blazing inside of him. "Two rules. No killing each other. And keep your teeth in your mouths, you're not that desperate, girls." Georg said. Stefan, Mikel,

Daniel and Joel stepped closer to the ring. Khoi kept his distance. "When then bell rings." Georg said, before nodding at the ring manager.

The bell rang once, metallic and muted. Paul started circling Marcel, never losing eye contact nor blinking. Marcel let out a single burst of disbelieving laughter and looked at Georg; his eyes could be seen asking "Really? This guy?" Georg met Marcel's eyes then looked away, not dignifying him an answer. Marcels attitude was a sign of inexperienced weakness. A flaw that not rectified might lose him his life one day. Georg's response, or rather lack thereof, clearly upset Marcel. He joined Paul in his predatory dance.

With the time ticking, Paul was unable to contain himself any longer. He leapt at Marcel throwing a punch towards the guts only to be met by Marcel's well-put iron fist in his face.

Paul fell on the floor. Marcel thought that was the end of it till he saw Paul get up quickly with his face now red from the initial impact and that was to be the tale of the match.

Paul kept trying to get at Marcel and Marcel kept punching Paul to the ground. It seemed that Paul was deliberately entering Marcel's fist, maintaining eye contact, keeping his face dead and distant despite the increasing number of bruises and the injuries.

After a few more poundings on Paul's face and he still remained unrelenting, Marcel began feel uncomfortable, secretly saying to himself, "this is freaking me out". What he didn't know was that Paul did not just want to win; he wanted to teach Marcel a lesson.

After a hard punch to the chin which made Paul fall again. He lay still on the ground for a moment, still except for a slowly growing smile. Marcel turned to Georg, forgetting the cardinal rule of "never turn your back to your opponent" with a questioning gaze asking "should I stop?" but Marcel's ignorance to the rule was about to bite him.

Paul slowly and silently rose and started walking silently towards an unobservant Marcel. Georg smiled, and then began to laugh, Marcel began laughing as well, at first unknowingly, failing to notice Paul's approach. Georg and the others could see Paul coming and started to laugh mockingly at the presumed winner.

Georg stopped laughing and smiled at Marcel. It was a fatherly smile as he shook his head knowing what was to come. Mikel tried to signal the imminent approach of Paul using his eyes, but Marcel didn't catch on in time and when he finally did, Paul proceeded to ram his fist into his groin.

With Marcel keeling over and falling on to the ground, Paul slammed a punch right into his face causing Marcel to fall backwards and flat on to the canvas. Paul went haywire, beating Marcel to a pulp. Georg asked for the beating to be stopped. Ralph and Mikel ran into the ring and pulled Paul off a now unconscious Marcel.

Paul looked around the room looking for some form of confirmation from the person he cared for, but Khoi had left, the blood was too much for him to accept but Georg was satisfied as he proclaimed "The kid's got character. I want him in. Tend to Marcel and send this guy to my office when you're done. I want a word with him."

Watching Marcel on the floor was satisfying to Paul. The thrill, the high, the respect, it was like a drug that flooded his senses. He looked around at the cheers, it was for him, and they were all exalting his triumph. This must be how David felt when Goliath hit the ground. Everyone commended his efforts and in the midst of the rejoicing, Georg confided in Stefan that though he wanted Paul in the group, it was Stefan's job to win Khoi over because he knew Khoi would never approve.

With his order given, Stefan climbed into the ring and lifted Paul off his feet. "That was fucking amazing!" He proclaimed. This was a feeling Paul never wanted to end.

Back home that evening, the conversation between Khoi and Stefan was rowdy. Paul felt frightened to come down from his room, afraid he may have let Khoi down. At one point, Stefan roared "Georg wants him!" to which Khoi instantly replied "NO! You want him! Go and tell Georg there is a change in plans!" They soon reverted back to their own tongue before the voices stopped.

Attracted by the happenings, Paul went down to the kitchen to find Khoi and Stefan in silence, but the resentment for each other could be seen simmering beneath. His presence was noticed; giving Stefan to opportunity put Khoi on the spot. "Well, he's here. Don't you think he has a say?" Stefan said to Khoi before turning to Paul and asking, "What do you want little one? Who do you want to be with?" Paul could felt the eyes on him and despite his initial thoughts; his gut feeling pushed him to the choice he made. "I want to join the gang." Paul announced.

Stefan smirked as Khoi shook his head and made his way to the door. As he passed Paul, he stopped to look at him and proclaimed "You're an idiot." before leaving the kitchen for his room.

Paul was taken aback by Khoi's remark as he turned to Stefan, who appeared more a person defeated than a victor. Still, Paul was forced to inquire "Why is Khoi such a bitch?"

Stefan took a deep sigh and replied "Because he cares about you. I have to talk to him." As Stefan left he too stopped and said to Paul "If I ever hear you insult Khoi again, I'll cut out your tongue."

Paul had never been as frightened as he was that evening as he heard steps approaching. Stefan came to his room, opened the door and said "We'll talk about this after your exams. Finish that first." Before shutting the door and leaving Paul sitting there, angered that Khoi had got his way again.

On hearing this, Jelena had to stop the story to find out why Khoi was held in such high esteem. Mikel explained that Khoi, though not a part of the gang, was probably the most powerful member. Georg, whom Mikel referred to as the big boss, trusted Khoi unconditionally to give him a clear and honest opinion. "The big boss made it clear what he thought about Khoi and he never stopped repeating it "You insult Khoi, you insult me. You disobey Khoi, you disobey me and if you disobey me, I'll cut you down."

Also, Khoi was seen as an independent judge. When Joel and Stefan couldn't agree on which direction to take, it fell on to Khoi to cast the decisive vote and his decision was not to be questioned. In other words, he was an integral part of the dynamics of the group." Mikel clarified.

Returning to the story, Mikel explained that the relationship between Khoi and Paul turned resolutely Antarctic, with Paul pinning the full label of blame on Khoi for his intervention. This led to no words spoken between them besides cordialities. Khoi ditched the art class all together. Paul didn't and wasn't delivering the goods in terms of his grades by the middle of summer, and he left the college with his classmates, smug as a cat that got the cream, having the highest score in the school that year.

So buoyed was Paul's confidence that he entered the art competition at the evening classes that very day. Paul had just left his night art class, his pad under his arm, trying to cap the end of his pen using his teeth whilst walking out of the building.

Upon stepping out of the building, he found Mikel waiting for him by a silver car, his mobile phone in hand. "Stefan said it's time." Mikel said as he opened the door to the back seat of the car.

They drove to the derelict part of Berlin that was going to be blown up in preparation for regeneration. Paul had feeling of suspicion running through his body. He didn't know what to expect as the car parked and Mikel ushered him out.

They entered a building that used to be old bank. Mikel walked Paul down some crumbling steps to the old basement. Paul followed Mikel down to a vault door that was closed shut. It was being guarded by Marcel, who bore the black eye Paul inflicted, taunting him "You think you are tough huh?" as he pushed the door open with great difficulty.

The room was illuminated by two large spotlights in the corners, upping the temperature. The light went into his eyes, making it difficult to see. Though he was temporarily blinded, Paul beheld a strange sickly smell. Then, as his vision adapted to the light, there was the sight of a naked man tied between two pillars.

The person had been stretched so far apart and so tightly bound that he had been stretched to the limits of human endurance, hovering above the ground, blood originating from various sections of his body.

The man's mouth was gagged and all that could be heard was Stefan's heavy breathing. Stefan, on hearing the door, turned and smiled at Paul. That was when Paul noticed Stefan was sweating, sleeves rolled up, a few needles held between his teeth and his fingertips stained reddish brown.

Stefan didn't have time to welcome him and it was ruining his concentration as to where to touch next. The man's whole left arm had already been occupied.

Paul looked at Mikel, Daniel and Ralph, all present in the room, mesmerised, as Stefan walked a few paces from the body. Like an artist, Stefan stood back observing his work to determine what more was required.

Stefan returned to the man, went on his knees and began to place a needle into the right foot of the man. One followed another till he near exhausted all the needles he had been holding with his mouth. "Ralph? More!" he ordered. Ralph grinned and handed more of them over to Paul instead "you give it to him. He's been waiting for you."

Paul felt a feeling he had never thought he could find, terror. Everyone in the room now had their eyes on him. He wouldn't let that tame him. Paul smartly walked to Stefan and placed a box of needles into his out stretched hand.

Stefan looked and set his eyes upon Paul's face, he smiled "Glad you could come. Open the box." Paul did as he was told. Stefan looked in the packet and found there was a 13cm stainless steel Needle Replacement kit for Airbrush Guns, each 0.5mm thick. "Hmm, I was saving it for later, better late than never" Stefan picked out the 20 in the box, got off his knees and went to the front of the man.

Looking him straight in the eye, he rammed the first needle into the gut of the man, slowly till its entire length entered the body. The agony could only be seen in the man's eyes as he was unable to toss and turn in pain.

4cm below, he inserted another. It entered in an angle and was inhibited half way. "Oops, I hit a rib." Stefan said pulling it out gently. "Let's try again." This time there was no hindrance and another piece of metal was stuck into the man's abdomen.

Finally, the pack of 30 was extinguished. The man had remained conscious through the ordeal, rolling his head back and forward, shaking it vigorously. "Ralph! I need you. Bring the small ones this time," he ordered with a hint of orgasmic euphoria in his wide dilated eyes.

Stefan took a moment to look at his blood covered hands and gave a short giggle before he did something unexpectedly creepy. He touched the bound victim's wound that oozed blood and in turn smeared it on Pauls face. He collected more and ran his hands through Paul's hair, staining his head. Looking at his result, Stefan laughed and commented to Paul "You look pretty in red." then turned to the bound man, who was wondering why his suffering was being prolonged and asked "Look at him? Doesn't he look pretty in red? Your red?"

"Needles." Ralph announced handing more to him before promptly returning to his place by the door. Stefan hurriedly opened the pack, some of the metal implements dropping to the ground. As he glanced down to see them, he noticed Paul, who seemed to just stand there, looking unmoved by the experience, bar the tears dripping down his left cheek. Stefan reached for his face, collected the tear with his index finger and with the drying blood of the double crosser; he proceeded to taste the tear drop. The disgusting display was not perceived by the others present in the room and in a soft tone, inaudible from the others he added "Let no one see you cry." He then turned to the man, "And since you have seen him, we must do something about."

The man knew what was coming and began to swing his head vigorously. "Oh please." Stefan remarked and then ordered "Daniel! Hold his head steady." Daniel with his large hands clasped hold of the man's head. Stefan didn't care if the man's eyes were opened or shut; the needles were going in anyway. And they did so, the slender metal tubes puncturing through the eye lids one after the other. When all the needles were spent, the left eye and its surroundings managed to contain 39 needles, out doing the right by 3.

Stefan carried on his grizzly act, inserting pointy metal objects into the man through every part of the body whilst aiming precisely to avoid killing him. But now, with over 900 external objects within his body and three protruding from each deafened ear, it was to no surprise to everyone that after 3 hours, the man had slumped into unconsciousness.

Stefan took a few steps back to admire his handy work. Paul had remained where he stood since handing the pins to Stefan "Can you see?" Stefan cried out to him "You want to join us; the books are just a bit too boring. Do you think you can stomach this?" Paul did not reply as he looked down at the concrete. Stefan thought he had his answer already, but to make sure he decided to provide one more test. Stefan ungagged the man, and then went to Ralph to collect his blade. "Here, shorty." he said, offering the knife to Paul. Stefan's eyes looked wild, filled with visions of possession by undesirable beings. "Finish him off if you dare. If not, you can go back to Khoi and take a fucking desk job."

Paul looked up, he wanted to clear the grin off Stefan's face with a punch, but that was just one of the many feelings he had at the moment. Paul didn't take the knife. Instead he snubbed the offer opting to walk to the vault door turning to Ralph, saying, "I want to leave please." Ralph looked at Stefan who nodded his approval. As Ralph turned the leaver to allow the door to open, Stefan asked "So where are you going?" Paul didn't look back as he replied "I'll be back soon."

Ralph opened the door and allowed Paul to exit. Once gone, Ralph raised his concerns "You don't think he'll call the cops?"

"No, I trust him." Stefan stated emphatically. Stefan looked around and found a few more needles, noting that the testicles had yet to be addressed along with the genitals. He was tired however and an hour of rest was required.

It was just as the hour was about to end that Paul returned with a rucksack on his back and a clean face. He placed the bag down and took out a pack of canned beer, leaving them on the floor. "Thought you might be thirsty." Paul said, picking out a can offering it to Daniel first. The group smiled and helped themselves to the refreshments. Daniel then made a snide remark "At least he's good for something."

It was then Paul produced the other items he had in his bag. Out came what looked like a small blow torch used in kitchens and some Crisco oil, drawing a bit of concern from those present. "This place is soundproof right?"

"Once the door's shut, yes." Stefan confirmed.

"Good." He concluded as he brought out the pack of 12 UK standard size 14 knitting needles made of stainless steel, the longest ones in the market. "I found your needles too small."

Paul proceeded to coat them in oil before approaching the nude man whose blood dripped onto the floor along with his urine, his head bent over from anguish and physical exhaustion.

Unconsciousness was the only relief he had had all night, but the buzzing sound and slight change in temperature suddenly brought him back to life. His sense of sight was now gone, and his left ear deafened but, by some miracle, he could hear a little using his right and caught the words "Close the door gentlemen, he's going to scream." Paul grabbed hold of the man's penis and shoved the tip of the long knitting needles, which he had heated using the blow torch, up his urinary track, emitting a sizzling sound from the skin within. It caused the man to screech like a girl as it progressed further till it perforated the organs within. "This is dark" remarked Ralph. Daniel stood there stunned and shocked, Stefan beamed his admiration as it was the most painful thing any of them had ever seen, and Paul was doing it agonisingly slow.

Paul had never been pretty, but now his face grew exceptionally demonic, with his tongue between his teeth and a crumpled brow of concentration. The needle made a soft hissing noise as it sank deeper into the flesh, but then it got stuck. Stefan whistled and said "I think you need to reheat it, if you want it to go in any further." the man himself was beyond the point of sobbing, and seemed to be frozen in an endless, soundless, bloody scream.

Paul looked at Stefan mockingly, and put his hand on the back of the needle. His muscles bulged, and he pushed the needle another 15 cm into the man's loins, by pure force. All onlookers except Stefan had to look away. As the tortured man shot up one last time, and then fell back, forever.

Paul wiped the blood off his brow with the back of his hand, took a can of beer and his bag, saying as he walked to the door. "Sorry I can't stay for more than one can, there is an art event I need to prepare for. See you at home Stefan."

Paul returned home but not to practice his shading. Having found a private place near the building to clear off all signs of blood on him, using wet-wipes and putting them in his bag, prior to setting off on his journey back.

Paul walked into the flat riddled with guilt. He heard the rattling of pots and pans in the kitchen and immediately raced there hoping to find Khoi there and he did.

Khoi gave him a quick glance and looked perplexed as he asked Paul, whilst searching. "What on earth is happening?" He said, "My memory must be on the blink. First, I couldn't find my knitting needles and now my blow torch is gone. How am I expected to make crème Brule for tomorrow?" As he crossed the kitchen to look at another compartment, he homed in on Paul's distress and asked "what happened to you?"

Paul immediately fell to his knees before Khoi and confessed all that had brought him the torment which had occurred just an hour earlier. He didn't know what to expect, perhaps a "laying of hands" upon his head to absolve him of his iniquities, or some words of reassurance, what he got instead was a heavy dose of reality delivered via a lament. "Oh Paul," Khoi began "why? And please don't tell me it was a lapse of judgment." It was true. Paul could not rely on that excuse. Facing the situation head on, Khoi declared "This is beyond me."

"Please Khoi, help me. Tell him I made a mistake, I got carried away..."

"No Paul. It doesn't work like that. You belong to him now." Khoi proclaimed.

The revelation was a body blow to Paul who seemed to plead for salvation "please don't tell me that, please don't say I am condemned..."

Every fibre in his being told Khoi to turn away, but the innocence of Paul's youth was a compelling counter argument. With a heavy sigh Khoi replied "No, I won't abandon you. I still see promise in you. But I won't fight for you either. If you still want to keep studying, I am here for you, but I won't shield you from your choices."

Khoi had seen enough of Paul grovelling and it hurt to watch a tormented soul, yet he couldn't help but conclude "Stefan may be my best friend but he is also the devil. You sold your soul to him and there is nothing I can do. You will never be free till he says so." Paul began to whimper, his soul ached more when Khoi added "I opened your letter. You got accepted in Bochum, Cologne and Berlin school of art. What are you going to do?" Khoi asked. Without waiting for an answer, he left for his room as Paul wailed.

Paul did not get any sleep, he sat in his room with constant "what ifs" buzzing in his thoughts. The sound of Stefan coming home brought out in a cold sweat. He quickly locked the door to his room and sat, fearful of what was to come. He didn't need to worry however, as Stefan gave Paul's room a miss, tired from the activities of the day, instead choosing the comfort of his bedroom where he turned on some rap music and was soon sound asleep, his snoring alerting Paul to that fact. Paul was completely astonished that Stefan could find rest.

Stefan kept his distance from Paul through the means of intentional avoidance for a couple of weeks as a result of another intervention from Khoi, but even Paul knew this couldn't last. Paul returned to the flat one evening after classes. He tried to enter the house as quietly as he could, hoping to avoid crossing paths with Stefan, who had successfully managed to avoid him for the past three weeks.

Observing the entrance, Paul noted that Stefan and Khoi's shoes weren't by the door. Paul relaxed and proceeded to the living room and froze upon seeing Stefan seated on the sofa, watching a wildlife programme. He was instantly spotted. "Paul! Long time man!" Stefan cried out.

With a lump in his throat, and feeling vulnerable in Khoi's absence, Paul replied "Yes."

"Cool! Come here for a minute." Stefan ordered. Paul dutifully complied and stood over Stefan who pointed at the screen "Look at that beast" directing Paul's attention to some stripped large rodent like creature chomping on a carcass "It's called a honey badger. Man that thing is fearless. I just watched them fend off a pack of hyenas five times their size and they didn't care, they are completely fearless, just like you… you take them down no matter their size…" Stefan looked briefly straight at Stefan's face but he didn't want to make eye contact, so he fixed his vision to the screen as Stefan added "No, I'm wrong, you are better than that oversized rat. Your upward pointed nose, misshaped lips, screw the badger, you are a rhino, my rhino. You will put out all the fires in the savannah, okay rhino?" Paul pretended not to hear him but Stefan was persistent "Rhino! I'm calling you." Stefan shouted. Paul turned to look at him "Did you hear me? You will be putting out the fires for me. Is that clear rhino?" Paul could feel his identity fading away as he capitulated, accepting his new place with the words "Yes Stefan."

So began the slow and progressive indoctrination of Paul into the fold. Stefan carefully crafted a role for him in the gang. Stefan took great pains to ensure Paul's studies weren't affected by only acting over the weekend.

Stefan would summon him; using the name no one else dared use at the risk of serious retribution from Stefan. "Rhino! Come..." You could see when he got the call. Paul would shudder and lose all colour before following Stefan obediently. Like a lap dog, he'd be there, waiting, unhappy and disgruntled, yet silently, he'd go.

Again he would be brought to a location and Stefan would do what he enjoyed best before inviting Paul to have a go. Gradually, Stefan began to take steps back, taking a supervisory role to his little protégé, allowing Paul to express his creativity with an ear being lobbed off or forcing a person onto a bed of burning coal, encouraging Paul to do more heinous and vile things.

Slowly, the light within seemed to diminish in Paul. Paul did manage to find sleep however by mentally blocking the events from his mind allowing him some peace. He would try to capture some normality through his education while waiting for the call to get his hands dirty. Thus his soul sunk deeper into hell.

Yes, Paul did prefer his own company, often spending time with his ever growing collection of books and articles, taking one course after another. He felt like his education was going to come to an end as his free time was becoming more occupied by Stefan's requests.

The fringe benefit of this interaction with the gang was the rare occasions when he got to socialize with the gang and hear the tales of their escapades. It was a small benefit for his bloody actions. The effect of this was that Paul's social circles became limited and he found it hard to associate with others, even those in his class.

Paul lived day by day between senses of self-loathing and anticipation, waiting for the moment he would be summoned. Fifteen months after his first encounter with the needles, Paul was eating a sandwich when the words "Rhino, I need you" flashed across the screen of his phone.

His mind seemed to shut down, all thoughts streamed to the text and a transformation occurred. He was now a lackey, the right hand man, subservient to no one but the person he considered his saviour.

Stefan had been looking for the right case for Paul to address. When the word got out that a shipment of alcohol had gone amiss in transit, there was only one suspect. Yes, he'd done it before. A few boxes here and there mysteriously taking flight, but they did no harm to the profit margins and thus could be over looked. It was clear that neglecting his actions had only made the thief more audacious as he had decided to whisk away a container of champagne from the port.

Again, it wasn't the cost of the theft that was the matter, this could be absorbed. It was the breezy arrogance and audacity of the thieving bastard who thought he could hoodwink them, especially when the man was indebted to them already to the sound of €84,000. Georg, dismissed it again, but did leave it to Stefan to decide what to do. This was a case of self-liquidation by the thief.

In Stefan's eyes, this was an abomination and he was obliged to cleanse the system of it. A perfect first case for Paul, Stefan concluded.

A text followed asking Paul to meet Stefan at OJ's at 34 minutes after one. Like a zombie, he left his classmates and walked all the way to Stefan's favourite place. The bar from outside seemed empty, with only one or two people sitting around the bar along with Stefan who was sipping his brandy.

Paul entered, the sound of the door being heard over the soft music being played. Upon setting sights on him, Stefan downed his drink and paid before putting on his coat and asking Paul to walk with him. Strolling down the boulevard, with no cordialities, Stefan got straight to the point. "Mister Lenz hasn't paid us what we are due for two months now and what's worse; he appears to have sticky fingers. I don't expect we'll see the money or items anymore."

"I am sorry to hear that, Stefan" Paul replied meekly

"It's irrelevant. His money is irrelevant. Lenz paying, however, is tantamount."

"Yes, Stefan, I understand." Paul concurred, even though he knew where this was going and despite how he deplored the wretched existence he now entrenched himself, Paul, nevertheless paid attention to what was to follow. "He wanted to handle the shipment of booze and buy it cheap. Well now we'll make sure he pays the full price. No death by steel for him, but a traitor's death. Drown him in the merchandise. Or smash in his head with it and pour it into his brains. Drench him in it and set him ablaze while he'd still breathing, but no knives or bullets. Traitors deserve a traitor's death" Order given, Stefan added "You will be doing this alone and you have a week. Call Mikel when you are ready. He will take you to the relevant place. Tell him what you need and do what you like, just don't fail me."

Paul went off to prepare his mind using a process that was to be a permanent ritual of his when needing to conduct his operations.

He sat in his room for two to three days, depriving himself of food, light and human contact, all to build his hunger which he needed to accomplish his set goal, regardless of how grizzly it was.

Paul did carry out his task in accordance with Stefan's wishes but using the classiest of manner with the use of long garden hose, a funnel and four crates of champagne. When Ralph and Daniel went to clean up, they found Lenz, seated at his desk, with his eyes bulging out his face and his entrails herniating from his anus.

Stefan was pleased and decided to show Paul his appreciation by having a tattoo with the word "RHINO" inked on his under left forearm and the picture of a rhino on the right. They all attended the honour being bestowed and despite Paul's smile, and expression of gratitude, He knew he wasn't too pleased to be branded.

Stefan never took part in any elimination again; Rhino did all the dirty work for him from then on.

Despite this, Khoi's influence on Stefan was what kept Stefan from having complete control over Paul. Some sort of quasi-parenthood had evolved in the way Khoi and Stefan treated Paul. Despite their cold frosty relationship, Khoi's influence could be seen in the way Stefan ensured his education was on track.

On his third Christmas in the household, Stefan came home with three advent calendars, one for each member of the household.

Three days after Christmas, whilst recovering alone in the flat from over eating, he got a text. "Rhino, I need you. Meet me at Alexandra Square." His heart sunk as put on his down jacket and left the flat.

He arrived at the square and a car pulled up before him with Stefan at the wheel. "Get in." he was told. Paul sat in the front beside Stefan who drove off quietly and remained so for over half an hour. As they got further out of town Stefan spoke. "Probably wondering where we're going right?" Paul said nothing. Then they parked in front of a building. Paul thought he was finished as Stefan wasn't one to drive him anywhere.

"Out." Stefan ordered. The pair entered a lovely, clean looking building. It was a private clinic. They were directed to a waiting room and found Khoi already waiting.

Stefan confessed that this was all Khoi's idea and he was dead against it because he didn't see anything wrong with him "But if it'd make you happy and get rid of your insecurities, then I'm all for it." Paul was going to have surgery that night to fix his lip and he actually cried out in glee at the prospect."

"You should have seen him" Mikel remarked "When he got his new face he began to smile all the time, it seemed no matter what Stefan told him to do, it was worth it for getting his face done. Though Stefan could show signs of kindness towards Paul, what he made that boy do often made me wonder if he had forgotten that Paul was actually a child when he found him and was still developing."

Mikel seemed troubled, pouting as he tried to stomach his own guilt "I think we better continue on our way, I've nearly finished anyway." He added as he got up. Jelena did the same. As they strolled Mikel continued. "I could see things were wrong, but who was I to butt in? Surely, where he was now was far better than where he could have been if Stefan hadn't found him... I never seriously thought or wanted to know how it affected him till the day Stefan died.

The way he reacted... I thought he was devastated, then he insisted on doing what he was sent to do and once we were finished, he didn't drive home, he drove to Ghent and found a bar there and gave me the keys. "You're driving" he said before diving into shots of strong spirits and leaving me to my own devices. I'd never seen him so courageous. He approached people, bought them drinks, had chats and even got a kiss or two from a hot girl and when he had his full at four in the morning, he called me over, and divulged everything I told you before he bought me a drink and cheerily gave a toast "To freedom." I didn't understand the significance of those till a few weeks ago.

I think with Stefan's demise he was truly free... and now that he got it, he doesn't seem to know what to do with it." At the junction of the road, Mikel pointed to the nice glass covered building "It's over there."

As they crossed the street to another small square near their destination, Jelena paused to ask, "Wait... How did you know all this? Paul doesn't look like the "woe is me" sort of chap is he?" Mikel smirked and confessed, "You're right. Paul wouldn't let you in even if he wanted to.... you'd have an easier time stealing some gold in Fort Knox. I guess in Stefan's absence he's felt he could open up a little and Ghent was the right setting. I'm pretty sure he chose to confide in me because of all we've been through together. Still, it didn't make it less weird hearing him tell me all about his life ... He made strange confession as well. He always considered the gang as a family and I could see where he was coming from... Khoi and Stefan, the bickering parents..." Then Mikel stopped looking up to check if the light was on in the flat when a follow up question came.

"And you?" Jelena pressed, "Where do you fit in the family unit?"

Considering the question for a moment, Mikel replied "I guess he now sees me as a brother."

"OK, so as a brother, you could say all that he told you came as a surprise? You must have seen all, if not some of this happening, was there no debate with Stefan about this?"

Mikel wished to rebuff the statement but hesitated for a moment. He had a flash back, it happened last spring at the flat. He and Paul had just returned from another task and he was invited up for a drink. Stefan had started before them. They found him in the apartment feeling sorry for himself and because of that Mikel sat to with him in the kitchen to have a beer.

Stefan was reeling, having sustained two major blows which he considered as challenges to his position and he didn't like that. The person whom he felt most aggrieved by was Khoi. "First, he moved out, and now he sides with that simpleton Joel!" Khoi had the casting vote over a particular matter and he had decided that Joel's approach was more reasonable than Stefan's and this was a body blow. "It's a bad time to be alive when your best friend is quick to abandon you." Stefan whined. He sipped his beer and looked at Mikel who sat there uncomfortably "Why do you humour me with your presence? All I need to do is turn my back and you'll sell me down the river too" Mikel found it better to gaze into the bottle he held. Stefan sniggered "I knew it. I can't trust anyone can I? Not even you rhino!"

There was the shattering sound of glass. Mikel and Stefan looked to find Paul with broken pieces of glass around his feet, his khaki trousers wet by the beer and his hand dripping blood. Paul had squeezed the bottle till it broke. "Everything ok rhino?" Stefan asked.

There was a hollow menacing look about Paul, but what he said was more ominous "Do you want me to die?" Paul asked "If you want me to die, I'll do it right away. Do you need my life? I'll give it to you." Mikel was genuinely frightened of the happenings of the night. He turned to Stefan hoping he wouldn't say anything to encourage Paul.

Stefan got out of the chair and walked up to Paul who, still seated, looked up at him. Stefan touched the side of his face, looking back at Paul in an intense gaze that lasted a moment "Let's hope it never comes to that." Stefan said, breaking the stillness. "Let's sort out your hand."

By the time they reached the door, Mikel's story had ended and the culpability mounted before he acknowledged "I guess we were all afraid of him…" Unable to take any more of the retrospective self-loathing, Mikel opened the main door to building with the key he had been given.

They entered into an art deco styled foyer towards a flight of majestic stairs, covered in emerald green carpet. Despite how nice it looked, Jelena enquired whether the building had a lift and was told that due to the age of the building and the special protection granted to it by the state, there wasn't a lift to speak of.

Jelena took off her heals before attempting to tackle all the steps leading to the seventh floor. It was hard work making it up to the flat. All the physical exertion made Jelena hot and as she caught her breath as Mikel opened the door and ushered her into the abode.

It was dark and distinctively cold. Jelena watched on as Mikel shook his head, turned on the lights in the entrance before moving to the last switch, the thermostat, which he turned up. Mikel apologised for the temperature and remarked "I believe Paul must have antifreeze in his blood."

They walked through the opened doors of the living room and were greeted by the sound of gunfire, the cries of people howling in pain and the faint smell of Dettol. There were no lights on. The only source of illumination was the flat screen mounted high on the wall.

Sitting upright, with a control pad firmly in his hands, gesticulating in line with the activities on the screen, was Paul, totally engrossed in his activities, spellbound and silent. "Hey?" Mikel called out. There was no response. "Jelena is here too." All he got was a grunt of acknowledgement from Paul. Accepting this was the most he would receive, Mikel asked Jelena if she wanted anything to drink, she chose water.

When Mikel went to fetch her order, Jelena took the time to observe the room. It was all decked out in the style of a gentleman's smoking club with the large, high backed leather arm chairs, a matching sofa and a brown bear hide placed over the finely polished wooden floor.

One of the walls was obscured by a large bookshelf. It was filled with hardback books from ground to ceiling with a drink cabinet crafted in the middle of the shelf. Though unable to read the brands, from the décor and their line of work, she was sure that the cabinet was stocked with nothing but the best alcohol available.

The other walls were covered in paintings that went beyond decorative and more into the area of fine taste with the exception of the wall which held the television.

Amongst all this splendour sat Paul with his ruffled blonde hair, biting his lower lip in concentration and wearing a singlet and torn jeans within nothing covering his bare feet.

Jelena caught sight of his left arm which was still bound in a bandage, with a slight stain, solving the mystery of the strange smell. It began to make sense. The biting of the lip and the wincing probably had a lot to do with the use of his wounded arm.

There was something about Paul that made Jelena feel maternal. She wished to sit by him, and ask if all was well, perhaps reassure him. "Paul?" She called.

He paused the game and looked straight at her with his strained, cold eyes, void of affection. But before she could open her mouth to speak, the utterance was stemmed by Mikel's arrival with a tray containing two plastic bottles of water and two glasses. "I didn't know if you wanted still or sparkling water, so I brought both. Need ice?" Mikel offered.

"Em... no." Jelena replied

Mikel concurred "You are right. It's too cold for that." As he placed the tray on the stool he remarked "What happened? You finished all the levels?"

"Jelena called me" Paul replied

"Fancy that? I call you when you are playing that thing and you make pig noises and ignore me." Mikel snapped "Why is that?"

"Jelena is a guest and a lady. Stefan always told me never to ignore such people." Paul stated, bringing a smile to Jelena's face. Mikel chortled "Listen to him? Such a charmer because you are here."

Despite the niceties, Paul remained cold. "Care to sit down?" Mikel offered, directing him to the arm chair closest to Paul. She felt she could have sunk into the soft yet hefty cushions. As he unscrewed the top of the bottles he asked "So, still or sparkling?"

"Sparkling please." She replied.

Mikel served her a glass whilst he, on the other hand, opted for the still water before taking his seat next to Jelena. He drank half of his water before reaching into his pocket for a small parcel of marijuana and cigarette paper. "Hey, tiny!" Mikel called out to Paul, who didn't respond, as he restarted his game. This caused Mikel to giggle, as he teased "you should see this guy in action. He's unstoppable. Aren't you Paul?" He licked the sealant of the cigarette paper, holding the flammable plant in place.

Concerned about the quantity of narcotics bound by the thin slither of paper, Jelena hinted "Shouldn't you have added some tobacco to that?"

"And add cancer into the mix? No thanks. Besides, it needs to be strong or Paul won't get his share of the buzz through the second hand smoke. It calms him." When Jelena asked why Paul couldn't just partake in the joint, she was told by Mikel as he lit his spliff "because Stefan told him not too."

Taking a deep draw of the weed, he asked Paul whilst exhaling "Did you change your bandage and dressing? Can't have you getting another infection" The stabilising effect of the drug began to silence Mikel as he sat back into the chair only remarking "wow, good shit." He then proceeded to close his eyes eventually passing out.

Jelena was amazed at how quickly the drug took effect. She reached over to shake him and was told by Paul whose eyes remained fixed on the screen "Don't bother. He's out for the count." When asked how strong the narcotic was, Paul informed her that that it wasn't the strongest they had in stock, rather the second strongest. "He comes here to take it and says it's for me. It's only because he hasn't been eating much lately and thinks it would help him find his appetite. Then he passes out. What a fool."

Although not even being given a glance, Jelena was overcome by interest in Paul's plight. "Does he always do this? All the time?"

"No, only around very close friends. You should be honoured." Paul highlighted, causing her to giggle. It was then she saw her chance to investigate and asked what Paul was playing. It was a game called "War at Dawn".

"Looks pretty hard." She remarked. Paul sighed and pressed a few buttons, halting his progression through the game to save it. Then he restarted the game and went to TV cabinet which held the console to fetch the second control pad and offered it to Jelena. "It's not that hard." He said "Give it a go."

Jelena was reluctant initially, but she saw potential in partaking in the game and for that reason decided to play. She was invited to take her place on the sofa next to Paul who instructed her on the aim of the game which was to kill all the enemies and accomplish tasks, like releasing a hostage, gaining some secret information, kidnapping and assassinations, all by using an array of arsenals that could be upgraded or changed as one advances through the levels.

Paul proved to be a great teacher and after just four restarts of the game Jelena was soon pulling her weight as the body count climbed. By level five, the instructions and words of encouragement stopped as Paul got drawn deeper into the game.

Soon a trait became abundantly clear as Paul would often cut down an opponent Jelena could easily have handled and would advance further leaving her behind. Paul was clearly not a team player. By level nine, Jelena had been blown up by a grenade and was out of it, not that Paul noticed.

She put down the control pad and watched as Paul pressed ahead in silence, slaughtering and maiming till he reached level 13. "You've clearly played the game countless times."

"It helps me relax." Paul replied whilst slitting the throat of a character that got in his way.

"Why don't you go jogging or take some Mikel's grass? Surely it's better than eye ache?" Paul took a minute to kill a few more enemies before responding "Stefan said it was bad for me… it could make me paranoid."

"Have you ever tried it?" Jelena probed, however Paul did not reply. Jelena continued "You seem to have looked up to Stefan didn't you?" Paul still didn't answer, yet she pressed on "why do you live off his every word?"

"Because… it's Stefan." She concluded.

Thinking of how silly the statement was, Paul chose to expand "Everyone has a role in the group…" he began as he sprayed bullets in a room filled with characters then sighed "You know what I mean? Stefan was the boss, Mr Wise and the brains, Joel was second in command and Khoi … well, he's just Khoi." Jelena saw the funny side of Paul's description of Khoi and asked "What about the others? Where do they fit in?"

Still with eyes fixed to the controlled animation Paul continued "Pretty boy there" referring to Mikel "He's the client facing schmoozer with all his poshness and shit. He can wine and dine the ass off most people. Marcel, he's more like the big stick you carry with you when you want to be persuasive during your negotiations. His stature was intimidating enough. Thus they worked more with Stefan, the commander of the import, export, customer services and enforcement unit."

"The two remaining meat heads are Joel's wards. Joel leads the 'rough em up', collection and sanitation crew. If someone needed a warning or reminding, you sent Joel. If they needed to be shown a preview of event to come upon failing to meet our requirements, Joel and Daniel will be at your door. And once the situation has been resolved, Daniel and Ralph would be sent to clean and ensure all traces are gone and to ensure no one comes looking for them either. Joel would grease a few palms, scratch a few backs and, where necessary, show them something the nosey individual didn't want the world to see to ensure their silence. Ralph also acted more as the bodyguard of the big boss too."

"All this happened under the hawkish eyes of Stefan, the most trusted member of the group and the mouth piece of the puppet master supremo, our boss's wife."

Then with a sigh, Paul concluded, and there is Khoi, "Mr Clean". He runs the legitimate side of the business which he helped start up using the money our leader earned before he decided to expand into the unsavoury side of business. So he is kept from the front-line and acts more as a consultant than an active participant."

Again, Jelena laughed but didn't let one notable absence slip. "You seemed to have neglected yourself. Where do you fit in this jigsaw puzzle?"

Paul, still glued to the screen, didn't immediately reply. In fact, Jelena had to wait seven minutes before Paul finally spoke. "Me? Well, there isn't much to say about me. I was the exterminator… Ralph and Daniel would get to work when I was done. I used to address the vermin that troubled us."

"So you reported to Stefan?" she interjected. Paul winced again in pain. Jelena picked on a particular detail "Why do you refer to yourself in the past tense? Do you think your position is in danger?"

Paul took a moment to give her a stern look as he answered "I don't know. You tell me… they hired you didn't they?" With his point made, he returned to his game.

Jelena wasn't going to be brushed off so easily. "I noticed you had a bag all packed and ready to go… got a trip planed?"

Paul laughed out loud "You went through my things? Damn you are good"

"I hope you don't mind?" She asked

"It's too late to mind… you've already done it." Paul's response was loaded with sarcasm.

Jelena chose to wait for a moment, gauging his body language. He didn't seem fazed or aggrieved as she continued with her game. Now confident he wasn't too peeved, she proceeded with her investigations "So tell me, why you have your bags packed?" Paul didn't flinch as he steadied his hand and played on "Are you really that frightened of being left out?" Paul remained silent, another tactic was required "So no drugs for you because Stefan told you… have you ever had a girlfriend?" Paul began to blink more frequently, struggling to maintain his concentration. She was getting to him "I bet you haven't… Stefan got in the way of that didn't he?"

He twitched a little, anxiety levels were rising in Paul's mind as he prayed Jelena would stop, but there was no sign of that happening "Did Stefan control you? Did you do everything he told you to do?" Paul grew more agitated, his avatar even got shot three times in the game … something that had never happened before to him, but Jelena didn't want to let it go "What would have happened if you ever said no? Have you ever disobeyed him?"

She drew closer as she asked "Tell me Paul, were you happy doing everything you were told to do?" Paul shook his head to confirm the truth he could never say "What did he make you do Paul? Did he change you?" Paul paused the game as his eyes welled up with tears. He didn't want to be seen crying. He covered his eyes with his left hand as the tears formed then fell; the angst of his life being sprawled out on the floor was proving too much. He gripped the control pad with his right hand so hard that it squeaked.

Jelena gave him a moment to recover, but as he moved his right hand, Jelena saw the fading tattoo on his inner right forearm. It was hard to make out the words at first, but when she did, she proclaimed "Rhino"

The reaction she received was completely unexpected. The name seemed to trigger a rage within Paul as the control pad was flung across the room headlong into the television screen, shattering it. The sound of the appliances clashing with each other caused Mikel to stir, groggily trying to take stock of what caused the noise.

Paul was seething, breathing through his teeth as he pointed at Jelena and growled "Don't you ever call me that name! No one calls me that!"

Though startled, Jelena maintained her composure even as Paul laughed as though under the influence of the drug he refused earlier. He gazed at her with the hint of unleashed insanity in his eyes as he began to unfurl the bandage that covered his healing wound, the gritted teeth exposed through his sinister grin he said "You shouldn't have said that."

With his binding removed, he held the material with both hands and strung them apart for a moment as his empty gaze grew devilish.

Jelena knew she was in trouble. Slowly she reached to for her shoe, whilst maintaining eye contact as Paul asked "you want to know what Stefan asked me to do? I can show you? I don't mind." He said as he held up the bandage, gripping it tightly "Please, let me show you" He began to lurch forward when Mikel called out "PAUL!"

Like a snap of the fingers, Paul's heaving lessened as he was stopped in his tracks, as though released from the powers of a hypnotist. Paul blinked tightly and shivered. When he opened his eyes, he appeared disorientated and puzzled by what he held in his hands. He caught sight of Mikel who look appalled as he asked "What are you doing?" Then there was Jelena, her stiletto in her right hand ready to strike.

Awash with guilt and shame, Paul could not stop shaking. He got up and tried to apologise but words failed him, there was just too much pain. The binding slipped from his hands with the tears dripping down his face, he raced out of the flat.

Mikel had sobered up, but was still baffled as he asked "What the hell is going on?" Jelena didn't respond as she quietly slipped on her shoe. "Did he just… was he about to strangle you?" she still said nothing as she stood up picking up her purse "Oh my God…" Mikel remarked and mumbled "I got to find him. Are you ok to make it home on your own?" She nodded as she watched Mikel collect his thoughts.

He reached for his phone and made a call as Jelena went to fetch her coat from the rack by the front door, hesitating in order to listen in on his call. Mikel had rung Khoi to explain how he woke up to find Paul in the process of attempted murder. She noted that there was a bomber-jacket missing from the rack and it got her thinking. It was then she decided to leave the flat, and Mikel who began to panic.

Mikel checked the flat and confirmed Paul was not there. Under strict instruction from Khoi, he was told not to inform anyone and meet him at the bar from where they would organise a search.

*10 December 2010*

Three hours and still nothing, Khoi returned to his hotel feeling cold, and deflated. He had conceded that he may need some additional hands in his search for Paul, but he desperately needed a change of clothes first having walked in the rain all that time for nothing.

As he opened the door, he noticed the light was on and sitting there on the chair, looking seductive, with her short dress and her long legs crossed, was Jelena. She was busy sniffing the complimentary cream left by the hotel. "Not bad." She remarked before smiling and said "hello Khoi".

His nostrils flared in despair, but he had to maintain his cool. He responded with a smile "Nice to see you." as he walked in, taking off his coat and leaving it a heap on the floor. He approached the bed and took one of the towels to dry his hair and face. "I guess I owe you an apology about

Paul's behaviour. I heard he lost it for a moment... he's been having a bad..."

"Let's skip the details." Jelena interrupted as she got up and approached him. Khoi seemed apprehensive about her intentions.

Jelena reached for his buttons and began to speak as she unbuttoned his shirt "Do you know what happens to hired guns once they have out lived their usefulness? They don't retire to a nice little villa in the Costa del Sol, most are eliminated and those who can't stand the taste of their own medicine kill themselves." She concluded once she reached the last button. "Now, take off your shirt before you catch something." She ordered. Khoi followed her instructions without question. Jelena took hold of a towel and began to caress his chest softly to dry it, as she added "they all know when their time is up... I guess it's a feeling we are all born with."

"Some go on the run, but what sort of existence is that? Besides you only make the end harder to bear. Some are lucky and have enough goods on their previous client to buy them a few more years... the more info they have, the longer they can keep their fate at bay."

"But what if they were an 'in house' assassin?" She asked as she progressed to dry Khoi's left arm. Khoi, allowed her, as though incapable to prevent her advances while still maintaining eye contact as she continued "They don't have the luxury of fleeing or snitching. As an in house assassin, you'd have to live day by day, wondering when they'd come for you... wondering when you'd be fitted for a coffin." Then she stopped and offered him the towel to complete his own drying process as she underlined "That's what Paul thinks this very moment."

"Why?" Khoi asked. Jelena raised an eyebrow, as though trying to hide her surprise at the stupidity of the question. She folded her arms and explained "The trigger is gone. Once you turn on the tap to the reserve of rage, using a specific channel, you must have a means of turning it off. Now imagine the trigger has been turned on, but the channels and means to shutting it down has disappeared... then you'd be left in limbo with no idea of where they fit in the scheme of things with no possibility of rehabilitation, no one to assure him that he's still wanted, with or without the trigger."

It took Khoi a minute to digest the information. "I understand." He confirmed. "But what can we do? We can't find him..."

"Have you ever thought of looking where he felt safest?" Jelena suggested as she made her way to the door. As she left, she gave a quick summary of the evening. Adding "By the way, the trap worked. Our friend from the bar sent me a text asking for another date. Good night Khoi." She concluded as she left, shutting the door softly.

Khoi sat there and looked at the door in silent contemplation. He knew she was right on all grounds and decided that he was going to change the search area, but before that, he decided to call reception to demand a new room, one with potentially added security.

The town house at Otto-Suhr-Allee was a lonely place to be at 01:23am on a rainy Friday, even the security guards were nowhere to be found. Yet, walking around, there were still the familiar sights of the drunks sleeping on the benches. It was odd to be back there, strolling around the large building till he reached his old spot.

He reached it only to find it occupied by a young looking boy, sleeping in a sleeping bag. He may have been gone for years, but to Paul, it still felt like someone had intruded in his territory.

"What are you doing here?" Paul asked the dirty faced teenager. Upon setting eyes on his face, Paul felt sorry for the boy, still he asked the boy who looked frightened "Do you drink?" The boy shook his head "Do you take drugs?" The boy shook his head again confirming he didn't "Did you run away from home?" The boy cautiously nodded, the fear in his eyes was immense. It touched Paul to the pit of his soul. "They beat you there?" The boy averted his eyes as he nodded again. Paul sighed and reached for his wallet. Upon opening it, Paul found he had €135 in notes.

In a sense of acceptance and trepidation, Paul took out all the money and handed it to the boy. "Here, take this and get out of here… find a hostel or something." The boy seemed to tremble "come on, take it!" Paul ordered. The boy grabbed it quickly "Now, fuck off! I said get the fuck out of here!" Paul ordered.

The boy quickly collected his things and took to his heels running in the rain. Paul watched him vanish amongst the rain drops and fluttering leaves. Now he had the place to himself, the spot on the east side of the building, next to the pillar, sheltered from the rain by the eaves.

Looking at the concrete step where he spent his nights in the past, he considered his blissful happiness before he joined up with the club. At least then he had hopes for the future, now he didn't know if he had one. Paul took his place on the ground and didn't know whether to scream or cry or do both.

Looking at his surroundings, he wondered how the elements could encapsulate his feeling so eloquently. The wind picking up, the rain coming down, the heavy rain, and then lightening followed by thunder. It made him shiver like some sign of impending doom. Affected by the moment, he began to sob. As he sat there, consumed in the emptiness of his thoughts, he could hear the sharp sound of wooden heels striking the pavement. The sound drew closer causing his stomach to churn. Paul was determined not to crumble, and kept his head down till the footsteps stopped. He could feel the person standing over him. Paul could not ignore the looming prospect anymore. He held back his tears and looked up.

Mikel stood there with a sympathetic look on his face. It was clear what had to happen. Paul got up and received an awkward smile from Mikel who placed his hand over his shoulder and led him across the square to the waiting car with tinted windows and the engine running.

Mikel opened the back door and stood aside to allow Paul to enter. Once seated comfortably, he noticed Marcel was in the driver's seat and with the press of the button, the doors were locked. Then Mikel opened the front passenger's side and once seated, the drive began, taking Paul on an unknown journey.

It took nearly forty three minutes to reach their destination, a building site with a near completed looking complex and various half-finished houses all around the field. The car parked and immediately, Marcel turned to point a pistol at Paul. "You know the drill." Marcel said, and Paul certainly did. He was expected not to move and, in his current submissive state, Paul was only too happy to oblige.

With Paul secured, Mikel got out of the car to open the boot and fetch some items they required for the procedure putting them into a back pack. Soon, he too reached for his gun and approached Paul's door. Paul looked at him and their eyes met, and Mikel read what his large blue eyes said "You don't need that" it cried. The gun returned to his coat pocket, before he opened the door and proclaimed "We're here little one."

Paul stepped out of the car and Marcel did likewise, his gun still aimed at Paul till Mikel called out "Put it away man. He's not going to bolt." Marcel slowly put the firearm away and warned "Don't try any tricks."

With his arm over Paul's shoulder, Mikel led Paul towards the building. He could feel the small man shiver as they approached it with Marcel following close behind. At the front of the large unpainted structure of steel, concrete and glass, Mikel unlocked the front door of the building and stood aside. It was time for Paul to go through the door, accepting the lurid, grim, inevitability.

Mikel and Marcel followed Paul inside. Once they were all in the cold unheated building, the door behind them was locked. They carried on their walk to the corner of the building and on to an open door with a flight of steps leading to a dark basement.

A switch was flicked as a light bulb came on, illuminating the steps. Ushered in, Paul walked down to the door of the basement. Another light was turned on and the fluorescent tubes flickered into life. There was an empty space and underneath the light were four stakes driven into the ground with rope inserted in them in preparation for the acts of the evening.

With the ropes before him, there was a table nearby where the items in the bag were laid out and a blow torch was produced, an alluring image that brought a rush of déjà vu, streamed through Paul's core. There were to be no pins, rather two bowie knives were set on the table and a large tub of antibacterial gel followed by several white latex gloves, three large bottles of water and what looked like white cotton sheets.

He had seen enough. Paul chose to focus on the ropes, pondering what delights were to be dished to him for his sins. "Paul?" Mikel called. Paul turned and tried to suppress his anxiety, but the beads of sweat trickling down his brow gave him away. "Don't worry little man. I promise it won't be long unless you choose it to be." Mikel touched Paul's face, it felt cold and his breathing was intermittent.

He knew Paul was afraid, but there was little he could do because despite how sorry he felt for him, Mikel still had his orders. "Take off your jacket, sweater and whatever else you got under there. Let's get things moving." Mikel said with an upbeat tone, a worthless attempt to sooth Paul's climaxing trepidations.

Paul did as he was told, quickly, taking the advice given, he never did enjoy letting others linger, so why try it out? He thought. Now standing bare chested, Marcel paused to remark "Didn't know he was that hairy." Mikel asked Paul to politely "lie down on the floor between the ropes please?"

The similarities to his first day on the job began to grow and as he lay there on the dirt covered floor, uncomfortably, with a pebble jabbing into his upper back, Paul considered, without the pins, what was on offer? Was he to be drawn and quartered? Disemboweled... there were so many things he could devise. Hence, there were many options available to those present as well.

"Stretch out your arms please?" Mikel asked.

Paul stretched out his arms and had a leather wristband placed on either wrist. The bands contained large metal hoops in which the ends of the ropes were inserted before being bound around the wrist band. The ropes were then pulled; stretching him till he felt his arms would be wrenched right out of their sockets. It was the expressions on his face that signalled that they had reached Paul's maximum elasticity.

Now firmly extended between two stakes, they proceeded to do the same to his legs. The agony of the ropes being so taut made it extremely hard to take a full lung of air, but this was just a frisson of what was to come and Paul knew it.

Paul was offered a gag, but politely refused. He wasn't going to face this as a weakling.

Unable to see what they were doing, Paul could hear them mumble amongst themselves as the sounds of coats being shed followed by the snap of latex gloves.

With the light in his eyes, Paul could hardly see till the shadow of

Mikel's body casted over him proclaiming "Alright, let's begin." Paul felt Mikel apply something cold over his right forearm. He wanted to ask what was being done, but yet, thought it was best to linger in ignorance.

It was when Paul felt Mikel's hand press heavily on his wrist that he couldn't turn away any longer. He turned and saw Mikel holding something that reflected the light into his eyes. Paul strained his vision and saw that Mikel held one of the Bowie knives and was slowly bringing it down upon his arm.

Paul began to twitch in fear, trying to muster his strength and see whether or not he could free himself. "Stop moving." Mikel ordered, but Paul wasn't keen on letting his flesh be cut without some resistance, hence he disobeyed the instruction. "Please Paul, stop moving!" Mikel begged, yet Paul was did not yield.

Now frustrated, Mikel called for an intervention "Marcel! Help please?" Marcel arrived, sat on Paul's chest, placed his large right hand over Paul's throat and started to squeeze, slowly depriving Paul of oxygen before landing a hard punch to his face. Paul could taste blood at the back of his throat as he fell into a heavy daze, slipping in and out of consciousness.

Paul, though groggy, soon felt a greater weight bearing down on his arm, rendering the left arm immobile ready to be addressed. The cold of the steel was a feeling that lasted less than a hundredth of a microsecond before the pain came rushing in via the cutting action of the knife as it sliced away the layer of skin which bore the tattoo with the word "Rhino" the size of which was about the length of a five euro note and the width of a standard chocolate bar.

Paul tried his best not to vocalise the agony he felt, but halfway through the process, he could take it no more and began to scream continuously till the procedure was completed.

The epidermis that carried the offending mark was removed in one go. Yes, there were bits of the ink remaining and some bits of flesh along with a tad bit of muscle. They weren't medics after all, but when Mikel stood up to look at the limp skin dangling from the blade, he considered that he had done a good job.

Paul, lay there, sweating profusely, as he moaned intermittently; blood from the opened wound oozing on to the floor. Marcel then left the arm alone.

Paul could hear Marcel ask "What next?" Mikel initially dithered before replying "The salt." Paul could only dread what was to follow. "Hurry up!" Mikel ordered.

Paul wanted to plead and beg them not to do what they had in mind, but it was too late. Mikel served a handful of salt and poured it on the wound rubbing it vigorously into the exposed tissue. Though some mixed with his fluids, the undissolved granules felt like scolding sandpaper causing Paul to yelp and cry out in pain till his voice went hoarse. It was a shame he went hoarse before the area went numb from the rubbing that had persisted for over four minutes. Mikel finished, sighing from all the effort exerted.

Paul began feel rather dizzy from all that had been inflicted on him. He wondered what was to follow as the light began to make his head ache, his thirst for water growing. This was where he was to remain with the whiff of burning tobacco filling his nostrils as Marcel decided to have a quick fag.

For half an hour, Paul remained on the cold concrete floor and throughout that time he remained dazed. He could hear the familiar buzzing sound of the blow torch. All Paul could wonder was what was to follow. "It's nearly done little man. I just need to wash the area." Mikel said returning with two large bottles of water.

The cool feeling of the water falling on the wound was welcomed, but then the rubbing out of the excess salt wasn't. This was repeated again and again till Mikel was satisfied that the opening was clean of ink. By now, Paul was so numb to the pain that he didn't feel Mikel drying the area to try and devoid it of moisture, but he did hear what Marcel was up to. Marcel had kept heating the knife till the blade was white hot.

"Done! Come quickly!" Mikel ordered

Paul could hear Marcel approach with the humming of the blow torch persisting as he drew closer. Paul turned away. He knew what to expect when Marcel arrived. Marcel turned off the blow torch and told Mikel in Dutch "We need keep him very steady"

"No, no… please" Paul begged in a soft voice resulting from his fatigue, his eyes averted.

"Don't worry little man, it'll be over soon." Mikel said, as Marcel knelt down and looked carefully at the area before placing the heated blade on part of the open wound. This sent Paul into a frenzy, screaming, "No…aaarggh!" as the skin sizzled from the heat of blade as any moisture that remained evaporated.

The burning action of the heated knife sealed the exposed vessels and stemmed the bleeding giving off a smell which made Mikel feel nauseous, but yet he stood his ground, begging Paul to remain calm as he tossed his head in pain.

This was repeated 3 times causing the most unpalatable discomfort to Paul, who had effectively began to struggle to stay conscious and had lost the will to resist any further. After the last infliction of the knife, it all grew too much. Paul's screams seemed to sound like a gargle as the blood from his injured nose collected at the back of his throat.

Mikel was quite concerned by the sound from Paul. Paul tossed his head from left to right as the others stood up to look at their handy work. Marcel was wiping his brow as he went to cut the rope that held Paul's left arm.

Paul felt he was shutting down; all he could remember was Mikel standing over him saying "It's finished little man, we're done." His lack of awareness gave them the opportunity to rub some antibiotic ointment on to the wound, followed by applying strips of gauze before a bandage was wrapped around the forearm.

Marcel completed the morbid task of packing the removed skin into a sealed plastic bag whilst Mikel went about cutting the remaining ropes and trying to get Paul to drink some water. It took quite a while to get Paul back into the room and without delay; Mikel forced the bottle containing water into his mouth. "Drink, you need to drink." he said. Paul remained encapsulated in a constant haze as he drank. The water went down too fast and with the blood clogging his airway, Paul nearly choked and coughed out some water tainted with blood before he wilted.

Paul had to be carried to the car where his body was left to lay in the back seat before it was taken Mikel's flat. Khoi arrived minutes later and was told the deed was done. Initially Khoi was offered to be shown the evidence, he declined. He asked them instead to pack it up in an envelope and bring it to him. While Mikel wondered why Khoi had made such a request, Marcel quietly whispered to him "He squirms at the site of ketchup."

Khoi's immediate concern was Paul and his current state. Khoi went to the room where Paul had been placed and found him sleeping. He sat by the bed side, allowing Paul to sleep for a while, before waking him, asking him drink some water and take some strong pain killers.

After taking half a litre of water with his pill, Paul looked and observed his surroundings, with Khoi standing there, gawking at him like a disapproving school teacher.

The light from the window hurt his eyes. The pain on his arm began to radiate. For some reason, he had a memory lapse and wondered why it ached. It was only when he set eyes on the bandage that he began to have flashbacks, but in patches… he couldn't really form a chain of events. "How are you?" Khoi asked, Paul didn't reply as he propped himself up in the bed. His nose was blocked, so Paul forced air out of his nostril, along with mucus that dripped down containing clotted bits of blood. His throat hurt and so did his head and back. "How's your arm feeling?" Khoi asked again. Paul confirmed that it "Hurts like hell" then asked "what happened?" Paul enquired. In response Khoi simply tossed a small brown bubble envelope onto the bed, resting next to Paul's thigh. As Paul picked it up, Khoi added "Rhino is dead." and turned on his heels quickly leaving the room.

Alone, Paul opened the envelope to find the slither of skin that once formed part of his arm in sealed transparent plastic bag. The word he hated was now gone and for some reason he felt concerned at the feelings which he had... he wasn't happy, he was angry, and that alarmed him.

Paul took his time to look at the skin again before realising what had been done to him and the effects began to creep in. He felt lighter, and then a smile grew on his face as he held up the skin for closer inspection. A knock on the door brought the moment to an end. Mikel entered holding clothes in his hands. "Hey little man," called softly "Khoi wants us to take you to the hospital. Says he needs you back at work by the end of next week... you think you can handle that?"

"Yeah... yeah I can." Paul confirmed before requesting a moment to get dressed. Mikel left the room giving Paul the chance to finally do something he had struggled to do in the past month, he began to grieve, he didn't know why, or what for, but it seemed the most appropriate feeling.

Once he had composed himself, Paul was taken to the hospital and given a skin graft which resulted in an overnight stay and additional doses of antibiotics. The only upside was this time the procedure was done using anaesthetics.

Mikel didn't leave his side throughout his stay in hospital and Paul was eventually allowed to go home late Saturday night. Sunday was for soul searching which ended by Monday when Paul reported back for work.

# 8

*11 December 2010*

Uhlandstr subway station was certainly an unusual place to meet anyone for a date. This oddity threw up a lot of questions in Robert's mind. It was well lit but quiet and a lousy place to be robbed if that was the plan. Robert was apprehensive. He had moved his dinner with his mother up to lunch just to accommodate his somewhat out of the ordinary rendezvous. He decided he might as well wait patiently since he was ten minutes early. Still, he hoped he hadn't made a mistake.

As he paced, Robert saw a flower stall across the road that was closing for the day. He rolled his eyes, chiding his inaction for forgetting to get something for the lady he was going to meet, even though he didn't consider her one.

Robert walked to the edge of the side walk and called for the florist's attention, pleading with her to suspend her departure for a few minutes. Crossing the road, he looked around for what to get her. There were slim pickings at the stall and it seemed that it was a choice between roses and chrysanthemums, and then he spotted something unusual, dark violet, near black tulips. He was informed that they were called "Queen of the night."

Roses were cliché, chrysanthemums were too big, but his mother liked tulips and what could be better than something out of the ordinary, particularly since the person shared his mother's name. Accepting that it was rather silly to deduce that every lady called Ulrika like tulips, Robert nevertheless took the risk and purchased a bunch for €16.50.

Robert crossed the road back to the station. As he placed the receipt into his pocket, Jelena walked up behind him unnoticed and said in his ear "Last minute purchase?" Robert was startled and nearly jumped as he turned to find her there, her dark brown fur hat matching her mink fur coat, standing still with a smile on her face as Robert revealed "Jesus, you startled me." Jelena said nothing, looking unimpressed. "You look good." He remarked only to get in return "thanks." She didn't even bother to acknowledge the effort he had made.

Robert felt aggrieved, he had spent an hour grooming and priming himself, only to be ignored. This never happened before. His sense of style was always his most effective weapon.

Ulrika wore a familiar scent, Robert couldn't recollect where he perceived it in the past, but it seemed to subdue his growing feeling of outrage towards her behaviour and how she made him feel.

Why was this woman making him nervous? Robert wondered. His

hands became clammy and he handed the flowers to her "For you." Jelena finally smiled and declared "Tulips, my favourite. Sadly, I don't think I can take it where we're going." Jelena then walked to the nearest bin and put the flowers away there.

That was it, that was why he anxious around her. She was the first lady he had ever met that didn't swoon or fall at his feet, for the first time he wasn't in control. Robert strained to keep the smile on his face and his hurt feelings hidden as Jelena walked up and kissed him on the cheek as she said, "It was still ever so thoughtful of you. Shall we go?"

"Sure… where are we going?" He asked

"The zoo." Jelena revealed.

This was something new indeed. Robert had never considered going to the zoo at night or, for that matter, in winter. He wondered if it was even open and it was the last place he expected to go on a date.

The zoo wasn't far, just a 10 minute walk. It gave Robert enough time to make small talk. Robert was keen to find out who this anomaly in feminine form was. By the time they reached the gates of the animal prison, all Robert could uncover was that Ulrika was a real estate agent in Slovenia. She was in Berlin to look at properties for her rich clients back home and to see where they could open an office. It was just a two week fact finding mission which she had extended to encompass a holiday which had started yesterday evening. "That's why you needed the company… I'm just a holiday fling." Robert concluded. He was unable to contain his horror at her impudence.

Jelena simply winced as she handed over the tickets to the man at the gates, brushing him off with the words "Don't be so surprised, we all do it. Now, let's go in there and have some fun."

With a nod from the guard validating their entry, Jelena led the way. Robert hesitated, hating the fact that he had been reduced to doormat status, yet, with the impulse of an intellectual heroin addict, he wanted to be with her, even though he knew it could lead to him being treated like dirt. Robert smiled accepting that he was infatuated.

Robert followed quickly after her, down the path leading towards the animal enclosure. Robert didn't know what to expect. Jelena decided to throw him a bone. Jelena gently locked arms with him as they approached the wood forest section. He turned to find her smiling at him and said "You look very good. I hope your clothes won't be too restrictive." "Restrictive clothing", the last time Robert heard such words being said he was in a back seat of a parked car struggling to unbuckle a bra. Robert felt his spirit lift at the prospect of a potential sexual encounter. "There was still hope for this evening" Robert said to himself.

As they walked past the stalls that featured hare and other forest animals, Robert casually spoke about his career as a model until he caught site of the ferrets. Robert wondered aloud why they were considered wild animals "My brother and I had a pair and the female was a nymphomaniac." He said laughing out loud at his own words. Again, it failed to hit the proposed mark. Jelena didn't even fake a smile this time. "What you may call nymphomania she calls a necessity. Female ferrets have to be stimulated every time they come into season or they start having skin and other related hormonal problems. So they basically have to have sex."

Unfortunately, Jelena could not keep a straight face and simultaneously they both burst out laughing as they walked further down to the reptile enclosure. This lifted the mood and allowed Robert to appreciate her gentle laugh.

The reptile enclosure was quite warm in some sections, an effort made by the zoo to emulate the animal's tropical environment. Jelena could feel a slight shudder from Robert. Passing by poof adder, he shuddered again. Concerned, Jelena asked if all was well with Robert. Robert divulged his general phobia for snakes and when asked why he replied "They are legless, make a horrid sound and most are poisonous."

"I think you are wrong there." Jelena rebuffed again. "Only two snakes are known to be poisonous."

This Robert refused to believe this fact and challenged Jelena on the point. "You have got to be kidding. Who told you that? Over half of them are poisonous."

"Let's make this interesting. You have access to the internet right? Why not check and if I am right we go on another date and I pick the place." She proposed

"And if you are wrong?" Robert asked.

Fluttering her eyelids flirtatiously, Jelena said "You pick the place and what we do after."

With his mind filled with all the potential fun he could have with her, Robert reached for his phone and typed in "List of poisonous snakes."

The slow reception meant they had to wait for a minute for information to upload, and once it did, Robert cried out "Aha! I told you, see?" He turned the face of the phone to Jelena with smug satisfaction as a list of legless reptiles was shown. Jelena raised her finger to halt his progress of pride and observed "The list says venomous, not poisonous."

"So? Same thing, right?" shrugging off her attempt to wiggle out of her deal.

"No, it is not the same thing." She corrected. "Venom is injected, so when a venomous snake bites you, it injects its venom into your body and there are hundreds of those. Poison, on the other hand, is ingested. Meaning, you have to consume it for it causes you any harm.

I could take you to a Chinese restaurant nearby where cobra is served under the table and I can tell you, you will leave there with a doggy bag. But if you ate a particular sea snake, I forget the name and the Japanese grass snake, you will be poisoned." Jelena snatched the phone from his grip, punched in some words of her own handing it back to him saying, "Clear your diary for Monday night. Wear something casual." And she walked ahead slowly.

It pained Robert to read it. She was correct. He decided to say nothing in his defeat as he followed her to the end of the enclosure, leading to the open area, set in a dip on the ground, where there was a marquee planted in the centre. Whilst on the far right was a frozen lake that had been converted into an ice ring.

Robert's thoughts turned to his skating skills which weren't so good. He had fallen one too many times, still he had a date and it could bring them closer to the possibility of bodily contact. He took some steps in the direction of the frozen body of water only to find he was going alone. Jelena was walking straight towards the marque.

Embarrassed, he ran after her. "So where are we going?" Robert asked. Jelena pointed to the large tent with multi-coloured light appearing on the white canvas, yet it was silent. "What is it? Some kind of light show?" Jelena chuckled, slapped his gut with the back of her hand and ordered, "Come on." as she jogged down the slope.

Robert was getting tired of the catching up, but yet there was some thrill to the chase. He caught up with her. Another ticket was handed over and the tent's entrance was opened, revealing a mass of people dancing almost in silence. There was no music on, all the people had were big headphones placed over their ears and a small device attached to their belt.

It seemed airily spooky, something Robert had never witnessed before. "What the fuck is this?" He asked. Jelena revealed he had been brought to a silent disco. The zoo wanted to organise something for the public at night without disturbing the animals and this was it, each individual listening to music with their headset on, changing tunes when they wanted whilst still being able to dance. The only thing available to drink was anything that didn't have alcohol.

Jelena then took off her heavy fur coat. It revealed a dress that was clung close to her bosom yet was free from the waist showing a loose knee length hemline enabling flexibility in movement. She was certainly prepared for dancing, hence the question about his attire. He was in a suit and looked out of place.

It was time for a radical transformation. With Jelena putting away her coat and hat, he took his outer coat off followed by his blazer then his tie, untucked his shirt and ran her hand through his slick hair to disturb it before proclaiming "Right, let's dance." Jelena smiled at him as though admiring his intent of making the best of an alien situation.

Jelena and Robert walked, doe eyed, to the desk where a bald young man with several metal studs nestling in his face. They were handed their headsets and large badges with a number written on them as he asked "Have you been here before?" They confessed they hadn't. The usher proceeded to instruct them on the principles of the evening. The head set plays music from various genres. All they needed to do was to select a channel using their digital remote, and press "0" if they needed help. Information would be channelled into their headsets. In particular, information relating to the forth coming competition and notifications of the closing time which was set for 9pm "even the animals need their sleep." he concluded as wishing them a pleasant evening.

As they turned to join the silent groovers, Robert pointed at the notice overhead which listed the 8 genres available. They were tempted to pick the 90's, they realised that there was a possibility they didn't live in the same world at that time as Jelena admitted that it was almost likely that what was set to be played as 90's music would probably be modern music. Yet they decided to take the plunge and filled their ears with "hammer time".

Having found their own private corner of the space to practice their moves, they initially took on the task of dancing in jest. However, soon they started swaying to Rhythm and Blues music. Within an hour, they had grown tired of practising, amongst other things, their "running man" dance step.

Following a quick drink of non-alcoholic red wine, Jelena proposed they try channel 3, the Latin music channel. Jelena quickly saw the fright in his eyes and she was right, Robert was afraid. He wasn't so light on his feet especially when it came to salsa or cha-cha. Jelena wasn't going to force him into moving, rather he needed a motivation.

She held his hand and looked into his beautiful baby blue eyes that almost made her lose her train of thought. Once back on track, she said calmly, "You don't have to do much, just look into my eyes and follow my lead and if you feel uncomfortable, we can change to another tune. Okay?"

Robert announced his perception, "You sure like making deals don't you?"

She giggled, led Robert by the hand and placed her hand on his shoulder and the other on his hip. His nerves returned and she could tell. To pacify this torrent of doubt, she simply said "trust me. Now look into my eyes and left forward, right forward, right to the side, left to the side and now me..."

Slowly, and without any music to follow, Jelena managed to instil a level of confidence into Robert that allowed them to put on their headphones and give the steps a try. Robert kept his gaze fixed to her eyes. Slowly they danced, bar the few trampled toes, things ran smoothly for most of the dance and they even tried a few spins. It was during a trial of a triple spin that Jelena tripped, falling to the floor landing on her backside.

Robert was near panic as he cried out to her "Oh my goodness are you alright?" Jelena laughed, pulled off her headphones and offered Robert her hand which he used to raise her from the floor. She kept laughing and remarkably enough; she held Robert's face and gave him a gentle kiss on the lips. "Let's try again." She proposed.

This time, Robert didn't slip up. The feeling of her body rubbing his caused chaos to ensue within him. He began to long for her, so he tried his luck. Robert's right hand crept slowly down to her rump. Jelena's instant reaction could not be read, Robert could not tell if she approved or disapproved of his advances. The dance stopped, she held his face and kissed him deeply with the music ringing in their ears.

This was it, this was what he wanted, perhaps he had tamed the shrew, sadly the blissful moment was interrupted quite cruelly by the announcement over the headsets which said "Ladies and Gentlemen, its 8:55pm, time to close." Unable to contain his frustrations, Robert found himself crying out "NO!"

The MC replied to Robert's cry with "Yes lover boy, carry on your duties in your bedroom and do it like they do it on the discovery channel!" This caused all those who had seen Jelena and Robert locking lips to laugh; point or applaud. Robert began to blush and Jelena said to him "I guess it's time to go."

They retrieved their belongings and left the tent. Robert proposed taking a taxi, only to receive in response "What's wrong with the metro?" that blew his plans for a quick snog in the back of a taxi.

Still Robert didn't regret the loss of physical contact, taking the subway turned out to be a good idea after all. Jelena and Robert had bumped into a few other people who had joined them at the silent disco. They chatted and laughed about how bizarre yet fun the event was till they got to Robert's stop. "This is where I get off." he said "Is this where I say goodnight to you?" Robert cautiously enquired.

She didn't reply, rather Jelena got up offering Robert her hand again and having said goodbye to their fellow travellers, together they walked out of the train, not letting go of each other as they strolled the seven minutes to Robert's building without a word exchanged between them. Each for their own reasons, feeling it would spoil the moment.

They reached the front of his building. Robert wondered how effective his charm was as he looked at her, she was smiling. Robert couldn't understand why he felt so nervous. As they stood there, the seconds ticking by, Robert was perplexed. He was an expert in these things, so why did he hands feel clammy? "Em… this is where I live." He announced. Jelena looked up at the building and replied "Nice place."

Robert took his chances and asked "Care to come in?" Again, she smiled and stood there, her teeth discoloured a slight hint of blue from all the "alcohol free red wine" they had tasted.

Robert was eventually caught by surprise when Jelena grabbed him by the lapels, drew him close and kissed him on the lips.

It was tender and quite a nice feeling, yet ,before he could inject some depth and passion into it by wrapping his arms around her and holding her close, she withdrew and took a fool step back as she replied "Maybe another time. See you on Monday." She called as she walked away. She didn't turn back; she knew Robert was there, marvelling at her, as the distance between them grew till she turned a corner.

He was hooked and she knew it, so she chose to enhance the magic by making the man who only needed to click his fingers to get what he wanted, wait. It was working, Robert kicked the air. His appetite had been wetted and yet he was in a desert.

She paced as quickly as she could till she reached the meeting point by the children's nursery, sending a text requesting her collection. Mikel was six minutes late and now she was cold and actually began to wonder why she had to be so frugal with sex, after all, she was like him, she got whom so ever she wanted but now she had been given a verbal chastity belt that prevented her from enjoying herself.

As Jelena lamented over her carnal deprivation, a black BMW parked a few feet in front of her. She noticed it but chose to ignore it, but the occupant found her difficult to avoid. The window of the driver's side and a chubby looking red faced man, curly black hair with bad teeth and scent of filth was about him and his intentions. "Hey, baby!" the man called out. Jelena looked at him for a split second then turned away with her hands behind her back "Hey. You are new to this corner."

'Corner', the word got Jelena's back up. Surely there was no suggestion that she was a lady of the night? And for his sake, she hoped he didn't. Then the man asked "Where are you from?" Jelena did not answer. The man remained persistent "So, how much would an hour be?"

Jelena's ears perked up, she was totally insulted. With her hands still behind her she back away from cruising fatty's view, Jelena reached for the flick knife she had hidden in the hem of her coat sleeve, pushing out the blade by pressing the button. "So you're looking for a good time?"

"For the right price, come closer and let me see what you got." He instructed.

Jelena walked forward slowly, trying to identify the best point of entry for the steel she held.

With just a step away, Jelena was given a shove by Mikel. Who said "Sorry for being late" as he grabbed her by the arm and said, as he moved her along.

"What are you doing?" Jelena asked as they walked. The man started to shout out loudly, complaining that Mikel had gazumped him. "I'm stopping you from making a mistake" Mikel replied as he and Jelena continued down the street, leaving the disgruntled man behind them.

"But the guy is a pig; the man thought I was a prostitute." She protested.

"Yes, he may be pig, but it doesn't mean he has to die."

Arriving at the car, which had been parked at the end of the road, Mikel ordered "Come on, let's go." Jelena stood, motionless with a stern look on her face. Mikel knew he had slipped "Please?"

With the magic words issued, she opened the passenger door and entered the vehicle.

They had arrived at Khoi's hotel. She knew why she was there, it was to be debriefed. Mikel didn't go in with her as he had some other business to attend to. Jelena walked into the hotel alone. She didn't have to walk far, Khoi was in the lobby.

Khoi looked crossed, yet she smiled and turned on the charm. "Hello my dear." She said, but Khoi did not respond in kind. Rather, he walked before her, leading the way to the dining area where a table at the back of the room awaited them. He was about to pull a chair out for her, when her patience ran out. "Look, I am not in the mood for cold conversations in a dull environment with even duller, gloomy clientele. I could easily write down for you what I found out on a napkin. If this is how the evening is going to be, allow me to leave and I shall return to my hotel and enjoy my own company."

Her brut candour cured Khoi of his foul mood which originated from his obsessive paranoia. He was consumed by shame as he pushed the chair back into place. "Let's not talk shop today. I promised to tell you more about myself, didn't I? Are you hungry?"

"Yes. Quite." She replied.

"Good. Get ready to get stuffed." Khoi proclaimed.

Khoi had a taxi ordered and informed the driver of their destination, as he and Jelena entered. Again, it was a quiet journey with Khoi looking out of the window. Jelena began to resent this stillness. She wanted to find out more about him, but could not bring herself to dig despite the volume of questions filling her mind.

It was a relief that it only took ten minutes to arrive. They had reached what seemed to be a residential district of old flats. The car had parked across the road from a busy brasserie. Khoi did the gentlemanly thing and opened her door for her and paid for the taxi. He stated "You wanted to know about me... we can start here."

Having waved the driver off, they crossed the road to the establishment. Again, Khoi opened the door for Jelena. They had barely taken a step inside before they were confronted by an exasperated waiter who turned to tell them "Sorry, we are fully booked."

"Is Clara here?" Khoi enquired "Clara is always here." The waiter replied, as he went to the reception desk and began typing on a computer before taking a payment portal in hand. "Well tell Clara Khoi is here please."

The waiter left hurriedly and initially stopped at a table to collect payment from a diner. As they stood, waiting patiently and in silence, Jelena and Khoi watched as the waiter went deeper into the restaurant.

After another minute, a woman came cutting through the crowd towards Khoi, clapping her hands in excitement .She almost leapt into his arms when they finally reached each other. "My boy! How lovely to see you!" Jelena could not help but be touched by such a warm and heartfelt welcome between Khoi and the lady whom she assumed was Clara. Then the small woman with a perm and an apron seemed to pause as she turned her attention to Jelena "Oh, you brought a friend."

"Hello, I am Jelena…" Jelena tried to shake her hand but was promptly embraced by a very enthusiastic lady who excitedly replied "So nice to meet you."

Once released, she turned to Khoi and said "Where did you get this one? She's stunning. Turn around." Jelena obliged. "My, you are such a lucky boy." Then she held them both by the hand and said "Come, I have a table for you. Oh I am so happy to see my little Khoi!"

Her enthusiasm was infectious, even Jelena was anticipating a pleasant surprise as they were led through the crowd of customers. Some were clearly regulars as they called Clara by name to get her attention. She would graciously ignore them or promise to return shortly.

When they finally reached the back there was a thick black curtain just next to the grand piano. The woman pushed them aside to reveal a small table. "For you." She said. Khoi went and took his seat only to hear Clara gasp "Where are your manners? I am shocked." Khoi jumped out of his chair like a child and raced to pull Jelena's chair out for her and gave a grovelling apology. "That's better. Wait here, I am going to make you full to bursting tonight." Clara promised, before she disappeared again.

Jelena picked up the menu from the table and she heard Khoi giggle. "I don't think you will need that." Taking his word for it, she placed the leather bound list on the table and made her observations. "It looks very nice. You come here often? And who is that remarkable woman?"

"I did come here regularly." Khoi replied "And you're right, she is remarkable. She's like a mother to me."

Then Clara's voice was overheard in the distance. Jelena turned to find

Clara greeting another guest, laughing with them and giving one a kiss on the cheek, it seemed she could be everyone's mother.

Then her attention was brought back to the table, as the waiter brought two drinks in a cocktail glass. The waiter informed them it was from Clara. A taste revealed that they had been served Melon Martinis and the flavour was wonderful.

This was followed by appetisers of asparagus and liver, as well as rabbit sausage with some dipping sauce. The spice used on the liver made it delectable and the sausage was so mild and mellow it made Jelena pine that she would much rather have this for dinner and she would have believed that when the main course arrived.

They could smell it before it even before it left the kitchen and the people applauded as Clara carefully carried it over. Jelena joined in the clapping wondering whom it was for. She didn't notice Khoi, who was just laughing as Clara approached. The waiters brought some flat bread, tomato and chilli sauces and carried away their cutlery leaving them only a knife and a pile of napkins.

Jelena soon stopped clapping when it dawned on her that the food being ferried by Clara was heading for their table. It was a tray carrying a shiny, well done whole suckling pig with the works, apple in mouth included. It was to be eaten by hand with the aid of a steak knife and some condiments.

Clara set it before Jelena and declared "Eat my dear and leave nothing behind, you are home." Jelena was not one to get frightened of anything, but this was enough to put her in shock. Yet she grinned and thanked Clara for her generosity. Intent on seeing her sample the meal, Clara cut a piece and divided it into two, fed a bit to Jelena and ate the other before remarking "Uhm, delicious. Khoi you are going to make me happy tonight. OK? Eat, eat!"

Clara was right, it was yummy and after two hours, Jelena found she had eaten most of the animal till nothing remained, the bone had been picked clean and she was full to bursting as more drinks arrived.

As the plates were cleared away, Jelena soon realised that with the certain oncoming indigestion, she still had not had the opportunity to speak to Khoi and she felt it was time to rectify that. Sadly, her attempts were put on hold when the background music stopped and Clara was helped up onto a chair by a waiter. She called for everyone's attention. "Everybody, I have to tell you, my favourite pianist is here tonight. My son is home. Khoi, come over here and play for your supper."

Jelena turned to Khoi and watched him turn red. It didn't take much coaxing to get Khoi to rise and walk past three tables to the piano while the customers applauded. Khoi sat at the piano, looked up at Clara and said "If I play, will you come down before you hurt yourself?" She laughed along with everyone else as she dismounted.

Khoi looked at the keys, thought for a moment before he wiggled his fingers and began to play. He drifted away as he played Chopin piano concertos one after the other, hypnotising everyone who could hear. Even the waiters stopped to listen. Clara wasn't so captivated; she had tasks to carry out. She quietly slipped into Khoi's chair. Upon noticing her Jelena smiled. "He's great isn't he?" Jelena nodded. "He wasn't lucky, with his mother dying when he was a kid, if it weren't for his brother God knows what would have happened.

"His brother used to work here whilst he studied; he had to be the mother and father figure. He sacrificed everything for him, and that's why I knew he was going to be fine. You know he always been talented... he's so gifted. God knows why he never followed the music to the end?" Clara's rhetorical question coupled by Khoi's flawless display got Jelena thinking the same thing. "I hope you will make him happy and bring him the peace he seeks... he hasn't had that for years and you seem a genuinely good person and he really likes you." Jelena asked for the source of this assumption to which Clara replied "I saw it in his eyes. Every time he looks at you... the way he struggles to speak when he sat with you, I can tell, and so can you." Jelena's heart melted. She reached out with her palms opened, Clara placed her hand in Jelena's and they held each other till Khoi finished playing.

The crowd rose to their feet and cheered, patting Khoi on the back as he returned to his seat. Clara got up and gave him a kiss on the cheek before directing his attention to Jelena "Look what you did. You made her cry." Jelena was busy clearing the tears from the side of her eyes. "Take care of her you hear?" Clara instructed, as she returned to work.

Khoi sat back down silently almost as though he had done nothing of significance. Jelena could not contain her admiration "That was beautiful" prompting a snide response from Khoi "The black widow has a heart after all." She threw the napkin she held at him as she laughed.

Khoi looked around and could sense the possibility that dessert could soon follow. He leaned forward and asked Jelena "Want to leave?" Jelena's mind wondered of the possibilities and agreed to the proposal.

They walked to the cashier and asked for the bill and were handed a small booklet. He didn't look at it, he took out his wallet and took out some money and turned to Jelena "Want to leave something?" She eagerly opened her purse and took out two €100 notes to add to the three Khoi had placed in the booklet. It covered the bill and left a €407 tip. Khoi left specific instructions that it be handed to Clara directly. As they waited for their coats, Clara accosted them. "You are leaving?"

"Yeah, we have work tomorrow." Khoi replied

"I hope you didn't pay. You never pay for mother's food." Clara warned. Khoi lied and said he hadn't.

Jelena had been touched by Clara's warmth and generosity which was further instilled when Clara instructed Khoi "You bring her back here." Jelena and Clara hugged one another tightly and soon they were out of the restaurant door and instantaneously Khoi ordered Jelena to "run" as he took to his heels forcing Jelena to follow suit as they laughed. It was then the door of the restaurant door opened and Clara burst out shouting at them as they fled "You are so stupid you know that? I told you not to pay you silly boy!"

Khoi was ahead of her, and took a quick turn hiding in the shadows as Jelena ran past him. She stopped for a moment and looked around for him. "Khoi?" she called out. He soon emerged from the shadow of the doorway and stood before her.

Their eyes meeting, Jelena yearned for him and this brought her thoughts into conflict, she wasn't meant to sleep with her employers, but she wanted him and she knew the feeling was mutual. Khoi walked up to her still refusing to speak as he held her hand and they walked together to Khoi's hotel.

In his room, with the seconds ticking by, dragging them towards the midnight hour, they stood like birds on opposite banks of the stream wondering who would move first. Khoi took on the challenge and kissed her deeply, placing his hand on her waist, moving and creeping ever closer to her breast when his progress was stopped, as Jelena held his hand, pushed it off her body and took a large step back.

"Sorry Khoi" she began as she collected her things and made her way to the door with the last words, "If I am not allowed to sleep with Robert, then I won't do so with you… not till the job is done. Good night Khoi." She blew him a kiss and left him alone knowing she had tantalised him to the point of frustration. Once on the other side, she waited by the door for a moment, knowing what to expect.

Khoi gritted his teeth wondering why he had been overwhelmed by this person whom he saw as a witch. He prided himself on his level headedness, but now he was suffering from raptures of the mind, this was not a reality he was not use to living in, he roared and shouted "What the fuck is wrong with me?" On hear his frustration, Jelena smiled, her plan worked.

# 9

*13 December 2010*

It was Tuesday, a rather dull day. Though the hand cream swap was a success, there was scepticism as to whether or not it was the way to go by Mikel, Marcel and Daniel.

Joel had to manage and control their bellyaching as they waited for Khoi and Jelena's arrival. They were late and with subversion bobbing up in the horizon, Joel hoped Khoi would arrive soon before it turned to a full revolt, goodness knows what his father would do to him then.

Joel fiddled with his phone. Paul was busy drawing a sketch on his pad whilst Mikel peeped over his shoulder to review the progress. "Hand Cream... we used hand cream." Mikel lamented just as Khoi and Jelena entered.

Khoi was carrying a suitcase. "Sorry we're late." Khoi began as he and Jelena took empty seats next to one another. "Jelena and I were delayed by the record's office." He placed his items on the table and began "we will have to move quickly today. Jelena has an appointment and I have some tasks which will need particular attention."

"Sure boss." Joel mumbled. That stray comment was unheard by Khoi but Joel had unwittingly begun to smash the established order.

Opening the folder he held Khoi proclaimed "Let's begin. I would like to congratulate you on the Nivea operation. It's been a great success and a week down the line, I can confirm that the tube has been exhausted."

"So when are we going to see the results?" demanded Daniel. Khoi raised his eyebrow and others had similar surprised expressions at such insolence, the group then turned to Khoi to see how he would handle it. "I applaud your enthusiasm, but I assure you your patience will be rewarded in the next couple of weeks." Khoi with one sentence had reasserted his authority as Daniel sat back in his chair and tapped the table with his fingers just before receiving a text on his mobile. It was from Joel who wrote "Don't ever do that again."

Deep inside, Khoi was relieved that others didn't take up Daniel's mantra and quickly proceeded turning to Ralph to ask, "So how is Max?"

"He's good... didn't know how white albino's could be, almost translucent." Ralph observed. It prompted the others to laugh except for Khoi who just remarked

"Good. Makes sure he's kept sweet. By the way, did you all see the news?" Khoi asked.

"You mean yesterday's drug bust? Yeah, absolutely fucking amazing. I didn't know that much stuff could be brought in on boats." Remarked Daniel.

"Not sure why you are surprised, they have been doing it for years." Paul droned as he carried on doodling.

There was an uncomfortable pause resulting from Paul's remarks. Khoi persisted, saying "Yes, now that the bust has happened, it's time to step up with the rest of the plan. It's only a matter of time before they find out the source of the anonymous tip and trace it back to us. It is time to act." Khoi declared. "We need to organise abduction." Khoi included as he took out the photo of "Mr F" from his folder and moved it to the middle of the table. He added "Mr F, real name Siegfried Weidman, will be going to Thailand for Christmas on Thursday the 15th. It is a night flight leaving at 21:40 to Bangkok. He must not be on that flight." He turned to Joel and asked "is there something you could organise to snap him up?"

"Sure." Joel confirmed with a sinister sneer.

This prompted Khoi to clarify "When I said snap him up, He must not have a mark on him and it should be that way till we are ready to dispose of him. Do not rough him up." Khoi asserted. "Once you have him let me know."

"Marcel, Mikel, can you handle this? We will discuss how we go about this later." Joel delegated. Mikel affirmed his interest, whilst Marcel kept his feelings hid.

With that concluded, Khoi proclaimed "Good. The next item on the agenda is to capitalise on the cocaine shortage and take out Mr C."

"Our red headed party animal." Joked Joel "What would you like us to do Boss?"

This time Khoi did hear what Joel's remark, but thought, perhaps, it was a slip of the tongue and carried on "From the information we have, he's got tickets to see Jompa at "Whyte" for Friday night."

"He got tickets? Ah man, I have been trying to get my hands on them. Jompa is so cool, lucky bastard" Mikel sulked.

"Joel?" Khoi called for his attention and at once suggested "For our next meeting, shall we establish an agenda?"

Getting the hint, Joel said to everyone "Shut up guys!" Like trained dogs, they all obeyed with the exception of Paul who made noise as he added shade to his drawing. That was a noise Khoi could tolerate.

As he restarted "I never heard of this DJ before, but from your excitement and that of the target, he must be good. Mr C is so excited, that he's been calling around for some cocaine since last week and with the scarcity, he's having a tough time finding some."

Khoi noticed Ralph raising his hand as he said "I have a question. If District 3 supplies the strong stuff, why does he have to ring around for it?" Everyone thought it was a good question except for Khoi, Jelena and Paul who, still not looking at anyone or showing any interest in the meeting at all, answered "He doesn't want to break the fundamental rule of the dealer. Never use your own stash."

"Correct Paul" Khoi acknowledged "and since he is not an avid user... the last time he did use it was..." Jelena came to the rescue, reaching into her bag for her tablet and after a few touches of the screen confirmed "August, and before that June."

"Thanks for that. So you see, he's not an avid user, therefore, he can afford to purchase it from the outside from time to time. But back to the plan"

Khoi was keen to keep to the allotted time as he had much more to say. "I organised the purchase of all the available cocaine yesterday and I was surprised how little was left. It seems as though many were really depending on the shipment. On this basis, we are the sole supplier of cocaine to the inner city at least for the week and we have a huge demand out there. We recently got word from one of our minions that Mr C is looking down there. It is time to use our network to fulfil the demand so we will sort out the distribution tomorrow. In regards to Mr C, he'll get his delivery on Friday." Like a child in class, Daniel raised his hand. Khoi nodded hi approval allowing Daniel to ask "Which one of us will organise the delivery?"

"I know what you are thinking. You think I will ask one of you to go out there and when making the delivery, take him down?" Khoi deduced "Nah, the bullet is not for him. And No, none of you will be making the delivery. I'll organise it. And if I have any piece of advice for you who may be a secret nose duster, try and go cold turkey for the next couple of weeks and I mean it." A disappointed look came on Daniel's face. Khoi decided to throw him a bone "But you could help me by finding me a very good looking pickpocket for hire. He must be German and tall."

Daniel perked up, happy that he had been delegated a task "Any other specifications?"

"No, get me a couple to choose from by tomorrow, Joel and I will make a choice then." Khoi concluded.

"Yes Boss." Daniel replied, surprising Khoi whilst Joel giggled.

Khoi choose to let it slide again. "Moving on to Mr D, please congratulate Jelena on her amazing recognizance exercise. We have managed to get the necessary information to execute another plan I have. To enable it, I will need Paul, Marcel and Mikel to wait behind if that's ok? The rest of you can enjoy the rest of the day."

Everyone not required left the room but Joel who remained seated next to Khoi and asked "So what's next?"

"Nothing for you. You have to take care of Mr F." Khoi stated.

It appeared not to be clear to Joel, "So why do you need them to stay behind?" he said, referring to the other three.

"I need their skills, as much as I need your in distributing the drugs on Friday." Khoi replied.

Joel was getting suspicious and started to speak in Jekorian. What the others considered gibberish; Khoi understood perfectly as Joel asked him "Are you keeping me out of the loop?"

Fearful of how things were going, Khoi leaned over and whispered in his ear using the same alien tongue "No. I need your help in getting the drugs out there, who else is best placed for such a thing other than you and Daniel?" Joel seemed unconvinced however forcing Khoi to pull rank. "You told me to take charge of the situation and ensure we manage to achieve all we can by the end of the year, I think you best leave me to it, ok?"

Joel managed to keep his shock in check; rather, he gave a grin. He still couldn't hide his thoughts from the others who saw that there was a stand-off unfolding as Khoi and Joel eyeballed each other. Joel blinked first however and replied in German "whatever you say Boss," slowly getting up and exiting the room.

Once he shut the door of the meeting room, he walked out to the back door of the building into the mild winter's day. His blood was boiling, unable to comprehend what had just happened. He was surprised at how callously he was pushed out. This was incendiary material in the hands of the innocent observer. His once assumed "God given authority" was being eroded by someone, regardless of how close they were, he considered a usurper. He was clearly losing his reason, Joel concluded. Khoi wasn't that sort of fellow. Joel decided to take Ralph and Daniel out for a few drinks.

With Joel out of the room, the others were a bit shaken by the potential schism. Khoi though, seemed oblivious, but cautious. Khoi waited for a moment before asking Paul to check if Joel and his team were actually gone. Once confirmed, Khoi began. "I asked you guys to stay behind because you have some intelligence and think outside the box, not so quick to use your fist like some others and because I feel I can trust you. But before I continue, I want you to all swear that anything we discuss today and all our actions resulting afterwards will be kept secret till I say so. That includes keeping it from the rest of the team. Any of you who feel uncomfortable about this can leave."

None of them got up choosing to stay for various reasons.

Each person took Khoi's statement differently. Mikel remained thankful for the flattery of being called intelligent and Marcel because he got a thrill from covert behaviour. Paul stayed out of curiosity.

Satisfied that he had them on side, Khoi announced "Jelena has been kind enough to put out a tender for us. As we were allowed one bullet, it makes sense that it shouldn't originate from our gun. Hence we are in the market for a sharp shooter. Once we find one, I will need you guys to take care of him till his services are required."

Marcel asked, "A sharp shooter, who is it for?" Khoi chose not to answer and changed the topic. "In the next few days, I may need your assistance in organising something." Khoi announced "Once I have it all worked out, I will let you know. Again, this is private and we need to keep it that way." Once again, they agreed with Mikel adding "If it relates to getting those bastards, you have my word."

"Good. Jelena, you have your work cut out for tomorrow." Khoi then rose and concluded the meeting "Well, good luck and keep me posted." And without as much as a goodbye, he left the room.

Jelena was puzzled as the others got up as well. "Is he always this rude?" She asked Paul.

"Only when he's got something heavy on his mind." He continued, "Would you like a lift anywhere?"

Upon departure, Khoi went to his hotel room and waited. Julien promised to call that evening. He sat, watching the television. As midnight approached, he soon realised the call wasn't going to happen. Not willing to be miserable, he turned on his computer, put on some porn and pleasured himself till he fell asleep.

*15 December 2010*

Sun! That's all Siegfried could think of, sun, sun, sun. It didn't matter that winter was initially mild. If the weather outside today was anything to go by, this was bound to change, but he couldn't care less, Siegfried was off to Thailand.

He had everything laid out on the bed. He ticked off the list to ensure he had all the items he needed. Once he was certain he had it all, Siegfried went to his drawer to collect the gift he had bought for his father's best friend.

The man had lived in Phuket for over thirty years and his father had pleaded with Siegfried to go and meet him. A quick call to the man proved he was friendly enough; however he made a request for an item that Siegfried considered a disgusting reminder of the past and which everyone he knew thought would be best left in the past.

Siegfried told his father of the man's request for a Nazi flag, his father reacted with shock initially only for him to renege, go out and purchase the item himself. "He's an old friend." That was all his father could say to keep his conscience clear.

It was an uneasy compromise, but one which Siegfried was comfortable with. Provided he was just the courier, he could live with it.

As he figured he was ready, he checked again for his most important possessions including his cell phone, his travel toothbrush, and his earphones and of course his passport. Siegfried had one more look around the room, making sure everything looked ok and no electrical appliances were left on. "Nice and tidy" he said to himself before deciding to draw the curtains shut and head out the door.

Siegfried was walking leisurely down the street, and was about to call out for a passing taxi when his phone rang. "Hey man, heard you were going for a trip?" He recognized Mikel's voice after a second and answered a bit baffled "Hi Mikel, no, I mean yeah, why?"

Although Siegfried knew Mikel through his own long-time friendship with Marcel whom he grew up with, they rarely ever spoke. Then he heard Mikel add "Yeah, I was just asking Marcel to come have a drink with me and on our way to the bar we spoke about going away somewhere warm and he mentioned he had heard you were on your way somewhere. He thought maybe we could catch up a little if you joined us? How about it?"

Siegfried hesitated; this wasn't in his sunny plans. "Well the thing is, I'm sorry, but I'm actually on my way to the airport right now." But Mikel wasn't budging "Come on! It's been so long, and it would just be one drink, I promise. I know Marcel would really appreciate it?"

"I don't know" Siegfried said as he considered the hour.

It was kind of early. He had more than four hours until he absolutely had to check in at the airport, as he had been eager to go and had gotten ready packing much faster than anticipated. "Just a beer to say hello, it would take the edge of the good old travel nerves... And besides, we shouldn't be too far away from your neighbourhood; actually, we're at The Maroon." "Alright," agreed Siegfried, "I do have time for one beer".

The Maroon was a mediocre bar at best, trying a bit too hard to be hip, which fit perfectly with their late-night clientele of middle-aged men trying the exact same thing. But now, at six in the evening, there were only a few tables sporadically occupied by small groups of people talking privately. Some looked like they might be discussing business of some sort, while others seemed more like the kind that just needed a place to hang out. The bar was located only 10 minutes away from Siegfried's flat, and so he decided to walk there with his luggage.

As Siegfried started walking, he failed to notice an inconspicuous man standing across the street from his building, sending an affirmative text message to some friends before hurrying off to prepare their evening. He had also failed to take note that Marcel had not called him personally.

As he walked through the first couple of back alleys lined with bins and skips that would lead him to The Maroon his mind was focused on sunny beaches and smiling waitresses.

Suddenly he felt a thud and a tingling feeling on the front of his right shoulder. This was accompanied by a stinging sensation, jolting Siegfried to an exclamation of pain. "Ow!" he shouted as he turned around to see if he had hit something sharp pointing out from the alley wall. There was a good two metres of absolutely nothing between him and the wall.

Siegfried felt confused, his adrenaline rushing from the sudden scare. He looked around to see if anyone had reacted to his outcry, but there were absolutely no one around that he could see. He grabbed his shoulder hard to suppress the sting when he saw it had a small syringe protruding from it.

Thirty metres down the same alley, behind a skip, Marcel scolded Mikel in a low but agitated voice. "What the fuck man, you said you could shoot this thing!"

Mikel in response shrugged "I hit him, didn't I?"

"Yes you did, barely. You were meant to hit him in the thigh, what if you had missed?' Marcel complained before he turned his attention back to the situation at hand, and dared a peek over the edge of their hiding place.

He got up just in time to witness their target leaning to the wall before slumping down on his knees and finally rolling over sideways on the concrete. "Quick, bring the car!" Marcel ordered to Paul over the phone before he ran over to check Siegfried's vitals. He was alive, but obviously heavily sedated and about to go unconscious as Paul pulled into the alley with the vehicle.

Mikel helped Marcel wrestle the now limp body into the back seat of the car, before Mikel ran back to where Siegfried fell to collect his bag. He took them back to the car while Marcel finished awkwardly trying to lay Siegfried down in as decent of a position as possible.

Mikel put the luggage in the boot, whilst Marcel, once satisfied that Siegfried was in no danger of respiratory blockage, was pushing their sleeping passenger to an upright sitting position in order to make room for himself. Mikel got into the front passenger seat of the car, and Paul drove away.

'Shit. Shit...' cursed Marcel as he turned to adjust Siegfried's sitting position in order to support his friend's head and to make sure he was breathing. Mikel didn't comment, he just glanced at Marcel and they made for their destination.

The car stopped outside the Marzahn-Hellersdorf district of the city in a residential area where modernity appeared to have given a miss. Tall socialist era apartment blocks stuck out of the greenery like isolated peaks.

The whole district had been slated to be demolished, with the buildings covered in graffiti, but a group of squatters had made a community there along with many of the old residents, who clung on tightly to the area. The "Old communists never die" spirit resonated there as the average age of the inhabitants was 67. Eventually the redevelopment process appeared to take a back seat and the tower blocks became another reminder of Germany's communist past.

Today, that didn't matter. The car parked before block three of the apartment buildings. Mikel got out and opened the back seat of the car. Siegfried slumped out and was quickly caught by Mikel before his head hit the ground. Marcel got out also and once Mikel had pulled out Siegfried from the car, he assisted him, grasping his friend's ankles.

Paul turned off the engine, and got out to take out Siegfried's luggage from the boot. Paul looked around to ensure they weren't being observed. 'Let's go.' Paul ordered as he led the way into the building straight to the lift, it was out of order.

Marcel and Mikel had to carry the slumbering Siegfried up seven floors. The first three were fine, but soon their arms got tired. It didn't help that Paul kept prodding them to hurry up before they were seen.

At the seventh floor Marcel and Mikel were about to drop. 'Open the damn door.' Marcel beseeched Paul as he tried each key to open the door. Once done opening the first lock, he had to go through the same time consuming process for the other two. Four minutes later, they were finally able to enter the cold flat

Marcel and Mikel entered quickly and placed Siegfried on the dusty rug covering the wooden floor before both of them went to recline on the sofa. As the others rested, Paul went about turning on the heating and drawing the curtains to prevent any prying eyes from the building across the road.

Paul went to the kitchen to check the electric metre, it was still running. He went through the cupboards and found they were bare. Walking back into the living room, Paul took out his phone to call Khoi reporting "We have him".

Later that evening, an old lady and her dog, whilst taking her walk, nearly bumped into Robert who was scanning the area nervously. Robert had been looking forward to his date with Ulrika, having ended his last meeting on a high. From then on, to the irritation of all who knew him, he had been totally preoccupied by his next encounter with the woman who stole his heart.

So consumed was he by thoughts of her that he found himself talking about her all the time even at the meetings with his colleagues where he was told to "Give it a rest man. She's just another bitch; you'll soon get over her. You usually do."

Robert defended his feelings by highlighting his belief that she wasn't another one night stand or good lay. He succeeded to make his point when he revealed to the doubters that he was going on an unprecedented third date with her. Most of his 'love' interests tended to fizzle out on the first date the longest of which ending on the second. He eventually shocked them into silence when he added that had yet to "get into her pants."

The initial downplaying by the doubters turned to grave concern. Some felt he had taken ill or suffered from a sickness of the mind whilst Richard was certain he had been bewitched. No one was able or willing to accept the faintest of possibilities that he may have fallen in love. Infatuation? Possibly, but Robert In love? This was unheard of. Robert ignored the naysayers and focused on the upcoming event with the enthusiasm of a teenager.

Although giddy with affection, he could not put his sense of style away and asked Ulrika what he was to wear to this surprise date. In return, he received a message that read "dress sloppy". "Sloppy" a word he didn't comprehend. He opened his closet, sifting through his collection of designer apparel before giving up. Robert chose to ask for clarification. She replied, "Sloppy, as in wear something you don't mind getting dirty." With a definition given, he chose to put on his old gym clothes which he had only worn six times. Luckily, he hadn't yet disposed of it which allowed him to fetch it from the charity bag.

Once happily sporting his rags Robert took a little time to make his way out of his flat to the address given for their date. It was to take place in a culinary college just a kilometre away from his home and he couldn't wait to get there.

His eagerness brought him to his destination twelve minutes early. He was lucky however. He drove into the car park and at the front of the building; she was waiting for him at the top of the stairs.

As he parked his car, Robert could feel his hands dampen with sweat and his heart begin to race. The feeling was near overwhelming. He had the urge to look at the mirror to check if he was presentable, but he really didn't care. He raced out of the car and worked gingerly to meet her.

As he drew closer, he could tell she was not wearing any makeup and her hair was cropped back. She seemed to carry the sloppy look very well in her hooded top and jeans, with her bomber jacket resting over her arm. She had a smile on her face, her high cheek bones lightly peppered with freckles, complimenting her emerald green eyes.

He ran up the steps and lost a bit of his footing causing him to trip. She laughed and t seemed carefree and from the heart. She then raced down to meet him, offering her assistance, but his pride got in the way. Standing up, Robert grinned and greeted her with a kiss on the cheek. "You look beautiful." He said to her. She didn't reply, rather, she held his hand and walked with him up the remaining nine steps to the door.

Once out of the cold, she spoke "I am sure you will like what I have planned for tonight." Robert didn't want to sound eager, so he chose to let her reveal what was in store. They walked down the stairs to the basement past a few rooms to what looked like an industrial kitchen. It was filled with what seemed like around two dozen people all chatting with a glass of wine in their hands.

Jelena was approached by an usher who asked, "Are you here for the baking lessons?" Jelena confirmed it so and once their name was ticked off the list, they proceeded to the table where the wine was set and she picked up two glasses of white.

As Jelena offered him one and found Robert unable to conceal his excitement. "Oh my God." He remarked "It seems you know me so well. I love cooking, this isn't what I had in mind for a date, but here we are again! You are so cool!"

"Thanks..." She replied, only to be interrupted by the organiser clapping loudly as she announced,

"Good evening everyone, thank you so much for coming, great to see such a good turnout for the charity baking classes and competition."

Robert listened attentively at the line up for the evening whilst Jelena was more concerned about the wine which tasted past is drink by date. It was only when she heard the words "and the winner will receive a box of champagne" that her ears perked up. Amongst the applause of those gathered at the prize on offer, she tugged on Robert's sleeve "Did she say the winner gets champagne?" He confirmed it was true. Jelena bluntly put it to him that she "wanted that prize."

Robert could see the conviction in her eyes and replied "We'd best get baking then."

Each of the person present were put in pairs, luckily, Robert and Jelena came ready-made. They were allocated a table which had all the ingredients and appliances to make and decorate a cake. In addition, there was a large box.

Everyone was required to watch the professional who stood at the table with the same appliances and ingredients as the others with the addition of an extra two boxes sitting alongside the prize for the evening.

She showed the participants how to mix the batter for the cake, all within twenty minutes. The jolly looking, chubby woman placed the mix into the baking tin and inserted it into an oven at 180c. She remarked that time was a factor, and produced from the box on her table, a cake she made earlier, which she cut up and offered to all those present to sample. It was universally agreed that the warm cake was quite delightful.

With the cake baking having been addressed, the lady proceeded to the next event of the evening, cake decoration. The second box was opened and another cake was produced. The woman proceeded to make cream, whilst calling out instructions with every step. Eventually she had created a floral decorative image on the cake, all within half an hour. There was another round of applause before she called them forward to come and marvel at her art before sending them off to their stations to put into practice what they had been shown.

One member of the team was allocated the task of baking the cake and the second was to decorate the cake in the box.

Everyone put on their aprons and was given an hour to create something. When the group was told to start, pandemonium began to reign. No one had written any of the instructions down and had been universally mesmerized by the instructor's activities as opposed to keeping track of the items being used. Everyone was blank with the exception of Jelena who seemed as calm and as cool as a cucumber. She had been delegated the task of decorating the cake. Having made the cream with her steady hand, she got to work. Her skill didn't go unnoticed by the organisers and instructors who commented on her concentration.

Jelena's professionalism and poise was in sharp contrast to Robert who had fallen into a panic, wondering what went into the mixing bowl first. He waffled a little till he eventually found his bearings starting with the butter and sugar.

Time flies when one is under pressure, Robert thought as time ticked away and he had only got as far as sifting the butter into the mix whilst Jelena was putting the finishing touches to her creation and most of the other people were placing their batter into the oven.

Eventually, he did make it and it was in the nick of time with just two minutes left. By that time, Jelena had already finished her cake decoration way before most of the others who had either given up or made do with their limited efforts. There was envy and admiration in equal measure from those who passed by the table to view Jelena's work.

Whilst waiting for their cakes to bake and the judges to inspect the decorated ones, they were offered snacks and more drinks. Robert found it difficult to relax, and he wasn't the only one, as many also wondered about their items in the oven.

Small talk didn't come naturally for Robert when he was anxious. He just wanted the time to fly by. When it finally did come time to check on the cakes, Robert was relieved to find his had baked all the way through. It was when he took it out and placed it on the wooden table he noted something... he had forgotten to add the vanilla. He could have screamed, but he didn't. Rather, he bit his tongue as the judges came along and placed a card in front of the Jelena's work. It read '1$^{st}$' she came first in the decoration task!

Elated, she cheered and clapped her hands in glee before embracing Robert who soon realised he may have let his side down. The cake tasting was to take place in half an hour. The teams were asked to cut the cakes into pieces to enable it to cool for consumption. It was as Jelena and Robert acted on the instructions that he revealed that he had missed using the vanilla essence.

Her glee turned to silent scornful rebuke "How could you forget the vanilla? It's a vanilla sponge cake, the clue is in the name."

"I'm sorry, maybe I could sprinkle some over the cake and they wouldn't notice..." Robert suggested.

"No, no... I want that champagne" She reiterated. The judges were just four tables away, she had to act. "I'm going to the toilet; get ready to bail out of here." Robert didn't comprehend what Jelena had in mind, yet he nodded like he understood. Jelena looked around and silently disappeared, leaving Robert to stand on his own as the judges approached.

Jelena did go to the toilet, she realised that there were security cameras everywhere, but none leading to the toilet. Jelena entered the men's toilet and took all of the toilet paper available. Reaching into her pocket, she took out her trusty lighter and set fire to the rolls of bum wipes and watched as the smoke rose slowly. Satisfied with the level of the flames, she left for the female toilet to do the same and this time she didn't wait to watch the progression of the fire.

Jelena returned to Robert's side just as the judges arrived to taste his creation. The plump lady and a lean man with a clip board as well as the organiser arrived, toffee nosed and suffering the delusions of grandeur as they poked the cake with a knife to see if it was cooked through as well as to gauge the temperature.

They tasted it, chewed it gently, making faces as they swallowed. "It appears to be lacking something." Robert was about to confess to his error when Jelena promptly replied "There wasn't any on the table." She lied. Robert looked around for the bottle of essence and found it gone. Jelena continued "We could have asked, but he was all thumbs and I was busy concentrating on my decoration…" Jelena stopped, interrupted by the lean man who sniffed the air loudly saying, "Does anyone else smell smoke?" The others stopped their probing of the cake to take in the air, each contemplating whether or not they could perceive what the lean man had.

His perceptions proved to be right when the fire alarm went off shortly before the sprinkler system did the same.

There were the usual shrieks, cries and commotion as people got wet and ran towards the exit. Shepherded by the organisers, Robert followed the crowd, out through the fire escape into the biting night air. He looked around for Jelena, but couldn't find her. He was set to panic if it weren't for his phone ringing. He checked the number, it was Jelena. Once he answered he was met with the order "Slip away as quietly as you can and meet me by your car. Hurry, it's rather cold."

With everyone chattering away to calm their nerves, Robert did as he was told. He walked from the side of the building to the front where he found Jelena standing by the car, slightly damp, shivering as she cradled a box in her left arm and doing the same with a box of champagne in her right. "Come on, we got to leave." She snapped. Robert was spurred into action. He opened the boot of his jaguar and placed the items into his car.

Jelena and Robert boarded the car and with a screeching of his wheels, they sped away from the cookery college. Robert was so filled with adrenaline that he screamed out and laughed declaring, "My God, what the hell just happened there? That was crazy! Did you set off the alarm?"

"Did you like it?" Jelena asked as they stopped at the traffic lights.

He hesitated, as he traded in his infatuations for deep affection. Robert held her hand and kissed it before responding "Yeah... I did. So what next?" he enquired. "We got 6 bottles of champagne and cake; I think we could make a night of it at your place?" She proposed. He smiled, confirming he liked the sound of the plan.

The journey went quickly as they reminisced about their recent experience, focusing their aim on the instructor, poking fun at her nasal voice and lisp.

Arriving at the building, Robert had a growing sense of expectation, yet he kept it hid. He led them in, punching a code that allowed them access. In the lift, they said nothing. He just looked up at the ceiling, doing all he could to avoid eye contact which was difficult since she was looking at him.

He felt relieved when they arrived at the fifth floor. Robert opened the door and invited his guest in. Once they passed the entrance into the kitchen, Jelena was rather impressed by the size of the open plan kitchen living room area.

The kitchen was fully fitted and there was a leather sofa by the circular bay window and a flat screen TV latched to the wall. "Wow... this is a nice space. Cute living room too. I like this lay out... but there is a faint smell of fish though."

"Oh I had tilapia this morning. I probably should have opened the window" Robert confessed "One thing though, this is just the kitchen, come with me." He led her to two doors and opened the left one and announced "This is the living room."

Jelena gasped. It was well planned, tastefully decorated and large. "Oh my goodness! How many bedrooms does this flat have? Do you occupy the whole floor?"

"Three bedroom and yes, I do have the whole floor... actually it's four, but I have a room for my gym and the other for …. Other things."

"What other things?" She asked. Robert was stumped. He hadn't been asked this question before and wondered if he was going to embarrassed or whether he should be proud, still, he didn't want to admit what the other room held. "I'll show you." He offered.

They walked to the end of the living room where there were another two doors. Once again he selected the left one. Jelena was speechless as she walked in slowly, mouth ajar. She stood there marvelling at the rack of clothes that hung everywhere and the shelves that contained numerous shoes.

Her silence brought the magnitude of his decadent home to him. "I guess it is a little too much."

"Leaving a €10 tip for €30 meal is a little too much… this, this… this is something else." She concluded. "I mean look!" She cried, going to the racks ruffling through them before proclaiming "They are all designers! How did you get all these?"

"From work… you forget, I am a model." He said in an attempt to explain it all away.

"So they give you all the clothes when you finish your photo-shoot?" Jelena asked

"Sometimes." He replied, watching her as she took out a navy blue pin striped suit and commented "You know; I bet you would look cool in that."

Placing it under her chin she asked "You think I could pull it off?"

"Why not? Put it on whilst I serve the champagne" He proposed. She seemed to blush as she replied "OK".

Shutting the door, Robert felt lighter and ran to the kitchen. He put the four bottles of champagne in the fridge, one in the freezer and opened the last one. He decided to cut up some of the cake. As he plated the second slice, he heard Jelena say "Well, what do you think?"

Robert almost dropped his plate. The clothes fit her well, due to her height and stature. He had to admit "You look great! You could seriously pull it off! You carry it with some grace, it actually looks better on you than on me…"

"Flattery gets you everything." She said, walking to the kitchen work top and helping herself to a glass of fizz. Robert seemed totally taken as he stuttered "C, c, cake?" She took one and proceeded to bite a large chunk away. With her mouth almost full she remarked "Um, good. So what's on television?" That was the cold water that doused his rising urge for sex.

"TV…" Robert began "Well, yeah, em… I think there is some football on."

"I like football. Which teams are playing?" "This was a bolt from the blue.

Although he was happy to hear that, like him, she was enthusiastic about the lovely game, he thought it was the most inappropriate time for such a common interest to rear its head. Yet, he had to play the host and thus, begrudgingly, he went to the sofa to get the remote and turned on the television.

The match on air was Mainz v Hamburger SV. Hamburger SV was his team and he had totally forgotten that they were playing today. They were just two minutes into the game then he heard the words that instantly rekindled his affections for Jelena when she proclaimed "Hamburg is playing? Cool!" She approached the sofa with the glasses of drink. Still unable to reconcile himself with what he heard, Robert asked "You follow the Bundesliga?"

"Yes, I do." She said bringing the pinched alcohol and cake to the coffee table, handing Robert his glass. "Let's enjoy the game shall we?"

This was remarkable, this was too good to be true and he was so taken it was evident in his voice as he replied "Sure… let's… let's do that."

They sat on the sofa and Robert grew nervous, wondering what to do next. He hadn't felt this shy before, he usually was full of confidence. There he sat, with his hands sweaty, his stomach filled with butterflies, as he contemplated. He didn't have to contemplate further. She rested her head on his shoulder and snuggled up close to him. Robert thought it was safe enough to place his arm around her. There was that smell again "What perfume are you wearing?"

"Oscar De La Renta. Do you like it?" She asked.

Robert felt nostalgic. It was the same scent his mother used. He kissed Jelena on the head and said "Yes, I love it." before taking another sip of his champagne.

As the Hamburger SV made an attempt for the goal, Robert began to feel woozy. His eye lids felt heavy as he struggled to pay attention, but he couldn't. Eventually, he succumbed to the call of sandman and fell asleep. Once he dosed off Jelena went to work.

She took Robert's glass from his hand, went to the kitchen area and tipped it into the sink. Jelena marvelled at how quickly the drug took hold. She ran the tap and rinsed the glass clean before she took the second bottle of champagne out of the freezer and poured it down the drain. This was followed by a third bottle which had the same treatment but only half way.

She then took the bottles to the coffee table, tipped over the empty ones and filled the glass halfway, placing it on the table.

Jelena took out her mobile phone and began to snap pictures of the flat, going from room to room to collect some images. Once finished, she forwarded the pictures to her contact. That done, she collected more information by going through his mail before venturing into his walk in wardrobe to pick a hat to conceal her features as she ventured out of the flat to investigate the building floor by floor.

Once satisfied, she returned to Robert's side, pushed him over to create more space for herself and proceeded to enjoy the cake and champagne whilst watching the football match which eventually ended in disappointment for Hamburger SV.

*16 December 2010*

At just after 4 the following morning, Robert awoke to find Jelena resting on his chest. He didn't want to wake her, but he desperately wanted to pee and his head felt rather groggy and heavy. Still, he didn't want to spoil the moment. He liked the feeling and the presence of this beautiful being.

Taking the chance available, Robert stroked her hair gently, causing her to stir. She raised her head and smiled as she said "Good morning" He would have replied, but his bladder could not wait any longer. "Excuse me!" Robert cried shunting her aside before vaulting to the loo, his need to urinate keeping him from shutting the door.

It was a blessed, pleasant sensation as his expelled the liquids from within, shutting his eyes as he drowned in pleasure.

Once emptied, Robert went about giving his member a shake. The ritual was interrupted when he felt a hand, other than his, holding his penis. He was about to turn round and ask what the hell Jelena was doing. "Don't turn around." She instructed, "Just enjoy it."

Jelena wrapped her left arm around his neck and began to squeeze. Robert didn't know what to expect, he didn't like surprises, especially one that obstructed his airway, but once she started working, he knew where it was going.

Initially it felt weird having Jelena choking him as she jacked him off, but he quickly overcame that and actually began to enjoy it. She had the perfect momentum, going fast initially while tightening her head lock, causing his face to turn red due to a lack of air, touching the tip of his now erect member then loosening her grip and slowing down just before he climaxed. His heart rate grew along with his breathing.

It was exquisite torture to be taken to the brink only to be brought back again, yet, it was mesmerising. Robert felt his knees turn to jelly due to the dwindling oxygen in his body. He rested his hand against the wall to keep him standing as he perspired and, where possible, moaned in ecstasy.

He couldn't hold it any longer, he was going to explode and announce the procession by howling, but just as he was about to erupt, she let go, causing him squirt and drip before losing his stamina and slumping on the floor in exhaustion, struggling to catch his breath, unable to speak.

Jelena went about washing her hand as though she had done nothing, not knowing that her assisted masturbation was the best sexual experience Robert had ever had. She walked out, leaving him alone to recover having sprayed his sperm all over the toilet tank.

Jelena changed back to her own clothes and as she stepped out, so did Robert who finally found the power to speak. "What was that?"

"My way of saying good morning properly." She replied as she cropped back her hair. "I'm late for a meeting and I have to travel to Denmark for a few days to see a friend. Will you be around when I get back?"

"When do you get back?" He asked

"Around the 19th… don't know, going by train." She said as she walked up to him and kissed him on the lips. "Then we can go out to dinner."

"No… I'll cook for you. I promise I won't leave any essential ingredients out." Robert promised.

"I trust, you…" She said kissing him quickly on the lips. "I have to go."

Jelena went to the kitchen, picked up one of the unopened bottles of champagne from the fridge and walked to the door.

Robert had a question he needed answering and she couldn't leave until he did receive some form of confirmation. "Ulrika…" he called. Jelena stopped as she turned the handle. "Did we… you know…?"

"Have sex?" she concluded. Robert blushed at her frankness but it got worse when she replied "No, you drank too much and you said you just wanted to cuddle, and then you passed out."

Shame consumed Robert. He never slept before a performance, but, according to Jelena, he had. She then compounded the feeling of self-reproach by adding "Maybe next time, when you are ready." He wanted to scream, "I'm ready now!" but it was too late. Jelena blew him a kiss as she exited the door.

Robert stood there shaking from his previous experience, observing his surroundings and accepting that he may have to wait a week for another chance. Somehow, even though he knew he could get a fix without issue, there were many numbers he could have called that would have brought a willing bed warmer to his door within minutes, but chose not to. He was going to wait for this one, she seemed wild. Hence it was best to conserve one's energy, Robert concluded as he started to clean up his flat.

The morning of the 16th was a cloudy day. Khoi thought he woke up early, but hadn't. He had been fooled by the dark clouds that promised some form of precipitation, but what type? Even the weather reports weren't sure. Luckily he didn't need to worry about his late rise. He had the day off.

A day off didn't mean he had nothing to do though. Khoi had a lot of additional research to complete. Before he began, Khoi was concerned that was being rude by keeping Han waiting in regards to her invitation, but it was short lived.

Having connected his phone to it, Khoi sat before his laptop looking at the pictures taken by Jelena along with the details of the items present. Khoi was more interested in the kitchen. If he was going to execute his plan, Khoi had to be sure that it is executed with as little detection as possible.

Someone could pop out from the ventilation shaft and kill him in his sleep then go back up... but there would be evidence everywhere.

Once again Khoi sat back, looking at the plan and the picture of the kitchen again and soon realised how nice it was.

Clearly Robert had taste. There was a quality solid oak floor, glass dividing walls, ceramic plates and stainless steel kitchen units. There was a leather sofa in the corner where someone could watch him cook before they proceeded to the oak dinning set.

Robert must have had a slight fetish for stainless steel. The room was littered with it. The kitchen units, the door handles, locks, pots, lighting and even the extracting fan were made of stainless steel.

All that steel must have cost him a fortune, let alone the amount spent on the induction hob cookers, Khoi contemplated. Then he took another look at the room and something began dawn on him. The room had just two, quite small, window dock windows. They were pretty, but wouldn't be quite effective as to let the air circulate freely.

Then he saw the solution over the door. There was a ventilation system, something to keep him cool in summer and warm in the winter. That was smart indeed… but not as smart as the idea that popped into his head. His deviousness grew with every second as he looked at the picture, it was then he remarked to himself "It just might work."

Khoi needed to examine viability of his plan. He walked around his hotel room, thinking and looking up at the walls to see if he could get an idea of what could be in the kitchen. It didn't work. He needed the more than his imagination.

He searched online for information from the planning office and it did say individuals could get plans of buildings for a small fee from the public records office.

There was no time to waste. Khoi didn't bother to shower. He put on his jeans, shirt, and bomber jacket and raced out of the hotel. He had already made it to the underground station when he realised that he hadn't take his mobile phone or laptop with him, nor did he have the address of the location concerned. First lesson of the day, don't get too excited. Once he got all his items together, Khoi continued his journey.

It must have been the time of the year that made it otherwise cold, uncaring, borderline inhibitive civil-servants to become ever so helpful.

It took them an hour to find him the plans for the building. After an additional two hours of reviewing the drawings, Khoi asked for a copy. There was a fee, he was happy to pay.

With the plans in a tube, Khoi returned to his hotel, stopping at the reception to ask if they had a tape measure, which after several minutes of searching, they provided him with one.

In his room, Khoi measured himself whilst taking into consideration the information he had jotted out from the plans, he didn't fit.

He sat there contemplating. Marcel and Ralph were certainly out of the question, they were much too big. Daniel was about his build, slightly bigger, so he too was out. Mikel was too clumsy and noisy, though he was smaller than him. He was a risk, reliable, yet a risk. It left one alternative and he was perfect.

With that sorted, Khoi began to investigate further. How could he tick Robert off his list without detection?

Again, he looked at the pictures of the kitchen as he had his late lunch at after six in the evening. He almost choked on his orange juice when he realised what he needed was staring him in the face.

Immediately he was back on the web typing out word after word, searching for the right item with the right density and effect. After seventy nine minutes, he saw the correct chemical formula and it put a satisfied grin on his face.

Time to celebrate, Khoi thought as he reached for the phone and asked for a bottle of champagne and a bottle of water to be brought to his room. "Would you like still water or water with gas?" asked the receptionist. "With gas please, definitely with gas." Khoi confirmed. Order placed, Khoi sat back before he noticed the advent calendar, he hadn't had his treat for the day and he totally deserved it. He took a piece and enjoyed the rich dark flavour.

Khoi was now confident that he had a fool proof plan. He sent a text to Jelena, Marcel, Mikel and Paul to request they come to his hotel for a meeting at 10 in the morning. He rolled his eyes when he got three responses with the word "Boss" in it and just one stating "I'll be there."

His pugnacious activities caused Khoi to over indulge but he didn't care. He could pick up rest tomorrow.

The alarm went off earlier than usual. It rang at 7. There was a lot to accomplish today by the entire team. Khoi got ready, taking a shower then going to breakfast.

Khoi summed up his courage before he picked up his phone making a call to the strangest man he had ever met. He genuinely didn't wish to speak to Callum, he considered him a sociopath who had ambitions of being an evil genius, but he had to settle as a pharmaceutical scientist instead.

After providing Callum with the relevant specifications, Khoi asked "Could you get something I can use?"

"€10,000" Callum demanded.

"€5,000 and you bring it to my hotel by lunch time. Besides, what are you going to provide?" Khoi parried. There was silence. Khoi waited to see if his counter offer was acceptable. Then he got his reply "You'll see. Where is your hotel?"

With the item on its way, Khoi could not be complacent. He extensively searched for a protective suit and gas mark and was astonished by how many were available.

Carelessly, he forgot the concept of time and was soon brought back to earth when there was a knock on the door. Looking at the time, he soon realised that he had spent the best of 2 hours browsing.

Khoi went to the door of his hotel room, looked through the peep hole and found the four invitees waiting. Khoi opened the door, ushered them in and proceeded to clear the table of empty bottles and other objects.

The others shared a private thought that Khoi may be hitting the sauce hard, but yet said nothing. Rather, Mikel decided to assist, placing all the items on the floor.

Khoi removed the top of the tube producing a large roll of paper which he unfurled. Paul took the ashtray and empty bottles and placed them on the edges to straighten out the sheet. They all gathered around the table.

On the paper were the floor plans of a flat, its ventilation system and stair plans of a building. Khoi took out a pen and wrote "Mr D" on the side of three drawings and proclaimed "This is the plan for Mr D"s building and his flat. He lives on the top floor of the building and the flat covers the entire floor. As you can see," said Khoi, directing their attention by pointing "there are two entry and exit points. The first leads you into a small living room and then you walk through there to a kitchen-dining area. There are two doors, one that leads to the large living room which then has access to the three bedrooms. The other door leads to the veranda."

"The second exit and entry is the fire escape which is the door at the end of the large living room. There is a door at the start of the third floor that prevents people from coming up to his floor through the fire escape without a key. Our focus is the kitchen. 5m x 6m x 2.5m, total volume of the room is 75 cubic metres" The other's nodded, faking their attentiveness, waiting for the moment the information would be relevant to them as Khoi carried on regardless "He had a hand in the building of his penthouse and the ventilation system to ensure it was not linked with that of the rest of the building."

"Being on the top floor, he had his own ventilation system made, the size of which is 85cm wide, 50cm high." He emphasised by drawing a circle around the area "We need access to the ventilation system of the kitchen, and the entry point is located at the top of the door of the fire escape." Khoi drew a cross on the area "That's where you guys come in."

"During her visit, Jelena observed the following. There are surveillance cameras on all floors except his floor and, surprisingly, the fire escapes are on either ends of each floor, one exiting from the service door at the back of the building the other from the front door. There is also a blind spot for the surveillance camera on the third floor in this corner." Khoi circled the relevant area again. "She also observed that the maintenance crew are set to arrive at 8am on Monday 21 December to service the lift and perform some checks on the ventilation shafts."

Pointing at them, Khoi added "You three will be there to observe their activities and watch carefully. They will need access through the front door and the service entrance at the back here." For any work, they need three people." Counting with his fingers "One to perform the task; the second to assist, pass the tools etcetera and the last who remains by the door acting as security with the key in the lock just in case."

"They have two distinct tasks to perform that day hence there will be six; three for the ventilation, three for the lift. The ventilation guys will need the service entry at the back. The lift guys will use the front door. In flat 5 on the third floor just in the blind spot area lives a devout Muslim couple. The man goes to work, she stays at home and never leaves the house unless in a burka. After he goes to work, she goes to the local market around 10 for some shopping which is not good."

Noticing that he may have thrown the others off course, Khoi insisted "Stay with me here, it will make sense in a moment. Jelena has the front and back door access codes which she will use to enter the building to leave a small condolence card for Robert… I mean Mr D, on the passing of his dear friend Mr C…"

"How are you certain that Mr C will die?" Khoi paused on the question delivered by Mikel and smiled "Don't doubt me again." Khoi said brushing aside the comment and soldiered on "Our subject would be out at the gym by that time, even if he isn't, Jelena will get into the working lift, go up to the fourth floor, place his gift by the door, get back into the lift and get off at the third floor. We will then walk to the end of the corridor to the blind spot here." Khoi said, pointing to the relevant place on the diagram. "She will then change into a burka before setting off a smoke canister a moment before she throws it down the rubbish shoot and presses the fire alarm. She will then exit from the closest fire escape which leads to the service elevator."

"Jelena will block the exit with a car lock which means that lady in the flat will not be able to exit if she is in. Once the woman in flat 5 realises she can't get out of that way, she'll use the other exit."

"This is where you come in Jelena. Once you see that she has given up, you take your lock and race out the other way. Since the ventilation team start from the top they would need time to get out… we would have approximately 5 minutes to get those keys."

"If all goes according to plan, the man at the door would race up to try and assist his colleague, you would run down and we hope that key is still by the door. If it is, you have to take it, meet with Paul and Mikel who will cut a new set as soon as possible. It would be best to get the original back to them, throw it on the floor whilst strolling past, meet them by accident and tell them you found it nearby. Though it's desirable, it's not a must. Marcel, you must be close to ensure that nothing happens to Jelena. If she doesn't show up after 15 minutes from entry, alert the others and go and get her out." Khoi concluded with a sigh

Paul, Mikel and Marcel were perplexed as they looked at one another, considering the complexity of the plan, prompting Paul to query "What if the plan doesn't work?"

"That's where Marcel's plan comes in. You guys will stalk the key keeper and organise to rob him on his way home." Khoi replied. See things could possibly be done much easier, Paul suggested "Wouldn't that be an easier option?" Paul statement of the obvious was shared by the two other men. Khoi winced "You are right. It would be easier, but this is more fun. Besides, Jelena wants to play too."

"I love danger" Jelena interjected. The team started to laugh and all agreed to give it a go.

However, Paul's curiosity had not been satisfied. "When we have the keys, what's next Boss?" Khoi frowned "Don't call me Boss." Having been scolded, Paul apologised "It's ok." Khoi assured him. "Once we get the keys, I'll tell you the next step."

Then, Paul noticed Khoi scrutinizing him. "Khoi, are you alright?" He asked. "Yes, yes…" Khoi confirmed "Can you tell me your measurements? I mean chest, neck, etc." Khoi probed "We need to fit you for a suit." Khoi brought himself back to the room and to the matter of the day. "Is everything set for our backpacker's trip?"

"Yes" muttered Marcel.

# 10

*17 December 2010*

Friday had finally arrived and Richard was in high spirits. Despite the setbacks of the last few days, he was glad to have something lined up to take his mind off the police raid. What had lifted his spirits was the tickets he held in the breast pocket of his coat and the fact he was seeing his best friend again after a long time.

Jompa, the Swedish DJ was playing tonight at the exclusive night club called "Whyte" and he had access for four to the private booths of the club.

He arrived home to his ground floor flat and once the door was shut, he concluded that it was time to get the party started. Richard took off his coat and didn't bother to hang it, marching into the kitchen to fetch vodka from the fridge.

Richard served himself a shot feeling the sharp heat of the alcohol inundate his senses. "Wow!" He screamed before going to the living room, turning on the sound system to play the second album released by Jompa. The beat mixed with words got him in the groove. Richard danced about a bit before reaching for some more vodka. It was already eight in the evening and the alcohol wasn't enough to give him the kick he craved.

The mule was late. Richard sent a text asking for the mule's location but all he got back were the words "Will be there in an hour". This was not good. Despite the disappointment, Richard knew he had to get ready for the night.

Power shower on, the heat and velocity was just right. Richard took off his clothes as he sang along to the music as it faded to another tune which he didn't really like so much. It prompted him to focus on his shower.

Richard enjoyed taking long showers. The water calmed his overactive mind and body.

"Crazy-tomato" they called him. He was always seen as stupid and disruptive, never paying attention in class. He was hot tempered and foul mouthed and it didn't help that he had bright curly orange hair. He was called the idiot and excluded from education. Parents would tell their children not to play with him because of his behaviour.

Everyone knew there was something wrong with him. Some called him crazy and for many years they were right. So Richard found himself abandoned by his parents in a boarding school for badly behaved children where he was made to take cold showers every day, regardless of the season and to go through near militaristic exercises every morning and night.

His parents would come when they could on the monthly visiting days but he was never brought home for the holidays, except for Christmas.

There were beatings, there was a lot of bullying and eventually you had to be tough or toughen up otherwise you would be eaten up by those who choose to use you.

The fall of the wall was the best thing that happened to him. Richard was liberated from the prison that was meant to help him. Four years after the wall came down and after 7 long years of boarding life, he was free and at 14 Richard was finally diagnosed with attention deficit disorder.

He was taken into a special school to try and salvage what they could of his ability to assimilate some form of education. It wasn't successful. Richard, though creative and intelligent, could only read and write at the same level of 7 year old and had to keep his temper in check via medication.

His time in the boarding school wasn't completely void of education. He was being groomed for the military, so he was extremely regimented and physically fit. Also, Richard had been exposed to the more unsavoury characters on the streets and soon mastered the art of criminality.

It was that knowledge which he gained in boarding school that brought him into the fold of the "District 3" gang and it was the time in the boarding school that made him detest cold showers and swimming pools. Yet, there was one thing he never did master. Richard's temper was often easily ignited and hard to quench. What the gang managed was to channel this destructive force for their gain.

Hell befell anyone that crossed the District 3 gang. Richard was not shy of doing the most grotesque and violent things to a person condemned to feel his rage. His most legendary moment so far was having steamed cooked the genitals of a member of a Ukrainian gang trying to muscle into their territory with low grade goods.

He thought of the idea whilst watching the home shopping channel where a geeky looking man with his even duller female assistant who had taken feigning amazement to such new lows, that he wondered if there might be a crime against it.

He wasn't interested in their personalities yet his attention was caught by the cleaning power of steam. He bought one of the products and found it annoying to use for its primary purpose so he began to think of new uses for it.

It was then he and his friend picked up their man of interest in his flat, right in the middle of intercourse that it came to him, if it is good enough for killing unwanted microscopic bugs, it should be effective against over-sized ones.

Being held down and gagged, Richard proceeded to cook the Ukrainian jewels whilst the gentleman was still alive, at least he was until Richard had his fill and decided to put him out of his misery by strangulation the body dropped off at the door of the offending gang's hideout.

The Ukrainian gang didn't last long though. A week later, their hideout was raided leading to half of them being imprisoned for criminal acts and the other half being deported for not having the right documents which proved that the law wasn't only for the innocent and wronged.

But he was growing weary of his fierce nature. Richard wasn't stupid. He knew time would catch up with him eventually. He was already 32, it couldn't last forever. So he planned to try and find a less physically assertive role in the gang by the middle of the following year. After all, he had made his mark and he was feared so he knew he was secure, yet he missed one thing, but to have it would be to take a bite from the forbidden fruit.

Richard's best friend was actually his first cousin, Simone. She and her mother never gave up on him. They would visit him in the boarding school and on two occasions came to spend Christmas with him and when he finally was let out, he didn't go back to his parents, he moved in with them.

They loved him, and Richard loved them back and to a certain degree he began to be infatuated by his first cousin.

She too had red hair but unlike her, had a great sense of humour of a sort to make people happy. That was why it was hard for Richard to meet her. They were of the same age, but very opposite and he often longed for the peace he found with her.

Simone was always helpful and when Richard moved in, she was the first to beg his mother to have Richard checked.

Richard remembered coming home glum and thoroughly distraught by the prognosis. He felt alone as he sat in his room whilst the others whispered around him. Simone walked in and sat next to him and held his hand. Richard looked away, feeling fragile. "What are you thinking?" Richard remembered asking "Your cousin may be crazy? There could be insanity in the family?"

"No." She began "I'm thinking 'my cousin is crazy, there is insanity in the family!'" it made him laugh and with a hug, it seemed that things were going to be well.

Sadly, like everything in his life, Richard was always his own source of woe. He found it hard to manage his emotions for Simone but he couldn't. Eventually he decided to leave the loving bosom of the family and head straight into the open arms of District 3.

Richard was menacingly hedonistic in his approach to being a gang member, with drugs and drink as his fuel for his first few years. This alienated him more from what was left of his family.

Even though Simone was advised to, she never abandoned him and initially pleaded with Richard to leave the gang, or at least stop the drugs. When that failed, she carried on with her life going to university, finding a good job and making a life for herself, yet she didn't turn her back on him. She chose to see beyond the darkness that cloaked him and always kept in touch with him even after she moved away, reducing their contact.

It hurt, but it was also a wakeup call. He wanted her back so he gradually reduced the variety and quantity of drugs he took until he stopped regular use two years ago, only using them maximum three times a year and on special occasions or very dark days. That was enough for her and with the new social media network Richard was able to return into the lives of Simone and the rest of her family.

As he combed his wet hair looking at himself in the mirror, Richard hoped he would have overcome the indecent affections he harboured having not seen her in three years since she got a job in Cologne and that made him nervous. That's why he needed a boost and it was infuriating that it was now an hour late.

No point worrying about punctuality. Richard brushed his teeth and trimmed his stubble. Then came the antiperspirant, and if the fragrance wasn't strong enough, he put on some cologne.

Richard went to his closet to select something smart but casual to put on. A dark blue blazer with a black collar, white t-shirt and a pair of black jeans along with some nice soft leather brown shoes would do.

He put on the shirt and saw his chest hair protruded over the collar. He plucked out the offending strands from their follicles using a tweezers till he was satisfied.

As he pulled up his jeans, the doorbell rang. Richard quickly put on his belt and raced to the door. Expecting his delivery, Richard had a disappointed face in preparation to pour scorn on the party concerned only to find his old friend from boarding school, Erik and his girlfriend Jenny, standing there, their smile fading once they noticed the reception they received.

"Are we early?" asked Erik.

"It's you." Richard replied giving his friend a hug. Then he turned to the lady and greeted her with a heavy handshake before he ushered them both in.

Richard played the host laying out some finger food and plying them with alcohol. Richard and Erik stayed with the vodka as Jenny sat bored sipping champagne as the two chums reminisced about old times; this helped to momentarily put Richard's nervousness at bay.

A vibration in his pocket told him he had a call. He looked at the number, it was the mule. Furious, Richard answered the call with a question "Where the fuck are you?" The mule was outside.

Richard excused himself and went to the front door of building. "You are fucking late." He shouted at the young, Mediterranean looking guy who showed his age by confessing that the reason for his delay was due to his father forbidding him to go out till he had done all his homework.

The courier apologised as he handed over a shopping bag containing the seven sachets of cocaine rather than six. The boy told him the seller gave him an extra one free.

Richard took out one of the small packets, opened it before he dipped his little finger into the white powder, and then rubbed the powder on to his gums.

A few seconds later, there was a tingling sensation followed by a buzz. It was confirmation enough of the authenticity of the product. Richard reached into his back pocket and took out €300 "I was going to give you

€250, but it's Christmas isn't it? Not that you guys celebrate it." The boy did not reply, rather he saluted him and walked to his bike before riding away.

Richard returned to the living room announcing "They're here." as he threw three sachets on the coffee table, one falling into the bowl of nuts.

Erik cheered, Jenny seemed uninterested. The men cleared the table before Richard went to his room, opened his dresser drawer and took out a small square mirror.

Back in the Living room, Erik emptied two sachets on to the mirror. Richard divided them into two long lines and challenged Erik as to who could snort the most in one go. With their €50 notes rolled in a tube, they were off. Richard lost by 6cm as Erik finished his line and then helped himself to what was left of Richard's. Erik cheered, celebrating his win; Richard clapped as the drug took effect. Meanwhile Jenny wondered if there was any champagne left having almost exhausted her bottle, she was not amused by the men's antics.

Buoyed by the narcotics, the pair started playing games that tested their strength in a flagrant display of machismo. All the exertion helped bring the effects of the cocaine down to tolerable level and it was enough for them to conclude that they were able to leave for the club now. A taxi was called.

Arriving around eleven, they walked past the queue to the ominous looking bouncer who turned from a grumpy looking hulk to a smiling friendly giant once he set eyes on Richard with whom he was acquainted and after a warm embrace, Richard and the rest were allowed in.

Their tickets were checked and they were led to their table where, waiting for them, was the person Richard longed to see again and in his eyes, she was a picture of loveliness. Her hair was wavy, long and as red as his, but now, she looked elegant and totally sexy as she rose to meet him, jumping bit in excitement as she raced into his arms. Richard realized they were now the same height thanks to her heels "So nice to see you." Simone said, but Richard couldn't reply, he was consumed by the fragrance of her hair.

Richard didn't want to let go, but he had to. Reminding himself they weren't alone, he introduced his friends to her and they all took their place around the table.

Drinks were ordered, and they toasted each other's advancement.

Richard had the opportunity to ask about the rest of the family "Mum asks after you all the time. I saw your mother too last month with your dad… they said hello." Richard's grin sunk. Sensitive to the complexities of his status in his family, Simone thought it was best to change the topic. "You know, I am so excited. He's my favourite DJ. Thank you so much for the tickets. You are so cool!" She then gave him a kiss on the cheek.

The stage was set and the DJ was going to make an entrance any moment, just enough time for another couple of lines. He sent an invitation by text to Erik who was only too happy to come.

Richard and Erik went to the toilet for their fix. Someone came up to them and asked if he could buy a sachet from them. Richard thought he had enough; besides, he needed to remain sane for Simone. He took out one of the last two sachets from the side pocket of his jacket and handed it over to them with the words "It's free, Merry Christmas."

Feeling warm from his selfless expression of the spirit of the season, they walked back into the club where they were met with a thumping beat. The DJ had arrived. Eager not to miss a beat, he raced to the table to request a dance from Simone. She was tipsy and he was hyper. Richard's jumping and erratic dancing made Simone laugh. It prompted him to act the fool further and soon she too joined him in his merry dance.

The strobe lighting and diverse colours gave their movements a rhythmic hue. She stopped jumping, approaching him. She missed him very much and wanted to show it by giving him a hug. Richard saw her coming and stopped bouncing as their eyes met making him wonder what was about to happen.

She held him close, resting her head on his shoulder as he stroked her hair. Richard kissed her on the head. Simone looked up. Again, eye contact, the old feelings he tried to suppress resurfaced, this time, Richard thought, she must feel it too.

It was now or never, to hell with everything. He held her face and kissed her deeply. She didn't protest at first… she sort of liked it. But this was wrong, forbidden for that matter, notwithstanding how mutual the lustful emotions were Simone couldn't go through with it.

Simone stopped kissing him and saw the disappointment in Richard's eyes. "No…" She stated. His heart was falling to pieces and it hurt more than the headache he was getting. She looked away from him and said "I'll be right back… I need to use the toilet."

Richard agonised as he watched her go. He never knew that love could be physically and mentally painful. The headache he tried to ignore seemed to increase dramatically. His leg began to feel weak whilst he felt pins and needles in his arms.

He found it hard to swallow and he tried to go after her but found it difficult to move as she pushed her way through the crowd, tears falling, as the feelings of guilt and nausea welled up from within. It was meant to be a happy reunion, now it was ruined.

There was no queue for the ladies toilet as one usually expects in such a venue. Simone walked into the room and headed straight for the mirror to check her makeup and restore some form of poise to her being. She looked at the mirror and was instantly drawn to the site of red stain that covered the upper part of her lip and the end of her nose. It wasn't lipstick. She touched it, it was blood.

Simone rinsed the stained area to check if it originated from her, it didn't. A scream came from the dance floor. She raced out and found Jenny shaking her hands and jumping, calling for help with Erik who had slumped over the table.

The music stopped, people's curiosity drew them to the centre of the situation, except her, she was not frightened. "Simone…" came the muffled voice, she turned and found Richard behind her, blood dripping from his nose, struggling to remain standing. "Simone." he begged as he fell.

She caught him in time and laid him on the floor. The lights came on and then she noticed he was slipping away 'Richard! RICHARD!" she cried "Stay with me!" She pleaded. She was shaking his head as people began to gather around her and she was becoming more distraught by the moment. "Somebody help me, he's not breathing!" She screamed. With no volunteers, she started giving him mouth to mouth resuscitation. "Stay!" she cried between breaths.

Finally someone came to help press on Richard's chest as she pushed air down his lungs. Richard wasn't responding. As Richard's chest was pressed, his blood sprayed into the air. It was obvious he was fading and was slowly turning cold.

The paramedics were soon on the scene along with the police. They requested space and placed an oxygen mask over his face to try and resuscitate him. They asked if he had taken anything, but she couldn't confirm. They kept trying, and each time the mask was lifted, blood would stream down from Richard's nose.

Simone was horrified when they stopped after ten minutes, they looked up at her and their looks said it all, he was gone. Her shriek could be heard outside the establishment by onlookers who didn't need to guess the outcome.

Outside, a person wearing his tuxedo and loosened tie, who had tried to help Simone with the resuscitation process, was being asked some final questions from the police. He got the usual, a request for his contact details if they had any further questions. The man was told it was unlikely they would be in touch and with a pat on the back from the police officer who said "You are a good man for trying. Not many would. Try not to let it spoil your Christmas." He smiled and replied "Thank you."

The man walked away from the area as the sounds of another scream and another person falling to the ground distracted him. He turned round and found another person being treated by the medics.

He had no time to stop and gape, he had an appointment. He walked on till he was out of site then began to jog to prevent himself getting cold. 10 minutes later, he arrived at the car parked by a closed florist shop.

The occupants saw him coming and stepped out. "Hi, are you Joel?" he asked.

"Yes" Joel confirmed as they shook hands. "And this is Khoi." The man turned to shake Khoi's hand, it was then Khoi noted the stain on his cuffs. "What's that?" Khoi pried.

The man looked at the cuffs of his right hand and callously remarked that it was blood "Must have picked it up whilst helping out the guy."

Khoi's mouth began to water uncontrollably. He was struggling to bear it, but he couldn't. Khoi didn't shake the man's hand, rather, he ran to other side of the car to vomit. Joel rolled his eyes in exasperation. "He's got a phobia for blood or something. Anyway, you got it?"

"Yep." answered the man as he handed over one sachet of cocaine to Joel and explained "It was all I could find on him."

"Cool." Joel replied, the backing track noise of Khoi gagging made it hard to savour the victory. "Here." Joel mumbled as he reached in his pocket, took out €1000 and handed it to the man "Have a good day."

"Thanks." The man said as he took the money from Joel.

As the thief went on his way, passing by Khoi, he felt someone holding him back by the tail of his coat. He turned to find it was Khoi holding onto him with his right hand. Khoi looked strained and was still bent over, but with his left hand stretched, Khoi demanded "The watch please." The man laughed and took out the watch he had stolen from Khoi's pocket and handed it over to him. "Now get out of here." The man did as he was told and Khoi got up and approached Joel who didn't comprehend what had just happened until Khoi handed him the watch.

Joel checked his wrist and sure enough, he wasn't wearing one anymore. He was amazed at having been hoodwinked. "Wow, thanks." Joel said. Then he advised "You know you got to see someone about this reaction you got to blood, it's embarrassing." Khoi did not respond as he walked to the passenger's side of the car where he sat.

"Did you get the text from Dad?" Joel asked as he started the engine.

"Oh yes, he's back on the 24th isn't he?" Khoi acknowledged.

"Yeah, that's just what I need right now. More pressure. We have to sort this out quickly and stealthily." Joel ordered as he turned on the radio set it to the local radio station and drove.

On their way to Khoi's hotel, the classic 80's music stopped as the news at midnight came on the air. "There is great concern as four more people have now died having taken what the police are suspecting to be a bad batch of cocaine. This brings the total number of fatalities to eight and the number is set to rise to eleven as others are in hospital now in a critical condition."

"There are believed to be several unconfirmed victims in the night club called "Whyte." It is in the south of the city and paramedics and police officers present claim it is suspected that several revellers may have succumbed to the effects of the contaminated cocaine. Frank Muller reports."

"The paramedics and police are incredibly concerned. With 8 people confirmed dead and more soon to follow, the police are appealing to the public to avoid using cocaine or any drugs for that matter."

"Victims have been suffering from nausea, abdominal pains, loss of balance and extreme haemorrhaging and internal bleeding. The warning from the police tonight is that if anyone has any cocaine with them don't use it, get rid of it or risk being another statistic. Whilst the police investigate, one thing is certain; four more families will be grieving this Christmas." Joel had heard enough and turned off the radio while he looked around sorting out a place to park the car.

Once the car was stationary, he turned to Khoi who wondered why they weren't moving. He asked "What the hell did you put in that stuff?"

"Warfarin." Joel didn't know what that it was. "It's blood thinner.' Khoi expanded, "you can find it in rat poison." Feeling smug, Khoi conceded "Yes, I know, it's a messy way to go, but it's rather effective don't you think?" Joel couldn't hide his disgust as he exclaimed "at least eight innocent people are dead man!" Khoi was indifferent to the plight and defined the slain innocent as "simple collateral damage."

Joel asked if Khoi cared to expand and so he did. "I think you fail to see the big picture." Khoi began, "Consider the events of this evening as a socially beneficial service. After this, people will be reluctant to buy cocaine from anyone for many months and many more will be deterred from trying the stuff. Subsequently, District 3 will find their profits disappearing and will spiral into terminal decline as the market for their key commodity falls."

"Oh sure, people will eventually return to the substance, but by then, it will be too late for District 3 since they won't be able to afford it, and besides, someone else would muscle in and they would have a fight on their hands."

"As we progress with our schedule, it is safe to say, if all goes according to plan, they will be decimated and we would exceed our goals by not only achieving our initial aims, that is justice for Stefan, but also reduce the number of addicts in the city in the long run. The police will consider it a contaminated batch of drugs which will be hard to trace, and even if they do, it all came from District 3. Everybody wins." Khoi concluded his explanation which is provided in a manner of primary school teacher explaining how photosynthesis worked to a receptive audience.

Though receptive, a feeling of fear washed over Joel as he sat there, mouth open in awe toward Khoi's mode of thinking. Seeing his reaction, sinisterly Khoi added "Don't get all sentimental, we're making an omelette after all, some eggs have to be cracked. Now, can you drive me back to the hotel? All that vomiting has put me off going out tonight."

Unwilling to be in his company, Joel drove to the hotel first, and just like Khoi, he too didn't feel like enjoying the Friday night, so he cancelled his plans and went home. Joel wasn't worried that people got killed, he just didn't see why the innocent should die and the fact that Khoi was comfortable with it was even more disturbing.

Joel got home, turned on the television and went to get himself a beer. He needed distraction and decided to watch a cartoon. Yes, he laughed a little, but after hours of slapstick and several bottles of beer, he still couldn't sleep, and he couldn't help but be drawn to find out more.

Joel turned to the news channel. The number of dead from their acts of calculated homicide had now risen to 13. Joel shut his eyes as the pictures of the confirmed dead were shown on television. He couldn't look at their faces and with numbers rising by the hour, Joel ended up sprawled on the sofa, mesmerised by the news channel till the sun began to rise.

Khoi didn't have such issues with sleep that evening. Once again, he resorted to his old friend, diazepam which kept the torment of his conscience away.

# 11

*20 December 2010*

Marcel used the map provided on his phone to find his way to the theatre. He was seething at the fact that he had been ordered to hang around the arrogant bitch he knew as Jelena whilst the others did the organising. A sneaking suspicion made him consider if it was just a ploy to keep him out of the way.

After thirteen minutes of searching, Marcel arrived at the theatre, feeling as uncomfortable as ever. He walked into the foyer, wondering why Jelena couldn't just take a taxi. He looked around for her but before he could give the room a proper scan, he heard her call out his name.

Marcel turned and there she was, elegant as ever in an emerald green dress and clutch bag.

As she approached him, Marcel asked "Are you ready to go?"

"Not really. I wanted to ask if you would like to watch the play with me." Jelena opened her bag and produced two tickets "I came here earlier today for the backstage tour and rehearsals, it promises to be good." Marcel didn't look convinced so she added "I spoke to Khoi already, he said you can stay."

Marcel began to loath Khoi and his new found power, hoping it would all end soon. Jelena saw he still distrusted her "You can check if you like."

"Tsk" was the sound Marcel made as he took one of the tickets and walked towards the entrance so quickly that Jelena had to almost prance after him.

Their seats were in row 35, seats K & L with the L seat just one away from the aisle. Jelena entered first to take seat 35K. "It's a beautiful theatre and I was happy when I heard they had a tour of the premises, it was so good I came twice." She said. Marcel was not listening. He was just waiting for the show to end before it had even begun, but she didn't shut up. As he took off his leather jacket, Marcel wondered if it was possible to feign sickness just to avoid any more contact with this woman.

Yet, somehow, her elation was infectious as she hammered on about the tour. As he took his seat, a man took a place on seat M next to Marcel. Marcel soon began to wonder what all the excitement was about. "The tour was really extensive" Jelena confirmed "You could see the costumes and the props and they are all life like, I couldn't even tell that the daggers were retractable props." she chuckled "You know, the actors are told to ram the prop knives in to their fellow actor's body as hard as possible. The tour guide said she found it near impossible to tell the difference herself. We'll soon find out. I saw the play yesterday and it was great, everything was great." She added as she sat down.

Marcel didn't bother to listen to her. All he could do was check his watch and the time stated on the ticket, hoping that nothing was running late.

The lights dimmed and bang on schedule, the play started. A lonely figure walked on stage and proclaims a victory for the great general Gaius Julius having conquered the Gauls. Others soon joined the stage to signify a crowd that cheered as the skinny, balding, wire faced man who played the all glorious Julius walked out to receive his acclaim in accordance with the script.

As the show progressed, despite his initial misgivings, Marcel actually began to enjoy the play. He had never seen a Shakespearian play being performed live and the actors were doing it justice with their gestures and facial expressions. They were communicating each emotion as the characters that once glorified and exalted Julius as a soldier now plotted and schemed against him as Julius Caesar. Marcel vaguely remembered the plot and knew that they were set to reach the crescendo soon. Regardless, he was captivated and began to enjoy the play whole heartedly.

Act 3 began. Julius had just been warned about going to the senate on a particular day and had chosen to ignore the counsel provided by the heavily made up lady who played the role of the soothsayer.

With one spin, the set changed. On stage were benches like those in a football ground but flanking either side of the set. Seated on them were men dressed in white, the senators. As they filed in, the traitors picked up their prop weapons one after the other before mounting the stage to take their seats on the front row of the bench.

The actor playing Julius strolled on to the stage, arms aloft, with a staff in hand initially to the applause of the senate. Then came a cry from one of the actors, pleading with Julius to spare his brother and allow him to return to Rome, Julius rejected his pleas and right on cue one of the actors rose from the front row of the bench from behind Julius and stabbed him. The actor playing Caesar gave a spiffy performance of someone experiencing the initial shock of dying as he oozed red liquid from his back.

Then came the second blow, after which the six of the actors playing the conspirators rose to their feet and began to stab him ferociously. Then, after the third blow the actor playing the victim screamed "Aaargh! Oh my God! Stop! Stop! Somebody help me!" He attempted to run but was held back by the scruff of the collar by another actor who proceeded to play his part, plunging the dagger into Caesar; regicide for the masses in full display as the victim cried again "Please stop! Aaargh! Fucking hell, somebody help me!" red fluid sprayed on the face of the actor playing Brutus as he stood there waiting to play his part and Caesar carried on screaming and begging for mercy.

Marcel's breath was taken away by the realism of the acting which made the occurrence seem to last much longer than the entire 47 seconds of the scene. The man in front of him was clearly a true fan of Shakespeare as he turned to the lady next to him and said in an English accent, "This isn't right, he doesn't swear."

It was orchestrated pandemonium on stage as the Senate ran around, exiting one by one. Marcel didn't think much of it until he noticed the actor playing Casca touch the tip of his blade and turn as white a sheet before proclaiming to the other actor play Ligarius "Oh Lord, there's been a mistake."

No one noticed, or perhaps they didn't care but they were spell bound by the acting and the screams to the point that the man seated next to Marcel grabbed his hand that had been resting on the arm of the chair in fright. Marcel didn't mind, he was equally amazed by the realism, especially the fake blood tainting the stage floor and darkening the purple worn by Julius on stage.

The highpoint came as the actor playing Julius, weeping, stumbled forward towards his counterpart acting as Brutus, mumbling the words "Help me, help me please... help me" before slumping on him. The actor playing Brutus looked uncomfortable, very uncomfortable, but he had his role to play and as Brutus he rammed the knife into the body of his friend. There was silence in the house as everyone waited for the famous line "Et tu, Bruté?", but it was never heard.

The actor playing Julius on stage, slid to the floor and lay there twitching with Casca being the first to run off the stage screaming the words

"Someone come quick!" The other actors stood around Julius, their hands stained red with the expression of various states of exertion and shock on their faces. The curtain came down marking the end of the act.

This spectacular display of acting dexterity was appreciated by all who witnessed it in the audience. The public, including Marcel, instantly rose to their feet and applauded loudly. Everyone clapped but Jelena, who got up only to put on her coat and pick up Marcel's leather jacket before shouting in his ear "Time to go".

"Go? It's not over yet." Marcel protested.

"You've seen enough, time to go." She said and with the applause still echoing across the hall accompanied by cheers, she scooted her way past the person on the end of the row, straight to the exit. With her gone as well as his jacket, Marcel was obliged to follow.

Back in the lobby, he commented as he approached her to take his coat "That was amazing. I didn't know I would enjoy it so much…"

"I'm glad you liked it." She replied, as she helped him into his coat.

"And the acting in that dying scene, the guy playing Julius was amazing." He added as he wrapped his scarf around his neck.

"Oh he wasn't acting." Jelena said in a cold manner as she pushed the heavy door and walked out into the breeze and softly falling snow. Marcel didn't really perceive her comment, assuming it was one of her cutting declarations. As he joined her for a slow walk in the direction of the station he heard her say, "Do you know why I brought you here?" "I hoped it was to make amends for how you've treated me lately… but something tells me that's not it, is it?" Jelena stopped and winced asking "are you a soothsayer too?" Sarcasm intended "If you are so in tune with my intentions, what else do you know?"

Having had his fill of dramatics for one day, Marcel bluntly asked "What do you want?"

He stood in front of her, staring straight into her eyes, hoping she would show some fear or any form of weakness, but it wasn't forthcoming. "I wanted to speak to you about tonight." She began. "I think you have to consider your options very carefully."

Marcel felt deceived and in this state of outrage queried "Is that why you brought me here? To watch a play about one man betraying his friend? Is this part of your sick twisted mind game? They warned me about you." Marcel's fury intensified as Jelena stood there, a grin on her face. The wind blew strongly as two police cars sped by causing her coat to flutter in the gust. He waited for an answer and wasn't going to leave till he got one. Jelena felt a chill and took out her gloves, putting them on as she revealed "I brought you here because I like you. I brought you here in solidarity because I have been in the same situation you are about to face in five hours. I wanted you to watch this play to show you that even Brutus had a choice as do you... You don't have to go through with tonight's plan."

Marcel stood there, the force of Jelena's words had nearly broken him and he hated her more for that as he began to heave. Nothing made sense anymore, he could hear his heart beating so loudly that it drowned the noise of the approaching vehicles whizzing by. He was being confronted by the magnitude of his uncompromising stance. He shivered as Jelena's steely eyes deepened his troubled mind. Marcel pointed at her "You can't stop me... It must happen!" his voice volleyed the doubts in his resolve. "No." she refuted in an equally louder tone "It doesn't. You have a choice!" Marcel wasn't prepared for this. His resolve was being tested and he was found wanting. It didn't help when Jelena stated the obvious, the solution he desperately longed for "You can back out."

This triggered Marcel's childish need to defend himself swinging his hand up and down as he snapped "Fuck you, you are nothing but an overpriced whore and fuck Khoi, you and that manipulative puppet master can go to blazes! Who the hell do you think you are telling me what I can and can't do? I can take Siegfried and I can take you out, you bitch." Marcel turned and began to walk away, turning once to check if he was being followed by Jelena. He didn't hate her anymore, now he feared her.

Once out of range, Marcel began to run and continued running till he reached the station. He found a small corner by the bicycle shed where he went to vent. Resting on a wall, he wailed and wallowed in mental agony, his soul was being antagonised. Marcel had already made his choice and he wasn't one for turning regardless of the consequences. He had fallen into a trap of his own making and with less than four hours to go, he wondered if it was too late.

Jelena now stood alone. She had done her part and had nearly reached her compassion quota which she had set to prevent herself from getting too emotionally involved in her work. The quota was two hours a week, two hours when she can reflect and either lament on the past or make a difference where possible. Now, even she wondered if she had been effective or had she squandered this window of humanity? Only time would tell. But for now, she had to report back to base.

As an ambulance approached, Jelena reached for her phone to call Khoi who was in the office doing the figures for the month. For Khoi, it was to be a month where they just barely made a profit since everyone was preoccupied with other matters. The fitness centre was still going strong though and he was getting prepared for the New Year's guilt membership rush.

Whilst providing a projection for the following month, Khoi's mobile rang, it was Jelena. As he answered, there was a howling sound of sirens blazing through. It soon subsided and Jelena spoke immediately. "I tried. I may have worn him down, but he didn't budge. It is up to you now."

Khoi rubbed his brow, infuriated by the failure, yet calm as he sniggered at the irony. He remembered how just a few weeks ago he was being told not to play. "People in glass houses shouldn't throw stones." He said out loud. Jelena was confused by the seemingly random statement. Realising what he said he quickly replied "Thanks for trying. I will see him tonight. You are coming out to the bar right?"

"Yeah. See you there." Jelena confirmed.

"Oh, you said you had an experiment to perform… are you still not going to tell me?"

"No." She replied.

"OK… was it successful?" Khoi chose to accept a less detailed response. Jelena looked as the ambulance parked in front of the theatre as the paramedics ran in with a stretcher and their kit whilst the police entered and spoke into their communication devices. Jelena was satisfied enough to conclude "A resounding yes. It literally got the audience on their feet." hanging up in the middle of a chuckle.

With the call ended, Khoi was left to contemplate if he should increase the pressure on Marcel to back down. He decided it could potentially be a counter-productive affair and he had a lot to do before tonight's main event and thus considered it best to focus all his efforts on the figures.

Khoi worked for hours trying to finalise the accounting till he heard a knock on the door of his room. He got up to look through the peep hole and found Mikel, Paul and Marcel waiting on the other side. A brisk look at the time showed they were actually a couple of minutes late.

Khoi immediately opened the door and confessed. "Hey guys, so sorry, I haven't had the time to get ready. Give me one minute and I'll meet you in the lobby." Mikel said it wasn't a problem but before they left, Khoi called on Marcel and on close inspection, Khoi could see the strain on Marcel's face. "You don't look too well." Khoi said to Marcel.

"I told him that." Mikel echoed.

"Perhaps you can sit this one out?" Khoi suggested.

Marcel knew his game plan and replied "Fuck you."

As Marcel walked away to the lift, the others were taken aback by Marcel's response as well as Khoi's restraint. Noting this, Khoi confirmed "It's cool guys. Give me five minutes, tops, OK?" The pair left to join Marcel in the lobby. Khoi went around looking for his gloves and wallet constantly being distracted by his aims to prevent Marcel from taking part in the evening's event.

Khoi could have ordered him to stay behind, but what good would that do? If Marcel was dead certain on participating, perhaps he would be forced to relent when he finally confronts the matter. The wallet was found under the pile of excel sheets he had printed out, as for the gloves, he couldn't be bothered to seek them anymore. Time was against him.

Khoi met with the others in the lobby and on the way sent a text to Paul "Please sit in the front, I want to sit with Marcel." When he arrived, he got a wink from Paul, who acknowledged he got the message.

At the car park, Paul walked quickly to vehicle standing by the designated seating whilst Mikel opened the door of the Land Rover. Marcel didn't care where he sat. He got in the back with Khoi, instantly choosing to ignore his presence by turning away. Khoi saw his plan crumbling before him.

Accepting defeat, he decided to enquire if all the items required had been purchased, going through the list with those listening. He had to speak loudly however, as the radio was on.

It was during the "news in brief" segment that it was announced there had been an incident at the Volksbühne theatre on Rosa-Luxemburg-Platz where an actor was accidentally killed by his fellow Thespians when the daggers used to portray his slaying in a rendition of Shakespeare's Julius Caesar turned out to be real. It had resulted in the actor playing the part of the Roman emperor sustaining fatal stab wounds to his back and front in the full view of the unwitting audience who thought it was all part of the play.

As eye witnesses gave their testimony Khoi ear's perked up. Khoi then noticed Marcel equally sit up listening in horror. Once the segment was over, Marcel could only turn to Khoi asking "What is wrong with that bitch? Did you know anything about this?"

"No… Oh my God!" Khoi proclaimed

"What's going on?" Mikel asked intent on finding out what so appalled them.

"Nothing… just mind your own business!" Marcel snapped

"What the hell is wrong with you man? You've been a grouch all day!" Mikel observed.

Marcel's response was impolite "Just shut the fuck up and drive."

"That's it… I am going to pull over and kick your ass…" Mikel threatened

"I'd like to see that!" Marcel challenged

"HEY, STOP!" Khoi proceeded to quash this unrest "No one is going to kick anyone's ass till the job is done ok?"

There was an uneasy silence in the car. Paul felt lost, yet was not curious as to the source of the anger. Marcel returned to listening to the music whilst Mikel turned up the volume of the radio. No one wanted to ask him to change the channel, even though they all hated death metal, so they bore it till they reached their destination.

They arrived in the Marzahn-Hellersdorf district and not a moment too soon Paul thought, considering the sense of ever increasing tension. As they stepped out Khoi gave the necessary instructions "Marcel and I will go up first. You guys park the car nearby and stay out of sight till we leave."

"Yes Boss." Mikel's accidental slip forced Khoi to give him a discerning expression which prompted an instant retraction "Sorry."

"Let's go." Khoi ordered with Marcel leading the way.

Ralph was bored. He had been on guard duty for the last twelve hours. With his captive bound to a chair and his mouth sealed, he had no one to talk to and he had covered every level of the game on his phone, yet he had an additional eight hours.

There was a knock on the door, Ralph reached for his pistol and made his way to the door, calling out "Who is it?"

The recognisable voice replied "It's me." Ralph unlocked the door.

Khoi and Marcel greeted him and when he asked how things were going, he wasn't too shy to confess that he was being driven to distraction with having nothing to do. "Then it's your lucky day. I have come to take you out for dinner and Marcel will relieve you." Ralph didn't ask twice. He raced to get his coat and gloves and was out the door before Khoi could give further details.

With the first hurdle crossed, Khoi wished Marcel luck before he shut the door behind him. Prior to taking another step, Khoi took out his mobile and sent Marcel a text which read "If you have any doubts, if you are uncomfortable, if you just don't want to do it, you leave." Khoi hoped and prayed that Marcel would follow his instructions. Ralph had already made it halfway down the stairs of the building causing Khoi to chase after him.

Alone in the room with the blindfolded and gagged man tied to the chair and his head slumped forward, Marcel spoke. "Hey Ziggy. It's me." Marcel walked up and knelt before him lifting the blindfold. He was met by a pair of eyes overflowing with dejection. Marcel couldn't help it, he began to sob.

Marcel ungagged Siegfried and asked him "how are you?"

Siegfried could only ask in return "why did you remove my gag?"

"I know you won't scream." Marcel replied. Marcel wanted to untie him as well, but he couldn't.

Siegfried was no fool, and his voice showed no sign of fear as he asked "So... It's tonight then?" Marcel didn't reply and Siegfried continued. "I'm glad it's you." Marcel could hardly find the words to convey his feelings as he choked. "May I ask you a question?" Siegfried begged.

"Anything." Marcel offered.

"Why am I here?" Siegfried put to him bluntly

Marcel began to feel disgusted by what he considered lies "Don't play stupid" He snapped "You know what you did."

"No I don't. I don't know why I am here. You have to believe me." There was a knock on the door. "One minute." Marcel whispered as he replaced the blindfold and reinserted the gag before he let the others in.

Paul and Mikel entered and went straight to the kitchen to prepare for their task. This gave Marcel time to steal a few more seconds with his friend and exchange a few words before the order of the day came to a head.

As Marcel, Mikel and Paul went about their work Khoi was on his way to his rendezvous with Jelena at the bar on Veteranenstrasse in Mitte. His conversation with Ralph turned out shorter than he thought. Ralph wasn't one for talking, but he did enjoy his food, ordering two of each course.

Though unable to speak freely with Ralph, Khoi was able to connect with him when he asked about his family. It was then Khoi had the great idea of telling Ralph to take the rest of the month off and visit his family in Konstanz provided he returned before the New Year. Ralph didn't even finish his meal before thanking him and walked out into the snowy evening to prepare for his holiday.

With things, hopefully going to plan, Khoi carried on with his day, returning to the office, then the hotel to get changed for his evening drinks with the team.

Khoi got to the bar seven minutes late, he asked where their reserved table was and was informed that one of the expected guests had already arrived. He guessed who it was as he was led to the private table.

Jelena was there pouring champagne into her flute before returning the bottle into the bucket of ice provided. Upon noticing him, she got up and when he reached her, kissed Khoi on the lips to welcome him and instantly perceived his mood. "So, did someone have a bad day?" Khoi sat down next to her and a look of disappointment was slapped across his face. "Is there something on your mind?"

"What did you do today?" Khoi asked

"I went to watch a play with Marcel, and then I had a meeting with Robert to keep him company whilst he grieved for his loss. FYI, he's really taking it hard. I am going to have to see him again tomorrow." She paused for a drink. "Now, where was I? Oh yes, after that I went shopping for a new dress. Do you like it?" She asked leaning back in her chair to ensure Khoi had a good view of her royal blue dress with embroidery on the bust area.

Despite conceding it was a nice dress, Khoi wasn't ready to believe her "Really?" he began cynically. "I thought you spent the entire time after the play washing the blood off your hands and from under your nicely manicured nails."

"You noticed. The girl did do a good job" she remarked referring to her nails.

This was proving to be annoying. Khoi leaned forward and pointed at Jelena chiding her softly "You said you were taking Marcel to a play, not an execution. Why do you think you can go about killing people willy-nilly? What do you have to say for yourself?"

"Jesus, you sound like my old school teacher. Can't a girl have some fun?" She picked up her glass of champagne and took a sip and flagrantly confessed "I've seen Cleopatra the movie and I saw the play yesterday and it was quite mind-numbing. I just thought that, since I was going to see it again, it might as well have a different ending..."

"So you orchestrated one for yourself?" Khoi interrupted.

"I couldn't exactly contact the writer asking him to change some parts could I? Shakespeare's been dead for four hundred years." She stated as she placed her glass down on the table.

"And I bet, being a daytime vampire like yourself, you had a hand in the great man's demise as well." Khoi sarcasm made her laugh.

"Oh Khoi," she called "you are so funny. Didn't your mother tell you never to ask a woman her age?"

Ignoring the short lesson in etiquette, Khoi continued to express his disappointment "Don't you ever consider the consequences of your actions? That man could have had a wife and a child."

"Children, he had five and no wife, more like three different mothers of his kids." She corrected.

"I guess you found this out as part of your job?" He enquired

"No, this was done outside office hours, so it falls more into the hobby category. Besides, you have more pressing issues to worry about."

"Like what?" he asked, Jelena directed him with her eyes. Khoi turned round to find Paul entering the room looking troubled.

Khoi waved to get his attention. Paul arrived and was given a glass. When asked where the others were, he explained that he had waited for Marcel and Mikel in the flat only to be told by phone that Marcel had driven off without him and he wasn't sure where he had went, hence the reason why Paul came by taxi to the bar to see if Marcel was already there.

Khoi instantly began to worry. He reached for his phone when Jelena stopped him, telling him not to make the call "He'll come here. I assure you. Don't fret. At least give him another hour, he has a lot to deal with."

Khoi took on her wise counsel and tried to relax by offering Paul some more champagne before asking "How did it go?"

"According to plan… It was surprisingly easy to be honest." Paul replied as he took a sip and proceeded to check the menu for something to eat.

Paul had a plate of chicken and vegetables and joined Jelena and Khoi in a discussion about the European Union and its recent expansion. This jogged Jelena's memory. She confirmed that she had found a preferred marksman, whom she referred to as a "tailor" from Serbia who came highly recommended. Jelena provided Paul with the details required and underlined his arrival date. "Make sure you are on time, he hates lateness." She stressed.

As Paul digested the information from Jelena, Mikel appeared, two hours later, looking furious. "I am going to kill Marcel!" were the first words from his mouth as he sat down with his coat still on, shivering. "Oh my, you look cold." Jelena observed and instantly ordered a cup of tea for him.

Khoi asked what had happened. "I don't know, I was tying up the boat, turned round and he was gone with the car and my wallet!" the tea arrived. Mikel took off his gloves and held the cup. "Bloody hell it's cold out there."

"How did you get here?" Khoi inquired

"I had to walk from the park to the station and caught a train. All my money was in the wallet, I had to keep looking over my shoulder! I can't believe this. What the hell is wrong with him?"

There was an uncomfortable silence between Jelena and Khoi who hoped Mikel wouldn't press the topic any further. Lucky for them, they didn't need too as Paul suggested "I think you can ask him yourself."

Having entered the establishment, Marcel had been directed to their sitting area. Aware of his guilt, he walked up to them slowly. Khoi could see him forcing a happy face. Marcel could see all eyes were on him and he wanted to run back, but it was too late.

As Marcel drew closer, hoping to strike a note of reconciliation, Mikel was in the mood for revenge and once Marcel got to the table, he got up and before Marcel could apologise for his behaviour, landed a punch flat on Marcel's nose so quickly that it was only observed by a few people around. Paul, Khoi and Jelena did see it and what a blow it was. Marcel covered his nose with both hands and staggered back in a slight daze. "That's for leaving me behind you dick." Mikel calmly said as he sat back down. Paul scolded Mikel "What did you do that for? Couldn't you take it outside?"

Jelena went to Marcel's aid, sat him down, urging him to uncover his nose. "Let's have a look." Marcel unveiled his sniffer prompting Jelena to remark "Oh dear you are bleeding. Pass me that tissue." Paul did as he was told and then went about collecting some ice cubes from the wine chiller, wrapping them in a napkin, offering it to Marcel to put it over his nose.

Mikel was enjoying his tea as though nothing had happened, keeping up appearances even though his knuckles stung. Jelena placed the ice over Marcel's nose but the bleeding wasn't stemmed. Turning to Khoi she asked "could you go and get some more tissues?" But Khoi had vanished, undetected by those gathered. Jelena decided to address Khoi's presence, or lack of it, later. She walked Marcel to the toilet to tend to him but when they got to the door of the men's room; he said he could handle it himself.

Accepting his wishes, she returned to the dwindling numbers to find that four shots of tequila had been ordered. She rolled her eyes as she sat and remarked "You guys are amazing." It was then she realised Khoi had evaporated.

Khoi wasn't far away. He had left the bar and turned to a corner street to address his irrational fear of blood. He proceeded to spew, trembling as he walked, the vision of the blood stained napkins used by Marcel haunting him. He couldn't breathe, and though he knew it was stupid to feel this way, he couldn't control it anymore. He vomited again, spitting to clear the taste from his mouth. It may have been -4 outside, but Khoi was sweating profusely. Perhaps distance would be helpful, believing that, Khoi headed back to the hotel.

Khoi wasn't the only one to leave early. Paul, Mikel and Jelena were on their third shot glass of tequila when the waitress came up to the table, asked for Mikel and presented him with the keys to the Land-Rover, passing on the news that Marcel had chosen to leave and would meet them the following day. With ever decreasing numbers, Jelena decided to call it a night. Mikel offered to drive her, but she declined, Paul then insisted to walk her, she accepted.

As they walked, Paul listened attentively as Jelena expressed her anger as to how unprofessional the team seemed to be, particularly Khoi. Jelena saw a change in Paul's decorum when she raised the issue of his departure and wondered the reason.

She took her chances and confronted him "but you know why, don't you?" Paul looked around for a moment, aimlessly trying to avoid eye contact. "Is it serious?"

"Serious? No... it's the blood you see? He's got a hemophobia. All the hankies stained with blood must have freaked him out." From Jelena's concerned expression, he realised he had said too much Paul warned "Please, please don't tell anyone."

"No, I won't. This is serious, he needs to address this or there'll be trouble." she warned "Something must have triggered it."

"It was an experience he had as a kid. Khoi used to play on the landing of their second floor flat right outside the door. He often left his toys behind there even though they warned him not to.

He must have been four or five when it happened. One day he left his toy car outside on the door of the flat again, his brother was running off to school, slipped on the car and rolled down the concrete steps. Khoi heard the noise and rushed out with his mother to find his brother at the bottom of the stairs, bleeding from his head and arm, not moving."

After listening to Paul's story, Jelena understood. "That could put the fear into anyone. He must have been traumatised. Did his brother live?"

"I heard he did. They don't talk anymore, but yeah, he's fine, no permanent damage." Paul substantiated. Curious, Jelena asked if anyone else knew, "No" Paul replied.

"How did you find out?" she asked

"From Stefan, he told me not to tell anyone." Jelena was puzzled and asked why he chose to divulge such information to her "Because you care about him and wouldn't use it against him, not like the rest... they're fuckers."

Jelena was moved "thanks for telling me" she kissed Paul on the cheek as they waited for a bus and as it approached, she reminded Paul to come over to the hotel the following morning as it was time to reel Robert in. The bus didn't take long to arrive and with a hug, they parted, leaving Paul to worry if he had said too much.

## 21 December 2010

Jelena returned to the hotel feeling exhausted. Looking at the time, she was surprised at how late it was even though it felt like she hadn't been out for long at all. She concluded it must because it was the longest night of the year.

With a sigh, she fought off her need for compassion. She didn't want to be alone tonight and wondered if it was brave or foolish to go and see Khoi. She took another look at the time, it was nearly three in the morning and to go see him would eat into the remaining thirty seven minutes of her compassion quota which she needed for later in the day. A text did arrive from Paul to request their meeting time, she replied "Noon, my hotel."

She undressed, cleaned off her makeup and put on her nightgown. It was an item she once thought old fashioned, but now couldn't do without. . Jelena crawled under her blankets and was near sleeping when there was a knock on the door.

Jelena could have ignored it, no one ever saw her if she didn't look her best, but she thought otherwise. Jelena took her flick knife, which lay by her bed, and walked to the door, It was better to be safe than sorry. "Who is it?" She called, but there was no response, just another knock on the door. "Perfect", she proclaimed internally, she had a door without a peephole. There was a knock again. "Who is it?" still no response.

Jelena placed herself by the side of the door in the direction where it opened, reached out and turned the handle, opening it slightly before standing still and silently, knife opened, set for attack. The door was pushed open and she held the knife firmly getting ready for a potential attack. The person walked in and she relaxed having recognised him "Oh, it's you." She proclaimed as Marcel walked in.

Marcel turned round and there he stood. She could recognise the strain and grief plastered on his person. She saw he had been crying and she noticed the gun in his shaky hand pointing at her.

Normally, Jelena would have grabbed hold of the hand holding the gun, twisted the arm and jab a knife into the neck of the holder, but this wasn't the time. Marcel was clearly in despair, but it was still a delicate and potentially dangerous situation. "Oh, I see… so you have come to prove your point. Look at me, Grr I'm a man, I can beat my own chest." Jelena taunted as she pulled back the blade into its holder and dropped it.

Marcel had tears forming in his eyes again. She could hear him breathing from his mouth due to his nasal injury. Jelena took a gamble. "So, if you are prepared, I am ready. Where do you want me?" It was a standoff, one she knew she could win if she wanted to or she could have raced out the door, but this time, she didn't want to. It lasted seven minutes before Marcel faced the barrel to the ground, shut his eyes, took a deep breath and spoke. "I'm sorry... I'm going crazy. Excuse me." Marcel was about to walk out the door when he felt a hand on his arm. He turned round and saw Jelena with a truly concerned look about her. He couldn't help it. He broke down began to weep.

Jelena hugged him before leading him to the bed. She sat him down but he was in such a state of distress that he didn't let go of her, resting his head on her bosom as she sat by him trying to soothe his troubled soul.

He didn't speak, he just wept for an hour and a bit. Eventually Marcel grew tired. Jelena proposed they go to sleep to which he agreed. Side by side on the bed, they slept together and besides the fact that Marcel was unable to let go of her hand, proof of his need for comfort, nothing happened between them.

Having set her alarm for eleven in the morning, Jelena woke with numbness in her fingers. She turned and found Marcel still asleep clutching hold of her right hand. She sat up and took back her hand, shaking it to return some feeling to her pale cold fingers.

Jelena realised that her appointment was looming. She nudged Marcel to wake him. She soon realised that she overestimated the size of the bed and underestimated her strength as Marcel rolled off, landing on the floor hard, flat on his face and his injured nose. "Ouch!" he cried.

"Oh my God, are you alright?" She asked, as Marcel got up and nodded. "Good. I have an appointment, you can stay here if you'd like, but I have to get ready."

"No, I'll leave." Marcel scanned around for his shoes. When he found them, he proceeded to put them on as Jelena got off the bed and went to the closet to select what she was going to wear.

Jelena clearly had no inhibition.

She took off her nightie and stood naked in nothing but her lace panties, revealing her lean yet shapely figure. Marcel finally knew why she was irresistible. Manners however made him avert his eyes and focus on his shoes.

"What are your plans for today?" She asked as she laid out a light blue polo shirt and jeans on the bed. Marcel didn't turn to look at her as he replied "I don't know… I've got nothing till tomorrow… guess I'll go and rest or something."

Satisfied with her selection, she proclaimed "OK, now I shall take a shower. We could meet for a drink if you want? You know I am leaving tomorrow? Would be nice to say goodbye?"

Marcel paused whilst tying his laces and turned to look at her. Their eyes met and Jelena could tell that despite their night together he was still incandescent with rage and based on what he had heard about her as well as what he witnessed the day before, only one question rang through his mind "How can you live with yourself?"

Despite being taken aback by the question, she squinted, then approached him to remove the feather from the pillow in his hair concluding "I guess that's a no to the drinks then?"

"That's not true…" Marcel rebutted as he got up "I would love to have a drink with you, but I want to know you… I want to understand how you make it through the day crossing between the boundaries of debouched, unfeeling, charismatically evil to compassionate, caring and protective good? Because I try, I really do, I hate what I do and I try to find balance and end up failing… So, what's your secret?"

Jelena had never been seen as a role model before, rather, she was deemed a person to fear at all time, yet if this was what being a role model was, she didn't like it. She decided to tell the truth. "I try to live through it day by day and it is not easy. I've had a lot of bad things happen to me when I was growing up and I bet most of you guys did too… but for me, the result was I stopped seeing the good, I stopped feeling for others, and used the demonic and bad as a drug. It was a means of sustenance and I stuck to it. But, and you must agree with me here, when you find people you care for, sometimes you have to bend the rules and try to save them from making the same mistakes as you did."

"I may be the devil, but I don't want people to join me in my own private hell, and if you feel drawn between both paths, I suggest you choose the one that bears fruit and brings true happiness to you and others, even if it is for a brief, fleeting moment. And now I only have 12 minutes left of my compassion quota for this week."

Marcel's hate for Jelena vanished that very second. In his eyes, she was no longer the femme fatale from the Balkans, she was someone he now found a place in his heart and he possibly loved.

"May I hug you? I promise to make it as brief as possible to keep your quota." he asked. She reached out and embraced him. Initially it was cordial but then his grip grew tighter, he really wanted to express how he felt but she had a schedule to keep and after a five seconds she said "I have to have a shower now."

"Oh, yeah" Marcel let go of her and kissed her on the cheek adding, "You aren't the devil."

Marcel then left the room still grappling with the grief of losing his friend yet happy that he made a new one.

Jelena could only spare a second to reflect, she had to get ready in forty-five minutes, definitely not enough time she thought. She left a message at the front desk instructing that anyone asking after her should wait in the lobby.

Jelena was in and out of the shower with just 10 minutes to spare, her agenda was full today. At 2 she had to meet Robert for lunch after which he promised her a surprise. She decided to give most of her focus on her hair as her make up could be applied in transit.

Bang on time, at noon, her phone rang. "Hi, I have a guest right? I'll be right down to meet him." She took a quick look around for what she needed and proceeded to meet Paul. As she approached him, she exclaimed "Count yourself lucky boy, you are one of the very few who have seen me without my makeup and lived to tell about it." She greeted him with a kiss and Paul honestly remarked "You actually look better."

Thanking him for, what she considered a shallow compliment, they made their way to Khoi's hotel room using Paul's car. She applied layers of makeup on to her face completing the transformation within five minutes.

Paul dropped Jelena off two streets from Robert's Penthouse with the words "Be careful."

Jelena walked with the wind blowing in her face. It caused her eyes to water. As well, it made her wonder what the weather was like back home.

Jelena had to stem her homesickness, she was being distracted. She took a quick glance back to see if Paul had gone, but he hadn't left yet. Jelena carried on till he was out of view. At the door of the building, she considered entering using the access code, but decided not to blow her cover.

Jelena pressed the busser to announce her arrival. She entered and felt a bit relieved since it was to be the last time she was going to visit Robert. She got into the lift and waited patiently till she got to the 4$^{th}$ floor.

The door opened and there was Robert with the pain only a great loss could inflict on a person imprinted all over him. His lower lip was quivering and his eyes so red, she questioned if he had slept at all.

This was annoying, very annoying. This was why she hated this. Jelena didn't want to have this on her mind. She hated the horrible sense of having to care for the target, it wasn't right, but she couldn't just leave him standing there. Again, she thought of her quota.

Robert began to sob, causing the weirdest feeling of déjà vu for Jelena, only this time it didn't involve a gun being pointed at her nipples.

Jelena decided to accept that she had to do it. She stepped out of the lift and gave him a hug as he broke down. "There, there…" she said patting and caressing his back

"Tomorrow is his funeral… I can't go. I can't bring myself to go." He sobbed.

"You don't have to go, let's go inside." She suggested.

Once in the flat, Jelena noticed the open bottle of brandy and the nearly empty glass on the coffee table by the sofa. She asked if he had been drinking, he replied "a little."

"No good wasting it then." She added, as she took off her coat and threw it on the chair. She helped herself to the brandy. Robert stood there as she filled the glass half way. She took a sip before giving him the glass as she said "here."

Robert didn't take the glass from her but instead held her hand, holding the tumbler and raising it to his lips to drink. He then kissed her deeply and when he stopped he gazed into her eyes longingly. "What do you want to do?" Jelena asked.

Robert was about to tell her how much he longed to have her in his bed and make passionate love to her. He had, for the first time, wasn't having a fling. He actually started to more than just like her. The fact that she was in his flat for the fifth time and nothing had happened yet was unprecedented for a person like him who always got his way. But now, that would be meaningless. He kissed her again and suggested to order some food and watch a movie.

Jelena was instantly deflated. It was true that she wasn't too interested in the emotional sense of things, but he was hot, super-hot and no red blooded heterosexual woman would ever say no to having sex with him and she was craving for it. So much for self-restraint to keep Khoi happy she thought. Robert was doing a pretty fine job to keep her out of his bedroom.

With her eye on the job Jelena smiled and replied "I have a better idea." She walked to the window to draw the curtains and have a quick look if Paul was around. Though she didn't see Paul standing by the bakery, she was reassured that there was a member of the team watching out for her.

For her plans to work she needed to do what she was told not to do. Jelena drew the curtains to darken the room. "Go and light some candles" she commanded. Robert didn't know what she had in store but he was only too happy to do anything to take his mind off his sorrow. Jelena went to her bag, took out her phone and sent a text as Robert gathered the wax lights.

"Going off line for now, don't worry, I am safe." she wrote to Paul. She then placed her phone on flight mode to prevent any disturbance.

She selected the music she wanted and walked to the docking station to insert her handset. The soft music infiltrated the room. Robert asked who the musician was "Noel Coward. You'll love him. He's funny." The song playing was called "Half Cast Woman." Though it was normally not what he would listen to, Robert did find it had some soothing qualities.

He then watched Jelena make her way to the kitchen, returning with some fruit, vegetables and a bottle of water, assembling them on the coffee table. She went off again; this time returning with a small knife clenched between her teeth, a bottle of vodka and two shot glasses as well as the heavy granite mortar and pestle and placed them on the coffee table as well. She sat on the sofa and patted the space by her side beckoning him to join her. "I noticed you have been drinking a lot and eating very little… let's combine the two shall we?"

Robert sat there and watched Jelena slice into some of the ripe yellow melon. She poured a shot of vodka into the mortar and began to pound away with the pestle, turning the fruit to pulp, forcing out the juice, allowing it to blend with the vodka. Then she served it into two shot glasses. "Cheers" she proclaimed as they both drank. Jelena downed hers but Robert kept it in his mouth for a while to savour the flavour and declared it was wonderful.

Jelena hadn't finished. She went to the kitchen to get a bowl and some water in a jug. She used it to rinse the mortar and emptied the contents into the bowl. From there, she proceeded to create various combinations such as crushing ginger and lime as well as a scotch bonnet pepper and lemon. She continued by mixing strawberry and lime with a pinch of sugar. If it was a vegetable or fruit it was cut, mashed and mixed with vodka and served in a glass.

Robert started to feel better as he knew he was having his recommended amount of vegetables and fruit for the week. Not to mention it was great to have company.

They ordered some Indonesian food which they had delivered. It was accompanied by water this time. Even Jelena was feeling the kick from the booze and decided to cut down her consumption but Robert had been taken by her skills and ordered more of the cocktails.

When dinner was finished, a song came on entitled "Louisa". Feeling the merriment of the alcohol affecting her brain, she got up and started to act out the lyrics, swooning when expected, making faces and mimicking pill taking to such great effect that it caused Robert, who was lying on the sofa, to laugh heartily. Whilst he appreciated her comical skill, her elegance of dancing was brilliant.

When it ended, Robert applauded and called her over. Jelena stood over him and reached out her hand. He kissed it. Jelena knelt before him, their eyes meeting. She was hungry for him and grabbed hold of his face, kissing him passionately.

She wanted him and couldn't hold her feelings back anymore. "Sleep with me." She said as she unbuttoned his shirt. However, she was halted. Robert held her hands at the third button. He stopped kissing her. "I can't. I am way too drunk. I wouldn't give a great performance." He replied. Jelena wanted to tell him it didn't matter, but it would make her sound desperate. It was one thing to be desperate, but it was another to show that you are. Robert sat up, kissed her on the lips and proposed "I promised you dinner tomorrow. Let's do it tomorrow. I'll cook dinner and we can have a romantic night in." Jelena let her guard slip "What if there isn't a tomorrow?" She asked with another kiss. With a reassuring grin Robert said "There's always a tomorrow."

Jelena dug deep into her sense of duty to prevent the rejection taking over because she knew herself. If she did let that happen, it would lead to anger and his handsome looks may be no more. "Want to cuddle?" he offered. Accepting that it was better than nothing, she lay next to him in his arms as she kissed him on the head.

After an hour, Robert fell asleep. Jelena left his grasp and accepted that there was little more she could do tonight. She sent a text to Paul to inform him that she was set to leave.

Now prepared, she nudged him. Robert stirred to find her with her coat on, ready to go. "Where are you going?" he asked. "Out, I need to make it to the shop to buy some gifts and a dress for tomorrow." She replied.

Feeling uneasy with her response Robert checked "You're not mad at me are you?"

"No, not at all." She lied. "It just makes it a whole lot more special. Besides, you need your sleep. I'll be here at 6pm tomorrow." Jelena leaned forward to kiss him again and walked slowly out of the door, a bit furious at herself for being so horny.

Jelena entered the lift heading down and remembered she had been followed. She decided to exit from the back door to avoid detection from the man across the road. Jelena returned to the drop off point and entered the car driven by Paul. Not willing to speak, Jelena greeted him and inserted her headphones into her ears, connected it to her iPhone and pretended to turn on the music. Paul got the hint.

They were on their way to the Dahlem gym for a debriefing when two minutes into the journey Paul's mobile rang. He checked who was calling, it was Joel. Paul considered his options. He took a glance to check on the passenger in the back. Jelena seemed preoccupied as she bopped her head presumable to what she was listening to.

Paul chose to take the call and inserted blue tooth headset before answering. Paul had presumed, wrongly, that Jelena couldn't overhear his side of the conversation. She knew it was Joel. After the pleasantries, Paul and Joel conversed about a folder "Folder? Yeah, I gave it to Khoi. It's in his office... I'll pick it up after Christmas." Evidently, it was perceived that Joel wasn't happy with the response as Paul appeared to try to appease him "OK, OK, I'll try and get my hands on it tomorrow, dependent on my schedule." The call ended with Paul taking off his headset, exasperated and muttering beneath his breath "Dick head."

As they went through the heart of the city, Jelena asked "Do you mind dropping me off at my hotel? I need to take a shower. I'll meet you at the restaurant. Please tell Khoi all is set for tomorrow." Paul did as she requested and dropped her off at the front of the building.

Khoi was seated in the meeting room with Mikel and Marcel. The latter of the two spending his time observing Khoi who fiddled with his phone, tapped on the table and was exhibiting a clear sign of nervousness. They knew why, Paul had stated he was going to be late without providing a reason and it was driving Khoi to distraction. Though concerned, the others kept it well hid.

Thirty two minutes later than expected, Paul strolled in with a smile on his face. He announced that Jelena's expedition had been successful and the plans can go ahead tomorrow. He also relayed Jelena's message to Khoi when he asked for her whereabouts. "She didn't think it necessary to come?" Khoi snapped in a reaction the others did not expect, not that he cared. He decided to focus his attention on the plans for the following day.

When the meeting was over and the others made their way out to dinner, Khoi took the opportunity to send a message to Jelena asking where she was. "In your office." was her response. It carried on with the words "I can meet you at the restaurant when I am done?"

Khoi broke into a sweat, wondering if it were a case of paranoia or genuine concern. There was no time to answer that question. Khoi left the others vowing he would join them shortly as he ran out of the building to his car before driving off to the other side of town where his office was situated.

Khoi walked toward the building via the usual side entrance. At nearly five in the evening close to Christmas, all the staff would be home by now since the finishing time was four today. However, he saw from the outside that the lights were on.

Khoi opened the door of the office and walked in to the sound of humming. He followed the sound past his office where the door was opened to reveal that his computer was on. He wasn't interested in investigating that though, rather, he carried on trailing the noise to the end of the office to the photocopy room.

Khoi opened the door and there she was putting sheets on the screen, placing down the lid before pressing the button. As the light slithered across the frame, she looked up at him and continued on her progress.

Inquisitively, he asked "What are you doing here?" As Jelena continued with her scanning, she stated "Not one to pry, because it's not my position nor am I being paid to do so, but I wondered if you ever took the time to review these?" Khoi didn't reply, he was still wondering why Jelena was there using the photocopier in a beautiful floral dress more suited for summer. The sight of her glossed lips and wavy brown hair made his heart race and his rage climb high on a wave of paranoia. He was too mad to reply.

Accepting his silence as a no, Jelena added "Well, if I were you, I would put my hang ups aside and take a detailed look at them. You might be in for a surprise. I certainly was."

Khoi finally decided to ask "What the hell are you doing here?"

Jelena finished off the last page and returned it to the folder as she answered "Joel was quite anxious that you still had this document and wanted it back urgently. That got me suspicious... kind of how you are right now." Jelena walked out of the room to Khoi's office, Khoi followed her.

She sat on his chair and took the USB stick from the desk. She inserted it into the dock of the computer and proceeded to do as she pleased right in front of Khoi.

When she was finished, she removed the USB stick, returned the document where she found it and locked it up. She then took out the key and walked up to Khoi handing it over to him along with the USB stick. "I have scanned them all and they are on here and have been emailed to you as well. Read it in your free time."

As he took the items from her, Jelena could feel his pulse vibrating in the room, his eyes fired up as he placed the items into the pocket of his coat and said "I am angry with you..."

"For breaking into your office? You'll thank me later." She interjected.

Her response infuriated him "Cut the crap!" he roared. Jelena's grin was goading him "What the hell happened today?" He asked. "Exactly what you paid me to do." She replied.

The intensity of her gaze didn't break him, instead led to him confronting her "You are lying!"

"Oh, you want to know if I slept with him." Jelena could smell his insecurity and thought she may enjoy capitalising on it "What do you think? Were you watching me? Would you believe me if I told you I didn't?"

"If you didn't, why did you draw the curtains?" he challenged

"Oh ho, so you were following me?" she drew closer to him, standing up to his face "So you were wondering what was going on... What were you thinking? Did it drive you crazy considering what we were up to? Wondering if I was making his final hours happy... did it drive you crazy?"

As she reached to touch his face, Khoi grabbed hold of her wrist, firmly squeezing it. It hurt but she didn't show it. Khoi, on the other hand, was tense and breathing heavily. He was a bomb set to explode and it didn't help that she kept her smirk "Could you bear the thought of me with him?" teased Jelena.

Then she reached to touch his chest, he trembled "So, you are curious." Her hand slowly creeping down to his member, touching it and raising an eye brow saying "Gay boy has a hard on. Did I convert you, or am I an exception?" Khoi loosened his grip on her hand "Tell me." She ordered "Tell me." She held his head and kissed him deeply.

Khoi wished he could escape but like a moth from the flame but he froze as though incapable to decide what to do next. Jelena was in control and she knew it. She unbuckled his belt and reached into his trousers and observed "hmm, you are cut. I like that."

Khoi couldn't help feeling vain over the compliment but it did nothing to expand his comfort levels. His personal space had been well and truly invaded and an army was aiming to conquer.

She turned him around and shunted him to the edge of the desk forcing him to sit. Jelena swiftly sat on his torso area. "You know I am not wearing any underwear" She revealed. Khoi tried to get up, but was shoved right back down, his head hitting the keyboard of his computer.

Her grin vanished, replaced by a fiendish appearance. "Do you want to know what Robert and I got up to?" she said pulling out his belt with a single pull, reaching into his trousers to take out his member. "No... please don't... please" he begged.

"I'm not the Nancy boy with a stiffy... is someone fibbing to himself?" She asked. Khoi accepted that it was going to happen whether he wanted it to or not.

Holding his penis in position, Jelena allowed it to enter her, shutting her eyes temporarily as the sensation reigned all over her. When she opened them, Khoi was afraid; it was as though she had been possessed by a demon as she cried out "Yes!', taking his hand and rubbing it against her breast. "Now you will know!"

She proceeded to ride him. Khoi was initially petrified, lost as to what to do. His concern soon began to dwindle as did his inhibitions. Khoi actually began to enjoy this aggressive form of conjugal encounter and could have derived more pleasure if his head weren't rested on a computer keyboard. He made an attempt to get up and change positions, but it failed.

Jelena used her thigh to tighten her grip on him, pushing him hard on table with the sound of glass breaking as the computer screen tumbled from the table shattering on the floor and the glass cup left there three weeks earlier broke on the table. Her actions forced Khoi back down.

"I stay on top!" She roared at him taking his hands and holding them over his head, pinning him down on the table.

Khoi was terrified, but there was more to come. The glass cup broke when Jelena accidentally pressed on it. Khoi could feel the wrist of his right hand, within the grip of Jelena's left hand, getting wet.

Initially he thought it sweat, but the left wrist remained dry. He wasn't the only one who noticed. In mid flow, Jelena slowed and let go to inspect her left hand and found she had cut the palm and she was bleeding. "Look." She ordered.

Khoi glanced up and found her dripping blood. His mouth began to water as nausea set in. Khoi looked away, hoping to avoid the reality of his phobia, but Jelena had plans for her fluids.

"You must look!" She ordered, but he wasn't forthcoming. She began to cackle, Khoi could see her about to touch his face. He shut his eyes tightly as he felt Jelena smear her blood on the side of his cheek.

Regardless of the fact that Khoi still managed to keep his member up, he was shivering and sweating in fear. Jelena could not stand being ignored. Jelena held his nose screaming repeatedly "Look, look!" He refused till there was a change in her voice "please look, please look."

Khoi gave in.

He turned slowly, and squinting, he looked at Jelena who was still pleasing herself sexually, as though her arousal increased with his irrational fear. She placed her bleeding palm over his face, a drop dangled, falling on his chin. He wanted to vomit, but was calmed by Jelena's voice "don't give in... don't give in..." And he didn't. Khoi was hypnotised, he looked up at her, their breathing synchronised as she continued. He felt nothing, not even the blood got to him anymore.

Khoi snapped out of it when Jelena cried out "Oh my God!" as she climaxed. Jelena had finished.

She dismounted him, pulled down her skirt as she caught her breath after her moment of exertion. Khoi just laid there, his now phallus penis dangling to the left over his pants and pulled down trousers, totally immobilised by his ordeal.

Jelena went to her hand bag to take out a paper handkerchief and pressed it on her wound. She put on her coat as she added in a flippant manner "I'll need to take a shower." Then her tone turned assertive as she added "I expect to see you at dinner tonight so go clean yourself up." Now ready to go, she gave her passing shot "By the way, I didn't sleep with him."

Jelena left the building. Khoi didn't see her leave though; he just heard her walk away and the door slamming. Now alone, he began to wonder how things could have escalated this far. He felt used and confused. He got what he wanted but now wished he never craved it.

Khoi slumped on to the floor like well-cooked spaghetti off a fork, surrounded by the wreckage of his computer screen and the items that once decorated his desk, a metaphor of his current position. He didn't know why he stayed on the floor, but couldn't find a reason to get up so on the ground he remained, tears falling and trickling to the end of his nose, till he heard the buzzer for the door.

Khoi didn't want to answer or check who it was. He wished they went away, he wished the whole world could go away. Khoi felt vulnerable, he didn't know how to classify what had occurred, had he been raped? Or did he let it happen? If this was the dish he wanted, he sure didn't want it served in this manner. The buzzer went off again and once again he ignored it.

Then his mobile phone rang. Khoi slowly reached for his handset, which had made it to the floor during the melee and rested just inches from his head, he checked who was calling, it was Paul.

Paul had been outside for a few minutes, and the cold was enough to give him a chill. With the light on, he knew someone was in, but with no response, he assumed it probably wasn't Khoi.

As Paul was about to hang up, the door opened to reveal Khoi, who was looking haggard with puffy eyes which held no feeling or emotion and his cheek stained with streaks of blood. "Khoi?" he called, but rather than responding, Khoi handed him the folder he came for and tried to shut the door. It was clear that something had happened. Paul quickly stopped the door from closing and walked in after Khoi.

Khoi was staggered back through the open office area and straight back to his private office. Once in, Paul looked around to see if he could deduce what had happened from the surrounding outer office, everything looked fine.

Paul then followed Khoi to his office to find him sitting on the floor in the corner, crouched down, arms folded over his knees, head bowed to conceal his face. The sight of the displaced stationery, broken computer screen and cup prompted to Paul to ask, "What the hell happened?" Khoi didn't answer. Perceiving the odour of the room, he noted "Smells like sex in here." Khoi remained unresponsive.

Paul knelt before Khoi and touched his shoulder "Are you alright?" Khoi looked up, his eyes streaming with tears. Unable to think of anything else, he got up and went to the kitchen to fetch a glass of water. "Here, drink this." Khoi didn't speak, but Paul coaxed him insisting he take the glass from him. Irritated, Khoi took it from his hand a flung it across the room, breaking it to pieces.

Paul was startled and Khoi saw it. This wasn't what he wanted. So he took a deep breath and forced a smile. "Hi." Khoi said.

"Hi… how are you?" Paul thought it best to approach this cautiously. "I'm fine." Khoi responded as he slowly rose to his feet. He had to put his mental state behind him for now. "Could you take me to my hotel? I need to quickly get ready for dinner."

Paul wondered if it was reasonable to notify Khoi of the splatter of blood on his chin and marks of it elsewhere on his face and decided against it "sure, let's go."

The trip was surreal from Paul's point of view. Khoi chatted as though there was nothing out of the ordinary about his appearance. They spoke about their forthcoming mission and what they had done to prepare themselves. This faux realism came to an end when they arrived at Khoi's hotel and he faced returning to his room.

Khoi's hesitation in leaving the car stirred Paul's concern. "You want me to come with you?" Khoi couldn't answer, he seemed frail and that answered Paul's question. Paul smiled and drove down to the car park.

He escorted Khoi to his room and when they arrived at the door Khoi seemed to regain his focus, running around, picking out the clothes to wear and changing his over coat. Then he went about finishing off his knitting and placing his creation in his coat pocket. All this took note more than 12 minutes.

Having organised himself, Khoi went to the desk where he had placed the advent calendar. He needed his chocolate. He seemed to relax as he chewed it, relieved as he stated "three more chocolates and it will all be over."

Khoi went to shower whilst Paul turned on the television to distract him from the fact that they were going to be late for their 8pm table. Paul was correct. By the time Khoi was done, they had just 10 minutes left which resulted in them arriving 10 minutes late.

Khoi and Paul entered to find Marcel, Jelena and Mikel at the bar drinking as they waited for their table. Khoi greeted them with a hug and when it came to Jelena, it was a hug and a kiss on the cheek. It was then she stole an opportunity to whisper in his ear "I'm sorry." Khoi looked at her. He didn't know what she was sorry about and assumed she probably didn't know either. Khoi kissed her on the lips quickly replying "Me too."

Realising they were being watched he turned to Paul and asked for his preferred drink and he went to order it. As he placed his order for whiskey sour and his glass of red wine, Khoi found it remarkable that with her two words, he forgave her. It was enough to confirm to him that he was indeed in love with the scary woman.

Whilst Khoi was busy, Paul took note of her bound left hand and asked what had happened to her. Jelena giggled. She gave a fleeting look at Khoi, and returned to their conversation. "You need not worry. It's nothing" she assured him, her initial action was enough to make Paul wary since he had noticed who she looked at.

At Dinner, Khoi ensured he sat away from Jelena and kept Paul well away from her as well. He may have forgiven her, but his trust needed to be rebuilt from scratch. For now, despite it happening just over two hours before, it was history. The dinner was for Jelena, to bid her bon voyage and to thank her.

Each person appeared to have their own reasons to thank her. Marcel for her compassion, Paul for being a confidant, Mikel for bringing back old memories and Khoi who was grateful for having simply met her.

Khoi watched silently as they all surrendered to Jelena's charm, allowing her to take all the attention, hanging on her every word even though she used the opportunity to tease each of them whilst slipping in elements of the truth.

Over their main course, Jelena decided to give each person their animal alter ego. Jelena started with Mikel, branding him a naughty fox, cunning and playful. And then she told him that he would be a fool to let a treasure like Brigette slip through his fingers.

With Marcel, Jelena likened him to a turtle, hard exterior, able to take the strain and role with the punches, but inside is a soft tender creature.

Paul in her eyes was an American pit-bull terrier. A fighter, dangerous when provoked, yet loyal to a fault and caring unconditionally.

Finally, and with great anticipation from the rest of the team, it was Khoi's turn "What about me?" he asked. Jelena paused for thought and replied "I don't know… What do you guys think?" They seemed to observe him and the first to come up with a suggestion was Mikel .He said Khoi was most like the owl. Marcel branded him a scorpion and Paul saw him as a shark.

When asked to elaborate, Paul explained with conviction "You're a shark because in your element. You are dangerous, swimming in the water, top of the food chain, once out of it, on a deck of a boat, you wiggle and die."

The analogy was enough to cause great contemplation by everyone who eventually agreed with Paul's view and though he smiled and brushed it off, it did hurt to be branded a cold blooded killer. Paul's razor tongue cut deep. An uncomfortable hush settled around the table. Paul was unflinching, one would believe he deliberately said it to provoke a reaction, but Khoi wasn't falling for it, he continued eating his pork belly.

Khoi was just chewing a bit of crackling when Jelena stopped for a moment to reach for her bag and took out her phone. "Ah" she exclaimed. With all eyes on her, she turned round to face the door of the restaurant and waved. The others looked at the direction to which she gestured "Is that Daniel?" Mikel asked.

"Yeah," Jelena rose to her feet and tapped the side of her lips "I have to go."

Marcel was surprised and just had to double check "With Daniel? Are you sure?"

"I am so sorry boy. I need his help getting Joel's Christmas gift. I did enjoy our moment together but I have something urgent to attend to." Jelena added.

Despite suggesting Daniel join them and pleading she stay longer, Marcel, having accepted that she was determined to leave, gave her a hug and gentle kiss and with sincerity thanked her.

"Good bye baby brother." She said bending over to kiss Paul on the cheek

"Later big sis" Paul replied. Mikel didn't need words; he got up and gave her a big hug, lifting her off the ground.

Once out of his grip, she walked round to Khoi who was already standing and waiting for her. She strutted towards him as he reached into the pocket of his coat and took out the scarf he had knitted, placing it around her neck. "I was going to give it to you tomorrow." He said, "But you are here now."

Jelena admired the royal blue coloured wool and noticed the little red heart crocheted into the corner of the base. "I love it." She proclaimed, kissing him on the cheek. "I have your gift for you too… but not here." She looked over to Daniel who pointed to his watch. "I've got to go."

Khoi had mixed emotions as Jelena went to meet Daniel. Khoi watched and observed. Jelena and Daniel appeared to be having a short, good humoured chat as Daniel helped Jelena into her coat. Then he seemed to have delivered some good news to her as she flung her arms around him and gave him a peck.

It became clear to Khoi that he wasn't the only one watching this oddity. Mikel remarked "It's amazing isn't it? Someone so elegant and smart cavorting with a bone head. Three weeks ago, they couldn't stand each other, now they are leaving together? Amazing."

Khoi didn't want to be told the obvious as Daniel opened the door for Jelena and they took their exit. Now they were four. Khoi sat back and tried to carry on eating. The food didn't taste so good anymore. Accepting that the evening was well and truly over, everyone took their leave.

Paul was Khoi's designated driver and it was during the ride that he chose to ask a question that nagged him. Whilst they stopped at the traffic lights as they drove up Alexander Strasse, Paul broke his silence and bluntly put it to Khoi "You hurt her didn't you?" Totally taken aback, Khoi could only remark "Sorry?"

Paul soon realised he may have over reacted. It was Khoi after all. "Nothing…" Paul said, driving to Khoi's hotel. There appeared to have been a faux pas based on unfounded suspicions.

Khoi thought it was best not to push the matter and once at the door of the hotel, he bade Paul goodnight and went straight to his room. With the door shut, Khoi was instantly consumed by a terror that he couldn't place.

He locked the door and pushed the desk against it to keep it shut. Khoi's rational side considered whether he was having an anxiety attack, but he didn't want to be over suspicious… how could he be? He had every reason to be afraid.

Khoi knew the source of his apprehension. He had been humiliated and emasculated. Looking at himself in the mirror behind the door, Khoi broke into a sweat, shivering, with a strong feeling of nausea. He couldn't stand the site of himself anymore.

He needed a diversion. Khoi ran to his bedside table for the sleeping pills he had become dependent on and soon realised he had moved the bottle to the bathroom.

Khoi went to the bathroom and found the medication by the sink. He filled a glass with water. Khoi began to tremble so much so that most of the water spilt from the brim of the glass. "Fuck!" Khoi cried out. He needed to calm down. Khoi placed the drinking glass and medicine bottle down and using his left hand, he took hold of his right hand to steady himself, it didn't work.

Khoi resorted to taking deep breaths, but as much as he tried not to, every glimpse of his reflection in the mirror disgusted him, forcing Khoi to ask himself "What's she done to me?"

Khoi felt the need to cry. He realised he had to take control of his emotions, but didn't know how he could escape this mental anguish.

Defeated, Khoi sat on the edge of the bath to avoid the mirror, vigorously running his hands through his hair till loose strands fell to the floor. It took him half an hour to feel marginally steady. Cautiously, Khoi returned to the medication sitting by the sink, for now, he thought, he could at least tolerate his image if it allowed him to get some relief.

Yet again, he only got as far as opening the medicine bottle before the shakes returned and as he poured out a tablet, the entire contents of the container dropped out, missing his hand completely, falling into the sink and rolling down the drain. "No, no, no!" he screamed in horror as he tried to rescue as many of the precious capsules as he could.

Khoi could only salvage three. He couldn't risk it anymore. Khoi popped one straight into his mouth and didn't even bother using water. Khoi felt an instant relief, safe in the knowledge that sleep was on its way. With the pill finally consumed, the two remaining pills were treated like diamonds. He stepped back into the sleeping area, as far away from any drainage system as possible and placed them in the bottle, closing the cap before putting them in the bedside drawer.

Another glance in the mirror placed on the bedside table begged the question as to why the hotel had such an obsession with reflective surfaces and even more pressing why he never noticed them before.

Khoi took the desk mirror and hid it under the bed. With it gone he hoped for peace, but it only made him more conscious of his behaviour. He wondered how he could have been so forlorn. Khoi saw himself as a wretched wreck and he said it to himself over and over that he was a weakling.

All this self-loathing crushed him. Khoi began to acknowledge that he might have had a bad deal when he sold his soul in exchange for respect and he didn't like it anymore. Sadly, all sales were final and now he craved normality so much that he wanted to weep but there wasn't any strength for that.

Perhaps if he spoke to someone, perhaps it could help. Khoi walked back to his room, reached for his phone and sat on the floor, resting his back on the bed. Khoi called Julien. He needed to feel appreciated, but it rang and rang with no one answering but the voice mail. It beeped, it was time to speak. Khoi procrastinated as he tried to suppress the shudder in his voice. "Hey Julien... call me."

That was all Khoi could muster. He curled up on the floor; near convulsing, as the shear force exerted by shame and guilt tormented him till sleep came.

Yet, as he dosed off, he wondered if sleep would be an antidote or if he the little Dutch boy putting his hand in the hole of the dam to hold back the flood of his own self-reproach which he created from lashing at his sanity with gumption. He would have to wait and find out in the morning.

# 12

*22 December 2010*

For those who lived to see it, 6am was a rather horrible affair. A strong gust wind of propelled dropping snowflakes on any object it encountered with force. Should the object be living, it hurt and stung any exposed areas, particularly the eyes. It was in this weather that Jan ventured out walking to work that day for his early shift.

Taking off his coat as he walked through the front door, he hoped to God that he would have a quiet day. The "all hands on deck" situation of the last week following the poisoned batch of drugs situation took the life out him. Yes, Jan was pleased to have helped Wolfgang.

With no one present in the office, Jan began to consider if his wish was coming true after all. He placed his lunch of cold pasta and an apple in the fridge. He found a large number of left over expired food forgotten by those who took flight for their holidays and now the food had begun to smell.

Jan took it upon himself to clean up, disposing of all the offending consumables. Once done, he placed his lunch box in the now empty fridge. Feeling contented, he went to his office, hung his coat and took his seat in front of his computer only to find an envelope there.

It was a white unassuming thing, and it was unsealed. He placed it aside and turned on his computer. As he waited for it to boot up, Jan took the moment to review the contents of the envelope, skimming through the papers inside having to read it once again to ensure he wasn't seeing things.

Once satisfied that his mind wasn't playing tricks on him, Jan calmly picked up the phone and called Kat to confirm what time to pick her up from the airport.

Kat answered in an enthusiastic manner "HEY! JAN! What's up?"

"Not much, what are you up to?" Jan sounded catatonic in comparison.

"Me? Nothing, but Julien is about to go bungee jumping!" She cried and as Julien stood at the ledge she showed her encouragement "Go baby, GO!!!"

"Where are you?" Jan asked out of concern

"In Macau. So how are you?"

"I got the promotion. "Jan responded

"Oh baby I am so happy for you, well done you deserve it… Oh my God he's about to do it" Then she fell silent.

"Hello?" Jan called, "Are you there."

"OH MY GOD! Julien, you are so cool! You are so cool!"

Accepting his news was no match to Julien's antics so Jan conceded defeat. "Maybe I'll call you later."

Replying quickly she said "Bye baby! I think I am going to do it, wish me luck!"

"Good…" And before he could complete his statement, Kat had hung up. Perhaps it was a bad idea to call during her holidays.

Jan decided to focus on his work. Twenty minutes after reading some news an email popped up from Julien with the subject "HEY!" He opened it and there was an attachment which when opened. It was a picture of Kat hanging upside-down from a bungee cord holding a sign which read "Well done Jan". That made his day.

At quarter to seven, at the hotel on the side of town, there was knock on the door waking up Khoi. Believing it was the room next door, he went back to bed, but it was his door. The knock came again much louder. He sat up, his body aching with every movement having slept on the floor. Lurching to the peep hole of the door he saw who was knocking, it was Jelena.

She was an unwelcome visitor, like a crow standing on a wedding cake. His heart raced as he stood still, hoping that, by not making a sound, she would go away. "I know you are there." She said "I came to say I am sorry about yesterday… I didn't mean to do that to you. So I came to say good-bye… and thank you."

She sounded sincere and apologetic, but he had been deceived once, why take the risk again? Then he heard her speak "Take care Khoi." He couldn't take it. There was no time to deliberate. He pushed away the desk and opened the door. She was just three paces away and Khoi called out to her "Wait!" She turned to face him, her luggage in hand. "Why should I believe you? Why should I listen to a word you say?"

"Because I like you…" She replied "I don't understand why… but I do and I understand if you don't believe me…"

Khoi had heard enough. He let his heart rule his head. He ran up to her and gave her a deep kiss, the pain of the night before was now a thing of the past, right now he wanted her and to hell with his sexuality. Once he let her go, Khoi held her by the hand and led her into the room. This time, no one will be on top, this time, he wasn't going to be submissive, this time, they made love.

Meanwhile, at eight minutes to seven, Robert woke. This was a late start for him after the night before which seemed to confirm that Ulrika might be a sure-banker. Shame he didn't get her into bed, now he had to resort to masturbating.

Once done, he sighed and checked his mobile and found three text messages waiting for him. The first came from Oliver asking if he intended to come to Richard's funeral.

The next was from Tatiana, a liaison of his, who thanked him for the good night and was looking forward to the next evening.

The last was from Oliver again who provided the detail of the church service, just in case he wasn't aware. This was too much for him and replied quickly to the last message "I'm not coming. I've got a date to prepare for."

Robert checked the time. It was 7 in the morning, time for the gym, but first, what to wear. He took a few minutes selecting what to dawn before settling for a great track suit with a hooded top to wear over his t-shirt and shorts. Robert took even longer to choose what he was going to wear for that evening taking half an hour to decide which of his fifty three pairs of shoes would match the baby blue shirt he intended to wear. A colour he selected because it matched his eyes.

Having decided on dark blue leather loafers, Robert packed his bag and exited the building.

Robert did his usual workout, and then did an extra hour and a half of cardio and weights to give the perfect finish to his abs, which he considered his best feature.

Having gone through what he felt was an intense workout; he went to the sauna for an hour before going for a chest and armpit wax. This was followed by a massage and body rub, then a facial, manicure and pedicure.

He got into the health spa at 8 am and had emerged at just after 2pm. It was now time to go shopping. He went to the wine dealers and after tasting over 13 samples of red wine in just under an hour, he settled for a case of "chateauneuf-du-pape 2004" at €45 a bottle.

Next, Robert moved on to his plans for dessert. It was to be chocolate fondant with sweet Muscat wine. This he had no time to make himself, so he resorted to go to his friend who was a pastry chef.

He had to wait a bit as the man finalised the items. Not that he minded because he had a chance to taste a strawberry cheese cake and found it quite enjoyable. After a half hour, he left with the items he came for and the cheese cake as well.

The next thing on his list was to buy the ingredients for dinner. Nothing but the best would do so he took his time to collect the items for his foie gras, goose and beef medallions which he planned to make from scratch himself. This would have been straight forward if he weren't so picky about the goose and its liver. It was quite a relief to the butchers when he made his selection. Sadly the butcher's ordeal was yet to end as Robert turned his attention to the beef.

After hour of gathering his ingredients, Robert finally got home. He walked through the entrance, taking off his shoes by the door and pulling off the hooded top of his jogging suit.

Robert was lamenting to himself on how quickly it got dark as he opened the door to the kitchen, passing under an unseen presence. He checked the time and realised that he had just over two and a half hours to get things ready.

Robert opened the dishwasher and crouched down to take out the crockery he needed. He was overheard remarking "Oh" as his emerged holding a large bright red dildo in hand.

Holding the sex toy appeared to rekindle fond memories. Robert was observed taking out his phone and making a call. "Patricia, how are you today?" Robert proceeded to chat about the depraved night he and the lady shared in such great detail that it would have made any one listening disgusted at the least. "One minute sexy, I got another call coming in." he then pressed a button before declaring "Ulrika, how are you today?"

"I'm fine, and you?" She asked

"Very well. Are you looking forward to this evening?" He said in a manner that made all those who could hear squirm.

"Yes. Want me to bring anything?" She asked.

"No, just your beautiful sexy self." On the other end of the line Jelena cringed.

"One must persist" Jelena said to herself as she replied "OK. Oh don't forget to turn on your extractor, last time I was there, the place smelt of salmon."

"Your wish is my command my lady." Robert acknowledged.

"See you soon." Jelena said as she hung up.

Once the call was over, Khoi turned to Jelena and sighed. "It's in their hands now." Following which they left the lobby of her hotel and progressed to the restaurant where Khoi had booked a private booth.

Robert never did call Patricia back; rather he turned his attention to prepare dinner. He opened a bottle of wine and helped himself to a large glass. After one large gulp, he took a deep breath before clapping his hands to mark the beginning of the food preparation process.

He washed his hands and drew out a knife. He began to prep the vegetables, chopping them fine. Once Robert had finished dicing the onions, he piled them next to the other vegetables. It was time to make the terrine of foie gras. It was quite easy.

The vapours of the onions filled the air causing Robert's eyes to well, flooding his senses. With his runny nose, he approached the cooker and reached to turn on the extractor fan. The unnoticed onlooker anxiously waited to see what Robert was set to do next and pre-emptively acted, but then, Robert chose not to turn on the extractor fan, rather, he left the room. The dispersal had to wait for now since Robert was no longer in the kitchen.

Robert was in the bathroom to rinse out his eyes and clear out the effects of the onions. Once satisfied, he put on a pair of yellow tinted glasses. This was his way of shielding him eyes from the onions.

He returned to the kitchen and was met with a faint pong which filled the air which began to get stronger. Robert wondered where it originated from and opened his fridge to check if his eggs had gone off. It wasn't the fridge. Then the smell vanished as quickly as he detected it, so he carried on.

It was time to make the sauce to go with the goose. Robert turned on hob of the cooker. Still taken by its novelty, he placed his hand on the cooking station, feeling nothing. He placed the frying pan on the stove and drizzled oil into it before adding the vegetables. Whilst the onions and garlic simmered in the pan, he decided to take the advice he was given on the phone and turned on the extractor fan which sat over his cooker.

That was the signal to strike. The unseen party turned from an observer to an assassin as they loosened a valve once again, allowing the gas to escape.

Robert added the peppers to the pan and then the ginger, lemon grass and chillies. He initially expected there to be a nice fragrant result, however the strange smell returned again and he was sure it didn't originate from the frying pan. Once again, it disappeared by the second breath.

By the third breath, he felt his throat dry out and a sharp pain in his diaphragm. This was unusual. His skin began to tingle and his eyes began to water.

The fourth breath brought Robert to his knees. He started to cough as the pain grew sharper and sharper to the point that it floored him.

He tried to scream but it turned into a gargle as his gullet filled with fluids. The agony was excruciating. He tried to crawl towards his mobile phone which he left on the work top but could only move a couple of inches before he was rendered immobile.

Robert tried to scream again but couldn't as he coughed and expelled some blood from his mouth. Everything seemed to burn, from his skin to his eyes. Robert made one last attempt at screaming but choked as the blood went down his throat.

Robert's body was now overcome. His eyes were shut as he trembled violently on the ground, distressing the person seeing him slowly expire. The last movement witnessed by the invisible watcher was Robert's left index finger that appeared to tap the floor as though transmitting a message in Morse.

The provider of the noxious gas that put an end to Robert's life wanted to be double sure so they waited till all the gas was expelled from the canister he brought with him.

Mission accomplished, the perpetrator crawled backwards towards the entry point. They were also struggling and fading fast from the heat resulting from being in near air tight protective gear for the last two hours, not to mention, in a confined space with warm air blowing over him whilst waiting for Robert's return. They successfully made it out through the vent but could not come down. They were so beat that he had to be helped down by

Mikel and Marcel.

Noting the assassin's frail state, Mikel and Marcel they sat the poor person down gently on the floor and took off gas mask, unzipping the suit to enable the circulation of air.

With the protective clothing off, Paul was covered in sweat and clearly dehydrated and was given a bottle of water to drink. As he caught his breath he remarked "That man was disgusting".

It took Paul twenty minutes to fully recover. Once able, he and the others, wearing their disguises, left through the back door of the building and went to their car. Paul opened the back door and spread himself across the seat, totally pooped. Once in, Mikel called Khoi placing him on speaker phone and confirmed "It is finished."

"Well done gentlemen, would you like to come for a late lunch with Jelena and me? We're having goose." Khoi invited.

"Not at the moment Boss, Paul needs a drink. After that we plan to go out later. Paul's kind of angry with you. The suit he wore today wasn't exactly the one he had in mind when you said he was going to be fitted for a suit." Mikel replied.

Khoi laughed "Tell him I will make it up to him… and tell him I'm glad he's back. Let me know where you are late this evening and I will join you once I drop Jelena off at the airport."

"Oh yeah, wish her a Merry Christmas for me." Mikel concluded

"Will do, and by the way, don't call me "Boss"." With that instruction, Khoi ended.

Content with the result, Khoi raised his glass to a radiant looking Jelena who sat across the table from him "Congratulations my dear, we couldn't have done it without you." He then took a sip of his drink.

Jelena, hiding her sadness at the news, appreciated the accolades but was still inquisitive, and asked what kind of gas was used. "Silly me, I forgot to tell you. It was H2S…" the look was enough to confirm that Jelena did not comprehend. "Hydrogen Sulfide?" he clarified yet nothing.

Khoi placed his glass down, leaned forward and explained "Remember you mentioned that "hot spring" you went to in Hungary and you said you didn't like the smell? Well, that smell is Hydrogen Sulfide." She nodded and concentrated on the information being provided. "At low levels, it's totally harmless. But if you increase the concentration, this colourless gas is very poisonous, not forgetting heavier than air, corrosive, flammable, foul smelling and explosive.

"Its effect differs dependent on the level of concentration. In an enclosed room at 1000ppm, it's lethal from the inhalation of a single breath. But at 100ppm, it destroys your sense of smell and hence becomes impossible to smell, slowly killing you by dissolving your insides."

Based on the lay out of the room you provided, we released the right amount of gas to allow the..." then as the waiter arrived with the menu, he stopped for a moment and continued once he was out of the room "the subject" choosing his words carefully "to be unconscious within 10 – 20 seconds and most certainly dead within 30 seconds after that. Also, none of the items installed in the kitchen could be corroded by the gas and, assuming the extractor fan is as good as the manufacturers claim, the room should be cleared of all evidence of the gas within a few hours to a couple of days … at least before the body begins to rot…Ah, here comes the waiter again, I think we best decide on our meals." Khoi said as he looked through the menu.

Then he remarked "Ah, they have foie gras too. Bar the chocolate pudding, and you could have your intended dinner after all." He teased before concluding "You know what?" Turning to a passing waiter "I will have the foie gras for starters thank you."

After their meal, Khoi escorted Jelena to the airport by taxi. Seated in the back, and since they were not alone, conversation was rather restricted to trivial things such as the weather in her final destination, whether she enjoyed her trip and, of course, if she had her passport. Then he told her that the guys had asked that she join them for New Year's celebration if she didn't have any plans. Jelena said would if she had no work obligations before then.

Unable to keep up the chitchat, they fell silent and reverted to looking through the window, watching the scenery pass them by. Khoi did have a lot to say but he felt there was no need to. Khoi thought they had bonded and it wasn't just what happened in the bedroom.

He could see her through the faint reflection of the glass. Khoi would have loved to hold her and smell her hair again, but he wasn't courageous enough to do so in public, even though there was just one person present.

The yearning was deep and he was relieved when they reached the airport. Having arrived, he paid the driver and walked away from the Mercedes to the automatic doors of the airport with Jelena slightly ahead, dragging her bag. Khoi's pulse raced and he didn't know why.

Once they got through the automatic door, into the airport, Jelena exclaimed, "thank God".

Khoi almost fell when Jelena swerved in front of him, left the handle of her trolley bag, allowing it to fall loudly to the floor before wrapping her arms around his neck, kissing him.

Khoi was happy. Clearly she had been tussling with her feelings as long as he had. Now they were locking lips in a state of undefined passion. He had never felt this sort of release before, especially not for a woman… it felt wrong, but he didn't care, he was going to enjoy it for as long as he could, yet it didn't last. She stopped and pushed him away and ordered "Go!"

"But… I" Khoi struggled with his words.

"Go." She ordered again as she picked up her bag and walked away.

Khoi was perplexed. Every fibre of his being wanted to follow her, but his rational side told him otherwise. Khoi stood there and watched her go up the escalator till she was out of sight.

After a split second of self-sympathy, Khoi sorted to keep his mind off his sense of loss by calling the others to find out where Paul, Mikel and Marcel were. He hoped to stop the onset of misery with company.

As a sombre Khoi made his way to join the others at Mikel's abode, Jan was trying to calm the temper of his colleague.

Wolfgang had been given the task to investigate the mass deaths resulting from the tainted cocaine. However he had gotten nowhere, which in turn made him mad.

Seated on the sofa at Jan's flat, the football match to which he was invited to watch, FC Bayern Munich v SC Freiburg, already 10 minutes in, did not much interest him. "I still don't understand how he could refuse!" Wolfgang exclaimed, in order to be heard over the commentary of the match to Jan who was in the kitchen opening several bottles of beers, placing them on a tray. "It's common sense."

Jan heard Wolfgang carry on as he returned to the living room. "'The only way we can get links is by granting an amnesty to all those in possession of drugs in exchange for information on who sold it to them', that's what I said, and our superintendent warned me that I could get disciplined for such thoughts!" As Jan came to sit, Wolfgang helped himself to a beer without being offered, yet finding the manners to thank Jan for the drink as he lamented further. "What is wrong with granting an amnesty?"

"I don't know. Perhaps Casper is putting his moral convictions above his common sense, as you put it." Jan explained. He took his place next to Wolfgang and proceeded to enjoy his drink. "But it can't be right, there are people still dying out there, it's up to 18 now!" Wolfgang protested, his throat now dry, forcing him to take a sip of beer as he ranted on. "I asked him to consider the potential number of lives to be lost and he told me "It's God's will." Hope his lesbian daughter comes across some during her travels. Then he'll understand what "God's will" is."

Exasperated, Jan turned to his guest and asked "Are you going to be like this all night? I had hoped we could take advantage of Kat's absence and our free day tomorrow to have some… as our friends across the sea put it 'Bro time.'"

"The English say that?" Wolfgang asked. Jan couldn't believe how unworldly Wolfgang was till he winked, signifying he was kidding and started to laugh. Noting he had gone too far, Wolfgang accepted "Yeah, you are right. I am taking this quite personally aren't I?"

"You said it, not me." Jan said taking a gulp of his drink.

Wolfgang kept quiet for a moment of reflection. He realised that he was getting worked up by the situation and thus being a bad guest. "Let's forget it for a moment." He conceded. "Thanks man." He said, lifting his bottle to Jan who replied "Don't mention it." They touched bottles and returned to the match groaning in disappointment as a player missed a potential goal.

Whilst the match progressed and the policemen lamented about the striker's missed opportunity, Khoi arrived at Mikel's flat.

Khoi didn't need to knock or press the buzzer; he had already been spotted by Marcel who stood alone in the cold on the balcony. Mikel was waiting for him by the door, holding it open for him.

"Hey, you made it." Mikel said, giving him a tight embrace which Khoi thought was a bit over affectionate of an otherwise distant fellow. "Glad you are here actually." Mikel led the way to the lift. "Marcel has been down since Monday… we don't know what's up. He's been moping about and standing out there all evening" Mikel explained as he called the lift.

Once in the lift they went up to the third floor, Khoi took the opportunity. "Was your Monday outing successful?"

"Yeah, everything went like clockwork." Confirmed Mikel.

"There's your answer." Khoi declared as they reached their floor.

Then it dawned on Mikel who remarked "Siegfried."

Feeling guilty for his lack of sensitivity, Mikel proposed speaking to him, but Khoi was quick to slam the idea down "Don't say anything to him, just let it go, ok."

"Sure Boss." Mikel said as they got to the door of his flat.

Khoi was about to turn around and tell him off for using the "B" word, but he was cut short as Paul opened the door and welcomed him with the statement "You owe me a suit."

"I owe you more than that." Khoi replied as he went to give Paul a big hug and congratulated him for his hard work and ability to fit into tight spaces.

By the time Khoi had been handed a glass of wine, SC Freiburg was one up against Bayern Munich with just thirteen minutes before half-time. Khoi was given a second drink and some pizza, but could not sit still whilst Marcel was out there on his own. Khoi waited till he wasn't noticed before slipping away to join Marcel. He pulled opened the sliding door and called "Hey Marcel."

Marcel didn't look back he simply replied "Leave me alone."

Khoi took the hint and chose not to pry. He returned inside the flat and to his seat to pretend to watch the match.

Whilst picking up a pizza a goal was scored, and once the jubilations were over, Paul asked after Marcel "He's ok." Khoi replied. "So who scored?" He asked faking interest in the game.

The night turned out to be fun for Khoi and the others who were pleased with the result of the match, arguing over the best player. Then everyone proceeded to play Xbox, trying out the dance game, everyone except Marcel, who remained outside the circle only returning to join in drinking vodka shots before walking out again.

No one left that night, hey all passed out drunk in the flat, all except Marcel who could not sleep due to his conscience.

Sadly, Marcel wasn't the only one who couldn't sleep as a result of conscience and alcohol consumption. Jan had to watch his night come to an end when Wolfgang got fried on 13 bottles of beer and dosed off on the sofa.

Jan covered Wolfgang with a blanket, check if he was comfortable before he went to bed himself, turning off his phone and alarm feeling too drunk to even take off his clothes before falling asleep under his blanket.

# 13

*23 December 2010*

The 23rd of December started off rainy and loudly for Joel as the doorbell rang. Rolling out of bed, he picked up his mobile to check the time. It was too early for the postman, who could be the person outside his door at 6:13am.

Sighing, he put a foot down when he heard his mobile beep again, it was a message. It was from Jelena and it read "I'm outside. Please get dressed. I want to give you your Christmas present." This couldn't be correct. Joel could have sworn that Khoi took her to the airport.

He raced down to the door, opened it, and sure enough, there stood Jelena, looking perfect even at an early hour of the morning, with a smile. "I told you to get dressed. We have to hurry."

Joel was too shocked to protest to being woken up. All he could say was "Come in."

When he was ready to go, Joel was driven to the construction site of the new spa resort that Georg was building by Jelena in a car she had hired. It had been closed for Christmas for the last two weeks and building was set to recommence on January 15.

As she parked, Joel asked Jelena, "What are we doing here?" She didn't reply. She walked out and he followed. Jelena led him to section of the building that was to be the Scandinavian sauna. The shell had been built and heating installed but it hadn't been kitted out for its purpose.

Jelena opened the door and allowed Joel to enter first. There he found Daniel looking excited and Ralph looking indifferent as they stood next to a structure that stretched to the ceiling. Jelena entered and shut the door to keep out the cold.

Joel wondered why there was a two and a half metre rectangular thing before him covered in a white sheet.

Jelena stood by him watching his expression as Ralph and Daniel proclaimed "taa daa!"

"What the fuck is that? And I thought you were on holiday?" Joel enquired, directing the second question to Ralph.

Jelena nodded. That was the signal for the grand unveiling. The sheet came down. The structure beneath was a two story shelf. On the top shelf was a small white water container about a meter and a half high with a tap at the end.

The tank was a fifth full of liquid with a hose attached to the tap nozzle leading down to another smaller thick plastic chest, the sort used to store gritting salt at stations. The hose went through a hole into the chest below just below the lid. The chest appeared bolted to the ground by a wooden frame, held in place by a padlock, which Ralph removed, to ensure it remained fastened to the ground.

The structure wouldn't have drawn much interest from Joel if it weren't for the odour emitting from the box below. "God, it smells disgusting, where is it coming from?" Joel wondered.

"Love that smell." Jelena said as she walked up to the shelves. "That smell is your Christmas present." Jelena walked and stood by the shelf and pointed to the water tank "We installed this last week. The tank above held twenty litres of water, I guess your gift was thirsty."

Then like a game show hostess, she gestured to the lower box. "The box! The box is simply a box. It is 60cm wide, 140cm long and 140cm tall; however, its volume is 45cm x 90cm x 90cm. Wondering why that's important?" She really didn't need to ask, Joel was already lost, yet she continued "A grown man, let say 185cm tall and of average build, would find it near impossible to fit themselves into this container except if they were a contortionist or if they had help. Even then, the box is just too small for that 185cm person."

"Now, pay attention, to fit in, you'll need a helping hand by being pushed inside, naked, in a foetal position, not exactly a foetal position, you would need your hands to either by your side and under your legs…" Seeing that Joel couldn't picture it Jelena cried "Daniel, be a dear and show him what I mean." Daniel obliged, rested on the floor lying on his side. He brought his knee right up to his chest and held his hands under his knees.

With a visual aid provided, Jelena continued "Before the person is inserted into the box, he is made to wear a gag, like this, we got it from a sex shop." Jelena opened her bag and handed Joel a black leather gag that was meant to be inserted into the mouth of an individual, forcing the person's mouth to stay opened and a hole, in the gag's mouth piece ensured entry into the mouth before the gag is tied behind the head of the person.

Jelena explained the purpose of the mouth piece with the short thick access hole to the mouth. It was to allow a tube to be inserted into the hole and held in place by duct-tape. She added that the wearer will not be able to close his mouth, but could breathe through their nose once the gag was in place, "I think it's for people who like golden showers." She added. "Daniel… you can get off the floor now, I think he got it." She instructed.

"Where was I? Yeah. So the end of the tube inserted into the mouth will contain two ball bearings, each two third the size of a table tennis ball, whilst the other end was inserted in the overhead water tank. With the tube containing the ball bearings has two ball bearings in the person's mouth, it acts like a hamster's water dispenser. To discharge water, the person will just press your tongue on the ball and water would flow. If they don't want anything to drink, they have to keep their tongue still. Are you still with me?"

"Em… yeah, I think." Joel confirmed.

"Good." She then walked to the structure pointing to the hose. "This pipe goes through this hole on the just under the cover of the container." She pointed to the relevant hole. "It's then put into the gag and tapped to ensure it doesn't pop out before it is inserted into the person's mouth. Then the person is carefully inserted into the box."

"With the person inside, we put a couple of sand bags on the body to fill in any excess space before the lid is shut tight and, as you can see, fastened to the ground."

"Now, the person within is totally immobile. The sand bag and fastened lid pushdown on every part of the person. Their back, neck and head, their movements are restricted to just millimetre twitches, and with the gag in their mouth, the head can't move at all, making it hard to breathe, let alone make a sound. Here is the air hole, allowing enough air to keep the person alive but not enough to keep it well ventilated, yet they will not suffocate."

"Of course the person has water and we have put nutrients in the water needed to extend the inevitable death which, as I explained, will originate from the dispenser in the mouth, almost stuck in there, a bigger version of what you would mount on a hamster cage… I said that before right?"

"Finally, we place a small piece of wood under here." She announced, directing Joel's attention to the slither of wood concerned beneath the plastic box "this causes the container to tilt slightly to an angle so that the corner where the person's feet is, is raised slightly higher by just a couple of centimetres than where the person's face is. This will ensure any liquids flow in one direction." She concluded with a grin at Joel who had frozen to the spot as he could imagine all that could happen to a person trapped in the box, but it was more graphic than he thought as Jelena delved deeper.

"At this point, the person in the box would be in an extremely uncomfortable place. Fast forward to a week or so, and their joints would soon begin to hurt; they are bereft of outside sounds and any light, and their senses would soon turn on them."

"They can't scream, each time they do, their tongue would press on the ball bearing and fill their mouth with water. If they panic, and feel they can't breathe, they won't be able to take deep breaths because their chest can't expand enough, worsening the sensation."

"So they have a choice, die of thirst and starvation or enjoy the water.

In reality, it's a no brainer. They'll get thirsty, and hesitantly drink. Of course, what goes in must come out and they will need to relieve themselves. Seeing as their face is at the lower end, their excrements, whatever comes out, will find its way towards their face."

"They will begin to scream perhaps, maybe they will try to twitch or push themselves out of the box, but at some point they will tire. They will try to rest but the pains will keep them awake for hours turning into a prison of panic and torment, which could include hallucinations of bugs all around them and a creeping sensation that they will die here. Maybe they'll wish to die? No, they're not there yet. After a couple more days they'll realize that the pain isn't just in the joints anymore. Their skin feels like its burning where it's pressed the hardest to the box, or rather it feels like that you are being gnawed on."

"If you know what bed sores are, you will be aware that the skin and other soft tissue, if being constantly pressed upon, will start dying; necrosis slowly begins to develop in it."

"Frantically, they try hard to wiggle, to move some of the tension around to relieve the pain, but as they do, they can feel themselves tearing their own dying flesh."

"Relief comes when they faint from the stress and pain, but it's temporary. The next time they wake, the person would have probably wet themselves again, and you can feel the liquid all over your face."

Then Jelena walked up to him and said "Close your eyes and imagine yourself in that box, you, trapped, cramped and hopeless. You scream, but you're hoarse and bereft of any real force to scream with. You have screamed before, no one came because no one heard. Why? You are nearly choked by the water each time you tried."

"You start to beg, but the pains are returning and you can barely make the words come out right. From here on, it's all up to your will to live. Will you keep yourself alive with the water? How will you get rid of the faeces and urine making its way to your mouth and nose? Will you try to die? What will you feel when you're not dying? For how long will you be alive? You've probably literally lost your mind by the time your body caves in. Maybe you eventually pass out resulting in you drowning in your own liquids or maybe a painful sepsis develops from your now irreversibly grave bed-sores... What degrading things have you thought, said or done in your final days alive?"

All this was scaring Joel and Jelena knew it. She could see the bead of sweat roll down the side of his face as she asked him to open his eyes.

Dramatically she pointed at the container, her voice rising steadily as she proclaimed "In that box was a man born in Darmstadt. In that box was a man who had four speeding tickets, one charge for assaulting his former wife and spent three months in prison for drunk driving. In that box was a man who, when released, became a welder, met the love of his life whilst on holiday in Croatia and had a daughter with her before they broke up and he came back to Germany."

"In that box is a man who, five years ago, found God, repented of his sins and became a born again Christian, devoted his life to charitable works, traveling to Gaza, Bangladesh, Congo, Tanzania, Haiti to build schools and help immunise children and feed the hungry aiming to be closer to his Lord."

Then Jelena held him by the hand and led Joel, who was struggling not to tremble, to the container. She instructed Joel to kneel and placed Joel's hand on the container.

The smell was near unbearable, but she still had the fear-provoking look in her eyes that frightened him as her voice softened and with a snigger announced "14 days ago, we placed that man in this box. Two days ago, the water level stopped dropping. Joel, in this box rests your Christmas present, in this box lays the remains of Jürgen Schmude."

Joel pulled his hand away from the box and scrambled backwards on the floor till he hit the wall and began to tremble in utter dread. The image Jelena provided was gruesome enough but to know it actually happened was enough to turn him into a quivering wreck. He didn't know why, but he began to weep. Jelena looked at her watch and remarked "I'm late, I need to get Khoi's gift ready."

She reached in her purse and took out a small vial held within a small plastic bottle, the content of the vial looked like a small amount of detergent, much less than a tea spoon. "Just imagine, all I need is a grain." Jelena remarked, eyeing her prize before she returned from her satanic haze, returned the item to her purse and said "You must thank Callum for me." Jelena approached Joel who just quivered like a leaf. She looked ghoulish as her hand approached his face.

Her touch felt cold to his cheek and her kiss on his head felt like his soul was being consumed, he began to know what the term heartless meant. She opened her purse, took out her compact mirror to ensure her lipstick was still moist and decided to add an extra layer she was now ready. "I am off to see Khoi. Merry Christmas, hope you like your gift. Let me know if we are still on for the New Year." She said as she reached into her coat, took out her gloves, putting them on as she left.

Once she was out of the room, Joel began to wail "Oh God… Oh fuck!" Ralph and Daniel didn't know what to do as they watched Joel slam himself unto the wall. "You ok Joel?" Daniel asked. Joel didn't respond, he could only sob and curse loudly. "That's it, I'll call Khoi."

"Don't fucking call Khoi. Just leave me here for a while ok… just get out!" Joel screamed. Daniel and Ralph left wondering why Joel reacted in this manner, it was what he wanted.

It was true, Joel wanted Jürgen Schmude to die, but the evil Jürgen Schmude, the one who didn't show remorse at the trial, the one who smiled as he walked out of the court room… not the Jürgen Schmude one who turned his life around and strove to make a difference. In Joel's mind, he had killed a man whom he considered innocent and this brought his conscience on a collision course with his ambitions because it wasn't the first time he had done this, but why did this death feel different? Why was he grieving? He couldn't find the answer and it upset him even more.

Three hours after Joel had received his gift, at the same time in Central London, there stood a robin sitting silently on the low hanging branch of a snow covered tree on the banks of the Serpentine in Hyde Park. The absence of its melody was enough to underline how cold it was that day.

The whole of the United Kingdom was blanketed in snow with temperatures dropping to numbers never seen in anyone's life time. -17 in Hampshire let alone to think of what was happening in Scotland.

The television was inundated with clips and documentaries showing the last time this happened in the UK. The grand frost of 1963 when the snow was thick, but at least the trains ran then. Today, a flake is enough to bring the commuter belt to its knees let alone the buckets of the white stuff which had accumulated over the last weeks. Not that this mattered to the robin who sat still watching the pond, but it did matter to it's observer, the 34 year old man who had to take the train that day, having seen on the news that the roads were blocked with stranded cars. It forced him to suffer the insensate rants of travellers comparing the train system there to that of countries with worse winter climates. What's worse, he arrived twenty minutes late.

Though he was happy to see the robin, the man's main interest was the bank siege taking place across the road behind him. He had decided to stand alone, waiting for his instructions to be carried out and to think and pray that his gamble would pay off.

He had been waiting for twenty three minutes when he heard the sound of footsteps approaching. It was enough to alert him that his time for reflection was up. He turned around and there was the uniformed officer, who had clearly been running, addressing him "Sir, the Deputy Consulate general is here."

"Thank you." He replied before taking one last look at the robin and venturing back to work.

As he approached the scrum of media and police cars, he was rather pleased that there weren't many pedestrians and onlookers flanking the wings, all too busy with their Christmas shopping and worrying about the weather to care about the four people being held hostage.

He sighed as he buttoned up his coat and shivered, not because he felt chilly, but because he had to meet an old university friend whom, despite studying the same law course had moved to the dark side and was now Deputy Consulate General for the Republic of Belarus. As he approached the car with a diplomat's licence plate, his old study buddy stepped out of the vehicle with a grin on his face. "Kirill," he cried, trying his best to mask his surprise.

When he knew Kirill 18 years earlier, he had wavy blonde hair, they were the same height at 176cm, he was slim, fit, a heavy smoker and had bad teeth, but when Kirill did smile this time, the teeth had been fixed, but that wasn't the only change he witnessed. Kirill was now a fat chubby man. Regardless his hair remained wavy and blonde.

Whilst embracing him he added "How are you? It's been a very long time!" Kirill nodded responding "Tom Evans" he called "how nice to see you. The last time I met, you were bigger, have you stopped going to gym?" Tom laughed and retaliated "So have you." They both laughed even though Tom had to force his.

As Kirill confirmed that all his instructions had been followed to the last letter, Tom surrendered his coat and was fitted with a bullet proof vest. Once on, Tom was handed the hamper basket containing the items from Fortnum and Mason. The eyes of those gathered filled with hope and excitement, all fixed on him as he walked to the entrance of the bank where a man stood behind the glass door with a balaclava over his head and gun in his hand.

"I've brought you lunch." Tom announced. "It's from a classy place and to show you it's all good..." Tom opened the basket, took out a spoon, and proceeded to taste all the contents of jars and the packs, even though some tasted vile. "As you can see, it's all safe"

The man with the balaclava called another of his accomplices to cover him by pointing a gun at the door as he opened it. Arms stretched and looking nervous, the man ordered "Give me the basket." Tom shook his head to refuse. "Not yet. I am here to negotiate with you to. May I come in?" The man turned to his cover who simply replied "Sure, one more hostage puts the value up." From his accent, Tom knew that was the man he was after. "Come in." Ordered the first man.

Tom picked up the basket and entered the bank. "Don't put down the basket till I tell you." Tom was told as he proceeded further. "STOP" commanded the man with a gun as the first man locked the door. Once secure, Tom was given a body search and it was discovered that all he had on him was his iPhone.

Having been certified clean, Tom set about looking for the weak link in the pair. And on closer inspection, he found him. The green eyes of the person who opened the door marked him out as Denis, and the other man taking the basket aside before picking up his gun and pointed it at him. Tom was ordered to keep his hands up and move forward away from the door whilst Brett locked it.

Tom found three people sitting on the floor huddled together. He looked carefully at each of them to confirm they were the right ones. "What are you looking at?" Brett shouted at him.

"Nothing... I came to talk." Tom proposed.

"We're not interested until our ride is here." Brett replied.

"Ah yes, your demands. For a pair of robbers, you do have exquisite taste." Tom remarked. "Caviar, two bottles of champagne, cranberries... you think this will be your last meal?"

"Go to hell!" barked Denis. Tom saw his opportunity to connect with him "Whilst I know it is potentially our final destination, let's try and slow down the journey to allow us to enjoy the scenery called life." Denis's pupil's dilated, evidence that he been antagonised by Tom. Regardless, Tom didn't have the time to loiter any further and switched to Russian. "Listen, Denis, your options are very limited." The fact that Tom could speak Russian and knew his name mentally disarmed Denis "They include killing everyone here, and the troops outside will storm the place and kill you and your friends"

"Speak English!" cried Brett who didn't like being left out. Tom ignored the protest and persisted "Or you could try and get away and I can assure you that you won't because we will get you. And when we do, the car you may be in could go missing, no one knows what you look like anyway, so who will care. Perhaps a little detour to the Belarussian embassy could be in order and there you can scream all you like as they torture you. We can't intervene because, technically you will be back home in Minsk. Look outside there, there is a man from the embassy waiting for you by the black jaguar." Denis did as he was told and caught a glimpse of the car with the Belarussian flag on the bonnet and Kirill leaning on the side of the car smoking patiently before his eyes met Denis. Kirill waved. Denis began to perspire and tremble ever so slightly.

Tom knew his actions were working. It was time to turn the screws "Do you know anyone at number 23 Druhaja Ziemliamiernaja vulica?" Brett was irritated by his exclusion "I know your game, you want to divide us!" He marched to the woman cowering in the corner and dragged her to her feet. Her protruding stomach showed she was expecting. With his arm forming a strangle hold around the woman's neck, pointed a gun to her stomach. "Speak English!" He commanded. The woman panicked "Please, Please, speak English. Don't let him hurt my baby." She wailed.

On the inside, Tom was alarmed as to how things escalated, he kept it well hid, choosing to sigh deeply, shrugging his shoulders in an unconcerned manner proclaimed in English "If I must, so Denis, do you know anyone who lives at number 23 Druhaja Ziemliamiernaja vulica?" Denis was unsteady on his feet and even more unsteady with his grip, he nodded to confirm he did know someone at that address. "A sister of yours I presume?" Denis again nodded.

Fearing Brett's trigger happy nature Tom put forward his hands "As you know I only have my phone, that's what I am going to reach for now." Slowly, he reached into his pocket for his phone, took it out and whilst facing the screen to Denis, made a call using face-time application. It rang for a few seconds before it was answered by a pair of men in the police uniform worn in Minsk one of them said in a soft voice "Priviet Denis" and then turned the camera around to show him the locality.

There was no doubt in Denis' mind; they were at Druhaja Ziemliamiernaja vulica. Then they walked to a door numbered 23 and then the camera of the phone was turned to another policeman holding a gun and waving in front of the phone saying in English "Hello Denis" again in a soft tempered voice.

"Turn it off" Denis requested. "I can't." Tom replied "It's out of my control now. If I do turn it off now, they will assume I am dead or something has gone wrong and they will... how can I put this? They'll make your sister and her three year old son, disappear." Looking him square in the face, Tom added "And you know they can."

Even from his breathing one could hear Denis trembling. Brett's apprehension was apparent in the clear look of fear on his face, worried that Tom's plan had worked. "But they are innocent!" Denis cried in Russian. "Just like our dear Philippa Wood who your friend is manhandling there." Tom rebutted, adding "What did this twenty one year old mother of five do to any of you? And by the way," Tom turned to Philippa, confident that he had nothing to fear from Denis anymore as he chided her "five kids before your twentieth, and another one coming? Haven't you heard of protection?"

"I had triplets!" She cried in an attempt to defend her virtue. "Regardless, you should try saying no." Tom added.

This was detracting from the matter at hand. Denis decided to bring things back on track "SHUT UP!" he screamed. His anxiety was visible and he couldn't even stand straight without fidgeting anymore. "So... What do you want me to do?" Denis asked in Russian. "Give up and get your friend to do the same and I promise you a jail term in this country and you won't get deported back home." Tom offered.

There was a tense standoff for a moment, prompting Brett to ask "What did he say?"

"It's up to you Denis, think carefully." Tom instructed in Russian.

"WHAT DID HE SAY TO YOU?" Brett asked again.

"You have a short period of time, all I have to do is turn off this phone..." Tom warned.

As Tom spoke, Brett had had his fill of Russia, pushed Philippa aside and pointed the gun at Tom and screamed "STOP SPEAKING RUSSIAN."

A shot was heard by everyone outside. The police were mobilised to storm the room. Kirill was fearful for his friend as the ambulance came rolling in but before the police could make it onto the steps of the building, the door opened and from instructions given within, the four hostages ran out with their hands in the air into the waiting arms of psychologists and their students who were brought in to help them cope with their experience.

The head of the armed response unit walked in to find Brett crying and rolling on the floor having been shot in the right shoulder, forcing him to drop his gun and allowing Tom to take the gun from an unmasked Denis. With the words "You made the right choice." Tom ordered the officers around him to deal with Brett for now, before addressing the officers via face-time with the word "Proceed".

Denis was startled yet petrified, he didn't know what was happening and could only hear knocking and his sister answering the door and finally her voice when she said "Hello?"

"Hello Mrs Ivanova, I have your brother here to speak to you." Tom said to in Russian her. He then offered the phone to Denis and advised "Tell her what you did." Denis took the phone from Tom and before he could speak began to weep, his sister asking if all was well. Tom ordered that Denis be given ten minutes before he was arrested.

Tom left the bank as the paramedic treated Brett. He received pats on the shoulder congratulating him for ending the situation so quickly. Tom went to his old school friend to thank him for his services. "I owe you one."

"Anything to save a life." Kirill replied as Denis was brought out in handcuffs to the waiting police car. Denis and Kirill's eyes met again, prompting Kirill to snap "You're lucky." Tom was transfixed as the frightened looking young man was being driven away. This made Tom down right miserable. He knew he was going to be haunted by his act of Christmas kindness.

Tom turned to Kirill to ask, "You're going to sort out his family's exit permits aren't you?" Kirill was slightly taken aback, as though Tom had committed blasphemy. Hoping to shake the staff of common sense, Kirill asked "Why are you so soft? You want to help such a man? He's a criminal."

"No, I don't think that's the whole story." Tom rebuffed. "Though he did wrong, he's more a victim of circumstance, you may be right that he is a criminal, but in reality, he's not lost.

So will you get his family the permits to visit him?"

"No problem." Kirill confirmed with his hand stretched. Tom took it and gave it a shake before Kirill drew him close for a hug. "Merry Christmas."

"You too old friend." Tom replied.

Tom waved Kirill off as he was driven away. It was then he began to feel the chill beating his arms. Tom wondered where his coat was. As he wandered around, a police woman came up to him absolutely excited. "Sir!" she called. "Oh Tiffany, you haven't seen Mathew have you? The dummy has my coat." Tom asked. "Sorry sir, I haven't, but I have some good news!" She said nearly jumping out of her skin "Go on." Tom urged

"They've tracked down Bozic!"

The chill Tom initially felt became the last thing on his mind. "Get my coat and find my phone, I have to hear this myself." Tom ran to the nearest car and asked to be taken back to the station for confirmation.

Upon arrival at the station, Tom made a B-line to his Assistant Commissioner's office radiating with glee. Ignoring formality, he opened the door and asked the lady sitting behind the desk "Is it true? Did you find her?"

"And good morning to you DAC Evans, I am fine thank you, and you?" Her underlying tone of sarcasm tamed his eagerness. "Very sorry ma'am." He apologised.

"It's ok." She replied. "Your Moby Dick has been busy and I think you had better rush home to pack. She has finally popped up for some air in Germany. You can find the brief waiting for you in your office.

I would have suggested you wait till after the holidays, but I am sure you aren't too keen on that.

So I guess you should go home, spend some time with little Tim and get ready for your trip. You have a ticket for the first flight out to Berlin for Boxing Day."

"When am I expected back?" Tom enquired.

"When you start to annoy them. And I believe I ought to congratulate you on your endeavour this morning, remarkable turn of events I must say. Yet I feel the need to slap you across the face for getting the Bela-Russians involved." Tom looked down in the manner of a naught school boy. "Well, you did what needed to be done." Remaining seated the Deputy Commissioner concluded "You can go now."

"Ma'am". Tom said as he left the office, closing the door gently trying to keep his elation in check. He walked quickly to his office, shut the door and there was the brief and the ticket on the top. It was true, it was all happening. He leapt up in the air and swiftly collected his belongings and left for home. DAC Tom Evans arrived home and to the warm embrace of his son Tim, his son who was only too happy to receive him.

Joel, on the other hand, was gradually coming back to reality. It had taken him a while to recover. The curse was on him now and there was no turning back. Joel had sat there for six hours amongst the smell and the thought of corpse, looking at the structure; he had been void of thought throughout that time. All he could do was just watch in tears.

Eventually, when he snapped out of his trance and made a call as he got off the floor to Ralph who was outside the building waiting for him. He smeared his runny nose on the sleeve of his coat as it rang. Finally it was answered. "Ralph, yeah it's me. You have to go to see Callum. We need some chemicals. We need to dissolve this body. I'll call ahead."

Ralph wondered why Joel didn't just come out and tell them himself. The fact was that Joel didn't want them to see the state he was in. Regardless, Ralph did not protest even though he had been kept waiting along with Daniel for nearly four hours without any refreshments causing Daniel to grumble incisively.

Joel called Callum to place his order. He requested acid only to be told by Callum that it was a common mistake was to believe that acids were needed to dissolve a body efficiently, hydrofluoric acid specifically as it is a highly corrosive acid, capable of dissolving many materials. However, this exact quality poses problems and many metals and most plastics are weak to the stuff, and it gives off strong fumes that can have negative effects on users.

A strong base on the other hand, like lye, is the stuff used in everyday maintenance at home, opening up clogged drains or wiping off areas covered in fat.

Callum explained, "Lye has the ability to transform flesh into thick murky goo that, compared to acids is a lot safer to work with and, more importantly, is easier to get rid of as you can pour it safely down the drain and rinse away with water. And it's a lot easier to get a hold of in large quantities."

Callum explained all this to Joel, who didn't understand and didn't really care. All this information reminded Joel of his secondary school days with his boring chemistry teacher. So when he said to use lye, he knew better than to argue.

Joel told Callum that the others will come to collect the items and he can call them directly if anything else is required.

An hour later, Joel went outside for some much needed air waiting for an update from Ralph or Daniel. It was already past 11 in the morning. Joel called Ralph and was told that Callum had instructed to get some other utensils. Hence they were going to be a bit late.

"But Ralph, we need this done quickly." Joel was getting stressed.

"I spoke to Callum, and he said not to worry. He said he had something for us that would more than half the process time. Come on Joel, it's Callum, he knows what he's doing."

"OK" Joel said as he hung up.

He really didn't want to hang around for much longer, but he would like it even less if anyone was to discover this inhumane crime scene by accident. It was not because he was afraid of getting caught, but because he was terrified of the idea of anyone ever finding out what had been done to a human being in here. It was getting quite cold outside, but he couldn't bear the idea of waiting back inside, so he called Ralph to return immediately and pick him up. "It would take about forty five minutes, we need to pick up a couple of things." Ralph warned.

"Whatever, just get here!"

Whilst he waited, Joel locked up the building. The car arrived fifteen minutes earlier than anticipated and it came with an attachment.

"He told us to bring a utility trailer for the car, so we went and hired one" said Daniel after they had been sitting in the car for a while, driving aimlessly. "I noticed" said Joel, his voice ladled with sarcasm.

Having picked up Joel, they started driving to a location selected by Callum. Ralph and Daniel had tried in vain to get some small talk going. When proposing to go get a warm cup of something, Joel declined without further explanation. With Joel's refusal, the others decided to bear their hunger pain and continued their journey.

They arrived at the agreed meeting point, an empty parking lot near a gravel football field for kids forty minutes earlier than intended. They were keen to find out what it could be that Callum had planned for the trailer.

As they came to a stop, Callum was standing next to three boxes, and a rather big metallic contraption, about 2 metres tall and one and a half metres wide. It was cylindrical, pointing up, looking a lot like a huge pot.

On the top, it had a lid sealed in place with eight big screws and a pressure release valve on the lid, and at the bottom it had four wheels for easier handling.

"Evening friends! I imagined you would be early" Callum proclaimed, greeting them with a conceited grin. "I gathered from your call you were in quite a hurry?" Ralph was about to answer when Joel spoke "Yes, we need to get this over with as soon as possible. I can't stand the thought of this shit much longer. Sorry about the language."

"I don't care if it's shit or cabbage you're cooking, just return this baby to me nice and clean will you? I need it back by Monday."

"Yeah, yeah." Joel snapped. "We really need to get this done with. What is this thing that you brought us?"

"This, gentlemen…" Callum replied as he gestured widely to the contraption with a smirk "…is what you would call a pressure cooker!" then pointed to the three large boxes "And this is your lye."

"We're not making dinner; we're getting rid of a human body!" Ralph exclaimed furiously as he thought this misunderstanding would be put on him. "Ach, your looks don't deceive after all. You are stupid." Callum concluded as he looked at Ralph with a disgusted expression adding "Sodium hydroxide, or lye as you say, works faster under high temperatures. You want it to be at just about 150°C for the optimal effect, and for that to work you need it pressurized. I really didn't expect I had to explain this part." Joel was beginning to get tired of Callum's condescension and asked "This isn't our field Callum. How will this help?"

"You should be done in three hours. It can hold almost three cubic metres, so you should have plenty of room to play around in as well. If I asked you to get one, I imagined you would turn up with the household kind…" Callum looked at them, and after a second of looking apprehensively back they nodded and passed him some currency. As they were about to start loading the trailer, Callum added "Oh, and FYI one of those boxes contains your protective gear. Try not to hurt yourselves will you?" And with that, Callum turned and walked away.

While moving the boiler with great effort, Ralph asked himself how this scrawny little scientist had brought the thing here in the first place, but thought better than to ask, rather he remarked "One day, I'm going to kill that guy". They loaded the boxes containing many cans of lye, and took off.

Returning to the scene, Daniel sprung to work, dismantling the frame to take it out of the box.

Joel walked out of the car to another side of the building. He was glad not to witness commotion and was pleased that there were no signs that anyone had seen anything. Ralph backed the car with the trailer as close as possible to the door, and went inside to join Daniel.

Despite trying to block it out, Joel could detect the odour from outside. The smell was even harder to deal with now that he had the images of what and who it was that was making it, and he felt almost physically assaulted as he went in with the others to get the box. He wondered if he would ever get the box out of his head.

Afflicted by the smell themselves, Daniel and Ralph didn't hesitate for a second, and carried the heavy, foul box back to the trailer and went straight to dump it inside the boiler while Joel kept the lid up. However, the lid didn't close all the way with the box inside. Joel started cursing and swearing at it while he jumped off the trailer. "Get that sorted will you?" he near shouted at the others while staggering towards some brush looking like he would throw up.

Daniel went into the car and got a crowbar they had in the trunk, and proceeded to strike at the offending corner of the box until he managed to force it into a less corner-like shape allowing the lid to finally close.

Joel was showing extreme signs of stress, but they couldn't hesitate. "We got to get out of here. We'll use the garage at my house… let's go, let's go!" he ordered.

Taking the back roads, they arrived at the mansion situated out of town, seated in the middle of a sizable plot of land, fenced off for maximum isolation. Luckily for them, Joel's family home wasn't too far from the construction site. Ralph and Daniel had never had the chance to look at the designated area, the detached building was a sizeable garage enough to accommodate the contraption and effectively utilise it for its purpose.

They parked the boiler and then the car inside, closed the garage door and got around to fill the boiler with lye. With the car safely indoors and out of site, the lid of the oversized cauldron was opened. Ralph and Daniel took out the box, petrifying Joel to the spot as it was placed to the ground.

The cans of lye were emptied into the large vat before they plugged the boiler in the socket, and watched waiting for it to heat up. Joel knew it would take about an hour before the adequate temperature was reached and they started the countdown.

Daniel and Ralph waited for their orders. Joel just stood there frozen to the spot. The smell didn't bother him anymore. What persisted was the fact that, yes, he did want revenge but not in this disgusting way.

"What do you want us to do?" Ralph asked Joel. "What time is it?" Joel enquired. He was informed it was just past five in the evening. Joel went pale. "Oh shit… she's going to have dinner with Khoi! I've got to warn him." He picked up his phone and called, it went straight to voice mail. "This is crazy." Joel proclaimed "We have hyena in our den." Looking at Ralph and Daniel, he instructed "Don't do anything till I get back ok? I got to find Khoi… I got to find Khoi…" Joel rushed to his car adding "One of you go back to that blasted place and dispose of the things and shut the door will you?" as he got into the car and sped off on his way to Khoi's hotel.

The 23rd of December started at just after 5pm in Mikel's flat. It was rainy, and then it hailed. The small pebble sized stones smacked the reinforced windows of Mikel's flat and didn't wake them. It took a ringtone from a mobile to force Paul to push himself off the floor, his head still spinning as he looked for the source of the noise.

Initially he thought it was his, but soon found, whilst searching through the coats hung by the door, that it wasn't. Regardless, he persisted and found that the phone ringing was Khoi's.

"Khoi! Khoi!" He called out. Khoi opened his eyes and groaned "Your phone… it's ringing." Khoi stretched and yawned as he ordered "Answer it will you?"

Paul, rubbing his eyes, ran his thumb over the touch screen phone and answered it "What?"

"Hello Paul…" responded the voice which he immediately recognised.

"Oh, Jelena, It's you." Paul began to yawn. "How are you?"

"I am well thanks, but I have a question, why haven't you bothered to meet with our friend from Belgrade?" Paul initially didn't comprehend what was being said as he looked at his watch "Belgrade… That's in Serbia right?" Then it clicked "OH SHIT!" he screamed as he ran around to waking the others "When does he land?"

"An hour ago, so best get your skates on. By the way, is Khoi there with you?"

Paul raced to Khoi, shouting his name as he tossed the phone, landing on Khoi's chest. The impact of the device certainly revived him.

Khoi took hold of his phone and was shocked when Jelena informed him that she was still in Berlin for another night and wanted to meet him for dinner at seven that evening "which, if you didn't know is in two hours." She reminded him. A look at his watch and the frantic manner in which Paul put on his coat was enough to prove that it was not seven in the morning. Khoi informed Jelena he was set to be an hour late. She didn't mind.

He rose, stretched and realised that he didn't have a hangover, unlike Mikel who couldn't manage to put on his shoes. A quick survey of the room showed that Marcel had already left and no one noticed he had gone.

Khoi, though concerned, needed to rush and get himself ready. He left the flat along with the others.

As Paul, Khoi and Mikel left the building, Joel was just pulling up to Khoi's hotel at the other side of town. Joel parked his car precariously on the curb and ran into the hotel, straight to the reception desk. "Is Mr Kyle Tabone, room 616, in?"

"Let me check sir", said the polite plump girl as she fiddled with her key board. "I'm sorry sir, but he didn't come back to his room last night. He is still checked in though. Would you like me to leave him a message?"

"Did he say where he went?" Joel asked in desperation which appeared to take the young lady aback.

"Em… I am afraid I am not able to disclose that information… if you have his mobile number, you could give him a call?" She suggested, making Joel feel so foolish that he remarked "Why didn't I think of that in the first place. Thank you."

He took out his mobile phone and placed a call to Khoi's number. It rang, and rang, but still no answer from the phone Khoi had forgotten on the sofa of Mikel's flat.

With no luck, Joel chose to try other avenues and called Marcel who informed him that he had left Khoi behind sleeping at Mikel's flat. There was no time to lose, he called Mikel but the call went to voicemail. "Mikel, call me now. It's Joel".

Joel drove to Mikel's place, wondering what horror could be befalling Khoi. At Mikel's flat he pressed the buzzer and waited. This was inconvenient so he walked around to check the balcony, still no sign of anyone. He growled in frustration and returned to his car, sitting for a moment, contemplating his next move.

Joel was ready to give up. He had a problem in his hands back home that needed addressing. He took a moment to think and making intermittent calls to Mikel, Paul and Khoi to no avail, losing track of time. When he finally looked at the time Joel realised it was already nearly eight in the evening. "Shit" he remarked realising he had been seated there for around two hours. He decided to call the only person that did answer his call and said to Marcel "I need you to find Khoi, cancel whatever you have planned and go and search for him. It's really important to see if he is safe... just check he is safe, please?" Sensing the urgency, Marcel agreed.

Joel hung up and punched his steering wheel blaming himself for bring danger into his circle. Still he didn't have time, he had to rush back to his task for the day. He had to pick up a coffee grinder before the shops closed.

As Joel drove away, Jan was also trying to prepare himself for Kat's return. Jan had also woken up late at around 5pm and Wolfgang was still in the living room. Considerately, Jan tried to clear around Wolfgang to prolong his guest's sleep, but he had to vacuum and that was going to be noisy, and the only humane thing he could do was wake him.

Jan woke the sleeping policeman who, despite not being asked, decided to give a hand. Wolfgang knew that Kat was house proud and with her flight arriving at 10:40 that evening, they had a lot of work to do. Both Jan and Wolfgang wondered what had happened. They certainly over did the beers and Jan didn't remember buying Chinese food. There was a chess board with a half played game set out which no party realised they had been playing. They both were suffering from a hangover and it took them a considerable period of time to clean up the house, about the same time it took Khoi to get ready.

Khoi initially didn't want to go out that night. It was still cold out there. Having checked the internet for directions to their rendezvous point he realised it wasn't that far after all and decided to take the bus.

Khoi got off the bus and walked and turn from Fehrbelliner Strasse up Chotiner Strasse. He wondered why Jelena had wanted to meet him at this small restaurant and what she was still doing in the city when only fifteen hours earlier, he had left her at the airport.

Khoi was very hungry and the information he got from the restaurant said it was a small, cosy place that served very good Italian food. Yes, he was not a fan of pasta, but they must have pizza and potentially good wine.

The name of the place was "Nicola's", and it should be on number 31, but soon noticed he had gone past it and had to walk thirty two doors back.

He arrived, walked in and was met by a black waiter with a strange accent asking if he had a reservation. Khoi mentioned his name at the door. The waiter smiled and asked for his coat.

Once his coat had been placed away, the waiter returned to lead him to the allocated table. There was the table, draped with a white and red checked table cloth, waiting for him right at the shop window which faced the street.

Though the table cloth was cliché, Khoi didn't like sitting in such areas. People passing by as he ate made him paranoid. He asked to be re-seated elsewhere but was told by the waiter that all the tables were booked.

Khoi looked around and noted there were only three customers in and twelve tables. Two of the customers sat at the back table kissing as their meal went cold, the other, an elderly man, reading whilst drinking his wine. "Are you sure?" He asked the waiter. "Yes, all the tables are booked." He replied with a grin.

Khoi decided not to make a fuss just yet. He thought he could wait there for Jelena to arrive. Before he could order some water, he received a glass of red, he looked up at the rather creepy waiter who had his hands behind his back "Your companion said I should serve you a Malbec, she is coming in five minutes."

Khoi couldn't argue with that. He smelt it pretending to know what he was looking for before drinking. It wasn't bad. So he waited, looking outside, watching people pass by. All the other small shops and businesses were closed except the kebab shop next to the tattoo parlour across the street which was also open.

A man, who appeared frail, walked his dog, nearly slipping on the icy pavement. Khoi wanted to race out and help him but another person had beaten him to it. A tall athletic young looking person caught the man from behind. Khoi could make out the younger man asking if the old man was alright and the geriatric seemed to thank him as he slowly made his way.

Though unsure, Khoi thought he may have recognised the helper but, he only caught a quick glimpse of his face, but that was enough to get his pulse racing. He hoped it wasn't who he thought it was, good job the wine was there he thought as he watched the helper walk into the tattoo parlour.

Khoi began to get nervous and slightly agitated. he didn't want to believe it could be the person he thought he saw, but yet, he couldn't shake off the feeling.

Khoi began to move his leg up and down, transfixed by the tattoo parlour. Khoi could see a bit through the shop window, part of his vision obscured by the name of the restaurant he was in and the sheets of designs on offer placed on the shop window of the skin ink merchants, exhibiting their trade of permanent marking. He could see the helper chatting with someone, yet not his face. Who could it be? Khoi asked himself.

Then emerging from the tattooist establishment was a face he did know. With her coat on and walking briskly over to the restaurant, their eyes met and Jelena waved at him. Khoi was confused but saved his questions for her arrival.

Jelena entered and walked straight past the waiter to Khoi. He stood up and received a hug from her and two kisses on the cheek "Hello Khoi."

"Jelena… nice to see you… so soon. I thought you left?" He asked bemused.

"I know darling." She said as she took off her coat and handed it to the waiter who had followed her. "Have you ordered yet? I am starving. What are you drinking?" She asked. Khoi grew more suspicious, yet replied "Malbec. You ordered it. What are you still doing here?" He enquired, but Jelena's priorities were set. "I'll have the Malbec too… would you recommend it?" She asked Khoi

"Yes, it's not bad." He replied calmly. "Now, what are you doing here?"

"Come Khoi, I thought you would be glad to see me." She snapped. "But if you must know, I forgot to give you your Christmas gift and thought it would be rude of me not to considering how nice you have treated me throughout my stay." Khoi was still not satisfied. Her wine arrived. Jelena thanked the man and took a sip. "You are right, it's lovely."

"Ok, I get the Christmas gift excuse, but what were you doing over there?" Khoi asked referring to the establishment across the road. She gave a disconcerting look

"What else do you do at a tattooist? Get a filling?" She responded rhetorically. "Am I going to be interrogated all night? I thought the Stasi were closed for business." Then she began to rise "Look if you aren't happy to see me, then I might as well go."

Khoi reached across the table waving her down as they drew unwanted attention from the other diners. He struck a consolatory note "Sit down, sit down, I am happy to see you, I swear, I was just surprised." She raised her eye brow, so Khoi added "Pleasantly surprised." She folded her arms and gawked at him "We are in a nice place, it's a nice evening and you are here. Please seat down, let's have dinner."

Jelena's frown disappeared as she sat down and added "You have to try the pizza, the crust is thin but not dry." She clearly knew his preference.

An order was placed and Khoi decided to put his reservations at the back of his mind.

"What tattoo did you get?" he asked

"If you are good, maybe I'll show you later." She alluringly replied then winked at him. "And the gift?" Khoi persisted. Jelena reproached him "Impatient child. You'll see it by the end of the evening, I promise."

The waiter arrived to take their order; Khoi seemed to relax as they bantered about their pet hates. Yet, despite how much he tried, Khoi couldn't help but steal a glance at the place across the road, the sign on the door read "Closed" and the helper wasn't there anymore. He had been ushered into the backroom for his appointment.

The good Samaritan, whom the tattoo artist, called Carl, greeted as "Ingi" took off his trousers in preparation for his inking. He was just there to have the rest of his art work completed.

The work concerned were the tattoos on his thighs. On Ingi's left thigh was a black unicorn with a crown around its neck and chain dangling down from it tattooed in gold. He initially insisted on a white tattoo, but soon realised it didn't show, only the outline of the unicorn appeared on his skin.

Ingi changed his demands and requested that a black unicorn be embossed onto his skin, but the lion was to stay brown, that at least could show on the skin.

He aimed to have both animals on his thigh to mark his links with his mother's home country, Britain by having the animals in their coat of arms published permanently on his upper thighs. The unicorn was finished and the outline of the lion had been created, time to colour it in.

Ingi was invited by Carl to lie on the examination table. The man picked the colour to be used and unscrewed the top and asked "You ready?"

"Sure, got any reading materials?" asked Ingi. That's why Carl liked Ingi. This man appeared to have no pain threshold. Most people wouldn't have the strength to stand being inked for hours on end, but this Ingi could do.

The first time he came for the outline of the unicorn, Ingi spent the whole time listening to his music. The second time, he sat through it reading a book as the colour was filled in. The third visit, for the outline of the lion, Ingi slept and that came as surprise to Carl. Indeed Ingi was the perfect customer because it meant he could finish things quickly.

Carl went to the front room to get a pile of magazines. He offered them to Ingi who selected the "Men's Health" magazine.

With his latex gloves on, Carl dipped the needle into the ink and began. Initially, Ingi felt the pain and it was awful but he didn't show it and he wasn't going to. It was a matter of pride for him because he was always been seen as the hard man.

Ingi flicked through the pages and saw an advert that caught his attention. It was for protein shakes to aid muscle development. Ingi turned the page and read on about a television hard man and his fitness regime, yet he felt something wasn't right. Ingi stopped his reading and though he heard the machine, rather than mounting, the pain appeared to be subsiding.

When Carl noticed he was being observed, he paused and asked "Is everything alright?"

"Yeah, everything is fine." Ingi replied as he carried on reading "How long do you think this will take?" He asked "Three, maybe four hours?" Carl replied trying to concentrate.

The machine hummed on with Carl stopping from time to time to clean off excess pigment as the needles entered his skin at a rate of 2365 time a minute.

Perhaps he was now accustomed to the pain, Ingi thought as Carl continued. "I think I will take a nap" He said to Carl who just gave him a thumbs up.

Placing the opened magazine over his face, Ingi shut his eyes, clasping his hand across his chest and trying to sleep. A further 37 minutes passed before a sensation, or lack of it, began to trouble Ingi. He didn't just stop feeling the machine, he soon realised that his leg felt very heavy. He tried to wiggle his toes and found he couldn't. It took tremendous effort to open his eyes and once done, he could not blink.

This was triggering a state of fear, Ingi wanted to sit up, but couldn't. He wanted to cry out for help and beg the tattooist to stop, but for some reason, his voice seemed to have left him. It seemed as though part of his body was being weighed down as though a heavy rock was being placed on his chest restricting him from taking in enough air to speak.

Ingi's lungs seemed to struggle to take in air and his heart beat slowed. His vision hadn't gone yet, and that made things all together more alarming. He was trapped in his body yet aware of his surroundings. He could hear it, feel it, even sense it but could not move or speak nor close his eyes for that matter, and he was left with the picture of a man covered in sweat whilst doing a sit up as potentially the last image he would see . Even worse was that the humming of the machine would be the last thing he would hear. It was strange because he genuinely thought that if this were the end, the noise would transition from that of the machine to that of harps played by cherubs.

Soon, even his sight, which he had clung to as the last vestige linking him to his surroundings soon began to fail him too, his breathing was shallow and his heart pumped at a snail's pace.

Ingi knew something was desperately wrong, he knew he was slipping away, but there was no pain, something he would have longed for. A feeling of pain, no matter how sharp would have given him some assurance, at least something to cling to, proving he was alive, but there wasn't any, just the sound of the machine.

Surely, Ingi thought, Carl would notice that his canvas was in desperate trouble, but the man was wrong. Carl assumed that Ingi was being his normal usual, hard, self and besides, he was too busy concentrating on the application of a darker pigment on to the lion's teeth and it wasn't as easy as Carl thought.

Carl worked on, blending different shades of the pigments to give the best colour and effect. He was lost in his work, this was to be his masterpiece and he was determined to make it dazzle above others.

Carl didn't spare the gold ink and he wasn't going to charge extra as he got the teeth just so. The eyes were tough. He gave the lion deep blue eyes and furnished it with a mane of wild fiery orange and brown. The crown needed to be perfect and he spent an extra 30 minutes more than he planned on getting it right. No time to take a break, he was almost done, Carl encouraged himself to continue.

Carl eventually gave up after three hours at work, his steady hand ached. He stopped, sat back in his chair and proposed "May be we should call it a day for now." He said . "I only have the left leg to go…" he added as he began to clean the area of excessive ink and it was then he noticed a yellow ting to the skin which seemed taut.

Carl began to feel the worry set in as he quickly took off his glove and touched the body, it was colder than normal. He pressed on the tattoo, it should at least hurt a little, he contemplated, but there was no response. Carl he shook his customer. "Hey man, Ingi? Are you still asleep?" He asked. Ingi's arm slid to his side, dangling off the side of the examination table, exposing his bluish discoloured hand.

Carl was shaking in fear as he lifted the magazine that covered his face, the sight of the blue lips and the eyes sinking into the skull was so horrifying, Carl leapt backwards and screamed.

At Nicola's, dessert was brought to the table where Khoi and Jelena sat. They had both ordered the panna cotta, but weren't impressed when it was served before them.

To hide their disappointment, a change in topic was needed. "We both grew up behind the iron curtain, what was it like having Christmas in Bulgaria before capitalism came rushing in?" Khoi asked. "During the communist years we lived in Romania." Jelena corrected "My mother is from Romania. We lived not too far from the presidential palace. Christmas was lovely, though austere."

"We made sweets and our own decorations" a happy glow ensued from her as the nostalgia of the time was evidently welcomed. "We exchanged gifts… shoes, clothes for the kids, wine and such for the adults." Then it disappeared, Jelena's smile dissolved as she continued "Then it happened. 1989. The revolution… People were being killed on the streets, some were starving and we could see it from our flat, all the killing because one man wanted to stay in power... I remember my mother coming to my room telling me "There will be no Christmas this year." Then we had to go, we had to disappear in the night, driving all the way to Serbia. Christmas was no longer fun for me, not after that..." Jelena soon realised she had lost Khoi's attention as he looked out the window concentrating on the happenings outside. She turned and realised what was the focus of his gaze.

Carl, the tattooist, was outside his establishment pacing franticly and speaking to a police officer as another stepped out of the parlour to join the conversation shortly before another police car arrived. "So, tell me about your Christmas?" Jelena asked in an attempt to divert his attention and his mind. Only the first worked. Khoi looked straight at her and asked "Why do I know that the happenings out there have something to do with you?"

She gave a sneer and pretended "I don't know what you are talking about"

"Don't lie to me! I saw you leave the tattooist and now there are two police cars and an ambulance out there. What have you done?" Khoi asked in assertive but lowered tone to avoid eavesdroppers. "Oh Khoi, you know me so well." She replied as she reached into her bag and took out a handful of colourful packets.

Baffled by the items, Khoi took hold of one and enquired "What is this?"

"Your Christmas present. Tattoo pigments. You told me of your tormentor, Ingbard, so I tracked him down and found out he was going to get a tattoo today and thought you might enjoy seeing his demise." She announced. He was still confused, so Khoi asked "His demise? What are you talking about?"

As Jelena collected the pigments, returning to her bag as she added "I read your notes. Very impressive. I must say your studies of lethal substances is quiet extensive." She dipped her spoon into the dessert progressing "From the list you made, I wondered what would be most effective. I chose to use Botox."

Khoi was swept by a tide of dread as he looked back at the activities across the road. Botulinum toxin was a substance he toyed with out of fallacy rather than with any seriousness. It didn't take a lot of effort to deduce what Jelena could have done. He pictured her going into the place, knowing the movement of her target; exchanging the pigments with the contaminated ones and with her taste for dramatics, she brought him here to watch the results.

Khoi imagined Ingbard receiving his tattoo, unbeknown to him that with every puncture and perforation of his skin, he was slowly being injected with a higher dose of the most lethal substance known to man. Heaven only knew what Ingbard must have gone through as the toxins slowly deprived him of the use of his limbs as his muscle relaxed, progressively attacking the body's most important muscle, his heart. Respiratory failure and cardiac arrest would have followed soon after, all in a manner, though possibly painless, evil and crushing.

A great mass of fury was rising in Khoi as he watched the perpetrator of the ennoble act chew on her treat remarking "This is delicious!"

Khoi could take no more, he picked up his half-filled glass of wine and threw at her face before storming away from the table, eager to get away from her before his unlimited rage was unleashed and he couldn't predict what he could have done.

At the front door, Khoi cried out "My coat!" Sensing the danger the small waiter leapt into action bringing the coat over to Khoi. As he wore it, Jelena came over to him and requested "Where are you going?" Khoi did not reply as he brought out his wallet and handed the waiter some money "Didn't you like you gift?" she asked as she drew closer. Khoi raised his hand out in palm facing her towards her stating "Don't come near me!" and stomped out of Nicola's. With everyone looking at her, Jelena said to the waiter "The meal was wonderful, but I think it's time to go. Could I have my coat please?"

Khoi walked away towards the station pausing momentarily to view the growing number of people around the scene, before continuing. There was no precedence to this feeling of outrage which he had.

He felt deceived and rather unsafe. The message was clear, she was not to be trusted and was a lady to be avoided, but it was impossible. Half a kilometre away from the restaurant, he heard his name being called "Khoi!" He turned and found her jogging towards him. He wasn't in the mood to expose himself to any further threats and began to pace away. "Khoi! Let's talk about this!"

"I don't want to!" he roared "I didn't ask you to fight my battles for me! I was over it already. It was in the past, fourteen years ago!"

Jelena caught up with him and overtook him, standing in front of him holding him back from progressing. "Listen to me!" She shouted

"Leave me alone you witch!" He retorted. Jelena was having none of it. No one calls her a witch. She slapped him across the face. As Khoi turned to face her, she could tell he had surrendered all opposition to self-restraint as his eyes flung open and flame seemed to have lit the fuse to his overriding anger.

Jelena took to her heels, dashing further away from the restaurant. She looked over her shoulder and found Khoi chasing after her. She approached the end of the road before she decided not to reach it, rather, she turned into a small pathway between two tall buildings. Khoi was just an arm's length away when she turned. He followed her but once in the dimly lit, narrow lane, there was no sign of her.

The pathway was lined with bins and doors which served as the back entrance of the buildings. Khoi was determined to find her. He walked cautiously, past a cat which was minding its own business, towards a skip when he was brought down by an extended leg tripping him.

Khoi landed on his side, Jelena pounced on him, turning Khoi over on his back and pinning him down using her knees. Khoi struggled but Jelena was able keep him down via a swift punch to the face. He was more surprised than anything. Khoi didn't know what was happening and that was principally why he did not resist her.

Jelena proceeded to kiss him on the lips. Khoi was instantly disarmed and aroused by her. He grabbed her by the hair kissing deeply. He felt a swell of passion developing, he couldn't understand where it came from but he wanted it.

The kiss lasted over a minute till she stopped it. They look into each other's eyes, Khoi wondered what was going to happen next, Jelena shut her eyes and drew closer, and Khoi thought it meant another kiss on its way and equally shut his eyes and raised his head, but his lips were met by another sharp blow from Jelena's fist which almost knocked him out cold.

Khoi lay on the ground dazed as Jelena got off his chest and boasted "the last person who called me a witch, didn't live to see the following day" Then she relented, her voice filled with feeling adding "… but I love you. That's why I am telling you this. You are not one of them, you aren't a killer…" Jelena warned. She picked up her bag walked away shouting "Goodbye Khoi."

Khoi found it difficult to raise his head. A mixture of a slight concussion and affections he had never felt before made him giddy. He struggled to get off the dirty, cobbled and snowy floor, propping himself up, he cried out to her pleading to her to return as she walked away. By the time he got to his feet and raced out to the main road, she had vanished.

He stood alone in the middle of the side walk, not far from where the night had started, wondering if he had entered a room where all the evils of the world had sat to eat and rather than turn away, he joined them and now he had to pay the price with his soul which felt destroyed.

Khoi stood under the street light, weeping. What was happening to him? He questioned himself. This wasn't what he needed, a conflict which tore him apart. His anxiety kicked in, Khoi's constitution began to crumble, and he had to prevent himself from breaking down.

He shut his eyes, summing up his reserves. He had to make it back to the hotel. Khoi dusted his off his coat, cleaning his hands on it before running all the way to his hotel, all 6km or more.

Khoi had been running for an hour when he stopped to catch his breath and cry again. He soon noticed he was attracting attention. He wasn't in the mood for that and continued his race.

Waiting at the airport, Jan stood nervously and patiently behind the metal rail, excited. He looked out for her and soon saw Kat emerging from the gates. She raced to embrace and kiss him. It was so nice to see her, so much so, he forgot the familiar stranger.

Their taxi ride home was a one sided affair as Kat could not stop talking about her amazing trip with Julien in Hong Kong. She showed off the pictures taken of the sites, the food, the lights, and the architecture ... it made Jan sick with envy.

To Jan's relief, they arrived to the flat. It soon evaporated when he totally had forgotten that he had left Wolfgang to work his magic. He intended to delay Kat's entry to the flat but couldn't, she needed the toilet and had run into the building, into the lift and up to flat, leaving him to pay the taxi driver and take up her bags.

"Please let her not kill me." He prayed as he entered the lift with her belongings. Reaching the door of the flat, Jan found it slightly opened. He followed, and there was no screaming, yet.

He dropped the bags and walked towards the dining area to find her sitting at the table, candles lit and placing an oyster on her plate. On the table sitting in an ice bucket was a bottle of champagne. By the candles were two roses, one red one yellow. Another platter of ice held several shells of oysters. Kat, noticing his presence turned and smiled "You always know how to make me happy. That's why I love you. Thank you" she said. Jan's mouth replied "You are worth it." In his mind, knowing what was set to follow, he said "THANK YOU WOLFGANG".

Khoi arrived at his hotel, panting as he walked through the automatic doors. He was greeted by the receptionist. He walked past her without as much as a smile of acknowledgement.

In the safety of his room, Khoi locked the door and was just about to continue his nervous breakdown when there was knock on the door. Khoi hadn't made it more than two paces away for the door so he turned to look through the peep hole. There, looking nearly as troubled as he did was Marcel, barely able to stand still.

Khoi opened the door to receive him and was met with the words "Boss, you look awful."

"Thank you, you don't look so good yourself." Khoi replied. There was a moment of hesitation before Marcel began to laugh. This prompted Khoi to do the same before asking him in.

"Joel called. He asked me to check up on you... everything alright?" Marcel asked as he walked further in, homing on the advent calendar. Marcel walked up to it and took out the chocolate for the day which Khoi had ignored. "He said something about you meeting Jelena or something like that. Is that why you didn't come out for drinks?" Marcel continued as he ate the chocolate then observed, "Your lip looks a bit swollen, and your eye... were you in a fight?"

Jelena was clearly the master of the mind games Khoi concluded and he wasn't intending to break. "I am ok... I just... I fell." He replied, going to the fridge for a bottle of water. Khoi opened it and drank it all at once, disposing of the bottle into the nearby bin. He was not in the mood of answering any questions so he asked for an update. "Haven't seen you since yesterday. How did it go with Siegfried?"

"Yeah." Marcel replied in down cast tone "It's all sorted."

Khoi seeking more details enquired "Was it smooth?" Marcel did not reply. "I know it must have been hard on you... Are you ok?" Khoi asked, in an attempt to show some concern.

"I'm fine, really." Khoi could tell Marcel wasn't fine as he sat on the bed, placing the remaining piece of chocolate by his side, clasping his hands and looking rather vacant for a moment. "The guy is... was a bastard anyway." Marcel adapted his words. "He saw us preparing his meal and he didn't beg, didn't even bother to show any remorse. He just watched. He knew what was coming." Marcel appeared to be grinding his teeth as though frustrated before turning to Khoi, "I asked him why he did it? You know what he told me?" Khoi shook his head to confirm he hadn't a clue. "He acted bravely, with the earnestness of an innocent child as he looked into my eyes and said I didn't do it. He took the meal without fuss or whimper and without a sign of fear. "When we were done, with no one looking, I don't know why, but I kissed him on the head and said I was sorry."

"But we had a job to do, that was all I could focus on and when we finished, I couldn't take it, I had to get away. That's why I drove off with the car to a quiet spot to think, I just didn't know why I was feeling like shit."

Khoi could tell Marcel was hurting and fighting back the tears, but he had to know. "Did you believe him?" Marcel sat there, running his hand through his hair. For the first time, Khoi saw Marcel's vulnerability as a tear rolled down Marcel face.. Marcel didn't want to answer, but he had to "Yes, I believed him." He confessed.

This infuriated Khoi and he promptly rebuked Marcel wagging his finger as he reiterated "Shit! I told you that if you had any doubt you should have called me, you shouldn't have done it if you were uncertain... why did you go ahead with it?"

Marcel stopped shaking, regained his resolve, as he ate the remaining chocolate he replied "I saw some Nazi memorabilia in his bag…" Then he got up and made his way to the door, walking past Khoi who stood there stunned. At the door, before turning the handle, Marcel chillingly added "Such people deserve to die. See you tomorrow Boss."

"Marcel?" Khoi called before he walked out the door halting his progress by placing his hand on his shoulder "You don't have to carry on if you don't want to?"

Marcel just looked at him and smiled "Nah, I'm cool. Besides, it's sort of fun." Marcel patted him on the arm before bidding Khoi "Good night, see you tomorrow Boss." Marcel walked out the door and down the corridor as Khoi called out to him "Don't call me boss!" In return, Khoi received a gesture telling him to fuck off.

As he shut the door, Khoi relaxed. Though strange, it was refreshing to see that he wasn't the only one with issues lately, but he wasn't interested in facing his right now. It was already close to eleven, so he chose to go to bed using his most trusted means.

Khoi slept, trying to keep his mind off the events of the evening. Joel, on the other hand, was still coming to terms with the events of his day which seemed unwilling to end. Having left Mikel's flat, he returned to the garage with a huge coffee grinder tucked under his arm.

Upon seeing him return with the appliance, Daniel jokingly asked "Now what is that for? Is the garage slowly turning into a kitchen?"

Joel was not amused by the Joke in the slightest. He had already his appetite for such hilarities to the ordeal and the overpowering smell of the substance made him dizzy. Quoting Callum, Joel explained "The lye will not completely break down the bones; it only makes them very brittle. Therefore, we grind them to powder with this and flush it down with the rest. Got it?"

The lye had been ready to use for a while. It was time to address the body. They put on their protective clothing, goggles and gas mask. They opened the box and the site of the discoloured being surrounded by different shades of yellow and brown excrement caught Daniel off guard.

He felt sick and immediately and raced to the large laundry sink nearby to vomit. He thought it was going to be a mild spate of time, but by pulling off his gas mask, the smell heightened his gag reflexes causing him to heave up so much of the contents of his stomach all he could produce was bile. Joel just shook his head, "Why Lord?" he asked.

"Come on, help me out here." Ralph called out to Joel who was eager to carry on with the job. They reached in through the muck and lifted the body that, even though rigor mortis had expired, appeared to have stiffened in that position, making it easy for them to lift to the vat. However, their hands were occupied and could not open the cauldron. "Daniel, please?

Could you give us a hand here?" Ralph called again.

Daniel turned round, sniffed for a moment before putting back on his gas mask and goggles. He opened the heavy lid as the others mounted the small step by the contraption. Joel, almost compassionately, was not willing to put the man through any more pain, ordered "We're not going to dump him in there. We'll put him in slowly ok?"

"Slowly, like he's going to mind." Ralph remarked sarcastically. Despite his lack of enthusiasm, Ralph lowered the sore covered carcass into the vat as gently as he could. Daniel didn't seem to care as much and shut the door of the vessel quickly, screwing down the clamps before returning back to the tub sink to continue spewing.

Two and a half more hours in, they felt they had finally surpassed the instructed time, and sure enough, the body and lye was transformed into a smooth pulp of brown-grey sludge, with no solid parts but bones left. Ralph, with some unexpected help from Joel, fished out the blackened bones using a pair of tongs and a net, rinsing them afterwards with some water before putting them in the grinder.

The grinder, under the supervision of Daniel, ground away at the ebony pieces it was fed. Meanwhile, Ralph and Joel carefully manoeuvred the boiler to the garage drain, and gently started tipping it over allowing the contents of the vat to pour out into the sewers below.

After some more tilting of the boiler and Joel cursing, they were done and started hosing down the garage, the boiler as well as the grinder and even each other a bit. It was now well past midnight, but Joel at least felt it made a difference that they were done. There was no longer a box, or a victim. All he needed now was a drink before heading off to sleep.

Ralph, Daniel and Joel sat in the living room, unable to speak. Even when the drinks were brought, the only one able to consume the beers was Daniel who was unable to understand the emotional turmoil that Joel was experiencing, it was just a job. Ralph felt guilty for participating in this depraved act in the first place and now had to clean up the mess.

At one in the morning with them all stretched out on the sofa, Joel's phone rang. It was Marcel who was off to Join Mikel and Paul at the bar. Marcel confirmed that he had seen Khoi and he was alright. That came as a relief to Joel and once he hung up, he got another call from Mikel.

"Where the fuck have you been?" Joel shouted instinctively. He could hear that Mikel was in a nightclub. Mikel Informed Joel that it had been a hectic day and he had been travelling with Paul to organise things on Khoi's orders. Joel was too drained to delve care. "We'll talk about it later." Joel hung up abruptly causing Mikel to worry for a moment, but it didn't last, he had three guests from Serbia who were led by a tall, dark hairy man called Darko Jamina. It was the perfect place to discuss the plans for the morning.

*24 December 2010*

The following day was Christmas Eve. Oliver woke up in an excited mood. After spending the last few days grieving over the death of his comrade, Richard, the day was finally here and his son was coming for Christmas.

Richard's loss was devastating to him. Yes he was a messed up sort of fellow but he was dependable, not like the others, and a fun guy. He knew he was going to miss him and the sense of loss was only heightened by the attitude of the others.

Siegfried seemed to have kept to his word that he didn't want to be reached during his holiday all attempts to contact him and break the news failed. On the other hand, Robert had always considered Richard's death a foreseen inevitability. "The guy was a junkie." Robert had proclaimed to him in private. "It was bound to happen."

It was ok that Robert did not consider the situation seriously, but Oliver thought by not attending the funeral on the account that he was busy Christmas shopping and the funeral coincided with a dinner date he had, that was just disrespectful. But that was yesterday. It was Christmas Eve and there was no time to despair. Christmas was to be spent at his parents in Cologne with his son Luke.

Luke was five and very spritely. He was the result of his failed marriage with a Danish lady called Mai who had no time for his way of life. She was intelligent, with a degree in economics. This should have bad enough to put things on the rocks due to the aspirational differences, but they were very much in love. What broke things up was the fact that on principle, she refused to be a gangster's moll and after five years and two weeks together, she upped and left with Luke.

Things remained cordial. They agreed on visitation and at no point did she ask for any monetary support nor was she combative or bitter and he was intent on keeping it that way by always being on time and never breaking any promises made to Luke. What always hung over Oliver's head whenever they met was her sneaking eyes of judgement and though she never said it, it was clear what she thought "You picked your gang over me."

Each Christmas brought back the memories of these troubling times and it didn't help that he was grieving too. But he had to cheer up, for Luke.

As Oliver got ready to go to the airport, he checked if he had all the gifts he had bought for all those who counted including Mai. Oliver hoped, this time, she would accept it. The year before, she sent it back with a note that read "I'm not going to wear jewellery bought from the suffering of others."

He got into the car and drove to the airport, arriving on time. He waited in arrivals for a glimpse of his family, his feet trembling in excitement since he hadn't seen Luke in four months.

After several minutes, they emerged. Luke cried out "Far" and ran into his open arms. He lifted him and tossed him the air, kissing his little son on the cheek several times before formally taking notice of Mia standing there with Luke's baggage.

"Hi", he said and gave her a kiss on the cheek. "How are you?"

"I'm fine. So how are you?" Her formality clearly hid something, and he knew it. Oliver replied "I'm ok, could be better."

There was an uncomfortable moment of quiet before he replied "I got a present for you." Oliver reached into his pocket and was about to produce it when Mai said "Don't make it difficult. Please keep it." Oliver was shot down again. Mai realised she was frosty and changed modes "It was thoughtful of you."

"Got time for a coffee?" he persisted. "Not really, my flight leaves in 70 minutes, so I best go back up and check in." She saw the disappointment in his face and revealed "I'll be back on the 30th for a night, we could catch up then? Like old times."

Oliver's smile returned as he replied "That would be great."

"Good. He's been to the toilet and I guess he's good to go." She then pulled on Luke's cheek and told him "You behave yourself Mister."

Luke returned with "You behave yourself madam. Say hello to Uffe for me." This was followed by a kiss.

Oliver's curiosity pushed him to inquire "So... who's Uffe?"

"My boyfriend." She revealed bluntly side stepping the matter by stating "Alright, have fun." Then she reached over and hugged him. Oliver struggled to let go, but he had to. Mai began to walk away toward the departure as Luke cried out "Bye Mummy." She turned back and waved.

Oliver's heart broke again but only momentarily as a kiss from Luke brought the joy to his day. "So you are excited to seeing Grand Pa and Grand Ma?" He asked the little one. "YES!" Luke cried. Off they went to the car park and began their journey through the city. He turned on their favourite songs causing the time to fly by.

They approached the high-rise district whilst listening to music, the song of choice was Elton John's "Goodbye yellow brick road" a favourite of Luke's due to the chorus. They turned left into Tiergartenstrasse and were making good time, but soon approached the traffic lights which turned red. They stopped.

Oliver took the opportunity to call his parents to inform them of their progress. He used his hands free mobile and it was answered quickly. The light turned green and off they went turning into Ben-Gurion-Strasse, and then left into Potsdamer Strasse driving flanked by the tall buildings of the Potsdamer area. "Hello? Mum?" exclaimed Oliver, "We have the VIP here and we are on our way!" His mother was eager to speak to her grandchild "Say hello to Grandma!" he urged the little one

"Hello Grandma!", Luke shouted as they got to another set of traffic lights which turned red causing them to stop again.

"Oh my little cookie, how are you?" she replied. As they chatted, Oliver's mother asked for their estimated time of arrival, the traffic lights turned yellow and Oliver was set to start the car and said "We are set to arrive…" Oliver fell silent.

Luke felt a spray of liquid on his face. He turned to look at his window. A hole had developed, splattered with blood. Luke entered a state of complete panic as he turned to his father, blood was pouring down the side of his face. He was slumped forward on the steering wheel

There was a hole in the side of Oliver's head the size of a tennis ball and for a moment, light streamed through it. The rest of Luke's father's face was sprayed all over the boy, the windscreen and the dashboard.

"Far?" Luke called. "Far? Far?" Luke began to shake. He began to sob "Stop playing Far, please?" he begged as the cars behind kept honking impatiently since the traffic light had turned green, oblivious to the boy's despair in the car ahead. Luke's grandmother was still on the line and asked what was going on "Daddy fell asleep. He's not waking up." She instructed him to get out of the car and see if he could fetch help.

Luke halfway fell out of the car and ran to the car behind theirs, frantically waving and banging on the door. The man stepped out of his car and at the sight of the boy, gasped.

The person followed Luke and opened the door to the driver's side of the car and on sight of the bloodbath, turned round and vomited on the car door. The man recovered and reached for his mobile phone holding Luke tightly as the boy started to shake.

Two pedestrians came running to the car and opened the door. The body slumped out onto the pavement as the pair tried to administer first aid, but it was too late.

From their vantage point on the roof of the Kollhoff Tower, Marcel and Mikel marvelled in awe as they watched the situation unfold through their binoculars. Khoi on the other hand, stood there, his back turned to the world, eyes firmly fixed to the ground asking "Is it done?"

"Straight through his ear" Marcel confirmed as the sniper got up and dismantled his gun. "Well done." Khoi commended and waved at Paul "Give the man his money. Mikel, call off the others."

Mikel took out his walkie-talkie and informed the other two snipers to stand down as Paul walked up to the man and presented him with a suitcase "It's all there." He confirmed.

"Thank you Mr Nyguyen." The sniper responded as he received the case from Paul.

"I don't understand why a bank transfer wouldn't suffice." Khoi remarked. He was still not keen to view the events of the day but more interested in walking towards the door "It is a Liechtenstein account after all, no one would ever check."

"It would take too long." replied the sniper.

"OK, thanks Mr Jamina for me and safe journey back to Serbia. Goodbye." Khoi opened the door and eagerly left the roof top. Leaving Paul to shake the sniper's hand and thank him for his services and the sniper to remark "Your leader is strange isn't he?"

"He's special." Paul corrected.

Mikel and Marcel came to shake the man's hand. Mikel described his actions as "absolutely awesome, just amazing." Wondering how he could do it with less than five hours sleep and having drank a lot. He got a chilling response "You have to live through a war to understand."

"I guess you have to." Mikel replied and with the others bade the sniper farewell. The rest of the gang left the sniper behind to collect his belongings and met Khoi by the lift.

As Khoi called the lift, the others approached. Marcel, in a euphoric haze proclaimed "That was amazing; I never thought he could get him. Is there any training available for that on our employment scheme?" Khoi gave him a disabling glance that silenced him.

The lift arrived. "So, where next Boss?" asked Mikel. Khoi cringed and then turned to give him a look that could silence a noisy child. "First, don't call me Boss. Paul?" He called as they boarded the lift. Paul put on his latex gloves before entering the access code that allowed the doors to close. People weren't allowed up or down from the top and roof floors without it. The doors closed. Khoi pondered silently till they got to the ground floor.

They stepped out of the lift into the reception hall. Muted pandemonium was the main stay with the echoes of "Oh my God" and "What's happening" being the chorus of the normally stoic business people in their suit, clients and visitors looking visibly upset at the sight of the cars across the road surrounded by people and police officers. Then they all watched through the large pane of glass in silence with only the sounds of their mobile phones ringing breaking the trend. None of them answered, they were too engrossed.

Khoi ignored it all and walked out of the building with his colleagues disregarded by all who should have been taking note. Now they were outside, people standing like statues blocking the way in silence or sobbing. The police had cordoned off the road to traffic. This was a crime scene now.

Khoi walked on up the pavement. His phobia and experiences had provided him with a defence mechanism that enabled him to mentally and physically block out such events when they happened around him. Once his foot hit the pavement, Khoi faced down looking only at the ground. He entered a self-induced state of hypnosis and walked straight ahead navigating through the stagnant onlookers, past the paramedics with their hands covered in blood as they brought out the body from the car and past the police taking a statement from the weeping Good Samaritan now covered in a blanket. He blocked out the screams of a child wailing at the top of his lungs "FAR! FAR!" as he was held back by a female officer, trying her best to keep him from running to his dead father's body. Khoi even managed to block out the feeling of the cold wind blowing mildly and the soft snow falling to the ground.

All this Khoi did with great success as he walked across the road to Leipziger Platz not paying attention to the traffic lights or the police cars speeding by until he heard a voice cry "KHOI!" followed by the fading sound of the horn of the car that missed him by inches.

He snapped back to reality and found the others still on the opposite side of the road surprised by his actions. When the traffic lights at the pedestrian crossing finally turned green, they jogged across to meet him "What happened there? Didn't you see that car coming? You nearly got hit!" Mikel shouted.

"What car?" Khoi asked.

"You must have been away with the fairies." Mikel concluded.

Ignoring the statement, Khoi carried on walking towards the Potsdamer Platz train and subway station. Still left with no answer, Mikel asked again "Where to, Khoi?"

Khoi turned to the them and condescendingly declared "It's Christmas Eve isn't" it? We've accomplished everything we aimed for, what's left? Go home to your families." He was met by stunned gazes and lack of movement. "Why do you look so surprised? Don't you celebrate Christmas?"

"We do, but we usually are told to come and spend Christmas with the boss." Mikel revealed.

"Who does?" Queried Khoi.

"Joel" Mikel answered.

Khoi rolled his eyes and with a sigh "Well, this year let's do something different. Go home to your families. I'll take the blame. Just go and have fun."

"Wow, thanks Boss" Khoi frowned at Marcel who promptly corrected himself "I mean Khoi. See you on the 27$^{th}$ then?" Khoi nodded and shook each of their hands as they parted company.

They all seemed eager to vanish with the exception of one. Khoi noticed Paul sombre position. It pulled on his heart strings and with the others now gone, he had the opportunity to ask Paul "Why the long face?" Paul initially said there was nothing to worry about, but Khoi urged him to confide in him. Paul finally gave in and replied "I don't have a family... I usually spent Christmas with Stefan and he's gone..." It all fell into place and Khoi placed his hand on his shoulder saying "I'm sorry." Paul's face fell again "Hey, you know what, I had an invite to a Christmas party, was going to spend the day on my own as well... but we could meet at my hotel room at about five tomorrow evening and we'll do something fun, ok?" Paul nodded "Now do us a favour and smile."

Paul's eyes lit up and he soon felt much better and discerned "You went from pussy to bad ass in a month, you're amazing man". Not knowing whether it was a compliment or not, Khoi replied as he left "We try our best. See you."

All the good tidings were infectious. Khoi decided, rather than go to his hotel room he would take the opportunity to go to the mall to pick up a few gifts.

As he approached the underground, his mobile phone rang. It was Joel who sounded perplexed. He referred to a call he had with Marcel in an attempt to invite them over to the house for Christmas lunch and was promptly informed of what Khoi had done. "Come on Joel, they've had a terrible winter with Stefan gone and all the activities of the week, I don't see the problem with them having time on their own?"

"They are heavies. They are meant to be tough as boots, now you are telling me we should be soft on them?" Joel rebuffed. Khoi stopped in his tracked, sighed, and challenged Joel "If you want them back, ask them back!"

"Oh no, the Boss has dismissed them." Joel said in a sarcastic tone. "Just to let you know, dad came back this evening, so things are bound to return to normal soon and perhaps you can then explain to him why there will be fewer people round for Christmas."

"Alright Joel, I will". Khoi called his bluff in an attempt to stop the conversation, but it didn't work. "And another thing, I was meaning to bring this up earlier. I spoke to Ralph two days ago and he told me that you called him and told him not to bother going to his guard duty today because there wasn't any need. Khoi, what have you done?"

Khoi sighed deeply "Look, I promise I will fill you in when I come over tomorrow. Right now I have to go get some presents. Talk soon." And with that Khoi hung up and tried to forget that last few minutes.

Khoi found peace in shopping, picking up confections and electronics and then stopping over for dinner before returning to his hotel room with the gift wrapped items.

He turned on the television and watched a movie on the local television channel which was then interrupted by breaking news. He didn't want to hear, but he couldn't find the remote soon enough. The report spoke of the killing that took place in the financial district. They interviewed a witness who spoke of the child who saw his father die and how horrible it was to find the child covered in blood weeping and begging his father to wake up.

That did it. That broke him. He found the remote and turned off the TV before sitting on the bed. He felt numb all over. That soon disappeared and was gradually replaced by grief. He didn't want to face it, not today. He ran to the jar for the pills, yes it was recommended that one be taken but this was an emergency, so he took one and a half. The grief did come and it consumed him. The only saving grace was the fact that the pills acted quickly and soon he was out like a light.

# 14

*25 December 2010*

Khoi woke up feeling ragged. He had a lot to do today and struggled out of bed, literally rolling himself on to the floor and crawling to the remote control for the television which lay on the chair by the set.

He switched it on and went to the twenty four hour news channel. There were joyous happy pictures of people getting ready for Christmas and the first signs of civil unrest in Tunisia was also making the news, not that he paid much attention.

Twenty minutes of warming up during the business segment was enough. He got up, raised the volume of the television set for the background noise and went to the bathroom to brush his teeth. He did the usual ritual, turned on the tap, let the water run free, placed the tooth paste on his brush and wet it before scrubbing his teeth. Though he didn't hear the details, a voice from the set caught his attention as it said "We are still investigating the tragic events of yesterday's shooting and we are going to ensure no stone is left unturned." He stopped brushing and walked back out to see who was being interviewed.

There, on the set was a glimpse of Kat's boyfriend looking stern as he was being asked if the police could verify if this was a gang related killing "The police are acting on all leads we have at the moment and I won't be drawn to speculate if it was gang related. Right now our attention is to find the perpetrator and to comfort the family of the victim and his young son. We should keep them in our hearts today having endured such horrors before Christmas."

Clearly not getting the response she wanted the reporter wound up the conversation "Thank you Polizeihauptkommissar Jan Harbeck for your insight." Then the cameras returned to the studio and the news caster.

Khoi's head was a basket of mixed feelings. He was proud of Kat's boyfriend who was going up the ranks so quickly to the point that remarked "Polizeihauptkommissar Harbeck, good on you man." Yet in a warped way, seeing him gave his mood a lift even though it was in the most abysmal of circumstance of his own creation. More likely it was because it was probably the first time he had seen his Jan in over ten years. This was a small consolation even if was on television.

He walked to the advent calendar and took out the last piece of chocolate and ate it. It was time to get ready to spread some Christmas cheer.

His started with Khoi going to the sanatorium. He greeted the nurses he knew and gave them chocolate covered in foil showing the image of Santa Claus. It put a smile on the face of all those there. Then it was time to see Jeroen.

Khoi stood by the door waiting for the nurse to return with the items he brought after their inspection to ensure it does not contain anything that could enable a patient to harm themselves. He looked through the opening above the door into the room as a nurse brought Jeroen in.

Jeroen still had the same slightly disorientated look on his face and looked much slimmer. Khoi's heart sank watching the nurse aiding him on to a chair.

Soon, an orderly returned with his backpack and confirmed that, provided he left nothing behind, he could take the items in. Khoi asked if the doctor was in, the orderly confirmed she was around and would show up when she could.

The nurse took her place in the corner of the room as the buzzing sound signified the door could be opened. Khoi entered and was welcomed with the most chipper set of eyes he hadn't seen in a while. "KHOI!" Jeroen cried as he got up and came to meet him, giving him a great big hug. Jeroen not only looked thinner, he felt it. Once out of his embrace, Jeroen held him by the hand and said to the nurse "Khoi is my friend."

"Hello." Khoi said to the lady who just nodded and smiled.

He led Khoi to the table and he sat him down on the chair opposite his. "I am so happy to see you." Khoi said to Jeroen who just had the grin plastered on his face as he rocked back and forward. "You know it is Christmas?" Khoi added.

"Christmas?" Jeroen asked in a puzzled manner.

"Yeah, it's Christmas. We are going to take a picture together. OK?" Jeroen nodded "But first you are going to have to look good."

Khoi produced from his bag a sheet, water sprayer and a pair of scissors. The nurse coughed to get his attention, Khoi turned to look at her and she said "He won't let anyone cut his hair."

"You're new here aren't you?" Khoi scoffed as he got up, took off his coat and proceeded to approach Jeroen with the sheet. "Time for a haircut

Jeroen." He announced. Jeroen clapped his hands gleefully as the sheet was placed around his neck. "So what will it be today sir? A short trim or would you like go bald?" Jeroen giggled. "Ok Jeroen." He said as he sprayed water on Jeroen's tangled long blonde hair to wet it.

Jeroen rocked back and forward initially and then Khoi began to comb his hair and started to tell him the story of "Trusty John". As Khoi narrated the tale, Jeroen appeared pacified as the blades of the scissors took off the excess hair. Khoi paced himself in order to ensure that the tale stretched as long as the trimming would, and when he finished, he replied "I'm done." Then he reached for a small towel from his bag and proceeded to dry Jeroen's hair saying "Rub, Rub, Rub" causing Jeroen to laugh.

Khoi styled and waxed Jeroen's hair and when he was finished, he took out a mirror and showed Jeroen how he looked. Jeroen smiled as Khoi said "Looking good huh?"

"Yeah." Jeroen replied.

"Look what else I got you for our photo". Khoi took out a new shirt and cardigan and proceeded to change Jeroen from his hospital clothing to his new attire. Khoi went to the nurse and asked if she could be kind enough to take a picture using his mobile phone to capture the moment.

Khoi returned to the bag and took out some pictures. "Let's make a movie for mummy and daddy ok?" He got a blank gaze but it didn't faze him. Khoi balanced his phone and pressed record. "The camera is on, say hi!"

"HI!" Jeroen shouted.

Khoi then sat by him and took out the first picture and asked "do you remember this person?" Jeroen nodded still with his smile on. "Who is it?"

"Mummy!" He cried

"That's right!" Khoi confirmed and showed the picture to the camera and proceed to show more of his mother and asked Jeroen if he would like to take one. Jeroen picked a picture then Khoi continued. He took out another stack and went through the same process. Jeroen confirmed it was his father and took a picture for himself. Then he went through the process with a third picture.

Presenting it to him, Khoi asked "Do you remember who that is?" Jeroen's smile turned to a look of confusion. "Do you remember this person?" Khoi asked again.

"Me?" Jeroen guessed.

"No, it's Joel." The blank gaze seemed to deepen "He's your twin brother. Remember him?" Jeroen appeared to get slightly agitated and started to rock forward and back again turning away from the picture "Come on Jeroen, have a look." But he refused "Want to take a picture?" Khoi asked however Jeroen shook his head and said "No."

As Khoi tried to convince Jeroen to keep one of the pictures there was a knock on the door and a proclamation "Merry Christmas" made by the doctor as she entered.

"MARY!" Jeroen cried causing Khoi to face the phone on her.

"You're being filmed" Khoi said as Jeroen got off his chair to give her a hug. "Say hello Mary!"

"Hello!" The doctor replied.

"I'll stop filming now." Khoi said as he turned off his phone.

After the preliminary chit chat to keep Jeroen happy, Khoi asked the doctor for a moment of her time. As they went out leaving Jeroen with the pictures, they stood outside the door. Khoi raised his concerns about Jeroen's weight. She smiled and said "I'm quite glad you mentioned that. He hasn't been eating regularly since your last visit. It's what keeps him going through the weeks.

But you haven't been here for a month and as bad as his memory may be, he does remember that you are meant to show up every Friday. Every Friday he would wait excitedly for your arrival and when you didn't show up, he would refuse to eat for two to three days before he returned to normal then Friday would return and it would start again. It seems that you are the only constant in his life and in his head of mixed signals and confusion, you bring a form of structure."

The revelation brought Khoi down, he felt ashamed that he may have been the cause of his friend's suffering. He apologised to the Doctor and requested if it were possible to take Jeroen out for lunch. She looked inside at Jeroen and replied "Well, provided you have supervision, then I don't see the problem."

"Want to come then? Don't think the nurse is pretty enough for Jeroen." Khoi offered. She laughed and replied "I am meant to be clocking off in half an hour anyway, if you can wait that would be great." The doctors replied.

Khoi, not knowing where anything would be open on Christmas day took them to the hotel restaurant. They arrived just in time for lunch and sat to have a meal. Jeroen seemed to calm as Khoi talked to him about old times as he cut and fed Jeroen some turkey and potatoes. Jeroen enjoyed it all, but not as much as when they brought out the pudding of chocolate cake covered in cream.

Khoi asked the doctor if she could film the moment and Jeroen feed himself. Slowly and a bit unsteadily, Jeroen used his spoon to eat the pudding. When he finished, the doctor cheered.

With dinner over, Khoi drove them back to the sanatorium. He said goodbye to his friend and promised to come back the next Friday. As he left, the Doctor walked him to the exit and confessed "It seems that Jeroen can progress and improve. I think we should try and see how he fairs at home for a couple of days before we make long term plans on his permanent return. What we should worry about is the period of adjustment. But he will need your help. You appear to be able to reach him even if we can't. Please remember that."

"Yeah, I've been a dick." he replied, then realised how ungentlemanly it was and added "Sorry for my choice of words. Hey, I'll drop off your gift at the front desk tomorrow. I have to hurry home. Take care yeah? And Merry Christmas." She wished him the same and waved him off as he drove back to his hotel.

Arriving just before five, Khoi entered to find Paul waiting in the lobby. "Oh, you're here." He said as he made his way to the elevator. "Come on." he ordered "we had better hurry, I think we might be running late." Paul followed him into the lift and once the eighth floor was pressed, Khoi relaxed and exclaimed "Merry Christmas. How was your day?"

"Boring." Paul's honesty was refreshing and made Khoi smile.

"I hope we can change that tonight" he said as the lift arrived and the door opened. "We are going to a house party hosted by a group of Chinese students."

Once in Khoi's hotel room, Paul was informed that "I bought some stuff." Khoi changed his shirt as he spoke "I hardly know them to be honest. I just bumped into Han, the girl who invited me, whilst doing some research. She seems harmless. Oh, you are a plumber and please, please don't call me Boss." He reiterated. Khoi waxed his hair, checked the mirror and concluded he was presentable in his black slick hair and blue shirt. A bit of cologne and that was it, allowing him to exclaim. "Let's go."

Khoi drove using the directions provided and eventually got to the student accommodations at the university complex. Paul looked nervous as they walked up the steps and was given a reassuring wink by Khoi. They arrived at the door behind which music emanated loudly. It was safe to assume this was the right place.

The door opened and they were received by a stocky Asian man who looked at them without saying a word. Khoi then broke the silence by asking, "Is Han in?" The man then called out in Chinese and then Han arrived with paper cut out antlers on her head. "You came!" she cried joyfully. "Merry Christmas! Come in, come in." the pair did as instructed.

Khoi introduced Paul to her and she replied "Nice to meet you." Khoi had instructed Paul to present the two bottles of wine to her and he did so. Han was quite pleased with what she got all under the gaze of the man who opened the door who didn't look particularly impressed. "This is for you as well. Don't open it till I am gone, ok?" Khoi instructed handing over the big box to her. Now the stumpy man looked impressed saying a few words in Chinese and pointing at the box. She waved him off. "He wants me to open it so he can see what's in it." She translated. "But I won't. Come, bring your coats, I will put them in my room."

They followed and once their over coats where put away, she led them to the living room where saw 10 other Chinese people sitting on either side of three joined up small tables. She introduced them to everyone, some having English names while others kept their original ones. Khoi sat at the end of the table next to a very cute good looking girl whilst Han had Paul sat next to her.

It was a noisy affair, everyone shouting over one another in a well-mannered but clearly vibrant conversational style. The girl sitting next to him did her sincere best to engage him, but for once Khoi was more interested in the food which was plentiful.

He spent the evening eating, impressing the others with his chopstick skills. Paul didn't have such luck in that department but it did give him the opportunity to learn and Han was more than willing to teach him. The sight of Paul struggling to pick up a dumpling made Han laugh and Paul seemed to enjoy the attention as well. She then proceeded to teach him some drinking games and he excelled challenging everyone at the table one after the other and making them drink. This was a different Paul, different from the quiet guy who stood at the back letting others take the lead and Khoi liked this new version.

Khoi looked at his watch and was amazed at how time flew by. It was already 8:32pm. He had one more stop before his night was through. He told Han he was about to leave and needed his coat. She looked disappointed, but walked him to her room followed by Paul. As she unlocked the door she asked "Can I open my present now?"

"If you want." Khoi replied.

As Khoi picked up his coat, he noted Paul doing the same. "What are you doing?" He asked? Paul thought that since Khoi was leaving he had to follow suit. "No man, have your fun. You earned it and I think you like her right?" He whispered. Paul blushed then they were met by a shriek. They turned and found Han holding her gift in her hand in shock. "For me?" She asked Khoi who just nodded. She jumped up and down in joy and ran to hug him. "You got me a new Laptop! Thank you so much!"

"And inside are some book and gift vouchers too. So check the box ok?" Instructed Khoi as she ran out to the living room to show off her new present. Watching in amazement, Khoi concluded "I've got to go." Khoi was followed to the door by Paul who could only say "Thanks Khoi."

"Anytime. Now go have fun." And with that, Khoi made his way down the stairs and to the car, on his way to his third and final appointment.

It took him about forty minutes to drive from Han's flat to the suburbs finally arriving at Georg's home at just after nine. He wasn't sure what welcome he would receive since he previously confirmed that he wasn't planning to spend Christmas with them.

He pressed the doorbell and could hear the chuckles of Anita as she approached the door. She checked the monitor as per usual before she cheered "I told you he'd come, I told you." She cried as she opened the door. Anita could not wait to give Khoi a huge hug and some kisses before leading him into the house.

As they walked through the sitting room, Georg had already made the effort of coming to meet them half way. He too gave Khoi a great cuddle that almost pressed the air out of Khoi's lungs. "My boy, how are you?" Georg exclaimed as he let him out of his encompassing and mighty grip.

"I'm fine. Glad to see you looking well." Khoi replied and he meant it. Georg did look more relaxed and healthy. The time away did serve him well. "How was Malta?"

"It was wonderful. I spent a lot of time swimming!" Georg boasted.

"Come, Georg. He must be starving. You can tell him all about it as he eats." Anita interjected, grabbing Khoi by the hand and leading the way to dining room. "Joel! Khoi is here." She called.

Khoi wasn't really hungry, but he could hardly refuse. She didn't even give him the opportunity to take off his coat and put down his bag and before Khoi knew it they were in dining room. He sat at the left side of the table whilst Georg took his place at the head.

They had clearly had a big dinner and hadn't cleared up yet. Anita carved some of the lamb leg, served it with vegetables and sauce. "Joel told me you gave the others Christmas day off. You told them to go home." asked Georg. Khoi was initially struck dumb, before replying "Em... yes".

"Good. I am glad." Georg concluded with a hint of disdain, promptly causing Anita to chide him, asking him to "be nice", but Georg added "Be nice? Don't know why they come, those parasites. This is the first Christmas I had alone with my family for years, it was wonderful and you said so yourself. They come here, eat everything leave a mess and disappear." Unwilling to getting into an argument, Anita made her way to the kitchen "I'm just going to heat up your food Khoi."

With Anita gone, a mischievous look emerged on Georg's face. "She's gone. Could you get us some port from the cabinet before she gets back? I haven't had a drop in weeks." Cautiously, Khoi wondered if it was advisable based on the doctor's advice on him abstaining "You sound like Anita. It's fucking Christmas. Come on, go it quickly. I won't tell if you don't."

Khoi went to the drink cabinet and took out two sherry glasses and the bottle of port. He filled up a glass and took it to Georg before he returned to the cabinet, filled the other glass and returned the bottle. Once the door of the cabinet was shut, he turned to propose a toast only to find that Georg had already finished his without a hint. "Now hide the glass." Georg ordered.

Khoi smirked as he placed the glass in his bag. Anita returned with the plate and cutlery and placed it before him declaring "Here you go. Enjoy."

"So what did you bring us for Christmas?" Georg demanded.

"Georg? What's wrong with you?" Anita scolded him, but Khoi calmed things by saying

"I do have a surprise for you." He reached into his bag and brought out the IPad tablet.

Khoi uploaded the clip he wanted to show then Joel arrived.

They greeted each other with a nod across the room as Joel took his place on the chair to the right of his father whilst Anita stood behind Georg with her hand on his shoulder, a means of keeping him in check.

With everything set, he handed the IPad to Georg for his, Anita's and Joel's viewing pleasure.

A glint developed in Georg's eye. "What a wonderful picture" Anita remarked at the still, "When was it taken?"

"This morning and it's not a picture. It's a video clip." Khoi corrected. Joel reached over and touched "play". The picture began to move. There was Jeroen with his crooked smile and styled hair. Joel's heart sunk. Khoi watched as the family drew closer around the tablet watching the missing member of the family.

They watched as Khoi cut Jeroen's hair, how calm and placid Jeroen was. Anita had her hand on the side of her face as the tears rolled down. "He's so thin…. Aren't they feeding him?" She asked, but Khoi didn't answer. The question did put what little appetite he had left at bay. Khoi was consumed by them watching Jeroen go through the family identification parade. Georg turned to Anita extremely pleased as he cried "See that? He remembers me, he remembers me." then reached over to kiss his wife on the cheek.

Joel was pleased with his brother's progress until it was his turn to be identified. Joel was visibly struggling to keep his distress at bay as his brother got agitated when shown his picture. Jeroen still could not comprehend that he had a twin.

Both Georg and Anita held hands, engrossed, while Joel sat alone with an increasing sense of guilt praying for the video to stop. When it did, he was not in for any relief as Khoi added "There's more." Khoi quickly took the tablet off Georg's hand and uploaded the next clip before pressing play and there was Jeroen in the restaurant, enjoying his pudding. It was delightful to see such a site, but it grew more uncomfortable for Joel who had since stopped watching and slowly slipped away, leaving the dining room.

When it finished, Georg was moist eyed whilst Anita was already in tears. They were so happy with the improvement they saw in Jeroen. "We want to watch it again. Can you go back to the previous video?" Georg asked. Khoi did as he was told and taught them how to replay and go to the other videos.

With them distracted, Khoi went in search of Joel. He walked around the house first checking the study, then the small living room and followed by investigating the stock room but Joel wasn't there.

Khoi walked up the steps going toward Joel's bedroom. He wasn't there either. Finally, Khoi was forced to approach the room he hadn't entered in over nine years. The door was slightly open already, so he pushed it further ajar. The light was on, and Joel was in the room, sitting on the sheep skin rug that lay at the foot of the single bed, sulking in silence in Jeroen's room.

"Hey." Khoi called. Joel looked up at him and saw Khoi.

"Hey." Joel replied.

"You alright?" Khoi asked.

Joel shook his head. "He doesn't remember me. He remembers everyone else, but me. I don't exist" Joel concluded. He sighed "I miss him. I really do. It's like there is a space… a death… but I can't grieve because he's not really gone." Khoi was about to enter to console him when Anita called out his name. "You better go. Your mother wants you." Joel remarked sarcastically.

Khoi brushed it off as a case of anger. Empathy had to wait for a moment. He walked down the step and found Georg and Anita waiting for at the foot of it with the IPad in hand and a grin on their face. "We wanted to ask if you had time to come with us to see Jeroen next week." Anita asked.

"Sure. I actually forgot to tell you, the doctor said he could come home on a trial basis next week, call them and fix a date and I'll come with you." Khoi replied.

"Oh that is good news." Anita remarked.

"Yes, we must celebrate. Let's have some port." Georg proposed. He was met with a shuddering glance from Anita which put that suggestion to rest. Khoi didn't feel at ease staying any longer and made excuses stating he had to organise some more paper work and so on.

Georg initially protested, but Anita knew how to put him in his place and told him that it could be the case that Khoi may be off to a date. Georg's initial protest turned to bewilderment as he brought up the fact that Khoi had a partner already and continued to persist until Anita told him to mind his own business.

Anita packed the remainder of the dinner up for Khoi and handed it to him who had been kept company in the meantime by Georg's tales of Malta.

With a kiss and a hug, Khoi collected his bag and made his way out of the door. As he walked through the front garden path lined with snow covered rose bushes, he heard his name being called. Khoi turned and found Joel coming out in his coat, shutting the door firmly behind him.

Joel paced towards him shivering slightly but this time he looked happy. "Thanks for going to see Jeroen. You know how much it means to the family don't you?"

"No problem." Khoi replied "Your dad looks great. He seems more robust than ever…"

Joel performed an 180c turn, executed in a manner a bipolar sufferer would consider harsh as his tone lowered as he said in their made up childhood tongue "Jekorian" "I was watching the news last night and this morning. What happened to Mr E?" Khoi could smell a confrontation brewing, he tried to be tactical in order to head it off but thought the best was would be with honesty. "You said one bullet, and I used it on him."

"Yeah. I heard. And what about Mr D? Is he dead too?"

It was clear that Joel was just asking to hear him say it, and he did "Yes, Robert has been neutralised." This wasn't the way Khoi had intended to inform him, but Joel was up for a battle.

"Really? When were you going to tell me?" Khoi could not reply. Joel persisted "I thought we were in this together. We are a team." Joel highlighted "Yet you went off and did all this and didn't consult me?"

"You had greater issues to worry about and we had a deadline. You told me your father was going to return on 24th and I thought it would be best not to put any further strain on you, so I decided to act to ensure we achieved our goal with as little stress to you as possible." Khoi explained. He hoped Joel bought it.

Joel nodded and growled "Never do that again. We work together. OK?"

"OK." Khoi agreed.

Joel soon realised he had been threatening, and recoiled. "Sorry about that. I just wanted to make sure this was done right. Is Mr F gone too?" Khoi nodded and confirmed "Last Monday."

Joel's sadistic interest surfaced as he asked how Khoi had gone about executing his plan.

Khoi explained how he, Paul, Marcel and Mikel came to the flat where Siegfried was being kept with the captive's supper and to relieve Ralph of his guard duty early. Ralph leapt at the offer. Khoi took him out for dinner and drinks.

Based on the report provided by Mikel and Paul, Khoi pieced together the chain of events.

With Ralph out of the door, they produced a large cup of soup. A straw was inserted into the cup containing the meal and having been starved for over fifteen hours, Siegfried made short work the soup and within minutes, the cup was empty. He consumed the entire contents which also had a tablet of flunitrazepam crushed in for good measure by Paul. Mikel thought it was more an issue of Siegfried being hungry, but Marcel knew better.

All that was left for those present to do was to wait and after two hours, they checked if the drug; famous for its use by dubious characters to have non-consensual sex with unknowing victims, had taken its effect by shoving a needle under his big toe. Siegfried did not respond even though his eyes were wide opened. One could only then imagine what went through Siegfried's mind, if anything, as he was untied from his chair and his unresponsive body placed onto the floor.

Mikel and Marcel cleaned Siegfried using a wet towel, and then dried him. Marcel went to the room and took out some clothes from Siegfried's bag, the one he had packed for his holiday and brought it to Mikel and Paul who proceeded to dress Siegfried in clean clothes, even putting on his watch and rings for him. Siegfried must have felt it and possibly knew he was being clothed. He likely heard them struggle as they put on his boots for him and tied up the laces, but probably didn't know why they were doing this.

Once done, they straightened his body, his hands placed by his side and his head facing up before they began. He must have heard them opening the packets and sense the feeling of the blood struggling to flow to his lower extremities as Mikel held them aloft as Paul bound them together starting from his ankles using a water-soluble alginate dressing slowly progressing upwards.

Yards after yards of the material were used as the body was gradually cocooned. Siegfried would have been propped up to address the upper part of the body until finally, after three hours, they created a living version of an Egyptian mummy, covered in dressing from head to toe with the exception of his nose to ensure Siegfried could still breath.

Blinded, inaudible and doubly immobilised, Joel could only envisage the anxiety and fear of the uncertainty that Siegfried must have underwent as he was placed into a hollowed out case of a large double bass. The sounds of the locks latching must have brought Siegfried close to easing himself if he hadn't done so already.

Then, the ground that supported his weight would have disappeared replaced by the grunts and groans of Marcel and Mikel as they tussled with Siegfried, carrying him up several flights of stairs in a gentle manner ensuring there was as little movement within the case as possible.

When they got out, Siegfried must have felt it; the cold air would have entered through the hinges. He must have known he was outside, but it wasn't for long. Marcel and Mikel slid the case into the back of the Landrover with the back seat folded down. With no space for him, Siegfried must have also heard Paul bidding Marcel and Mikel safe journey. The start of the engine must have struck horror into the heart of Siegfried as the vehicle started to move.

With the drug wearing off, Siegfried's constriction must have been evident, sweating, possibly weeping, but such tears made no difference, he still couldn't move.

The fifty nine minute journey must have seemed like a lifetime. The ticking sound of the turning indicators in the car would have been the only clue as to which direction the car was about to take. The sound soon became scare and it was enough to tell the man in the musical instrument case that they were now out of the city as their speed increased. Siegfried would have trembled if he could and would have screamed if he could open his mouth, but he couldn't.

They came to a full stop after fifty seven minutes of navigating through Berlin, using the autobahn, past Potsdam before arriving at their destination. Marcel and Mikel brought Siegfried's temporary tomb out of the boot of the car. Mikel walked down the banks of Templiner Lake in search of their next mode of transportation. It wasn't far from where they were parked. It was a row boat, the only one at the small pier.

The oversized cello case was opened and the cargo was taken out. He was lifted over Marcel's shoulder and carried a few paces before being set gently on to the vessel. The pair wore their life proof vests hoping for the best. Regardless of how strong a swimmer they both could have been, one dip into the water, would give them a nasty cold at least if not kill them, considering the air temperature was 2c. Mikel held the boat steady whilst Marcel placed the body in a more convenient position and then boarded. Mikel did the same and took hold of the oars. He began to row with Marcel holding a light.

Siegfried must have realised by now that he was nearing the end. He began to feel his arm and wiggled it a bit. Some form of movement, yes, but useless nonetheless. Then the rowing stopped after twenty minutes. Then, with a heave, Siegfried would never feel dry again for as long as he lived. He entered the water with a modest splash. The sudden loss of weight made the boat rock, causing a bit of a stir to those still on board. Eager not to go for a chilly nightly swim, they rowed quickly back to shore.

Whilst they were home and dry, Siegfried didn't have that luxury. Rather he was soon to realise why drowning is known as the most terrible way to go. His first gasp saw his nostrils fill with water. Siegfried must have held his breath for as long as he possibly could and hoped beyond hope that someone out there would save his life, but at 11:07pm on a cold December's night, it was never going to happen.

As the carbon dioxide built up in his body, his lungs yearned for oxygen. His reflexes kicked in and he drew a breath. His air sack filled with water. It was most unfortunate for him that evolution could not work in reverse within nanoseconds giving him gills, now he was choking as water was drawn into his larynx.

He'd want to open his mouth but couldn't, it was bound tight. He was sinking and he began to panic as his lungs filled with water. It was diminishing any space his organs had to do what they were created to do as he sunk ever deeper into the bottom of the lake.

Soon, he would have begun to feel high, Siegfried wouldn't feel the need to struggle anymore and by the time he reached the bottom of the lake, Siegfried would be dead.

"Marcel confirmed that they waited for another twenty minutes and he certainly didn't float back up." Joel seemed so impressed by how detailed Khoi's description of the event was that he remarked, "Cool. So we are done?"

"Yeah." Khoi confirmed.

"Wow... I have to hand it to you, you are efficient." Joel conceded then added "One more thing, don't we are going to have a New Year Day party, the guys and I have a surprise for you. I'll come get you. OK?" Khoi hated surprises, but he wasn't in the mood to argue with Joel and accepted the offer "Oh, here." Khoi said as he reached into his bag and handed him the sherry glass.

"Dad made you get him a drink too? The man is amazing. Well, for all it's worth, Merry Christmas." Another hug and this time it was Khoi who felt distant as Joel walked to the door.

At this point Khoi remembered that there was something else he needed to know and he called out "Joel, Marcel came over to my hotel room two nights ago... he said you were looking for me. What's up?" Joel wanted to confess his thoughts and concerns about Jelena but couldn't, rather he replied "You're here, you're safe, and that's all that counts. See you later."

Joel returned into the house. Attempting to avoid the sight of his parents, he made his way up the steps but Joel was stopped in his tracks by his phone. A text had arrived from a loyal friend. It informed him of a slip up which had now left Joel and his team vulnerable, particularly as there was foreign interest involved. The message ended with the ominous words "The British are coming."

This was enough to convince Joel that something had to be done about the Jelena situation once and for all.

Khoi, on the other hand, had returned to his hotel, eager to see the end of the day. It was hard to understand how one could go through such a merry day, only to come out feeling like shit?

Christmas would be over within the hour, but why wait any longer. His advent calendar was empty, no need keeping it around anymore. He put it in the bin and sat back on the bed. His phone buzzed, a text arrived. "Merry Christmas Mate, sorry I took my time. Will call you tomorrow." wrote Julien. The guilt returned again, he had forgotten about Julien all this time. This didn't help him or his spirits. Khoi wanted to reply but didn't, he wanted to be alone, but also hated every moment of it.

That was it, he needed to escape again. Khoi reached for the pill bottle, only two pills left. He took one, waited patiently, allowing the effects to take over.

# 15

*26 December 2010*

As Christmas day came to a close for Khoi, out of choices, Jan wondered if his yuletide nightmare could ever get worse.

It was now three in the morning. Jan considered whether the Gods had conspired against him, preventing him from spending enough time with Kat since her return. Luckily, she decided to spend the day with her family, so she wasn't alone, not like him.

Jan was just on his second day in his new role and he already regretted being pushed to apply for the post.

He had been provided with pictures of the deceased but it wasn't much help because the ballistic experts had stated that, thanks to a shortage in staff, they wouldn't be able to produce an accurate report till the 27th of December. That would be a slight issue as it meant that the area remained a crime scene until the ballistics team did their job. This meant that the cost local businesses were growing.

All Jan was left to do now was review the information on the dead man and wait for further information regarding his background. Even though he knew of Oliver's criminal links it had to be confirmed formally.

Now, he had to sift through more paper work and review the witness statements and they were all the same. Everyone saw the car come to a stop and a frantic screaming child with no information about the perpetrator, yet he needed to go through each and every one of the seventy three statements on his own due to the reduced number of staff. Jan was so preoccupied he didn't even notice his emails as they arrived; only checking the subject matter to determine if they were important enough to be opened and none fit the bill.

Whilst trying to keep his sanity, Jan's phone rang. It was the receptionist, calling to inform him that he had a visitor waiting for him at the front desk. The visitor was determined to speak to the person in charge of the murder investigations. With no one available to meet the man from his designated team, he was forced to leave his batch of work for now and go to the front desk, hoping and praying to God that this wasn't a hoax; he'd had enough of that already. Still, like any other lead, he had to take this seriously.

Jan walked out to the reception area and over to the space where the officer at the counter was separated from the public by bullet proof glass to find a man standing there who had evidently tried to look presentable but had failed.

To Jan, man looked dishevelled, weak, distracted and was holding on to the outer part of the desk with his latex glove covered hands to assist his balance. His hair appeared to be dwindling in number having fallen out in patches, leaving just strands behind. His cheeks and nose were quite pink, his face was covered in a rash and his breathing seemed laboured, a clear sign that he needed medical attention.

Jan approached the desk and the officer pressed the button to the speaker allowing Jan to proceed. "Hello, how may I help you?"

"Are... are you... Jan Har... beck?" the man asked in a laboured tone. The man was a troubling site to behold, yet Jan kept his composure and confirmed he was indeed the person being sought. "Good, good. It's him..." the man said to himself in a schizophrenic manner before he laughed began coughing. He tried to continue, but his words were intermittent on account of his coughing fits. "I am... I am Andreas Thill... I... I am ... I am the leader of the Dis... District 3 gang... you have to help me... They are out to kill us..."

"Andreas, please slow down..." Jan pleaded

"No... you have to help!" Andreas cried out. "You have to find the others... find Robert and Siegfried, you have to warn them, or they will get them too!"

Although he could see the man was visibly in distress, Jan could only query, all the names being mentioned didn't help. "Robert and Siegfried who? And who is coming after you? Please could you clarify?" Now coughing more violently and struggling to breath, Andreas added "Robert Steger and Siegfried..." Then the coughing returned causing the man to vomit on the floor. The colour drained from his face as he added "They will kill us all! They've killed Richard and Oliver... Help us..." then he slumped on the floor.

"Oh my God, get help!" Jan screamed as he ran out to man who was sprawled out on the cold marble floor, his phone, wallet, pen and inhaler lying next to him having tripped out of his pocket when he hit the ground. Andreas was in an awful state and his breathing was shallow prompting Jan to think he might be having an asthma attack.

Jan knelt next to the man and held his hand and he could feel Andreas' heart racing. "Andreas, we are going to get you some help!" he said. However Andreas was sweating profusely, his opened mouth showed he had lost a few of his teeth and though his eyes were open, they seemed to wander around the room with his head shaking side to side "Andreas, can you hear me?" he wasn't responding as he continued with his quest for air. "Andreas, listen, help is on the way…"

Jan took the inhaler, placed the mouth piece in Andreas' opened mouth and pressed on the top to release some of the contents, hoping it would sooth his distressed airway, it failed. Now even Jan was frantic. "Where's that fucking ambulance?" Jan cried out. "Help us… help us…" Andreas repeated continuously and no matter how hard Jan tried to get more information out of him, all he got in return was the continual plea for assistance.

It didn't turn out well for Andreas. Jan had followed the Andreas to the hospital and minutes after arriving Andreas kept slipping in and out of consciousness. His breathing became distressed to the point that he had to be attached to a respirator. Jan called Wolfgang. Despite the late hour he needed to ask for his guidance in order to confirm that the man he had followed to the hospital was who he said he was.

*27 December 2014*

At twelve minutes past four in the morning, having waited for several hours, Jan was happy to see some reinforcements arrive. Wolfgang appeared with three officers and having looked at the information contained in Andreas' wallet, his identity was confirmed.

Standing outside Andreas' hospital room, the doctor stepped out to meet the waiting officers. Jan and Wolfgang were informed that the man had been showing symptoms of poisoning and they were in the process of trying to find out what it was. "Harbeck, I want to speak to Harbeck!" Andreas cried at the top of his lungs.

"Can I go and see him?" Jan asked. The doctor reluctantly agreed on the strict instructions that he didn't touch the patient.

Jan cautiously entered and stood by the bed post as a nurse injected a drug in Andreas' veins. "I'm here." Jan said to the suffering man. Andreas fought hard to speak and coordinate his thoughts but managed to say "Find Robert and Siegfried… find him… find them… he knows about May…" Andreas went unconscious again and his heart rate began to drop, causing alarm.

Jan was hurried out of the room to a waiting team "We have to find Robert Steger and fast."

Wolfgang ordered the three police to stand guard outside Andreas' door and he spoke to the doctor asking him to provide a list of those who will allocate to treat Andreas and ensure no one else is allowed in.

Jan was taken to the empty waiting room by Wolfgang who remained sceptical about Andreas. Jan decided to play devil's advocate. "Why would he lie? He got one thing right. One of those killed by an overdose and our gun victim were in his gang and now they were gone within weeks of each other. I'd be suspicious too. I think it's worth looking up on Robert. I have his phone." Jan brought out an old nokia phone which required the person to press the centre key and the pound sign to unlock. They sifted through the man's address book; there was a Robert Steger, but four Siegfried's.

Jan returned to the ward and asked if he could try to speak to Andreas again, it was then he was informed that Andreas had slipped into a coma. Wolfgang decided to assist and made a few enquiries till they were able to locate Robert Steger's address and all evidence showed he hadn't left town. Jan insisted that things could not wait. He feared that Andreas would not make it, hence the sooner they got hold of Robert and Siegfried, the better.

Support was summoned. Police within the vicinity of Robert's flat were told to pay him a visit and keep him there till they arrived. Wolfgang and Jan drove to the west of the city in separate cars. All Jan could contemplate at that moment was whether there was any substance to Andreas' pleas.

They arrived at the place and found three police cars parked outside the venue. Jan and Wolfgang raced to the top floor on foot without using the elevator. They could hear the two policemen knocking on the door and calling out Robert's name but no answer.

Wolfgang asked one of the officers to speak to the neighbours to ask if they had seen him of late. They informed them that one of the neighbours below, awoken by the noise said that Robert's car had been in the drive way for three days and he hadn't been seen or heard from. As they chatted, Jan heard a humming sound. "Shh." He told everyone. They fell silent as Jan placed his ear on the door.

There was a humming sound indeed. He was convinced that Robert could have been reluctant to answer knowing it was the police after him. Jan knocked. "Robert? It's the police. You aren't in trouble. We have some news about your friend." There was still no answer.

There was no need to wait. "Break it down." Jan ordered. Voicing his objection, an officer replied "But we don't have a permit…" Wolfgang pushed back "Do what the man says and leave the permit issue to use." The battering ram was brought and after four hefty slams on the door, it flung open. Upon taking their first step in, they were met by a strange smell of lightly burnt product and decaying matter.

Wolfgang drew out his gun along with another officer "Robert!" he called again. "We only want to talk." The second door had not been shut properly. Wolfgang pushed it open with the end of his foot. The door opened, the humming grew louder and the smell stronger. Wolfgang entered first, leaping out and pointing his gun whilst the others watched. He drew down his gun shaking his head "Shit."

Jan followed along with the officers. Robert was in, on the floor, discoloured and bloated, congealed blood around his head as he lay on the ground on his front side, head facing to the left. "Guess the guy was right" Wolfgang observed. "We have to find this Siegfried he was talking about." All Jan could do was to place his hand on his head, discouraged on having failed to reach Robert in time.

Although he was interested in returning to the station and lead the hunt for Siegfried, protocol had to be addressed. They all left the room and waited for forensics to arrive and they were very late adding hours to the limited time they had to find the next potential victim and, if possible, prevent another death.

Jan was exhausted. He had been up now for twenty hours and was nearly burnt out. Seeing the dead body that morning, so soon after Christmas, spooked him, forcing Jan to confront his own mortality.

Dragging his feet into the station at 8:53am, Jan made his way to his office. He was demoralised. He had to find this Siegfried. Wolfgang offered to take some of the weight and coordinate things and pass on the numbers to the trackers and have the results relayed to him, but it didn't lighten the load of failure on his brow.

As he passed the desk of his assistant, he initially didn't notice that the assistant was there and took a second take. "What are you doing here? I thought you were off?" His assistant was equally amazed that Jan asked. "Did you forget about the email? Your guest, from the British police, is waiting for you in your office."

"Guest?" Jan repeated. Before his assistant could fill him in, Jan marched off to his office. The idea of someone in his space made him weary.

Jan opened the door to his office and found a man in a blue Calvary coat with a red rose in the lapel, hands behind his back, brown curly hair, angular nose, clean shaven and smartly dressed, looking at the picture of Kat on his desk. Noting he had been detected, the man looked up at Jan without a smile. The visitor was clearly cutting the size of him.

It appeared that one person was waiting for the other to make the first move. Jan was going to be courteous and was about to instigate the discussion but was beaten to it. "Tom Evans. London metropolitan police, nice to meet you." Said the stranger in English as he stretched out his hand to shake Jan's with his black leather gloves still on. This was odd, Jan thought, normally people take them off. Ignoring that hiccup in etiquette, Tom continued "And you must be Jan Harbeck. Nice to meet you."

Jan cautiously shook the hand of the man from London with a clean cut British accent and distinct feature that could not be missed, he had purple eyes. His lips may have been stretched to show a smile, but his eyes remained firm. "Yes… Nice to meet you." Jan replied.

After the brief but firm shake, Tom added "I believe it is safe to assume from your reaction that you weren't expecting me and I believe I must apologise on two counts. The first being for the short notice given for my arrival, and the second being that we didn't get to speak sooner, I just found out myself."

"The man is speaking in riddles" Jan remarked to himself before sort clarity "Found what out?" ask Jan. "Ah." Tom remarked, showing he was rather let down. "I see they haven't communicated much to you. Two weeks ago a tender was placed in the long range shooting market, i.e. someone wanted to hire a sniper."

"Thank you for clarifying." Jan interjected in an acerbic manner.

Though he didn't fail to notice it, Tom proceeded as if he didn't and mockingly replied "You are ever so welcomed. Where was I? OK, there we are. The tender was sent out to all criminal snipers within Europe to find the best value for money. I know you might think that the British are the most Eurosceptic of our fine bunch of nations, and you would be right, but I am sure you too would agree that tendering to perpetrate a felony is taking the European ideal of the free market economics a step too far, wouldn't you?"

"The tender was to kill an individual in Berlin, on the 24th of December, which has already occurred and for that I and my team are sorry because we found out who was awarded the contract. I was only informed myself yesterday. The man, who is wanted in Den Haag, for his part in the siege of Sarajevo, a man by the name of Denno Jazic from Pale, but he uses the alias Darko Jamina, carried out the murder with his team."

Jan's eyes flipped open "Please tell me you came to tell me you know where this man is?"

"Our friend, Darko should be the least of your concerns right now; the person you and I should be worried about is the person who hired him. This person is very dangerous. She's wanted in the UK, Russia, Kenya, Nigeria, Argentina… in about thirty four countries." Jan watched in amazement as Tom didn't move from his spot almost standing still with his hands remained firmly behind his back and only his mouth was animated as he continued "She's been known by many synonyms, Maria, Ronica, Daisy, and most recently Izabela, but, like most people in her line of work, she does have a real name. She is called Jelena Hoffman Bozic."

"A Serb of Hungarian ancestry, she appeared on the radar in 1993, in her late teens, when she was snapped up by the State Security Administration of Yugoslavia, who took over from KOS, the Counter Intelligence Service. We thought they died in 1992 with the end of the war, evidently, they just changed coats."

"She was found beating up some man who tried to assault her and ended needing hospitalisation to deal with his life changing injuries. She was used to exterminate opponents of the government within the Balkans. For that she was tolerated, so long as she didn't touch people who were deemed too important to disappear, we frankly didn't care what she or her organisation got up to. "

"Everything changed though in 1998 with the Kosovo war. She vanished for over a year only to surface in Israel offering her services to their

The Institute for Intelligence and Special Operations, better known as 'Mossad'. Even though she shined and was seen as one of the most effective tool in their box, she was let go for reasons our friends in Tel Aviv have chosen not to reveal but they did state it was a great loss."

"Now their loss is our regret because she decided turn her back on defending the free world to pursue a career in the lucrative gun for hire business where she has done very well for herself, moving from country to country leaving corpses with every step. Now you have the angel of death within your borders. She is very dangerous."

"How dangerous?" Jan asked.

Finally the talking statue moved. Tom went and helped himself to the seat on the opposite side of the desk where Jan sat. Crossing his legs, Tom replied "When she pops up in a city, she leaves a mark. It took Brno three years to get a good review from Trip advisor after her initial visit that saw several people disappear. And now she is here, and you are in trouble." Jan looked rather unconvinced, prompting Tom to scoff. "Come now, you honestly didn't think she would come for just one target, the middle ranker in the gang of drug dealers? I can assure you, if you look at the current spike of deaths in your city, her fingerprints would be all over it and from what I heard, your dead drug dealer isn't the only one of his team being brought before the scale of justice to determine his place in heaven or hell..."

"ENOUGH!" Jan cried. Jan shut his eyes for a moment and took a deep breath. And when he opened them, Tom was still there, same posture, some unflinching resolve. Still Jan had to make amends. "I'm sorry about that. Just too much information and too little sleep. Could you just summarise what you want?"

"OK. I am here to find Jelena. If we do find her, I am sure, with some persuasion, she would lead us to those who procured her services and thus everyone wins." Tom closed with a flicker of his left eye brow.

Although it made sense, Jan was frazzled and hoped to discover some common ground between them. "You must be tired... want a coffee?"

"Tea, green, no milk, no sugar, please?" Tom dictated.

Jan considered whether Tom thought by putting the word "please" at the end of his statement it would negate the display of superciliousness in his approach, it didn't. "One moment please." Jan replied as he picked up his phone and placed an order for the refreshments with his assistant.

As they waited for their drinks, Jan took the time logged back on to his system via his computer. There was an email from Wolfgang with the names and addresses of the individuals named Siegfried found on the phone and their current and potential whereabouts. Three have been found. One was in Bochum and was Andreas' brother. The other was Andreas' brother, Siegfried senior's son and they both spent their Christmas together. The next one was the plumber and the other couldn't be reached because, according to the records and his parents, he was off to Thailand.

Seeing Tom seemed bored, Jan loosened up and smiled for a moment. "Once again, I am so sorry. I had a death to attend to." Jan repeated. He took the time to quickly sift through his email to find the one relating to Tom's presence in his office. Taking quick glances at him, he decided he wasn't going to like this person.

Eventually, he did find the email from Gerhard. It did mention Tom's arrival and mentioned his investigations on a transnational criminal. All was fine till the last line which stated that Jan and his team must ensure that they cooperate with Tom and his team and there should be full disclosure and openness. His moment of peace evaporated having read that. "It says you have a team coming. How many people please?"

"Five." Tom replied. "So, tell me, the death you mentioned, does it relate to our situation with Jelena?" Tom asked with a sneer.

The man was beginning to grate on him. Yet, orders were orders "Possibly." Jan began. "But we can't be sure. We have one more lead to follow before we can officially join the dots."

"Please, tell me what that may be?" Jan grudgingly explained that there was an individual of interest who they are trying to track down but he had just heard that the person was on holiday. Tom laughed "Oh how I admire your faith. The man is dead."

Jan sat there in utter disbelief. "And how can you be so sure?" he asked

"I know the person I am dealing with. If he were on that flight, I promise you, the plane would have been blown up. Why not find out if he did make it to his destination?"

Taking on the challenge, Jan picked up the phone and made a call as their caffeine fixes arrived. Tom thanked the assistant, took off his gloves and served himself the tea from the pot.

As Jan spoke in German, a language his guest hardly understood, Tom tasted the tea, it was awful. Having painfully swallowed the mouthful, he placed the mug back on the tray, sat back and crossed his legs as Jan completed his call.

Jan notice Tom had crossed his legs. At least he was making himself comfortable Jan thought. Jan served himself some coffee and took a sip, though he was aware it was nothing more than placebo effects, the taste made him relax a little. Hoping to end the silence, Jan tried to strike up a conversation with his guest. "So how was your trip?"

"Uneventful." Tom answered. It was short, a clear sign that this man was not one for small talk.

Perhaps a conversation on the reason for his visit could increase the flow of words. "So, how dangerous is this woman?"

"Very... she is a walking weapon of mass destruction. You want to cause mayhem, you hire her. Would you like examples?" Tom teased

"It could be enlightening." Jan replied, hoping Tom would get to the point and end this dance.

Tom uncrossed his legs and sat up as he began. "In the UK, we were touched by Jelena on three occasions. Twice within our borders and the other, though outside it, hit much closer to home.

Late winter three years ago, two bodies were discovered on 12:35 train from London Kings Cross to Cambridge at the final destination."

"They were both on seats that backed each other, they were both returning from the Arsenal football match, they were both wearing the trade mark red football shirt of Arsenal and had both been killed with the same bullet with the entry point for first victim, let's call him "V1" being from the right side of his chest, puncturing a lung and hitting a few other things on the way exiting from his back. The bullet then went through the seats, entering the second victim, hence called "V2" from the behind and went straight to his heart where it lodged itself."

"On first inspection, it was rather an odd setting to have someone killed but then, why not? The train was packed as it set off from London, but steadily, the passengers reduced in number with every stop. Regardless of that, it was said by many passengers that even as they got to the final stop it was hard to speak or hear themselves think because Arsenal had won and their supports had been drinking heavily and forgot to leave their chants at the stadium and proceed to carry on singing their loyalty in fine form throughout the journey. Coupled by the sound of the train on the tracks and if a silencer was employed then it was possible and it was easy for someone either not hear or dismiss the sound of a gun being fired."

"Putting that aside, the question was who did it and how did they get the opportunity. Of course, V1 got the bullet, so who would want to kill him and why? He was a common bricklayer, cheating on his girlfriend, but I hardly think that merited his execution. Yet eye witnesses said he had boarded the train, quite drunk with his friend at Finsbury Park train station. They sat opposite a young woman and an elderly lady, they got chatty with the young one and some thought V1 and the young woman were getting flirtatious."

"V1's friend got off at Stevenage. The woman moved to the other side and sat next to him and by Letchworth, they were cuddling and stealing kisses from one another. The old lady opposite got a bit uncomfortable and moved to another seat. By the next stop, Hitchin, their side of the carriage was almost empty and the couple were now making out like crazy, she was seated on his lap, many thought it was near obscene. The next stop was Baldock, the numbers lessened again, the kissing continued till Ashwell & Morden where it stopped and the woman left the train having shot V1 and covered the wound by pulling his black coat over it.

It made sense that at the time she was seated on him, she wasn't aiming to get her knickers off, she was pinning him down and the kiss was to silence him, if he intended to scream that is."

"The alarm was only raised when the pair didn't get up to leave the train at its final stop.

The local forces spent hours, days, months combing through every scenario they could think to determine why anyone would want V1 dead. It wasn't his girlfriend or his mistress or the bank that he owed some money to and it didn't help that the family of V2, a medical student from Malaysia were demanding justice and were only too happy to appear on any news outlet to complain that they weren't getting enough information from the British police." Tom's voice went up by a near unnoticeable decibel which Jan did hear.

Tom was surely having trouble containing his rage as he persisted. "We kept in touch with V2's family and each time we received a tirade of claims of incompetence. Then, one day, we called, and they said we should stop calling and not bother continuing our investigation. You never say that to the British police. With everything relating to V1 coming to a dead end, someone, just out of interest, took a background check on V2. It turned out he was the child of an opposition leader in Sabah where his family had entered a blood feud with another family from the ruling party as they vied for the governorship. There had been attempts on that family for ages."

"We were fools. She wasn't aiming for V1, it was V2. She took her chances and realised that if she couldn't get to him directly, then it would have to be indirectly and to hell with the cost.

V2 had gone to the match with his friends. The good Muslim boy decided to enjoy a few pints, turned out to be light weight and fell asleep once he got on the train with his four friends. The students nodded off and slept all the way ignoring all that occurred around them, unaware their friend was about to be killed as he rested his head on the shoulder of the girl he had told someone he fancied. All the more reason why we had to track the killer down and we thought it wouldn't take too long. We already knew who it was, we had her on CCTV, yes it took us some time to identify the face but we discovered it was Jelena. However by then, she had left the country and thus the hunt began."

Jan summed up his thoughts with the word "Interesting. You said there were two incidents?"

"Oh yes, thank you for reminding me. I'll make this one brief." Tom promised "One of our officers, my partner, tracked Jelena down to Lisbon. He tailed her to the port and before he knew it, he had been received a blow to the back of the head, knocking him out cold. He was then sedated for good measure before being bundled up into a container holding books and papers and some provisions and water to keep him alive throughout his three week boat ride on a container ship to Sao Paolo."

"When he was discovered, he had begun to show some symptoms of a disease that the region in Brazil he arrived in had long thought was eradicated. Our man, my friend, hand been injected in several places around his head and neck with a virus and when they discovered he was unwell, he was too far gone for treatment. He died within weeks all alone in an isolation unit. She had injected him with the rabies virus or as you say in German, tollwut." The lack of response and the open mouth proved the impact the tale had on Jan. Always one to capitalise on opportunities, Tom went about winning him over. "When I said she was a very dangerous person, I meant it."

"Wow." Jan exclaimed in shock.

"Wow indeed." Tom then decided to strike a consolatory note. "Listen, I know I may I have come off quiet standoffish, I blame it on my upbringing, but I need your help, it may be a local affair at the moment, but it's only a matter of time before it goes beyond Berlin, and perhaps it has." Tom waited for a response. Jan quietly mulled over the information he had received.

Eventually he accepted that more help wouldn't do any harm provided they are not obstructive and it was safer for him to accept it than be forced to. Jan took another sip of his coffee. It had gone cold and tasted bad. He put it down and forced a smile as he announced "Based on the information you provided, I see no reason why we can't work towards the same ends. I think my colleague would also have to be involved. I think he might be interested in hearing about Jelena. I'll organise a meeting. Would you like anything? More tea?"

"No, no... thank you but no." Tom quickly interjected. "I need to check into my hotel. Your assistant has been informed as to where I am and my contact details are in the email sent to you. There isn't much I can do today anyway, the UK is also on holiday."

"Perhaps we could meet this evening around 7pm? Over dinner and we can look into the matter further?"

"Certainly." Tom agreed "see you later then?" Tom said as he stood up and stretched out his hand for a shake again. Jan got up and gave it a more confident shake and grip. "Get some rest." Jan instructed when he remembered something. "Oh, I forgot to ask, you seem to have described this woman's actions with such great detail, yet I have no idea what she looks that." Tom guaranteed Jan that he would forward him a picture by email.

Tom left the office with confident strides. Despite his misgivings, Jan began to warm to him. They clearly had the same work ethic. There was a growing respect for the man from London up until he got a phone call that confirmed Tom's convictions, the missing Siegfried did not catch the flight. The respect turn to a slight case of loathing for the "know it all".

As Jan battled with his jealousy for this stranger, Joel was yawning, wondering if he should get out of bed today having survived the most boring Christmas he had ever experienced in his life so far. He never thought his father's return could put a stop to his momentum, but it did.

Joel turned around in the bed, his leg heavy. The wall clock said it was past ten in the morning, the time his mother would be on the tread mill, the sound of it humming through the building. But the house was rather silent, a bit too silent.

It was customary that during the winter months regardless of the time, at 10am to 11am, his mother would be huffing and puffing trying her best to keep in shape, but there was none of that today. It raised Joel's anxiety, the only times it stopped were when they were on holiday and when his father took ill.

Fearing it could be the latter; Joel got out of bed and raced down the steps. The airy silence still prevailed. Joel wondered if the house was empty. He walked through to the living room. The television had a comedy show playing and on the side table rested a cold cup of coffee.

Joel walked in and turned off the set. It was then he could hear the faint sound of chatting. It was his mother's voice. It carried a sense of calm with undertones of stress and disappointment. It originated from the dining room; it lured Joel to investigate further.

As he entered, Joel found his mother seated at the far end of the dining table with the phone to her ear, his father standing over her gripping his cane, his face ridden with anguish as she said "Yes, I understand, it was excessive." This didn't seem right. "Dad?" Joel called.

His parents looked at him and on sight of him Georg appeared to glow with fury as his eyes widened. Georg started walking towards his son which in turn prompted Anita to end the call quickly with the words "I have him here. We will clean things up. I promise." As Anita thanked the person on the line, Joel had frozen to the spot. He knew his father was angry but wondered why. Both his curiosity and fear grew at the same time.

Georg stood before Joel, who could hardly speak let alone move, and landed a punch square into his chest which sent Joel crashing to the floor. Before Joel could begin to query what merited his father's actions, Georg began to bring down the cane he held on Joel with all the strength he could muster, landing heavy lashes on Joel several times before he was brought to heel by Anita whom, whilst still seated and in a normal tone intervened "Georg, I told you I will handle it. So stop that before you give yourself another heart attack."

Like an attack dog being brought to heal, Georg halted his assault on his son. "Go watch some television or something… I'll update you." Anita instructed. Georg did as he was told and walked out of the room cursing under his breath and remarking in an audible tone "Why did God take the smart one?"

Joel wanted to get up, but he couldn't. Those words said by Georg proved to hurt Joel more than the physical pain he felt. He knew it was meant to put him down, and it worked because he stayed down. All he could see were the legs of the table and chairs and those of his mother, and the fluff on the floor.

Then his mother came to him in her running shoes. She stood there for a moment to watch Joel sob silently on the floor looking at her feet. "Look at me." She ordered. Joel turned his gaze at her. Once assured of his attention, Anita, in a calm and collected voice, proceeded "Frankly, I too have the urge to kick you in the face, but sadly, I am not wearing the appropriate shoes and too many people have already been hurt by you already. In thirty years of running our operations, I have never seen such incompetence, what makes this worse is it's from my son."

"I gave you one simple task and you couldn't do it without raising unnecessary attention and suspicion. It was meant to be easy and straight forward, allowing us to stroll in without objection or hindrance but you couldn't help it could you and you replaced one obstacle with another in your usual style by going over the top."

"Not only did you go over the top you invited a third party which I had selected for a one off assignment outside Germany and brought into our business. The scale of retribution you and your friends have inflicted is unbelievable and now the British police and Interpol are involved because they are looking for that woman."

"You invited the fox into the house and now the hunters and their dog are following the scent to our door. This is your mess, you clean it up. I don't care how you do it, I just want this problem gone and things returned to the way they were. You must remove the scent the fox left behind. Is that clear?" Joel, with his bruised cheek and bleeding brow nodded, to confirm he understood. "Good. Now I have to organise your father for a meeting with his friends to find out what they know. You better pray to God they are all in the dark about this." Then she glared at him "Get up, you have a lot to do." Joel got himself off the ground with soreness across his left side. "If I were you, I would go to the living room and reassure the old man that you will deal with this."

"Yes mummy." Joel replied.

Taking her advices, Joel hobbled on to the front living room where his father sat in his big arm chair barely visible. Joel didn't get too close, afraid of what his father could do. "I'm sorry Dad… I promise I will sort things out."

"You'd better." Georg replied without turning to look at his son. Joel walked up to his room to look at himself in the mirror and take stock of his bruises and wounds as he drafted plans in his mind to resolve the problem before it resolved him.

Meanwhile, Khoi returned to the empty office with some mixed feelings. With everyone still off on holiday and it being a weekend, Khoi was on his own. He entered the room which had not been touched since the night Paul found him. It was time to move on.

Khoi cleaned up and returned things back to their place. He took his place behind his desk, turned on his computer and watched his hand tremble. Even though he was calm and had come to terms with the incidents that occurred in the room, it was clear his subconscious hadn't.

Unwilling to let it inhibit him any further, Khoi threw himself into his work totalling up the figures and expenses of the operations of the month, trying to offset it with the profits of the gym. It took several hours and by four in the afternoon, he was close to finishing when he heard footsteps. Khoi was apprehensive. He got up and went to the door of his office to lock it. It was then he noticed that the person approaching was Joel. The site of his friend approaching brought him great relief even though Joel appeared cross as he got to the door.

Khoi opened the door and welcomed him with a hug. "Hey, how are you?" Khoi enquired. On closer inspection, Khoi observed "What happened to you?"

"Let's ignore that for now. Got a moment?" Joel asked. Khoi ushered him into the room. Joel sat on the desk whilst Khoi went back to his seat. Joe decided to cut to the chase "We need to talk about Jelena."

"Alright…" Khoi was about to ask what the conversation as about when Joel proceeded.

"Three days ago… or was it four? It doesn't matter, on the 23$^{rd}$ I got a visit from Jelena, the person who I thought you saw off at the airport the day before. Apparently, she had forgotten to give me my Christmas gift. A nice gesture and all, but it was six in the morning and I wasn't interested till she insisted, telling me that I would love it. So I followed her and the gift she gave me was quite a surprise, it was one of those things that you wished it came with a receipt. I bet you couldn't guess what it was?" "No, tell me." Khoi urged pretending to be interested as he carried on with his calculation on the desk top computer.

Joel reached over and turned off the monitor, signal to Khoi that his attention was required and when Joel noticed he divulged "The gift was Jürgen Schmude, dead, in a box marinating in his own excrement." Khoi went pale with astonishment "Oh, I see I finally got you to sit up."

Khoi demanded confirmation "Are you serious?"

"Why would I be joking? She got Ralph and Daniel in on it and I saw the corpse with my own eyes! We spent the whole evening disposing of him. And I wonder why you are surprised? I heard you got a present too. Would it have something to do with the 8 grams of Botox she ordered from Callum?" Khoi squirmed "something to do with Ingbard?" Joel asked

"If you know this, why do you ask?" Khoi snapped

"Fuck what I know. This woman is crazy!" Joel stressed his point by slamming the table. "She's out of control and yeah, I am worried, fuck worried, I am scared. What if she comes for us? I called our friend in Serbia and do you know the bitch didn't go straight home? She took a detour to Bratislava, guess what she did there?"

Khoi hated Joel's rhetorical questions and roared "Just tell me!"

Joel got over off the desk and walked behind it to where Khoi sat instructing him to move over as he commandeered the computer and accessed YouTube. Joel punched in some words so quickly that Khoi didn't have enough time to read it. After a few clicks of the mouse, the clip began to play. Joel expanded it to fit the screen and raised the volume. On the screen was footage from an aquatic centre. From what Khoi could make of it, it was just about to be opened as a fat, bald, suited man with a pair of scissors, and a lady in a floral dress and a pretty hat to his left and a familiar looking young woman in a red bathing suit to his right. Surrounding them were a crowd of children who lined the edges of the pool, Khoi managed to count seventeen of them but there were much more.

The camera zoomed out to show the size of the pool. It was large indeed. Khoi initially struggled to detect the language but soon realised from the flag in the footage was from Slovakia. Once the countdown to the grand plunge was over, the ribbon was cut. The fat man was loudly applauded as he walked away from the water's edge allowing the eager children making gleeful noises to jump feet first into the pool most in the deep end led by the athletic lady in a tight swim suit.

The crowd cheered as the splash sound filled the arena which slowly began to die down as the children dived in the deep end and did not return to the surface. Then came the sight that caused the crowd their greatest concern. The children that had jumped in the shallow end appeared to fall silent and, one after the other, they began to wilt, submerged into the water. This turned the concerned chatter of the crowd into screams as peopled rushed forward and jumped, wading into the water to fish out the children.

What followed was the horrifying sight of bodies floating to the surface, motionless. The cry of a mother is a universal thing as the chorus rang out through the centre. There was a peculiar situation where those who went to get the children out either did not return immediately from the deep with bodies or, having tried to assist, collapsed, adding to the body count themselves.

If Khoi could speak Slovakian he would have heard the person behind the camera screaming the most sensible thing one could day at that moment "Don't go into the water! It's the water!"

The call soon came out and those who were wading or still swimming and hadn't succumbed returned to the banks of the pool to get themselves out.

There was a heart wrenching moment when a life guard in the deep end of the pool reached out to the others on the shore and when he was pulled out, he slumped to the floor, totally immobile. Khoi watched in horror as parents wept and ran around in distress as the body of their children were brought out of the water.

Even those who came to save lives began to lose theirs from just going in to fish out others. It was worrying to watch the site of a woman who was giving mouth to mouth resuscitation keeling over and twitching till she stopped moving. The situation was absolutely hopeless, yet the camera kept rolling as pandemonium reigned.

Eventually, all attempts to retrieve the bodies stopped as the lifeless, discoloured corpses of children and adults drifted on the surface of the water and finally, he spotted the bright red swimming suit, resting amongst the bodies, joining the number of the dead.

With the soundtrack of tears and wailing, Joel considered that Khoi had seen enough and stopped the video. Pointing at the frozen picture, Joel declared "There's where the left over Botox ended up, in the chlorine dispenser of the pool. Do you consider that thing human?" Joel remarked relating to Jelena.

"Oh my God..." Khoi stood up and paced for a moment, his mind drew a blank, his thoughts consumed by the devastation he had just witnessed. Having made up his mind he confirmed "What are we going to do?" Joel then underlined "We? You wanted us to hire her. She's your avenging angel. Just for your information, her employers told me she mentioned she met someone nice and warned that, if I knew this person, they should leave the fucking country! I don't like how this is going man, you have to deal with this and end our relationship with her!"

Khoi paused for a moment; he could see the fear in Joel's eyes, something that seldom occurred. He too began to ask himself how it came to this, but with Joel needing reassurance, he replied "I'll handle it."

"Yeah? But how?" pressed Joel.

Irritated, Khoi lashed out "I said I'll handle it ok? So leave it!"

Having drawn out a commitment from Khoi, Joel stated, "You'd better." then made his way out of the room, then hesitated "Oh, the next time you want to have sex in the office, turn the fucking security camera off, you sleaze."

With Joel gone, Khoi watched the clip again and again and it didn't fail to shock every time. With each viewing, he seemed to pick up something new. The most moving was a mother desperate to touch her son laying there on the floor, shrieking and reaching out to him, inhibited by two people. At the end, no one wanted to help. It was like a replay of the medieval times when a person touched by the plague was left to perish without assistance.

Khoi's horror festered and fermented eventually turning to anger that he never knew he had. All his misgivings about Joel's demands no longer existed. There was no time for figures anymore and something indeed had to be done. Khoi set to work by sending a text to all the numbers he had for Jelena with the question "Are we still meeting for New Years?"

Once sent, he waited patiently, but he didn't have to wait long. Within seconds, his phone vibrated. The message from Jelena read "Nothing will stop me my love." The word she placed at the end of her message, "love", went some way to melt his heart and tame his anger, but didn't force him to turn a blind eye to her killing spree. Once again, he reached out to the one he trusted and called Daniel.

Another person receiving a call that time was Tom who had spent the first half of eight hours sleeping and the other half catching up on some work. Whilst finalising his report on the Christmas Eve attempted bank robbery, the hotel phone rang. Upon answering it, Tom was informed that he had Jan waiting for him in the reception area of the hotel.

Tom halted his progress with the report, raced for a bottle of cologne and after three squirts on his person he put on his coat and went to meet him in the lobby; where, with Jan was Wolfgang who looked glum.

Following a quick introduction, the German policemen took their British counterpart to the Policeman's bar. Seated in the isolated corner of the venue and with Wolfgang off to buy the beer, Jan took the opportunity to speak candidly to Tom. "I have a confession." Jan expected Tom to show some interest, yet Tom didn't flinch. Regardless, Jan pressed on "I got the picture of the lady you sent... Daisy?"

"Jelena." Tom corrected.

"Yes, her. Have you ever met her before?" Jan asked. He waited for a reaction but there wasn't any. Tom just sat there comfortably, hands placed loftily on the armrest with the same emotionless expression.

This made Jan nervous and he was ever so happy to have the attention move on to Wolfgang who delivered the pints of beer and a shot of Gammel Dansk to accompany it remarking "Here you go.", placing the items before each of them. "Heavy drinking on a Sunday; isn't this novel." Tom sarcastically said. "It's fine, Old Jan here is getting tomorrow off and I don't have to be in till much later in the day." Wolfgang explained.

Jan noted Tom giving a cautious look to the drinks and thought it would be best to cast aside Tom's reservations. "Found out about this drinking practice in Denmark, some say it's an acquired taste."

"Oh, no, not these.... They're awful." Jan whined.

"Oh shut up." Wolfgang ordered as he took his seat and enthusiastically picked up his shot glass and proclaimed "Call this Danish tequila. Cheers!"

Tom picked up his shot glass toasted them without touching their glasses and amazed his drinking companions by not sipping the herby bitter drink, rather, he downed it, and unlike them, he maintained his steely resolve whilst they couldn't bear another taste of it without washing it away with their beers, Tom didn't touch his.

Having recovered from their self-inflicted torment, Tom took the chance to speak. "Wolfgang, I am sure you are aware of my quest here?"

"Yeah… but I have a question… why haven't the British police been able to get this woman?" Wolfgang asked, taking another sip of the beer. "It's more complicated that you think. She isn't your common heavy for hire, she is well connected, feared or has enough information on individuals to ensure their loyalty. Germany is one of the very few states that seem to be evaded her touch… until now. After many years of chasing her, we have decided to take a different approach. Why chase a fly when it's the poop that attracts it. It is time to place extra impetus on finding the person who hired her here in this country and I wouldn't be surprised if the recent unexplained deaths are all connected in some way."

"You still haven't answered my question." Jan interrupted "Have you seen her in the flesh?"

Shrugging his shoulder, an act that Jan translated as belittling his question, Tom replied "Yes, on more than one occasion. But that's a story for another day. I want to underline, this isn't a situation of a British policeman walking onto your patch, this should be your case, your arrest and I would like to assure you that I have been authorised to provide you all the assistance possible and grant you access to all our assets on the basis that I remain present and given full disclosure of how your investigations are going as agreed by our superiors."

Jan could only bite his tongue in anger. It would clearly be too much to ask for the, now annoying, bobby to return to his island defeated. More was yet to come as Tom suggested "I hope you don't mind, but would it be too much to ask if I could see the reports regarding the spate of murders?"

Jan was appalled, this, in his eyes, was a clear incursion into his territory, but before he could reject the offer, Wolfgang replied "I don't see why not, I'll check with the chief tomorrow." And with all sincerity, Wolfgang raised his glass as he added "Hey, welcome to the German police force."

Tom finally cracked a smile and touched glasses with Wolfgang and Jan. If the evening couldn't get any more sickening, Wolfgang and Tom appeared to connect. They chatted over the dinner served by the bar, a meal of sausage and potatoes with the all the condiments and sauerkraut. Wolfgang wasn't to blame. He always got along with others easily and he even managed to get Tom to laugh whilst he just watched, dreading with greater intensity the prospect of having to work with the foreigner. All Jan wanted to do was to punch the man in face and tell him he was an unwanted distraction, but he couldn't. He hoped was that Tom would be able to catch his disapproving glances and read what he could from that.

Drinks and dinner were over and it was time to go home. Jan felt increasingly isolated as he got to the door of his flat. Once inside and after hanging his coat, he found Kat watching television in the living-room. She was alerted to his presence and gingerly asked "Hey, you're back. How was it?"
"I hate him." Jan declared, not in the mood of discussing the matter any further, went straight to bed.

As Jan pretended to sleep to avoid any interrogation, it came to pass that on the other side of town, he wasn't the only one feeling discouraged. Khoi had just left his room on his way to the lift, to go down the six floors to the lobby, with his neck hurting as a result of trying to address the matters that troubled him.

Having been confronted earlier in the day by Joel and given his marching orders, Khoi decided to leave work early. He felt fragile and crushed.

With the death of the innocent children weighing heavy on his mind, Khoi returned to his hotel room, shut the door and crumbled onto the ground in tears and agony. He hit the floor several times cursing and impugning his part in the tragedy based on one line, if it wasn't for him, she would never had had access to Callum and those kids would still be here, they would have seen another year, they would have had a future.

Now they wanted him to terminate her. He had been given the task, and despite how much he knew she deserved it, Khoi could not stomach another life ending, even if it were that of the angel of death in carnet.

The reproach in his soul grew too loud. His mind was being overwhelmed with voices telling him he was no better, if not worse than Jelena. Khoi could only think of one way to silence the voices.

Khoi got off the floor and looked around the room to weigh his options. He had three pills left, the best he would get from that would good night's rest and washing it down with spirits would lead to him vomiting... besides, he could be saved.

The fruit knife would have been a better option, if his phobia didn't get in the way and it baffled him why such a hotel would bolt the windows, thus allowing them to only open only 20 cm and no more.

Having walked around the room, Khoi found a solution in the bathroom, but it needed testing first. The bar that held the shower curtains was sufficiently high enough from the ground to be effective. Jumping and grabbing on to the bar, he dangled just centimetres from the floor. After ten chin-ups, it was confirmation enough to him that the bar could support his weight. It was now time to choose which would make the best ligature, the belt, the sheets, or his trousers? Khoi selected the sheets.

Having created a suitable noose which dangled in anticipation from the shower curtain bar, Khoi brought in the chair from the room. Khoi stood under the bar, placed the sheet around his neck. He took a deep breath, shut his eyes, and even before he pushed the chair away, he actually began to feel much better, and peaceful, it almost seemed certain that it was the right thing to do.

A deep breath before his final thoughts turned to his mother and then he kicked away the chair. The initial tug around his neck was choking and chafing but it didn't hurt as much as when his hip touched the ground and the bar landing on his head. The bar had given way, breaking from the wall and foiling Khoi's plans.

Now surrounded by broken bathroom tiles and dust from the walls, Khoi lay on the ground for a moment to consider how pathetic he was. He couldn't even get his own suicide right. It was this attempt at his own life that intensified his disheartened state, causing him a great deal of pain. It caused him to limp into the lift and brought Khoi out of his room, urgently in search of a drink stronger than those he possessed to give him enough time dreams up another means of ending it all.

As Khoi entered the lift, Tom was going through the automatic doors of his hotel. He didn't feel confident that he made friends. Although Wolfgang was all "bon ami" Tom couldn't help but feel that it was all superficial, unlike Jan who fitted every German stereotype, humourless, non-smiling, cold as steel and wasn't afraid to show his disdain which was effective even though he never said a word throughout the dinner.

It was enough to make anyone uncomfortable and Tom was no exception, all he hoped was that no one noticed and Wolfgang's pledge of assistance could be relied upon.

Now back at the hotel, Tom felt he could finally relax choosing to make a little detour to the hotel bar as opposed to his room. He propped himself on the bar stool and browsed what was available on the shelf, none of which made his mouth water.

As he struggled to make his selection, the bartender dressed in his bow tie and flamboyantly decorated waist coat, obstructed his view and initially spoke in German. Even though Tom could deduce the man may be asking what he would like to have, he nevertheless asked in English if the man could clarify. "What would you like to drink sir?" asked the bar keeper. With nothing that caught his interest, he asked for a glass of champagne.

Whilst waiting, Tom realised there was no one seated in the area. Usually, such a hotel with a high reputation should have a few lingering businessmen swigging some strong booze on their company's expense. It made him have second thoughts on his order, but it was too late. The flute containing the fizzy glass of white wine arrived. With reluctant acceptance, Tim asked the cost be charged to his room.

He was about to take a sip when a tall slender Asian man, with rambled looking hair that seemed dusty and containing tiny bits of unidentifiable items amongst the stands of hair that crowned his worried looking head, sat one chair away from him at the end of the bar.

The man ordered a Campari and soda. More out of boredom than of genuine interest, Tom decided to comment on the angst of the man. "You look like you've had a terrible day." The man turned to Tom, smiled and replied "hmm... you're right. Hey?" The man called to the bartender and said in German "May be something stronger than Campari and soda please... Vodka, two shots please?"

Feeling a bit intrusive, Tom apologised for making such an observation, but the man shrugged, smiled and stretched out his hand offering Tom the full double shot glass "For you. Join my misery." Accepting the offer, he raised his glass and in unison with the gentleman, downed his drink but Tom beat the man in finishing, prompting the Asian looking chap to remark, "Clearly you had a bad day as well." Tom snickered as he nodded replying "Sort of."

"What's causing you grief? Asked the man who now had a smile which gave him seem approachable glow.

"I think my associates don't like me." Tom replied.

The man laughed out loud before remarking "You don't seem like someone who gives a shit what people think about them."

"You thought wrong." Tom replied, sipping his champagne before squirming as a result of the taste. Once recovered, he asked "Your turn. What brings you down here?"

"A woman." The man replied. Tom took a sharp take of breath and conceded by calling out to the bartender "Get this man two shots on my bill. He wins hands down." The man laughed in an infectious manner.

With two shots before him, the man insisted that Tom take one. Tom refused on the grounds that he already was drinking champagne before highlighting the risk of mixing his drinks.

To shut him up, the man ordered himself a glass of champagne to even things out. Now they were equal, Tom took the vodka and downed another shot with his new drinking partner.

Following the vodka, the man took a sip of champagne and cringed before remarking, "This is awful. I've got better stuff in my room… want to try some?"

With enthusiasm, Tom leapt at the offer "If it's better than this, why not?"

They left for the lift and once in, Tom introduced himself and it was then the man, who seemed to hesitate before take Tom's outstretched hand, proclaimed "I'm Martin, nice to meet you."

They arrived at the seventh floor of the building, whilst strolling to the room, Martin sang the praises of the drink he had available till they reached the door of room 715. Martin opened the door and welcomed Tom to his plush temporary abode and raced to fetch two bottles of champagne.

Tom took the moment to look around what was clearly one of, if not the most expensive room in the building with a living room, dining area, an oversized television set. There was a door ajar to his left leading to the bedroom and further down was an open door to what looked like the bathroom.

Looking through into the bedroom, Tom could see the unmade bed and he could hear the faint sound of the television set that was left on. Tom noted the blue ball of yarn at the end of the bed. A string dangled down from it to the floor where it was connected to knitting needles and what looked like half finished work.

Tom initially didn't know what to make of that until he glanced further down the room and saw there was something out of ordinary in the bathroom. He could see the metal bar, sheets and the shower curtain, which should have been up above the bath, on the ground and he could just see the hole in the wall where the bar once stood. As he pondered why there was so much disruption, he was interrupted when Martin placed two bottles under his nose, asking Tom to make a choice.

Martin was right, he did have better stuff. He picked the champagne in Martin's left hand, bottled in 1998. "Good choice. Open this whilst I get the glasses." Martin said, literally shoving it into his hands. Tom was uncomfortable being given such an honour, so he waited for Martin to return with the glasses and when he did, Martin didn't seem to note the bottle hadn't been opened, rather, excitedly, he took the bottle from Tom and popped the cork with a cheer.

This near optimistic U-turn, did lift Tom's mood as his glass was filled to the brim and proposed a toast to happiness. "This is fantastic." Tom remarked.

"Please sit down." Martin asked directing him to the lounge area. As Tom obliged his host, Martin proceeded to ask "So, what's causing you grief?"

"Before I tell you," Tom began "May I commend your English, it's really good." Martin laughed, waving off the compliment and pressing Tom to answer his question. "Well, you are right, it's not the being jilted that's dampened my day, to be honest, I miss my son and my ex-wife."

Martin laughed as he replied "Well that's novel. I never heard anyone say they missed their ex-wife, they often curse their name, what makes this so different?"

"It was my fault we are no longer together." Tom's response was ridden with guilt.

Martin then asked "You slept around?"

"No." Tom said increasing the quantity he consumed "Work."

Martin followed his question "And what do you do?" Then he paused shook his head, angered by the irony of the situation of doing the thing that Jelena did so well, and it was infuriating. "I'm sorry for prying."

"No, no. it's ok." Tom dismissed "I'm a criminologist."

"Wow, my job isn't as exciting as yours; I'm a simple wine merchant." Martin added before seeking clarification "Criminologist. You mean like you investigate crimes?" Tom nodded "Wow, interesting." Martin added with a hint of suspicion. He felt like a chicken who had invited the fox in for tea.

Then his reckless side took over and decided to enjoy the situation. "You must be very perspective." Feeling he was at the receiving end of an interrogation, Tom braced himself and placed down his empty glass and said "Go on". As he served Tom some more alcohol, he asked "Well, if you are a criminologist, why not try and pry out some information from me."

Tom smirked, reached for his champagne and before taking a sip asked "So you say it's a woman. She must have done a number on you to rely on medication to sleep." Surprised, Martin turned and looked around and it took him a few moments to find the bottle hidden behind the lamp. "You're good." He acknowledged "Thank you. Now the lady?" Tom pushed.

Martin served himself some more of the now half empty bottle and took a deep gulp to sure himself as he began "I met this woman, we kind of had to work together, then I did something stupid."

"You started having a relationship." Tom assumed. Martin raised an eyebrow as he tried to tiptoe around the answer "You could say so… I guess it was a mistake wasn't it?" He expected an answer but didn't get one. All he got was a comfortable looking Tom egging him on with his grin.

Martin sighed "I don't know what happened. I fell in love with… I don't know if I could call it love, but it's something, I feel so consumed by the want of her. She's in my thoughts, a constant distraction and what's worse she knows it and plays on it." Martin took another drink from his glass adding "It happened over night. One day I was happy and now I am fucking miserable. I cheated on my lover, and for what? Bringing volatility to my life by being unable to get my mind off this woman." Then he laughed as he leaned forward wagged his finger saying "you know what's funny? I'm gay." This threw Tom who sat up and asked "Wait, you're gay and have a partner?"

"Didn't see that coming did you?" Martin said taking another sip.

"No, but wait. Are you physically attracted to her?"

"No, I don't… but oh I want her. There is something seductive, so familiar, so intriguing about her that draws me like a moth to a light bulb." Tom then raised his hand to halt Martin's progression and once he had the attention required, Tom asked "You used the word "familiar" What do you mean by that? Does she remind you of someone in any way?"

Martin began to feel exposed, running his hand through his hair as he nodded; he took a deep drink before replying "Yeah, she does… My friend." Tom was about to ask what gender the person was when he got his answer "He was my best friend… and they are so much alike." His face being held by his hands, his hair draping down his ears, Khoi added "He was a bastard, one crazy, shameless, fucked up kid with no fears… they are so alike. Both have the same crazy sense of humour that makes you love and hate them at the same time…"

"And that turns you on?" Tom interjected. Martin paused and looked up as though he hit a realisation "Sort of… yes, I don't know why but it does and that's what drives me insane."

"What drives you insane? The fact that you have feelings for her? Or your feelings are more drawn to the features she shares with your friend? Did you ever have any feeling for this friend of yours?"

Tom could see his host seem more and more uncomfortable and thought it would be best to halt his examination.

Fiddling with his glass Tom drew on his own experience and confessed "A few years ago, this woman crossed my path and I found myself in need of her attention and like you, I found myself feeling trapped. I couldn't get her out of my head. It affected my work as well as my life and I thought it was taking a toll on my sanity. It turned out to be a brain tumour." Martin couldn't help laughing causing Tom to do the same.

Martin apologised, Tom saw the funny side of the statement. "Anyway" he continued "I had my surgery, and even after they took out part of my brain, the bitch is still in there." This caused another round of laughter, and when it died down, Tom took the opportunity to ram his point home "The thing is, even though she haunts me, I knew I needed to move on before I lost it all.

Will I ever get over her? Most unlikely. Would I ever forget her? Might take additional surgery to do so, but is she worth killing myself for? No."

Martin felt ashamed. His heart was heavy as his eyes misted over. He tried not to cry, but couldn't help it. He got up. "Excuse me" he said, leaving for the study area to allow the tears to fall for a moment. He had hit rock bottom, but he didn't have time to wallow in self-pity, he had a guest.

Using his hands to clear away his tears, he returned. By the time he got there, Tom was on his feet, buttoning up his coat "You're leaving?" he asked.

"Yeah," Tom confirmed "It's late and I have a meeting in the morning, can't arrive there with a hangover. Thank you for the champagne. It was lovely indeed." Martin looked sad to see him go

Offering his hand to Martin who didn't take it, rather, he chose to run to the box by the fridge to fetch a bottle of the drink they just had. He placed it in a plastic bag and presented it to Tom "Christmas may be over, but I hope you can accept this present?"

Tom took the bottle and was moved. "That's really nice of you. Thank you very much."

"No, no... thank you." Martin stressed.

Feeling a bit worried, Tom enquired "So... what are you doing for New Year? Going to party the night away?" Martin shrugged his shoulders and winced as he replied "I don't have any plans. I'll see how it goes." Astonished, Tom asked "Wait, you have no plans? Won't you go to your family?"

"No... I have a brother? Vania." Khoi confirmed.

"Why not spend it with him?" Tom suggested.

"Vania and I don't talk anymore." With that dead end, Tom asked about his friends "I haven't asked them, perhaps I will find out what they are doing."

"Good." Tom said as they walked to the door giving Tom another chance to catch another glance of the wreckage in the bathroom, prompting him to reiterate before crossing the threshold sternly to Martin "Please take on board what I said."

"I already have." Martin replied before they both shared a hug.

Tom went to his room hoping that he reached the man whom he thought was a nice guy, but with the doors shut, Khoi stood there feeling repulsed by the fact that he lied. Why did he choose the name Martin, why couldn't he use his real name? Khoi asked himself.

Yet, Tom did have a point. There was no point ending it all, the world would never forgive him. Rather, Khoi went for his phone. It was time to address the situation once and for all.

# 16

*28 December 2014*

The morning wasn't too good for Tom. He had felt slightly woozy having had very little sleep. He was consumed by concern for his fly-by drinking partner, so much so, he stopped by reception on his way out to ask if they could check on room 735, but there was no need to. Tom was informed that the occupant of the room had come down for breakfast that morning and made his way out of the hotel.

Now he could relax, Tom told himself as he too left for his task for the day.

Walking into the police evidence storage site, Tom beheld a car with a large sheet placed over it. Jan and Wolfgang were with him. Jan remained stone-faced towards Tom as Wolfgang introduced him to the forensics team.

Introductions over, they proceeded to unveil the car. The light shone over the metallic silver Audi. Tom was invited to inspect the vehicle. As he pulled on the latex gloves, he felt rather out of place being on his own. He couldn't believe his ears when he was informed by his superiors that most of the relevant staff wouldn't be able to make it till after Christmas having signed for a long holiday. It was code for "your case isn't really a priority right now". Still, he couldn't say no and he was genuinely interested.

He walked around the car. He could see the fine layer of powder dusted on and around the car door handle and windows and then the two entry points of the bullets. The first one came through the upper part of the windscreen on the driver's side. It was extremely clean as though drilled.

Then as he came to the door of the driver's seat and noticed the window of the driver's door had shattered as a result of the projectile. All that remained were the small, yet sharp edged shards protruding at the base of the window, which, under close inspection, was void of blood.

Tom approached to take a closer look. The front of the interior of the car was stained by dried blood, particularly the steering wheel and inner part of the driver's door. A child's shoe lay on the floor of the passenger's side along with a toy car. More dust could be detected on the steering wheel. Tom decided to take a picture.

Using all the modern technology at his disposal, which was less than what he would have had back home, Tom gathered as much data as he could, putting all he had learnt into use only to be left perplexed. Having spent the whole evening reading through the report and making some notes, he concluded that the report simply explained that the bullet that struck the man on the head, taking, upon entry, most near all the left side of his face before leaving a gaping hole in the right as it exited. He surmised it must have originated from the roof of the building at 15 Potdamerplatz.

Tom had been past the area before many years ago whilst hung-over following a stag party. And after two hours of examining the car, he asked to be taken to the part of the city where the event took place.

Armed with a tube containing a map with bird's eye view of the area, a pair of binoculars, his camera, six road cones and a can of bright luminescent spray paint, Tom methodically stood on the pavement, next to the point where the assassination took place.

With five tall police officers lording over him, he gave the word. The policemen walked into the street. Two diverted traffic from the designated area whilst the cones were placed.

With room created, Tom proceeded to spray a large "X" on the pavement before leaving the section of the road. A police van pulled up and parked just behind the cones. Now that the section was well and truly sealed off, two of the officers went into the van to shelter themselves from the cold.

Tom then put the remaining police in their positions. He took one of the officers and asked that he stay in the cordoned off section at the upper corner of the "X". Then, from the van, a chair and an umbrella were produced. The tall lean female officer seemed to find the bright side of things being told to sit on a chair in the middle of a busy road with an open umbrella, but Tom was certain the other officers wouldn't be so good humoured as they were to take turns doing this till he was content with the results.

With everything in place, Tom stood looking at all the tall buildings and their structures, wondering which of the many was high enough, far enough and architecturally sound enough to enable a person to take such a shot.

He walked around the area for several hours amongst the pollution from car exhaust pipes, till he was certain he was going to catch a cold. With Wolfgang having called ahead, Tom approached each and every tall building and was given access to the roofs. Each time, at the top, he would take out his binoculars to look at the officer seated and then take a picture.

It was when he got to the roof of number 13 that Tom noticed something. The breeze on top of this 23 storey building was strong enough to bring a tear to his eye, and he wasn't able to see what he wanted and reach the conclusion on the action he needed to take. He examined every floor till he was satisfied and yet angered. He thanked the janitor and the office staff for their assistance before he left to collect his thoughts.

Tom settled in a café, sitting there with his map and his coffee circling his observations and jotting down his findings. He was drawing circles in the relevant areas of the map when his phone rang. It was Wolfgang who asked "It's 6:45pm. Can my officers take their leave now? They are beginning to feel stupid." Tom had completely forgotten about them and raced to the nearest fine food store to fetch bottles of expensive whiskey to present to the officers This was followed by him offering to take the officers to dinner the following day for their efforts. With feelings mended, Tom returned to station to collect the next file he needed to review from Jan's office.

Lumbering with all his equipment, Tom walked through the busy station. His first point was to submit the folder and sign off the relevant documents confirming its return before making his way to Jan's office.

As he approached the door with the office assistant, he could hear a conversation in German. From the voices, he realised it was Jan speaking to a woman. "Maybe I should come back later?" He suggested, but the assistant ignored him, knocked and opened the door. Popping his head through, the assistant announced Tom's presence. "Oh, Tom, come in please." Jan called.

Tom entered and found there was a lady standing there with a sombre expression. She was a wide eyed lady with light hazel eyes and her hair tied in a bow and was dressed in bomber jacket and jeans. She watched as Jan went to the coat rack to pick up his jacket. "Hello Tom. I heard you had a very interesting day…" Jan began "Oh, this is my girlfriend, Kathrin."

Putting on the charm, Tom replied "Hello Kathrin. I can see why Jan never mentioned you. You are very pretty and he is lucky." She smiled and before pointing at Jan and directed Tom "could you repeat that last bit again? He seems to forget that very often."

"Don't mind her. She's just angry I have to back out of bowling match she organised." With his coat on, Jan turned his attention to Tom "You can collect the folder from the filing clerk. It was translated in haste, so sorry about that, but right now, I have to rush to the hospital to try and get something out of our poison victim. He's fading fast." With a kiss on his girlfriend's lips, he whispered "I'm sorry."

Jan then rushed out of the room, leaving Tom alone with Kat. Tom snickered as it reminded him of his good old days with his wife. He was about to bid Kat goodbye when she asked "Do you bowl? I know it's forward, but I have my friends from the Austrian and Swedish embassy… we were to play in teams of two but with Jan gone…" Tom raised his hand to stop the rambling and when she finally fell silent replied "Sounds lovely." Kat beamed and went about to call her friends to confirm that the night had been saved.

*29 December 2014*

Tom woke up with a hangover the following morning. He had embarked on a bridge building exercise via the girlfriend which had resulted in sore head. Reason being, having got the highest score ever recorded in the alley, everyone bought him a drink and there were 11 people there.

Yes, the company Kat kept were a nice and interesting bunch and Kat herself was indeed a genuinely open and nice person.

The spotty memory of the night before had now become the painful lament of the present as he struggled to keep awake.

Once he finally to get out of bed, he found he had slept in the clothes he wore the night before with the buckle of the belt leaving an imprint on the skin of his stomach. The foul taste of tequila lingered on his tongue; with his head still spinning he knew he was still, if ever so slightly, drunk.

Tom reached to check his phone and realised it was three past eleven in the morning. "Oh fuck!" he remarked as he tried to jump out of bed, but his throbbing head and wobbling feet slowed is progression.

Finally, he got his feet out from beneath the covers, placing them on to the floor, the hotel phone rang, an unwelcome noise that irritated all his senses. Tom reached to pick up the receiver answering "What?"

The receptionist, voice trembled with nervousness "Em, good morning Mr Evans, we have Herr Harbeck from the police here." He sat up and wondered if he had the strength to face anyone, but he had no choice, after all, he did make the trip. "Send him up." Tom ordered.

With the receiver down, Tom calculated that he had about two minutes to at least get some sort of civility in his appearance. Tom went to the toilet and looked amongst the many toiletry products left by the posh hotel and found a bottle of mini mouthwash. A quick swish of that around his mouth and a splash of water on his face didn't do much to aid his situation or his headache, nor did it diminish the colour of his eyes.

There was a knock on the door. Too late to turn him back now. Tom went to the door and found Jan there carrying a suitcase. He was stone faced as usual, but this time with an added imprint of a hint of loathing in his eyes. "Good morning" Jan said "May I come in?"

"Of course." Tom replied.

Jan took it upon himself to open the window and allow the air to circulate asking "I heard you had a good time yesterday?" in a less than interested manner. "According to Kathrin, you were a crowd pleaser. She said she had 'never seen a person so charming. We must have him around sometime soon.'" Jan seemed to turn slightly green as he delivered a message to Tom "I have been told to ask if you had plans for New Year's Eve? Because if you don't, she would like you to join us for the evening." Then followed a moment of silence, causing Tom to worry what answer to give. Jan prompted him for an answer "Well? Are you free?"

"Yeeees." Tom cautiously replied.

"Good. I'll inform her accordingly." Tom thanked him. An unnerving silence soon followed as Tom sat on the bed, his feet still unable to hold him up. He watched as Jan paced up and down. His slightly long blonde hair swung about when he turned.

This persisted for two minutes, putting Tom on edge before Jan finally stopped, looked straight at him before pointing his finger to Tom's face proclaiming "You were right you know. They are all connected. I spent the whole of last night with a man who arrived at the station needing medical attention. He isn't getting better; he had more hair on his pillow than on his head.

His skin was so translucent, I could see the green veins on his face… and his breathing… it was rattling… it was so strange."

"They thought he may have had something contagious. So I had to be covered up like a surgeon and I sat there next to him with the pictures of the people. The man could hardly speak, or move. He could only raise his finger ever so slightly, tittering on the line between sleep and consciousness, but still he remained determined, perking up when he thought I was about to leave.

I put the pictures in front of him and asked if he knew the people. He pointed out three of the people and then seemed to gather his resolve. He tried to tell me everything."

"He and the three people he identified were part of a gang that peddled hard drugs all across the city. The sick man in the bed, the quirky, mild mannered man with OCD who didn't have a drop of narcotic in his blood, doubt if he ever used it in his life, was the leader of the largest purveyor of cocaine in Berlin." Jan proclaimed, raising his tone as he added, exasperated "We have been looking for that man for years." Shaking his head in some form of self-rebuke, Jan added "But his determination was certainly admirable. He went into detail about their activities, how things get in and so on, but when I asked who their associates were…nothing.

"I asked who was most likely to want them out of the picture. Again, he said nothing. I then asked 'what was the significance of the month of May', which he mentioned on his arrival. He, as you say it in England, bit his tongue but he did say something before he fell into a coma. He repeated again and again, 'Find Siegfried.'"

Tom didn't look surprised as he remarked "The code, you don't snitch on your fellow criminals."

"Snitch? What is that?" Jan asked.

"It means you don't go telling the police or anyone about your criminality or that of others, even if it kills you." Tom clarified.

"Oh. Thank you." Jan said, whilst remaining his emotionless self even though Tom could tell he was disappointed.

Jan opened the case he held and presented Tom with the folder containing papers and a memory stick. As Tom received it, Jan asked "Do you really think one person could have caused all this carnage?"

"If paid enough, she could have done far worse." Tom confirmed.

Jan momentarily fell silent again as he bit his lip. Tom held on to the folders in anticipation of some instruction, yet Jan still asked in disbelief "She would really have so many people killed to get to her target?" Tom didn't reply. Jan could tell the answer and sighed "Well, we'd better find Siegfried." As he walked to the door, he stated "The files are for the three people he identified. I trust you with them. If you need access to anything, let me know and regarding the New Year's Eve events, please dress smartly and we will pick you up at 10."

"Will do and thank you for the documents and the invitation to the party." Tom acknowledged.

Jan, who had made his way to the door, paused, turned and gave a scathing remark as he underlined "You're welcome for the files. About the party, you can thank Kathrin when you see her." And with the record well straightened, Jan left, shutting door behind him.

Tom could have sworn he heard Jan cursing in German, but for now, he was too weak to let Jan's grumbles bother him. He needed to rest a bit more but he couldn't. The files were too alluring. Tom decided to sit up in bed to begin his reading for the late morning.

Meanwhile, walking down Hollywood road in Hong Kong with his old friend and father of two called Jack, Julien had been mulling over the lack of communication he had had with Khoi. It was more for his part, missing calls and forgetting time zones, but as he and Jack walked towards Lan Kwei Fong, he thought it was just about a reasonable time to get in touch with Khoi whom he had missed so much.

Using his mobile, he dialled away, whilst Jack watched on patiently. After ten rings, the line was disconnected. "No Khoi?" asked Jack, Julien shook his head, leaving Jack to observe "You've been trying for the last two days now; sure he's not banging another guy? You know, cat's away…?" he said with a wink.

Julien gave Jack a shove as they laughed. He then ordered "shut up you bitch and let's go." As they approached the famous land mark hotel, Julien couldn't help but try to connect again, this time by text with the words "call me".

The text was received at noon when Khoi's phone rang, but it was dismissed. In his office, Khoi could hardly concentrate on the work piling on his desk. The many applications from rich clients and companies for special rates and specific treatments, all for the right price, did not thrill him the least.

He had a deadline and yet he was unable to conceptualise what to do. All the stress of the past few days was driving him up the wall and he could use a distraction. It was then his thoughts turned to Jeroen.

Khoi always found the visits to the sanatorium very therapeutic and he could sure use something to ease his tension about now. He didn't know why he always left relaxed. Perhaps it was the mundane nature of their communication. But perhaps it was teaching Jeroen how to read and write again and enjoying the signs of improvement, or the many board games he often had to play with Jeroen time and time again, such as monopoly or snakes and ladders.

It was like a flash of lightening, Khoi was struck by an idea. His excitement levels were so high, he could have danced. First, he wrote out what he had in mind and once content it was considered fool-proof, he reached for his phone and called Joel whom he woke at two in the afternoon.

He informed Joel that he would need to meet with Daniel without delay in his office and it should all be incognito. In addition, he passed on what he considered some good news. "I think it is time we changed our fleet of vehicles. I am going to get the papers going today and you guys should get one before the New Year. What colour do you like?"

*30 December 2010*

The last formal meeting of the year was convened and the first between Joel and Khoi since the ultimatum was given. It was also to be the first meeting of the group since completing their quest. There was a change in the general tempo. Everyone was genuinely happy to be back in each other's company. Joel and Khoi waited for the mutual appreciation to die down before they got to business. The topic of the day was bonuses. Khoi distributed the envelopes containing the token of appreciation to the rightful recipients.

"Regardless of the reduction in our numbers, life must go on. We had a bumper year and it was all thanks to you, please remember to pass it on to your helpers." They all applauded "That's not all, we still have our New Year's Day celebrations to look forward too."

"Jelena is coming too right?" Mikel interrupted "Let's get her a gift."

"Already done." Khoi concluded.

"You did?" Joel asked "What did you get her?"

"The company needed some new wheels, so I got us a deal on some Land-rovers. It was a buy two get one free deal, so I bought four, we got two extra, so I thought we could give her one."

Joel was aghast by the generosity "You are giving her an off road vehicle? Why? Aren't we paying her enough?" Rubbing his brow more out of fatigue rather than frustration, Khoi replied "Daniel will fill you in."

Insulted by being skirted aside, Joel screamed "In other words, shut up Joel!" then he got up and pointed at Khoi "I've had enough of your arrogance." Joel stormed out of the meeting room. Khoi was now seated amongst a sea of bewildered uncomfortable faces. Eager to end the situation, he wound up the meeting. "I guess that's all for today and I hope ever. I will return to my humble desk as your faithful bean counter but before I go, thank you all for taking me in." As he got up to collect his belongings leaving behind a set of stunned faces, he turned to Daniel "Oh, don't forget to bring Joel up to date will you." Daniel nodded and without as much as an expression of affection to them. Khoi walked away crying out "See you at the New Year's party."

As he shut the door behind him, leaving them to come to terms with his departure. Khoi walked out of the building feeling a bit misty eyed. It was painful to see the dawn when sleep deprived. Ever since Joel showed him the video, he had been haunted but the images of the dead, particularly the woman in the red swimming suit who turned out to have been a gold medallist swimmer at the Beijing Olympic Games for her home country, Slovakia. She had come as the special guest, leading the big dip.

Stepping out through the automatic doors, Khoi felt the cold wind on his face and the hint of tobacco wafting through the air. Khoi turned to the direction from where the smell originated from and he found Joel standing at the other end of the door, taking in the nicotine deeply into his lungs. Their eyes met and they watched each other without speaking till Joel finished his cigarette.

Joel threw away the bud and pushed out the last bit of smoke from his lungs. Khoi could feel Joel's insecurities and said "I'm done now. You won't need me." Khoi hoped his words would ward off Joel's envy, but it didn't. "That's a lie, we'll always need you. And that's the problem; we can't get rid of you." Joel replied. His words were sadistic and serious enough to demonstrate that he wasn't pleased. Khoi managed to keep his thoughts on the matter to himself before reaching into the pocket of his coat and producing a pair of green hand knitted glove and handed them over to Joel.

Joel inspected it and remarked "You dick. Why must you always place that red heart on everything? Some gay code or something?" Accepting that this was the closest to a "thank you" from Joel he was going to get, Khoi walked on to his waiting taxi. He was more concerned about the bonuses of the ninety plus members of staff of the gyms and resorts with the piercing eyes of Joel aimed at him as he was driven away.

*31 December 2010*

Tom had been reading the folders and reviewing the information provided to him over and over again in his room and he was even more eager to look deeper into the matters he noted.

Tom made some calls to his team in London to confirm their arrival. He still felt uneasy with the completion date he had been provided.

It was during this conversation he, in passing, raised the issue of his concerns with the German's investigations and was promptly chided "Evans, your job is to find Jelena and not sniff out the skeletons lurking in the German Police Service's cupboard and by God I am sure there are plenty.

I know it's hard not to pry, it's your job, but you need to keep your distance from their internal affairs and try to make friends. It's important we have them on side. Understood?" Taking his orders, Tom thought it was no best to focus on what to wear for the evening and the paperwork on the bed as he had just two hours to prepare.

At 10pm, Jan and Kat arrived at the hotel where Tom was staying. They requested that Tom be informed of their arrival, but were told that Tom was aware already l and apologised that he could be fifteen minutes late.

They were offered a place to sit in the lobby area on the nice royal blue sofa opposite a low coffee table. Placing themselves on the chairs, anyone reading the body language of the couple would have detected the friction that was clear to see as they both sat at the extreme ends of the long chair that was meant to seat four.

This friction was created when Jan decided to be honest and asked if

Kat and Tom could ring in the year without him since he wasn't comfortable being around the foreigner and his idiosyncrasy of his nature. This was next to heresy in Kat's eyes and she didn't hesitate to make it clear what her thoughts on his offer were, calling him bloody-minded and used several curse words to bring him to heel.

Now they were seated together, uncomfortable with their own company, waiting for protagonist of their current misery. Kat was gradually losing her patience with Jan whose constant fidgeting with the packet of gum he had in his possession drove her crazy. Jan would toss it up and catch it on most occasions. He was trying to see how many times he could throw and catch the pack without dropping it, mumbling the numbers as he propelled the item in the air.

Unable to stand it any longer, Kat caught the gum in mid-air and stated "The fact that you are bored does not give you the right to annoy everyone else." Kat got up and looked around for a moment before putting the gum packet into a bin.

As she returned to her position at the far end of the chair, Jan sat frightened by her response. He was afraid to move let alone speak. Kat didn't have such restrictions. "You are such a bull head dick." She said in a soft voice. "The man is here alone, and you can't see the potential? By just being friendly to him, your possibilities could be endless, don't you think of the future? Don't you think about climbing further up the ranks? And you think all your piety would keep you warm through the years you vindictive man."

Jan said nothing in response. He knew better not to because she was correct, but he still found Tom a pill too bitter to endure, so he looked away, revealing the small strands of feathers imbedded in his hair. Kat reached out and ran her hand through his hair to rake them out "Didn't you wash your hair? It's dry." She complained.

Jan could feel Kat about to start another onslaught of humiliation, when he heard Tom asking the reception where his guests were. It was time to keep up appearances. Kat quickly raced to sit next to Jan and ordered "Stop looking like a child who lost his sweets."

As Tom appeared from around the corner, Jan and Kat forced a smile. She stood up and greeted Tom with two kisses on the cheek "Nice to see you again." She proclaimed. Tom shook Jan's hand, but it a cold limp movement of the wrist.

Tom noticed that Kat wore a long royal blue coat and a royal blue scarf, whilst Jan came in his leather jacket, and wore what one would regard as smart casual apparel; Tom remarked "I feel rather over dressed in my tuxedo. I wasn't too sure what sort of event we were going to attend." "Oh don't worry, you aren't overdressed. Jan never bothers to make an effort. See?" She said unbuttoning her coat, revealing she wore a knee length formal dress of shimmering blue, marked with studs. "Heavens, you look stunning in that." Tom said. Kat thanked him. Tom then added jokingly "Many people seeing us walking down the street would think we are a couple."

"Let's hope they do." She said. Tom and Kat laughed, Jan stood there feeling more and more isolated as it was clear that the pair did have the same sense of humour.

Confirming it was time to go, they decided to walk the six blocks to the venue. Tom began to shiver. Kat insisted Tom wear her scarf to keep his neck warm which he gratefully received and wrapped round his neck giving Kat the opportunity to find out more about Tom.

Kat uncovered that Tom had been in the Police since he was 24 and studied whilst he was in service. She learned he had recently attained a PHD in chemistry. Tom was candid enough to tell them about his private life. He had a son called Tim who was now 7 and whom Tom described as his "everything". Tim was a product of a nine year marriage which ended only two years after his birth.

Kat thought it was refreshing that Tom could be so open. On the other end of the spectrum, Jan wondered if Tom would ever shut up.

Finally they arrived at the venue. They walked down the steps to a basement door. There was a woman dressed in a tuxedo with her hair slicked back looking very androgynous if it were not for her protruding breasts.

Kat mentioned their name and they exchanged words as she opened the door allowing them in. Kat quickly walked to Tom as the piano music filled the air and whispered to him "She said, we have to find the tranny to find our place."

Tom was a little concerned as he wasn't too keen on surprises, but it didn't take too long to find the transvestite, a broad shouldered person donning a tight fitting dress and approaching them. She gave Kat a kiss on the cheek and then Tom and Jan before she led the way to their chairs.

The venue was dim due to the candles used to illuminate the room. It caused the air to smell of burning wax and perfume which was worn by the forty or so other people seated in the space. Kat sat in the middle of the two men at their allocated tables before the stage, prompting Tom to enquire what was in store. "I hear it's a cabaret of some sort, so it should be fun." Kat said without detecting the joint scepticism on Jan's and Tom's face as a bottle of champagne was placed before them along with some snacks.

Then came the announcement that rang through the sound system announcing the commencement of the show. The first act called "Savanah" pranced on to the stage. She was two metres in height and wearing 15cm pink heels. She was also dressed in inflated bin bags for a skirt and nipple tassels and a microphone in hand.

At first sight, she was a tall, elegant, stunning specimen of womanhood, although on the giant side of the spectrum. On came a popular track that made it big that year around the world called "Bad Romance". The Adonis began to sing instantaneously, causing utter confusion in the minds of Tom and Jan as the noise produced was not at all feminine.

The performer then came down from the stage to engage the audience. Kat was consumed by the atmosphere and began to sing along. It seemed that all the women were enthusiastic about it whilst Tom and Jan were speechless.

What came next was totally unexpected. Savannah walked to their table and caressed Tom's lapel, pushing away the table and placing her right foot in the space in between his thighs. The performer demanded "MAKE LOVE TO MY LEG!"

Tom looked around him and there were eyes of anticipation gawking at him "Go for it!" Kat cried. Accepting that he had to perform, be proceeded to kiss the hairless leg, then licked it from the ankle to Savanah's knee. "OH! Naughty boy!" Savannah cried then reached for his tie and loosened it and kissed him on the lips as she sat on his lap and sang the chorus. Once done connecting with Tom, she returned to the stage to finish the song by raising up her arms revealing how successful the surgery to create "Savannah" had been because, without the scars under the well mounted silicon breasts, she had a sexy body that could not be ignored.

As the next act came on, Kat commended his efforts in letting his wild side loose, Tom called the waiter and ordered three double shots of vodka, he needed it to steady his nerves and when Kat refused to drink since she was driving, he divided her glass between him and Jan who reluctantly drank it.

As the night progressed, the show became even more flamboyant with a strip tease number, feathers, contortionists, a fire eater, and sword swallower, all before the first half of the night was over. By that time, Kat had found some other friends, two women, and increased the number on their table to five.

Whilst mingling and chatting in German, Tom took the opportunity to go to the toilet. As he used the urinal, two men came running in, clearly frisky as they went into the toilet cubical and shut the door, bolting it for privacy. He didn't need to guess what they were planning to do in there, but he did consider the general feel of the table. Yes, he was having fun, barely, but the lingering cold war between him and Jan put a pea under his mattress. He thought it would be best to try and rectify the situation.

Having washed his hands, he thought of how to reach out to Jan. He went to the bar and asked for the drinks list. Looking over at the table there was something considerably wrong with the picture. There was Kat, the centre of attention, the queen amongst her courtiers, with them hanging on her every word.

That was nice, but at the end of the table looking rather lonely and squeezing his face with every sip of the champagne, was Jan, not enjoying himself, praying for this moment to end. Tom reviewed the drinks list and was surprised by the variety of wines, spirits and cocktails with flamboyant names he had never heard of, and whilst some sounded appealing, they weren't going to assist him in his mission for peace.

Accepting that there was nothing palatable available, he walked to the table, trying his best not to be detected. He succeeded and got to Jan, placing his hand on his shoulder calling out "Hey." Jan turned to face him giving Tom the chance to make a proposal "I wanted to ask, I kind of saw a pub about 200 yards from here and I could kill for a beer. The bar doesn't have any, I checked… you up for it?"

Jan looked at the glass in his hand, he found champagne a bitter substance to take and the show was equally a rape to his senses so a break, even with unwelcome company, would be a welcomed distraction.

Checking his watch, Jan noted that he just had fifty minutes to have the beer. He tapped Kat on the shoulder "Tom and I are going out for a moment. We'll be back soon."

Kat looked at him with suspicion before glancing at Tom who was already standing and waiting "Don't kill yourselves and be back for New Year." Kat instructed.

Jan kissed her on the cheek and left with Tom to the bar.

Once out and into the last winter's night of the year, they walked briskly to reach the bar before the cold became unbearable. Jan decided to strike a consolatory note "Thanks for that. I am not a fan of champagne."

"It's nothing. Besides, I need the beer to wash the taste of man's leg out of my mouth." Tom replied. Jan laughed and it was a great starting point to their conversation. They mocked most of the show. In particular the burlesque where the performer was seen as having too small breasts even though they were real.

At the bar, they two men soon found that they had something else in common. They both had Russian grandparents who were both from St Petersburg. There were more similarities to reveal, such as their pet hate for formality and the difficulty in comprehending why women insist on men showing some form of emotion.

They were knocking back the beer quickly and on their fourth glass, Tom decided to add another thing he had experienced with Jan. "I was meaning to tell you this. You don't need to worry much about having met Jelena, I've met her before, actually, she came looking for me."

"What did she want?" Jan asked

"Nothing. I was sick in hospital and she came over when there was no one looking to check up on me and then left."

Jan got curious and though normally he wouldn't be so forward, he decided to take his chances "I hope you don't mind me asking… but what were you in hospital for?"

"A brain tumour." Tom said passingly as he took a gulp of his beer. The response forced Jan to be inquisitive and posed the question "Is this a personal crusade?"

Tom fell silent and appeared more interested in looking at his beer than Jan. As he took another sip, Tom contemplated. This was a question Tom had asked himself over the years and each time he did, it drew him back to a particular moment in his relationship with Jelena.

It happened shortly after his surgery. Tom was resting on the sofa in his home watching another round of day time television which contained the usual drivel of repeats of comedies and home improvement programmes.

It was all so mind-numbing and having to watch it on his own while his wife, Caroline, had gone to pick up Tim from the nursery. She had confiscated his phone complaining that it irritated her with its constant ringing.

People from the station kept calling to find out how he was or ask for advice, which kept him busy. Now that the phone was gone and all he had was the television, he was at the mercy of the pretentious presenters who were just hoping to find some daft individual, with more money than sense, only to ignore the options offered by the presenters. Tom began to wonder if it had been such a good idea to discharge himself from his hospital bed early to convalesce at home.

He pressed the remote control to check the time, it was 3:15. Caroline and Tim will be back soon, and then he would have some company. Yet, adding to his televised misery, he resented them both for their mobility. He had been house bound by his surgery. His doctors told him to avoid going out in public areas, the sun and extreme heat because of the possibility of infection. This was easier said than done. It was 36c out there with the sun high in the sky and the house had no air conditioning.

Poor him to be ill on such a perfect day, Tom thought to himself. Everyone was in the street and their dogs took flight to the local lido as they went to the park or even the beach for a tan or to keep cool. All he had was his living room, with the sliding door opened to the garden where he couldn't venture out to enjoy it.

Still it was too hot and the heat was causing him a headache and pain in the stitched area of his scalp. He needed relief. Tom got off the sofa and staggered to the entrance that connected the living room to the kitchen. This was the second means of reaching the kitchen, the first being through the hallway.

He stepped on the marble tile of the kitchen. The cooling effect of his bare feet on the stone revived him as he made his way to what he considered to be the greatest modern invention known to man, the ice dispensing mechanism attached to the fridge.

Tom took hold of a plastic cup and approached the chrome coated fridge when he perceived something. He didn't know what it was or where it originated from but he did feel something. He'd been having a lot of these perceptions lately, particularly after Tom woke up from his surgery convinced he had seen Jelena. No one believed him.

Everyone told Tom it was either the morphine, or just a rear case of post-operative delusions. His boss simply put it down to having been over worked. The doctor promptly added another six weeks to his three month recover time.

The heat prickled his skin again, bringing him back to reality. Perhaps they were right, perhaps it was just an illusion, but why did they have to be so real? Tom wondered. He decided to take the world's word for it that his mind was simply playing tricks on him, either that or the onset of paranoia.

Tom placed his cup under the dispenser and pressed for some cubes. As they landed in the base of his cup with a clatter, there was a distinct noise that stopped him retrieving the ice. He waited for a moment to confirm his suspicion, and he didn't have to wait for long. There was a reflection that went across the metallic fridge door.

To hell with the concept of paranoia, Tom concluded, his home was being invaded and he had to do something. Tom crept to the magnetic strip over the sink that held the three sharp butcher's knives. He took the two largest blades and returned to the side of fridge to stand as still and as close as he could to the object to prevent being seen.

He could hear someone coming down the hall way entrance to the kitchen, but it wasn't the most alarming thing so far, that award went to the shadow forming on the wooden floor, the signs of someone who was about to enter from the garden.

Tom was torn on what to do, who would come for him first. Tom placed his bet and he won. As he expected, a person leapt into his living room with a pistol in hand pointing at him.

As though by reflex, Tom threw the blade he held in his left hand, which went through the air and, prior to being able to pull the trigger, perforated the intruder in the chest. The injured man must have been quite determined to pull the trigger. He fired a shot through the silencer nozzle attached to his gun. The bullet struck the floor causing a sound to ring through the house, alerting the second intruder.

Tom did not move from his post. The second intruder asked as he walked towards the kitchen "Did you get him?" as he drew closer. Tom counted the steps to determine when to strike and at the fifth step, when the person crossed the threshold, Tom launched the blade forward in a stabbing motion at the man.

Tom underestimated how tall the man was. The knife was forced through the gullet of the would be assassin causing the huge man dressed in black to stumble backwards with a horrible gargling sound as he attempted to gasp some air. The man leaned on the wall, the gun dropping from his hand as he slid to the floor in a sitting position, oozing blood that bubbled as it mixed with air.

Tom trembled. He hoped to God that this was one of those psychotic-induced episodes and that all this was imaginary, but he had to know. Tom reached to touch the man sitting on the floor gasping and received the shock of his life as with his last bit of strength, the man grabbed Tom by the wrist tightly. This was no imagination. The man's grip gradually loosened as the last signs of life left his big frame.

He could have panicked, but Tom made the conscious decision not to do so. He calmly walked to the front living room and used the handset to call the police. Tom gave his name, rank and number and this caused the person handling his call to cry out "What?" when he revealed that he had killed two who broke into his house bearing arms.

Having checked his details, the call handler transferred him directly to the rapid response unit. They took the situation seriously and ordered him to leave the house and wait outside with the assurance that help was on the way.

Who was he not to follow orders? Tom duly hung up and ran to the front door which had been shut. He opened it and took a step out when he was stunned to find a man standing on the other side. He was dressed in a black jogging suit with a hood over his head obscuring his face, not that it mattered though as he too had a gun which he pointed at Tom.

The world went still. Tom accepted that his luck had ran out and decided not put up anymore resistance. Frankly, he was too tired to fight. Tom blinked but before he could open his eyes, a shot rang out, but there was no pain.

When his lids rose, Tom felt his face, touching the warm matter which had fallen upon it. Bits of flesh, bone and grey matter splattered everywhere and across his face. Tom's would be executioner now had part of his head decimated and fell as a heap on the ground.

With the man no longer obstructing his view, Tom could now see his saviour. She was seated in a blue BMW convertible car with the top down, and a scarf wrapped around her head to keep her hair in place. Jelena looked satisfied as she put her gun away, placed her sunglasses on her face and blew him a kiss before driving off. Tom's eyes followed her till she disappeared in the horizon.

Jelena was gone, but there was another presence. There was a loud scream. Tom turned, Caroline was across the road with Tim who was asleep in the pram, totally oblivious to the happening just metres away.

Caroline stood there, her mouth ajar revealing the gum she was chewing before being overcome by the effects of watching a man die at her door step causing her to faint.

The summer's day didn't seem too happy anymore. Tom no longer felt the heat or the sun's rays beating down on him. He had no clue what to do anymore, but he had to be with his family. Tom crossed the street to his wife and son. He stood over Caroline for a moment to contemplate whether or not to revive her. Tom chose not to, he wasn't in the mood of talking or explaining anything at the moment, particularly when he couldn't. Rather, he calmly sat on the pavement and waited for the police.

It was airily quiet; Tom could not believe that there was no one around. This was a sobering thought. Tom struggled not to break, he need to be strong in order to relay the events of the day as the police car approached.

Now that it was firmly and gruesomely established that he wasn't crazy after all, the police acted swiftly to move Tom and his family into hiding.

During the course of the investigation, it was revealed that Tom had received warning of the forthcoming attempt on his life that afternoon. There were several missed calls and a text from a Dutch number that read "They are coming for you. Leave the house now. SMS when you do." But he received none of it because his phone was out of reach as it lay at the bottom of his wife's bag.

Such an incident was not to repeat itself. His phone never left his side after the incident.

There was to be no prosecution for the deaths, self-defence and the use of appropriate force was not a crime, but such information gave little comfort to Tom and Caroline who were now on the same medication to help them sleep and handle the state of depression that followed.

Tom shook off his down trodden spirits and used the time he had off to focus more on spending time with his son which inevitably had a negative knock on effect for his marriage.

With Jelena still at large, Tom could not rest easy and by the time of his first day back at work after an eight month hiatus, the events at his old home in Harrow had left behind four casualties. In addition to the three dead, Tom's marriage equally gave up the ghost. The love had gone and both parties didn't speak to each other anymore.

Tom returned to work with little fanfare and even a lower morale, yet he was glad to be back and appreciated it. The only thing that blighted his first day was the manner in which he was treated. People acted as though he were an egg, too frightened to address him in person. Tom didn't take it personally, he knew it was just temporary and he would have to prove his return to strength on his own.

During his lunch break, Tom decided to take a brisk walk. Despite the offers to have someone come with him, he declined them all even though he knew that once he stepped out of the building, he would have at least two people following him ten from ten paces behind.

Tom entered a store to buy a sandwich when his mobile phone rang. It was an unknown number. Tom answered it cautiously and before he could speak a voice came out "Purple, don't say anything. I know they are watching you. Listen, I am sorry they tried to kill you. I didn't know of the plan until too late. One of my clients whom you are investigating found out you were going to get back on the case and they wanted you out of the way. Don't worry; you will never hear from him again, I can assure you that. No one kills you unless I do."

Tom almost flew into a rage. He could feel his head hurting again as he asked as calmly as he could "How reassuring. Am I expected to be grateful?"

"No… I expect you to note that you owe me one." She replied bluntly

Tom looked around and saw his minders entering the store. He quickly covered his mouth as he spoke "And when do you plan to collect?"

Jelena answered "When I am dead… goodbye Purple." She cut off the call leaving Tom feeling hollow and lost.

He could have ran to his office, hand over his phone and ask that they trace the call, but Tom couldn't bring himself to it, not so soon in his return. He feared they would assume he had a breakdown. For the sake of his pride, he begrudgingly let her win this one.

With that memory of her activities to preserve his life flooding his mind, he decided to use them as the basis of his answer having kept Jan waiting for over a minute "Is it personal? No, no it's not."

Tom felt uncomfortable. Luckily, he had a diversion.

He reached into his pocket and placed a small box on the table proclaiming "Merry Christmas." That was information out of the blue and Jan was moved by his candour, forcing him to look more closely at Tom. Then he noticed as Tom looked at the wall clock a six inch scar running on the side of his head, faintly visible through his short cut hair. "We better go; we have less than three minutes." Tom took out his wallet and placed €40 on the table. Jan took the money and handed it back.

"It's on me." He said.

Tom smiled, appreciating the kindness but said "I buy the drinks here and you buy the drinks when you come to England. Deal?" Jan didn't want to insist, so he accepted and took the gift off the table.

Tom returned his money to the table. Making their way to the door, Jan could not hold back his concern any longer. He halted Tom's progress by holding his arm "Your cancer... you're going to be alright?"

Tom smiled at him, Jan didn't like that smile and he didn't like the answer either. Tom looked at his watch and remarked "Bloody hell man, we have to get our skates on!" and he began to sprint causing Jan to follow.

They returned to venue the in the nick of time. Jan meeting up with an anxious Kat fifty six seconds before the clock struck midnight. The performers of the first half were on the stage and to Tom's horror Savannah spotted him and cried out "English boy!" and ran down to meet him as the countdown began. "You didn't think I would like to spend the start of the year alone did you?"

With the crowd cheering in 2011 Jan said to Kat "I'm sorry." All was forgiven and the two kissed in the first few seconds of the year. They were interrupted though when the announcer said over the sound system "Look at Savannah!" The spotlight was shone on Savannah who had bent Tom backwards and was kissing him on the lips with much force for over a minute. The crowd whistled and cheered.

Tom seemed helpless in Savannah's arms and once Savannah had had her fill, Tom was left stunned as Savannah adjusted her large brown wig and remarked "Happy New Year baby." and returned to the stage to sing the song that brought the Eurovision back to Germany. Tom was traumatised and was helped to a chair by a snickering Jan who ordered him a vodka to help steady his nerves.

The rest of the evening turned out to be a blast. They watched the rest of the performance, drank heavily and danced the night away, eventually ending the night at Jan and Kat's flat. All this time around Tom allowed Jan to believe that he could find a friend in Tom.

# 17

*31 December 2010*

Khoi's Sylvester began an hour before Jan and Kat went to collect Tom.

Khoi got dressed and took a final glance at himself in the mirror. He still had misgivings about attending the New Year's party organised by the gang. It had been Otto's advice that it was important for the unity of the gang. Left to his own devices, he would have preferred spending it alone, regardless of how sad it may have seemed.

Khoi was angry because he had completely forgotten to dispose of the card Joel gave him. The words tore into his soul and replayed in his mind over and over again "One bullet". He checked his tie grateful that it would all soon be over. Just one more and he can return to his place in the shadows.

Despite that relaxing prospect, had he known the consequences to his state of mind that his participation would inflict, Khoi would have certainly refused. Now he couldn't sleep unaided and it didn't help that the pills were all gone.

He looked at the time as he applied the wax to his hair. There was a knock on the door. He knew who it was. He opened the door to find Joel looking merrier than of late.

"Hey, how are you man?" Joel asked.

"I'm cool. Come in" Khoi ushered. "Give me a couple of minutes. I won't be long."

Joel smirked and refused the offer rather, he told him to meet him by the bar as he wanted to try an apple martini.

Once done, he took the lift down and was met by a lady who tried to enter as he exited. They bumped into each other and both apologised. For some reason he thought of how easy it could have been to kill her without suspicion. Then he shuddered, frightened that he had been infected by the evil he had unleashed.

At the bar, Joel looked happy with his purchase as he sipped his drink. He noticed Khoi and proclaimed "You have got to try this. I thought cocktails were a girly thing, I am officially a convert."

Khoi took a sip and confirmed it was rather pleasant. Joel offered him a glass but he refused. "You look dapper in your tuxedo" Joel observed. "You are right, we best hit the road, and we've got a long journey ahead of us."

Joel led the way to the lift with Khoi following sheepishly. They went down to the car park in the basement where Joel presented "Here's our carriage." As he patted a forest green Land Rover bonnet. "Nice huh? It arrived yesterday." He added as he went to the driver's side, unlocking the door. Khoi wasn't too impressed; he was too exhausted for that. The diazepam shortage had taken a punishing toll on him.

He got in the passenger's side as Joel started the car and found that the seat was heated. If anything was going to put him to sleep, this certainly would and he knew it. Although he wasn't really concerned, he did think it was necessary to ask where they were going. "Not far, just out of the city." Joel confirmed "Jelena is going to be there too." Small consolation, Khoi thought as he yawned. "You're tired? I got some red bull in the back if you want one." Joel offered. Khoi declined and asked if he could sleep a little. Joel confirmed it wasn't an issue as he watched Khoi adjust his chair and use his coat as a blanket.

"Mind if I turn on the radio?" Joel asked as he did so. The station of choice was "Classic FM", the music from which was like warm milk, luring Khoi deeper and deeper into sleep and before they were five minutes from the hotel he was out like a light.

As he slept his mind wandered off. All he could see were things that made him happy, times gone by such as playing with Joel and Jeroen and having his mother read to him; playing football with his brother and eating at the bistro "Tiff" as his brother watched over him… all the things that made him happy, all the things that had now gone. They returned like episodes of a television show and he would smile as he slept.

The re-runs finally came to an end when the ride began to get bumpy. The shaking of the car woke him. He looked outside the window and found that they were now on a dirt road driving through what looked like a forest on a dirt track that was heavily covered in snow.

He thought it may have been an isolated route if it weren't for the fact that he could see some tire tracks imbedded in the snow which continued to fall as they progressed. All around were snow covered trees as the road grew steadily steeper.

"Hey! You're up." Joel proclaimed. Still disorientated, Khoi was forced to ask "Where are we?"

"Poland." The response was enough to prompt Khoi to consider how long he had been asleep for. He looked at the clock on the dash board, it was 10:43, Berlin time. He realised he had been out for two hours "We're nearly there. Another 10 minutes. The guys are waiting with their champagne." Khoi speculated if this was the surprise.

After 13 minutes they found three other Land Rovers parked by the side of the road with a shivering Ralph standing by one of them smoking. Joel parked the car and as he stepped out remarked "It's bloody cold."

"-12" Ralph added as he went to Khio's side to open his door "Hello Boss." He said as Khoi disembarked. "I got all the clothing waiting." Ralph added leading the way to the second jeep where he opened the door and presented them with snow boots, followed by heavy duty down jackets with fur trimmed hoods and Russian style fur hats. Khoi was unsure what it was for, but said nothing as he put them on. "You got the GPS set?" asked Joel. Ralph gave him the gadget. "How long have they been out there?"

"Daniel, Mikel, Marcel and I arrived with the surprise an hour and a half ago, Paul came with Jelena half an hour ago and now you are here, so you are good to go."

As he put his coat into the back seat, Khoi spotted something he could not ignore. "Whose clothes are those?" Joel and Ralph looked at one another grinning "You'll find out soon enough." Joel's tone was sinister.

Ralph then handed them flashlights, two fully charged mobile phones and then gave them a hand gun each. Before he could query the purpose, Joel pre-empted him "The guns are for the wolves. We're going to go through the forest before we reach our destination. Don't worry, I'll be with you, nothing is going to get us." With the GPS on and having spent twenty minutes getting prepared for their trek it was time to go. Ralph lamented that he was sad he was going to miss all the fun but assured Khoi that he would love the gift.

With the GPS on, Joel led the way. They marched through the forest which grew thicker the deeper they progressed and the dark winter sky gave the forest and ominous feel. Khoi pondered if the sounds he could hear were creatures or his mind playing tricks on him. Then there was a distant howl confirming the fears that there were wolves about. Khoi put his hand in his pocket which held the gun, gently feeling it, fearful he could need it.

"Turn left." Joel said as he repeated what the GPS instructed, calling the directions loudly.

After forty-five minutes of the march the trees had thinned to a clearing. Khoi could see lights ahead. Joel called and it was confirmed that it was the gang. They picked up the pace as they approached and about a hundred metres away, Joel's pace turned into a sprint through the thick snow that had settled up to a foot on the ground leaving Khoi behind as he leapt on Daniel forcing him to fall on the ground and in a show of childishness tossed snow on one another.

Khoi drew closer; the others had taken lanterns with them for lighting. He saw Jelena standing there almost motionless, watching something while the others talked amongst themselves with Marcel holding his gun. Then emerged a sight that struck Khoi with horror. There appeared to be a naked man, on his knees with a black hood over his head and his hands bound behind his back.

"Hey, you are here!" Paul called. The others cheered his arrival as he went to stand by Jelena. Jelena turned to him and looked as shocked as he was.

"You OK? Boss?" Mikel asked. Everyone fell still and the man on his knees in the snow could be heard sobbing and shivering struggling with his words.

"What is this?" Khoi asked

Joel got off the floor and said "Ah, it's your surprise. Our way of saying "well done"." Then he walked over to the man and pulled off the hood and illuminated the face of the person with his torch. It was Max, the one who gave information about those who ended Stefan's life.

Max's lips were discoloured, he struggled but Khoi could hear him begging that his life be spared. "We were going to give this to you at Christmas but you know what happened there."

"Ppp- please, don't kill me…I didn't do anything!" Max beseeched.

"Don't be silly, we aren't going to kill you." Joel said reassuringly. "We've already expended our bullet and we promised we wouldn't. No Max, you are our guest for the evening as we enter 2011 together. Oh I am cold. Brandy? Paul?"

Paul proceeded to a picnic basket and brought out some shot glasses and the bottle.

"What the fuck is going on?" Khoi asked Jelena in a soft yet frantic voice. "I didn't know anything about this, you have to believe me." She pleaded as Paul approached. "Here you go." He said handing them a shot glass each and was about to fill it when Khoi said "I don't want any." Jelena wasn't so reluctant and asked for her glass to be filled to the brim.

She tried to drink it, hoping it would steady her nerves but decided otherwise. She was amazed by the approach taken. Marcel and Mikel walked in circles at opposite ends. It wasn't clear the purpose for this, but if it was to further intimidate Max, it seemed to work.

"Just three minutes to go people!" cried Joel who stood 10 metres behind Max and next to Daniel "But before we toast in the New Year, I propose one for the brains behind this operation. To Khoi, the greatest criminal mind I know!"

The others raised their shot glasses and downed their drinks as then proceeded to chat amongst themselves pretending not to hear the wails of the man which grew more silent and less frequent, whilst Jelena and Khoi stood speechless in disgust.

Khoi tried hard to reach his coping mechanism, but Max wasn't bleeding and he couldn't walk away. He was trapped and could only look into Max's eyes as the tears fell. Khoi watched them trail down Max's face and hit the snow prompting him to protest "I thought we agreed we weren't going to make them suffer? We promised we wouldn't kill him!"

The others fell quiet again as Joel left his conversation with Daniel and handed him his drink. He walked towards Max. He took out the knife he always had strapped at the back of his belt, knelt on the ground behind him pulling up Max's bound wrists. He proceeded by cutting the plastic cuffs as he replied "You know what Khoi, you are right." And once he had cut through the cuffs, he got off the ground, dusted his knees to clear it of snow, then shoved Max on to the snow covered floor and watched him curl up into a foetal position trembling.

Then Joel continued "We..." He said pointing to the team "all agreed that we wouldn't make him suffer and we won't. We are all here to ring in the New Year" He added as he walked up to Jelena and took the drink out of her hand and polished it off "and to watch him suffer. After all, it's -12c, we don't have to do anything do we? All we have to do is stand here and watch nature take its course" He ended as he walked and stood behind him.

Khoi looked at Max who began to scream as the cramps kicked in. His teeth gnashing was so loud that it drowned out every other noise in Khoi's ears. Khoi felt a hand wrap around his arm, it was Jelena.

He couldn't take it anymore. Khoi turned away only to find Joel there standing there behind with anger in his eyes as he raged in a soft voice beyond the hearing of others "Don't you, for one minute, think you can escape this. You expect everyone else to do all your dirty work putting their lives down to the single imperative of eliminating others whilst you stay tucked away in your sanitised world, safe in the knowledge that all these things are beyond your visual sphere?

You too have blood on your hands; you too have to face the consequences of your handiwork, now it is time for you to see it for yourself. Look. I said Look." Joel ordered. Khoi reluctantly turned to face the naked man on the ground "Good." Joel said in his ear.

Joel looked at his watch and walked back next to Daniel and proclaimed "Bring out the champagne boys, one minute to go!" As the year was drawing to an end, Khoi struggled to keep his composure. Paul raced around with plastic cups and champagne, quickly filling the cups and ramming one into Khoi's hand. "Alright, twenty, nineteen, eighteen…" Joel's countdown seemed to be one for Khoi's melt down as he struggled not to break, but it was clear it was going to happen. Joel could see it coming as well from across the way and so did Jelena. She held his hand as they got to 11 and said "Don't cry.", but there was no use, by three the tears appeared to be forming as he visibly began to cringe "don't cry, it will finish you." she begged again, but it failed.

Then came the cry "Happy New Year!" Jelena quickly grabbed his face and kissed him deeply, holding his face and using that opportunity to clear his tears away. The rest of the gang, still circling the man on the floor began to cheer them on. Jelena pulled Khoi's hood of his jacket over his head. "Aah, they want their privacy. Get a room!" Daniel shouted.

"Shut up!" Joel cried as he continued watching enviously, grabbing the bottle of champagne from Daniel and taking a deep swig.

Unbeknown to Joel, the kissing had stopped and it was a race against time to stop Khoi from crying. As she cleared away his tears she whispered "You have to look."

"No" he mumbled.

"You have to…"

"Why?"

"To prove you are strong. A weak man is never respected." Then she looked him straight in the eye and could see the fear in them. "You have to look. I'll be here with you, please look. OK?" She could see she got his trust and added "Now hold my hand and look." They held hands and turned round to witness the squirming struggles of a dying man as the elements took their toll as his breathing began to slow.

For Khoi, everything seemed to fall silent. He didn't feel the cold anymore and as the others continued their festivities. He noticed none of it as he continued to watch Max slowly give up the fight.

Another forty minutes passed by before Joel walked up to Max and raised his arm which fell to the ground limp. Then he pushed the body with his boot, tapping it once again before being satisfied by the lack of response. "It's done. Let's go" Joel proclaimed as he proceed to restart his GPS. Puzzled Mikel exclaimed "Are you sure? What if he gets up?" Still fiddling with the GPS, Joel replied "He's not going anywhere other than into a coma, besides, he'll be wolf food soon. It's time we go before we join him. Leave nothing behind"

Joel turned on the GPS and led the way as the others laughed and joked drinking as they went. In the middle of it all were Khoi and Jelena still holding hands. "Look?" She called in an attempt to break the silence and distract him "I'm wearing the scarf you gave me." It didn't work. Khoi didn't bother to take a glance.

They got to where the cars were parked and greeted Ralph who had stood guard all this time before they started entering the vehicles except one which stayed empty. Jelena and Khoi still stood together as she asked him "You are going to be ok?" Whilst saying words of encouragement she was interrupted by Joel. "Hey!" he called out to as he walked towards the pair.

Joel reached into his pocket and handed Jelena the keys to a Land Rover, then pointed to the last one "That's for you. There are two brief cases in there. One is for your superiors and the other is yours to keep, and the car too, you earned it." And with a wave he added "Good luck and safe journey. Come on Khoi, time to go."

"I'm not going." She said stubbornly, fearing more for Khoi's welfare. She then turned to Khoi and said "I want to stay."

Joel had that sneer on his face again and it seemed he delighted in the situation. "If you want to stay, then it's totally up to Khoi. What's it going to be Boss? Can she stay?" Joel asked Khoi who was immobilised as he witnessed the longing in her eyes. Chaos reigned in his mind, but she said he had to be strong and on that basis he raised her hand, gave it a kiss and said "I'm sorry." before he walked away from her towards the first car. "You're not one of them! Remember that!" She cried out. "That's enough now, thanks for your services, off you go." Joel instructed, but she didn't move. Joel shrugged his shoulders, went to the first car and without looking back, took his seat in the back with Khoi before giving the instruction to Paul "Drive."

Paul started the car and as they drove past her, Khoi could see her sobbing in the cold watching them drive away. Khoi's heart ached and his mood was not lightened as Joel patted him on the shoulder and said "It's business, you'll live."

Left on her own, Jelena felt defeated, but it was no longer her problem and it was time to go. Instinctively, she crouched down to check under the car for any suspicious items or leaks there was nothing there. She proceeded to open the boot followed by the bonnet, and like under the car, there was nothing there to blow her sky high.

Jelena entered, sat in the car they had left for her, and turned the key to the ignition, it was time to go. For a moment she sobbed as she began to hate herself for letting her heart rule her head.

The engine made a less than satisfying sound before it stalled and Jelena cursed the cold weather as she gave it another go with the choke on. This time she had more luck, and after having revved it a couple of times, the engine started running with a steady purr.

Jelena moved the car slowly forward then brought it to an abrupt stop, confirming the breaks were indeed working.

She turned on the heating to let the car warm up, as she watched the dim lights from the other cars disappear into the moonless night. All Jelena could see now, was what was lit up by the headlights of her car, whilst the rest of the world turned into a maddening void of darkness around her.

She put the car in gear and turned the steering wheel, setting off down the abandoned dirt road, beginning her trip back home. As the familiar monotony of the empty country lane began, Jelena wondered what Khoi would do next and whether she should take one last shot at convincing him to leave the gang. She didn't know why she felt like this but for some reason she imagined him as a child whose innocence should be protected, and she felt as if she wanted to be the one protecting it.

Her chain of thoughts faded as she noticed she was going a bit fast, and slowed down to a more comfortable speed, because she knew the absence of people in the area probably meant wild animals were prone to cross the road. She fiddled with the car radio hoping she could tune it to a working channel, despite being all the way out here. She didn't really appreciate radio anymore. She felt it had lost the charm it once had. But for some reason she felt lonely, a feeling she hadn't felt in a long time, and some music would definitively help.

As she was doing so however, she was caught off-guard by a swift motion coming from behind her. Looking at the road, the motion was at the outer edge of her field of vision and she wasn't sure what had happened, but the scare jolted her enough to make her swerve over in the oncoming lane.

Grabbing the wheel with both hands again, she managed to keep control of the car and barely avoided a full blown spin-out on the icy road. Good thing this road was completely empty, or things could have ended a lot worse. With the car under control again, she took a look in the rear view mirror but there was no-one there. "What a silly idea, of course there is no one there" she thought, but her nerves were not relaxing. Then she noticed a dull pain in her lower right arm, feeling as if she might have pulled a muscle in the recent turmoil. Trying to stretch it out to the side didn't make it better; on the contrary it made it hurt more. She needed to gather herself and decided to pull over.

As she began to slow down, she started feeling a stinging pain in her abdomen, followed by a numb sensation all through her body. Suddenly she was not able to break as efficiently as expected, nor did she feel she had control over the car. Her heart started beating hard in her chest, so hard she could feel it in her temples. Was she panicking? She imagined Khoi, and how he looked when he panicked, but she couldn't understand why she would be.

A sudden hissing noise emitted from the backseat, immediately followed by the sound of the car rushing off the road towards the nearby trees. Jelena realized the car was going too fast and slammed on the brakes with all the force she could muster. It caused the car to spin sideways into a young pine. The force of the impact threw her upper body out of the seat belt and across the passenger seat making one of her arms bang hard on the passenger side door.

The car fell silent as the engine died, all except the sound of Jelena's frantic breathing and, again, the hissing noise from the back seat. The impact had broken one of the doors making the lights come on inside the car. Stretched out across from the driver seat to the passenger seat, Jelena turned to see what was making the hissing noise. She had definitively broken a rib or two, which was obvious from the pain that her movement cost her. But more than just the pain, she was beginning to feel rather sick, and before she could get around looking behind her, she started throwing up.

There was something very wrong with her, she knew that much. The pains in her stomach were getting worse, and she felt like the world was spinning around her in a sickening way. She threw up again, her stomach involuntarily contracting hard causing her ribs to hurt even more.

As soon as she had stopped vomiting, she tried to prop herself upright. Jelena was perspiring intensely. She knew she needed to get to the phone in her pocket, her survival instincts now kicking in. The last time she had had this happen, had been during an attempt to get to a drug lord's black book. While in the drug lord's office, one of his armed guards had walked in on her going through his things.

Back then, her immediate instincts and a set of lucky blows to the guard's head with a paper weight had saved her. Unfortunately, this time she wasn't facing an enemy she could see, let alone hit with heavy objects. The enemy was in her blood. Thus, all her energy was now focused on figuring out what had happened and on getting help.

Jelena managed to get back to her own seat, but the strain on her body made her feel even dizzier. Breathing was getting heavy, as if she had a weight on her chest. She tried to get to her phone, but her hand was not fully responsive and it proved difficult to get her hand into the pocket at all. To her side, the shattered window was letting in a drizzle of snow along with the icy air, and the one still functioning headlight lit up another tree in front of the car. And then she saw it.

Reflected in the tilted rear view mirror, Jelena saw a scaly, olive coloured creature stretching across the back seat, swaying with its head displaying a bright underside. Jelena's resolve strengthened as she managed to pull out her phone. To this sudden and threatening movement, the creature's mouth extended wide open, displaying its nasty ink-black interior only decorated by two slightly extended fangs dripping with venom. Jelena immediately recognized this from previous jobs in east Africa; it was the common black mamba.

Her heart sank, but she wasn't going to give up. Her heart was beating in an erratic, heavy, painful beats. She was feeling very sluggish now, her stomach and chest aches clouding her mind. She tried to unlock her phone, but took two failed attempts before painstakingly managing on the third. Behind her she saw one of the planet's most aggressive snakes, the mamba looking right back at her. It had been awoken by the heating, but now it was getting uncomfortable again, and it started slithering down on the floor and towards the front of the car.

Jelena's mouth felt thick as she started drooling, her head hung at an awkward angle, as she desperately tried to find a number to call. Her motor skills were now at a bare minimum, and she realized the only one close enough to help her in time, was practically being held in a car with the person responsible. Still, he was all the hope she had.

She could barely move her fingers, making it seem impossible to make the call. She was not panicking, but the thought of not talking to Khoi again seemed unbearable. She finally managed to mark his number and call, but she could barely speak and by now she was too weak to lift the phone up to her face. "The speaker!" she thought as she desperately struggled to move her finger a bit to the left and hit the correct button.

She felt dizzy, her body in agony on several levels and she didn't know how much longer she could last. But at least she knew she would get to make this call. Khoi needed to know. The glow of the phone illuminated the yellow belly of the snake, as it moved across her limp arms towards the broken window. The phone call completed dialling. "We're sorry. The number you have dialled is not available, please try again later. We're sorry. The number you have dialled is not available, please try again later. Beep-beep-beep"

Disaster, the cold began to get her. She mustered the energy for one last act. She wrote one worded text message and as her vision blurred, she sent it to the number required.

In a wreck on an otherwise empty road, a body started shaking as it was no longer capable of providing oxygen for its brain, eyes squarely fixed on a cell phone resting in her hand.

Several miles ahead, the gang continued to drive on. Once again they were on their way to another destination unknown to Khoi. Paul drove with the radio on, not a word was exchanged amongst those in the back seat as Joel finished a bottle of champagne and opened another one offering Khoi a sip but he declined. "Stop sulking". He chided Khoi who spent the entire time looking out the window as the landscape changed from woodlands to semi-rural before finally reaching the outskirts of a city.

They drove past a sign that read Gorzow Wielkopolski and as they entered the city, it had a particular feel of regeneration, just like East Germany did when the wall came down.

Passing the centre of the town, they turned down a narrow road and parked in front of shop window with a neon light which read "TATTOO". Before they stepped out of the car, Joel remarked "Time for you to join the inner circle." Khoi, initially snickering at the irony of situation, was unimpressed by the idea of being indoctrinated into the "inner circle" by being permanently branded. Under normal circumstances, he would have protested, but he had lost the will to fight and with a sigh replied "Let's get it over and done with. Paul, you stay in the car." as he stepped out of the car.

Joel led the way and there were three empty chairs with three tattoo artists chatting amongst themselves till they noticed their presence. Khoi observed that the artists had used themselves as a canvas, covering their skins in various designs. Joel then instructed "We're all getting the same thing and we'd like you to choose what we're going to get. So Khoi, you pick."

Everyone seemed to laugh as they looked at him, but Khoi looked indifferent as he was presented with the book containing the various designs.

Khoi's independence was on constant attack as the others would peer over his shoulder and suggest, often sternly, that he select a particular pattern of their choice. It was annoying. Khoi shut the book and handed it back to the female tattooist and asked "Can you give me a noose?" She didn't speak German and it seemed things were likely to be lost in translation as she turned round looking for clarity. "Noose? You know?" Marcel gestured a hanging and it appeared to click as the woman ran and picked up her pad and doodled with great concentration before presenting her drawing. It was rather nice but he said nothing, rather, he shrugged his shoulders and said "I like it." Then turned to the others "What do you think?"

Everyone seemed to be consumed by a haze of sycophancy and all agreed without protest with the exception of Joel who seemed unconvinced but kept his tongue as democracy prevailed. Everyone then decided what part of their body to have the mark. Khoi chose to have it on the upper part of his chest area. Joel then decided to have it on the inner part of his left forearm whilst Marcel insisted he have it put around his neck "That's where a noose should be" he insisted. Mikel and Daniel appeared more inclined to conceal theirs and had it put on their lower leg and upper thigh respectively. Ralph asked for it on his back.

They were very swift and good and by quarter past two, they were done, even though they felt bloodied and blue but there was one thing that was one unifying factor, they all loved it.

Yet the night wasn't over and Joel took them to a night club just a street away from the tattoo parlour, there was no need for the car. Joel knew the owner and upon entry, they were warmly greeted by owner who took them to a private room where there were some girls were waiting as well as a lot of bottles of Champagne and vodka.

The boys dove into their lusty surroundings and frolicked. Joel was cupping a feel and teased Khoi by tapping him to get his attention. Khoi just sat there, not drinking anything, lost in thought. Joel was persistent, unwilling to leave Khoi in a stupor and left the lady he was interested in to offer Khoi a shot of vodka and a bit more.

He sat next to Khoi and called for his attention. Their eyes met and Joel appeared consolatory as confessed "I know I pissed you off, I know you're angry with me and I am sorry... but it had to be done." Then he handed him the drink which Khoi took "Brothers?"

Khoi nodded as they touched glasses and replied "Brothers." Paul watched as they drank together then Joel slapped Khoi on the shoulder and told him he was off to the toilet. Khoi smiled as Joel made his way and once out of sight, took the shot glass and spat back the drink he had been offered and hid the cup under the table.

Marcel, Mikel, Paul and Ralph watched from a distance trying to assimilate what had just happened. Ralph caught everyone off guard when he said "All is won, but the king is mad and the queen is dead. Makes our victory rather hollow doesn't it?" It was probably the most eloquent thing he had ever said before them, and though no one seemed to perceive the meanings between the lines, Paul replied "Speak for yourself."

Paul decided to leave the bunch and placed himself next to Khoi and asked "How you doing?" Khoi nodded and confessed "Could be better."

"I saw what you did with your drink... why?" Paul asked

"He spiked it." Khoi bluntly replied. He seemed edgy as he fidgeted with the cork of the champagne bottle and eventually proclaimed "Why are we here? What are we doing here?"

"You want to go?" Paul asked. Khoi's look said it all. "I'll round up the others."

Paul went and informed the others; one after another those who were receptive began to collect their things. Paul brought Khoi's coat to him and helped Khoi into it just as Joel returned, baffled by what was happening "What's going on? Where are you going?" Joel asked Khoi who sighed and replied "Home"

"You can't leave, we're just having fun" Joel protested loudly.

Calmly Khoi said "You can stay if you want, I just want to go." He walked to Mikel and asked for the keys to the Land Rover but Mikel refused "It's ok, I'll take you." Khoi refused and tried to encourage him to stay and enjoy the evening but Mikel wasn't for turning and insisted "I want to."

Joel stood there dumbfounded by the phenomenal happenings unravelling before his eyes and his defeat was final when Marcel came up to him presenting his coat with the words "We can continue tomorrow." Joel didn't take his coat until Khoi asked "Are you coming?"

Joel snatched the coat from him and staggered in a drunken manner towards the exit without bothering to thank the owner and went straight to the back seat of one of the vehicles.

Khoi went over to do the diplomatic thing and thank the owner, offering to pay but was informed that the amount had been covered already which was a relief. He didn't like the man, he was worm like.

As they gathered outside, Khoi decided to share some words of encouragement. "You guys are the best. I am proud of all of you."

"No, no." Marcel interjected "We are proud of you."

"Thanks, very kind of you. Daniel, you can take Joel home. Mikel, Marcel, Ralph, you live in the same area, makes sense you travel together. Paul and I will take the last one. Tomorrow is Sunday, so I guess you have the day off, we have the pickup on Wednesday, Mikel, Paul, Daniel? You guys sort it out taking some of your gang. Marcel, you better take care of Ralph, he looks like he's about to develop a cold." They all laughed "Next Friday, we take Ralph out, he deserves it after spending his New Year on his own."

"Good old Ralph." Daniel supported.

"What about Joel?" Mikel inquired.

The expression on Khoi's face was as cold as stone as he replied "What about him?" There was an uncomfortable silence which he failed to notice "We've done our best. Happy New Year guys."

Everyone entered their allocated vehicles and drove away. Daniel drove along at the end of the convoy and noted through his rear view mirror Joel struggling as he bit his nails. He thought Joel could do with some reassurance. "Don't worry. Things will return to normal once we get back."

"No it won't… things will never be the same." Joel concluded as he took out an ecstasy tablet and washed it down with some vodka and demanded "We need to go back to the woods, our work isn't over."

*1 January 2011*

Paul parked the car somewhat glad that the entire journey was over as Khoi had been silent throughout the drive. Now they were back in Berlin, all Paul wanted to do was go to bed. Once the ignition was off, Khoi opened the door, but hesitated before disembarking. He then asked if Paul would like to come for a drink. Something told Paul that Khoi clearly didn't want to be alone.

Despite feeling sorry for him, Paul was too exhausted to be good company, hence he declined the offer. Khoi's face fell, but he tried to mask it with a smile. Khoi had no need for the vehicle so told him to take it. In addition, Khoi made him promise that he would take Han out for dinner. That's why Paul liked him, he was always so considerate. They shook hands. Khoi cut a lonely miserable figure as he waved Paul off.

Paul had made it just a couple of kilometres down the road when he heard a beeping sound which he recognised. On the passenger's seat was Khoi's mobile which he had forgotten. He returned to the hotel. Paul entered the lift, almost dozing off as it went up. Once at the relevant floor, Paul walked to the door and was set to knock when he discovered that the door was" slightly opened with the sound of water running.

Something seemed amiss. Paul reached for his gun and entered, carefully creeping in. He leapt forward and pointed his gun, there was no one there. Then he walked towards the bathroom and heard some wailing, he paced to the door, opened it and found Khoi sitting at the foot of the bath, still in his clothes, clearly intending to take shower, but something had happened to cause him such great anguish. Paul knelt before him; placing the gun away "Khoi…?" he called. Khoi kept blithering unable to make sense before he broke down.

Paul helped him up off the ground and took him back to the bed room and allowed him to flop on to the mattress. Paul went back to the bathroom to shut the water and returned to Khoi who by now was howling in pain. Paul was perplexed. He didn't know what to do, so he followed his instincts and climbed into the bed, holding Khoi from behind and cuddling him. Khoi initially put up some resistance but Paul wrapped his arm around him fast. "Shhh, shhh. It's going to be ok." Paul said in an attempt to calm Khoi down and continued doing so for over an hour till fatigue caused them to both of them fell asleep.

Paul was deep in a state of sleep when there was a faint sound of a German euro-pop song playing the background. He stirred for a moment, he couldn't decide, he was too tired to care and sure enough, the music stopped.

A couple of hours later the phone rang again, this time, he couldn't ignore it. Paul stumbled out of bed, followed the sound to his coat which he had left on the floor. Paul recovered and answered the mobile phone which generated the music "Yeah?"

"Hello?" responded the caller.

"Who is this?" Paul asked

"I should be asking you? This is Julien. What are you doing with Khoi's phone?"

Still confused by sleep, Paul struggled to recollect the name and proclaimed "Oh, Julien, Happy new year."

"Happy new year to you to, now who is this?" Julien's patience was clearly wearing thin.

"It's Paul. Khoi is here but he is asleep…"

"Khoi slept with you?" Julien asked

"Yes…" realising how that came across, Paul quickly changed his response "No, no. I mean he's sleeping here…"

"Sleeping where?" pressed Julien

"In the hotel room." Paul replied "With you?" Julien pried

"Yes, no!" Realising he was digging himself a grave, he paused and sighed and explained "Khoi had a panic attack last night and had to stay with him because I was worried he was going to hurt himself, so I stayed behind."

There was a still silence from Julien before he asked "Where's the hotel?"

Paul told him of their location and within half an hour, Julien was at the door.

Paul ushered him in and tried to explain what had happened, but Julien wasn't interested as he walked to Khoi and tried to wake him. "Khoi, Khoi?" He called, Khoi woke up gradually. He looked awful and Julien noticed he had a temperature. "Get up, you're leaving." Julien ordered as he walked around and hurriedly gathered Khoi's things into his suit case.

Khoi was tired and strived to wake up, looking at Paul who seemed unwilling to speak as he stood by the door. "Where am I going?" He asked. "Home." Julien shouted with a tint of anger within his voice. Once he gathered all the items he could find, Julien cried "Well come on? I got a taxi waiting."

Khoi slowly rose and put on his coat and other clothing. Julien walked up to Paul and in a soft voice thanked Paul for his help "I hope he wasn't too much trouble?"

"Nah, we all have our bad days." Paul said "Would you like me to give you a lift?" Julien declined. Then Paul asked "Could I give you my number or something? Just give me a call if he needs anything."

"Sure." Julien brought out his mobile phone and took down the number. "Are you part of the group?" Paul knew he meant and nodded. "I couldn't have guessed. Do you need him this week?"

"I don't think so." Paul replied.

"Good. He looks like he could do with a rest." Julien's concern was evident as he watched Khoi sluggishly move towards his things.

Impatiently, Julien went and picked up the bag. "I'll take it." He snapped at Khoi. Khoi had the look of shame about him, Julien touched his cheek to reassure him, but he wasn't sure it worked. Still it was time to leave. "Paul?" Julien reached to shake his hand. Paul did the same and as Julien walked out, he was followed by Khoi like a puppy. All Paul could do was pat Khoi on the shoulder as the pair departed. On his own, Paul felt ashamed and guilty as he went to collect his items and left the room.

Initially, he drove with the intention of going home. However, two blocks from his home, he made an illegal turn and drove towards another direction.

Han and her friend Miranda were playing on an X-box. They were playing an interactive dancing game where they were meant to follow the moves. They were trying to dance to a tune, when there was a knock at the door. Han paused the game she was playing to check who was there.

She opened the door slightly and peeped. There was Paul, looking flummoxed and sad. "Paul! Happy New Year!" She said opening the door. "Have you been partying?" Han asked?

"Yeah, I just came to say hi…" Paul replied, and then he noticed she was still in her pyjamas with giraffe prints. "If it's a bad time I could come back?"

"No, are you crazy? We're playing a game. Come in! You must try it." Han insisted. Her cheerful manner and welcoming smile was enough to lighten his mood and put his cares away for another day. "I have dumplings?" she added alluringly.

"For the dumplings then." Paul replied as he followed her into the flat.

In an automated state, Khoi entered the gallery like a puppy. He waited by the door for directions. Julien unlocked the door that gave access to the flat above. "You want to go up and sleep some more?" Khoi nodded. Julien left the door ajar and went back to the front door to lock it and prevent a draft. "Go have a nap." He instructed Khoi as he knelt on the floor collecting the pile of mail that lay by the door.

Khoi walked away, dragging his feet till he reached the steps leading to the flat. Indeed he was tired, but he was afraid to sleep. In the bedroom, he turned on the lights, stripped naked and went under the sheets. It was bitterly cold in the flat. The heating hadn't been switched on yet, but it didn't matter. Khoi didn't notice. His head was heavy, and as the light shone brightly he blinked for a moment to rest them, but when he opened them, Khoi could hear the wind blowing gently on his face. It intermittent gust irritated him. And he wondered if he had left the window open. If he was going to get any sleep, he had to do something about that. Khoi opened his eyes and saw the night sky, slightly lit by the moon which teased the illumination available as the cloud passed across it's full face.

As he lay there, Khoi could see white dots coming towards him. When the first white dot landed just below his left eye, it gave him a chill. Another followed, adding more and more to the cold he felt. He touched where the dots fell, it was wet. Khoi sat up and put out his hand out allowing a white dot to fall peacefully on to his opened palm. The dot melted, it was snow.

Khoi looked around him and found his bed lay in a forest dusted by snow. This was strange. How could he wake up here in the open, in the middle of nowhere? He asked himself.

Khoi pushed off his duvet and placed his right foot on the floor. It gave a crunching sound as it pressed on the snow. Yet, unlike the rest of his body, his feet didn't get cold. He placed the second leg on the ground, looking around his surroundings.

A light shone in the distance, Khoi considered it was shelter. There was only one way to find out. Khoi covered himself in the bed sheet and duvet and took a pillow with him. The purpose of the pillow was more as an assuring presence as he ventured towards the light.

Khoi walked, passing beguiling trees with low reaching branches, causing him to bend a few times to dodge them. He heard nothing as he progressed, not even his footsteps. There was no sound coming from the brook, even though it glistened as it ran near him, emerging momentarily before flowing back into a darker part of the forest.

Khoi was close. The light grew brighter. It was then he realised that the light didn't radiate from any form of accommodation, rather, it was paraffin lantern and finally, he could hear something, it was the sound of sobbing.

Khoi ran towards it, clutching tightly at the duvet which hid his nudity. Khoi arrived at clearing, it was familiar, then it came to him, he was in the same clearing the night before. The sobbing grew louder. Khoi looked down, and there were two people on the ground next to the lantern. The first was a woman, seated on the snow; her long curly blond hair concealed her face.

Khoi drew closer. The woman was still sobbing. She had a naked man lying on the snow by her. She had his head pressed to her bosom as she rocked back and forward, sobbing. "No." she said, "Please stay". The voice was familiar to Khoi. "Mother?" He called. The woman looked up and it was her, it was his mother, sitting in the snow, looking up at him with eyes showing the strain of grief.

As she shivered, she said "He's dead." She let go of the man with a blue tinge to his skin and white hair. He rolled out of her arms and fell on the floor. Khoi heart stopped as Max lifeless gaze focused on him. "How could you?" She asked.

Khoi wanted to scream, he wanted to defend his actions, but couldn't. She was clearly beginning to freeze. Khoi couldn't bear to see her suffer. "Mother, please" he pleaded as he took off he duvet and placed his over her shoulder "please wear this."

"No." She said. Then he tried again, causing her to roar "NO! Why didn't you give it to him when he needed it?"

"Mother, please, take it." Khoi begged.

"No Khoi. No." She repeated over and over till she got up and stepped away into the darkness.

"Don't go mummy, please? Mummy!"

Julien had to get up from the edge of the bed where he sat, having had to fight off Khoi attempts to smother him. He had only come to check up on Khoi and as he checked his temperature, Khoi, without notice, tried to cloak him with the duvet calling him "Mother" and begging him to wear it as to keep the chill away.

Having calmed him, Khoi remained on the bed, sweating and crying, mumbling and begging his mother to stay. Julien checked the thermometer and commented "Oh my God, you're burning up." Khoi body temperature was 41c and he clearly was either dreaming or hallucinating.

Julien ran to down to the medicine cabinet for some the strongest painkillers he had and by the time he returned, Khoi was barely conscious.

It took a while to get Khoi to down the two pills, he kept falling asleep. Once Khoi swallowed them, Julien stood vigil to ensure he didn't regurgitate them. After an hour, Khoi was sound asleep and had not reproduced the drug, but his temperature remained stubbornly high. Julien resorted to cooling him down with a towel drenched in cold water which he dabbed on Khoi's skin.

Occasionally Khoi would grunt and moan, a couple of times he cried out "I'm so sorry" and on one occasion he asked "Why didn't I help him?" Clearly whilst the still body slumbered, his mind was active.

Jet lagged and sleep deprived himself having just flown over 17 hours only to arrive to have an ill person on his hands, Julien sought assistance by dialling Kat's number.

The phone rang several times before it was answered. "Hello?" Kat said. Julien observed that it wasn't her usual cheery self "Kat? Are you ok?"

She hesitated and struggled as she responded in her trembling voice "No… I'm not feeling too good."

"Anything serious? Or was it too much of a good thing?" He teased hoping to encourage a giggle, what he got was a deep sigh.

"I'm pregnant." Kat stated.

Julien had thought of how delicately to travel this situation. He knew that Kat desperately longed for a child of her own, but the two miscarriages and the doctor's warnings must have made her edgy, he thought. "Where are you? Are you ok?"

"I'm at home… in the bathroom, looking at the pregnancy test kit, the fourth one that confirmed it and yeah… I'm fine… Don't worry about me." She sighed deeply. "Who knows, it may all be alright. Happy new year by the way."

"Same to you darling. Is Jan with you?"

"Nah, he had to go to work. Something urgent I guess." She replied.

Julien offered to come over to keep her company but she declined and moved to end the call "Let's talk later."

"OK. Bye."

Julien could only imagine what Kat would be going through after she had hung up. She was strong indeed but there is just so much anyone could tolerate and that also applied to him.

Julien was running on empty. He walked back up to check on Khoi's temperature and found it had gone down by two degrees and was still sound asleep. Julien decided to address the mail he received and his hunger, but he didn't get far. At his desk, surrounded by applications, a sandwich and coffee, he succumbed to fatigue and dosed off in his chair.

# 18

*1 January 2011*

Jan was getting to grips with the prospect of another long night ahead. Andreas, his one possible link, had died hours earlier. He had been in the office with Tom who was still struggling with the New Year's Day hangover to discuss how the information sharing process was to be implemented, when the news came and with little time to reject the offer, he found Tom in the car with him, speeding to the hospital.

Walking through the corridors, with Tom a few steps behind him, struggling to keep up, Jan was eager to speak to the nurses and doctors hoping Andreas had left a clue, regardless how little, as a parting gift for prosperity, but first he had to find the room and if the numbers were to believed, they weren't too far.

Tom hated being in hospitals. The smell of disinfectant and viewing the sick didn't appeal to him. Tom saw Jan progress to a jog, clearly they were close. Finally at the end of the corridor was an officer by the door of the room looking rather bored.

Jan greeted the man in German and after a brief discussion, Tom saw Jan hunch over with disappointment. Jan placed his hands on his head and shut his eyes as though a headache was coming. "He died saying nothing." Jan shared in English.

Jan seemed defeated, the officer seemed befuddled and whilst Tom observed this spectacle, he queried "Have they discovered what the cause of death was? I understand that a pathologist would give us a conclusive finding, but it could help?" Jan blanched for having let that slip him. He thanked the officer standing guard and began marching on.

Tom was getting exhausted having to trail along with a hangover that wouldn't go away. The next stop was the reception desk. More German rang in Tom's ears, but he did get the gist of it as a passing nurse was called up and asked to take them to the doctor's. To Tom's relief, the pace was slower.

As they progressed, Jan remembered and shared the fact that the doctor claimed that Andreas was being treated for mercury poisoning. Tom was intrigued and decided to probe further just as they reached the door of the doctor's office. "Did this Andreas work in a condition where he was exposed to mercury?"

From his recollection Jan confirmed Andreas was an accountant. This wasn't a line of work where an individual would come across hazardous substances. Before it could be knocked, the doctor's office door opened and behind it was an exhausted man. "Hello Doctor" Jan greeted. "Officer, Happy New Year, please come in."

As they entered, Tom was immediately taken by the life size skeleton in the corner of the room whilst Jan proceeded with his questioning asking when the man died, were there any final words, was there anything unusual. After five minutes of the background conversation and the novelty of the bones gone, Tom asked for a translation.

Jan informed Tom that he was at loggerheads with the doctor at the plausibility that mercury must have been the method of the man's demise. "Even I know you need a prolonged exposure to it and even the doctor said that things moved too quickly…"

"How quickly?" Tom asked

"Less than a week." Replied the doctor

"Let me guess, and by that time, there was nothing you could do right?" Tom concluded. The doctor nodded. "It's mercury alright, Dimethylmercury to be exact. That stuff is nasty."

The doctor was stunned and turned to Jan who replied "He has a master in Chemistry or something.

The doctor seemed to be alarmed. "Oh my God!" He exclaimed changing to English "We could have a public health situation on our hands. If your friend is correct we have to find everyone he has been in contact with!"

"Hold on." Tom ordered. "We don't know the means by which the metal entered his system and you know it's something that's quickly absorbed into the body, so it wouldn't really linger around for long and even if did, the incubation period has well passed. Why not call all the hospitals to confirm if they have had anyone turn up in a similar condition as our departed friend out there before we raise the alarm?"

Tom's words appeared to startle the doctor, who agreed and proceeded to make enquires, at ease. Tom took the opportunity to ask if he and his team could have access to any information the German police had on Andreas. Tom also requested incognito access to Robert's flat and the items taken from the flat.

Every fibre of Jan's being still wondered if Tom was doing this for his own selfish interest whilst the situation at hand perplexed everyone, but decided not to ask. "Regarding the files, I'll ask for permission. About access, let's talk about it later."

Jan dropped Tom off his hotel which had turned into his hub having had the entire sixth floor vacated and taken over by the his colleagues who finally arrived post their Christmas break.

Having conveyed a meeting with his group to inform them that, so far, he hadn't made any progress, a call came informing him that permission for him and his team to examine the crime scene with the added bonus of reviewing their findings. Tom was so pleased his luck had changed.

## 3 January 2011

Khoi arrived at the sanatorium eight minutes late. He parked the car and ran straight through to the waiting area. Initially terrified for keeping them waiting, he soon relaxed when he was saw the smiling face of the eager parents.

This welcoming smile he received was a far cry from the angry look he left behind at home. Julien was furious at Khoi for choosing to leave the house even though, according to Julien, Khoi wasn't ready to go out considering the state of mind he was in. Khoi was so fed up of constantly being asked what was the source of his angst was from Julien, that coming to a sanatorium was a welcomed relief.

Anita welcomed him with a kiss on the cheek but as she held his face, her maternal instincts tingled. Whilst holding his face she looked into his eyes. Brushing aside the facade of his smile, she asked Khoi "Are you alright?"

"I'm fine." Khoi replied.

Khoi's lack on sincerity made her inquisitive "You don't look fine. Have you been sleeping well? Is everything ok?" she asked holding his hands.

Khoi felt the need to be honest, the smile was slowly fading, he was about to crack again but was saved when Georg cried out "For heaven's sake, the boy said he is fine."

Khoi looked and found Georg approaching, using his cane for support. Taking his chance to escape, Khoi went straight to him and shook Georg's hand greeting him with a "Happy New Year."

"Same to you son." replied Georg. Unwilling to have Anita's prying eyes on him, Khoi suggested they proceed with their plans for the day.

First stop was to see the doctor who bid them welcome and informed them that Jeroen was looking forward to their visit and had been very busy being creative. Georg wasn't interested in a progress report, he wanted to see his son and he didn't hesitate to make that clear.

The doctor took her robust approach in stride; she understood the reasoning behind his approach. To prevent a repeat performance, she took them to the room where Jeroen was. The doctor instructed the parents to wait behind the door till they were called in.

The doctor entered followed closely by Khoi who left the door slightly open behind him to allow the parents to peep through the gap. Once in the room, Khoi was mesmerised, taken by the paintings that had adorned the space. The terrific artistic display was breath taking, but they were too much to take in initially, until he noticed a familiar theme.

The paintings were of things linked to Jeroen, such as the family home where they lived. There was a striking picture of Jeroen's room, just as he left it, right down to the cricket bat that hung over his bed. There were paintings of his parents, tastefully done, depicting them sitting in a living room, his mother reading a newspaper and his father drinking something in the sun.

They were so real and so life like, just like the paintings Jeroen made in the days of old when he doodled and created his comics of well-formed super heroes.

Khoi was brought back to the room when the doctor called out "Jeroen?" Jeroen was busy painting. With his attention drawn, he turned and upon setting sites on Khoi, dropped his brush, got up and in his jovial manner ran to give Khoi a huge hug. "Happy New Year Khoi!" "Happy New Year man. I see you've been busy." Responded Khoi as he drew closer to the work he was working on. Jeroen rushed quickly to cover Khoi's eyes with his hands "Don't look. I haven't finished." He begged, pressing on Khoi's face till he gave in. "Okay, okay, I won't look. You idiot."

Then followed a bit of rough housing as the two tickled each other like children till the doctor stepped in to move things along. "Enough now, you're going to miss your surprise." Jeroen paused as the doctor beckoned his parent's into the room.

Anita and Georg entered the room not knowing what to expect. They were filled with anxiety because Jeroen seemed to look upon them as though strangers had walked into the room. The parents stopped their advance. Khoi and the doctor wondered what was to follow as the quiet standoff between the hopes of his parents and reality on the ground as no one could predict if Jeroen would remember his own family.

Jeroen took a step forward, there was progress. He proceeded till he was at arm's length from them. Jeroen reached out and touched his mother's long curly brown hair, feeling them between his fingers. Anita and the entire room held their breath as Jeroen finally stopped fiddling with her hair. Anita and Georg remained still as though being confronted by a beautiful creature that could bolt at any moment, easily spooked by sudden movement.

Then, after six minutes of patience, a smile emerged on Jeroen's face and though sounding unsure, Jeroen called out "Mother?" The relief was evident as she Anita replied "Yes, I'm your mother." the tears followed as she fought her urge to launch herself at her son and hold him tight. Jeroen turned to his father who was close tears himself and cried "Hello Georg." The big man couldn't help it, he broke down responding "Father, I'm your father, but Georg is fine."

Jeroen approached his mother and carefully wrapped his arms around her, hugging her. As the connection between mother and child grew, so did the strength of their embrace. "Come on George" She called. The old man put aside his manly pretences and joined the family bonding moment.

It was that sense of togetherness, being cocooned by the love of his family which his brain trauma had robbed him of that spurred Jeroen to act. Yes, it was all fuzzy, yes, it felt strange, but like a fungus hidden deep underground, the mushroom love for his family emerged from the dull dead soil of his confused damaged mind. As the smell of his mother's hair triggered a state of confusion within him, he didn't remember why, but there was one thing Jeroen was certain of, he loved these people and it was a feeling he hadn't had before, or could recollect himself experiencing. It consumed him, and it led Jeroen to sob.

Anita heard Jeroen whimpering. She drew back from the hug and held his face kissing him on the forehead "Don't cry. We're going home."

"OK, bye bye." Jeroen bade them.

"No, no, we are going home. You are coming with us. You are coming home Jeroen." Georg clarified.

Jeroen was initially stunned and repeated the word "home" before it settled in and he replied "Okay." More hugs followed.

It was a sight to melt the coldest of hearts. Even the doctor commented "I never get tired of this." The doctor reached for a handkerchief from her pocket to dry her eyes.

Watching on, Khoi received the gratitude he deserved from Georg who said to him "You did this, you made this happen. Thank you." It filled Khoi with a sense of accomplishment so much so that he could not respond.

The doctor had insufficient time and called the parents aside to discuss how they can manage Jeroen's return to his stead, leaving Khoi to keep Jeroen's attention. Jeroen relented and brought Khoi to his latest work. It was a painting of Khoi and what a striking likeness it was. "I haven't finished... so stop looking." Jeroen ordered, but it was too late, Khoi was taken by his skill, yet he needed to be sensitive, so he turned away and proceeded to change the topic. "So what would you like to do when you get home?" Jeroen went blank, then he looked around him as though in search for the appropriate reply till he found it. "I don't know." Jeroen said. "I don't know where it is." Khoi could only ponder what difficulties Georg and Anita were going to face now that they had their son back after nearly a decade as a 28 year old man in body alone.

The driving arrangement was interesting. The doctor suggested that Khoi take Jeroen home alone. There were concerns that being driven by his parents would be too much for Jeroen's delicate state.

Upon arriving at home, Jeroen initially looked out of place but relaxed when he realised Khoi was by his side.

The doctor informed that Khoi that he needed to be in charge to ensure Jeroen's adjustment was smooth.

First step was to take him somewhere familiar. Khoi led Jeroen to his room, which was left virtually the same way it was on the night of his accident, whilst his parents stayed alone downstairs to discuss the changes to be made.

"Here you are" Khoi announced. Jeroen appeared to accept his surroundings with a mix of trepidation and excitement. Khoi could only relax when Jeroen finally smiled. Khoi thought it would be best to allow him to immerse himself to his old room.

With the door slightly opened, Khoi went down to join the parents for a coffee. Anita dispensing a large number of pills prescribed to keep Georg ticking on as Jeroen ventured around the small space, feeling things in this strange peculiar land which promised possibility of discovery.

Jeroen took it all in with glee as there were treasures to behold. Some he remembered, like the comics left by his bedside whilst others were obscure and interesting, so much so, he couldn't believe they were his.

In the opposite room, his twin was sleeping, having spent another hard night sorting out deals and sealing them with drinks. Normally the alcohol would keep him pleasantly in bed for a long time, but for some reason, at that very moment, his sound sleep was being disturbed by his mental activity. It was an odd uncomfortable feeling that beset his mind like an invading poltergeist stroking his soul.

As Joel's slumber was being interrupted, Jeroen went to his shelves and found his collection of miniature action figures of amply muscled men. He knew they were superheroes, but couldn't determine who they were.

Jeroen's eyes caught site of a yellow box with a crank to the side. He went to pick it up and when he did, a gentle tune emitted. He shook the cube and more noise came. Jeroen's curiosity, coupled with his power of deduction made him turn the crank. More music was produced, exciting Jeroen, prompting him to roll the crank even faster. Jeroen was enjoying it till he was startled when the top of the box flipped open and out popped a puppet causing him to drop it to the floor.

The noise of the metal item crashing to the floor wasn't perceived by those downstairs deliberating on what adjustments were required to accommodate Jeroen's needs, but it was overheard by his twin.

Joel's troubled sleep came to an end that instant. Joel discovered he had been sweating. He didn't understand why he was so fearful, but he was. Joel looked round his room and there was nothing out of the ordinary to set off any alarms. Perhaps it was a dream and he tried to go back to sleep.

On the other side of the corridor, Jeroen picked up the toy, it made the noise again. This time, Joel was certain it was not a dream and got out of bed.

Joel slowly crept out of his room wearing nothing but his pyjama bottoms. He took a couple of steps forward down the corridor, it was then he noticed the door to Jeroen's room was half opened.

Joel heard movements in the room and approached the door stealthily till he reached the opening. There he beheld a sight that lifted his heart. It was his twin, a person he hadn't seen for many years. He thought he was still dreaming, having another one of his nightly hallucinations stemming from over consumption of whiskey.

Joel continued to watch to confirm if this was reality. He asked himself if it was Jeroen trying to force back the puppet back into its container. Jeroen didn't know he was being watched and when he finally succeeded inserting the toy into its den.

The uncertainty was killing Joel. He had to know. "Jeroen?" Joel called out. Jeroen looked up and upon seeing Joel, stood still, turning white as a sheet as the colour was flushed out from his skin.

Joel had failed to perceive this, he was just ecstatic to see his brother again. "Droit… it is you. You're home." Joel moved forward to touch his brother and hoped to embrace him, but Jeroen took a step back.

Jeroen's reaction was puzzling. Joel then remembered what he had seen in the clip as strove to assure him. "Hey droit… are you alright?" Joel asked taking another step forward which was met by the same but opposite reaction. "Droit… it's me." Joel reached out to touch him again. Jeroen shuddered as though he was in the presence of an evil spirit. "Jeroen?" he called again.

Joel had prayed for the privilege to hear his brother's voice, things seemed interminable and he was set to give up when Jeroen spoke out "Georg!" initially in a soft voice. Thinking it was a mistake, Joel corrected him "No, no Droit, it's me, Joel."

Then Jeroen shrieked out as though tormented at the top of his lungs "Khoi! Georg! Aargh!"

Alarmed, Joel raced towards him in an attempt to calm Jeroen, yet with one touch, Jeroen dropped to the floor, cowering in a foetal position. Joel knelt and finally got the chance to touch his brother giving him a shake calling on his brother "Jeroen, it's alright, it's me." Before Joel could proceed further, Joel felt a hand on his shoulder that yanked him away from his cherished other half by Khoi.

Joel got off the floor and became a spectator and a stranger as Khoi and his mother tried to silence and sooth Jeroen distressed state. "Could you leave please?" Khoi ordered him.

"What's going on?" Joel asked, but no one was in the mood of explaining, he was only told by his mother "Just get out!"

Joel soon began to partake in the feeling consuming his brother. All the uncertainty upset him and he wanted to be with his brother but his brother didn't want him. This rejection saddened him deeply as he left the room.

Once he stepped out of the door, he found his father standing there with the look of seething fury about him as he asked "What did you do to him?" Joel hadn't seen his father in such a state before and he was struck by terror, causing him to stutter as he replied "Nothing... I just wanted to say hello"

"Don't lie to me! What did you do to him?" his father asked again.

"I swear I did nothing!" but before he could finished his words, Joel was hit across the face by his father as the old man roared "Stop lying to me!" That was followed by another punch that brought Joel down on his behind.

Joel wanted to run, but couldn't get up fast enough to escape another assault from the heavy oak his father used for balance on his shoulder, this was followed by a quick succession of lashes which only ended when Khoi rushed between the father and son and took a blow to the leg.

To prevent another strike from Georg, who was overtaken by a temporary state of anger induced madness, Khoi restrained Georg by holding his hands. "No, Georg! Stop this!" Khoi ordered.

"What did he do to my son?" asked Georg as he struggled to continue his onslaught.

"Nothing, he did nothing!" Khoi replied. "Please Georg, Jeroen needs you. Stop trying to give yourself a heart attack!"

Khoi's words seemed to appease the man. The cane came down, the fire diminished and slowly, Georg regained his senses. Silently, he walked away past the son he had assaulted without acknowledgement into the room to attend to the other in need.

With Georg gone, Khoi helped Joel off the ground. Joel was shell shocked, trembling from the acts inflicted on him. Joel shook off Khoi's hand, limping back to his room, falling on his bed not knowing what hurt the most between his bruised body and his battered spirit.

Khoi longed to speak to him and promise him all would be fine, but he didn't have the time. Jeroen drew on his mind. As he returned to Jeroen's room, the adrenaline that coursed through his veins appeared to diminish as the pain from the blow he received grew.

Once he had entered the room he looked at Jeroen in the midst of the love of his parents. He looked comfortable and Khoi felt he was intruding in their moment of bonding. As he tried to escape, Khoi was spotted by Jeroen who called his name. "Come and sit with me." Jeroen pleaded.

Khoi was no longer interested in that or censoring his thoughts. The elephant in the room could not be given the cold shoulder any longer. Khoi chose to be blunt. What he witnessed worried him. "Georg, can we talk for a moment?"

"Let's talk later." Georg' proposal was not acceptable.

"I think we need to speak now please?" Khoi insisted.

Georg gave him a scornful look.

A confrontation was brewing. Noting this, Anita stepped in to defuse the situation. "Darling, go and speak to him. I am sure it won't be long." She said. Reluctantly, and with some difficulty, Georg got up from the ground. Mumbling as he passed Khoi "It better be quick boy."

Once outside the door, Khoi knew he had to speak first before Georg got a word in and verbally suppress any sense of decency he noticed, he always did that. Khoi quickly began "I think you have to understand that Jeroen's reaction to Joel wasn't based on any actions of Joel. It's all in Jeroen's mind. To him, Joel doesn't exist… he thinks he's an only child so the sight of someone who looks just like him is hard for him to comprehend and that display, what was that? I have to say you need to take it easy. Jeroen needs you and he needs Joel too. You don't want to alienate him… you can't do that." Georg stood there with a sneer on his face. For Khoi, the initial relief of getting his thoughts off his chest followed by an intense apprehension. He didn't know what Georg would say or do.

Georg looked for a moment stamping the base on the wooden floor several times before he looked up and sighed then conceded "You're right… I was out of order. I just need to come to terms with the changes around me. I used to be strong… I used to be capable…"

Khoi interjected "You had a heart attack. You should count yourself lucky you survived. Slowing down is the natural progression of life. I know it's hard to take, but the second chance you have should be used to reconnect with Jeroen and Joel... your family."

Georg seemed to soak up all the words. He reached out and patted Khoi on the shoulder and with his silent nod seemed to accept Khoi's advice and finally said "Thank you. I'll talk to Joel later."

Feeling he ought to make the best of the opportunity available to him, Khoi brought forward his own needs. Cautiously, he asked "Georg, I was meaning to ask you this... but I need some time off... if you don't mind?" Georg's response was to ask in a lowered tone "Are you trying to take advantage of a man when he's most vulnerable?" Khoi froze and stumbled over his words, wondering if it had been a good idea to ask the question in the first place. Then Georg grinned and responded "It's alright, how much time do you need?"

Khoi was pleased to have his wish granted and now he had to quantify his request, but he was totally demoralised with his life and his place within cooperate structure. Unable to provide an answer by asking what he truly wanted, he asked "May I get back to you tomorrow?"

"Yes, let's speak tomorrow." Georg agreed and patted him on the shoulder again "You've done a lot to be proud of, we owe you a great deal."

Khoi considered this the best time to leave. He joyfully bid them all a good day as he left the house, but once the door was shut, his pain returned with full force. He had feigned a good natured attitude but it was all empty talk directed by his need to keep up appearances.

Without need for the elaborate display, he felt weak at the knees and physically sick to his stomach. He rushed to his car and drove just a few meters away into the woods, parked it and progressively declined into an anxiety attack. Everything around him seemed to scare him. The wind seemed to mock him using Jelena's voice, calling him weak, defective and a murderer.

Khoi accepted that he was living in darkness, slowly marching towards insanity, but the mocking had to stop. Khoi turned on the radio and found the rock channel. He hated the music, but it served a purpose. Eventually, a heavy metal tune was discovered blasting out rambling words to the strumming of electric guitars and drum beats.

Khoi raised the volume to the highest level as he could and with the music blaring in the background, he let his emotions free as his world collapsed around him. Khoi screamed out loudly as he banged his steering wheel and pulled on his hair. He kept screaming till he was hoarse and broke down in tears, weeping till he made himself sick and till he was totally exhausted, all before two in the afternoon. After he had time to let his rage subside he drove home to his medication and his bed.

As Khoi prayed for peace of mind, Tom was walking up to the flat of the now deceased Robert, with the snow falling on his head.

Tom felt nervous. The anxiety didn't stem from the task ahead; rather, it came from the event of the morning when he tried to brush his teeth only to find he wasn't able to use his right hand to exert enough pressure to eject the toothpaste from the tube.

Tom had to shake his arm vigorously to bring it back to full flow. The knock effect of such actions was that now he noticed his right hand trembled in intervals. Hoping to keep the involuntary movement from view, he kept his hands in his pockets at all times.

At the door of the building, he was met by some officers who were to act as his four German chaperones, however they seemed aloof the approach taken to by the Germans to cross border cooperation was picked upon by a member of the forensic team who sought an explanation from Tom.

Tom could only use the fear of communicating in English as an excuse and promptly told his team to ignore it and should they be hindered in any way, report it to him. Then Tom had second thoughts. He decided to attend to the scene with them.

Once the door of the flat was opened, Tom looked around. He had been privy to the autopsy report of the deceased prior to arrival and was aware that when Robert was found, he had been dead for about two days with congealed blood from his mouth and other orifices. The poor man had had his innards dissolved from inhaling the noxious gas that killed him.

Although the information was well laid out and even though poorly translated, what surprised Tom the most was the German's inability to deduce where the gas had originated from. Yet, he wasn't intent on judging the report till he saw what was at play.

They took the lift to the relevant floor and with the required protective clothing on, they entered the flat. Moving to the kitchen, there was the stained floor, brown with hints of dark red. Tom stood aside to allow his team to do their job around the crime scene, whilst he occupied himself by inspecting the rest of the flat.

Tom wandered from room to room, trying to uncover any sign of Jelena's presence, but he couldn't find anything. He wasn't astonished by the lack of evidence, so he decided to divert his energy to assisting the others.

Tom walked into the kitchen just in time to watch his team, under the squinting eyes of the German officers, leering at them with suspicion, as they sprayed the surroundings of where the body was found to detect which areas had had the highest exposure to the gas.

The results proved that it was evenly distributed, meaning that the gas could not have been applied directly to the person by another being. Again, though not surprised, Tom did begin to see a pattern forming.

Tom then instructed his team to scan the immediate area again and pay particular interest to the white goods to find any defects. Noting the gas used, Tom expected some corrosion to be found on the furniture, but there was none. Amazed, Tom took personal charge to actually review the environment himself only to marvel. The killer, or killers, had certainly done their homework noting that the appliances were made out of material that wouldn't be affected by moderate exposure Hydrogen Sulfide.

The area of inspection was widened to cover the rest of the flat, but they didn't need to go far. The painted wooden doors that divided the kitchen from the entrance at one end and the other that divided the rest of the flat from the kitchen did show signs of corrosion with the paint peeling off slightly, but more from the door by the entrance to the flat.

Then it clicked. Tom turned to the portly moustached German officer and asked "You said the extractor fan over the cooker was on, is that correct?" Tom had to explain his question in detail to aid the man's understanding. The man confirmed that it was found on. Tom then asked if the grid that covered the extractor fans could be removed. The German officer had to make a call before permission was granted.

With the screws removed, a flash light was shone on to the blades and wires and there the saw that the coating covering the wire had been eroded and the plastic blades did show signs of corrosion.

Now Tom was able to confirm that the report provided was right. With the absence of fingerprints and multiple DNA from many different women detected all over the place, the killer wasn't in the flat when the gas was released.

Everyone in the building was alive, so the gas must have come from somewhere. Tom promptly fell to his knees and crawled around, baffling those present as he went to the wall, checking the air vents at ground level with his flash light. Content that they weren't the source, he got to his feet and turned his head upwards, scanning around till he found the three air vents that were overhead. It was then Tom smiled, beckoned his assistant and said "look up there and see if there is any corrosion."

As the others went about asking their German colleagues for a ladder, Tom asked another one of their attendants if he could be shown the access to the ventilation shaft.

The janitor was summoned and he took them to the two access points, one close to the door and the other in the fire escape area. Once the covers were removed, Tom asked for another ladder and attempted to enter, it was then he realised something, if a man of his frame could just squeeze in and then would able to move a few centimetres let alone the whole length required to reach the flat, then it was impossible for Jelena who was bigger than him to do the same.

Tom then asked why there was no CCTV present anywhere. It transpired that the deceased owned the building and ensured that there was none in activity, they were all for show.

Having had his fill of the reluctant, glum faces of his foreign counterparts Tom left the building to give Jan a call.

In excitement, when the call was answered Tom didn't wait for Jan to speak and went straight to the point. "Jan! Hello, the air-conditioning! That's the key. We need to check who services the system. Could you get in touch with them and ask the following; is the flat's ventilation system connected to the main system for the rest of the building? Have they ever needed to go through the vent to service it or for whatever reason? If yes, how do they go about it? I assume they would need a person of small stature. If it is a person, find them; check their size, data and their whereabouts during the relevant period.

Based on your report I would be thinking from the last time the man was alive and two days after that, confirm with your pathologist, but you need to track their movements, review all their equipment. We need to have them eliminated from our list of suspects.

Once that's done, I think I can tell you more of my findings. I will get the rest of the team to the area where the guy was shot in the head and will be back in the office by hmm... let's say 5 or so? See you later." Then he hung up then dashed up to the flat and rounded his team.

Despite the arrogance in the delivery of the request, Jan forgave Tom. He could tell the Brit had a hunch and it would have been counterproductive to stick on ceremony.

Tom returned to the hotel at quarter to seven that evening. He had organised a meeting with his team to review the events of the day in forty five minutes, so he had a short time to rest for a moment, but it seemed not to be.

As he slipped off his shoes, his mobile phone went off. Initially, he was going to ignore it till he checked the number and found it was his boss. He picked it up answering "Ma'am?"

"Evans, glad you are there. I need you to go to British Embassy right away. There is some important information waiting for you." Not one to argue with his superiors, Tom returned his feet into his shoes and did an about face to the Embassy.

Arriving at the building, he walked around wondering where the entrance was when someone came out from what looked like the closed gate "Excuse me, Mr Evans?" Tom turned and found a man, clearly a security guard, walking towards him. "Are you Mr Evans?" The man asked. Tom simply took out his identification and handed it to the man. As he returned it, the man said "Sorry about that. The building is closed, but you were expected. Please, this way."

Tom followed the man through security into the building and then to a meeting room. The door was opened and there seated around a table with a laptop and project were two smartly dressed women seated on opposite sides of the table, flanked by a man in uniform on the left and on the right, was a man in a suit, all with their eyes fixed on Tom as he walked in.

The woman in her beige office wear with a flowery silk scarf around her neck stood up, smiled and approached him and gave Tom a warm handshake. "Ambassador Ruth Lawson. Nice to meet you." She said, "Your excellency." Tom replied, she seemed embarrassed by being called that and told him to skip on formality "Call me Ruth. Please, may I introduce you to Ambassador Maria Pijanowska from the Polish Embassy?" She said, directing Tom to the lady in the red dress.

Tom greeted her with the respect due and he was quickly introduced to the man in the uniform "Mr Ewa Fabirkiewicz, chief of Police of Lubusz Province, Poland." A stern handshake and eye contact was made before Tom was introduced to the man in the suit "and this is Mr Bruce Arrowsmith. Our Consular General in Warsaw."

"Pleased to meet you all." Tom replied as he was shown to his seat next to the Ambassador who seemed very statesman like as she began "Thank you for coming at such short notice. I really appreciate it. Before I pass it on to my counterpart, I just wanted to inform you that I and Mr Arrowsmith, have been brought up to date by London and we are here to provide you with as much help as you require. So, madam, over to you."

"Thank you" said the Polish Ambassador, "but my position here is to act more as an interpreter for the Chief of Police." She then prompted to the policeman to speak.

The sturdy Polish policeman clasped his hands on the table and leaned forward as he began, the Ambassador conveying his message "Yesterday, a body was found in the Ujście Warty National Park district, alone, fully clothed." He then gave a signal for the projector to be switched on and on came the picture of a frozen, bluish face. It prompted Tom to sit up from his previously relaxed position. Pointing at the picture Tom remarked "You found her where?"

"In the woods" replied the policeman "I see you clearly recognise her and once we looked through our records, so did we. We checked the phone she had and found only one number saved on it, yours Mr Evans." Tom struggled to mask his astonishment as the Polish policeman carried on. "Have spoken to London, it was confirmed that you have been looking for Ms Bozic. Now that you have found her, the Polish government would like you to come and identify the body if possible and take it out of our country as soon as possible."

"I'm sorry?" Tom was surprised by the demand being made "Aren't investigations required?"

The policeman decided to deliver the message in person and in English "If you want to do an investigation, do an investigation, we don't have money and time for that or any interest for that matter. We know about this woman, we don't want trouble. Just come, see if it is the person you are looking for, take the body, do what investigation you want and leave, we won't stop you but we don't want to help you either."

"I'd like to add Mr Evan's" interjected the Polish Ambassador "That is our government's stance as well. We feel this is a British matter and in the spirit of cooperation, we are granting you free reign and jurisdiction over the relevant areas. Tell us what you need, and so long as it's not man power, you shall have it."

This was an unexpected turn of events. Whilst wrestling with the blow inflicted by the news, all Tom could say was "Okay... thank you for the offer. I and my team will be in Poland as soon as I can. So we meet in Lubusz?"

"No Mr Evans. The body has been transported to the Capital." The Ambassador confirmed.

"I guess I best find a ticket to Warsaw then. Thank you for the information." Tom replied.

The rest of the meeting was to underline the rules of engagement and what the British Embassy and Consulate would do to assist Tom and his team. Tom sat there, nodding in pretence that he was assimilating all that was being said when in reality, all he heard were words that were repeated in his mind "She's dead...? That can't be right... she can't be."

Returning to his hotel at just after 11pm, he instructed the team to pack their bags and prepare to take the first flight to Warsaw the following morning.

Tom didn't even try to sleep. In his mind, it was all a practical joke or a strange mistake, or even worse, a ploy by Jelena to throw him off her scent. Yet he couldn't help but wonder, if not worry about the consequences if the information proved true.

*4 January 2011*

Khoi woke up prematurely again at 3 in the morning thanks to his now nightly torment. Again he turned to the other side of the bed and for the third day in a row, Julien wasn't there.

Khoi felt cold, even though he was drenched in sweat, what's more, the bed was equally soaked. Concluding that he hadn't lost so much water from sweating alone, Khoi felt the mattress and then his groin, he had wet the bed.

This was unprecedented, not to say extremely troubling. Khoi couldn't even remember the last time he had ever urinated in his sleep. This caused him to panic. Khoi jumped out of the bed. He took off all his clothes and pulled off the sheets.

Khoi thought fast, taking hold of the hair dryer, using it to evaporate the damp in the fibres. It caused a horrible smell and the noise echoed through the silence. As he intermittently paused to feel the patch, Khoi was rumbled. Julien walked in with the sleep still in his eyes and Khoi stood over the bed, hair dryer in hand and totally naked.

Khoi had expected Julien to say something, but he didn't. With the sheets on the floor and from Khoi's actions, Julien easily deduced what had happened. He walked in and collected the clothes together and carried them away. On his way to the door, he pulled out the hair dryer's plug and in a sleepy tone ordered "Please go and sleep in the guest room." Julien left and went to the kitchen where he placed the clothes in the washing machine.

Khoi felt humiliated. He wandered about the room for a while considering what to do next. He decided to put on his clothes, the next thing Khoi had in mind was to speak to Julien. Khoi went to the living room and found the television on and Julien fast asleep on the sofa.

Julien was the lucky one to be able to slumber so quickly. The fact that Julien had to sleep on the sofa made Khoi's heart sink in a deep sense of guilt. Khoi returned to the room to think but there was nothing in his mind except grief. He needed a distraction and fast.

Khoi decided to start the day early. Having been granted some time off, he need to organise his hand over notes for whoever would fill his shoes. Khoi took to the shower, put on some clothes, got into his car and left for the office at five in the morning.

He immediately threw himself into his work. Reviewing more figures, devising more savings and calculating where more resources should be allocated. All that transferred focus worked. He was able to forget his sorrows even though it was for the briefest of time. At 9:15am, his alarm clock went off. It was time to check on Jeroen.

The post-holiday traffic significantly added to his journey time turning a 35 minute drive in 73 minute ordeal, confirming why Khoi hated driving in general.

Parking his car just outside Georg's mansion, Khoi brought out his backpack and made his way up the drive way to the front porch. It had started to snow again, but the flakes refused to settle. As he reached the steps, he found Joel sitting on the stairs by himself, wearing his shoes, a pair of jeans and a light sweater, considerably little for this time of the year.

Khoi could tell Joel must have been outside for a while due to his shivers and a slight blue tinge to his lips and now, he was smoking. This was bad, Joel gave up smoking five years earlier and even then it was not a usual occurrence, he only smoked when stressed and it was limited to just one or two, but from the number of buts littering the ground, he'd had more than two, it was closer to eleven, things weren't bad, they must be terrible.

Khoi walked up to him, his shadow falling over Joel who didn't bother to acknowledge his presence. Khoi decided to sit by him. A closer look at Joel revealed the bruises on his face, his cracked lower lip and black eye.

Joel drew hard on his cigarette, still unwilling to look at Khoi as he spoke "Came to check on Jeroen?" Khoi didn't say anything, he just reached out and turned Joel's face to see if there was more to be seen and there was.

There were more bruises on his face and the skin his left eyebrow had been broken. "Are you alright?" Khoi asked. Joel grinned and looked to the ground as he smoked on before confirming "yeah, I am fine... at least it's safer out here."

"What's happening?" Khoi asked

"I don't know... things are changing. My father who had never once raised his hand to me has now done it twice in ten days. I think he's forgotten I am not 12 anymore." Joel said as he finished his cigarette and threw the end away. Khoi suggested Joel speak to his father and in turn was asked "And tell him what? Dad, have you checked your medication? Lately you've been out of character.

Don't be silly. Besides, I wouldn't be able to reach him. He's in heaven. Busy taking care of fucking Droit." Joel paused to light another cigarette. He sucked in the fumes before adding "You know I dreamt of this day. Droit would come back, I'd have my brother again... we'd deceive the girls , get into trouble... things returning to normal with him being the responsible one and I being the naughty one." Joel paused, Khoi thought he was going to cry, rather, he stubbed out his cigarette and reiterated "Like I said, it was a dream. The reality I got was a mirror image of me with the

IQ of a potato who screams every time I go near him."

"Come on Joel, he just needs to adjust and adapt a little… he'll be gone by Monday, maybe we could tell the doctor to find out why he reacts that way." Khoi suggested.

"Don't bother." Joel snapped "I already know why, we all better cut the act. Droit hasn't forgiven me… Just like dad. They both haven't forgiven me, no one has. I spent years hating myself…" Joel began to sob.

Khoi felt truly sorry for Joel, but also considered that Joel wasn't doing his health any favours by sitting out there in the cold. As he rose, Khoi took off his coat and placed it over Joel's shoulders and proceeded into the house using the key he was given announcing his entry by crying out "hello everyone"

"We're in the kitchen!" responded Anita. Khoi went to join them.

There was Jeroen sitting at the head of the table, his parents on either side patiently watching him slowly eat whilst their meal was left untouched. Jeroen's progress was halted once he set eyes on Khoi and with the usual cry of his name, Jeroen got up and went to embrace him and led him to the table.

Anita got up to allow Khoi to take her place. She offered him some food, he didn't refuse and as Khoi ate, Jeroen appeared to grow in confidence and ate at normal speed. Deciding it was time she and her husband also had some food and took their plates to the kitchen to warm it up again. This gave Georg an opportunity to commit some mischief. "Khoi, now that the lady is away, you wouldn't mind…"

"No, Georg, I won't get you a glass of port. It's not good for you." Khoi interjected.

Georg knew he had been sussed out and admitted defeat "Smart kid. So what about the dumb one, still sulking outside?" Khoi was caught in the process of eating his egg, but he quickly swallowed the pieces and took the chance to voice his concerns. "I think he's feeling left out. Jeroen doesn't remember him and I don't know what's going on, but you need to calm down and not jump to conclusions…"

As Georg's casual style turned stiff with a frown developing, Khoi wondered if he had made a mistake bringing up the topic. "You annoy me sometimes, but you are right. I wouldn't be so hard on him if he wasn't such a cock up!"

"Who's the cock up?" Anita asked having just caught the last part of the conversation.

"Nothing, dear… by the way, Khoi asked for time off. I said he could have it. Mind taking over the accounts whilst he's away?"

"Not at all darling." Anita replied kissing her husband on the lips. "Are you off to anywhere nice?" Anita asked Khoi

"No…" Khoi soon realised that he had been put on the spot, but his candour was expected "I just need some time…" his statement did nothing to settle Anita's apprehension.

"How long are we talking about? A couple of days…?"

"I don't know." With all eyes on him Khoi's heart began to race.

A vale of gloom fell over Anita's face and her voice didn't hide it either "what about Jeroen?"

"I thought about him." Khoi went to his bag and took out an iPad. With everyone gathered round, he showed his solution to the problem. Khoi could face time Jeroen at any time or even Skype him. After a small demonstration using his phone, Khoi definitely won Jeroen and Georg over to the point that Georg also wanted to get connected himself.

Anita, on the other hand, hadn't been convinced by the use of technology. Taking him aside to the study using the guise of reviewing the work load she was to take on, she shut the door and without hesitation said "Now, tell me the truth, what's going on?" Khoi could not lie to her, nor could he hold it back anymore, he struggled to look her in the eyes as prior to confiding in her, swore her to secrecy then confessed "I can't take it anymore… I just need to go … I…"

"It's ok." Anita interrupted. "If you need time off, you should take it."

"Thank you." Khoi replied giving her a hug.

"No, thank you for not giving Georg a drink." She replied. He had exposed his underbelly and didn't get it sliced open, Khoi felt a weight lifted off his shoulders.

Khoi took his time to walk Anita through the system she helped develop and once done, chose to speak with Jeroen who had gone to his room. Khoi went up to join him and caught him painting.

"Hello Jeroen." Jeroen beckoned Khoi in as he remarked "I've finished." And he had. It was a great likeness of him and he was so pleased. Yet, it wasn't the main reason for his visit. Alone with Jeroen, he managed to get his attention and asked him "Jeroen, do you know Joel?" From Khoi's point of view, Jeroen didn't comprehend anything. "Do you remember your brother?" Khoi tried again and soon concluded that he might be fighting a losing battle. He threw his hand over him and drew him close making Jeroen laugh. It was a beautiful innocent laugh which gave Khoi some cheer "I love you, you crazy boy."

"I know Joel... he hurt me." Jeroen replied with his smile still beaming. Khoi caught the statement and immediately reacted

"Jeroen, look at me, look at me." He ordered. Jeroen did as he was told still snickering, but Khoi had to get this message through to him "Joel is your brother and he loves you. He will never hurt you. OK? Say ok."

Jeroen just nodded. Khoi hugged him tightly, his heart wrenching with fear that Joel could be right.

Khoi kissed his friend on the head. Jeroen offered him the painting, but as the painting was wet, Khoi said he would collect it later. It was time to leave, but prior to his departure; he stopped at Joel's room to collect a coat.

Khoi exited the building and Joel was still there, smoking and shivering. Khoi retrieved his jacket and replaced it with the one taken from the room. Joel looked up at Khoi as he put on his jacket. Joel shrugged his shoulders "isn't it funny how things turn out? Sitting out here reminds me of when we first met. You were in the playground, sitting on the swing all by yourself, as gloomy as ever because your mum had just died. Stefan, Jeroen and I noticed you. I told him 'That kid looks lonely, let's invite him over to play.' And you know what Jeroen said? Jeroen said no. He thought you would steal our toys, but he was out voted so we called you over and throughout that time one thing ran true."

"What's that?" Khoi enquired

"Jeroen was right. You are a thief. Before you leave tell me, how does it feel now that it's all over? The rush of adrenaline, the constant attention, the feeling of authority, how does it feel now that it's all gone? Do you get haunted? Can you sleep at night?"

Khoi wanted to cry out "No, I can't... is there anything you could recommend to help me through this?" but he didn't. Rather he considered Joel's inquiry as a rhetorical question and decided not to reply. Joel carried on smoking, avoiding eye contact. Khoi touched Joel on the head as a sign of solidarity and left for the flat.

Upon arrival, Khoi searched for Julien but he wasn't home. Khoi felt the need to sleep, but he was afraid to do so, unwilling to confront his nightmares, yet he went to the guest room laid on the bed, looking at the ceiling till he fell asleep again.

As Khoi returned home with his troubled conscience, Paul had been waiting nervously for his encounter with Julien.

Three days had passed since Paul met Julien. Over that time, Paul used the break from business to get closer to Han. He was fond of her and was certainly keen on her... she made him happy. If only he could sum up the courage to show her that, the problem was, Paul wasn't too sure Han was interested in a relationship... and this was to be his first.

He was soon to find out what occurs in a relationship when he got a call from Julien asking for a meeting immediately.

At 9:57 in the morning, in an art café, Paul sat there waiting, sketching the old lady with her beagle watching her. The dog was longing for the scraps from her plate as she sat reading a newspaper and drinking her tea.

As he shaded in the colours of her fur coat, he didn't notice Julien pull the chair up in front of him. He looked up and smiled but got a cold "good morning" in response as Julien sat down.

The first thing Julien noticed was the sketch. "May I have a look?" he asked. Paul initially felt uncomfortable showing his work, but now he was cornered, he handed it over to Julien.

Julien flicked through the pages. Paul tried to make some sense of Julien's facial expressions. He l didn't like being judged in this way and began to regret handing his sketch pad over to him. Half way through, Julien remarked "this is good, bloody hell!" He looked up and asked "You did this?" Paul nodded. "Wow. Well done my friend. Ever thought of exhibiting?"

"Are you serious?" Paul could hardly believe his ears as Julien added

"Yeah. This could be what I need. I was going to reopen the gallery next week with two new up and coming artists, but one of them pulled out at the last minute... I could exhibit these. They are so... detailed." Julien gestured touching his chest. "You captured the character of the subject in your drawings. I am seriously impressed." Then he reached into his laptop case and brought out his card. "If you have any other drawings, bring them over, it would be great to see more of your work."

All this encouragement was rather uplifting adding to the luck he had with Han who seemed equally as interested in him. In his mind, Paul concluded that he would take up Julien on his offer.

Once Julien handed the pad back, his expression changed and so did the atmosphere. He gave Paul a stern look as Julien asked "Now, the reason I am here is to ask you what the fuck happened whilst I was away?"

"Sorry?" Paul was surprised by the abrupt change in tone. Julien sat back on his chair and pointed at him "Before I left, Khoi was fine, eccentric, but fine. Now he's a nervous wreck. Every night, without fail, he wakes up screaming covered in sweat. When I wake him, he starts to cry uncontrollably.

What worse is the steady rise in my energy bills; he keeps turning up the heating and when I ask why, he says nothing and that's been the norm. Each time I ask him what's up, he says nothing, acting all weird and cold."

"I know he took Stefan's death hard, but something has definitely spooked him and I want to know what it is, because I don't think this can persist. I need my sleep."

It was the first time he had ever been confronted about his business in a long time, his upbringing in state institutions where no one was interested, it seemed alien to him that here was someone whom, despite stating it was more for their own selfish interest, this was someone who genuinely cared about someone else.

Paul jostled between his loyalty to the gang and his responsibility to the wellbeing of an individual who deserved better than his lot in life.

A café was not the place to address such matters. Paul then asked "Could we go outside for a walk? There is a park nearby?" Julien rolled his eyes before he collected his things.

They walked to the park and once at the gate, Paul decided to take the side of loyalty and chose to lie. He explained that, during the New Year festivities, Khoi began to miss Stefan and before they knew it, he flipped out, ran away to his hotel room and that was where he found Khoi, whimpering. Julien was speechless for a moment as he tried to comprehend what he just heard asking "You mean Khoi just lost it and started crying and no one else went after him but you?" Paul's look was enough to confirm his words "What bastards."

"Please, please, don't let on that you know." Paul pleaded.

"No, don't worry."

Julien shut his eyes for a moment to consider what he needed to do. He then shook his head as he thanked Paul for being so kind. "No problem." Paul replied. Prior to their parting, Julien asked Paul if he could borrow his Pad. "You can have it."

"Thank you." And Julien left him in the park. As Julien left, he chided himself as he appeared more concerned with who Khoi may have met, rather than Khoi himself. It was time to focus.

Julien returned home to Khoi who was resting on the bed, exhausted from his third night of interrupted sleep. Each time he tried to sleep, he'd wake up within the hour screaming. Khoi was now officially afraid he was losing his sanity.

Khoi heard the front door open and shut. Some more movement below followed. Khoi deduced it was probably Julien, not that it mattered.

Khoi hugged the pillow tightly trying to block out the noise of the approaching footsteps and hoping it was not coming his way, but it was.

The door opened and in marched Julien. Julien followed the advice he was given and went to draw the curtains, allowing the last rays of the day to come in. Khoi hid his head under the pillow. Julien sat next to him and called his name. Khoi decided to sit up and pay some form of attention to Julien who still hadn't taken off his winter coat and was holding a small cup of water in his hand. "Are you feeling better?" Julien asked.

"Yes." Khoi lied, but shortly recanted "No, I'm not."

Julien gave him a smile as he reached into his pocket. He brought out a bottle of medication. "I spoke to my friend, he's a doctor. Here… there enough for a week. You take one every eight hours."

"Xanax?" Khoi remarked. "Is that it? You think I need drugs?"

"Yes! You haven't seen yourself in the last few days, you've been acting crazy! I saw Paul today"

"You met up with Paul?" Khoi interrupted "For what?"

"To talk about you!"

"Why the hell did you do that?" Khoi snarled

"Because I care and I am afraid you'll hurt yourself. He told me that you're missing Stefan and no matter how bad it is you need to get over it but you can't because you never talk to me, you never talk to anyone. So this is all we got." Julien said referring to the pills.

Khoi still looked unconvinced, but he appreciated the situation as getting serious. "It's only for 7 days and after that I promise no more, but you have to talk to me when you are ready. I promise I won't judge you, but you need to stop this, stop building this up. OK?" Khoi, embarrassed, nodded. Julien then offered him the cup of water "please take one."

Khoi opened the bottle, shook out a tablet and swallowed it before taking the cup of water and washing down the pill. Julien could see Khoi still required some encouragement. "Tell you what, I went to Tiffs and got you some of those pastries you like. We can have some ice-cream and stay in bed all day and perhaps tomorrow, if you have some time, you could help me with the exhibition."

"That would be nice." Khoi agreed with a grin.

As promised, they sat in bed, television on and all the treats on offer, but they hardly touched it. Khoi fell asleep due to the side effect of the drugs whilst Julien was just plain exhausted and equally fell asleep. Thanks to the pills, Khoi wasn't tormented and slept through out for the first time in several days.

# 19

*5 January 2011*

In Warsaw, Tom had just arrived at a mammoth sized grey building from the communist era, with a high door which was opened wide exposing an automatic revolving door. Tom hated such entrances. They often got jammed if one accidentally touched it or looked at it in a manner the automated item hated.

Tom took his chances and succeeded in entering the building where he beheld a grand lobby which could easily accommodate an army, but it was bare, nothing there other than a gigantic chandelier hanging overhead, the light shimmering on marble floor. At the end of the large lobby were eight steps leading to another pair of large wood and metal doors which were shut.

Tom looked around and found in the corner an empty counter with a small door behind it. Tom approached it, the stomping sound of his wooden heels touching the stone floor and echoed loudly, causing him to consider whether he should step more lightly.

Once at the desk with no one behind it, Tom found a bell. He felt that this oversized concrete temple of death was probably as dull and as lifeless as most it's occupants. Since it invited him to do the obvious, Tom pressed the bell and waited patiently, feeling slightly guilty for not just failing to say goodbye to Jan and the team, but also for leaving without returning Kat's scarf which he was still wearing.

He paced back and forward, where he deduced that it took approximately sixty six long strides and paces to make it from one end of the hall to the other and a minute to complete it. After fifteen minutes of noting, Tom decided to look for some form of directions or sign to aid him.

Tom finally discovered a large sign over a door. That was a start, but it was in Polish. Tom took a picture of the sign and sent it by text to his colleagues back in London requesting a translation since he couldn't be bothered to look for the special characters. A few minutes later, he received a reply. It read "Toilet."

Feeling irate, Tom was set to give a call to his team to ask them to address the situation when, finally, a slender looking middle aged woman emerged from behind the small door at the back of the counter. Tom walked quickly to the desk, pleased to have finally spotted someone.

The lady said some words in Polish, perhaps a greeting which he didn't understand since he didn't speak Polish.

He asked if the lady spoke Russian. "Only a little" she replied. Unwilling to wait any further, he brought out the printed email he had on his person and handed it to her. She skimmed through the text and proclaimed "Ah, Pawel Jurzcak!" she picked up her phone, made a call and after a few exchange of words, she hung up and said "Wait one minute please?" in a cautious manner.

Tom thanked her and carried on waiting. After 18 minutes, his legs began to hurt from all the standing and it didn't help that he was hungry. Why was this "Mr Pawel Jurzcak" taking such a considerable period of time? As a pathologist, his patients weren't going to complain if he left them for a few minutes, even if they had their rib cage opened.

Tom sighed deeply as he checked the time. His stomach growled in anticipation of sustenance. He reached into his pocket for the chocolate he purchased from the airport. His favourite, Ritter sport hazelnut chocolate.

Tom broke a square and placed it in his mouth, hoping it was enough. One was not enough when you were this famished. Tom proceeded to break five more squares. It turned out to be a case of his eyes being bigger than his stomach. Having stuffed the large chunks into his mouth, Tom tried to force his teeth down on the chocolate when a man emerged from behind the large metal and wood door that separated the public from the inner sanctum of the building.

A spritely, slim, silver haired gentleman in a three piece pin stripped suit and a large smile walked quickly to him and reached to shake his hand announcing "Hello, I am Pawel."

Pawel could not have picked a more inappropriate time to make an appearance. Tom had to gesture that he had something in his mouth which inhibited speech and begged for Pawel's patience.

Pawel's grin dissolved to a stern look. Tom could hardly believe the audacity of the man. If the change in appearance related to having to wait for a few minutes whilst he finished what he had in his mouth, then Pawel would have to just stick it, Tom thought as he carried on chewing. Once finished, he apologised and admitted "I was very hungry."

"Understandable. I am so sorry for keeping you waiting. I wasn't aware of your arrival. Once again I am so sorry."

"It's ok." Tom replied even though he was aggrieved by Pawel's lateness.

"May I offer you something to drink and some sandwiches?" Pawel suggested.

"That's very generous of you, but no thank you."

With the signal fully received, Pawel ushered Tom through the heavy doors revealing a hive of activity. "I hope you didn't find it hard to get here?" Pawel enquired, snapping Tom out of his distracted state. "Oh yes, it was straight forward. Heavens, it's rather busy today isn't it?" Tom observed people running around with files and some dressed in medical gowns and no one talking to one another. "It's been very busy this winter." Pawel confirmed. "Thanks to the extreme cold, the death rates have gone up. However, from what I heard, ours is not an isolated situation but, unlike your country where it's the old and infirm that fall victim to the cold, here it's alcoholics, over merry students, the homeless and farmers trying to save their livestock, or as we city people call the livestock, their girlfriends!" Pawel laughed at his own joke which Tom found a bit morbid to say the least. Then, considering Pawel's line of work, perhaps it was his way of coping with the situation. In line with that rationale, Tom laughed along even though it was forced.

They proceeded further down the long corridors flanked by offices and after a few turns, the number of people began to dwindle significantly. There was a smell of embalming fluid and other chemicals in the air which grew stronger as they went further into the bowels of the building till Tom could taste it. With the temperature steadily ebbing away, giving Tom a chill, they reached another heavy metal door with a large handle.

Pawel pushed it open and in the room was a table. On the table covered by a white sheet was a body. The sight of the dead did not faze Tom, yet something about entering the room to this view had butterflies reproducing in his gut. It was a strange mix of excitement, anticipation and unwillingness.

There was no point turning back and asking for photographic evidence now. Standing by the corpse, Pawel picked up the ends of the sheet and unveiled the catch, the discoloured body of a woman with swollen blue lips and her hair spread around her head like a flamboyant crown.

Tom could not fathom why, but he found himself utter the words in

Russian "Ti onchi krasivia"

"Yes, she is indeed beautiful." Pawel responded exposing his comprehension of the Russian language. "Is this the person you are looking for?"

"I'm not sure." Tom replied as he drew closer to inspect the body. The smell made him want to hurl, but it had to be done. Having not found what he was looking for, he asked Pawel "May I see behind her right ear please?" Pawel retrieved some latex gloves and slowly reached over to hold the head and turned it to the right and lifted the ear. There was nothing there. "Could I see the left?" Pawel obliged him. There was still nothing. Pawel returned the head to a central position, but Tom's curiosity wasn't stemmed. He went forward to look again and noticed something. "I know this may be a strange request, but could you get something to clean the skin behind the right ear? Like mentholated spirit or Turpentine?"

Using forceps to hold a ball of cotton wool soaked in chemicals; Pawel rubbed around the ear area for a moment and after a few seconds proclaimed "Oh, what have we here?" Pawel carried on rubbing till content. The paint thinner had removed a strong coat of skin coloured foundation which hid a tattoo of the number 6 behind the ear.

Tom exhaled, he was relieved but yet, his hand began to tremble. "It's her." Tom announced. Spurred on by curiosity, he asked "I know I could find out in the report, but can you tell me… what killed her?" Pawel pulled the sheet lower, revealing her naked torso. He called Tom to come around to the left side of the body where he raised her left arm and placed it across her before pointing to the middle part of her torso. Six inches beneath her breast, were two puncture wounds which brought her to this place. "It was a snake. The police found it a few metres from her body, frozen to death."

Tom's stomach began to ache as he stood there puzzled. He should have felt content, he should have derived some sweet pleasure from seeing Jelena's lifeless body spread on the table and delighted in the delicious irony of it all, the bite of a cold blooded killer ending the life of another, but there wasn't any of that. No "hurray! She's gone." None of that seemed appropriate. At that very moment, Tom didn't know what to feel or how to accept this.

Tom was suffering from an age old malady which had afflicted many who had triumphed. From conquering generals, to politicians and many others who had to face adversity at the hand of one particular foe. It was the affliction which arose when a goal had been achieved at a great cost or via a stroke of luck, the emptiness that followed the vanquishing of a nagging foe. Yet his was doubled as he had played no part in her demise nor did he get the opportunity to bring her to justice, what compounded things further was the fact that the bitch was right. He never did see her again alive.

Tom wondered how, if there was one, God would judge her? Most of the people she targeted did deserve to go. It was then Tom remembered receiving a call from his French counterpart on the Maundy Thursday of the previous year, where the Frenchman complained not about the fact that three Russian agents had been found dead on a boat outside Nice, rather, he protested that Jelena clearly had no limits. "The woman is plain evil!" Protested the Gaelic inspector as he informed him that Jelena had been seen leaving a church looking and walking normally having been the only one of the congregation who had not partaken in the holy Eucharist and thus did not drink the communion wine which she had spiked with a large dose of LSD. This had caused a 93 year old woman to declare herself Joan of Arc with the intent of saving France from itself and also saw the choir boy ride the procession cross which was placed on the staff, up and down the knave like a stick horse.

What would happen to Jelena now? Would God have a sense of humour and let her in? Or would the devil have a contender for his spot in hell, and if it every came to blows, Tom knew where he would put his money. It was most unlikely Satan would be able to handle her.

Tom didn't know if it was the way she died or the fact that she was dead that stirred up the emotions that clobbered his soul. Despite how hard he tried to prevent his urges from overriding his common sense, Tom actually felt sad.

Tom remembered the moment when their paths finally crossed. He remembered lying on the hospital bed in his private room, his head hurting as per usual. They definitely picked a bad time to take him off the morphine. Having endured the tumour for the last seven months, he had been promised that the surgery to remove the non-cancerous growth and that could probably alleviate his condition or at worse kill him. Either way, it would bring this constant pain that blurred his vision, caused him to have fits, affected his balance and slurred his speech to an end. Whatever the outcome, he was just fed up.

Tom had had enough of having his blood pressure taken, his blood tested, his heart rate monitored and more. He just wanted it over and done with so he could get back to his life and find out what happened to Darren. It had been a week since they heard from Darren. Darren went to Portugal in his place and never returned.

Besides being worried about his colleague, Tom was bored and frightened. His family had come to visit as well as his ex-wife and son. All his son did was cry constantly, upset on seeing his father unable to play with him and that hurt. All these thoughts were driving him to distraction and he welcomed the entry of the doctor and the geeky looking nurse who pushed in a trolley in her large glasses and blonde hair.

It was time to get him ready for the operation. The doctor explained that the nurse was there to shave off his already short hair. Glancing at the nurse the doctor noticed her pretty face was one he hadn't seen around the wards. Looking at the name badge, the doctor said "Nurse Hillary? Are you new?" The nurse replied politely "Yes doctor, I only started last week." Thinking nothing of it, the doctor proceeded in handing down the necessary instructions which was to prep the patient for surgery by shaving off his hair. Once bald, Tom was to be taken straight to the theatre to have his skull opened.

Tom wasn't paying attention to the doctor's attempt to assure him that all would be fine; he was distracted by the tall stunning nurse who just smiled at him. There was an air of familiarity about her, as though he knew her even though he accepted that they had never met.

Having completed his speech, the doctor left the tall, elegant looking nurse with her hair tied back, to perform her task. Their eyes met, the nurse knew she was being observed, yet seemed to brush off the gazing eyes as she went about her business. She picked up a syringe from the kidney dish, removed the protection cap, and flicked the syringe before pressing the pump, releasing some of the liquid it held from the mouth of the needle all without saying a word.

Tom began to doubt her bed side manner. He expected some words of comfort, but there wasn't any emerging from her lips as she inserted the needle into the peripheral venous catheter on the back of his right hand. As she pressed on the pump, forcing the tranquilliser into his system, he could feel the fluid rushing in. She took her time and did it attentively till the entire content of the syringe was emptied.

Then followed the annoyance of waiting for the drug to take some effect. The nurse stood there at the corner of the bed watching him as he watched her observe the effects of the drugs. It was slow progress but after seventeen minutes, Tom could no longer fight it. His eyelids, like his limbs where heavy. He began to giggle and there was a building sense of uncontrollable euphoria.

Wishing he could feel like this every day without the limp limbs, Tom could only remark "Oh my, this is bloody good."

"Amazing what medical science can do these days." Remarked the nurse.

"I have yet to find out." Tom said in an attempt to be sarcastic.

"Yes it is. That's why you swore Tom." Said the nurse in Russian. "Don't worry, you are in safe hands."

Normally, Tom would have reacted quickly, but he could barely remember where he was, yet Tom managed to respond in Russian "How do you know I speak Russian?"

"Oh, I know a lot about you my purple eyed monster and you know a lot about me. We just never met, till now." She replied as she went to the trolley to take a large bib which she placed around his neck. Then she returned to the trolley to retrieve a spray bottle and the kidney dish holding a razor. She sprayed some water on his head and pulled the razor out from it's case. Tom was frightened even though all he could do was smile. He didn't know why, but he sensed he had a lot to fear about this woman.

The first movement of the blade and some of his hair came off. The nurse continued speaking "You know I was disappointed that we didn't meet in Lisbon. You sent that silly Darren who stuck out like a sore thumb. Still, it is nice to finally meet you in person after all these years, despite the circumstances. We're practically family."

Then it clicked "Je... Jelena?" Tom called

"The one and the same." She confirmed, moving his left ear to reach the hair around the area, her bosom grazing his nose allowing Tom to have a close look at her as she added "Darren was a nice guy though."

"Yeah, he is a great person. Did you say was? So... so where is he?" The drug was clearly taking a greater grip on him as he struggled to stay awake.

Jelena cleaned the blade and carried on shaving "The last time I caught sight of him, he was on his way to Brazil."

"You witch… so you came to kill me too? You… you better kill me… or I'll come after you."

Tom's question stopped her in her in the process of shaving the back of his head. Jelena looked him straight in the eye and asked "Kill you? Where would the fun be in that?"

She could feel his heart racing, sensing his need to try and apprehend her but he was thwarted by his lack of mobility. This spurred on the philosophical side of Jelena. "We are both alike aren't we? We both have a self-destructive thing about us. Fate brought us together to show us that."

Tom tried his hardest to stay attentive and in his woozy state parried "You… you don't know anything about me…"

"That's where you are wrong." She said having finished shaving the left side of his head and proceeding to take on the right. "You, Thomas Evans are a broken man, brought down by self-doubt. That's what ruined your marriage. You don't trust anyone, not even yourself, let alone your wife. Behind all this bravado is a man who lacks confidence, unable to stand by the decisions he makes… just a follower, you're not your own person."

"So your wife left you because you lacked a backbone and now you see your life as being in the gutter, a failed marriage, failed at achieving your goals and now you are looking for success to make your life seem worthwhile and redeemable, to prove to yourself that it wasn't a total waste after all. And now, battle scarred, you see yourself as uninteresting, not worth knowing. But it's a lie, the problem is you believe those lies because you think that way, you anticipate that no one would be interested in a failure like you."

"Now you're are stuck in this cycle, this self-degrading mind set which has turned you cold to your friends, your wife, your son and to the world to ensure that nothing disturbs your obsession with achieving one goal, trying to find the opportunity to prove everyone wrong. And I am that opportunity. Catching me would show them wouldn't it?"

Jelena's words were all true. To Tom, it was like being stripped naked before the public with Jelena directing the audience to marvel at all his imperfections. The euphoria brought by the medication was long gone, but the effects on his body persisted. He could no longer speak or move, but he could still blink and feel. Tears began to fall from side of his eyes as Jelena finished. She touched a falling drop of tear and tasted it as she mockingly asked "Is that why you weep? It's silly to cry over something within your control. Granted, at the moment, you can't move or speak… but what's the difference? You never speak your mind anyway; you believe everything you have to say about yourself is worthless or not fit for people's attention.

Have you ever wondered if you have lost your path in life or do you honestly believe that if you catch me, you will be able to find your way back to normality and find a way to continue?" Jelena used a damp cloth to wipe Tom's bald scalp before removing the bib adding "Do you honestly think your tattered life will mystically mend if you caught me? Is that why you have been after me for the last three years? Hoping it would make everything all better. At the risk of sounding like an old western, you'll never catch me alive and even if you did what then?" She got him and she knew it.

Jelena giggled as she stroked Tom's face. Even his vision was failing him now, her touch made his skin crawl, but what could he do? Tom considered whether it was possible that Jelena could read his mind when she concluded "Don't worry, like I said, I didn't come to kill you. I never take advantage of the sick and the dying, even those who are dying inside." Jelena gave him a kiss on the lips before she collected the implements and placed them on the trolley. "I'll get you some roses. Do get well soon. Life is more fun when you are on the run."

Her final words rendered, Jelena pressed the call button to announce that the patient was ready for surgery and then she left the room, vanishing amongst the staff and into obscurity. The unexpected meeting left Tom to wonder if it would have been better if she killed him now that his life was exposed in such a graphic manner whilst in his most vulnerable state. He would have done it himself, if he had the strength, now all he could hope for was that the surgeon to make a mistake.

Regardless, Tom vowed that if he did recover, things would change for the better, he'll even show more compassion to criminals if he could, but he also promised that he would certainly get Jelena.

Tom stopped his walk through the past to focus on the present. There she was, he got what he wanted but now she was dead and again, she proved herself right, he didn't get her alive. Unbeknown to Tom, a tear that had formed and trickled down his face fell to the ground as he moaned out loud "Oh Jelena."

This outburst of grief prompted Pawel to enquire "Were you close?"

This was an awkward question, yet he found himself responding "Yes, we were."

"I am sorry for your loss."

Tom laughed as he cleared away another tear. "Don't be." he fought to take his eyes off her. He had one last act to perform. Tom reached for the rose attached to his lapel and placed it next to Jelena's head. His heart was confused and raced again.

Finally, Tom began to focus on the future. He finally owned up to his obsession regarding Jelena, was hunting this woman worthwhile? Why did it drive away other pursuits like the family life he once hoped and prayed for in the past?

Feeling sympathetic and having watched Tom stand vigil near five minutes Pawel offered "Would you like to be alone?"

"Perish the thought. If I had had a moment with her in the first place, she wouldn't be here." Tom added as he finally composed himself allowing his professionalism to take back control. "Do you have a certified translated copy of the pathology report?"

"It's being finalised and should be with you in twenty four hours." Pawel assured.

"Good." Tom concluded. He could not take another minute in the presence of Jelena. His nose was running slightly, so he reached for a tissue to clear it before taking a deep breath of chemical infused air, shutting his eyes and reflected on how stupid it must seem to weep over a stranger who deserved what she got in the end. Once he opened them again, Tom seemed to have regained his resolve. "Thank you so much for your help. I will be in the consulate waiting for the report. Please let me know if you find out anything."

Tom shook Pawel's hand and made his way out. As Tom turned, he realized that the trip to the exit would symbolize the end to his frenzied search. This crazed manhunt had kept his life in a vice. He turned his head slowly to look at the person who nearly cost him his sanity, his family, his only source of warmth and love. Death claimed Jelena, as her maniacal life had caught up with her. Tom realized that Jelena didn't look so daunting; to him her death, as well as her life, were both meaningless. He sacrificed so much for so little. As Tom reached for the door handle, he was filled with regret and questioned the righteousness of his deeds. What now?

Tom exited the mortuary and was confronted by the words that the local graffiti artists had tagged on the building opposite to the mortuary, as an act of defiance. Some were in English, but most didn't make sense. However, one word stuck out of the unimaginative clutter "Sophrosyne". Tom left the area pondering what it meant. Then he found himself laughing, he finally got it. He remarked to himself "A snake, how cool." as he walked to the nearest street to hail a taxi.

At the consulate, Tom spent his time sitting in the office provided to him watching his phone. He knew it was stupid, but he was really reluctant to call London to inform them of his finding. Tom took a deep breath, and held his head, it began to hurt and he wondered if divulging the information would be the solution or only make things worse, but there was only one way to find out.

Using the secure line, he rang his office and passed on the news. The Superintendent seemed unmoved as she replied "Oh. I guess that's good. Better inform your team and drag to… where are you again?"

"Poland" Tom confirmed

"Yes. The job isn't done yet. We still need to identify her clients… just because she avoided justice, doesn't mean they should. Do you need anything?" She asked

"No Mam"

"Very good. Enjoy your time in Warsaw."

Despite being given his orders, he didn't think being commanded to do so would enable him to enjoy his time in the city; he simply didn't have the will. As required, a call was made to Berlin and tickets and hotel rooms for the next day were booked via the British diplomatic representatives. Tom wasn't planning to spend more than a day in Poland, now it was to be extended. Hence he had to ask his colleagues to aid him by bringing his belongings to Poland.

The people at the embassy were gracious enough to take him out for a meal, which he played with rather than ate, and then they drove him to his hotel.

Tom had a bed, but could not find any sleep. He was kept awake by the rhetorical questions that ran through his mind. There was one that gnawed on his soul. Having reviewed the last time he ever saw her, he knew if he had made an effort, a concrete effort, rather than paying attention to the needs of Caroline and her mental state, he could have been able to go in some way to find her and perhaps apprehend her and bring her to justice and none of this would have happened and his mind would have been at rest.

Now he lingered in the torture chamber of the castle of "what if". He was too tired to cry, but to trouble to sleep. He longed for some company, but he wasn't sure it was right to call Caroline on the matter.

Accepting his fate, Tom spent the whole evening wondering how she died. The report stated she was found on the ground in the middle of a snow covered field. She had been placed there by very intelligent individuals who dragged their feet as they walked to ensure no foot print indented the snow. Rather, a trail was made like those of the wheels of a train from where they left Jelena to the vehicle that brought them.

There were tire tracks, yet, annoyingly enough, they came from four different tire companies and that's where the Polish police left it.

Tom now had a reason to stay awake. He had the tire numbers. Hence he looked through the available database trawling through the information available only to find out five hours later that each tire was sold in four different countries and each had been reported stolen over the past weeks. "Foiled again!" Tom screamed, having stayed awake till 6 in the morning only to find he could not finalise the information on his own. He had to wait an additional 4 hours for his team's arrival and now that he knew he couldn't get any information, fatigue did begin to creep in. Tom walked to his bed, took off all his clothes and went to sleep in the hope that the short slumber would bring him a clearer frame of mind.

*6 January 2011*

Morning broke. It was beautiful bright day that failed to deliver the clarity Tom sought. Tom took the moment to call his son, a voice he hadn't heard in over a week. The boy's giggle and the childishness revived him and kept him going till it was time to work.

At noon, with his colleague in the same hotel and having been so kind enough as to have brought his belongings, he set about taking a shower and making his way to the new outpost of the London Metropolitan police in the basement of the British Consulate Warsaw.

The two small rooms, one for police work and the other kitted out for the forensics team were where they were meant to work amongst the smell of damp walls and moulding files. It was bitterly cold and even the staff felt it. Hastily they raced to provide the team with electric heaters which, though warming the air made it dry.

Accepting the happy medium was never to be found, they set to work collecting information from the belongings delivered by the local police. This was only after Tom had to fill in a 20 page form all in Polish.

The coroner's report was extensive and detailed, listing the bruises and cracked ribs which was evidence that she may have had some impact, most likely a car accident. It provided a narrative of her potential last moments and even cited the level of toxins in Jelena's blood. In sharp contrast, the police report was slim and lacked information. It simply read "Lady found in field dead after snake bite." According to the police, she made her way to the field in search of help.

The team from forensics rummaged through Jelena's belongings whilst Tom read the pathology report again. Two things stuck out there were bits of glass found in the tips of her thumb and pointing finger and what's more, it wasn't pressed in, it appeared to have entered the skin in an angle. The other thing was the scarf she wore. It looked familiar, but he couldn't pinpoint where he had seen it.

The lack of sleep made Tom's head hurt. He had enough of the reading and decided to find out what the forensics team had discovered from Jelena's belongings which the Polish police handed over to them.

The first was looking through Jelena's bag. Amongst the items spread out on the table were gloves, two tampons, a bank card and fake identity card which had Tom as the next of kin written on its back. There was also a St Christopher's pendant and a Gucci mechanical wrist watch which, upon seeing it, caused Tom to shudder. He saw that watch in the pictures of the body taken by the Polish police. Excusing himself, Tom quickly went to review the pictures again, using a magnifying glass to detect the time on the face of the time piece. It said 9:23 as it did now. Tom assumed the watch wasn't working.

Tom requested for a pair of latex gloves allowing him to handle the evidence. It wasn't battery operated, so it was fair to deduce it had to be wound to start it working. Tom tried to get the mechanics working by a couple of twists of the knob to see if the hands would move, but they didn't. The watch was a dud. Tom decided not to mention this discovery; rather he put it back down on the table.

Tom then proceeded to the next table where the clothes were to be examined. He was pleased to hear that a few strands of hair had been found that did not match her on the shoulder of her coat and a couple on her gloves and the scarf.

Tom inspected Jelena's choice of wear and something seemed out of place. Everything on the table was very expensive and made by the finest fashion houses in Paris, so what was this simple, unbranded knitted scarf doing amongst all this finery?

Tom picked up the scarf and looked carefully at it. It was well woven using a specific pattern and style, made from royal blue yarn.

The neck warmer held a familiar spell over him. He turned to his one of the officers "Sean?" He called, "could you please dawn a pair of gloves and pick up my scarf from the coat rack?" The junior officer was hesitant by the request till Tom added "Today?"

Sean did as he was told, fetched the item and presented it to Tom, who didn't wish to touch it, rather, he picked up the scarf worn by Jelena and looked at the one in Sean's hand. "Tell me... are these the same colour?" Giving a brisk look Sean confirmed they were. Tom then examined Jelena's scarf in search of a tag and failed to find one. "Could you check if my scarf has or had a label?" Sean examined it briskly and replied "Not really, I don't assume there would be. They're hand made." Tom's ear's perked up. He pressed Sean to explain how he could be so certain. "My grandmother knits me a scarf every year; it's always the same finish at the end the extra stitching. See?" He said, raising the end.

"Does this one have it as well?" Sean squinted and said pointing to the base. "Yeah. See?" directing Tom's view using his little finger.

Tom sixth sense was giving him a stomach ache, but he needed to follow it. "Sean, could you carefully bag my scarf for me and I will sort this one out. I want you to send it back to London and ask them to urgently look for any DNA that could be on them."

"Sure." Sean replied before Tom snapped "And don't take any crap saying that it'll take two weeks. I want it back in one week at the latest...." Tom's orders were interrupted when his phone rang.

Assuming it was London, Tom raced to the room next door to answer the call. He ran his thumb against the touch screen without taking the time to review the number as he spoke "ASI Evans." Then a voice came on he recognised and said "Hello Tom, how have you been?" The caller was Jan. The sound of a familiar voice allowed him to relax. "Hey Jan," Tom cried "How are you? So sorry for not being in touch of late."

"Seems like you've been busy. I understand. I just wanted to know if you had an update on our late lady?" Tom explained that he had nothing as of yet but would get back to him, yet he vowed to contact him if he had anything.

It was as Jan passed on Kat's greetings that scales fell from his eyes. He decided to make an unorthodox request encasing it in a courtesy. "That's ever so nice of her. I should call her. What's her number again?"

"Oh, she would like that." Jan replied as he passed on her number. With the number in hand, Tom hung up and returned to the forensics room and asked if he could take the watch with him. The team agreed to, provided he gave them a DNA sample in order to eliminate him from the list of suspects. Finally, Tom handed over his keys and granted Sean permission to go through his belongings to find the bottle of champagne he had been given days earlier asking it be given the same treatment as the scarves.

Tom's aim was to find out if what he had in his hands was indeed a watch without having to smash it. He took a taxi ride to the British Embassy where they had an airport style x-ray machine.

Tom requested if was possible to use their appliance. The item went through the scanner and the picture came on the screen. The watch didn't have the usual mechanics within them; rather, it contained a rectangular shaped object, like a chip.

Now he had no choice but to open it. A small screw driver was provided to him. With this, Tom forced the back off the watch. Tom's hunch was right. It wasn't a watch after all; it contained a small USB storage device.

Tom was in his element. Convinced that he had something of value in hand, he raced back to the consulate, his morale high and barely able to contain his excitement as he evicted his assistant in order to be alone with his laptop, into which he inserted the data storage unit into the device.

His computer detected the presence of a drive and asked if Tom wanted to open it. He wondered why the computer needed to ask. He clicked it open and found a folder that held a video file labelled "EnD" that was 1.09gb in size.

Tom knew he was on the verge of something big and with two left clicks of his mouse, the video file opened. It started with Jelena sitting before the camera over a wooden table with a smirk on her face that Tom wished he could slap right off. "Hello Purple" Jelena began from the grave.

It was almost a reflex reaction that caused Tom to reply "Hello Witch" before realising he had greeted a non-interactive movie.

Tom rolled his eyes as the video carried on. "Well Purple, if it is indeed you, but I am 100% sure it is. I thought I would leave you this before I left." She then giggled as though she found the prospect of death an amusement. "Remember I told you that you owed me a favour? I have come to collect by giving you some information that could aid your investigations, but you will need to go and get it in person from my lawyers."

"You have a lawyer?" Tom remarked in astonishment

"I know what you are thinking, and yes, I do have lawyers." Jelena replied, exposing how predictable Tom had become. "The law firm is called Jovanovic & Dobik. They are situated at 26 Vladimira Popovica, just down the road from the Crown Plaza hotel where there is a room booked for you for a month's stay. All you need to do is show up. At the Law firm, you need to ask for Biljana Dobik. She is expecting you and she won't release anything to anyone other than you. There you will find what can most certainly help you. It'll be no use to me now." Jelena slowly began to look glum as she proceeded "If it hasn't been stolen, please find my St Christopher's medal and take it with you.

Thank you Purple, You are a true gentleman and brilliant person.

Don't miss me." Jelena was finished. She reached across to fiddle with the camera, blurring the vision of her face, eventually putting an end to the recording.

Tom sat there, furious at the message left behind. Then there was a knock on the door. He called the person in and found it was his colleague. "We could hear the recording from the next room." She began. "Sorry, but who is "Purple"?"

"Me." Tom admitted as he got off his chair and paced about a bit to calm his spirits. It didn't work. "This just stinks!" He cried rubbing his brow. "She thinks she can just play around with people?" when finally asked whether or not he was going to take Jelena's quest seriously, trying to avoid eluding his misgivings that it could all be a trap, Tom threw his hands up in the air and proclaimed "We'll never know will we? I guess I have to go to Serbia."

Tom returned to the hotel quite late and he had to go through the paper work of filling out forms regarding the body and the belongings which were to remain in Poland till he gave the word.

He nevertheless took one item with him from Jelena's belongings in addition to the chain Jelena told him to carry. Tom opened his bag to extract and examine the scarf it held once again. Why did it call to him? And why was his hand shaking and feeling cold?

Tom had a scare, he remembered the first signs of the growth in his brain, and they were quite similar. He didn't need this right now, an additional problem to add to his many woes including an ever growing feeling of melancholia he couldn't shake off and even though it wasn't a long term solution, Tom decided to seek company from the bottom off a bottle. However where was he to find spirits at thirteen minutes before midnight? He rang the reception and was soon reminded that he wasn't in England and he could get himself whatever he fancied if he just walked up the street to the nearest off-licence.

This was pleasing to the ear and without hesitation Tom took the short trip to retrieve his panacea of choice, Vodka. Initially, Tom tried to pace himself, but seated in his hotel room on his own left him haunted with his thoughts and taunts of guilt. He had lost count on the number of times he had read and reread Jelena's passing words, each time feeling her watch, subconsciously wishing he were closer to her.

Tom knew what the right thing to do was, but yet he found it stomach churning. He knew he was being played, but he couldn't help falling for it. Tom needed support, a sharp slap to tell him to get real.

The vodka didn't help, all he got was more confusion wrapped in a cloak of tipsiness and the ever growing need to vomit. The only thing greater was the urge to review Jelena's words for the thirty-third time but this time, it made him rather emotional. He couldn't determine what he felt; it was an uncomfortable cross between anger, loathing, guilt and sympathy.

Tom finally accepted he couldn't continue without assistance. He took his mobile and sent out a message that read "Are you awake?" to the only person who told him what they thought. Tom was getting agitated. He shook impatiently, needing another shot of vodka. He was fighting the march of nausea or alcohol poisoning but he couldn't take his eyes off the screen in anticipation for a response. It came four minutes later; Caroline replied "I am now."

Looking at the time, he realised it was already three in the morning. Tom got an added dose of embarrassment and responded with the words "Sorry for waking you up. Let's talk later." But before he could press the send button, Caroline called him.

Tom answered all apologetic "I am so sorry."

"It's okay; it's not the first time I had to talk to you at one in the morning. What's eating you?" She asked. Tom sighed and wondered if it was wise to reveal all to Caroline, but he couldn't take it any longer, again he repeated "I'm sorry."

Brushing it off, Caroline said "We've past that dear. What's up?"

Tom sighed as he replied "I'm in Poland … Jelena is dead."

There was a pause. One would have thought that this would have been an excuse for a rapturous spontaneous rejoicing, it would have been justified, but rather than celebrating, Tom was left speechless by Caroline's response. "I'm sorry to hear that." She began "Are you OK?"

"Yeah, I'm fine. A little drunk though… okay, very drunk." Tom confessed. Caroline asked if he was celebrating, Tom replied "I wish. The cow continued her mind games to the very end! She named me as her next of kin, can you believe that? That's why I am here. I had to come to bloody Poland to come and identify her body. And if that wasn't bad enough, she decided to leave behind a "tell all" exposé video where she kind of excised her demons. In the end, all she said was she did it for her son! Can you believe it? She even asked me to help organise her funeral…"

"She has a son?" Caroline sounded shocked by the revelation. Tom wondered why she homed in on that fact. "Does he know?" Caroline enquired.

"I don't think so…" but before he could finish his statement Caroline cut in and asserted "You have to tell him. You have to find him and tell him." Tom instantly sobered up and wondered if Caroline was insane. "Tom? Are you there?" she called.

"Yeah, I am… are you alright?" Then he whined "This is crazy. Why should I go find the kid of a criminal? He'd be better off not knowing. Tell me why I should even consider helping her?"

"It's not for her Tom, it's for you. You need to do this." Caroline highlighted.

Tom nearly voided his bowels when Caroline smites him with the truth. He wanted to ask why he needed it, but didn't want to face reality anymore. Tom was forced to admit "I hate it when you are right."

"But you love me because I'm honest." Caroline's sassiness made him laugh. Then she continued "listen, could you do me a favour? When you have everything organised, will you let me know?"

Jokingly, Tom asked "Why? You want to come?" Again, his heart was put through his paces as it skipped a beat when Caroline confirmed "Yes. You're not the only one who cares for others… even if it's not always reciprocal." Whether or not she knew, Caroline had inevitably detonated the bomb of guilt and Tom had been hit again by all its shrapnel. Yet, he felt reassured that he would have someone to stand by him "I'd Love to have you there… thanks again."

"Yeah. I'm going to bed and you are going to stop drinking. Good night Tom and remember, let me know."

"I will." Tom wanted to say how he felt, but before he could thank her, she already hung up. It was clearly time to go to bed, but first he needed the toilet to vomit.

# 20

*8 January 2011*

Tom stood in the airport. He was tired and absently stared at the rain soaked runway while his mind went through the last 24 hours. The vodka and the conversation with Caroline still had a grip on him when his telephone woke him up after only 3 hours of sleep, especially the vodka. His presence was required at the police station and judging by the tone of the police commissioner it was better sooner than later.

He rushed dutifully there with his mind filled with the melancholic numbness of a drunk, a skull-splitting headache and alcohol sweating from every pore only to find heaps of paperwork waiting for him. They really wanted him, correction, Jelena, out of the country.

Arriving at the station he went to the office to be met by a broad smile. "So, Serbia." said the police commissioner matter-of-factly. "We've arranged a flight for tomorrow morning. The Serbian authorities require you or one of your colleagues to escort the body and take care of business as soon as you arrive. I don't really care about that. I just want you and that body on that plane when it leaves." Tom asked for a glass of water and sat down by the desk.

After half a day of signing papers, double-checking, keeping his team at it and making phone calls in and out of the country being kept alive only by coffee and Ritter Sport, he went almost unwillingly back to the formaldehyde-drenched warehouse of human bodies. Dr. Pawel greeted him as soon as he came through the doors. "I've been waiting all day!" the annoying doctor said impatiently relaying his frustration on to Tom. Tom appreciated the irony but he could sense the good doctor had been leaned upon.

They went to the same fridge as 2 days before. "Here she is, your…krasavitsa." he said almost mockingly so. She was still beautiful and for a moment Tom forgot about his headache. "Sign here and here, the forensic report has been sent to the consulate, here's an extra copy for you, we'll have her transported directly to your flight tomorrow morning". Tom's headache was back worse than ever. Massaging his right temple Tom asked, knowing the doctor really didn't have a say in this, "Would you mind if I had my team come over to study her…the body?"

"Suit yourself!" the doctor answered carelessly "It's being transported tomorrow by 8; I want you out by 7. There will be a night guard, but that's it. I will be enjoying my wife with a glass of wine and my cell phone off." Tom looked at the thin, grey doctor. "Just…clean up after yourselves!" the doctor said terminating their conversation and rushing out of the chilling room leaving Tom alone with Jelena.

Half an hour later the room was filled with a handful of his people professionally chatting away in their own language, not really minding Tom nor the morbid nature of their work. Tom had to step out of the room. He found a couch in the waiting area and situated his corpus horizontally without ever closing his eyes or really finding comfort. He didn't care. His headache had been replaced by a growing feeling of loss. Almost like sorrow. Heck, it was sorrow. "Fuck" he muttered almost inaudibly to himself. At 3 am his team was done and after being shown the fridge was clean he went back to the hotel where he hoped he could get some sleep, but he didn't.

Now he was leaving Poland with a cargo that was being carried in a white heavy casket carried by six men who seemed to labour under the weight. Tom didn't know if it was due to the moisture of the rain on the steel handle that caused it, but the man at the right end appeared to lose his grip, causing the casket to fall on the ground with a loud clank.

The men laughed before continuing, only to be stopped by a person who was running around to get the paper work signed and the hull opened. The men charged with ferrying the body appeared bored. A pair of them sat on the coffin whilst another rested his foot on the box as he lit his cigarette offering another a stick.

This lack of respect for the dead was deplorable in Tom's eyes, but there was little he could do about the manhandling other than watch as the men were finally given the O.K to transport the body.

It was almost 10 and Tom was snapped out of his staring contest with the rainy, grey environment by Sean's hand landing on his shoulder. He turned around and looked Sean right in the eyes. "Yes?" he said with all the formality he could muster. Sean quickly put his hand down. "Sir, we…I hope you have a pleasant flight, we're heading back now."

"Thank you for your effort, Sean, I'll see you back home." Sean extended his right hand and as Tom extended his he felt a slight but otherwise unnoticeable tremor. Putting it aside he grabbed Sean's hand. His grip was slightly weaker than usual and his hand seemed to be suffering from involuntary spasms and this Sean clearly noticed.

"Sir?" Sean said, inquiringly.

"Have a nice flight." Tom said and turned around. The thoughts of Jelena evaporated. Emptiness filled him and from an almost instantaneous unfathomable solitude, one thought emerged: "It's back."

The flight to Belgrade's Nikola Tesla Airport was smooth and not eventful, but it didn't stem the growing sense of monotony that could only be appreciated by someone who is constantly on the move, just like Tom whom, as he walked towards immigration, began to acknowledge that there was an element of truth in the statement that all airports and hotels start to look the same the more you frequent them.

Handing over his passport to one of the immigration officer behind the counter, the official took one look at the picture and then at him. The officer squinted and said in English "One moment please." He then got off his seat and left his cubical taking Tom's travel documents with him.

Tom didn't want to turn around.

As the minutes passed, He could feel the eyes of his fellow travellers waiting to be seen tearing into him for causing a delay, even if it wasn't of his own making. It took seven minutes before the officer returned. Then, out from the door on the side of the wall came a police officer. Tom observed he was holding a British passport in his hand. Tom assumed it was his and wondered what was next.

The man's stone face turned into a smile as he reached Tom. "Hello Mr Evans. I am Zoran Antic. Please come with me." Tom obeyed and followed Zoran into the office where there was a desk and three chairs and a lady seated wearing a formal police wear with her cap resting on the table.

She rose to her feet with her face grinning from ear to ear. "Hello Mr Evans, or shall I call you sir?" she reached out to shake his hand saying in English "I am Sargent Danijela Leko. Everyone calls me Dani. Welcome to Serbia and although it's a day late, I would like to wish you Merry Christmas"

"Thank you. Pleasure meeting you Dani, you can call me Tom. For a moment there, I thought I was in trouble…"

"Sorry about that. We thought it would be best to keep things stealthy in accordance with the instructions sent from London." Dani then rose, picked up her cap and announced "If you come with me, we have a car waiting for us."

Tom was flattered to be in the care of someone so charming. There was the usual chit chat as they made their way to the car, but Tom was more interested in the instructions Dani had received.

Tom was impressed that his luggage has already been brought to the car, but before he could carry on, Tom asked what had become of Jelena's body. "Don't worry sir. It will be transported to a mortuary awaiting your instructions. By the way, we have circulated the information about Jelena and gathered a few of the people we think are linked to her and will proceed with the necessary questioning."

Tom felt he could trust this gentle looking lady, a reminder to Tom that not all Serbian women were like Jelena. Having entered the car, Dani drove away from the airport. Passing by the parked planes, Tom asked what she was told to do with him. Dani informed him that she was meant to take him first to the Embassy and then to anywhere he wanted. This was his expedition and Tom was in no mood for set plans and promptly requested if there could be some deviations, he was pleased to hear that it was not a problem. Immediately Tom provided Dani with the address for the law firm "Jovanovic & Dobik" on Vladimira Popovica.

Dani knew the company; it was a law firm by name alone. She stated that it was a firm that specialised in conveyancing; wills and probate with a list of clients who were as exclusive as one could get in this corner of the world.

Tom didn't need to plead for the detour. As they approached the law firm, Tom passed the Crown Plaza hotel, just as Jelena had said. Eventually they reached a tall monument of metal and glass called Ušće Tower, the top of the building poking its head way above the other structures that surrounded it.

Tom and Dani ventured on to the 23rd floor where the reception area for the law firm was located. "Perhaps we should have called first to check if the lawyers were in." Dani suggested.

"We're here now." Tom replied as the lift door opened presenting them with a temple of white and green modernistic furniture. Even the two receptionists stationed at the desk wore the matching colours befitting of the decor.

Tom and Dani went to the desk. The woman who welcomed them in Serbian had bleached not only her hair but her teeth as well. Dani was kind enough to ask if the woman spoke any English, she replied "a little". Not willing to risk anything being lost in translation, Tom asked Dani to act as the translator. He asked for Biljana Dobik. The receptionist appeared reluctant to call one of the partners particularly when the person requesting her presence didn't have an appointment.

When Biljana's secretary was informed that a "Mr Tim Evans" was here to see her, the receptionist relayed the message that it would best if they booked an appointment. Dani decided to step in "Tell her Sargent Leko from the Police is here to see her as well."

Tom added "Tell her "Purple" is here."

The receptionist didn't mask the fact that she thought it was an odd name, yet she told the secretary that the police and someone called "Purple" had come to pay Biljana a visit. Perhaps it was the police being mentioned that drew an automatic reply, but rather than being allowed to go and meet the lawyer, the receptionist informed them that Biljana was on her way.

Tom and Dani were offered a seat and some snacks, Tom declined but Dani was more willing to indulge. It took 4 minutes for Biljana to emerge from the lift, enough time for Dani to take two sips of her piping hot coffee and consume three biscuits.

This slim, elegant looking middle-aged professional walked out with scepticism on her face, even though she tried to hide it with a courteous smile. She approached Dani first and greeted her warmly. Dani then introduced Tom who said "How do you do" but rather than receive a direct reply, Biljana gawked at him in silence for a moment, as though examining him. Finally, when she seemed to find the power of speech, she turned to Dani and remarked in Serbian "One su ljubicaste…Da li on ima kontaktna sociva?"

This prompted Dani to also stop and inspect his face before she declared in English "Oh my God, they are purple… and they are real."

The two ladies then looked at one another in amazement completely ignoring the awkwardness being felt by Tom, who could only wince as they chatted amongst themselves in Serbia. He could only guess what they were saying. Either they were calling him a freak or they liked his eyes.

Having recovered from her momentary lapse of manners, Biljana smiled, a sign that her professional face was back on. "Sorry about that. I am Biljana. Please come with me." Tom was getting used to being asked to trail behind others. As he was walked to the lift, he noticed he was going alone. "Aren't you coming?" He asked Dani.

"I thought it was private?" She replied.

"Nope, come on, I might need your help." Tom said.

Dani dusted the crumbs off her skirt, took hold of her hat and followed them into the lift to the very top floor. The door opened to a more sedate setting with old style wooden furniture and paintings. They walked past a secretary who rose from her seat to greet them as they entered into Biljana's large office with tall glass walls giving a spectacular view of the entire city. Tom was impressed but he soon took note that Dani had lost her colour. "Vertigo?" He quietly asked Dani, she nodded. Tom smiled and asked "Excuse, would you mind drawing the curtains? It's a lovely view but it's rather distracting"

"Oh, sorry." Biljana replied as she went about pressing the button that operated the blinds. "Most people love it, and it gives the client something to look at as I work." Once the blinds were fully drawn, Dani appeared to relax a little.

Biljana ushered them to her desk, sat before them, clasped her hands and announced "So Ms Bozic is dead."

"A surprising deduction, how did you know?" Tom asked whilst masking his amazement.

"Sir, it's not every day a client comes to your office, requests your services and says "If a man called "Purple" with purple eyes from England comes to see you, know that I am dead and act accordingly", it's something you seldom forget."

That was it; he was the messenger. Jelena had made that official. Still, Tom didn't care much about that, rather he pressed on why Jelena had wanted him to meet her lawyer. Biljana rose to fetch her coat as spoke "Jelena left something behind for you. It's in a safe deposit box in a bank nearby. I suggest we go by my car, if you don't mind?"

"Police transportation bad for business?" Tom replied.

The lawyer laughed out loud "Jelena appears to be right about you. You're hard to deceive."

As she dressed herself, Tom was still suspicious and even though he opted to go with the lawyer, he asked Dani to follow in her car at a distance.

Having driven through the more affluent part of town, the Lawyer parked her car in front of a branch of French bank. As Biljana, took out her key, Tom felt a slight pain that ran down from the left of his head down his back like moving tremor of an earth quake. It wasn't bad, but Tom was scared. He had not felt this pain in a while, further affirmation of his fears, but he didn't have any time to worry as Biljana announced that they had arrived at their destination.

Entering the bank with Dani, he was informed that they were there to access a safety deposit box held by the institution. Some papers were brought which Biljana had to sign. She then passed on the document to Tom "These are the release forms… you need to sign for it please? Don't worry, it's in English." Tom was not keen on signing without reviewing.

A quick glance showed that it was indeed a standard release form with his name inserted as the party and Biljana signing as a witness. Having placed the ink on the paper, the bank manager was summoned. The nice jolly looking man, who could have passed as Santa Claus if he donned the apparel, greeted them and led them to his office where they were made to wait with the usual complementary refreshments on offer. Tom was now officially getting sick of the sight of biscuits and the smell of coffee which only served to agitate him further as the bank manager appeared to take his time.

An hour passed before the man returned with a metal case and a sealed envelope. The man then handed over the contents of the case to the lawyer who then passed it on to Tom with an evident sigh of relief. "There you go, all yours." Biljana proclaimed.

Dani had provided a swift interpretation of the conversation between the lawyer and the bank manager which seemed was along the lines that the manager was somewhat saddened that he and Biljana wouldn't have their meetings again. This prompted Tom to ask why the visits were so frequent. Biljana underlined client lawyer privacy and added "It's just my job. Almost every month or so she sends me a package with the same instructions, "give it to the bank manager who will destroy the previous package". I am paid to perform a service."

Accepting the lawyer's explanation, Tom glanced at his name on the back of the envelope and quickly opened it with the enthusiasm of an excited child at their birthday. This caused the contents to fall to the floor and skid under the table. It triggered a universal response with everyone bending down to see where the item went.

When it was discovered by the leg of the chair it was found to be another USB memory stick. Tom examined it to ensure no damage was inflicted by the fall before thanking the bank manager and the lawyer, leaving with Dani to the police station.

The station seemed rather subdued by the post-Christmas dip. It was oh so common amongst any European public service. Having been ushered to his allocated desk, slap bang in the middle of everyone there, Tom requested if there were a room where he could review the information contained in the memory stick.

Tom was presented with a small meeting room which was literally a fishbowl style where everyone could easily look in to observe the goings on within. "So much for privacy." Tom sighed in exasperation, conceding that the best place he could do what he wanted in confidence would be in his hotel room.

Collecting his things, Tom excused himself and rejected the offer of Dani to ferry him to his hotel, preferring to take a Taxi they called for him.

Once in his room, Tom didn't even bother to take off his coat and settle down; opting to take out his laptop and proceed to review his gift, praying it wasn't some kind of virus.

Hi patience was being tested as his portable computer took its time to load up, only to inform him it needed to perform updates, Tom could have screamed. Finally, he was able to slot the appendage into the device and once it was detected, opened the folder and double clicked on the file labelled "For Purple_2".

The clip began and once again, seated on a chair in a white sweater, her hair falling over her shoulders was Jelena with a smile on her face. Tom wished he could reach into the screen and slap her, but then she began to speak. "Hello Purple. I guess by now you are in Serbia. Thank you for making the journey. Now, since I am the only one doing the talking right now, I might as well clarify a few things."

"This isn't going to be some sob story about why I did things. Yes I regret a few things I did, but even you have to accept that most of those that have joined me today should be here. There was an element of excitement that egged me on, prompting me to test the waters and see how far I can go, oh, FYI, better contact the Slovak authorities and tell them I did the pool murders before some poor janitor is made a scape goat." She then laughed prompting Tom to give a short giggle himself at the morbidity of her request.

"Anyway," she continued "There is no point dwelling on my past actions. I know you want me to spill the beans… or as you say in England "rat some people out" and you are not too far from it, but it's not on this episode, you have one more journey to perform. There is a priest at the Church of the Holy Virgin. His name is Velkjo, but I am sure, upon your arrival, you would not need to ask for him. He has what you are looking for, but to get it you have two more tasks to perform.

The first is mandatory, the second optional."

"The first is to find my son. He lives with my grandmother. He needs to hear it from you that I am gone. The second will be revealed to you by Velkjo when you meet him. I know you are frustrated right now." Tom realised that she chimed with his emotions at the moment and could only roll his eyes as she added "but you always liked the chase."

"Now, Velkjo is available Mondays and Wednesday, Friday and of course Sundays. So you better go and find him and one last thing, when you do get the information you want, at the end of the day you will have a choice. You could either continue this chase that has wrecked your life… wrecked your health, wrecked your marriage…" Tom seemed to detect Jelena's confident voice quiver with a slight strain of sorrow and he wondered if her eyes were welling up as she stressed "wrecked everything that I envied you for and proceed with your hunt? Or you can choose to make your own happy ending? I may be wrong, but if 'following on the leads' provides you with a happy ending, then go for it. But do you think it was worth continuing on with this thankless task?" And on that note, Jelena finished her broadcast.

Tom sat there with a lump in his throat and a great weight on his heart. He literally felt offended by Jelena's last statement, "I mean, who was she to give me such ultimatums?" he asked himself. Yet he knew she knew he wouldn't let such a challenge slide and that was what irritated Tom to the core. Tom put down the screen of the laptop and went down to the reception to ask for the whereabouts of the church Jelena referred to.

With paper work being addressed and having to confirm with the Serbian police that he could sit in on the interrogations of individuals identified as the associates of Jelena, Tom went to bed. He tried to sleep but was troubled by a reoccurring dream where he walked through a field of dandelions and heather toward an old cottage with moss on the roof. It was the type of house Tom had always wanted before having to settle for a vanilla flavoured life of suburban London.

Arriving at the door of this perfect house, the faint smell of bread was inviting. Miraculously, he had the key to the door in his left hand. He ventured in and was pleased with the furnishings and layout with the old wooden floor creaking after ever third step as he always imagined it. The smell of bread only heightened the level of the idealism of his imagination, following the smell to the kitchen, hoping it would be the baker was the person he hoped for and it was. It was Jelena.

Jelena, dressed in a floral summer's dress, was just taking out a freshly baked loaf, putting it on a wooden work top to cool before she placed another tray of dough into the oven. She turned, smiled and said "So here we are. You finally got me where you want me." Tom was overcome by desire and raced to grab her face kissing her deeply.

Before he knew it, their clothes were off and in their embrace, he took her to the kitchen table and began to aggressively have sex with her till he climaxed.

When he stopped Jelena took the opportunity to ask him a question "Is this what you wanted?" and with that question, he seemed to be pulled away from her. Now standing two metres away, she began to laugh, and he started to be consumed by shame which only intensified when he heard a voice call out "Dad?" he turned and found Tim behind him and Caroline looking on, weeping, they had seen the whole thing. All Tom could do was "It's not what you think! It's not what you think!" Then Tom turned to face Jelena who was cackling as the walls began to bleed. Her body turned grey and the puncture mark of the snake bite just under her left breast was visible.

The horror of it all caused him to wake up in a sweat, struggling with a full blown anxiety attack, something he had never encountered before.

## 10 January 2011

Driving through Belgrade did all it could to test Tom's patience. It was amazing that the tailback that went on for nearly two miles was caused by two cars colliding with one another. The unhurt drivers decided to settle their score in the middle of the street whilst leaving their cars stationary.

The police did turn up, but when they did, the disgruntled drivers were aimed on getting their voices heard. Some left their vehicles to take a side and eventually fighting ensued. Thus, the whole situation required backup. Now, at 11:17am, there were two broken cars, three police cars, 15 people fighting amongst themselves whilst the 6 policemen tried their best to calm the situation and from Tom's perspective, it wasn't working.

A theme Tom had noted that seemed to persist throughout the force having spent the whole of the day before watching the interrogation process and after eight hours and 14 individuals, Tom concluded that the group questioned fell into two camps. The first being too frightened to speak and the second being unwilling to speak. What was more remarkable to Tom was the Serbian official's ignorance to Jelena's notoriety till that very day when the head of the force actually called on Tom to explain how a woman could instil such fear into the country's most hardened criminals and yet remain undetected by the local forces.

Brushing away the misogynistic undertones of Belgrade's Chief inspector, the answer was simple, her activities were never local, but her reach was.

Lamenting the fact that the previous day was a complete waste, Tom wasn't too keen on repeating the same event twice. Popping his head out of the car window he could see the church in the distance. Judging it was about 900 yards away, coupled with the fact that they hadn't moved more than half that distance in an hour, he turned to Dani and said "I think I'll walk it. See you there."

Tom opened the door and put out his right foot which only just touched the ground before it went through a puddle of slushy snow. Tom cursed internally, but no sounds ventured out his lips as he turned to smile at Dani who grinned back, having heard what occurred. Tom proceeded to walk on the pavement, past the polluting diesel cars that all seemed in need of servicing. The fumes caused his eyes to water and stung the back of his throat.

The wintery weather had a taming effect on his anxiety in regards to his growing concern for his health. He was pleased with his progression, reaching the church before Dani progressed an inch.

Tom stood to admire the building for a moment. It was a rather pretty, average sized church, painted white with its golden onion domed roof. It reminded him of his times visiting family in Russia.

Tom got to the heavy, hardwood door. He noticed the tale of Lazarus was carved upon it. Tom turned the large ring handle and opened the door slightly before it halted. Tom thought something must be obstructing its movement so he gave the door a push causing it to open a little more but still not enough to allow him access to the building.

Tom gave it another push, but this time, it didn't budge. He knocked and waited for another few minutes with no response. He decided to give brute force one more go and it worked. The door flung open, hitting the wall behind. The absence of the door to support him saw Tom crash to the ground landing on his shoulder on the cold stone floor. As he got off the ground, reeling in pain, Tom brushed off the dirt and dust from his coat when he heard a crumbling sound. Before Tom could look up, the dislodged snow from the roof fell on his head.

This was the last straw, unable to contain his rage Tom cried out "Fucking hell! In God's name, what's wrong with this city? Damn church. Couldn't they just oil the…" Tom's rant was stemmed when he turned to find the church's chaplain standing there looking appalled when had come to check what the commotion was about. Flustered with shame, Tom thought the man required an explanation. "I'm so sorry about that. I mean the swearing. The door was stuck you see…" The chaplain didn't seem interested in the words emitting from Tom's mouth, rather, he squinted. Noting he was being observed, Tom stopped his explanation to ask "Is everything ok?" The chaplain smiled and used the only words in English he knew gesturing to Tom "Come, come. Please?"

Tom followed, as the man led the way, turning to take curious glances at him. Once in the heart of the church, amongst the icons and candles that raised the temperature of the room, the chaplain added in poor English "Wait please. I come back." Tom watched the man pace off quickly to the door leading to the back of the church and soon the priest vanished.

Tom waited, pacing around the room for a few minutes, taking the time to review the icon of St Joseph when he heard the door open. Tom turned and saw the chaplain emerge followed by a portly man with a long grey hair, dressed in a black robes with a staff and a mounted cross in hand which made a stomping sound as the end hit the stone floor with every step the man took.

His crucifix was balanced on his belly, jingling as he drew closer. There was an air of wisdom and dignity about the man who smiled as he stood before him beaming as he proclaimed in fluent Russian "It is true, it is you Tom. I am father Velkjo. Welcome to the house of God. The lord has brought you here to do his bidding and for that, we must praise his name." The man offered Tom his hand. Tom wasn't too sure what the etiquette was. Tom took the hand and kissed the back of it. "A handshake would have been sufficient my son." The priest replied before commenting "you looked troubled my boy."

"I have had very little sleep." confessed Tom.

"Rest comes to those who follow the teachings of the lord and the calling of their heart." Velkjo proclaimed. Tom blushed slightly as the man added "She was right, your eyes are a lovely shade of purple." Tom rolled his eyes as it dawned on him that Jelena had done it again. The man had been briefed. Tom replied "Thank you father for taking the time to meet me."

"No. Thank you for coming. I know it must be difficult for you to come. Please follow me and let's prepare our sister for her final journey."

Velkjo led him to his office, which doubled as his private praying room. Seated together, Velkjo announced "I know why you are here." Tom had to keep the pretence but nevertheless asked "You do?"

"Yes." said the priest. "She entrusted me with an item for you. Our sister told me you need not carry out her wishes if it made you uncomfortable."

"That bitch" Tom remarked to himself. He felt that Jelena had deliberately done this challenge to his resolve, to goad him into doing what she wanted. Sadly, blaming it on the fatigue, it worked and Tom found himself asking the father "What wishes are those?"

Velkjo explained what Jelena had put in place for her funeral, all paid for in advance by her and after two hours of what was a very detailed explanation which included some words of wisdom and humour, it was all boiled down to two things, a date for the funeral and when the body could be released into his care.

Tom could have said no, got up, demanded the item and returned home to his life, but he didn't. Tom left it to the priest to decide the details. It turned out to be a mistake when the man flicked through his dairy and selected the 14th of January. Tom knew it was an auspicious day to select; it was New Year's Day according to the orthodox calendar. He raised this point with the priest who simply replied "God doesn't care what day it is, why should we?"

This didn't leave Tom a lot of time to complete his investigations, but Tom didn't let it on. Rather, he sought Velkjo's assistance, asking if he had an idea where Jelena's grandmother lived.

Luckily for Tom, the lady use to be part of Velkjo's congregation prior to moving to his new place of abode. Tom was provided the number and address along with a bottle of spirits Jelena had set aside for him, and after three hours, Tom was set to leave and was walked to the door by the holy man just as Dani finally entered. She was huffing in frustration which only grew when she heard that it was time to go. To abate a potential melt down, Tom asked if it weren't better if he drove.

## *11 January 2014*

Julien was stressed. The refurbishment meant that he wasn't able to locate anything, including some of his equipment. Normally he'd have three assistants running around giving him a hand, but due to an outbreak of influenza, only one could come and they had been slowed by constant sneezing.

The framers had failed to return the works in time and three of the works from Italy had sustained some damage. In addition, the wrong drinks were delivered.

Along with Khoi's constant need of attention, it was enough to put his stress levels up. Hence the site of Marcel and Paul looking through the gallery window did nothing to reduce his worry. Yet he had to remain civil. Julien waved at them and wanted to intercept them before they got to the door, but he tripped on a box and yet managed to maintain his balance. As he recovered, he had inadvertently allowed the peeping toms to reach the door and help themselves in.

Keeping his outrage under wraps, Julien put on a smile and proceeded to welcome them. "Paul, nice to see you again. Marcel, happy New Year."

Julien proclaimed as he shook their hands. The pair looked more nervous than he did so he tried to put their minds at ease. "Would you like to come in for coffee?"

"No thanks… we just came to see how Khoi is doing." Paul replied. Although he didn't consider it a good idea, Julien thought it would be best to be obliging and went to the flat to check if Khoi was able to accommodate the company.

Julien went upstairs leaving the two in the gallery area with the assistant who was struggling to pull out a large painting from a box. Marcel decided to help and with his height and strength, he pulled out the artwork in one go.

The frail assistant would have normally struggled to hold the heftily framed work with both hands due to the length and weight which was 27KG, near 40% of her own weight. She would have struggled to carry it alone. Marcel on the other hand, held the painting in one hand and looked at it "Hmm, not bad. Where do you want to hang it?" Seeing his potential, she smiled and pointed to the space on the wall where it should be placed.

Over the past few days, Khoi had steadily been improving from his initial dip when he couldn't even face himself let alone being around Julien or anyone for that matter. His lack of sleep and constant night terrors had taken its toll and it was a relief when they started to reduce in the last three days and Khoi seemed to be catching up on all the sleep he had lost. Entering the bedroom, Julien woke Khoi up gently and told him that he had guests. On hearing the names of those who had come to see him, Khoi promptly became defensive "I swear I didn't invite them…" "It's ok." Julien confirmed. "You think you are strong enough to see them?" Khoi was more interested in seeing Paul as opposed to Marcel. He just wasn't ready for some heavy jokes.

Julien then went back down to the gallery to find his assistant ordering Marcel about as to where to put a sculpture. "Renata, what are you doing?" He called out. Marcel confirmed he didn't mind giving a hand which made the delivery of the news easier as Julien relayed Khoi's wish to see Paul.

Julien led Paul to the flat. Khoi was there waiting in the living room, sitting on the sofa, drinking some tea. Sensing they needed their privacy, Julien left them alone, physically. Julien didn't go down the stairs. Rather, he went to the next room, to the toilet and placed a cup on to the wall to eavesdrop on their conversation. Paul thought he had to cautious, but sadly couldn't help but remark on his observation. "You look terrible."

"I know." Responded Khoi as he reached for a glass.

"You're shaking." Paul added. Khoi confirmed it was a side effect of the medication he had been given. The thought of Khoi being so frail and in need of drugs made Paul's heart sink. Paul finally sat opposite him and tried to smile, but what confronted him was just too powerful. "We miss you." Paul said as he tried to get some eye contact which wasn't forthcoming. "Joel is driving us crazy. He doesn't know what he's doing anymore."

"I'm sure he'll be fine." Khoi snapped. Realising he was being harsh, he changed the topic "How's your arm?"

"It's healing." Paul replied, wondering what sort of action he could take to snap Khoi out of his lull. Frustrated by the lack of ideas, Paul asked "What can I do? How can I help you?"

Khoi looked at Paul and could see the genuine concern in his eyes. It began to depress Khoi and after a quick sip of tea, he stood up and announced "I am going to bed."

Khoi exited the room without even saying goodbye, returning to his bed to cry.

Paul sat there for a moment, saddened by the experience. He got up and was about to leave when Julien walked in with an envelope in hand. Paul watched as Julien reached him and presented the envelope to him. "It's an invitation to our first exhibition of the year." Taking it from Julien and without opening it Paul made his excuses "I don't think I can come…"

"Oh you will come, you must." Interjected Julien "The event can't happen without you. Think about it." Paul thanked him and placed the envelope in his inner pocket.

The pair went back to the gallery and found one of the three rooms had already been decked with the relevant art works and now, Marcel appeared to be giving his own interpretation of a painting by the Swedish artist J. Elizabeth Berg. It was of a boy, resting on a large orange yoga ball, reading a book on green grass with a dark skyline touching the sky. They caught Marcel in mid-flow as his hand moved around "You can see that it's a process of anticipation. The boy seems to have been forced to read a book, like to do his homework and stuff, but he'd rather play with the ball, but that has to wait till he finishes his reading… can't you see the boredom in his eyes?"

Renata seemed to take Marcel's critic of the work seriously, nodding along confirming she could see the listlessness in the boy's eyes.

Julien was amazed and before he could applaud Marcel's ability to appreciate art, there was a noise at the door. The Framers finally arrived. He quickly had to address the delivery, leaving Paul alone. Paul asked if Marcel wanted to come, he refused underlining that Renata needed to move things about. Marcel stated he would catch up with him and find his own way back.

Getting the hint, Paul ventured out. Once in the car, he drove down the road before stopping at the traffic light. This gave him the opportunity to read the invitation and under the name of Elizabeth Berg was the name "Paul?" He turned the card around and on the back Julien had written, "I don't know your surname. Hope you can come see your works shine." Paul smiled and if he hadn't had a task to do, he would have returned to thank Julien, but it'd have to wait.

# 21

*12 January 2011*

Having spent the whole of the day before telling his boss that there was strong chance that his entire trip to Serbia may have been a waste of time, Tom felt deflated. The conclusion was based on the fact that he had spent all of the day before and half of the day before that sitting in their interrogation process.

Some parts of the process were a bit heavy handed to say the least only to be met by a wall of silence with the exception of one who clearly explained that the reason for this was that Serbians didn't take kindly on Westerners coming to town, snooping around for information on their own countrymen, especially if it meant bring them to book in a western forum. Then he had to actually explain why he wanted to stay an added few days and the reason, to which his superiors commended him for being honourable if not crazy, they didn't object, provided it was taken out as a holiday.

With the large amount of paperwork looming, Tom wasn't initially looking forward to his trip that morning but driving down a clean gritted street within a small gated community, Tom marvelled at the stark change from the slippery roads of the main street ridden with potholes like a skin scared by the pox. Clearly this was a more affluent area, the cars alone proved that. "So this is where all the money went." He remarked as he arrived at the tall temple of steel and finery along with Dani who insisted on coming.

"I've never been here before." She added whilst locking her car. "A first for both of us." said Tom as they walked up the steps to the front door manned by hefty rock of a man with a grumpy exterior. He was dressed smartly in a tailored suit which was a bit too tight, exposing the wires that led to his earpiece and the belt that held the gun. One look at Dani and her uniform turned his stone face into a smile, giving them a courteous welcome as he opened the door allowing Tom, Dani and the interpreter they brought along to facilitate communications with Nicola in.

Dani gasped whilst Tom was quietly astonished at the large fountain planted firmly in the centre of the lobby, flanked by boutiques selling chic designer items and imported food items. It seemed more like a five star hotel than a block of flats. Dani finally realised she had spent too much time gawking when she noticed Tom wasn't by her side anymore. He had gone to the lift and approached the bellboy and they were conversing. She hastily followed as the door of the lift opened. The bellboy punched in a code that allowed him to press the button labelled 19, the top floor. Once in, Tom informed Dani that he had gone to ask the receptionist if they were expected and they confirmed they were and directed to the lift.

On second inspection, he noticed that even the lift's minder was armed. Out of curiosity, he asked Dani why the man was armed. Dani almost seemed surprised by the question. She informed him that it wasn't just the lift operator that was armed but the receptionist, the shop attendant and probably everyone who lived in the building. The reason being was because five ministers, an ex-president, two former acquitted war criminals, in Serbian eyes, national heroes all resided in the very same building. This made Tom hypothesise; were Jelena had one of the parties mentioned as a target; would the building still be standing?

At the top floor, the lift door opened to wall covered in crimson wall paper with golden leaves pressed lavishly on the strips. "Turn right please." instructed the bellboy before he vanished behind the sliding door. Ever so nosy, Tom turned left and found it ended with a wall. He knew Dani considered his action a waste of time, but his cautious nature overrode his obedient side. They walked to the end of the corridor and found a simple white door which had a cross hammered on to it, right above the doorbell.

Dani did the honours of pressing the doorbell to announce their presence. They waited for a moment during which Dani asked "Are you nervous?"

Taken off guard by the question, Tom paused then enquired "No, why?"

"Your arm's shaking." Tom paused to notice, but before he could make an excuse, a voice came from a speaker in Serbian asking who at the door. Dani did some talking and within a couple of seconds, the door opened. There stood a young lady who gave what appeared to be a curtsy, welcoming them to the flat, leading the way down the hall of an opulent corridor holding the pictures of an old lady and that of a boy in his various stages of development till he became a man, no picture of Jelena though.

At the end of the corridor, they walked through a blue living room. Tom noticed it wasn't a flat at all, it was actually a two story penthouse with a stairs leading up to more rooms above. But it wasn't their destination. Their destination was beyond the living room with its plush carpeting and latest modern conveniences, it was the dining room located in the room behind, the room seemed larger than his living room and kitchen combined.

The young lady opened the door and introduced them to the sombre elderly lady seated on a chair. Her left arm rested on the table holding a handkerchief, with her long wavy shoulder length hair, her face etched with the tracks of time and its toll and now they wished to add more to it. There it was, this was where Jelena got it all from. The same wavy hair and height. If one looked beyond the effects of ageing, Tom concluded she most probably took her looks from the woman as well. Yet, she looked dignified in her simple floral dress and sweet. She didn't have the iniquity her eyes he had so associated with Jelena.

She reached out with her right hand and in soft tone said "Good morning. Thank you so much for coming to see me. I would rise, but my knees are not friendly with me at the moment, I must wait for my medication to work. Do forgive me." As Dani went to shake her hand, Tom felt weak at the knees. The elderly woman didn't just look sweet, she sounded genuinely nice, welcoming and distinctively regal in her approach.

Tom shook her hand and said respectfully "Good morning mother I…"

"I know you are Mr Evans." the old lady interjected speaking in Russian. "I am Diana. Please take a seat."

As they rested their posteriors on the well-crafted chairs, Diana ordered the lady to fetch some refreshments. Once alone, she continued "Jelena said you would come, Mr Evans. So it is true, my darling Jelena is no more." Her tone showed that behind her dignified stance, Diana's heart had been shattered to pieces yet Tom nodded to confirm her suspicion. Diana could no longer conceal her grief. She sobbed silently for a moment prompting Dani to ask if Tom had this effect on people where ever he went "Are you the angel of death?" she queried. Tom soon began to feel that way in reality.

Diana finally regained her composure and put on a stiff upper lip that would give an officer in the First World War a run for its money. "I'm sorry." Diana began, dabbing away the tears "It's such a great blow. You were the man I never wanted to meet… and now you are here."

There was an uncomfortable stillness which followed that statement and it lingered till the old lady called out "Maria? Where is the tea?" The young lady hurried back in to set the table and serve them all a cup. Tom didn't even touch his. He was too upset. Diana persisted "Jelena told me that one day you would come, the man with the lavender eyes. Tell me, was it painful?"

"I cannot say mother… but it was quick." Tom responded, feeling more self-conscious than ever since his trembles were noticed a moment back.

"At least that's a small consolation. Please Mr Evans, drink your tea, we won't have long to wait, Nikola is set to arrive shortly… as will his mother." Although taken by the information since the mother hadn't been invited, Tom smiled and thanked her. Diana explained that Jelena wasn't a fictitious figure in her son's life. Yes, she never did visit, but with the advancement of technology, she would talk to him using web cams and chat.

Diana thought adolescence would dull the need to maintain such connections. Most of those she knew at that age wanted more time with their friends than her family, but Nicola, she proudly boasted, "Was different" he was always punctual and Jelena was never failed to attend. Diana explained Nicola's disabilities and how he overcame them and being three minutes into his second cup, the sound of the door followed by stomping footsteps coming their way. Diana beamed and announced "He's coming. Go and get him." she ordered the maid.

The lady briskly ran out of the room leaving a silence that unsettled Tom as the old lady fixed her eyes on him. Nervously, he picked up the cup of tea and tried to take a sip only to realise the cup was empty. Emerging from the corner was a tall, young man, with short black hair and blue eyes. He didn't look like Jelena though. He was about 5feet 11 inches, about four inches shorter than his mother. He had a slightly square jaw, in contrast to his mother's slim face. The maid was dismissed to the kitchen.

The boy looked around at the faces present and with the police there, he frowned and sighed, saying to Diana "Hello, what's this?" Diana sighed, and replied "Nicola, this is Tom Evans, a policeman from England." Tom rose to give the boy a handshake when the teenager's lower lip began to quiver. "Is that him?" he sighed to Diana who just nodded. Nicola began to shake his head in disbelief and asked "Is she dead?" Tom was informed of the question being asked by the cross translation from the signer via Dani who shook her head as she passed on the message.

Tom could tell Dani was thought that perhaps he was the angel of death again. Diana answered but the boy insisted on hearing it from Tom who, even though he had passed on bad news on many occasions, found this the most difficult situation ever, so he simply nodded his confirmation.

Nicola didn't move, freezing with an absence of emotions in his being. This lack of animation raised concerns "Are you alright"? Diana questioned. Nicola nodded and said "Thank you for coming." Then another moment of silence before Nicola sighed and asked "what happened?" Tom turned to Diana as though seeking permission only for the doorbell to ring.

The maid opened the door and found standing there a woman draped in fake fur. She was tall, slim and elegant. "Good morning. Is Madame Bozic at home please?" The maid looked her up and down before, oozing with scepticism confirmed that the old lady was home. The visitor asked if the maid could announce her arrival, the other Mrs Bozic. The maid shut the door and raced back to the dining area to pass on the news. Diana rubbed her brown hair in trepidation. "Let her in." she said "that's Jelena's mother. Her name is Irene." Diana confirmed.

The second Mrs Bozic was led to the meeting. Momentarily, she halted her progression to marvel at the furnishings. At the dining room, the maid ushered her in. Without a word of thanks, she entered to a pool of gazes of those present which ferried loathing, bewilderment and amazement. The latter emitted from Tom who was in no doubt that this woman was certainly Jelena's mother. She was tall, lean, same slim face, evidence of the once red hair mixed with the grey and the full pouting lips.

The eyes didn't discomfort her, rather, Irene fixed on Diana and said "Hello old woman. Why did you summon me?"

"Please, let's leave our animosity behind." Begged Diana "Your daughter is dead.". To all there, the announcement seemed to mean nothing to Irene; she stood there, stone faced until she replied "Thank God. I hope the devil takes her." Once conveyed to Tom, he thought this was quite extreme as did Diana who chided "Dear, I did not expect that from you. She was your child…" "My child?" Irene snapped "She stopped being a person of significance to me when she did away with her father and tried to kill me!" It was then Irene noticed the presence of the teenager in the corner, the cold exterior melted at the sight of Nicola.

She approached him and declared "My, you look so much like your grandfather." Upon reaching him she touched his face. Nicola seemed to shudder from the woman's caress, glancing at Diana for security which Irene detected. "Interesting" Irene remarked "You don't know who I am, do you? That witch didn't tell you, did she?" Turning to Diana with a scornful look she snarled "You did this. You never told him about me." Choosing to rectify the situation, Irene turned on the charm "Nicola, I am your grandmother…" The boy looked confused as Irene added "Yes, I am. I am your mother's mother." She reached to touch his hair "You look so much like your grandfather. You have the same eyes and skin…" Nicola could take it no longer. He took a step back away from Irene.

Irene gave a cackle that preluded her demand, pointing at her mother-in-law as she demanded "You must tell him what his mother did!" Diana shook her head, begging Irene to leave the past where it should be, but Irene wasn't to be silenced. She spotted the interpreter and with that tool at her disposal, she walked up to the lady, frightening her as she asked "Could you make sure he get this?" The frightened, plump nerdy girl nodded, Dani informed Tom that she would be his guide.

Irene began "Did you know your grandfather was a bee keeper? He made the best honey in all of Zlatibor. People would come for miles for it. You know his secret? Elderflower and Pear trees. The bees took their nectar and the honey created was simply delicious. But your mother didn't think that was enough for her. We tried to bring her up right, but she was nothing but evil."

"Lies!" Screamed Diana. "Shut up!" snapped Irene as she continued "There was nothing we could do. She hated us so much, she ran away and we never heard from her for years. She didn't even want us to meet you. We searched for you and her, but we couldn't find you. Then the day that she finally came home, we were asleep in our bed when the door opened and there was a person wearing a bee keeper's suit, carrying a hive with them. I didn't know who it was till your mother spoke. It was her voice that gave her away."

"You know what she said? She said 'Good morning father, I hope you suffer.' Then she threw the hive on the bed where your grandfather and I were sleeping."

"The bees flew everywhere. Your mother left, locking us in. The insects went into our noses, our hair, and our mouths. Despite his years of managing them, your grandfather was stung to death by his own wards!" It was then Tom realised that the sign language interpreter was busy ferrying on the tale. In terror, Tom screamed at her "Stop translating!" Dani had to pass on the order and the interpreter blanched and apologised when Nicola signed something back which Tom caught.

Whether or not she had someone to pass on the information, Irene persevered. "I was lucky. I picked up the blanket and threw it over myself and jumped out the window. We were one storey high! I broke my leg! Now you know, your mother killed her own father."

"You know what your mother did for a living? She killed people. They paid her to do so. That's why you can live like this." Irene added. The devastation in Nicola's eyes was prevalent. He turned to Diana for reassurance but she was too distraught to provide the comfort he sought. Unable to stomach the news, Nicola raced out of the room and the sound of the door slamming showed he was no longer in the flat.

Irene looked smug by her activities but she still wasn't content. She turned to Diana and commented "What a nice flat. This should all be mine, my daughter taking care of me, but now she is gone. Still, you can keep it. I am happy just knowing the girl is dead." With that passing shot, Irene left.

With everyone recovering from their trauma, Dani took the time to console the old woman who made it clear that Irene didn't tell the full story. Eagerly she shared her version, inserting the bits which Irene chose to leave out. The fact of Jelena's rape, the fact that Jelena's father had plans to traffic her into prostitution hadn't it been the saving grace that Jelena had fallen pregnant and more. Diana concluded "Jelena may have done wrong but I believe in salvation. Every day I pray for her, I pray she finds peace and that she may have sought forgiveness before she died... I pray she did."

A growing sense of empathy developed in Tom for Jelena, but it didn't negate the fact that Jelena was a killer. Tom could stomach this family drama no longer. He got up as he answered "Me too mother." He leaned over and kissed her on the cheek "God bless you." It was time to leave.

Once out of the building, everyone seemed to take a moment to reflect. It was the most confrontational, intense and unpredictable situation any of them had ever been in and quietly, they were all pleased it was over.

As they walked to the car, Tom noticed from the corner of his eye, Nicola marching towards him. Dani observed "He looks angry." And she was right. Tom braced himself as Nicola walked up to him and gave him a shove and began to sign frantically. "Why did you come?" he asked. "How could you do that to an old woman? We were happy! We didn't need to know! Why were you so heartless?"

"I'm sorry." Tom said as Dani translated to the interpreter who didn't move. Concerned, Tom asked why the interpreter wasn't doing her job. It was then revealed that Nicola could read lips in Serbian only. Relying on Dani, Tom told Nicola "I didn't mean to cause you harm, but you had to know."

The torment Nicola was experiencing was obvious as he ran his hands through his hair. Then he signed "Is it true? Is my mother a murderer? Was my mother a good person?" Once he got the question, Tom was hesitant to respond, his heart sinking as looked Nicola in the eye and replied "No, she isn't a murderer."

Nicola anxieties seemed to reduce, but he had one more quested "Did she kill my grandfather?" This time, with conflicting information swimming in his mind, he opted for diplomacy "She had her reasons." Tom hoped it would be enough for now, but Nicola could not stand the sight of Tom and his company anymore and sought distraction by averting his eyes, staring instead at the ground.

Tom asked Dani to jot down some relevant addresses on a paper. Once done, Tom took it and walked up to the teenager, handing the paper to him. "The funeral will take place here on 14 January... come if you can." Nicola looked up and took the paper; he glanced at it, before crumpling it up, throwing it on the ground and walking away.

Accepting there was little else to be done; Tom asked to be taken back to his hotel.

# 22

*13 January 2011*

The morning arrived. In twenty four hours he was going to bury his foe and it seemed rather unreasonable to be asked to take the day off by his boss who believed Tom deserved it after all his efforts. He declined the offer, opting for a half day off instead.

He concluded his report on the computer before turning his mind to another document he had to draft. Deciding to use the old method of paper and pen, Tom drafted and redrafted the words he wanted to express but nothing seemed to convey his feelings correctly.

After twenty nine crumpled papers and a growing headache, he paused. There was a tapping sound that began to irritate him. Tom looked at the source of the noise and what he witnessed caused his heart to sink. His left hand which was rested on the table was trembling so quickly that his nails were hitting the surface of the table so hard it caused a tapping noise.

He reached out to hold his shaking hand with his right, hoping it would stem the sound, and it did. Tom didn't want to face his involuntary movements anymore and decided to take a nap. Caroline wasn't set to arrive for another four hours anyway, perhaps a two hour nap would help calm his nerves.

Tom woke up a bit sprightlier, buoyed by the prospect of seeing Caroline. He yawned and stretched and was only caught out in the middle of his activities when he realised it was 3pm already, Caroline's plane was going to land in fifty minutes, he was going to be late.

Jumping out of bed, the first thing Tom decided to do was to draw the curtain to let the natural light in only to discover there wasn't any available. Storm clouds had smothered the sun, and rather than its rays reaching earth, the only thing that came down was large flakes of snow at an astonishing rate. The vision of cars skirting and sliding from side to side, their tires unable to grip to the road was evidence that the storm had caught the authorities by surprise. It took him a few minutes to pull himself away from the window. The whole city, at least what he could see of it, was virtually white.

Having called reception, Tom was relieved to hear that the airport shuttle bus was not affected. He took a ride in the coach through the streets as he watched people slip on the ice covered pavement and cars which were marooned on the side of the road. He prayed for luck and a safe journey and was delighted that he got what he wished for even though he was twelve minutes late.

Running on the only piece of gritted earth he had seen so far, Tom entered the arrival area. He didn't need to look far. He saw Caroline immediately and she was holding her luggage in one hand and a suit carrier in the other. As he drew closer, the sight of travellers and their companions halted him from running to her and grabbing her in a great big hug, he noticed that Caroline seemed baffled and was looking around.

Upon reaching her, he greeted her with a kiss on the cheek. It was then Caroline exposed what had her stumped "Is Serbia an anagram for Siberia? The plane struggled to land"

"Siberia has an additional "I" dear, so I doubt if it would be an anagram." Caroline's bent brow proved the joke had failed to hit its mark. "Sorry... still, it's so nice to see you."

"You too." She reiterated and hugged him tight before proclaiming "Your son wants to know when you are coming home?"

"How is he?" Tom asked holding her hand. "He's with his aunt. Amazing how people without children tell you how to feed your kids." Caroline remarked checking her phone. Turning it off, she said "So, let's venture out into the cold!" Approaching the exit, the automatic doors slid open, the gust of wind slamming the coin size flakes on them. It caused Caroline to let out a shriek. Luckily, she wasn't the only one, sparing her from blushing.

Tom took hold of the luggage, held her free hand and led her to the bus with the wind lashing at their faces. Once in the bus, the heater failed to warm Caroline up. Taking sympathy on her, Tom took off his coat and allowed her to use it as a blanket. "Thank you. How long before we get to the hotel?" she asked and he replied, "Just under 40 minutes." Exhausted from her early morning flight and six hour stopover in Frankfurt, Caroline got herself into a comfortable position before nodding off for a short nap. Tom had made a mistake. An additional two hours had to be added to the journey due to the adverse weather conditions and the havoc it had caused.

With his back aching, Tom helped a now well-rested Caroline off the bus. Caroline checked into her room, an act that brought his loss home in a big way. Once they would have checked in together and booked the same room, now they sleep alone in two different beds.

The time now 8pm and the weather were not adequate for an evening stroll, they suggested they ordered room service and waited to eat in Tom's room. With the food to take 35 minutes, Caroline took the opportunity to take a quick shower. Tom thought it would be best to clean the room, making his bed and arranging his things. It took him back to his university days when he had a girl coming to see him.

This moment of blissful reminiscing was interrupted by more present matters. With his phone vibrating on the coffee table, Tom glanced at the number. It was British but it wasn't one he recognised, yet he decided to answer the call. "Hello?" A shaky yet light voice replied back "Mr Evans?"

"Yes? This is he. Who is this?"

"Good evening, I'm Dr Sands from the forensic department." With evident relief Tom proclaimed "Oh yes. Good evening, how are you?"

"Very well thank you. I was instructed by your colleagues to call you relating to the DNA search you requested on the two scarves along with the other items brought to us." The man added, his tone telling of his displeasure in making the call. "Thank you so much for making the effort. Pardon my eagerness, but could you quickly summarise your findings?" Tom asked looking at the time in anticipation of dinner. "Certainly. One moment." Tom could hear the stroking of keys on a computer and the rustling of papers before the Dr returned "Here we are. Now, since the items were of similar nature, I have labelled them Scarf "A", the one found on the deceased, and Scarf "B" the one provided by yourself. First thing you may wish to know is that the scarves are handmade. In addition, they are made from the same source of wool."

"On scarf A, the following were found. The was DNA from two individuals on the material with most coming from the hair and skin samples found on the scarf originating from the deceased and the other DNA found from the hair samples recovered from the scarf, originated from a man."

"Dr Sands, could you please tell me more about the man's DNA, anything distinctive?" Tom pressed.

"Well, we know it is a man, we can't tell his exact age but we can place him being in his twenties or thirties, of mixed Caucasian and Asian origins…" On hearing that detail, the hair at the back of Tom's neck stood to attention.

Quickly, Tom interrupted again seeking clarification "Asian… South Asian? Central Asian?"

"South East Asian, like China, Thailand, that region of the world." The doctor responded. "That's amazing." Tom remarked, content with the information on the first scarf,

Tom asked "Setting that aside for one moment, could you tell me what you found on the second one? Scarf 'B'?" Taking a moment to assimilate what the doctor considered to be rude behaviour, he persisted "With scarf 'B', excluding the hair and skin sampled belonging to you, we found an abundance of hair and skin fragments belonging to a white Caucasian woman potentially in her thirties and it was by chance we found two strands of hair belonging a man."

"Let me guess, the same man as that on Scarf "A"?" Tom asked. Unable to contain his annoyance any longer, the doctor replied "Mr Evans, could you possibly be patient please?" Tom promptly apologised allowing the man to continue. "No Mr Evans, it did not belong to the same man. It belonged to a white Caucasian man with blonde hair." Tom's heart sunk at this point, but the doctor's synopsis was finished. "However, it appears that both the men, i.e. the men of scarf "A" and "B" are related."

This information stuck Tom like a brick. Out of interest he asked "How related? Distantly?"

"No, quite close. They are brothers." The doctor specified. Tom voice evaporated as the news sunk in. He couldn't believe it and begged for clarification. The doctor initially was sceptical to go into detail, but when Tom explained he had a science degree, the man proceeded "We all inherit the "X" chromosome from our mothers and it's the other chromosome, the "X" or "Y" that determined if we become a boy or a girl. The other means of deducing this is via their mitochondrial DNA which is passed down by the mother and would be the same in individuals with siblings from the originating from the same mother. In this case, it all matched. The two men are brothers from the same mother."

Tom's heart seemed to sink. His instincts had failed him, causing him a mixture grief and anger. "I'm such a fool." Detecting the emotions, the doctor noted "I guess that it wasn't the news you wanted to hear."

"No doctor, but you were doing your job" Tom sighed "But you were doing your job. One last thing… the champagne bottle?" The doctor confirmed that the DNA on the bottle matched those on the scarf "A". Tom almost screamed at the prospect of being hoodwinked but was stalled by the knock on the door.

Tom decided to wrap up the conversation. "I have to go. Thank you so much doctor. Please could you send me a summary of the report via email, please?"

"No problem and take care." The doctor said as he hung up.

Tom began to struggle. He was struggling to move and struggling to find his appetite. He also struggled to see the need for company. The second knock at the door forced him to put his reluctance aside and he opened it, he had more of an urge to rush to the airport and return to Berlin, but he couldn't.

The food had arrived ten minutes early. Tom had the meal set on the table in the centre of the room by the bed. He mustered some courage, wondering what to do, but the food wasn't going to stay warm forever. Tom called Caroline to join him for their meal of duck, vegetables and dumplings with a bottle of water and a rose on the side.

A knock at the door, heralded Caroline's arrival in a bathing robe with her hair still wet. Upon opening the door, Tom's previous distress melted. He was captivated by her natural beauty of her short blond hair and baby blue eyes; he was taken. "Em… Why are you looking at me like that? It's rather creepy." She remarked. "Oh, sorry." He said stepping out of the way.

Caroline went straight for the food and didn't wait for Tom before tucking in. Tom went to join her.

At the rate at which she scoffed her meal, Tom feared she might choke. He reached for the bottle of water and served her a glass. Caroline vocalised her thoughts on the water "We order a big meal and we are going to wash it down with water? Don't they have some wine? I hear it's good here." Tom seemed to be enjoying the somewhat open Caroline; it beat the old version, the silently watching and nodding Caroline that didn't speak till it was too late. "I've got something better." He proclaimed. He went to his bag and took out the bottle of drink he had inherited and placed it before her. "Courtesy of Jelena."

Whilst chewing on her goose, Caroline picked up and inspected the bottle and gave up trying to comprehend what was written "What is this?" "Viljamovka it's a rakija. It's made out of pears." Tom explained. Caroline's unimpressed look made him smile. "And you say this is from Jelena, and you want us to drink it? What if it is poisoned?" Caroline put forward. "There's only one way to find out." Tom said as he opened the bottle, served himself some and gave it a taste. He let it settle in his mouth for a while before he drank it. "Hmm, it's pleasant. Not as sharp as I thought it would be." Caroline looked over Tom's shoulder to glance at the time set at end of the news channel. "May be later." She said, leaving the liquor alone as she carried on eating.

The pair ate in silence. Since the booze complemented the meal, Tom consumed more of it. With the bottle a third empty, Caroline looked over his shoulder once again for the time. "Thirty minutes and you are still here. It should be safe." She downed her water and served herself some of the rakija, raising her glass and saying "Thanks Jelena." Before downing the drink.

Tom laughed when he realised that was the canary in the mine. "Yeah, to Jelena." He repeated before downing his glass. "So, what did she look like?" Caroline's question caught him by surprise, and he was rather confused. For clarity sake he asked "What did who look like?"

"Jelena of course." Tom wondered if it was the case that he may have already had too much to drink to have missed such an obvious reference.

He left the table for his dresser where he sat and turned on his laptop. He called Caroline over to come and watch the video Jelena had left behind. Tom waited for a reaction, but there wasn't any, Caroline stood over him, watching attentively even though it was all in Russian, a language that meant nothing to her. When the clip finally came to an end, all she could do was sigh, returning to the table where the food was and helping herself to a triple shot of Viljamovka. She downed half of it and remained silent, leaving Tom in on tenterhooks. Unable to bear it any longer he asked "Well, what do you think?"

"I think you need to see a doctor when you return. Your shakes are back." Her response directed Tom's attention to his trembling left arm. He held it to still it before brushing his potential health problem aside to press his question home "No silly, I meant Jelena!"

"Oh, her..." Caroline remarked as she finished the remainder of her glass, served another triple shot and topped up Tom's glass which she brought to him as she continued "Now I understand how she could get away with it for so long. She's sexy, no red blooded man and most women would be able to resist her, let alone want to kill her... whoever did it must be blind or gay..." handing over the glass to Tom she asked, "Let me know if this is confidential, but do the police know who did it?"

"Nope?" Tom replied taking a sip of his drink. Then came the look again, the "I know you are up to something" look she always gave him. In the past it was just a look, this time she asked him "Do you?" Tom never liked being put on the spot, especially by her. He could have side stepped the question but he chose to face it head on, but first he required some courage. He emptied his glass with one gulp before confessing "Yes... I think I do."

Tom braced himself for the questions to follow, those he didn't want to face yet. Looking into her eyes, he waited patiently, but they never came, rather, Caroline went back to the table, took hold of the bottle that was just a third full. Caroline took half of what was left of the bottle and gave the remainder to Tom. "This is officially a wake, you know that?" She remarked, Tom gave short laugh "Seriously, we have to have a toast." Tom tried to put on a straight face as, the laugh wasn't real, it only masked something stronger which soon bubbled up to the surface as Caroline, looked up to the heavens, glass raised as she spoke "To Jelena, you were one hell of a woman. Sleep well babe." Immediately she downed her drink and shuddered from the effects of its strength. "That was good." It was then she noticed Tom had gone into a haze, as though disorientated. "Aren't you finishing yours?" She asked, and then Tom's eyes misted over and swelled with tears. "Tom?" She called. It all proved too much for him, he was grieving and yet he couldn't explain why. Tom began to sob.

Caroline quickly took the glass out of his hand and embraced him. There was a gush of sorrow that could no longer be contained and it took a few minutes for Tom to regain his demeanour, yet he failed. Still he got a grip on his senses, letting go, reaching hold of some tissues to blow his nose. The tears still did not stop, yet he spoke "I'm sorry, I just don't know what happened to me."

"I guess it's a release of pent-up pain after all that time. You have had a horrible six years." Placing her hand on his shoulder, Caroline asked "Are you going to be alright?" Tom nodded. She kissed him on the head, and advised "you better go to bed. You need your strength for tomorrow."

"Thank you." Tom said. Caroline didn't reply, she just smiled and left the room, leaving him to fester in his own misery. There was one thing he took from the dinner; he did need his strength for the morning.

Tom cleared the table and left the trays outside the door before finishing the water left in the bottle. Again, his gag reflexes came to the rescue. Tom vaulted for the toilet and vomited most of his dinner and the Viljamovka. The strain on his gut was the sign he needed to go to bed and it was the gift from Jelena that ensure he slept soundly even though he feared the forthcoming events.

*14 January 2011*

It was New Year's Day morning in Serbia, according to the Orthodox calendar that is, and, though cold, it wasn't as cold as the day before. It had been snowing ferociously throughout the night making Tom wonder if the ground wouldn't be too hard to be dug. Now that the snow stopped, the sky seemed to open, allowing the sun to shine brightly through, a redemption from the darkness of the day before.

Peering out the window, Tom fiddled with his cufflinks, the final part of his attire before he put on his jacket. Tom was lumbering with a great deal of misgivings on his mind. As the odd bird flew by in the cold, he asked himself why he was burying an undeserving sinner like a saint, as though there was some sort of redemption to be found through the expense of church burial.

He genuinely hoped the snow would save him the task of having to attend the funeral; it seemed that the weather had conspired with Jelena to ensure the funeral took place.

With a heavy sigh, he accepted his fate as mourner in chief of the day. His cufflinks were on and so was his blazer. He took a look at himself in the mirror one last time. Dressing in a black suit pushed away the frustration that slowly crept, satisfied with Caroline's choice. Tom reached for his coat, turned out the lights and shut the door to his hotel room, walked down the corridor, two rooms away, to fetch the occupant of room 310.

Tom gave a knock and after a few seconds, the door opened. There she was. A sight to behold, Caroline stood there. Her hair cropped back, her face made up to make her look flawless and a black cloak draped over her. "Good morning." She said. Tom could not hold his admiration "Good morning. You look beautiful." Caroline blushed, not that one would notice under the skin coloured foundation applied to her face. Caroline shut her door and the pair walked towards the lift together.

Caroline decided to check on the arrangements. "So what's the deal for the day?"

"We go to the funeral director's reception room for a small wake and some prayers, head off to the church, service, and stick her in the ground." Summarised Tom as he called the lift.

"Nicola still didn't contact you?" Caroline enquired as she put on her white elbow length gloves. Tom shook his head to confirm Nicola hadn't reached out to him. "Oh well, at least you are here. By the way, what is she wearing?"

"The little black number she asked for." Tom replied as the lift arrived at the ground floor and opened as he added "Now she can meet her maker dressed like a show girl." Caroline laughed even though it was in bad taste, and it was the guilt that made her give Tom a gentle shove as they got to the lobby.

Quickly, they put on faces of sombre contemplation as Tom approached the receptionist to ask if their car had arrived. They were informed that their car and the driver had been waiting for them outside for the last fifteen minutes.

It was then the couple realised the time, they were already twenty minutes late. Quickly they raced out to apologise to the man called Zoltan who didn't seem much bothered with their tardiness and made it clear when he told them "No worries, I get paid by the hour."

With little time to lose, the requested they be driven to the funeral parlour as quickly as one could on the icy roads. As they were driven on, Caroline pressed on with her inquiries. "So what's the service going to be like?"

"I'm not too sure. Could be similar to a Russian orthodox one… so I guess a lot of icons and making the signs of the cross." Tom guessed. Caroline then asked where the church was "4 Rajaciceva Street, I think it's 10 minutes from here. Zoltan, where is the church?" Zoltan confirmed it was actually 15 minutes from the funeral parlour. All this was of little interest to Caroline who was curious about the name of the church. "Oh, that?" Tom remarked to the questions "It's called the Church of the Holy Virgin." Upon hearing the name, Caroline's eyes flung upon and began to laugh "The Church of the Holy Virgin! That whore certainly has a sense of humour."

Though late, Tom finally got it and joined her in the laughter. This was the first time they had shared a joke in a long time and once again, they had to compose themselves as they arrived at their destination.

They were ushered into a small private room where Velkjo and two other deacons were waiting for them. Velkjo was dressed in his black cassock, floor-length robe with long sleeves, a blue band around his portly belly, an epanokamelavkion, a klobuk over his shoulders and a medal worn around his neck that hung down to his naval with the icon of the Madonna and child encased in gold.

The deacons were more modestly dressed with just a black inner cassock and their cross around their neck, but it seemed a competition between Velkjo and his assistants to determine who had the longest beard with Velkjo losing by centimetres. There was also the dark brown mahogany coffin and a large bunch of calles flowers placed on top of the casket in a very tasteful way. Tom seemed not to notice it as he entered, but Caroline was taken by the site. Caroline never got the chance to see what this woman looked like, and she was rather disappointed that casket was closed.

Velkjo, with his long grey beard, round glasses and generous looking smile, stretched out his arms and greeted them most merrily with a "Welcome" in English, Russian and Serbian as he advanced to them. Velkjo shook Caroline's hands as he spoke in English "I am glad you made it. Good morning, my son." He said to Tom "Good morning Pop how are you?" Tom replied in Russian. "God has made this day glorious and I am grateful for his mercies. But we best not stand still."

Velkjo seemed a man bursting with energy as he walked around putting on his scarf and changing his cape for one with strong colours, principally of gold and blue.

Out went the warm man and in came the holy man. The ceremony began with a short wake and the first panikhida, the prayer service for the deceased. Tom was right, it was pretty close to a Russian orthodox service and immediately he seemed to be in his element. Caroline, on the other hand, could have been left in the middle of the woods in Siberia, that was how lost she was, yet she appreciated the melodic way the prayers were delivered by Velkjo.

It was a very short wake and soon they had to progress to the church. Again, in the car, with the body being transported in a hearse behind them, Caroline noticed that Tom had fallen quiet. Caroline wondered what he was thinking, yet, she didn't want to pry. So they sat in silence till they arrived at the church.

The pair got out of the car and were met by another church deacon also with a beard who introduced himself, in fluent English, as Kirill. Kirill was there to walk them through the service.

They stood out of the church for three minutes as Velkjo's Volkswagen driven by one of his deacons arrived railed by the pallbearers in the hired minibus and then the body.

Kirill hurriedly ran back into the church and opened the door. The body was then taken out of the hearse and a procession was formed led by Velkjo with cross mounted staff in hand. He walked in in front of the coffin with the censer singing the hymn "Trisagion" as Caroline and Tom followed from behind.

The door was then shut behind them, depriving the church hall of a large amount of light. Then she beheld an amazing sight. The candles were lit, illuminating the icons that covered every conceivable space on the walls from the alter to the other parts of the church. There was a choir waiting patiently all in black as the pallbearers set the casket on the plinth and walked away backwards in respect, leaving the coffin alone at the centre of attention once again. Tom and Caroline left to stand a few feet away.

A church deacon proceeded to place a dish of boiled wheat with honey with a lit candle placed in the middle. Caroline was told that it symbolized the cyclical nature of life and the sweetness of heaven and the candle was to remain lit throughout the service.

Once the Trisagion was finished, Velkjo spoke "Welcome to the house of God. As your friend had made a special request that you pick the first hymn, I turn to the choir to sing the song you selected for our late daughter." Caroline whispered "Is this the one she said you should choose?" Tom nodded. She didn't need to wait long as the choir belted out the hymn "To God be the glory" by Fanny Crosby.

Caroline swooned. It was her favourite hymn. Tom gave her a wink. It was touching that he could be so considerate, tapping into her thoughts. So buoyed was she that Caroline sang along with gusto.

When the choir finished the first English song ever sung in the church, Velkjo began the service by leading the Divine Liturgy as a deacon brought forward the decorated bible, holding it above his head before presenting it to Velkjo to give it a kiss. After the Liturgy, Velkjo began saying prayers which seemed to have a lot of points where it was required to make the sign of the cross. It was difficult for Caroline to keep track of when to make the sign and when not to and then it came time for the bows. Tom seemed to be on the ball, but the rituals got rather confusing for Caroline who eventually decided there was nothing wrong with just standing respectfully still.

Caroline began to regret wearing her heels. There was no sitting in an orthodox church and all the standing was wreaking havoc to her calf muscle. Caroline met the news with immense joy that Velkjo was leading the Divine Liturgy which was to be followed by the recital of the Memory Eternal after which the service would come to an end.

With the Divine Liturgy concluded, Velkjo called Caroline and Tom forward for a blessing. As they approached, there was a sound from the entrance and the candles flickered as a cold breeze came in. Caroline then noted that the priest stopped speaking and his eyes seemed to divert away from them towards the door.

She turned and Tom did the same to find Nicola, dressed in a black suit, white shirt and black tie, shutting the door behind him as he entered the chapel. With all eyes fixed on him, Nicola did not proceed any further. Believing the funeral had been gate crashed, Kirill said "One moment." Kirill was about to go to meet the youth when Velkjo chided him, ordering him to stop, then he hailed Nikola, gestured and called him forward to join them.

Cautiously, Nikola approached. He had a stern look on his face which appeared to unnerve Tom who took it upon himself to walk forward to meet Nikola. Now standing face to face, Tom smiled and noting the potential communication barriers, Tom instinctively waved and said "Hello."

Nikola did not respond to his gestures. Rather, he reached for his android phone, turned it on and typed away. Once done, he handed it to Tom. Caroline and Kirill came over to read over Tom's shoulder.

On the phone screen of the smart phone was a language translation application with the some Serbian words on the upper half of the screen and some English on the lower part which read "You didn't answer my question. Was my mother a good person?"

"What did he say?" Velkjo asked eagerly. When Kirill passed on the information, Velkjo looked appalled. Tom and Caroline looked at one another totally stumped, but the question had to be answered.

Tom decided to let Nikola reach his own conclusion. Tom asked via Kirill if the coffin lid was locked. It wasn't. Tom typed his answer to the phone before gesturing Nikola to come closer to the casket and once by each other, Tom opened the top half of the casket revealing Jelena's face, chest and arms, folded over her stomach. Tom then handed the phone back to Nikola with the words "Look at her and see if she was a good person."

Tom stood aside to give Nikola the space he needed. There before him was a face of a person he recognised, yet it was unfamiliar, almost mystical. The person in the coffin wore a smile on her beautiful face, but, despite how he tried, he could not remember seeing her smile. Nikola crossed over the norm into the morbid as reached in to the casket and held her hand hoping something would return. Nikola shut his eyes and the church was dead silent as everyone wondered what he was thinking. Then he was overcome by a chaos of emotions and despair. Slowly, the tide began to turn, he began to remember.

Nikola remembered as a child, lying on a pillow. He had just lost his hearing, but he remembered her smile as his mother tickled his stomach and blew on his face and he laughed. He remembered reaching to touch her face to feel what she said. He hadn't yet mastered the technique, and he didn't know what she actually said, but he knew, Nikola didn't need to hear it, he knew his mother said "I love you".

Nikola opened his eyes and touched her face, hoping he could feel her words again, but there was none.

Hate, that's what he should have felt but he couldn't because he didn't know her, he never got the chance and that was what infuriated him. She was as beautiful as he always imagined her to be, the sort that he would have been proud to point out to his pubescent teenage friends, but again, he never got the chance.

Nikola stopped feeling his mother's face; he took a step back with a clear look of dissatisfaction written over his brow. He appeared to resign himself that he needed to perform his duty as opposed to anything else when he took out his phone and typed for the translation the words "May I stay please?"

Tom smiled and typed in response "Yes, please."

The casket was closed, the bouquets of calles returned over the mahogany, and Nikola stood one step behind the couple. Caroline didn't consider his position as acceptable. She turned, reached for his arm and ushered him forward and even though she knew he didn't understand her, she said "Your place is here" and moved him forward a step ahead of her and her husband.

With things somewhat back to normality, Velkjo, having confirmed that Nikola could lip read in his native tongue, moved on, but rather than progressing with the blessing, he turned to look at Nikola and addressed him directly. "Welcome home my dear Nikola." He began. "You have come here to seek answers, particularly to the questions of whether the woman who bore you was a good person. You may already have an inkling of an answer by just counting the number of mourners here, but my boy, don't let the absence of the weeping and the grieving lead you to assumption.

Nikola, you may not know me, but I certainly know you. I remember that winters night in 1991 when we all thought our world was coming to an end; your mother came here to seek refuge and to fight for your right to see the world, even though many opposed your existence."

"Your mother knocked on our doors, a child herself, afraid and lonely. She was being coerced to abort you, but she was determined not to let that happen. She pleaded for sanctuary from those who were dutifully bound to protect her. They promised they wouldn't harm her, but she was not having any of it. She stayed put. She had been traumatised by your conception and was determined that no harm befell you. She was determined not to leave until she had you in her arms."

Velkjo pointed to a corner of the room and proclaimed "It was there, not far from where we are standing that she gave birth to you having refused to leave the church to go to the hospital. She was such a stubborn child, but she was right to be. She called you Nikola after her grandfather whom she doted on. You mother left the building with less than $100 in her pocket and hope in her heart, stepping into the city as the drums of war grew ever louder. You mother swore prior to her departure that you would never want for anything. To keep that promise, she left school, went about doing her best to provide for you."

"As years past and the jets flew overhead, the bombs falling all around us, your mother braved the fires from the sky and dashed across the city bare foot to return to this church cradling you in her arms. The building you lived in had been hit and you were both injured. Fearing you may die, she demanded you were baptised. I remember her words 'Pop, I beg you, I may be doomed but let him not share my fate.'"

"I was alone that evening and had to request a nun join us quickly at great risk. We baptised you and prayed for you and once we were done, she didn't wait, she ran out again into the night to find a hospital even though the sky was illuminated by falling bombs like a spectacular firework display, no one dared venture out, but she did, you had to live, you were her everything.

"When the heavens stopped falling and the world's wrath had stemmed temporarily, your mother brought you back to me when you were five and asked for me to pray for you again. She was weeping bitterly that day for her prayer was for reconciliation with your grandmother so she could take you into her care, thus enabling your mother to do what many young people did then and now which was to venture beyond our borders to make money for those at home. She took another oath before God that she will ensure you wanted for nothing and your impediment would not be a hindrance to your development."

"That night, I walked her to her grandmother's home. Your mother was inconsolable as she let you go. But, again, she knew it had to be done."

"Nikola, your mother did not abandon you, she did what was needed to make you the man that you are today. And here you are, not locked away, poor and helpless like many people with your condition in this country. In a world without sound, you have dreams, hopes and ambitions for the future because of her and yet you ask if your mother was a good person? Turn around Nikola, turn around and look. Though the church may be empty, these two people came here because of her. They are like candles in a dark room devoid of light, shining and shimmering brightly. Their presence here bears testament to the fact that the good she has done for you trumps all her evils."

Once Kirill finished translating, Caroline marvelled at Velkjo' eloquent speech and how, with his last sentence, he summed up everything. It moved her to tears. Tom gave her his handkerchief and put his arms around her as Velkjo continued giving his blessing and prayers.

Nikola stood there, affected by the tale of his mother's struggles. He felt remorseful and longed more than ever for the chance to see his mother's face again, but he didn't want to delay the service any further, besides, it appeared the Velkjo was bringing it to an end.

The holy man followed by his three helpers gave the blessing, sprinkling holy water over the casket then proceeded to use the water to put the sign of the cross of the heads of those people present and upon reaching Caroline, he placed his hand upon her shoulder and said "Don't cry my dear, she is with the lord." Taken by his faith, she asked "Do you really believe that." The man grinned as he placed the sign of the cross on her head and replied "Yes my child, for it is God's will."

The man's belief brought her the strength she needed to regain her composure as Velkjo, followed by his two helpers made his way to the front coffin and walked to the four corners swinging the smoking incense burner back and forward as he prayed and bowed at each axis.

Once done, he stretched, exposing the full glory of his embroidered robes as he told them to love each other, live in peace and pray for the soul of the departed. The choir broke into song, singing "O mladosti". It was the signal to the pallbearers to perform their duty.

They all stood as the six young men came forward for Jelena's earthly remains. As they stood by the handles, Nikola could not take being parted from his mother in such a cold informal manner. He walked forward, tapped the shoulder of the lead carrier on the right. Nikola raised his hand to signal that the man stop before waving his hand and said "I'll do it." Due to his lack of hearing, the man couldn't comprehend what Nikola was saying, but when he noticed Nikola reaching for the handle, he tried to stop him by holding his hands, "No, no, it's ok. I'll carry it."

Nikola was reluctant and reached for the handle again, but again was refused access "No" he said as he tried again, and was again refused. Nikola grew increasingly agitated, evident by his failed attempts to speak his mind which only came out as noises as he was prevented from touching the coffin again. Tom could tell what he could do and quickly intervened.

Tom rushed in between Nikola and the man and cried out "Hey!" The man stopped. "Kirill, could you tell him that it's ok to leave the casket?" Kirill said the necessary words that allowed the man to smile and stand aside. Once settled, Tom turned to Nikola who was now red with anger, then smiled and stepped away from the coffin along with the man.

The two mourners were then invited to go to the coffin to say their farewells. Tom and Caroline decided to go together and gave a short bow and took the flowers off the casket before stepping back.

Velkjo then went before the coffin to lead the procession holding the cross mounted on his staff to the church cemetery. Velkjo gave the nod and along with the others, Nikola carried his mother. As they left the protection of the church, the Trisagion was sung by the priest, the canon and the choir sang once again.

The body was taken from the church to the cemetery nearby where a hole awaited the box's arrival. The grave yard's ground was not smooth and the slippery snow didn't help either. Nicola and the other pallbearers moved on with difficulty. Velkjo walked behind them reading psalms with Tom and Caroline tailing behind. The sound of Velkjo's reading only made Nikola's journey to the grave more daunting. There was once he lived in hope that he would see his mother again to ask her the questions that niggled him, like why she left, now that hope was gone, stolen from him by the destructive yet inevitable hand of death.

When Nikola caught site of her designated grave, he paused for a moment, the enormity of his loss acted as a wrecking ball to his resolve which crumbled to the floor, crushed like the snow under foot.

He promised he wouldn't do it, he promised he wouldn't feel sad, but that too was gradually being attacked by the heavy weight of grief and eventually, like an elephant seated on a stool, his promise broke, destroying the delusion of his false strength. Yet Nikola stopped the tears streaming down his face, he had to carry on, even though it was painful. Once at the grave, Nikola accepted that it was time concede to the victory of the grim reaper.

With Velkjo standing at the head of exposed earth, the three grave diggers standing a few feet away with their shovels at the ready, heads bowed, the pallbearers were finally to carry on with their task without Nikola's intervention with prayers continually being said as the body was lowered into the earth. It must have been her maternal intuition that prompted Caroline to take the bold step of standing between Tom and Nikola and as the last rights were said, Nikola felt a hand slip into his. He didn't look at her, rather, Nikola latched on to Caroline's hand. It was a welcomed support during this emotional time, support he clung to tightly causing some considerable discomfort to Caroline as the body was finally commanded to the earth with the final words "Ashes to ashes, dust to dust"

Caroline observed that both Nikola and Tom seemed hypnotised as their eyes remained transfixed on the casket in the ground. Then one of the grave diggers scooped some of the excavated soil on to his shovel and brought it to the mourners.

Nikola was the first to have it presented to him. He looked at the soil and then Velkjo, who just smiled. There was no confirmation as to what to do from him. Cautiously, Nikola turned to the foreigners. Caroline indicated by her hand movements that he was to pick up some of the dirt and throw it in. Caroline was taken aback by the expression on his face. Nikola had the look of a person who had been told he was going to be eaten alive. For the first time, he showed a visible sign of grief.

With his hand's trembling, Nikola picked up a hand full of dirt. Again he looked around, he didn't want to do it; he didn't want this final confirmation. It was a symptom of the moment which he endured with Tom who equally fought to accept that the present situation was real. With a track record like hers, Tom hoped beyond hope that Jelena would jump out screaming "I got you!" If not for the comedy factor alone, at least for her son who was now facing the unnerving task of coming terms with the fact that Jelena was never coming back.

Nikola took a deep breath and tossed the soil in. He and Tom watched as the clumps of sand allowed gravity to do it's bidding and even though it took a less than a second, the soil's descent seemed like an eternity of torment to them both which only came to an end when it landed on the coffin. The sound of the dirt on wood rang like a gong to their ears. Nikola seemed to freeze to the spot, a tear rolling down his face as the grave digger progressed down the line.

It was Caroline's turn. She handed over the flowers she had been holding to the grave digger and took a large handful. Before she threw it in Caroline gave a smirk because in her mind, it seemed that Jelena got what she wanted after all, she had two men she cared about the most together in one place and one thing was for sure, they would never forget her. "Good bye Jelena." She said as she too disposed of the sand in her hands.

Finally, it was Tom's turn. He too felt the reluctance that Nikola had just a minute earlier felt, but he knew he needed to do this, this door must close. Bravely, he took some of the soil and threw it in and as he did, he said to himself "I'm going to miss you, you crazy bitch."

It was over; they had done their duty and fulfilled the wishes of a dead woman. It was time to go. Tom excused himself in order to go and thank Velkjo for his assistance and help and to collect what he was due, leaving Nikola and Caroline alone. She searched with her eyes for Kirill, lucky for her he wasn't too far away but during that time she noticed Velkjo handing Tom something small and shiny, probably a crucifix, she assumed. Caroline called Kirill over to enable her to deliver her statement to Nicola.

She reached into her bag to take out her purse and she produced a small passport photograph of her son. "This is Tim, my son. He's going to be eight this year but sometimes I think he is fifteen the way he behaves." Her words, relayed to him via Kirill's lips, made Nikola smile whilst he brushed off a tear. "He's learning sign language too… and I want you to meet him. Don't worry about the visa, don't worry about the cost, don't worry about anything, you tell me or Tom when you are free and we will organise everything. We may be far away, but you always have us. OK?" Nikola nodded.

It was then Tom joined them. Tom was pleased to finally see Nikola smiling. "I told him to come and visit. Can you give him your card?" Caroline asked as she reached into her bag for her jotting pad and pen. Tom did as he was told and provided Nikola with a card whilst Caroline finished writing out her details before ripping off the sheet and handing it to Nikola. "Give me a missed call or send me a text and I will have your number. Please promise you will come and see us?" This sudden gush of generosity was nearly overwhelming and Nikola had to try hard to keep the tears bay as he nodded to confirm he intended to keep the promise.

With the car waiting, Tom asked Nikola "Do you want us to take you anywhere?" Nikola turned to look at the grave before declining the offer, he wasn't exactly finished yet.

It was time to go. Caroline leaned over and kissed Nikola on the cheek and rubbed his shoulder as she said "See you soon Nikola" before she made her way to the car. Now alone, Tom looked at Nikola, he wondered what he could say to him, but he didn't need to worry much, Nikola spoke first. Yes it wasn't too clear and wasn't pronounced properly, but the effort was enough. Nikola said in English "Thank you." This was no time for a formal handshake, Tom leaned forward and the two embraced each other tightly. Tom felt close to the boy and wished the best for him as the let each other go.

Tom walked to the car with Nikola watching them. Tom turned to wave goodbye as he entered the vehicle and he couldn't help but notice Nikola's face. All the "tough guy" stance was bravado, the boy was truly heart broken. Still, Tom smiled and waved as he took his place in the back seat of the car next to Caroline.

Before the car started, Caroline asked "Do you think he will be alright?" shrugging his shoulders Tom replied "If he's anything like his mother, he'll blossom."

As the car moved, Caroline waved at Nikola and gave the sign that he should call her to which Nikola smiled, nodded and waved them off. "Ah, what a nice kid." She remarked as she looked at her hand, her white gloves were now dirty. "Well, this will need a wash. Wasn't that silly of me, picking up dirt with them on, look?" As she showed her hands to Tom, she realised that he wasn't really interested in what she had to say, rather, he just looked at her, grinning, before leaning over and kissing her on the cheek. Tom then said "You are a wonderful person. What you did over the past few days was nothing short of amazing. You are truly a good human being."

"It's nothing... I did what had to be done." She replied as she reached in to her bag and took out a folded piece of paper. "Here, for you." Tom took the paper and opened it.

On the sheet, written in Caroline's hand, were the words "Come home." The words caused Tom to sweat, it resulted from the shame he felt, the shame that stemmed from the revelation that despite all the neglect, all the strain and pain, she still found it in her heart to forgive him. This realisation weakened him. Tom could not look at her anymore. She noticed and thought it was best not to make things more awkward for him, so she pretended to top up her makeup as Tom dissolved into silent contemplation.

# 23

*14 January 2011*

Back in Berlin, Julien was close to a meltdown. With the time now 17:24, and just over two hours before show time, the caterers called to say they were not able to provide the items till about nine in the evening because the batch of food they had produced were now on the streets due to an accident with their catering truck.

Now he had to prepare food for over 70 to possibly 100 people, all who expected to be wined and dined before opening their wallets.

Julien had to accept that he couldn't handle this all on his own. Upon returning from the store with his assistant, Renata and all the ingredients needed for the finger food, he went up to the flat and insisted that Khoi stop wallowing and pick up a peeler and address some potatoes.

It was then there was a buzzing sound at the door. Julien could only hope that it was the caterers, ready to point, laugh and proclaim it was one big joke. But it wasn't, it was just Paul with a small Asian girl whose glasses loosely fitted her face. Paul began to speak English "Hi, Julien, sorry we are early, this is Han…" all the words flew past Julien's ears as he smiled and ushered them in.

As they entered, Paul could observe Julien's fretfulness and remarked "What's up? You seem shaken." When Julien exposed what had happened, Han and Paul's face seemed to light up. Han proposed that she give him a hand and asked "Would steamed and fried dumplings be appropriate?"

"Honey, if it's quick and easy to make, let's do it." Julien replied. In support of that, Paul added "Yeah, you can try and make some sushi too." Only for the smile to be cleared off Han's face as she rightfully corrected him "I'm Chinese, not Japanese. But sushi is a good idea. Why not go and buy some?" Feeling he had firmly put his foot in it, Paul decided to go out in search of a good Japanese restaurant that could produce enough sushi for an army. Once a red faced Paul left, Han's smile returned and in a reassuring manner, she placed her hand on Julien's shoulder and said "Take me to the kitchen and I will see what I can do."

Come show time, Han actually saved the day as the food she made went down as a treat along with the sushi. People started arriving ten minutes earlier than the stated time, but they were ready. Khoi was in the kitchen with Paul organising the drinks and the food on trays which Renata and Han served to the punters, whilst Julien did his best to schmooze the public into purchasing the works in room one, but no so much efforts were required for those in the second room, which was a relief. And then Renata's date arrived. The giant frame of Marcel dominated the room sucking up the attention to the detriment of the painting. Of particular interest to the people were his elaborate tattoos.

Julien initially had a sinking feeling till Marcel seemed to ignore the eyes on him and walked to the painting he liked, the boy and his ball. He stood there before it for two minutes as though hypnotised causing others to wonder what he thought, drawing some concern from Julien who walked up to him and asked if he was alright. "Yeah... I'm cool." Marcel replied "I want this..." Looking at the plain, not very impressive work, Julien had to ask why the strong interest "What not to like?" Marcel asked in turn "It's childhood encapsulated. The cross of being made to learn conflicting with a child's urge to play? We've all been there, it's something we miss. How much?"

Julien saw the potential and told him the price to which Marcel shrugged his shoulders and asked if Julien took credit cards. Noticing that the people around had overheard Marcel's critic of the painting, Julien brushed away the query and led Marcel to another painting of ladies breast feeding in a café, surrounded by others with some looking in disgust and others ignoring the ladies and their activities. "So tell me, what you do think about this?" Julien challenged. Marcel looked for a moment and before proclaiming "Nurturing. The reality of our lives today what's wrong with breast feeding? It's the most natural thing anyone can do. It's a depiction of our problem with being human, showing ourselves. The women aren't being brave, they are being normal. It's those who are looking that have the problem." Then some of the eavesdropping women could be heard swooning.

At that very moment, Marcel was the most eligible straight man in the room and the best means of selling the works as a renewed interest was placed on the paintings as Julien took him from one painting to another.

At the end of the evening, people were bidding against each other of the paintings available, even the one Marcel wanted to buy, but Julien made sure it was remained his.

With all the food finished and everyone watered, Paul and Han eventually joined the people in the gallery leaving Khoi alone in the kitchen. He had been receiving text messages from Joel who was outside.

Julien coaxed him out of the kitchen to join the crowd, but Khoi began to sweat. He felt himself falling into panic mode again, not that anyone noticed. Another text appeared. Khoi looked at his phone "Come on man, it won't be long I promise. I just want to talk." Again he tried to ignore it as a lady stood next to him admiring the work. "Can't believe he just sat there and did that in one day. Such detail" Khoi tried to humour her and replied, "Yes, impressive indeed." another text arrived "It's cold out here man. Don't keep me waiting."

Khoi felt his heart racing, he was near breaking point. Things began to fall out of focus, but he wasn't in the market for such feelings at the moment. Khoi walked up to Julien who was in the process of finalising a sale and whispered in his ear "going out for some air." He didn't wait for Julien's response before he walked up the stairs to the flat to fetch his jacket.

Khoi went through the back, via the office and the kitchen then out through the delivery door. Once out, he could feel Joel's presence. Khoi walked down the steps, the snow fluttering gently down on to his hair. He looked around and from the shadows emerged Joel, hunched and shivering under the chill.

Joel had his left hand in his pocket and holding a cigarette in his right, he said "Hello Khoi. Glad to see you could make it." Joel took a draw on his cigarette as he added "Long time no see." Khoi said nothing in return. Joel could feel the venom of Khoi's thoughts with his look, yet he persisted" Are you feeling better? Dad told me to come and check up on you…"Khoi was heaving, his posture and stance was as aggressive as the season.

Seeing his tactic wasn't working, Joel changes the subject." Julien sure knows how to pull a crowd, doesn't he?" he took a step forward only for Khoi to take one back. He decided not to approach further. "We missed you at the last meeting."

"I did ask for some more time off…"Khoi finally spoke.

'Oh yeah, you weren't feeling well. Or were you busy assisting your boyfriend put on his show?" Joel goaded but noted he had gone too far "I'm sorry, didn't mean to come out that way…'

"What do you want?" Khoi snapped.

"Wow… someone is angry." Even though it was obvious, Joel changed his tongue and reverted to using their made up language of "Jekorian" "Are you mad at me?" Joel asked. Khoi looked away avoiding any eye contact. "Are you?"

Khoi returned his gaze at him and asked in Jekorian "What do you think?"

"Is it about your girlfriend because we followed your instructions to the last letter, so don't get all remorseful on me."

"It's not that." Khoi said through gritted teeth.

"Is it about the surprise? "Khoi said nothing and began to heave again. Joel could see he was right. "I don't understand why you are upset? It was just business."

"Business? Is that what you call it? How much did we make from dragging someone to the centre of a forest in the middle of a snow storm? You gave me your word!" Khoi asserted pointing at Joel. "And don't give me that crap that it was nature not you that did him in…You are heartless!"

"You should talk. We only had 5 people in our sights and you added 22 more to the body count. You left 6 in a vegetative state and God knows how many grieving people and let's not forget a traumatised child that will need many years of therapy, all under your watch, all under your direction and you call me heartless? Mr 'socially beneficial collateral damage'" Joel taunted causing Khoi to snap at him

"We promised him and we broke it." Joel shook his head snickering as Khoi continued "I trusted you!"

The bickering pair didn't notice that they were being watched by Julien who had come to pick up another bottle of wine. Although he didn't understand, he followed the sound to the door and watched, unnoticed as Joel grew more animated. "You see? You don't understand. Max was a witness; he was dead from the start. If the others knew of his existence they would hunt him down and us too. You saw how quickly he squeaked, we didn't even have to touch him. If he had gone to the police, he would have sung like a bird and we know they wouldn't do anything; hell, they would have just kept him away…"

"So you thought he should die in one of the most horrible ways imaginable?" Khoi interrupted. The statement threw Joel, forcing him to reflect as Khoi added "That was wrong. He had a family…"

'So did Robert and you didn't have any issues there. So did Richard and that didn't matter to you. What about Oliver? You sorted him out in front of his own son. What about Jelena… what about the only girl you ever slept with? You didn't worry about her. Perhaps we should tell your man in there, tell him that you actually like eating carpet before you gave the word and killed her. You turned her into an idol for all of us to worship." Khoi raged in silence and it grew as Joel pulled on Khoi's heart strings and in a calm voice asked "What about Stefan? He had a family too. We were his family, or did you forget that? Don't you think he deserved some justice?" The memory of Stefan was still badly felt by both of them. It caused Joel to be philosophical and doubtful of his approach. "Oh Khoi, let's not fight. I miss you man, I miss our good times. What happened to that?"

In an unfeeling pitch, Khoi responded "It died in Poland."

Having had enough, Joel made his frustration heard "I was trying to be consolatory here! The man deserved to die!" Reverting back to German, Khoi remarked "You're a monster" and in the same language, Joel rebutted "And you're a coward."

Julian from his vantage point saw the moment when Khoi's simmering blood came to a full boil. Khoi was heaving, and a fist was forming. Fearful of things escalating, Julien moved in. "Khoi?" It caused the pair to turn round with anger in their eyes. "Khoi, I need your help with the music please? My compilation seems to have been corrupted. It's rather urgent." It seemed to work, the feuding pair seemed glad to leave things where they were. "Sure." Khoi said as he went up the steps into the kitchen and rested on the work top to calm his nerves.

Now, it was Julien and Joel alone. Feeling uncomfortable, Joel took the first step and waved "Hello Julien." Julien didn't bother to gesture back, but he did raise his left eyebrow as he replied 'Joel.'

This was more than Joel could bear. Joel turned and walked down the alley cursing beneath his breath. He knew Julien was watching him and once out of sight, he leaned on the wall under the window of the gallery to light a cigarette and compose.

Julien shut the door and went to Khoi who looked distressed. He held his hand and asked "Are you alright?" Khoi looked up at him with tears forming in his eyes, literally being eaten by self-rebuke as he asked "Why do you keep me? Can't you see I am just a no good?" Feeling sympathetic, Julien ran his hand through his hair and said "Because one day, you'll do the right thing. But right now, I really do need your help with the music.

Could you please play something on the piano to entertain the guests?" Khoi kissed him on the cheek and gave him a hug before taking off his coat and handing it over to Julien. He proceeded to the gallery unnoticed and sat by the piano and began to play Bach's Goldberg Variations.

As he stroked the keys, everyone fell silent as they listened attentively, almost hypnotised. Not all the listeners were in the room though. Julien stood by the door of the office, watching, whilst beneath the window, having just finished his cigarette, Joel waited in the cold to listen to his friend play.

Joel swung between his affection for his friend and his irrational anger brought on by jealousy and it made him ache. He wanted to leave, but he couldn't tear away. Like a moth to a light bulb, he stayed even though it hurt and after an hour of the ordeal of listening to the beautiful music, he walked away feeling alone in this cruel evening choosing to go to a bar where he sat, drinking by himself.

The evening came to an end just around half past eleven, but it took more than an hour to get the last guest out. Marcel left with Renata and his painting under his arm, causing others to demand the same, which was great for Julien as he was happy to ensure they left.

Paul stayed behind to help clean up with Khoi as Julien was in the office organising the invoices. Han had initially waited for a moment but decided to return home as she had to prepare for an exam. Paul, with sleeves rolled up, and Khoi, gathered the used cups and bottles whilst commenting on the individuals who graced the evening in their own special way. As Paul tied up a bin bag outside the front door, Julien summoned him to the office.

He entered and found Julien sitting behind the desk, licking envelopes. "You called master?" Paul teased. Having finished, Julien put the envelopes aside and picked up another before offering it up to Paul who was baffled. He opened it and found the check for €6000 with the name space left blank "What's this for?"

"It's the proceeds from the sale of your sketches." Julien confirmed. "I didn't know if Paul was your real name or what your surname was, but if you give it to me, I can fill it in. Nice tattoo by the way."

Still confused, Paul queried the situation "Thanks. Khoi chose it. Excuse me, but what's this for? I sold something?"

"Didn't you notice? What do you think all those orange dots stuck to the name of your works were for?" Julien asked "Everything you drew was sold at €500 each and a total of 20 works, minus 30% gallery fee and 10% for the cost for all the frames that is your cut.'

Paul was struck dumb with amazement. "I don't know what to say?"

"Thank you? Or is this the first honest € you ever made?" Julien teased only to have Paul confess that it was. "Oh... Well you were a hit and I would be glad to represent you if you have any more works. I would link you to my friends outside the country; we should see what we can make out of your skill. You see, there's always another way." Still feeling giddy with joy, Paul pulled out the cheque and looked at the figure again and smiled at Julien "It's not a joke right?"

"You want it in cash?" Julien asked "Yeah!" Paul said in a gleeful state.

With a sigh, Julien pushed back the chair and walked to the safe. "Turn away!" He ordered with Paul complying. He entered the pin code and took out the necessary amount, before shutting it and handing over the funds to him. Paul had in his hand, twelve €500 notes and remained stunned. Julien then placed his hand on Paul's shoulder shaking him gently saying "Well done buddy!"

"Thank you." Paul said.

"It's nothing. Now go home and do me favour, please don't give up you skill for financial gain. Your work was generated from you being observant, you being you and that's what was special about your work. People saw what you saw. OK?" Julien begged.

"OK.... Sure you don't want me to help out?" Paul offered.

"No, no, go and enjoy your evening, just don't spend all your money at once."

Paul laughed a little, then asked Julien "May I hug you?"

"If you must..." With permission given, Paul gave him a great bear hug.

Paul then gathered his coat and walked out of the office literally floating past Khoi as he swept the floor with a broom. Paul pointed at the direction of the office and proclaimed "What a guy you got there... he's amazing. You're really lucky." Paul didn't even bother to say goodbye as he left. Khoi was left alone to consume the words that were served.

Julien was busy totalling all the sums for the day to see if he made a profit other than that originating from the sales of Paul's works when a shadow fell over him. He looked up and found Khoi there, broom in hand, looking committed as he declared "We need to talk". Khoi entered the room. Julien offered him a chair which Khoi rejected.

Khoi seemed agitated, gripping the broom handle as he proclaimed "Whilst you were away I did things... terrible things I am not proud of... things that would make you hate me..." Raising his hand to stop Khoi's progression, Julien said "I don't want to hear." When asked why he was reluctant, Julien admitted "you said I would hate you if you told me... I don't think I can live with that. All I want to know is what I can do to stop this torment you are going through." Being given the option, Khoi realised he had the opportunity to be honest. He rested the broom on the wall before taking the seat opposite Julien.

Khoi began to sweat, he didn't know why, but his nerves were all over the place. His resolve almost failed him, but with Julien looking at him with his concerned eyes, he said "I have to leave... I can't be part of the group anymore; it's turning me into something I am beginning to hate. But I don't know... I just don't know."

"Why?" Julien asked again. "Because of what I did... you are now in danger and if anything happens to you, I just wouldn't know what to do... I wouldn't forgive myself. I just have to go." Khoi answered as he began to cry.

Julien never liked to see Khoi cry, under general circumstances, he thought Khoi's connection with his feelings was rather annoying to say the least, something he often ignored, but with the genuine fear he witnessed, Julien couldn't help but act. "Where do you want to go?" He asked "I don't know." Khoi responded "Somewhere far away from Berlin, far away from all this!"

Julien paused for a moment to think. He proposed somewhere in Europe but Khoi revealed a fact that gangs are interconnected and thus he wouldn't be safe on the continent.

With very little options available, Julien reached for the phone and dialled a number he knew by heart. With the phone on speaker, Khoi and Julien listened to the dialling tone of the phone. Khoi was terrified and it showed. It rang again. He wished Kat answered quickly before he chickened out. Another ring before an engaged tone followed.

Julien turned off the speaker "Perhaps she is busy?" It was the only excuse Julien could offer. Now Khoi was certain it was a bad idea and was about to confirm that he had changed his mind when the office phone rang.

Khoi and Julien looked at each other to see who would answer the call. It rang the second time and Julien thought he best grab the nettle and pressed the answer button, putting the call on speaker phone. "Kathrin, how are you?"

"I'm fine. Sorry I missed your call, I was in the toilet vomiting. I must have eaten something that didn't agree with me." She replied.

"Are you alright? Want us to call you back?" Julien proposed but she said all was well. However Kat was observant enough to see he used the word "us" and asked why. "I have Khoi here with me. Are you alone?" With Jan out for the late Christmas lunch which was meant to take place on the 17th of December but had to be postponed due to the spate of murders, she was. "Cool, Khoi wanted to tell you something."

Julien sat back and allowed Khoi to take the floor. Khoi's anxiety levels were sky high as his trembling voice showed "He… he… hello?'

"Hi. How are you?" There was a still moment. Khoi felt his mouth dry up as he stumbled. "So you have something to tell me?" Khoi opened his mouth but the words never came out. Impatient, Julien assisted "Khoi wants to take you up on your offer in regards to a potential career change."

"Khoi? Is that true?" Kathrin enquired. Cornered, Khoi corroborated that the information. "Wow. That's good news. It's going to take three to four months or so, but I will get to work right away.

You do know you will have to leave the country?'

Khoi had totally forgotten about that fact and rubbed his face as the ramifications hit home. Yet he signed "Yeah, I understand."

Julien reached out to him as he added "Yeah, we understand." It was refreshing to hear that Julien wasn't going to abandoned him.

"OK. I will make a few calls… where are you planning to move to?" Kat lamented.

"I don't know… I still have family in Christchurch… who knows."

"Shit, that's far." Kat remarked.

"One question…"Khoi interrupted "what do I do till then?"

"You carry on as per usual till I tell you when."

Kathrin's reply wasn't what Khoi wanted to hear. "I was hoping I could stop immediately… I don't know if I could bear being there another day!" He protested

"Calm down Khoi!" Julien begged

"Khoi, you need to stay there. If you leave now they will note something is up. Trust me on this. Just try and manage till I am ready. OK?" With no other option, Khoi conceded. "I am proud of you Khoi, I know it's tough to move on but it's for the best.'

"Yeah… thanks." Khoi sounded totally demoralised.

Once they were off the call, Khoi broke down and wept. Julien didn't really understand what was happening or what he was going through. Was it guilt; anger; pain? He didn't know. What Julien was sure off was that Khoi needed a hug and that's just what he got, allowing him to vent on his shoulder in the hopes that it would calm him.

*15 January 2011*

Morning came with a knock on the door. The smell of used prophylactic merged with bodily fluids made for a nauseating atmosphere.

Joel's head hurt and light at the same time, a terrible combination. There was another knock on the door again. Joel tried to get up, but found his right arm pinned down by a body of a naked woman. Now it was totally numb.

There was another slightly louder knock on the door again. Annoyed, Joel pushed the lady off his arm, sat up, shook it hard to get some feeling back into it before getting out of bed. The lady didn't even stir.

He walked slowly, hung over and groggy. Joel opened the door and found a hotel worker with a trolley. The hotel worker gasped initially before maintaining her decorum. "What?" Joel snarled having been dragged out of bed by her knocking. "I brought you your breakfast sir." She replied trying her best not to blush. Joel, having realised he was too exacting, mumbled "Thank you."

"You're welcome sir." The worker said and promptly walked away.

Joel wondered why she didn't wait for a tip as he reached for the trolley. As he drew in the trolley, he had the strange feeling of cold metal touching his upper thigh and then his penis as he dragged the trolley over the threshold.

It was then he realised why the hotel worker was laughing. He was totally naked and so was the lady on the bed… The night came flooding back. Following his confrontation with Khoi, he went on a stopper, throwing himself in all iniquities. That was why he had a dead arm which was now tingling back to life which originated as a result of the prostitute in the bed sleeping on it.

More of the night began to flood back to him. They had taken speed and had gone about enjoying one another all night. Embarrassment was the feeling that consumed him. Joel was desperate to get out of the hotel room without exposing his shame.

He put on his clothes as stealthily as he could. He was trying his best to ensure he didn't wake her and he succeeded. Joel reached for his wallet and took out €250 and left it on the bedside table. Joel departed the room, paid for her board and an extra night at reception and left, walking briskly.

Joel took a taxi home dreading what he was going to face upon his return. He failed his father and he was certain Georg was going to kill him.

It couldn't be avoided any longer. Arriving at the door Joel summoned up his courage which appeared to be whittling away quickly. He unlocked the door and entered and was met by his mother who was just about to set out for a jog. She informed Joel that his father had been waiting for him and was currently in the living room watching the news.

It was time to take the blame. Joel walked to the living room hoping his mother would not leave, in case things got heavy, but the sound of the door shutting meant he was now alone with his father. At the entrance to the living room, he noticed his father in his arm chair watching a cooking show. "Dad?" Joel called. Georg leaned forward to look at him before proclaiming. "You are home. Good. Khoi called today he will be back next week. Get the others ready for a meeting." Then in an ominous twist, Georg added "You were lucky." as he returned to his position to watch a chef chop ginger finely.

In Belgrade, a slightly hung over driver was waiting outside the grand hotel waiting patiently for Tom and his wife. Tom was struggling to find the space in his bag for the gift of alcohol given to him by Dani. He frankly would have left it behind without sentiment if it weren't for Caroline's insistence.

Based on that, Tom gave up moving around his luggage and went to Caroline's room and handed her the bottle "You want it, you can have it." He said before returning to his room to collect his items and when he was done, he lifted the bag off the bed and went to put on his coat.

The jingling sound in his belt alerted Tom to examine the contents to ensure he had his house keys. As he dipped his hand in, he pulled out not only the house keys, but also the purple memory stick left behind by Jelena and handed to him by Velkjo.

Satisfied with knowing he had all his things, Tom shut his eyes and though he had a heavy heart, he was pleased to be leaving and vowed never to return to Serbia for as long as he lived.

Eagerly, he went to Caroline's room to find she was ready.

Tom and Caroline walked out together in silence to taxi with the shivering driver showing he was only too happy to see them. With their items in the boot, they took their seat in the back. As the car man powered on to the main road, Caroline remarked "The booze is in my bag." The only response Tom could make to the announcement was "I'm happy for you." The silence continued. It seemed as though it was mutually agreed with Caroline taking in the sites whilst Tom looked out the window to ponder on his next move.

Driving to the airport, they approached the Ada Bridge. It was then Caroline noted the flowing body of water. The car slowed down thanks to the traffic. Caroline then took the chance to ask "Is that the Danube?" Tom didn't reply, so she asked again, "I didn't get the chance to see it. Is that the Danube?"

"Sava." Tom replied. "Sorry?" She asked, wondering if she misheard "It's the river Sava!" Tom shouted unable to contain himself. "I'm sorry, I need some air." He said opening the door of the slow moving car, alarming the driver, before he stepped out and ventured out towards the side of bridge. This behaviour frightened Caroline who followed Tom out of the car and chase after him. "Tom!" she called as Tom paused at the side of the bridge, his hand in his pocket.

He watched the river flowing, the memory stick felt like a pocket of radium, infecting him and he knew if he pushed further he'd end up by the element's discover, killed by his own activities. He was fed up, he couldn't take it anymore. Tom scoped out the contents, and he heard Caroline cry out his name. He turned to face her, the veins on the side of his head pulsating, causing Caroline some great concern wondering if it were a prelude to a stroke.

Avoiding the car as the driver sorted out a place to park, Caroline ran towards him. He was not to be deterred with all the content including the memory stick in his hands and threw them all into the middle of the river.

Now that she was next to him, Caroline could see the items flying through the air before descending into the river with a splash. "What did you do that for?" Tom turned round, walked up to her and gave her a deep kiss before remarking "That was for my happy ending." It was then Caroline revealed "Is that why you threw your house keys away?" the revelation prompted him to check his pockets and, as per usual, Caroline was right, it prompted him to cry out "Shit" till he saw the smile on Caroline's face who consoled him with the words, "Don't worry, you can move back in."

Tom could have floated home. His decision had been made for him and with a kiss on the cheek; he took her by the hand and led her to the taxi, to proceed with their journey.

As Tom and Caroline made their way to the airport, Biljana was finishing for the day. As she walked out the office to the lift, she held in her hand an envelope containing a memory stick, addressed to "Mr Nicola Bozic" which she handed to the receptionist on her way out. "Could you please post this for me via courier?" Instructions given, Biljana boarded the lift, looking forward to returning home to sleep off her excessive indulgence of the Orthodox New Year.

Printed in Great Britain
by Amazon